THE GUNS OF
THE SOUTH

THE
GUNS OF THE
SOUTH

A NOVEL OF THE CIVIL WAR

HARRY
TURTLEDOVE

BALLANTINE BOOKS · NEW YORK

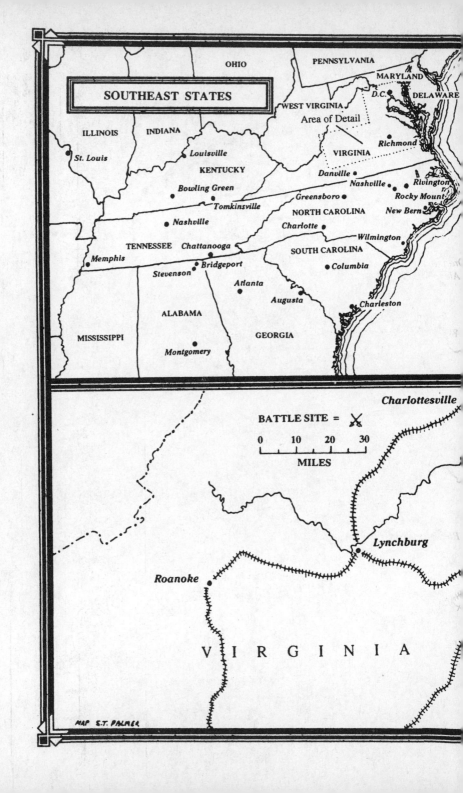

SOUTHEAST STATES

OHIO

PENNSYLVANIA

MARYLAND

D.C. DELAWARE

WEST VIRGINIA

Area of Detail

ILLINOIS   INDIANA

VIRGINIA

Richmond

St. Louis

Danville

Nashville   Rivington

KENTUCKY

Bowling Green

Greensboro   Rocky Mount

Louisville

Tomkinsville

NORTH CAROLINA   New Bern

Nashville

Charlotte

TENNESSEE   Chattanooga

SOUTH CAROLINA   Wilmington

Memphis

Bridgeport

Columbia

Stevenson

Atlanta

ALABAMA

Augusta   Charleston

GEORGIA

MISSISSIPPI

Montgomery

Charlottesville

BATTLE SITE = ✗

0   10   20   30

MILES

Lynchburg

Roanoke

V I R G I N I A

MAP S.T. PALMER

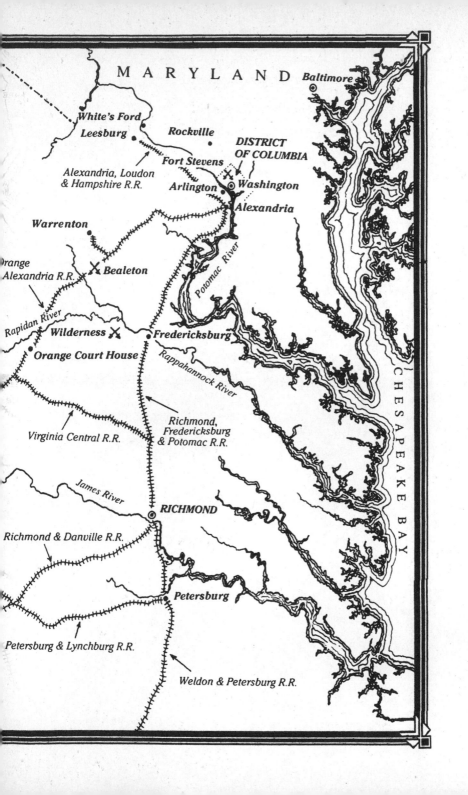

THE GUNS OF
THE SOUTH

Headquarters
January 20, 1864

Mr. President:
I have delayed replying to your letter of the 4th until the time arrived
for the execution of the attempt on New Berne. I regret very much
that the boats on the Neuse & Roanoke are not completed. With their
aid I think success would be certain. Without them, though the place
may be captured, the fruits of the expedition will be lessened and our
maintenance of the command of the waters in North Carolina uncer-
tain.

Robert E. Lee paused to dip his pen once more in the inkwell. Despite
flannel shirt, uniform coat, and heavy winter boots, he shivered a little.
The headquarters tent was cold. The winter had been harsh, and showed
no signs of growing any milder. New England weather, he thought, and
wondered why God had chosen to visit it upon his Virginia.

With a small sigh, he bent over the folding table once more to detail for
President Davis the arrangements he had made to send General Hoke's
brigade down into North Carolina for the attack on New Berne. He had but
small hope the attack would succeed, but the President had ordered it,
and his duty was to carry out his orders as best he could. Even without the

boats, the plan he had devised was not actually a bad one, and President Davis reckoned the matter urgent . . .

In view of the opinion expressed in your letter, I would go to North Carolina myself. But I consider my presence here always necessary, especially now when there is such a struggle to keep the army fed & clothed.

He shook his head. Keeping the Army of Northern Virginia fed and clothed was a never-ending struggle. His men were making their own shoes now, when they could get the leather, which was not often. The ration was down to three-quarters of a pound of meat a day, along with a little salt, sugar, coffee—or rather, chicory and burnt grain—and lard. Bread, rice, corn . . . . they trickled up the Virginia Central and the Orange and Alexandria Railroad every so often, but not nearly often enough. He would have to cut the daily allowance again, if more did not arrive soon.

President Davis, however, was as aware of all that as Lee could make him. To hash it over once more would only seem like carping. Lee resumed: *Genl Early is still in the*—

A gun cracked, quite close to the tent. Soldier's instinct pulled Lee's head up. Then he smiled and laughed at himself. One of his staff officers, most likely, shooting at a possum or a squirrel. He hoped the young man scored a hit.

But no sooner had the smile appeared than it vanished. The report of the gun sounded—odd. It had been an abrupt bark, not a pistol shot or the deeper boom of an Enfield rifle musket. Maybe it was a captured Federal weapon.

The gun cracked again and again and again. Each report came closer to the one before than two heartbeats were to each other. *A Federal weapon indeed*, Lee thought: *one of those fancy repeaters their cavalry like so well.* The fusillade went on and on. He frowned at the waste of precious cartridges—no Southern armory could easily duplicate them.

He frowned once more, this time in puzzlement, when silence fell. He had automatically kept count of the number of rounds fired. No Northern rifle he knew was a thirty-shooter.

He turned his mind back to the letter to President Davis. —*Valley*, he wrote. Then gunfire rang out again, an unbelievably rapid stutter of shots, altogether too quick to count and altogether unlike anything he had ever heard. He took off his glasses and set down the pen. Then he put on a hat and got up to see what was going on.

At the tent fly, Lee almost collided with one of his aides-de-camp, who was hurrying in as he tried to leave. The younger man came to attention. "I beg your pardon, sir."

"Quite all right, Major Taylor. Will this by any chance have something to do with the, ah, unusual gun I heard fired just now?"

"Yes, sir." Walter Taylor seemed to be holding on to military discipline with both hands. He was, Lee reminded himself, only twenty-five or so, the youngest of all the staff officers. Now he drew out a sheet of paper, which he handed to Lee. "Sir, before you actually see the gun in action, as I just have, here is a communication from Colonel Gorgas in Richmond concerning it."

"In matters concerning ordnance of any sort, no view could be more pertinent than that of Colonel Gorgas," Lee agreed. He drew out his reading glasses once more, set them on the bridge of his nose.

> *Bureau of Ordnance, Richmond*
> *January 17, 1864*
>
> *General Lee:*
> *I have the honor to present to you with this letter Mr. Andries Rhoodie of Rivington, North Carolina, who has demonstrated in my presence a new rifle, which I believe may prove to be of the most significant benefit conceivable to our soldiers. As he expressed the desire of making your acquaintance & as the Army of Northern Virginia will again, it is likely, face hard fighting in the months ahead, I send him on to you that you may judge both him & his remarkable weapon for yourself. I remain,*
>
> *Your most ob't servant,*
> *Josiah Gorgas,*
> *Colonel*

Lee folded the letter, handed it back to Taylor. As he returned his glasses to their pocket, he said, "Very well, Major. I was curious before; now I find my curiosity doubled. Take me to Mr.—Rhoodie, was it?"

"Yes, sir. He's around behind the tents here. If you will come with me—"

Breath smoking in the chilly air, Lee followed his aide-de-camp. He was not surprised to see the flaps from the other three tents that made up his headquarters were open; anyone who had heard that gunfire would want to learn what had made it. Sure enough, the rest of his officers were gathered round a big man who did not wear Confederate gray.

The big man did not wear the yellow-brown that was the true color of most home-dyed uniforms, either, nor the black of the general run of civilian clothes. Lee had never seen an outfit like the one he had on. His coat and trousers were of mottled green and brown, so that he almost seemed to disappear against dirt and brush and bare-branched trees. A similarly mottled cap had flaps to keep his ears warm.

Seeing Lee approach, the staff officers saluted. He returned the courtesy. Major Taylor stepped ahead. "General Lee, gentlemen, this is Mr. Andries Rhoodie. Mr. Rhoodie, here is General Lee, whom you may well recognize, as well as my colleagues, Majors Venable and Marshall."

"I am pleased to meet all you gentlemen, especially the famous General Lee," Rhoodie said.

"You are much too kind, sir," Lee murmured politely.

"By no means," Rhoodie said. "I would be proud to shake your hand." He held out his own.

As they shook, Lee tried to take the stranger's measure. He spoke like an educated man, but not like a Carolinian. His accent sounded more nearly British, though it also held a faint guttural undertone.

His odd clothes aside, Rhoodie did not look like a Carolinian, either. His face was too square, his features too heavy. That heaviness made him seem almost indecently well fleshed to Lee, who was used to the lean, hungry men of the Army of Northern Virginia.

But Rhoodie's bearing was erect and manly, his handclasp firm and strong. His gray eyes met Lee's without wavering. Somewhere in his past, Lee was suddenly convinced, he had been a soldier: those were marksman's eyes. By the wrinkles at their corners and by the white hairs that showed in his bushy reddish mustache, Rhoodie had to be nearing forty, but the years had only toughened him.

Lee said, "Colonel Gorgas gives you an excellent character, sir, you and your rifle both. Will you show it to me?"

"In a moment, if I may," Rhoodie answered, which surprised Lee. In his experience, most inventors were wildly eager to show off their brainchildren. Rhoodie went on, "First, sir, I would like to ask you a question, which I hope you will be kind enough to answer frankly."

"Sir, you are presumptuous," Charles Marshall said. The wan winter sun glinted from the lenses of his spectacles and turned his normally animated face into something stern and a little inhuman.

Lee held up a hand. "Let him ask what he would, Major. You need not forejudge his intentions." He glanced toward Rhoodie, nodded for him to continue. He had to look up to meet the stranger's eye, which was unusual, for he was nearly six feet tall himself. But Rhoodie overtopped him by three or four inches.

"I thank you for your patience with me," he said now in that not-quite-

British accent. "Tell me this, then: what do you make of the Confederacy's chances for the coming year's campaign and for the war as a whole?"

"To be or not to be, that is the question," Marshall murmured.

"I hope our prospects are somewhat better than poor Hamlet's, Major," Lee said. His staff officers smiled. Rhoodie, though, simply waited. Lee paused to marshal his thoughts. "Sir, since I have but so briefly had the honor of your acquaintance, I hope you will forgive me for clinging to what may be plainly seen by any man with some knowledge and some wit: that is, our enemies are superior to us in numbers, resources, and the means and appliances for carrying on the war. If those people"—his common euphemism for the Federals—"use their advantages vigorously, we can but counterpoise to them the courage of our soldiers and our confidence in Heaven's judgment of the justice of our cause. Those have sufficed thus far. God willing, they shall continue to do so."

"Who said God is for the big battalions?" Rhoodie asked.

"Voltaire, wasn't it?" Charles Venable said. He had been a professor of mathematics before the war, and was widely read.

"A freethinker if ever there was one," Marshall added disapprovingly.

"Oh, indeed," Rhoodie said, "but far from a fool. When you are weaker than your foes, should you not take the best advantage of what you do have?"

"That is but plain sense," Lee said. "No one could disagree."

Now Rhoodie smiled, or his mouth did; the expression stopped just short of his eyes. "Thank you, General Lee. You have just given much of my sales talk for me."

"Have I?"

"Yes, sir, you have. You see, my rifle will let you conserve your most precious resource of all—your men."

Walter Taylor, who had seen the gun in action, sucked in a long, deep breath. "It could be so," he said quietly.

"I await the demonstration, Mr. Rhoodie," Lee said.

"You will have it." Rhoodie unslung the weapon. Lee had already noted it was of carbine length, stubby next to an infantry musket. Because it was so short, its socket bayonet seemed the longer. Rhoodie reached over his shoulder into his haversack. That was made of mottled cloth like his trousers and coat, and looked to be of finer manufacture than even a Union man carried. Most of Lee's soldiers made do with a rolled-up blanket.

The tall stranger produced a curved metal object, perhaps eight inches long and an inch and a half or two inches wide. He clicked it into place in front of the carbine's trigger. "This is the magazine," he said. "When it's full, it holds thirty rounds."

"In fine, the rifle now has bullets in it," Taylor said. "As all of you will no doubt have noticed, it is a breechloader." The other aides nodded. Lee kept his own counsel.

With a rasping sound followed by a sharp, metallic click, Rhoodie drew back a shiny steel lever on the right side of the rifle. "The first round from each magazine must be chambered manually," he said.

"What about the others?" Venable whispered to Taylor.

"You'll see," Taylor whispered back.

Rhoodie reached into the haversack again. This time he drew out some folded papers. He unfolded one of them. It proved to be a target, a cutout roughly approximating the shape of a man's head and body. He turned to Lee's aides. "Will you gentlemen please put these up at different ranges out to, say, four or five hundred yards?"

"With pleasure," Taylor said promptly. "I've seen how fast your rifle can shoot; I'd like to learn how accurate it is." He took some of the targets; Rhoodie handed the rest to the other aides. They stuck low-hanging branches through some, leaned others against bushes, both in the upright position and sideways.

"Shall I have them straighten those, sir?" Lee asked, pointing. "They will make your shooting more difficult."

"Never mind," Rhoodie answered. "Soldiers don't always stand up, either." Lee nodded. The stranger did not lack for confidence.

When the aides were through, a ragged column of thirty targets straggled southeast toward Orange Court House a couple of miles off. The knot of tents that was Lee's headquarters lay on a steep hillside, well away from encamped troops or any other human habitations. The young men laughed and joked as they came back to Rhoodie and Lee. "There's General McClellan!" Charles Marshall said, stabbing a thumb in the direction of the nearest target. "Give him what he deserves!"

The others took up the cry: "There's General Burnside!" "General Hooker!" "General Meade!" "Hancock!" "Warren!" "Stoneman!" "Howard!" "There's Honest Abe! Give *him* his deserts, by God!"

Lee turned to Rhoodie. "At your convenience, sir." The aides fell silent at once.

"One of your men might want to look at a watch," Rhoodie said.

"I will, sir." Charles Venable drew one from his waistcoat pocket. "Shall I give you a mark at which to begin?" Rhoodie nodded. Venable held the watch close to his face so he could see the second hand crawling around its tiny separate dial. "Now!"

The rifle leaped to the big stranger's shoulder. He squeezed the trigger. *Craack!* A brass cartridge case flipped up into the air. It glittered in the sun as it fell. *Craack!* Another cartridge case. *Craack!* Another. This was the same sort of quick firing as that which had interrupted Lee's letter to President Davis.

Rhoodie paused once for a moment. "Adjusting the sights," he explained. He was shooting again as soon as the last word left his mouth. Finally the rifle clicked harmlessly instead of blasting out another round.

Charles Venable looked up. "Thirty aimed shots. Thirty-two seconds. Most impressive." He looked from the rifle to Rhoodie, back again. "Thirty shots," he repeated, half to himself. "Where is the smoke from thirty shots?"

"By God!" Walter Taylor sounded astonished, both at the lack of smoke and at himself. "Why didn't I notice that before?"

Lee had also failed to notice it. Thirty closely spaced shots should have left this Andries Rhoodie in the middle of a young fogbank. Instead, only a few hazy wisps of smoke floated from the breech and muzzle of his rifle. "How do you achieve this, sir?" he asked.

"The charge in my cartridges is not your ordinary black powder," Rhoodie said, which told Lee nothing not already obvious. The big man went on, "If your officers will bring in the targets, we can see how I did."

Taylor, Venable, and Marshall went out to retrieve the paper men. They laid them on the ground, walked along the row looking for bullet holes. Lee walked with them, quiet and thoughtful. When he had examined all the targets, he turned back to Rhoodie. "Twenty-eight out of thirty, I make it to be," he said. "This appears to be a fine weapon, sir, and without a doubt very fine shooting."

"Thirty-two seconds," Venable said. He whistled softly.

"May I show you one thing more?" Rhoodie said. Without waiting for a reply, he loosened the catch that held the magazine in place below the rifle, stuck the curved metal container into a coat pocket. Then he pulled another one out of his haversack and clicked it into position. The operation took only a moment to complete.

"Another thirty shots?" Lee asked.

"Another thirty shots," Rhoodie agreed. He drew back the shiny handle with the *snick* Lee had heard before. "Now I am ready to fire again. But what if the Americans—"

"*We* are Americans, sir," Lee broke in.

"Sorry. The Yankees, I mean. What if the Yankees are too close for aimed fire?" Below the handle was a small metal lever. Rhoodie clicked it down so that, instead of being parallel to the handle's track, its front end pointed more nearly toward the ground. He turned away from Lee and his staff officers. "This is what."

The rifle roared. Flame spurted from its muzzle. Cartridges flew out of it in a glittering stream. The silence that followed the shooting came hard and abrupt as a blow. Into it, Lee asked, "Major Venable, did you time that?"

"Uh, no, sir," Venable said. "I'm sorry, sir."

"Never mind. It was quite rapid enough."

Rhoodie said, "Except at close range or into big crowds, full automatic fire isn't nearly as effective or accurate as single shots. The weapon pulls up and to the right."

"Full automatic fire." Lee tasted the words. "How does this repeater operate, if I may ask, sir? I have seen, for example, the Spencer repeating carbines the enemy cavalrymen employ, with a lever action to advance each successive bullet. But you worked no lever, save to chamber your first round. The rifle simply fired, again and again."

"When the charge in a round explodes, it makes a gas that rapidly expands and pushes the bullet out of the muzzle. Do you follow me?"

"Certainly, sir. If I may remind you, I was an engineer." Lee felt irked at being asked so elementary a question.

"That's right. So you were." Rhoodie spoke as if reminding himself. He went on, "My weapon taps some of the gas and uses it to move the bolt back so the magazine spring can lift another round into the chamber. Then the cycle repeats itself until the magazine has no more ammunition left in it."

"Most ingenious." Lee plucked at his beard, not wanting to go on. Southern inventors had come up with a great many clever ideas during the war, only to have them prove stillborn because of the Confederacy's feeble manufacturing capacity. Nevertheless, the question had to be asked: "With how many of these repeaters could you supply me?"

Rhoodie smiled broadly. "How many would you like?"

"I would *like* as many as you can furnish," Lee said. "The use to which I might put them, however, would depend on the number available. If you can provide me with, say, a hundred, I might furnish them to horse artillery batteries, so they might protect themselves against attacks by the enemy infantry. If, on the other hand, you are fortunate enough to possess five hundred or so—and the requisite ammunition—I would consider outfitting a cavalry regiment with them. It would be pleasant to have our horsemen able to match the firepower those people are able to bring to bear, rather than opposing them with pistols and shotguns."

Andries Rhoodie's smile grew wider still, yet it was not the smile of someone sharing something pleasant with friends. Lee was reminded instead of the professional grimace of a stage magician about to produce two doves from inside his hat. Rhoodie said, "And suppose, General Lee, suppose I am able to get you a hundred thousand of these rifles, with their ammunition? How would you—how would the Confederacy—use them?"

"A hundred thousand?" Lee kept his voice low and steady, but only with a distinct effort. Rather than pulling two doves out of his hat, the big stranger had turned loose a whole flock. "Sir, that is not a piker's offer."

"Nor a likely one, if you will forgive my saying so," Charles Marshall said. "That is nearly as many weapons as we have been able to realize from all of Europe in three years of war. I suppose you will deliver the first shipment by the next northbound train?" Irony flavored every word.

Rhoodie took no notice of it. "Close enough," he said coolly. "My comrades and I have spent some time getting ready for this day. General Lee, you will be sending General Hoke's brigade down to North Carolina over the next couple of nights—am I right?"

"Yes, that is so," Lee said without much thought. Then all at once he swung the full weight of his attention to Rhoodie. "But how do you know of it, sir? I wrote those orders just today, and was in the process of informing President Davis of them when interrupted by you and your repeater. So how can you have learned of my plans for General Hoke's movements?"

"My comrades and I are well informed in any area we choose," Rhoodie answered. He was easy, even amused. Lee abstractly admired that; he knew his own presence overawed most men. The stranger went on, "We do not aim to harm you or your army or the Confederacy in any way, General. Please believe me when I say that. No less than you, we aim to see the South free and independent."

"That all sounds very fine, but you did not answer the general's question," Marshall said. He ran a hand through his slick, dark blond hair as he took a step toward Rhoodie. "How did you learn of General Hoke's movements?"

"I knew. That's enough." The stranger did not back down. "If you order the northbound train's engineer to stop at Rivington, General Lee, we'll put aboard the first shipment of rifles and ammunition. That would be, hmm, about twenty-five hundred weapons, with several magazines' worth of rounds for each. We can supply as many again the night after that, until your army is fully equipped with new pieces."

"A hundred thousand rifles would oversupply the Army of Northern Virginia," Lee said.

"The Confederacy has more armies than yours. Don't you think General Johnston will be able to use some when General Sherman brings the whole Military Division of the Mississippi down against him come spring?"

"General Grant commands the Military Division of the Mississippi," Walter Taylor said: "all the Federal troops between the Alleghenies and the river."

"Oh, yes, that's right, so he does, for now. My mistake," Rhoodie said. He turned back to Lee, this time with a hunter's intent expression on his face. "And don't you think, General, that Nathan Bedford Forrest's troopers would enjoy being able to outshoot the Federals as well as outride and outfight them?"

"What I think, sir, is that you are building mighty castles in the air on the strength of a single rifle," Lee answered. He did not care for the way Andries Rhoodie looked at him, did not care for the arrogant way the man spoke, did not care for anything about him . . . except for his rifle. If one Southern man could deliver the fire of five or ten Unionists, the odds against which Confederate armies had to fight in every engagement might all at once be set at naught.

Rhoodie still studied him. Lee felt his cheeks go hot, even on this icy winter's day, for he knew the stranger could see he was tempted. The book of Matthew came into his mind: Again the devil taketh him up into an exceeding high mountain, and sheweth him all the kingdoms of the world, and the glory of them; And saith unto him, All these things will I give thee, if thou wilt fall down and worship me.

But Rhoodie did not ask for worship, and he was no devil, only a big, tough man, who was not too tough to wear a cap with flaps to keep his ears warm. For all that Lee had not taken to him, he spoke like a reasonable man, and now said, reasonably, "General, I will stay here and guarantee with my person that what I say is true. Give the order for the train to stop and pick up the rifles and ammunition. If they do not come as I say they will, why, you can do whatever you please with me. Where is your risk in that?"

Lee searched for one. Try as he would, he could not find it. To no one in particular, Charles Venable said, "The fellow doesn't lack for brass, that's certain."

"No, he doesn't," Lee agreed. The major's remark helped decide him. "Very well, Mr. Rhoodie, I will give that order, and we shall see what arrives on that northbound train. If you make good on your claims, the first rifles will go to General Stuart's cavalry. After that, well, the divisions of General Anderson and Henry Heth are quartered closest to us here. Those men can have first call on the rifles among the infantry."

"If he makes good," Charles Marshall said heavily. "What if he fails?"

"What would you recommend, Major?" Lee asked, genuinely curious.

"A good horsewhipping, to teach him to brag no more."

"How say you to that, Mr. Rhoodie?" Lee inquired.

"I'll take the chance," the stranger answered. Despite himself, Lee was impressed—whether the fellow could do as he said remained to be seen, but he thought he could. Rhoodie went on, "With your permission, General, some of my comrades will ride north with the rifles. You'll need instructors to teach your men to use them properly."

"They may come," Lee said. Afterwards, he thought that moment was the one when he first truly began to believe Andries Rhoodie, began to believe a trainload of fancy repeaters and ammunition could arrive from North Carolina. Rhoodie was just too sure of himself to doubt.

Walter Taylor asked, "Mr. Rhoodie, what do you call this rifle of yours. Is it a Rhoodie, too? Most inventors name their products for themselves, do they not?"

"No, it's not a Rhoodie." The big stranger unslung the rifle, held it in both hands as gently as if it were a baby. "Give it its proper name, Major. It's an AK-47."

Lee returned to his tent to finish the delayed letter to President Davis, then went back outside to see how his staff officers were dealing with Andries Rhoodie. Rhoodie, for his part, seemed perfectly ready to wait to be proved right. Either from that commodious haversack of his or from the pack behind his horse's saddle, he had taken out and erected a neat little one-man tent and was now building a fire in front of it.

Majors Taylor, Venable, and Marshall stood around watching him. Each of them kept a hand close to his side arm. It occurred to Lee, though, that with such a quick-firing repeater, Rhoodie might take advantage of a second's inattention to take out all three men before they could shoot back.

The notion was unsettling. But the extraordinary repeater was inside the tent at the moment, and the big stranger showed not the slightest sign of hostility. He got his fire going on the first match, and proceeded to warm his hands over it. Lee smiled a little. Rhoodie did not have the air of a man about to attack everyone around him.

He ducked into the tent, but emerged with nothing more lethal than a pot and a folding metal stand. He dipped up some water from a little brook that ran eventually into the Rapidan, then returned to his fire and put the pot over it to boil.

Lee's servant came up. "Supper be ready soon, Marse Robert."

"Thank you, Perry. What do we have tonight?"

"Possum soup, all nice and thick with peanuts," the black man answered.

"That sounds very fine." Lee walked over to Rhoodie. "Would you care to share supper with me, sir? Perry has not much to work with here, but one would never know it by the meals he turns out."

Rhoodie's eyes flicked toward Perry. "Your slave?"

"He's free," Lee answered.

Rhoodie shrugged. Lee could see he did not approve. The stranger started to say something, then evidently thought better of it, which was just as well. When he did speak, it was about supper: "Will you let me add to the meal? I know you're on short rations here."

"I wouldn't want to deprive you. Times are hard everywhere."

"It's no trouble. I have plenty." Rhoodie peered into the pot. "Ah, good; it's boiling." He set it on the ground. "Excuse me." He went back into the tent. When he came out, he was holding a couple of packages whose sides and bottoms reflected the firelight metallically. He peeled a lid off each of them. The insides of the lids looked metallic, too. He set down the packages, poured hot water into each of them. Instantly, savory steam rose.

Lee watched—and sniffed—with interest. "Is that desiccated stew you have there? The Federals use desiccated vegetables, but I did not know anyone was preparing whole meals that way."

"Desiccated stew it is, General." The tall stranger's voice was oddly constrained, as if he'd expected Lee to be more surprised. He passed him one of the packages and a spoon. "Before you eat, stir it about a little."

Lee stirred, then tasted. His eyebrows rose. "This is excellent. Were they to taste it, the wits in the army wouldn't joke so about 'desecrated' vegetables." He ate another couple of spoonfuls. "Very good indeed. Now I find myself embarrassed at having nothing better than possum soup to offer in exchange."

"Don't fret about it, General," Rhoodie said. He held out his metal packet as a bowl when Perry came by a couple of minutes later with the kettle. Perry ladled the container full. He smiled. "You have nothing to be embarrassed about. Your black is a fine cook."

"He does seem to work miracles, doesn't he? He has to, these days, I fear." Lee finished the last of his stew. Even desiccated, it had more and finer ingredients than he was used to; he could still feel their rich savor in his mouth. He said, "Mr. Rhoodie, you've spoken glibly of all the rifles you can furnish us. Can you also supply desiccated rations of this sort, enough to hold hunger at bay in this army until spring?"

"Our, ah, firm, is chiefly concerned with weapons. As far as rations go, I will have to inquire before I tell you how many we can bring in."

"I wish you would," Lee said. "A soldier who cannot march and fight is as much a loss to his country as one without a rifle."

"I'll do what I can," Rhoodie said. "I don't know how much that will be. We're ready to move with the rifles now. For food, we would have to begin to make special arrangements, and they might take some time."

"You know your own affairs best, I'm sure. I merely say that, if practicable, rations would be of material benefit to us." Lee got to his feet. So did the big stranger. He started over to the brook with his pot. Lee said, "Surely you aren't still hungry, sir."

"I was going to boil water for coffee. Would you like some?"

"Real coffee?" Lee asked. Rhoodie nodded. With a rueful smile, Lee said, "I almost think real coffee might be too potent for me, after so long drinking chicory and scorched grain masquerading under the name. Still, I will gladly hazard the experiment, provided you have enough for my staff as well. I would not see them deprived of what I enjoy."

"They're welcome," Rhoodie said. "They need their own mugs, though."

"By all means," Lee called his aides, gave them the good news. They exclaimed in delight and hurried back to their tents. Lee went off to fetch his own mug.

By the time everyone converged, mug in hand, on Rhoodie's shelter, he had his pot back over the fire. With his free hand, he passed each Confederate officer a small, flat packet. Rhoodie said, "Tear it open and pour it into the bottom of your cup."

FOLGER'S INSTANT COFFEE, Lee read on the packet. Below that, in much smaller print, was something he could not make out. He put on his glasses. The words came clear: MADE IN U.S.A. He returned the glasses to his pocket, thinking he should have been able to guess that without reading it.

As Rhoodie had directed, he poured the contents of the packet into his cup. The stuff did not look like ground coffee. "Is this another of your desiccations?" he asked.

"You might say so, yes, General. Now if you'll hold out your cup—" Rhoodie filled it to the brim with hot water. All at once, it smelled like coffee. "Stir it about to dissolve it all," Rhoodie said as he filled the aides' mugs in turn.

Lee raised the cup to his lips. It was not the best coffee he'd ever had. But coffee it unmistakably was. He took a long, slow sip, closed his eyes with pleasure. "That is most welcome," he said. One after another, the staff officers echoed him.

"I'm glad you enjoy it," Rhoodie said.

Charles Venable had been examining his packet, too. "Instant coffee," he said musingly. "An apt description, though not one I've heard before. Is this little envelope made of tinfoil, Mr. Rhoodie?"

"I think so," the big stranger answered after a slight hesitation, which Lee believed he recognized: it sounded like the pause of a man who was not telling everything he knew. Andries Rhoodie seemed to know a fair number of things he wasn't telling. The things he had already spoken of and shown were quite remarkable enough. Lee wondered what secrets he still kept.

Walter Taylor pointed to Rhoodie's coffee mug. "What is that emblem your cup bears, sir, if I may ask? At first, seeing the red background and the white, I took it for a Confederate symbol, but now I see it is not."

Rhoodie held the mug close to the fire to give Taylor a better view of it. Lee looked, too. Inside a white circle on the red background was a spiky, black emblem that reminded him of a caltrop:

Under the emblem stood three letters: AWB. Rhoodie said, "It is the sign of my organization." He was good at appearing to answer while actually saying little.

Lee asked, "What do the initials signify?"

"Our motto," Rhoodie replied with a smile: "America Will Break."

Taylor raised his mug in salute. "I'll drink to that, by God!" The other aides followed suit. So did Lee. He had stayed in the Federal army as long as he could, but when Virginia left the Union, he went with his state. It counted for more with him than did the idea of the United States.

"Another cup, gentlemen?" Rhoodie asked. "I have more coffee."

The staff officers said yes in a chorus. Coffee won them over where even Rhoodie's repeater had left suspicion in its wake. Lee declined: "After so long without, a second cup would surely leave me wakeful. At my age, I find I must be careful of my sleep, for I need it more but have more trouble winning it."

Nodding to Rhoodie, he turned to go. His aides saluted. He returned the courtesy and walked slowly back to his tent. He took off his boots and jacket, lay down on the cot, and pulled several blankets over himself. Even with them, the night would be cold. Most of his men had but a single cover, many had none. The surgeons would see frostbite and catarrh come morning sick call. That happened every day.

The coffee did not keep him from falling asleep. It woke him a couple of hours later, though. He stood up to use the chamber pot. The ground chilled his toes through his socks.

Before he went back to bed, he glanced out through the tent flap. Andries Rhoodie had kept his fire large and bright. He was sitting in front of it in a folding chair of gaudy canvas webbing and wood. He did not notice Lee, being intent on the book in his lap.

"What are you reading, sir, at this late hour?" Lee called softly.

Rhoodie looked up and peered into the night. With his eyes full of firelight, he needed a few seconds to catch sight of Lee. When he did, he stuck a thumb in the book to keep his place, then shut it and held it up. A golden cross gleamed on the black cover.

"Ah," Lee said, all at once feeling easier about Rhoodie than he had since the moment he'd met him. "You could find no better companion, by day or night. May I ask which verses you have chosen?"

"The story of Gideon," the big stranger answered. "I read it often. It seems to fit."

"It does indeed," Lee said. "It does indeed. Good night, sir. I hope you sleep well when you do seek your bedroll."

"Thank you, General. A good night to you, too."

Lee went back to bed. As he'd told Rhoodie, he often had trouble sleeping. Not tonight, though—he dropped off as smoothly and easily as a child. Just before he stopped thinking altogether, he wondered why. Maybe it was hope, something that had been in short supply since Gettysburg. He slept.

The next couple of days went by in something close to a state of anticlimax. General Samuel Jones of the Department of Western Virginia sent a letter promising cattle and beef for the Army of Northern Virginia. Lee wrote effusive thanks, but the promised animals were slower arriving than Jones's letter had been. As he'd feared, he had to reduce the army's rations.

Just after he'd finished drafting the general order for the melancholy necessity, Charles Venable poked his head into the tent. "Telegram for you, sir." He paused for dramatic effect. "It's from Rivington."

"Read it to me at once, Major," Lee said.

"Yes, sir." Venable unfolded the flimsy sheet of paper. "Stopped at Rivington northbound per your orders of January 20. Many crates of two different shapes taken on board. Townsfolk helpful and well organized. After departing, opened two crates at random, one of each type. Contents, metal cartridges and carbines of curious manufacture. A dozen men also boarded. Asbury Finch, First Lieutenant, C.S.A."

"Well, well," Lee said, and then again, "Well, well. Our mysterious Mr. Rhoodie does indeed have the rifles he promised, or some of them, at any rate. Despite his certainty, I wondered, I truly did."

"I did more than wonder, sir," Venable answered. "I doubted, and doubted strongly. But as you say, he seems to have kept the first part of his promise."

"So he does. When General Stuart sees what these carbines can do, he will want no others. The repeaters, which ever more of the Federal cavalry employ, have hurt his troopers badly. Now he will be able to reply on equal—or better than equal—terms. And if Mr. Rhoodie was not spinning a tale all out of moonshine, there will be rifles for our infantry as well."

"I wonder how much the Bureau of Ordnance is paying for these—what did he call them?"

"AK-47s," Lee supplied. "Whatever the price, it may well mark the difference between our liberty and suppression. It would be difficult to set that price too high."

"Yes, sir." Venable hesitated, then went on, "May I ask, sir, what you think of Mr. Rhoodie?"

"Well, I certainly think a good deal better of him now that I know for a fact he is not a solitary charlatan with a solitary, if marvelous, carbine," Lee said at once. Then he too paused. "But that wasn't the whole of what you asked, was it, Major?"

"No, sir." Normally a fluent speaker, Venable seemed to be struggling to put what he thought into words: "I do believe he is the most *peculiar* man I've ever met. His carbine, his gear, even the food he eats and the coffee he drinks . . . I've not seen nor heard of their like anywhere."

"Nor have I, and with their uniform excellence and convenience, I should hope I would have, the better to wage this war," Lee said. "There is also more to it than that. The man knows more than he lets on. How could he have learned of my orders sending General Hoke south? That still perplexes me, and worries me no small amount as well. Had he been exposed as a fraud, I would have had some hard questions to ask him about it, and asked them in a hard way at need. As is—" Lee shrugged. "He is manifestly a good Southern man. How long do you suppose we could have lasted, Major, had he chosen to go north and sell his rifles to the enemy?"

Venable made a sour face, as if disliking the taste of that idea. "Not long, sir."

"I quite agree. They outweigh us enough as is. But he chose our cause instead, so for the time being the hard questions can wait. And he is a pious man. No one who was not would read his Testament late at night where nobody could be expected to see him."

"Every word you say is true, sir," Venable said. "And yet—I don't know—everything Rhoodie has seems too good to be true somehow."

"The Union has had the advantage in material goods all through the war, Major. Are you saying we are not entitled to our share, or that, if fortune should for once choose to favor us, we ought not to take advantage of it?"

"Put that way, no, of course not, General Lee."

"Good," Lee said. "For I intend to wring every drop of advantage from it that I may."

A plume of woodsmoke announced a train heading up the Orange and Alexandria Railroad to the little town of Orange Court House. Lee pointed to it with the eagerness of a boy who spies his Christmas present being fetched in. "If I have calculated rightly, gentlemen, that will be the train from Rivington. Shall we ride to meet it, and see this first consignment of Mr. Rhoodie's rifles?"

His aides hurried off to get their horses. Andries Rhoodie went with them. Perry brought up Traveller. Lee swung onto the gray. The staff officers and Rhoodie soon joined them. They rode down from the hills to Orange Court House together. Lee and his aides were all fine horsemen. He soon saw Rhoodie was not, though he managed well enough.

Old civilian men, walking or riding along the streets of Orange Court House, lifted their hats in tribute to Lee as he passed. He gravely returned their greetings. Few young male civilians were to be seen—in the town or anywhere else in the Confederacy. There were a fair number of soldiers, seeing what the shops had to offer: not much, probably. They saluted Lee and his staff officers. Some pointed at Andries Rhoodie: his size, his strange clothes, and the fact that he, a stranger, rode with Lee drew their notice to him.

The train station was not far from the courthouse that gave the hamlet half its name. For that matter, nothing in Orange Court House was far from anything else. The train had already arrived by the time Lee and his companions got to the station. Under the watchful eye of the crew, slaves loaded cut logs into the tender for the next trip south.

Other blacks were starting to unload the freight cars. Some of the men who supervised them wore the Confederate uniform; others were dressed like Andries Rhoodies, in caps and mottled jackets and trousers. Even their ankle boots were the same as his. Lee rubbed his chin thoughtfully. What one man wore was his own business. When a dozen men—a baker's dozen, counting Rhoodie himself—wore similar outfits, that suggested the clothes were a uniform of sorts. Indeed, Rhoodie's colleagues looked more uniform than the Southern soldiers with them, whose pants, coats, and hats were of several different colors and cut in a variety of ways.

Behind Lee, Walter Taylor turned to Rhoodie and remarked, "Your friends are all good-sized men, sir." He was right. The smallest of the men in spotted clothes had to be five feet ten. Most of them were six-footers; two or three were as big as Rhoodie. They all looked well fed, too, in spite of the war and the hard winter. The Confederate soldiers came to attention when Lee and his aides rode up. The men from Rivington did not. A few of them greeted Rhoodie with a nod or a wave. Most just kept calling orders to the slaves, who were taking crates off the train.

"Your fellows here have the same interesting accent as you yourself," Charles Venable observed.

"We are countrymen," Rhoodie said blandly. Lee smiled at the major's polite probe and at Rhoodie's equally polite but uninformative reply. Rhoodie had given a lot of polite but uninformative replies, the last few days. Lee told himself that a trainload—maybe a great many trainloads— of repeaters and cartridges gave him the right to hold his tongue.

Lee dismounted. His aides and Rhoodie followed him to the ground; Venable hitched Traveller to the rail. A soldier with two bars on either side of his collar walked up to them. His face, Lee thought, was too thin for the whiskers he'd chosen, which were like those of the Federal general Burnside. He saluted. "Asbury Finch, sir, 21st Georgia."

"Yes, Lieutenant. I received your telegram."

"Yes, sir." Finch sent a glance to Andries Rhoodie, who had gone over to greet his comrades. "So you've already met one of these all-over-spots fellows, have you, sir? They've purely done wonders for Rivington, that they have."

"I commanded in North Carolina a couple of years ago, Lieutenant, but I must confess I do not remember the town," Lee said.

"A couple years ago, General Lee, sir, wasn't nothin' worth remembering, just a town barely big enough for the train to bother stoppin' at it. But it's growin' to beat the band now, thanks to these folks. A big bunch of 'em done settled there, bought a raft o' niggers, and run up new houses and warehouses and I don't know what all. And all in the last three, four months, too; I heard that from one of the folks who's lived there all his life while we were takin' on these crates. They pay gold for everything, too, he says."

"No wonder they're welcome, then," Lee said. Confederate paper money had weakened to the point where a pair of shoes cost a private soldier three or four months' wages. That was one reason so many men in the Army of

Northern Virginia went barefoot even in winter. Another was that there were not enough shoes to be had at any price.

"Pity they couldn't have come a year ago," Walter Taylor said. "Think what we might have done with those rifles at Chancellorsville, or up in Pennsylvania."

"I have had that thought myself a fair number of times the last few days, Major," Lee said. "What's past is past, though, and cannot be changed."

"The guns, they're as fine as all that, sir?" Finch asked.

"They are indeed, Lieutenant," Taylor said. "With them, I feel we truly may hold in our hands the goose that lays the golden eggs."

"Or it holds us," Charles Marshall said, his voice sour.

Lee looked at him sharply. Marshall had not taken to Andries Rhoodie, not at all. But after a moment's thought, Lee decided he had a point. Trainloads of repeating carbines might save the Confederacy. But if Rhoodie and his friends were the only source for them, they held a hand to the throat of the South. They were not squeezing now—far from it. If, however, they chose to . . .

"Major Marshall," Lee said.

"Sir?"

"Please draft a letter to Colonel Gorgas in Richmond. I would like his opinion on the practicability of our manufacturing copies of these weapons, as we do now with the Springfield and Mississippi rifles. When the first shipment of rifles reaches our headquarters, you might also send one and a stock of cartridges to Colonel G. W. Rains in Georgia, who is, I think, the man most expert in the Bureau of Ordnance on matters pertaining to powder. Perhaps he can enlighten us on how these rounds produce so little smoke."

"I will attend to it, sir," Marshall said. His spectacles' wire frames could not hide a raised eyebrow. "Your trust in Mr. Rhoodie is not perfect, then?"

"The only perfect trust is in God," Lee answered. Marshall smiled and nodded. A relative of the great chief justice, he had been a lawyer till the war began, which gave him another reason besides religion to place perfect trust in no human institution.

Just then, Rhoodie came back to Lee, his staff officers, and Lieutenant Finch. Several of his friends were right behind him. He said, "General, let me introduce some of my comrades. Here are Konrad de Buys, Wilhelm Gebhard, Benny Lang, and Ernie Graaf."

"Gentlemen," Lee said, extending his hand.

They came up one by one to shake it. "An honor to meet the great

General Lee," Ernie Graff said. He was about Lee's height, and wore a neat, sandy chin-beard, which only partially hid a scar that ran up to the angle of his jaw. As Major Venable had noted, he and the rest of the men in mottled clothes spoke with the same not-quite-British accent as Rhoodie, and the same harsh undertone—if anything, that was stronger in his voice than in Rhoodie's.

"You needn't say my name as if you'd found it in some history book, sir," Lee protested mildly. All of Rhoodie's comrades smiled or laughed at that, rather more than the small joke deserved. Even so, Lee was pleased to put them at their ease.

"General Stuart is the man I want to meet," said the one who had been introduced as Konrad de Buys. Most of the strangers had a businesslike look to them, but de Buys's tawny eyes held a gleam that reminded Lee of a cougar. This man fought for the joy of it.

Then Lee remembered how Rhoodie rode. De Buys would have to do better than that to satisfy Jeb Stuart. "You are a horseman, sir?" Lee asked. De Buys nodded in a way that left no doubt. Lee said, "Then I am certain General Stuart will be pleased to make your acquaintance as well. Colonel Mosby also, perhaps, with his partisan command." By the way de Buys grinned, Lee knew he had judged his man aright.

"General Stuart is by—Fredericksburg?" Wilhelm Gebhard asked.

He turned the soft g of general hard, as a German might have. Behind Lee, one of his aides whispered "Dutchmen" to another. Lee guessed it was Marshall; he seemed most dubious of Rhoodie, and the bulk of Germans in America—including a good many who lived in the Confederacy— were Unionists.

But these men were far too open—and far too strange—to be spies, and in any case, General Meade knew where the Army of Northern Virginia's cavalry was passing the winter. "Yes, around Fredericksburg," Lee answered. He would sooner have had Stuart's troopers closer to hand, but getting horses through the winter was harder and required more land than men did.

Gebhard turned to Rhoodie, asked him something in a language that sounded close to English but was not. Rhoodie replied in the same tongue. *Dutchmen they are*, Lee thought. In English, Rhoodie said, "He wants to know whether he and de Buys should arrange to go to Fredericksburg to show off our guns, or whether you will call General Stuart here."

Lee thought about that. At last he said, "With the cavalry spread out on the countryside as it is, the more efficient course would appear to be convening General Stuart and his divisional and brigade commanders here at Orange Court House so they can judge your repeaters for themselves."

"Fine," Rhoodie said. "When we shoot, though, better we go back up to your headquarters, to keep word of what these guns can do from reaching the enemy."

"A sensible plan," Lee agreed.

Talking to himself as much as to Lee, Rhoodie went on, "Since this will be the center from which we give out guns to your army, we ought to rent quarters here, and warehouse space, too. We have a lot of work to do before spring, getting your men ready."

"The officers of the Army of Northern Virginia should prove of some assistance to you," Lee said drily.

Irony bounced from Andries Rhoodie like solid shot off an ironclad's armored hull. He looked Lee full in the face and said, "Some will help us, General; I don't doubt it. But if I were on the other side of the Rapidan and dealing with the Federals, say with General Burnside or General Sigel, they might not even have given me a hearing. They have their Springfields, after all, and once a routineer settles in with something, it's hard to boot him loose from it."

"You will be treating with better men in this army than the two you named," Lee said. "I should certainly hope so, at any rate."

"You vouch for every brigadier, every colonel?" Rhoodie persisted. "My comrades and I haven't enough manpower to do more than show the basics of how to shoot and clean the AK-47, regiment by regiment. Getting your soldiers to use it afterwards will be up to those commanders. Some of them will mistrust anything new and different."

"I see what you are saying, sir," Lee admitted. There was some truth to it, too. The Confederate States themselves had banded together in the hope of preserving their old way of life against the growing numbers and growing factories of the North. But here— "You get my men these repeaters, Mr. Rhoodie, and I shall undertake to see they are used."

"That's what I wanted to hear, General Lee."

"You have heard it."

Singing as they worked, slaves carried long crates with rifles in them and square crates of ammunition out of the freight cars and stacked them beside the railroad tracks. The stacks grew higher and higher and higher.

★ II ★

"What else, Alsie?" First Sergeant Nate Caudell asked patiently.

Private Alsie Hopkins furrowed his brow, as well as a man in his early twenties could. "Tell 'em I feel good," he said at last. "Tell 'em the arm where I got shot at Gettysburg don't hurt no more, and the diarrhea ain't troublin' me, neither."

Caudell's pen scratched across the page. Actually, it wasn't a proper page, but the back of a piece of old wallpaper. He wrote around a chunk of paste that still clung to it. He was sure he wrote more letters than anyone else in Company D—maybe more than anyone else in the whole 47th North Carolina. That went with being a schoolteacher in a unit full of farmers, many of whom—like Alsie Hopkins—could neither read nor write for themselves.

"What else, Alsie?" he asked again.

Hopkins thought some more. "Tell 'em we had us a rip-roarin' snowball fight the other day, and one feller, he got two teeth knocked out of his head when he got hit with a snowball with a rock in the middle of it. We all laughed and laughed."

"Except the man who got hit," Caudell said drily.

"No, him too."

Caudell thought that likely to amuse Hopkins's family, so he started to write it down. Just then, though, a bugle call came through the open shutters of his cabin's single window. He put down his pen. "Have to finish this another time, Alsie. That's assembly for officers, sergeants, and corporals."

"Everybody but us privates," Hopkins said, happy at the prospect of his superiors working when he didn't have to. "Can I leave this paper here, First Sergeant, and we get it done maybe some time later on?"

"I suppose so," Caudell said resignedly. His battered felt slouch hat lay beside him on the bed. He put it on, got to his feet. "I've got to go now, though."

He and Hopkins ducked out through the cabin's low door. With nothing better to do, the private ambled away. Caudell hurried up the lane that ran through the cabins and lean-tos and tents of the regiment's winter quarters. His cabin, which he shared with the other four sergeants of Company D, lay farthest from the open space at the center of the encampment. Closest to that open space was Captain Lewis's tent; being captain, he had it all to himself. The company banner stood beside it, the words CASTALIA INVINCI-BLES picked out in red silk on a blue ground, pierced by more than one bullet hole.

Men with chevrons or collar badges converged on the parade ground. They did not begin to fill it up; they were perhaps one part in seven of the six-hundred-odd soldiers who regularly drilled there.

Along with all the officers and noncommissioned officers was one private: Ben Whitley of Company A. As usual, the teamster perched on his wagon. With him sat another man, a stranger, whose cap, coat, and trousers looked to be made of nothing but patches, some the color of dirt, some of grass, some of mud. Slung on the stranger's back was a carbine of unfamiliar make.

Excitement ran through Caudell. The cavalry had got itself new rifles the past couple of weeks. So had Major General Anderson's infantry division, whose winter quarters were even closer to Orange Court House than those of Henry Heth's division, of which the 47th North Carolina was a part. If half—if a tithe—of the stories about those rifles were true—

Colonel George Faribault limped around from the far side of the wagon. He moved slowly and with the aid of a stick; he'd been wounded in the foot and in the shoulder at Gettysburg and was just back to the regiment. By his pallor, even standing was not easy for him. He said, "Gentlemen, it is as you may have guessed: our brigade and our division are next to receive the new repeater, the AK-47 they call it. Here"—he pointed to the stranger in the suit of many muddy colors—"is Mr. Benny Lang, who will show you how to operate the rifle, so you can go on and teach your men. Mr. Lang."

Lang jumped lightly down from the wagon. He was about five-ten, dark, and on the skinny side. His clothes bore no rank badges of any sort, but he carried himself like a soldier. "I usually get two questions at a time like this," he said. "The first one is, why don't you teach everyone yourself? Sorry, but we haven't the manpower. Today, my friends and I are working with General Kirkland's brigade: that's you people, the 11th North Carolina, the 26th North Carolina, the 44th North Carolina, and the 52d North Carolina. Tomorrow we'll be with General Cooke's brigade, and so on. You'll manage. You have to be more than stupid to screw up an AK-47. You have to be an idiot, and even then it's not easy."

Listening to him, Caudell found himself frowning. Camp rumor said these fellows in the funny clothes were not merely from North Carolina but from his own home county, Nash. Lang didn't sound like a Carolina man, though, or like any kind of Southerner. He didn't sound like a Yankee, either; in the past two years, Caudell had heard plenty of Yankee accents. The first sergeant kept listening:

"The other question I hear is, why bother trying anything new when we're happy with our regular rifles? I'd sooner show you why than tell you. Who's your best chap with Springfield or Enfield or whatever you use?"

All eyes swung to the regimental ordnance sergeant. He was a polite, soft-spoken man; he looked around to see if anyone else would volunteer. When no one did, he took a step forward out of line. "Reckon I am, sir. George Hines."

"Very good," Lang said. "Would you be so kind as to fetch your weapon and ammunition for it? And while he's doing that, Private Whitley, why don't you move the wagon so we don't frighten the horses?"

"Sure will." Whitley drove the team perhaps fifty feet, then jumped down and walked back over to watch what was going on.

Ordnance Sergeant Hines returned a minute or so later, rifle musket on his shoulder. He carried the piece like a part of him, as befit any man who wore a star in the angle of his sergeant's stripes. Benny Lang pointed to a tall bank of earth that faced away from the soldiers' huts. "Is that what you use for target practice?"

"Yes, sir, it is," Hines answered.

Lang trotted over, pinned a circular paper target to the bank. He trotted back to the group, then said, "Ordnance Sergeant Hines, why don't you put a couple of bullets in that circle for us, fast as you can load and fire?"

"I'll do that," Hines said, while the men who stood between him and the target moved hastily out of the way.

Watching the ordnance sergeant handle his rifle, Nate Caudell thought, was like being back on the target range at Camp Mangum outside of Raleigh, hearing the command, "Load in nine times: load!" Hines did everything perfectly, smoothly, just as the manual said he should. To load, he held the rifle upright between his feet, with the muzzle in his left hand and with his right already going to the cartridge box he wore at his belt.

Caudell imagined the invisible drillmaster barking, "Handle cartridge!" Hines brought the paper cartridge from the box to his mouth, bit off the end, poured the powder down the muzzle of his piece, and put the Minié ball in the muzzle. The bluntly pointed bullet was about the size of the last joint of a man's finger, with three grooves around its hollow base which expanded to fill the grooves on the inside of the rifle barrel.

At the remembered command of "Draw rammer!" the long piece of iron emerged from its place under the rifle barrel. Next in the series was "Ram," which the ordnance sergeant did with a couple of sharp strokes before returning the ramrod to its tube. At "Prime," he half-cocked the hammer with his right thumb, then took out a copper percussion cap and put it on the nipple.

The next four steps went in quick sequence. "Shoulder" brought the weapon up. At "Ready" it went down again for a moment, while Hines took the proper stance. Then up it came once more, with his thumb fully cocking the hammer. "Aim" had him peering down the sights, his forefinger set on the trigger. "Fire," and the rifle roared and bucked against his shoulder.

He set the butt end of the piece on the ground, repeated the process without a single changed motion. He fired again. Another cloud of fireworks-smelling smoke spurted from his rifle. The two shots were less than half a minute apart. He scrubbed at the black powder stain on his chin with his sleeve, then turned with quiet pride to face Lang. "Anything else, sir?"

"No, Ordnance Sergeant. You're as good with a rifle musket as any man I've seen. However—" Lang brought up his own rifle, blazed away at the white paper target. The sharp staccato bark, repeated again and again and again, was like nothing Caudell had ever heard. Silence fell again in less time than Hines had needed to fire twice. Lang said, "That was thirty rounds. If I had this weapon and the ordnance sergeant that one, whose chances would you gentlemen like better?"

"Goddam," somebody behind Caudell said softly, stretching the word out into three syllables. It seemed as good an answer as any, and better than most.

Benny Lang drove the point home anyhow: "If *you* had this weapon and the Federals *that* one, whose chances would you gentlemen like?"

For a long moment, no one replied. No one needed to. Privates came dashing onto the parade ground, drawn as if by magnets to learn what sort of rifle had fired like that. Then somebody cut loose with a rebel yell. In an instant, the shrill, hair-raising cry rose from every throat.

Caudell yelled with the rest. Like most of them, he had come back from Pickett's charge. Far too many of their one-time comrades hadn't, not in the face of the barrage the Federals poured down on them. He was all in favor of having the firepower on his side for a change.

Colonel Faribault waved the private soldiers off the drill field. "Your turn will come," he promised. The men withdrew, but reluctantly.

While that was going on, Benny Lang walked over to the wagon, lowered the tailgate, and began taking out repeaters like the one he had reslung. Nate Caudell's palms itched to get hold of one. Lang said, "I have two dozen rifles here. Why don't you men form by companies, two groups to a company, and Private Whitley and I will pass them out so I can show you what you need to know."

A few minutes of milling about followed, as men joined with others from their units. Caudell and his messmates—Sergeants Powell, High, Daniel, and Eure—naturally gravitated together. That left the Invincibles' two corporals who were present for duty grouped with Captain Lewis and his pair of lieutenants. "It's all right," Lewis said. "We're all new recruits at this business."

"Here you go, First Sergeant." Ben Whitley handed Caudell a repeater. He held it in both hands, marveling at how light it was compared to the Springfield that hung from pegs on the wall back in his cabin. He slung it as Lang had done. It seemed to weigh next to nothing on his shoulder. Toting this kind of rifle, a man might march forever before he got sore.

"Let me have a turn with it, Nate," Edwin Powell said. With a twinge of regret, Caudell passed him the carbine. He brought it up to firing position, looked down the barrel. "Fancy kind of sight," he remarked. His grin turned rueful. "Maybe I can nail me a Yankee or two without gettin' hit my own self."

"Goin' up to the firin' line without your 'shoot me' sign'd probably be a good idea, too, Edwin," Dempsey Eure said. The sergeants all laughed. So far as anybody knew, Powell was the only man in the regiment who'd been wounded at three different fights.

Ben Whitley came by again a few minutes later. This time, he gave Caudell a curved, black-painted metal object. Caudell had no idea what it was until he turned it and saw that it held brass cartridges. "Talk about your fancy now, Edwin," he said, handing it on to Powell. "This looks to beat Minié balls all hollow."

"Sure does, if there's enough of these here bullets so as we don't run out halfway through a battle," Powell answered—anybody who'd been shot three times developed a certain concern about such things.

"Does every group have an AK-47 and a banana clip?" Lang asked. He waited to see if anyone would say no. When no one did, he continued: "Turn your weapon upside down. In front of your trigger guard, you'll see a catch. It holds the clip in place." He pointed to it on his own carbine. "Everyone finger that catch. Pass your weapon back and forth. Everyone needs to put hands on it, not just watch me."

When the AK-47 came back to him, Caudell obediently fingered the catch. Lang had the air of a man who'd taught this lesson many times and knew it backwards and forwards. As a teacher himself, Caudell recognized the signs.

The man in the patchwork-looking clothes went on, "Now everyone take turns clicking the clip into place and freeing it. The curved end goes toward the muzzle. Go ahead, try it a few times." Caudell inserted the clip, released the catch, took it away. Lang said, "This is one place where you want to be careful. Warn your other ranks about it, too. If the lips of the magazine are bent, or if you get dirt in there, it won't feed rounds properly. In combat, that could prove embarrassing."

He let out a dry chuckle. The laughs that rose in answer were grim. A rifle that wouldn't shoot hundreds of rounds a minute was less use than one that would shoot two or three.

In the group next to Caudell, his captain stuck up his hand. "Mr. Lang?"

"Yes, Captain, ah—?"

"I'm George Lewis, sir. What do we do if the lips of this—banana clip, you called it?—somehow do get bent? I've been shot once, sir"—he was only recently back to the regiment himself—"and I don't care a damn to be, ah, embarrassed again."

"Don't blame you a bit, Captain. The obvious answer is, switch to a fresh clip. If you haven't but one good one left, you can load cartridges into it one at a time, in two staggered rows, like this. As I said when I fired, the clip holds thirty rounds." He pulled a clip and some loose cartridges from his haversack and demonstrated. "We'll come back to that later. You'll all have a chance to do it. Now, though, let whoever's holding the gun put that magazine in place."

Caudell was holding the AK-47. He carefully worked the banana clip into position, listened for the click that showed it was where it belonged. "Good," Lang said. "Now you're ready to chamber your first round. Here, pull this handle all the way back." Again, he demonstrated. Caudell followed suit. The action worked with a resistant smoothness that was unlike anything he had ever felt before.

"Very good once more," Lang said. "All of you with rifles come forward and form a firing line. Take aim at your target and fire." Caudell pulled the trigger. Nothing happened. No one else's carbine went off, either. The instructor chuckled. "No, they're not defective. Look at the short black lever under the handle you just pulled. See how it's parallel to the muzzle. That little lever is called the change lever. When it's in the top position, it's on safety, and the weapon can't fire. That's how you'll carry it on march, to avoid accidents. Now move it down two positions—make sure it's two, mind—then aim and fire again."

Caudell peered down the sights. They seemed close together; he was used to a longer weapon. He squeezed the trigger. The rifle barked and spat out a cartridge case. Compared to what he was used to, the kick was light. "Lordy," someone halfway down the line exclaimed, "I could fire this piece right off my nose." The kick wasn't that light, but it wasn't far away, either.

"Fire another round," Lang said. "You don't have to do anything but pull the trigger again." Caudell pulled. The repeater fired. Intellectually, he had expected it would. Intellectually expecting something, though, was different from having it happen. The chorus of whistles and low-voiced exclamations of wonder that went up from the firing line showed he was not alone.

"Thirty rounds to this thing?" somebody said. "Hell, just load it on Sunday and shoot it all week long."

Lang said, "Each time you fire, the spring in the magazine pushes up another round, so you have one in the chamber again. Take off the magazine, why don't you, then fire that last round to empty the weapon and pass it to someone in your group so he can have his three practice rounds."

Caudell moved the lever up, thumbed the catch that held the magazine where it belonged. When it separated from the carbine, he did not know what to do with it for a moment. Finally he thrust it inside the front of his trousers. He aimed the weapon, felt the light jolt of its kick when he fired.

"My turn now," Allison High said, tapping him on the shoulder.

High was half a dozen years younger than Caudell, two inches taller, and several inches wider through the chest. Not only that, it *was* his turn. Even so, Caudell said, "I don't want to give it to you, Allison. I want to keep it to myself."

"It ain't your wife, Nate. It's only a gun," High said reasonably. " 'Sides, from what this Lang feller's been sayin', we'll each get one all our own 'fore long."

A little embarrassed, Caudell surrendered the rifle and the banana clip.

High clicked the magazine back into place. The sound reminded Caudell of a faithless lover's laugh as she slipped into the arms of someone new. He laughed, too, at himself.

Benny Lang took the new firing line through the drill of working the change lever, chambering a round, and firing the rifle. The instructor had the knack of repeating his lessons without sounding bored. Caudell listened just as hard without the carbine in his hand as he had when he held it. Soon enough, he'd be teaching privates. He wanted to make sure he could stay ahead of them.

Lang kept at it until everyone had had a turn shooting an AK-47. Then he said, "This weapon can do one other thing I haven't shown you yet. When you move the change lever all the way down instead of to the middle position, this is what happens." He stuck a fresh clip in the repeater, turned toward the target circle, and blasted away. He went through the whole magazine almost before Caudell could draw in a startled breath.

"Good God almighty," Rufus Daniel said, peering in awe at the brass cartridge cases scattered around Lang's feet. "Why didn't he show us that in the first place?"

He was not the only one to raise the question; quite a few shouted it. Caudell kept quiet. By now, he was willing to assume Lang knew what he was doing.

The weapons instructor stayed perfectly possessed. He said, "I didn't show you that earlier because it wastes ammunition and because the weapon isn't accurate past a few meters—yards—on full automatic. You can only carry so many rounds. If you shoot them all off in the first five minutes of a battle, what will you do once they're gone? Think hard on that, gentlemen, and drill it into your private soldiers. This weapon requires fire discipline—requires it, I say again."

He paused to let the point sink in. Then he grinned. It made him look like a boy. When he was serious, his thin, sallow features showed all his years, which had to be as many as Caudell's own thirty-four. He said, "Now we've done the exciting things with the weapon. Time to get on to the boring details that will keep it working and you alive—cleaning and such."

A groan rose from his audience, the sort of groan Caudell was used to hearing when he started talking about subtracting fractions. Benny Lang grinned again. He went on, "I warned you it wasn't glamorous. We'll get on with it just the same. Watch me, please."

He held up his repeater so everyone could see it. "Look here at the top of the weapon, all the way back toward you from the sight. There at the end of the metal part is a little knob. It's called the recoil spring guide. Do you see it?" Edwin Powell had the rifle in Caudell's group. Caudell looked it over with his fellow sergeants. Sure enough, the knob was there.

Lang waited until he saw everyone had found it. "Now," he said, "every chap with a weapon, push in on that knob." Powell pushed, a little hesitantly. Caudell didn't blame him for being cautious. After all the marvels the AK-47 had displayed, he would not have been surprised to find that pushing that knob made it sing a chorus of "The Bonnie Blue Flag." Nothing so melodramatic happened. Lang was also pushing the knob on his repeater; as he did so, he went on, "Lift up the receiver cover and take it off the receiver."

More clumsily, his students imitated him. Caudell peered curiously into the works of the weapon thus revealed. "Never saw a rifle with so many guts," Dempsey Eure observed.

"I never saw a rifle with guts at all," Caudell said, to which the other sergeants nodded. A rifle was a barrel and a lock and a stock, plus such oddments as sight and ramrod and bayonet. It had no room for guts. But this one did. Caudell wondered what the unschooled farmers who made up the bulk of the Castalia Invincibles would think of that.

"Don't panic," Lang said. Caudell remembered that the instructor had seen other soldiers' reactions to the complicated interior of an AK-47. Lang continued to take the carbine apart, lecturing all the while: "We've already taken off the receiver cover, right? Next thing to do is push the recoil spring guide in as far as it will go and then lift it up and take it out along with the spring itself. Then slide the bolt carrier, the bolt, and the piston back and lift them out."

He held up each piece as he named it so his inexperienced pupils could see what he was talking about. "Now watch how I turn the bolt—the lugs here have to line up with the grooves on the carrier. Then the bolt slides back until it comes off the carrier. You only really have to worry about the spring, the bolt carrier, and the bolt. You need to clean them every day the weapon is fired."

Lang pulled a rod out from under the barrel of the AK-47. The carbine's stock had a hinged compartment. He took from it a little bottle of gun oil, brushes, and cloth patches. With meticulous care, he ran a patch down the inside of the barrel, then wiped the black spring and silvery bolt and carrier clean. When he was done, he resumed his discussion.

"Reassembly procedure is the exact reverse of what we've just done. The bolt goes on the carrier"—he deftly matched action to words—"and they both go into the receiver. Then the recoil spring and its guide fit in back of the bolt carrier. Push 'em forward till the rear of the guide clears the back of the receiver, then push down to engage the guide. Then you put the receiver plate in place, push in on the spring guide, and push the plate down to lock it." He grinned at the North Carolinians. "Now you try it. Don't bother cleaning your weapon this first time. Just get it apart and back together."

"That don't look too hard," Edwin Powell said. Caudell wasn't so sure. He didn't trust the look on Benny Lang's face. The last time he'd seen a look like that, Billy Beddingfield of Company F had been wearing it in a poker game. Billy had also had an extra ace stuck up his sleeve.

The spring, gleaming with gun oil, went back where it belonged with no particular argument. The bolt was something else again. Powell tried to fit it into place as Lang had. It did not want to fit. "Shitfire," Powell said softly after several futile tries. "Far as I'm concerned, the damn thing can stay dirty."

He was far from the only man having trouble. Lang went from group to group, explaining the trick. There obviously was a trick, for people looked happier once he'd worked with them. After a while, he came to Caudell's group, where Powell was still wrestling with the bolt. "It goes on the carrier like—this," he said. His hands underscored his words. "Do you see?"

"Yes, sir, I think so," Powell answered, as humbly as if speaking to one of the Camp Mangum drill sergeants who had turned the 47th North Carolina from a collection of raw companies into a regiment that marched and maneuvered like a single living creature. Lang carried the same air of omniscience, even if he didn't display it so loudly or profanely.

He said, "Show me." Powell still fumbled, but at last he got the bolt into place. Lang slapped him on the back. "Good. Do it again." Powell did, a little faster this time. Lang said, "When you get your own weapon tomorrow, you'll practice till you can do it with your eyes closed, first try, every try."

Powell grunted. "Been usin' guns my whole life. Never reckoned I'd have to put puzzle pieces together to make one work."

Oddly, that complaint cheered Nate Caudell. When he was a boy, his father had carved puzzles for him to play with. Thinking of the AK-47's works as a toy rather than something strange, mysterious, and threatening let him attack them without feeling intimidated. When his turn came, he got the bolt back into place after only a couple of false starts.

"Do it again that fast, Nate, and I'll believe you really can," Allison High said. Caudell did it again, and then, just to show it was no fluke, one more time. High whistled, a long, low note of respect. "Might could even be a reason you're wearin' that first sergeant's diamond to go with them stripes of yours."

"First time we've seen one, if there is," Dempsey Eure said. A grin eased the sting from the words; Eure had trouble taking anything or anyone seriously.

"To hell with both of you," Caudell said. He and his messmates all laughed.

"Wonder what Sid Bartholomew would say if was here to get a look at this repeater," Edwin Powell remarked. Everyone nodded. Nominally a member of Company D, Bartholomew was a gunsmith by trade, and had spent the whole war on detail in Raleigh, doing what he did best.

"Reckon he'd say good godalmighty like the rest of us," Rufus Daniel said, and everyone nodded again. The AK-47 brought on remarks like that.

By the time everyone was able to clean and reassemble the repeater, morning had given way to afternoon. As he'd promised, Lang showed how to load cartridges into the rifle's magazine. After the mysteries of the bolt, that was child's play. He also showed how to open the catch at the bottom of the clip and clean the spring inside.

"That's a once-a-month job, though, not once a day," he said. "But do remember to see to it every so often." He paused, looked around at his audience. "You've been very patient chaps, the lot of you. Thank you for your attention; I've said everything I need say. Have you any questions of me?"

"Yeah, I got one," somebody said immediately. Heads turned toward him as he took a swaggering step out of his group. "You got your fancy-pants rifle there, Mr. Benny Lang, kill anything that twitches twenty miles away. What I want to know is, how good a man are you without it?" He gazed toward Lang with insolent challenge in his eyes.

"Beddingfield!" Captain Lankford of Company F and Colonel Faribault barked the name in the same breath. Caudell said it, too, softly.

"How'd Billy Beddingfield ever make corporal?" Rufus Daniel whispered. "He could teach mean to a snapping turtle."

"You don't want to get on his wrong side, though," Caudell whispered back. "If I were a private in his squad, I'd be more afraid of him than of any Yankee ever born."

"You got that right, Nate," Daniel said, chuckling.

"Back in ranks, Beddingfield," Captain Lankford snapped.

"I don't mind, Captain," Benny Lang said. "Let him come ahead, if he cares to. This might be—instructive, too. Come on, Corporal, if you've the stomach for it." He set down his repeater and stood waiting.

"Is he out of his mind?" Edwin Powell said. "Billy'll tear him in half."

Looking at the two men, Caudell found it hard to disagree. Lang was taller, but on the skinny side. Built like a bull, Beddingfield had to outweigh him by twenty pounds. And, as Rufus Daniel had said, Beddingfield had a mean streak as wide as he was. He was a terror in battle, but a different sort of terror in camp.

He grinned a school bully's nasty grin as he stepped forward to square off with Lang. "That man's face is made for a slap," Caudell said to Allison High.

"Reckon you're right, Nate, but I got ten dollars Confed says Lang ain't the one to slap it for him," High answered.

Ten dollars Confederate was most of a month's pay for a private. Caudell liked to gamble now and then, but he didn't believe in throwing away money. "No thanks, Allison. I won't touch that one."

High laughed. Edwin Powell said, "I'll match you, Allison. That there Lang, he looks to have a way of knowin' what he's doin'. He wouldn't've called Billy out if he didn't expect he could lick him."

One of Caudell's sandy eyebrows quirked up toward his hairline. He hadn't thought of it in those terms. "Can I change my mind?" he asked High.

"Sure thing, Nate. I got another ten that ain't doin' nothin'. I—"

He shut up. Big knobby fists churning, Beddingfield rushed at Benny Lang. Lang brought up his own hands, but not to hit back. He grabbed Billy Beddingfield's right wrist, turned, ducked, threw. Beddingfield flew over his shoulder, landed hard on the frozen ground.

He bounced to his feet. He wasn't grinning anymore. "Bastard," he snarled, and waded back in. A moment later, he went flying again. This time he landed on his face. His nose dripped blood onto his tunic as he got up. Lang wasn't breathing hard.

"You fight dirty," Beddingfield said, wiping his face with his sleeve.

Now Lang smiled, coldly. "I fight to win, Corporal. If you can't stand it, go home to your momma."

With a bellow of rage, Beddingfield charged. Caudell watched closely, but still didn't see just what happened. All he knew was that, instead of flying, Beddingfield went down, hard. He moaned and tried to rise. Benny Lang stood over him, kicked him in the ribs with judiciously calculated force. He stayed down.

Still unruffled, Lang said, "Has anyone else any questions?" No one did. He smiled that cold smile again. "Colonel Faribault, Captain, I think you'll find I didn't damage this fellow permanently."

"I wouldn't have blamed you if you had, sir. He picked the fight," Captain Lankford said. He plucked at his chin beard. "Maybe some hours bucked and gagged will teach him to save his spirit for the Yankees."

"Maybe." Lang shrugged. It wasn't his problem. "Good day to you, gentlemen. Private Whitley, do you mind giving me a lift back to Orange Court House?"

"No, sir, not a bit, sir, Mr. Lang." Whitley hadn't sounded nearly so respectful before Lang knocked the stuffing out of Billy Beddingfield.

"Good." Lang ambled toward the wagon. "I could walk it easily enough, I suppose—it's only a mile and a half—but why walk when you can ride?"

"I don't know who that Lang feller is or where he comes from," Edwin Powell declared, "but he thinks like the infantry."

The other sergeants from Company D solemnly nodded. Caudell said, "Talk has it, he and his people are from Rivington, right in our home county."

"You cut out that 'our' and speak for your own self, Nate," Allison High said; unlike his messmates, he was from Wilson County, just south of Nash.

Rufus Daniel said, "I don't give a damn how talk has it; and that's a fact. Here's two more facts—Lang don't talk like he's from Nash County"— he exaggerated his drawl till everyone around him smiled—"and he don't fight like he's from Nash County, neither. I wish he'd learn me that fancy rasslin' of his along with this here repeater. Old Billy Beddingfield, he never knew what hit him. Look, he's still lyin' there cold as a torch throwed in a snowbank."

The wagon started out of camp, harness jingling, wheels squeaking, and horses' hooves ringing against the ground. It swung off the camp lane onto the road north. Billy Beddingfield still did not move. Caudell wondered if Lang had hurt him worse than he thought.

So, evidently, did Colonel Faribault. He limped over to the fallen corporal, stirred him with his stick. Beddingfield wiggled and moaned. Nodding as if satisfied, Faribault stepped back. "Flip water in his face, somebody, till he revives. Then, Captain Lankford, along with whatever punishment details you give him, have the stripes off his sleeves. A raw brawler like that doesn't deserve to wear them."

"Yes, sir," Lankford said.

"That's fair," Caudell said after a couple of seconds' thought. No one in his group disagreed with him. A corporal from Company F ran off the parade ground, returned a minute later with his canteen, whose contents he poured over Beddingfield's head. The fallen bully spluttered and swore and slowly sat up.

Colonel Faribault said, "Each of today's groups will hold its rifle and practice as much as possible until the full regiment's rifles arrive, which, I am told, will be tomorrow." His phrasing drew ironic chuckles—the time of promised shipments had a way of stretching like India rubber. He went

on, "Try not to actually shoot, except at our target here, for safety's sake—
especially not when the rifle is on—what did Lang call it?"

"Full automatic, sir," someone supplied.

"That's it." Faribault's mouth set in a grim line that his little mustache
only accented. "A fool with an Enfield can hurt one man with an accidental
shot. A fool with one of these new guns can mow down half a company if
he starts with a full banana clip. Bear it in mind, gentlemen. You are
dismissed."

Dempsey Eure carried the AK-47 as the sergeants started back to their
cabin. He slung it over his shoulder, then said, "I'd sooner tote this than
my old rifle, any day."

"Don't hardly weigh nothin'," do it?" Rufus Daniel echoed.

"Stubby little thing, though," Allison High said critically. "Wouldn't
want to get into a bayonet fight or have to swing it like it was a club."

Daniel spat. "I leave the bayonet off my own rifle now when I'm goin'
into a fight, Allison. So do most of the boys, an' you know it, too. You
don't hardly ever get close enough to a Yankee to use the blamed thing.
With these here new guns, they ain't goin' to get that close to us, neither."

As was his habit, High kept looking at the darker side of things: "If they
don't break down from use, and if Benny Lang and however many friends
he's got can keep us in cartridges. I ain't never seen the likes of these
before, not even from the Yankees."

"That's so," Daniel allowed. "Well, we'll use 'em hard these next couple
of months till we break camp. That'll tell us what we need to know. And
if they ain't to be trusted, well, George Hines can put Minié balls in the
ammunition wagons, too. We still got our old rifles. Be just like the first
days of the war again, when the Springfields and Enfields was the new
guns, and a lot o' the boys just had smoothbore muskets, an' we needed
t'carry bullets for both. I don't miss my old smoothbore, and that's a fact,
though I did a heap o' missin' with it when I carried it."

"You got that right," Dempsey Eure said. "Dan'l Boone couldn't hit the
side of a barn with a goddam smoothbore, an' anybody who says different
is a goddam liar."

"Goddam right," Rufus Daniel said.

Before the war, Caudell would have boxed the ears of any boy who
dared swear in his hearing. Now, half the time, he didn't even notice the
profanity that filled the air around him. These days he swore, too, when
he felt like it, not so much to fit in as because sometimes nothing felt better
than a ripe, round oath.

He said, "Can't be sure, of course, but I have a notion we'll get all the
cartridges we need. That Benny Lang, he knows what he's doing. Look at

the way he handled Billy. Like Edwin said, he knew he could take him, and he did. If he says we'll have repeaters here tomorrow, I'm inclined to believe him. I expect he and his people can manage cartridges, too."

"Double or nothin' on our bet that them guns *don't* come tomorrow," High said.

"You're on," Caudell replied at once.

"I want my ten now," Edwin Powell said.

High turned around as if to punch him, then looked back to the parade ground. He pointed. "See, Nate, there's one man who doesn't know if you're right about them cartridges." Caudell turned too. George Hines was on his hands and knees, picking up spent cartridge cases.

"He's a good ordnance sergeant," Caudell said. "He doesn't want to lose anything he doesn't have to. Remember after the first day at Gettysburg, when they told off a couple of regiments to glean the battlefield for rifles and ammunition, both?"

"I remember that," Powell said. His long face grew longer. "I wish they could have gleaned for men, too." He'd taken his second wound at Gettysburg.

The sergeants ducked back into their cabin one by one. Rufus Daniel started building up the fire, which had died to almost cold embers while the five men took their long turn on the parade ground. Caudell sat down in a chair that had begun life as a molasses barrel. "Pass me that repeater, Dempsey," he said. "I need to work with it more to get the proper hang of it."

"We all do," Eure said as he handed over the carbine.

Caudell practiced attaching and removing the magazine several times, then pushed in on the recoil spring guide and field-stripped the rifle. To his relief, he got the pieces back in the right way without too much trouble. He did it again, and again. He'd told his students that reciting over and over made each subsequent recitation easier and better. He was glad to find the same true here. His hands began to know what to do of themselves, without having to wait for the thinking part of his mind to tell them.

"Give me a go with it now, Nate," Powell said. "You're slick as butter, and I was all fumble-fingered out there on the field."

Not too far away, a man started banging on a pot with a spoon. "Mess call," Allison High said. "Edwin, it's your turn to fetch the grub. You'll have to fiddle with that repeater later on. Who gets the water tonight?"

"I do," Rufus Daniel said. He picked up his canteen, a wooden one shaped like a little barrel. "Give me yours too, Nate." Caudell reached onto his bunk, tossed his canteen to Daniel. It was metal covered with cloth, taken from a Federal soldier who would never need water again.

The two sergeants went back out into the cold. Dempsey Eure said, "Don't hog the rifle just on account of Edwin's gone, Nate. If wagonloads of 'em really do show up tomorrow, we'd all best know what we're doin' or we'll look like godalmighty fools in front of the men. Wouldn't be the first time," he added.

Fear of embarrassment, Caudell thought as Eure ran his hand over the chambering handle, was a big part of the glue that held the army together. Send a man alone against a firing line, with no one to watch him, and he might well run away. Why not, when going forward made getting shot all too likely? But send a regiment against that same line, and almost everyone would advance on it. How could a man who fled face his mates afterwards?

Rufus Daniel came back a few minutes later. He set the canteens down not far from the fireplace. "Reckon Edwin'll be a bit—you don't have to stand in line by the creek the way you do for rations," he said. "While we're waitin', how about I try that there repeater?" Everyone was eager to work with the new rifle as much as he could.

"What do you have, Edwin?" Dempsey Eure demanded when Powell returned. Caudell's stomach growled like a starving bear. He'd known some lean times before the war—what man hadn't, save maybe a planter like Faribault?—but he'd never known what real hunger was till he joined the army.

Powell said, "Got me some cornmeal and a bit o' beef. Likely be tough as mule leather, but I won't complain till after I get me outside of it. We still have any o' that bacon your sister sent you, Dempsey?"

"Little bit," Eure answered. "You thinkin' o' makin' up some good ol' Confederate cush?"

"I will unless you got a better notion," Powell said. "Ain't none of us what you'd call fancy cooks. Why don't you get out that bacon and toss me our fryin' pan? Here, Nate, you cut the beef small." He handed Caudell the meat, the hairy skin still on it.

The pan had once been half a Federal canteen; its handle was a nailed-on stick. Powell tossed in the small chunk of bacon and held the pan over the fire. When he had cooked the grease out so it bubbled and spattered in the bottom of the pan, Caudell added the cubed beef. After a minute or two, he poured in some water. Meanwhile, Allison High used more water to make the cornmeal into a tin of mush. He passed the mush to Caudell, who upended the tin over the frying pan. Powell stirred the mixture together, then kept the pan on the fire until the mush soaked up all the water and a brown crust began to form along the sides.

He took the pan off the fire, set it down. With his knife, he sliced the cush into five more-or-less-equal pieces. "There you go, boys. Dig in."

"I hate this goddam slosh," Rufus Daniel said. "When I get home from this damn war, I ain't goin' to eat nothin' but fried chicken and sweet-potato pie and ham and biscuits and gravy just as thick as you please. Aii, that goddam pan's still hot." He stuck a burned knuckle into his mouth. While he'd been complaining, he'd also been using belt knife and fingers to get his portion of supper out of the frying pan.

Caudell tossed his slab of cush from hand to hand till it was cool enough to bite. He wolfed it down and licked his fingers when he was through. It wasn't what he would have eaten by choice—it was as far as the moon from the feast Rufus Daniel had been imagining—but cornmeal had a way of sticking to the ribs that made a man forget he was hungry for a while.

Dempsey Eure lit a twig at the fire, got his pipe going. Daniel did the same. Caudell lit up a cigar, tilted his head back, and blew a smoke ring at the ceiling. The cabin filled with fragrant smoke. "Glad we're not short of tobacco, anyhow," he said.

"Not in this regiment," Eure said. The 47th drew its men from the heart of North Carolina's tobacco country; half a dozen soldiers had been tobacconists before the war.

"Almost makes me wish I was on picket duty up by the Rapidan," Powell said, shifting a chaw from one cheek to the other. "Might could be I'd find me a friendly Yank on the other side, trade him some tobacco for coffee and sugar and maybe some o' them little hard candies they have sometimes."

His messmates sighed. That kind of trading went on all the time. Confederates and Federals winked at it. *Why not?* Caudell thought—*it isn't going to change who wins the war, only make both sides more comfortable.* At the moment, with some food in his belly, a cigar in his hand, and a warm cabin around him, he was comfortable enough. He took another drag. "Picket duty's *cold*," he said reflectively.

"That's true," a couple of the other sergeants said. Dempsey Eure added, "To hell with your coffee and sugar, Edwin. I ain't gonna freeze to get it."

They talked awhile longer, and smoked, and passed around the new repeater. One by one, they went to bed. The last thing Caudell saw before he fell asleep was Edwin Powell sitting close by the fire, assembling the AK-47 and taking it apart again.

Reveille the next morning hit Caudell like an artillery barrage. He threw off his threadbare blanket, scrambled out of bed, and put on his shoes, tunic, and slouch hat. Everyone else was getting dressed at the same time.

The hut wasn't really big enough for five men to dress in all at once, but they managed; by now they'd been doing it for three months.

Dempsey Eure's black felt hat was even more disreputable than Caudell's, but he kept a gaudy turkey feather in the band. "You walk out wearin' that bird, somebody'll shoot it off you," Rufus Daniel said. He cracked the same joke about once a week.

Caudell went outside. As always, he had mixed feelings about that first breath of early morning air. It was sweet and fresh and free of most of the smoke that built up inside the cabin, but it was bitterly cold. When he exhaled, he breathed out as big a cloud as if he'd started another cigar.

Soldiers came scrambling out of their shelters to line up for morning roll call. In the Federal army, their appearance would have given apoplexy to any noncommissioned officer worth his stripes. Not all of them had shoes. Their torn trousers were variously blue—Union booty—gray, or butternut. No one wore a blue blouse, for fear of being mistaken for a Yankee troop, but that was as far as uniformity went there. Some wore forage caps, others slouch hats like Caudell's. The only thing of which that imaginary Federal sergeant would have approved was their bearing. The Castalia Invincibles might have been in rags, but they could fight.

"Dress ranks!" Allison High shouted. The men shifted a little. Company D, as a whole, numbered between five and six dozen men, which total included two corporals, four sergeants, First Sergeant Nate Caudell, a couple of lieutenants, and a captain. Right after Gettysburg, sergeants had commanded some companies of the 47th North Carolina; at the moment, the Invincibles were oversupervised.

Captain Lewis limped up. "Call the roll, First Sergeant."

"Yes, sir." Caudell took from his pocket a much-folded piece of paper. After so many repetitions, he hardly needed to look at it as he called the men's names: "Bailey, Ransom . . . Barnes, Lewis D. W. . . . Bass, Gideon . . ." He finished a few minutes later: "Winstead, John A. . . . Winstead, William T." He turned back to Lewis with a salute. "All present, sir."

"Very good. Sick call?"

"Sick call!" Caudell said loudly. A couple of men took a step forward. "What's your trouble, Granbury?" he asked one of them.

"I got the shits—beggin' your pardon, First Sergeant, the runs—again," Granbury Proctor said.

Caudell sighed. With the bad food and bad water the regiment got, diarrhea was a common complaint. This was Proctor's third bout this winter. Caudell said, "Go see the assistant surgeon, Granbury. Maybe he can do something for you." Proctor nodded and walked off. Caudell turned to the other sufferer. "What about you, Southard?"

"Don't rightly know, First Sergeant," Bob Southard answered. His voice cracked as he answered; he was only eighteen or so. He bent his head and coughed. "I'm feelin' right poorly, though."

Caudell put a skeptical hand on the youngster's forehead. Southard had already deserted the regiment once; he was a shirker. "No fever. Get back in line." Dejectedly, the private went back into his slot. The cook banged on his pan. Caudell said, "Dismissed for breakfast."

Breakfast was corn bread. The meal from which it had been made was ground so coarse that some kernels lay in wait, intact and rock-hard, to ambush the teeth. Caudell plucked at his beard to knock crumbs loose. He heard a wagon—no, more than one—rolling down from Orange Court House. "You don't suppose—?" he said to Rufus Daniel.

"This early? Naah," Daniel said.

But it was. The wagon train turned off the road and rumbled toward the regimental parade ground. Benny Lang rode beside the lead wagon's driver. Slaves accompanied the others. Caudell held out his hand, palm up, to Allison High. "Pay up."

"Hell." High reached into his hip pocket, drew out a wad of bills, and gave two of them to Caudell. "Here's your twenty. Who'd've thought anybody'd move so quick? Hell." He walked off scowling, his head down.

"Easy there, Allison," Caudell called after him. "It's only twenty dollars Confederate, not like before the war when that was a lot of money."

Benny Lang leaped down from his wagon and started shouting like a man possessed: "Come on, get those crates off! This isn't a bloody picnic, so move it, you lazy kaffirs!" The slaves started unloading the wagons at the same steady but leisurely pace they usually used. It was not fast enough to suit Lang. "Move, damn you!" he shouted again.

The blacks were used to letting such shouts roll off their backs, secure in the knowledge that the work would eventually get done and the yelling white man would shut up and leave them alone. Lang met that quiet resistance head on. He stamped over to one of the slaves, threw him to the ground with a flip like the one he'd used against Billy Beddingfield. "Ow!" the man cried. "What'd I do, boss?"

"Not bloody much," Lang snarled, punctuating his words with a kick. The slave cried out again. Lang said scornfully, "You aren't hurt. Now get up and work. And I mean *work*, damn you. That goes for the rest of you lazy buggers, too, or you'll get worse than I just gave him. Move!"

The black men moved. Boxes came down from wagons at an astonishing rate. "Will you look at that?" Rufus Daniel said. "If I had me enough niggers to hire an overseer, that there Lang'd be first man I'd pick for the job."

"Maybe so," Caudell said. But he watched the sidelong glances that were the only safe way the slaves could use to show their resentment. "If he treats 'em like that all the time, though, he'd better grow eyes in the back of his head, or else he'll have an accident one fine day—or lots of runaways, anyhow."

"Might could be you're right," Daniel allowed.

Once the wagons were unloaded, Lang ordered the work crew to carry a share of the crates to each company standard. When the slaves again didn't work fast enough to suit him, he booted one of them in the backside. They moved quicker after that.

Lang followed them from company to company. When he came to the Castalia Invincibles, he picked Caudell out by his chevrons, handed him a length of iron with a curved and flattened end. "Here you are, First Sergeant—a ripping bar to get the crates open. We found some of your units had a spot of trouble with that."

"You think of everything," Caudell said admiringly.

"We do try. You'll have two magazines per weapon there, more or less—enough ammunition to get a start at practicing. Your ordnance sergeant needn't fret. We'll get you plenty more as you need it." With a nod, Lang was off to Company E.

Caudell watched him go. After yesterday and this morning, he believed Lang's promise. This was a man who delivered. But then, the Army of Northern Virginia always got the ammunition it needed, one way or another. Caudell wished Benny Lang or someone like him would take over the Confederate commissary department.

The soldiers gathered round the stacked crates. "Those the repeaters the bad-tempered feller was showin' off to y'all yesterday?" asked Melvin Bean, a smooth-faced private with a light, clear voice.

"Yup." Caudell attacked a crate with the bar. The lid came up with a groan of nails leaving wood. Sure enough, an AK-47 lay inside. Caudell said, "Anybody with the tools to give me a hand, run and fetch 'em. We'll get the job done that much quicker." Tom Short, who worked as a saddler, left and returned shortly with a claw hammer. He fell to work beside Caudell. Before too long, all the Castalia Invincibles held new repeaters.

A heavyset private named Ruffin Biggs gave his weapon a dubious look. "We're supposed to whup the Yankees with these little things?"

"It ain't the size of the dog in the fight, Ruffin," Dempsey Eure drawled, "it's the size of the fight in the dog. These here puppies got plenty of fight in 'em, believe you me."

Captain Lewis said, "Break into groups of six or seven men each. That way, everyone who learned about these repeaters yesterday will have one group to teach."

The division, into groups smaller than squads, went rather awkwardly. Eyeing the soldiers in his group, Caudell suspected that the sergeants and corporals—the company's regular squad leaders—had stuck him and the officers with the men they wanted least.

He shrugged. Everyone would have to learn. He held up his rifle, pointed to the lever below the charging handle. "This is the change lever. See, it has three positions. For now, I want you to make sure you have it in the topmost one."

"Why's that, First Sergeant?" Melvin Bean asked.

"Because if you don't, you're liable to end up shooting yourself before you find out how not to," Caudell answered drily. That made everyone sit up and take notice.

He went through the lesson Lang had given him. The soldiers practiced attaching and removing a magazine. He showed them how rounds were arranged inside the clip and had them practice putting rounds into it.

A rifle cracked, over in another company. Shouts of alarm rose after the gunshot. "That's why I want that change lever up top," Caudell said. "As long as it's there, the repeater can't go off by accident. It's called the safety."

Paschall Page, the regimental sergeant major, came up to Captain Lewis and saluted. "The colonel's compliments, sir, and the companies will practice shooting at our targets one by one, in order."

"Very good, Sergeant Major. Thank you," Lewis said. Page saluted again and marched off, every inch a gentleman. His blue sergeant's stripes were joined above by an arc that showed he was the most exalted of all the regiment's noncommissioned officers.

The lessons went more smoothly than Caudell dared hope. For one thing, Benny Lang had done a good job with his instructions the day before, and Caudell had paid careful attention. For another, despite being different from a rifle-musket, the AK-47 was an easy gun to use. Even Ruffin Biggs and Alsie Hopkins, who had not a letter between them, soon got the hang of the repeater. Caudell wondered how they would do when time to clean the weapon came around. He intended to hold off on that till his pupils had fired.

The soldiers were learning how to chamber the first round in the banana clip when a volley of shots came from the parade ground. Company A was shooting for the first time. Almost at once, the gunfire rang so thick and fast as to remind Caudell of a whole regiment on the line, not just one understrength company.

"The Chicora Guards got new guns! Run for your lives!" Henry Joyner yelled out toward the practicing graycoats. Like the Castalia Invincibles, the Chicora Guards were mostly recruited from Nash County, which made the rivalry between them all the fiercer. For that matter, each company currently boasted three Joyners. The relationships between them were too complicated for Caudell to keep straight.

One of the soldiers of Company A—maybe one of the Joyners—yelled back, "Shame we ain't got the bullets to waste to turn these here fine new repeaters on you all!"

"Couldn't hit us if'n you did," Henry jeered. He thumbed his nose.

"Enough," Caudell said. Horseplay was fun, but horseplay between men who carried rifles had to be controlled before it got out of hand.

Companies B and C—neither of which had a name—took their first turns practicing with the AK-47. The men came away from the firing line exclaiming and shaking their heads in wonder. Some of them slung the new repeaters on their backs. Others carried the carbines in both hands, as if they could not bear to let them go. Three or four men from Company C started a chant: "*En*field, *Spring*field, throw 'em in the *corn*field!" Before long the whole company, officers and all, was singing it.

Captain Lewis said, "Form column of fours . . . to the parade ground, march." A couple of new men just up from North Carolina started off on the wrong foot, but growls from the sergeants soon had them in step with everyone else. "Shift to the left from column to line . . . move," Lewis said.

The company performed the evolution with mindless precision born of unending practice. Caudell remembered the first day of marching down at Camp Mangum, when an irate drill sergeant had compared their ragged line to a drunken centipede in an ass-kicking contest. Even that drill sergeant, assuming he was still alive, would have been satisfied to see them now.

"Load your rifles," Captain Lewis said. In one motion the men drew back their charging handles, and each chambered a round. "Fire!"

Not every repeater spat flame. "Check your change lever!" Caudell shouted, along with everyone else who had had instruction the day before. Soldiers checked. Some of them swore at themselves. The next volley was fuller; in a moment, a fusillade of shots made separate volleys impossible to distinguish.

The company's privates shouted in wonder and delight at how rapidly their repeaters fired and how easy they were to shoot. Caudell knew how they felt. The AK-47 was so different from any other rifle that hearing about it wasn't enough. Even after you shot with it, it was hard to believe.

"What happens if you put this here change lever thing on the middle notch?" Henry Joyner asked. "If it's as much different from the bottom one as that there one is from the top, reckon this gun'll march out and shoot Yankees all by its lonesome. I'm for it, I tell you that."

"Sorry, Henry." Caudell explained about full automatic fire. He also explained about how much ammunition it chewed up, finishing, "Shooting fast can be bad if you run out of cartridges before the battle's over. That's not easy to do with a rifle musket. With one of these repeaters, especially on full automatic, it's easy as pie. You'll want to be careful about that."

Melvin Bean said, "I got shot in the arm the first day at Gettysburg after I'd used up all my cartridges. Even if I'd seen the damnyankee who nailed me, I couldn't've done nothin' about him." The new men listened and nodded solemnly. Caudell reflected that a wound on the first day had kept Bean out of the third day's charge and very possibly kept the private from being captured or killed.

Ruffin Biggs fired one more round at the paper target circle, which by now looked as if it were suffering from measles or smallpox. He yelped out a rebel yell, then said, "Next time the drummers play the long roll, them Yankees is gonna wish they was never born. This here rifle shoots like hell-beatin'-tanbark."

"Is that good?" Joyner asked.

"Cain't be beat," Biggs answered positively.

"Clear the parade ground," Captain Lewis said. "Time for Company E to have their turn. Form column of fours."

Grumbling, disappointed they couldn't shoot more, his men obeyed. Somebody sang out, "*En*field, *Spring*field, throw 'em in the *corn*field!" The chant ran down the column like wildfire. The men from the other companies that had already fired took it up again, too.

"Whole army's going to be singing that before long," Caudell predicted.

"Hope you're right," Dempsey Eure answered, "on account of that'll mean the whole army's got themselves repeaters."

Once they were back by their own shelters, the Castalia Invincibles regrouped around the men Benny Lang had instructed. "Now for the dull part: cleaning," Caudell said. The men groaned. They groaned again when he showed them the cleaning rod and the kit in the stock compartment, and then how to open the receiver plate and extract spring, bolt carrier, and bolt. "It's not as bad as it looks," he told them. "They go together like—this." He reassembled the mechanism, closed the cover plate. "Now you do it."

They tried. The bolt proved reluctant to go back where it was supposed to. "Maybe for you it goes like *this*," Melvin Bean said. "For me it just goes straight to the devil."

"Practice," Caudell said smugly. Willingness to practice was a virtue teachers needed. His voice got deeper, more serious. "You all'll keep practicing till I see you can do it. Watch me again." He went through the process, very slowly. "You take another lick at it."

A couple of them succeeded in getting it right. Melvin Bean kept failing and swearing. Caudell walked over, took the private's hands in his, guided them through what had to be done. "There. Do you see now?"

Bean smiled. "Reckon so."

This time, everything went smoothly. "That's a good job," Caudell said, smiling himself. "Anyone else still having trouble?" Nobody said anything. "Good. Just don't think that because you did it once, you have it by the tail. Keep working at it tonight. We'll go over it again tomorrow, and the day after that. By then, I want you to be able to take that repeater apart, clean it, and put it back together in your sleep. If you can't, maybe you should be toting a billet of wood instead." The soldiers' expressions sobered. Carrying a billet wasn't onerous punishment, but there were better ways to pass a morning.

Caudell hesitated before he taught the privates how to clean the magazine spring—why burden them with something they might not need to know? Benny Lang had said it was only occasionally necessary, and there looked to be plenty of banana clips about. But on second thought, Caudell did demonstrate the technique. What passed for the Confederate supply system could turn plenty into famine without warning.

"More questions?" he said at last. "All right, then—dismissed." Most of the men drifted away, still talking excitedly about the new repeaters they were carrying. The other groups had already broken up, some a good while before. Caudell cared nothing about that. Thoroughness counted here, and he was used to repeating himself any number of times until students caught on to what he was saying.

Melvin Bean did not wander off. The private removed the receiver plate, took out the rifle's works, tried to put them back together. Caudell watched. They proved balky. Bean swore softly, then said, "I just can't make the pesky thing fit. Do you want to come back to my hut with me and show me what I'm doin' wrong?"

"I'd be glad to do that," Caudell said.

They walked down the straight muddy lane between rows of shelters. Bean's cabin was small but neat; its one window even boasted shutters. No one else lived here, which was unusual, if not quite unique, in the regiment.

Bean opened the door. "Go right on in, First Sergeant." Caudell did. The private followed, closing and barring the door behind the two of them. "Now show me that trick of puttin' this fool rifle back together again."

"You really were having trouble, then?"

"I said as much, didn't I? Thought I had it when you showed me before, but I lost the knack again." They sat together on the blanket-covered pine boughs that did duty for a bed. Bean watched intently as Caudell went through everything. "So that's what y'all were doin'! Here, let me have a go, Nate—I reckon I really have got it now." Sure enough, the pieces went back together smoothly.

"Do it some more. Show me it wasn't a fluke," Caudell said.

Bean did, twice running. Caudell nodded. Bean checked to make sure the repeater's change lever was in the safe position, then set the weapons aside. "Good. I need to be able to do that." Mischief sparked in the private's eyes. "And now, Nate Caudell, I expect you'll be lookin' to find out how your own bolt fits."

"I'd like that a lot." Bean had not waited for him to reply, but was already opening the seven-button private's tunic. Caudell reached out and gently touched one of the small but perfectly feminine breasts that unbuttoning revealed. He smiled. "You know, Mollie, if you were one of those bosomy girls, you'd never get by with this."

"If I was, I could bind 'em up, I suppose," she said seriously. "It'd be as uncomfortable as all get out, though, an' I do enough pretendin' as it is. Melvin! Took me a goodish while even to get used to answerin' to it."

Caudell's lips followed his fingers. Mollie Bean sighed and pulled the tunic off altogether. A long, puckered scar marred the smooth skin of her left upper arm, outer mark of where a Minié ball had gashed the muscle. An inch or two lower and it would have smashed the bone and cost her the limb.

"Here now." She reached for him. "Ain't hardly fair for me to be the only one gettin' out of my clothes. 'Sides, it's chilly in here."

He held her close and did his best to warm her. He certainly forgot about the cold himself, at least until afterwards. When he sat up again, though, he found he was shivering. He dressed quickly. So did Mollie. Back in Confederate uniform, with her forage cap pushed down so the brim covered her eyebrows, she seemed just another private, too young to shave. The 47th North Carolina claimed more than a few of those. But she had been all woman in his arms.

He studied her as if she were a difficult problem in trigonometry. She was very different from the hard-eyed Richmond whores to whom he'd occasionally resorted when he got leave. He supposed that was because he saw her every day and knew her as a person, not just a convenient receptacle for his lust, to be forgotten as soon as he was out the door. "Ask you something?" he said.

She shrugged. "Go ahead."

"How come you did—this?"

"You mean, how come I came up to the fightin'?" she said. He nodded. She shrugged again. "I was bored down home. Wasn't hardly nobody comin' by the bawdyhouse where I was at, either, what with so many men bein' away to the war. Guess I figured I'd come up and see it for myself, see what it was like."

"And?"

Her face twisted into a wry grin. She still wasn't pretty in any conventional sense of the word, especially with her black hair clipped off short like a man's, but her wide, full-lipped smile made her seem much more feminine when she smiled. She said, "Didn't like gettin' shot worth a damn, I tell you that, Nate."

"I believe you." He thanked his lucky stars he was still unwounded. Few bullets were as merciful as the one that had found her. The ghastly piles of arms and legs outside the surgeon's tent after every fight, the screams of men shot in the belly, the dying gurgles of men shot through the chest—

He was glad to forget those images when she went on, "But for that, though, y'all in the company are more like family 'n anything I ever knew 'fore I got here. Y'all care about me like you was my brothers, and y'all keep th' officers from findin' out what I am"—her wry grin flashed again—" 'cause you know blamed well I ain't your sister."

He laughed at that. He'd never asked before, though she'd been with the regiment a year. He didn't know what he'd expected to hear—perhaps something more melodramatic than her plain story. He took out the twenty dollars Confederate he'd won from Allison High, gave the bills to her.

"Wish it was Federal greenbacks," she said, "but it'll do, Nate, it'll do. Want to go another round?"

He thought about it, but shook his head. "I'd better not. I can't afford the time; I've been away too long as is."

"You care about what you're doin'. That's a good thing." Mollie made a face at him. "Or is it just I'm gettin' old? Cain't think o' many who would've turned me down if I'd asked 'em when I was down in Rivington."

"You're a damn sight younger than I am. You—" Caudell stopped.

"You were in Rivington before you joined up? They say these new repeaters come from there, and the people who make them or sell them or whatever it is they do."

"I've heard that, too," Mollie said. Caudell reflected that she'd probably heard it well before he did; she usually got news even before Colonel Faribault heard it. She went on, "Don't know nothin' about it, though. Them fellers weren't there when I left the place a year ago. Not much else was, neither, 'specially not men, so I got out. Sure you don't want to go again?"

"What I want to do and what I have to do are two different things," Caudell said. "This is the army, remember?"

Her laugh followed him as he returned to the cold and military world outside her cabin door. He looked down the lane toward the parade ground. George Hines was out there on his hands and knees, gathering up brass cartridge cases.

★ III ★

The locomotive snorted and hissed as it slowed. The shriek of the locked driving wheels against sanded rails reminded General Lee of the cries of wounded horses, the most piteous sound on any battlefield. The train stopped. There was a last jolt as the cars came together with a clanking clatter of link-and-pin couplings.

Lee and the other passengers got to their feet. "All out to Richmond!" the conductor called before hurrying down to the next car to repeat the cry.

Carpetbag in hand, Lee descended to the muddy ground outside the Virginia Central Railroad depot at the corner of Sixteenth and Broad. The depot was a plain wooden shed, much in need of paint. A banner on the door of the tavern across the street advertised fried oysters at half price in honor of George Washington's birthday.

The banner made Lee pause in mild bemusement: strange how the Confederacy still revered the founding fathers of the United States. Or perhaps it was not so strange. Surely Washington, were he somehow to whirl through time to the present, would find himself more at home on a Southern plantation than in a brawling Northern factory town like Pittsburgh or New York. And, of course, Washington was a Virginian, so where better to celebrate his birthday than Richmond?

A young man's brisk voice brought Lee out of his reverie and back to the here and now: "General? I have a carriage waiting for you, sir."

He turned around, exchanged salutes with a lieutenant who wore a uniform nattier than any still to be found in the Army of Northern Virginia. "I hope you were not waiting long for me?"

"No, sir." The lieutenant pulled out a pocket watch. "It's but a few minutes after four. The train was due in at a quarter past three. I arrived then, on the off chance it might be on time." Both men smiled, knowing how unlikely that was. But a wise lieutenant did not take chances, not when he was meeting the senior officer of his army. He held out his hand for Lee's bag. "If you'll come with me, sir—"

Lee followed him to the carriage. Its black driver tapped a finger against the brim of his tall silk hat as Lee got in. "Evenin', Marse Robert."

"Hello, Luke. How are you today?"

"Oh, middlin', sir; I expect I'm about middlin'."

"That's a fair enough place to be," Lee said judiciously.

The lieutenant put a snap of command in his voice: "Back to the President's office, Luke."

"Yassuh." Luke flicked his whip. The two-horse team started northwest up Broad Street. Like the lieutenant, both animals were in finer fettle than the beasts Jeb Stuart's troopers rode. It was the same in Washington City, Lee had heard. He believed it. The farther one drew from the front lines, the easier one found comfort.

Train tracks ran down the middle of Broad Street, connecting the Virginia Central depot with that of the Richmond, Fredericksburg and Potomac eight blocks away. Lee heard an engine coming their way, puffing at full throttle to haul a fully laden train up steep Shockoe Hill. The horses heard, too, and tossed their heads to show they did not approve. Luke calmed them with a few soft words.

Before the bellowing, cinder-belching monster appeared, the carriage turned left onto Twelfth Street. It rattled through Capitol Square on the way to the new building that had been the customhouse before Virginia left the Union.

Off to the left, twin rows of oaks led to the governor's mansion. To the right, Lee got a quick glimpse of the equestrian statue of George Washington before it vanished behind the severely classic bulk of the Virginia state capitol, now also the home of the Confederate Congress. The white columns and walls were remarkably handsome in spring and summer, when set against the rich green of the lawns and shrubbery and trees that surrounded them. Now the lawns were dead and yellow, the trees skeletal without their cloak of leaves.

The Confederate flag waved bravely over the Capitol, red canton with blue saltire cross and thirteen stars on a white ground. The Stainless Banner would come down soon; sunset was near. It was both like enough to the Stars and Stripes and different enough from it to stir conflicting feelings in Lee. He remembered the day, almost three years gone now, when he had gone into the House of Delegates to take charge of Virginia's forces. He shook his head. Four days before that, Winfield Scott had offered him command over the armies of the United States, to lead them against their seceded brethren. He still thought he had made the right—for him, the only—choice.

The massive rectangle of the former customhouse took up a whole city block. Built from concrete and steel, it might have served duty as a fortress. Unlike most of Richmond's major buildings, it was in Italianate rather than neoclassic style, its three stories shown by the tall windows with arched tops.

Luke hitched his team to the rail in front of the building. The lieutenant said, "He will be at your disposal for the length of your stay in the city, sir. Now I will take you up to President Davis. Let me have your bag there, if you would."

"That's very kind of you, sir." Lee followed the lieutenant inside.

The first floor housed the Treasury Department. Most of the time, busy men there would pause to look and point as Lee walked to the stairs. Those men needed to be busy, he thought with less than perfect forbearance, to print all the paper money that was pushing prices in the Confederacy to the sky. But even they had Washington's birthday as a holiday.

The second floor was always quiet, today no more so than usual. That floor belonged to the Department of State; no foreign nation had recognized the Confederate States of America, nor did any seem likely to unless the South won more victories than she had thus far.

President Davis's offices were on the third floor. The lieutenant tapped on a closed door. "Yes?" Jefferson Davis called from within.

"I have General Lee with me, sir."

"Excellent. I will see him. You may return to your other duties." The lieutenant opened the door, saluted Lee one last time, and hurried away.

"Mr. President," Lee said.

"Come right in, General. I'll be with you directly." Davis was going around with a tallow dip, lighting lamps. His bearing was military—indeed, extraordinarily erect; he was a West Point man himself, from the class a year ahead of Lee's. He came back to his desk last, and lit two lamps there. "Go on, sit down. Make yourself comfortable."

"Thank you, sir." Lee waited for Davis to seat himself before he sank into an overstuffed armchair. The lamplight played up the hollows in Davis's gaunt cheeks, lit his pale eyes within the shadows of their deep sock-

ets. He was aristocratically handsome, while Abraham Lincoln had no claim
to either breeding or good looks, but the two presidents, Lee thought ir-
relevantly, had faces of similar shape and leanness.

Davis said, "How was your journey south?"

"Well enough, sir," Lee answered with a shrug. "I left this morning and
am here now. If I am a trifle later than the railroad men claimed I would
be when I set out, well, what train ever runs dead on time?"

"None, I think; none on our railroads, at any rate." Davis glanced to a
tall clock that ticked in a corner of the office. His nostrils flared with
exasperation. "Nor is Mr. Seddon. I had hoped him to be here half an
hour ago."

Lee shrugged again. The Secretary of War had doubtless expected his
train to run even later than it did; unlike the young lieutenant, he was
sufficiently important in his own right to take such chances. In any case,
President Davis was for all practical purposes his own Secretary of War.
Lee knew he would sooner have been commanding Confederate armies in
the field than governing from Richmond.

As luck would have it, James Seddon walked into the office not fifteen
seconds after Davis had complained about him. Lee rose to shake his hand.
Seddon was tall, thin, and resembled nothing so much as a tired vulture.
He wore his gray hair combed straight back from his forehead (it was thin
in those parts anyhow) and long enough on the sides to cover his ears. At
the president's murmured invitation, he drew up a chair beside Lee's. They
sat together.

"To business," Davis said. "General Lee, I've heard great things of
these new repeating carbines the soldiers are being issued. Even General
Johnston has written to me from Dalton, singing hosannas in their praise."

If anything, praise from Joe Johnston was liable to make the President
suspicious about the new rifles; if Johnston said it looked like rain, Davis
would expect a drought, and the lack of affinity was mutual. Lee said
quickly, "For once, Mr. President, I would say the reports are, if anything,
understated. The repeaters are robust, they are reasonably accurate with
adequate range, and they and their ammunition appear to be available in
quantities sufficient to permit us to take the field with them. When spring
comes, I intend to do so."

"They improve our prospects by so much, then?" Seddon asked.

"They do indeed, sir," Lee said. "The Federals have always had more
weight than we, could they but effectively bring it to bear. These repeaters
go far toward righting the balance. Without them, our chances were become rather bleak. In saying this, I know I catch neither of you gentlemen
by surprise."

"No, indeed," Davis said. "I am most pleased to hear this news from you, General, for some of the counsel I have had from others approaches desperation." He rose from his desk, strode over to close the door that led out to the hallway. As he turned back, he went on, "What I tell you now, gentlemen, must not leave this room. Do you understand?"

"Certainly, Mr. President," said Seddon, who usually said yes to whatever Jefferson Davis wanted. Lee bent his head to show he also agreed.

"Very well, then, I shall hold you to that promise," Davis said. "To give you the full import of the remedies which have been contemplated out of anxiety for our future, let me tell you that last month I received a memorial from General Cleburne of the Army of Tennessee—"

"Ah, that," Seddon said. "Yes, that needs to stay under the rose." He was familiar with the memorial, then.

"Cleburne is an able officer," Lee said. "He fought well in the Chattanooga campaign, by all accounts."

"As may be. He stirred up a fight of his own, among the generals of his army. You see, in his memorial, he proposed freeing and arming some portion of our Negroes, to use them as soldiers against the Yankees."

"Many might say, what point to the Confederacy, then?" Seddon remarked. "What point to our revolution?"

Lee's brows came together as he thought. At last he said, "The Federals let some of their Negroes put on the blue uniform. They will surely take away ours if we are defeated. Would it not be better to preserve our independence by whatever means we may, and measure the cost to our social institutions once that independence is guaranteed? Fighting for their freedom, Negroes might well make good soldiers."

"Put that way, it might be so," Seddon said. "Still, the agitation and controversy which must spring from the presentation of such views by officers high in the public confidence are to be deeply deprecated."

"I agree. We cannot afford such controversy now," Davis said. "Cleburne's memorial is a counsel of the last ditch. At the last ditch, I would consider it—at the last ditch, I would consider any course that promised to stay our subjugation by the tyranny in Washington. What I hope, however, General Lee, is that, newly armed as we shall be, we succeed in keeping ourselves from that last ditch, and thus preserve our institutions unblemished by unwelcome change."

"I hope so, too, Mr. President," Lee said. "It may be so. That our prospects are better with these repeating carbines than they would be without them cannot be denied. Whether they will bring us victory—God alone can answer that. I shall do my best to foster that victory, as will your other commanders." That was as much as Lee felt he could say. He wished

Davis would trust General Johnston further, wished the two of them could compose their quarrel. He was not, however, in a position to suggest it. Both proud, touchy men would surely take it wrong.

Davis said, "General, am I to understand that these amazing rifles spring from Rivington, North Carolina? I had not thought of Rivington as a center of manufacture. Indeed"—he smiled frostily—"up until this past month I had not thought of Rivington at all."

"I'd never heard of the place, either," Seddon put in.

"Nor had I," Lee said. "Since it was brought to my attention, my staff officers and I have inquired about it of train crews and soldiers who pass through the place. Their reports only leave me more puzzled, for it has not the appearance of a manufacturing town: no smelting works, no forges, no factories. There has lately been a good deal of building there, but of homes and warehouses, not the sort of buildings required to produce rifles, cartridges, or powder. Moreover—Mr. President, have you had the opportunity to examine these rifles for yourself?"

"Not yet, no," Davis said.

"Among other things, they bear truly astonishing gunsmiths' marks. Some proclaim themselves to have been manufactured in the People's Republic of China, a part of that country no one has been able to locate in any atlas. Others say they were made in Yugoslavia, a country which appears in no atlas. And still others are marked in what, after some effort, we determined to be Russian. I have learned they were made in the SSSR, but what the SSSR may be, I cannot tell you. It is, I confess, a considerable puzzlement."

"By what you are telling us, Rivington seems more likely a transshipment point than one where the weapons are actually made," Seddon said.

"So it does." Lee looked toward the Secretary of War in some surprise. Why couldn't Seddon make such cogent suggestions more often? Or was it cogent? Lee went on, "From where could the rifles be transshipped? Granted, Rivington is on the Wilmington and Weldon Railroad, but the blockade runners are not bringing them in at Wilmington. They seem to originate directly at Rivington, coming, I cannot tell you how, from these unknown places I have mentioned, and travel from Rivington to us and, I gather, to other armies."

"You have interrogated the railroad workers and our soldiers, you say," Jefferson Davis said. "Have you not also questioned the men of Rivington, the ones who are with your army as instructors?"

"Mr. President, I have, but I confess only circumspectly," Lee said. "They turn aside all significant queries; they are as closemouthed a band of men as I have ever encountered. And without your order, I have been unwilling to do anything that might antagonize them, lest the stream of carbines dry up as suddenly as it began to flow."

Davis rubbed the smooth-shaven front of his chin, plucked at the beard that grew under his jaw. "I dislike our nation's dependence upon any single small group, let alone one about which we know so little. Under the circumstances, though, General, I must reluctantly concur with your judgment."

"Perhaps we should send agents to this Rivington, to learn of it what we may—circumspectly, of course," Seddon said.

"A good plan. See to it," Davis said. Seddon took a pencil and a scrap of paper from his pocket. He leaned forward, made a note to himself on the President's desk, and put away the paper.

"Is there anything more, Mr. President?" Lee asked, hoping the Secretary of War would not forget until the next time he chanced to wear that waistcoat.

"No, General, thank you very much. You may go; I know you'll be eager to see your wife. Please convey my greetings to her. She and her ladies have been of material benefit to the soldiers of the Confederacy, and I would not have her believe herself unappreciated," Davis said.

Lee stood to go. "I will give her your exact words, Mr. President, as best I can remember them. I know she will be grateful to hear from you." He nodded to Seddon. "I hope I see you again, sir."

It was full dark outside, and cloudy, with a feel of rain in the air. Lee put on his hat and buttoned the top buttons of his coat as he walked out to the waiting carriage. Luke looked up at the sound of his footsteps. The black man quickly stowed away a small flask. Lee pretended he had not seen it. If Luke wanted a nip against the nighttime cold, that was his affair. "Gwine home now, Marse Robert?" he asked as he got down to untie the team.

"That's right, Luke, to Mrs. Lee's house." It was hardly home. His proper home, Arlington, lay just across the Potomac from Washington City. It had been in Federal hands since the beginning of the war. For the last two years, he had lived with the Army of Northern Virginia. Anywhere away from it, he felt like a visitor.

"Have you there soon." Luke returned to his seat. "It only be a couple blocks."

The horses snorted eagerly as they began to walk. They had been cold, too. The carriage clattered northwest along Bank Street, the lower boundary of Capitol Square. When Luke got to Ninth Street, he turned right. Half a block later, at the corner of Ninth and Franklin, he went left again, onto Franklin.

Despite the holiday, lights burned at several windows of Mechanic's Hall, which stood at the corner of Ninth and Franklin. Seddon no doubt had come from there: the building housed the War and Navy Departments. Before the Confederate capital moved to Richmond, the convention that had taken Virginia out of the United States had met there, too.

Past Mechanic's Hall, Franklin Street was quiet and almost deserted. Two blocks away, on Broad Street, another train roared along between the depots of the Virginia Central and the Richmond, Fredericksburg and Potomac. Its racket was in marked contrast to the serenity that seemed to flow from every brick of the United Presbyterian Church on the corner of Eighth and Franklin.

Lee smiled and shifted forward in his seat as the carriage rolled past the church. The house Mary Custis Lee was renting lay halfway down the same block, on the opposite side of the street.

"Yours is the middle house, am I right, Marse Robert?" Luke said.

"Yes, and thank you, Luke." Lee descended from the carriage before it had quite stopped. Luke flicked the whip over the horses. As they began to move faster again, he reached down for the flask he had put away. He swallowed and sighed with pleasure.

The house across the street from 707 Franklin had in front of it a young maple in a planter painted with chevrons. "As you were, Sergeant," Lee told it, smiling slightly. He opened the gate to the cast-iron fence in front of 707 Franklin, hurried up the short walk to the porch. There he paused to wipe the mud from the unpaved street off his boots before he knocked on the door.

He heard footsteps inside. The door opened. Lamplight spilled onto the porch. Silhouetted by it, Agnes Lee peered out. "Father!" she exclaimed, and threw herself into his arms.

"Hello, my precious little Agnes," he said. "You must be careful with your knitting needles there behind my back, lest you do me an injury worse than any those people have yet managed to inflict on me."

She looked up at him with a doubtful smile. All her smiles were doubtful these days, and had been since her sister Annie died a year and a half before; she and Annie had been almost as close as twins. After he kissed her on the cheek, she pulled herself free and called, "Mother, Mary, Mildred—Father's here!"

Mildred came rushing up first. "Precious life," he said indulgently as he hugged her. "And how is my pet this evening?"

"Father," she said, in the tone of voice any eighteen-year-old uses when her elderly and obviously decrepit parent presumes to allude to the unfortunate fact that she was once much younger than her present peak of maturity.

Lee did not mind; his youngest child *was* his pet, regardless of what she thought of the matter. "How is Custis Morgan?" he asked her.

"He's happy and fat," she answered. "Acorns are easier to come by than human provender."

"Such a happy, *fat* squirrel had best not be seen in camp," he teased, "lest he exit the stage in a stewpot-bound blaze of glory." She made a face at him. He shook his head in mock reproof.

His eldest daughter came into the front hall a moment later, pushing his wife ahead of her in a wheeled chair. "Hello, Mary," he called to them both. Mary his daughter bore a strong resemblance to his wife, though her hair was darker than Mary Custis Lee's had been when she was young.

He took three quick steps to his wife, bent a little so he could clasp her hand in his. "How are you, my dear Mary?" he asked her. She stayed in her chair most of the time; rheumatism had so crippled her that she could hardly walk.

"You didn't write to let us know you were coming," she said, a little sharply. Even when she'd been young and pretty and well—more than half a lifetime ago, Lee thought with some surprise, he could call up in his mind the picture of her then as easily as if it had been day before yesterday—her temper was uncertain. Years as an invalid had done nothing to soften her.

He said, "I was summoned down to confer with the President, and took the first train south. A letter could hardly have outrun me, so here I am, my own messenger. I am glad to see you—glad to see you all. Your hands, I note, dear Mary, are not too poorly for you to knit." He pointed to the yarn, needles, and half-finished sock that lay in her lap.

"When I can no longer knit, you may lay me in my grave, for I'll be utterly useless then," she answered. She'd loved to ply the needles since she was a girl. Now she went on, "Since you are here, you may take the next bundle back with you for the men. Between our daughters and me, we've finished nearly four dozen pairs since we last sent them. And with them in your hands, the count should be right when they reach camp."

"Times are hard for everyone," Lee said. "If a railroad man is needy enough to filch a pair of socks, I dare say he requires them as badly as any of my soldiers."

His eldest daughter said, "Mrs. Chesnut visited not long ago and said we were so busy we reminded her of an industrial school." Mary tossed her head to show what she thought of the blue-blooded South Carolina woman. At the same age, her mother would have done the same thing.

"I don't care what Mary Boykin Chesnut thinks of us," Mary Custis Lee declared. "It would be altogether improper for me to lead in any entertainments of the social sort when the men you lead are all half-starved, and when you yourself live like a monk in that tent of yours."

"President Davis's opinion of you is rather higher than Mrs. Chesnut's." Lee passed on Davis's compliment. "Tell me, then, whose approbation would you sooner have?"

"Yours," his wife said.

He stooped to kiss her cheek. However her body troubled her, she was loyal to him to the bone, and he to her. They were part of each other. After more than thirty-two years of marriage, he had trouble imagining things being otherwise.

"Julia, turn down the second bed in Mother's room, please," Agnes called. The black woman started up the stairs.

Lee said, "That's thoughtful of you, but I don't plan on turning in quite yet. I should like to sit up awhile and listen to the doings of the city from the lot of you. If you can stand to hear me, I may even go on a bit about affairs at camp."

"I'm going to go hide Custis Morgan, so you don't take him back to Orange Court House with the socks," Mildred said. "What's your daughter's happiness, set against the prospect of squirrel stew for your men?"

Chuckling, Lee told her, "Your pet is safe from me, precious life. He would not go far enough, divided among hungry soldiers, to be worth absconding with. If the Scriptures spoke of the miracle of loaves and squirrels, though, instead of loaves and fishes—"

Everyone laughed at that, even Agnes, briefly. Mary Custis Lee said, "Let's go back into the parlor, then, and talk." The wheels of her chair squeaked as Mary turned her around.

"I don't want to talk about squirrels anymore," Mildred said.

"Then we shan't," Lee promised.

The women's needles clicked busily as they resumed their interrupted knitting. The war touched them in Richmond almost as hard as it did him with the Army of Northern Virginia. One of the stories Lee's eldest daughter told was of the mass escape of Federal officers from Libby Prison less than two weeks before. Over a hundred men had got loose, and fewer than half of them were rounded up again.

"Our own soldiers suffer in Northern prison camps," Lee said, "though the North has more to spare for captives than do we. The North has more to spare for everyone." He sighed. "I have said that, thought that, wrestled with that for too long. I wish this war had never come; it wastes both sides."

"I said as much when it began," his wife observed.

"I know you did, nor did I disagree with you. I wanted no flag but the Star-Spangled Banner, no song besides 'Hail Columbia.' But once here, the thing must be fought through." He hesitated, then continued: "It may even—may, I say—have seen a turn in our favor."

The knitting needles stopped. His wife and daughters all looked at him. He had always done his best to sound hopeful in his letters and to act so when he saw them, but he was not one to be falsely or blindly optimistic, and they knew it. His daughter Mary asked, "From where has this good news come?"

"From Rivington, North Carolina, as a matter of fact," Lee said. The name of the place meant no more to his family than it had to him a month before. He quickly told the story of the new repeaters and the curiously accented men who supplied them, finishing, "We cannot outnumber the Federals; if we outshoot them, though, that may serve as well."

His daughters seemed more interested in his account of the strangers and their gear than in details of the carbines. Mildred said, "I wonder if those are the same men as the ones who not long ago rented a whole floor in the building across from Mechanic's Hall."

"Why do you say that, precious life?" Lee asked.

"Any time anyone pays his bills in gold these days, word gets around, and by what you said, these—what did your lieutenant call them?—these all-over-spots fellows appear to have an unmatched supply of it. And if I were selling guns to the War Department instead of making socks, I should like my offices close by theirs."

"None of which necessarily proves a thing," he said. Mildred's lively features started to cloud up, but he went on, "Still, I think you may well be right. It could do with some looking into, perhaps."

"Why, Father?" Agnes scratched her head. Her hair, now tightly done up with pins, came closest of all his children's to matching the rich yellow that had been her mother's. "Why?" she asked again. "From all you've said, these men from Rivington mean us nothing but good."

"The old homely saying is, look not a gift horse in the mouth. If you follow that saying, you will end up with a great many old, hard-mouthed horses in your barn," Lee answered. "When the gift is of such magnitude as that which these men are giving us, I would examine it as closely as possible to learn if it is in fact as fine as it appears and to see if it comes attached to strings."

"Even if it does, you will have to accept it, Father, won't you?" Mary asked.

"You always did see clearly, my dear," he said. "Yes, I think we must, if our Southern Confederacy is to survive, which God grant."

"Amen," Agnes said softly.

The slave woman brought in a tray with cups and a steaming pot. The spicy scent of sassafras tea filled the parlor. "Thank you, Julia," Lee said as she poured for him. The tea made him think of the "instant coffee" Andries Rhoodie had brought up to the headquarters near Orange Court House.

"Coffee," his wife said longingly when he spoke of it. "We've been some time without it here."

"Surely it would come to Richmond more readily than to a small town like Rivington, North Carolina, especially if, as you say, Father, it was made in the United States," Mary said.

"That's true, and I should have thought of it for myself," Lee said. "Still, with gold, a great many things become possible. Rivington is on the railroad up from Wilmington; maybe a blockade runner brought it in there, rather than something more truly useful to our cause. Maybe." He found himself yawning.

Mary Custis Lee put down her needles. "There; this sock is finished, and a good enough place to call the day's work finished as well. Knitting by the light of lamp and candle is hard on the eyes."

"Which does not stop you from doing so, Mother," Agnes said reprovingly.

"Not on most nights," her mother agreed. "But tonight we find Robert here, so halting early is easier to square with my conscience."

"I wish I were here with you and my girls every night, both for the pleasure of your company and because it would mean the war was over and our independence won," Lee said. He yawned again. "Tonight, though, I own myself tired. Riding the train with the rails in their present sadly decrepit state is hardly more enjoyable than driving a light buggy headlong down a corduroy road."

"Then let us seek our beds," his wife said. "Surely you will rest better in a real bed and a warm house than in your tent by the Rapidan. Mary, dear, if you would be so kind?" Mary got up and wheeled her mother to the base of the stairs.

Lee rose quickly too, to go with them. As he stood, he felt a probing pain in his chest. That pain had been with him now and again all through the winter. Doctors thumped his chest and made learned noises, without finding its source or doing him any good to speak of. He endured it stoically; Mary, he knew, suffered far worse.

At the foot of the stairs, she used her left arm to push herself out of her chair and upright, then grabbed the banister with her right hand. Lee stepped up beside her, slid his arm around her waist. The feel of her body against his was strange from separation, yet at the same time infinitely familiar. "Shall we ascend, my dear?" he said.

He took most of her weight as they climbed to the second floor. "You are smoother at helping me than anyone else, I think," she said. "You have a gentle touch."

"Who is likely to know you better than your husband?" he replied as he guided her down the hallway toward the bedroom. He had nursed her many illnesses through their marriage whenever they were together; before that, his mother had spent her last years as an invalid. He was long practiced in dealing with the sick.

He helped Mary change into a warm flannel nightgown, then put on the pajamas Julia had left out for him. "And a nightcap, too," he exclaimed as he set it on his head. "Such luxury is bound to spoil me." His wife snorted. He walked over to her bed and kissed her. "Good night, dear Mary." He went back to his own bed, blew out the candle by it. The room plunged into darkness.

"Sleep well, Robert," Mary said.

"Thank you. I'm sure I shall," he answered. After so long on his cot, the bed felt almost indecently soft. But the room was warm, at least compared to a tent in the hills close by the Rapidan. He had no trouble dropping off.

Luke and his carriage showed up in front of the house on Franklin Street at breakfast time. When Lee went out to him, he seemed none the worse for wear for however much drinking he had done the night before. "Where to today, Marse Robert?" he asked.

"The armory," Lee answered. "I need to confer with Colonel Gorgas."

"Whatever you say, Marse Robert." Luke, plainly, could not have cared less whether Lee went to the armory to confer with Gorgas or with George Washington's ghost. But he flicked his whip over the team and got them moving, which was what mattered.

The carriage rolled down Seventh Street toward the James River. The armory sprawled at the foot of Gamble's Hill, diagonally between Seventh and Fourth. The Kanawha Canal ran behind it. Luke pulled up to the columned central entranceway; the dome that surmounted it did not seem to be of a piece with the rest of the long, low brick building.

The armory rang with the sounds of metalwork and carpentry. Drills and lathes and dies and punches and molds turned wood and iron and lead into small arms and bullets. No other Confederate arsenal came close to matching its production. Without the machines captured at Harper's Ferry and moved here in the first days of the war, the South would have been hard-pressed for weapons.

"General Lee." Josiah Gorgas came up and saluted. He was a heavyset, moon-faced man in his forties, his close-trimmed beard just starting to be streaked with gray. "I'm very glad to see you, sir. I'd hoped to have the opportunity to speak with you, and here you are."

"And I with you, Colonel. I suspect we have in mind a similar topic of conversation, too."

"Likely we do, sir. Will you come up to my office, where we can talk more comfortably?" He led Lee up to the second floor.

Lee took the stairs slowly, worried that the pain in his chest might recur. To his relief, it did not. He sat opposite Gorgas, pointed to the AK-47 on the ordnance chief's desk. "Yes, there it is, the marvel of the day." Gorgas looked at him sharply. "I meant no sarcasm, Colonel, I assure you. I am in your debt—the Confederacy is in your debt—for sending Andries Rhoodie on to me."

"I hoped you would feel so, General, after seeing it demonstrated. I certainly did, and I am glad to have my judgment vindicated by a soldier in the field. I do endeavor to give satisfaction so far as arms go." He spoke with some diffidence; a shipment of cavalry carbines the summer before had been almost as dangerous to the men who held them as to those at whom they were aimed.

Lee said, "My only possible reservation about these repeaters is that they have not yet seen combat. But I think they will answer. Though they are so different from our usual rifles, they are easy to learn and use and maintain, and the troops are much taken by the volume of fire they deliver. I like men to be confident in their arms; it makes them more belligerent."

"General, I think you yourself are the most belligerent man in your army," Gorgas said.

Lee considered. "Henry Heth said something to that effect to me once," he remarked. "It may be so. Hemmed in as I am by responsibility, I have few opportunities personally to demonstrate it, if it is. But I would surely rather strike a blow than either flee or remain quiet, waiting to be struck. Enough of my ramblings now, sir—to business. I thank God for these gentlemen from Rivington and for the arms with which they are supplying us. I am not, however, eager to forever depend on them for weapons. If anyone, if any establishment in the Confederacy can manufacture their like, you are the man, and this is the place."

Gorgas looked baffled and unhappy, like a hound that has taken a scent and then lost it in the middle of an open meadow. "General Lee, I do not know. I thank you for being thoughtful enough to provide me with more of these carbines and a stock of ammunition. I already had one, and a couple of magazines, from Andries Rhoodie. I have been puzzling at it since before he departed for Orange Court House. And—I do not know."

"What perplexes you so about the rifle?" Lee asked. He had his own list; he wanted to see what the Confederacy's ordnance wizard would add to it.

"First, that it springs *ex nihilo*, like Minerva from Jove's forehead." Colonel Gorgas evidently had a list, too—he was ticking off points on his fingers. "Generally speaking, a new type of weapon will have defects, which may in some cases be amelioriated through modifications made in the light of experience. The next defect I discover in this AK-47 will be the first. The gun *works*, sir, which is no small wonder in itself."

"I had not thought of it in those terms," Lee said slowly. "You mean it gives the impression of being a *finished* arm, like, for example, a Springfield."

"Exactly so. The Springfield rifle musket has a great number of less efficient ancestors. So, logically, must the AK-47. Yet where are they? Even a less efficient rifle based on its principles would be better than anything we or the Federals have."

"That is the case, I have noticed, with much of the equipment borne by Andries Rhoodie and his colleagues," Lee said, remembering a tasty tin of desiccated stew. "Carry on."

"From the general to the particular." Gorgas reached into a desk drawer, took out a couple of rounds for the AK-47. He passed them over to Lee. "You will observe that the bullets are not simply lead."

"Yes, I had seen that," Lee agreed, putting on his glasses for a clearer look at the ammunition. The cartridges were surely brass. As for the bullets— "Are they copper all the way through?"

"No, sir. They have a lead interior, sheathed with copper. We might be able to match that, though it is expensive, and we are short of enough copper even now to be commandeering coils from whiskey cookers' stills. Then again, unsheathed lead might serve at need. But do you see the cleverness of this ammunition? It all but eliminates lead fouling of the barrel."

"Less need for Williams bullets, then," Lee said. The Williams bullet had a zinc washer at the base of the lead slug, which served to scour away fouling from the inside of a rifle barrel when it was fired. Lee went on, "But would a copper-sheathed bullet not be too hard to take rifling well? And would it not wear away the interior grooves in short order?"

"With any normal barrel, the answer to both those questions would be yes." Gorgas ticked off another point. "The steel—or whatever alloy it may be—in the barrel of this weapon, however, is hard enough to lessen the difficulties. Again, I doubt we could produce its like, let alone work it once manufactured."

"They seem to manage in Rivington," Lee said.

"I know they do, sir. But—I—don't—know—how." The colonel ground out the words one by one through clenched teeth. He was a man of sanguine temperament and great resource, as he had to be to keep the Confederacy supplied with armaments in the face of an ever-tightening Federal blockade and its own inadequate factories. When he said, "I am thwarted; I admit it," it was as if he threw down his sword to surrender to superior force.

"Tell me what else you do know," Lee urged, not liking to see such a capable officer so downhearted.

"Very well, sir. You mentioned the Williams bullet. As you must know, the chief fouling problem it is designed to alleviate comes not from the lead of the Minié ball but rather from the powder which propels it. Whatever powder is in these AK-47 cartridges, it produces far less fouling than even the finest gunpowder with which I was previously familiar."

"Has that a connection with the lack of smoke from this powder upon discharge?" Lee asked.

"Exactly: fouling consists of smoke and tiny bits of unburned powder that congeal, so to speak, on the inside of a gun barrel. With this powder, there is next to no smoke and, thus, next to no fouling."

"I have sent a good deal of ammunition down to Colonel George Rains at the powder works in Augusta, Georgia," Lee said. "With his knowledge of chemistry in general and gunpowder in particular, I thought him the man best suited to penetrate the mystery of these rounds, if anyone can."

"If anyone can," Gorgas echoed gloomily. But after a moment, he brightened a little. "As you say, if anyone can, Colonel Rains is the man. Without his expertise, we should be much the poorer for powder."

"There I quite agree with you, Colonel. Chemical knowledge is too uncommon in the Confederacy. Of course, the same also obtains among the Federals." Lee smiled at a memory. "When I administered West Point a few years ago, I had to dismiss from the academy a cadet who informed his instructor and fellow chemistry students that silicon was a gas. Do you know, Colonel, were silicon truly a gas, that lad would likely be a Federal general today."

As Lee had hoped, Gorgas also smiled at the story. His amusement, though, soon faded. He said, "And now, General, I come to the particular most baffling of all, and when I speak of this weapon, that is no small claim. Do you know, sir, what these Rivington men charge the Ordnance Bureau for each AK-47 carbine? Fifty dollars, sir."

"It hardly seems excessive. A Henry rifle goes for a similar price in the North, I understand, and this weapon is surely far superior to a Henry. Of course, the Treasury Department will doubtless be anguished at the prospect of discovering sufficient specie to purchase the number of carbines we require, but—what is it, Colonel?"

Gorgas had lifted his hand, as if he wanted to speak. Now he said, "You misapprehend, General, not that I can blame you for it. The asking price is fifty dollars Confederate paper per carbine."

"You must be mistaken," Lee said. Gorgas shook his head. Lee saw he knew whereof he spoke. "But how is that possible? While I love our country, I am not blind to our financial straits. Fifty dollars of Confederate paper will not buy two gold dollars."

"Nor much of anything else," Gorgas said. "Save these AK-47s. The asking price for their ammunition is similarly, ah, reasonable."

Lee frowned ferociously, as if facing foes in the field. "You are correct, Colonel; the cost of an AK-47 is even more perplexing than any of its mechanical aspects, extraordinary as those are."

"Yes, sir. The only thing I thought of was that these Rivington men are such strong patriots that they insist on our dollar's equality to that of the North. But no one is that patriotic, sir."

"Nor should anyone be, with the manifest untruth of the proposition demonstrated every day of the year," Lee said. "Yet the Rivington men, despite the money they surely lose on every repeater they sell us, seem to have plenty of it. When they came to Rivington, they paid gold for homes and warehouses and slaves, and I am given to understand they have also put down gold here in Richmond for offices across from Mechanic's Hall."

"I'd heard that, too," Gorgas said. "Even the rumor of gold, let alone the sight of it, will set tongues wagging here. What are we to make of it, though? That they have so much money, they care nothing for how much these carbines bring them? The notion is logical but not reasonable, if you take my distinction, sir."

"I do indeed, Colonel." Lee started to rise, then paused and sat down again. "May I please have a pen and a scrap of paper?" Gorgas passed him pen and inkwell. He sketched rapidly, gave his drawing to the ordnance chief. "Are you by any chance familiar with this emblem that Rhoodie and his comrades use?"

"Yes, I've seen it. Funny you should ask, for it interested me. Not long after I first made Rhoodie's acquaintance, I made a copy of it and showed it to a friend of mine who knows something of heraldry. He said it reminded him of the arms of the Isle of Man, save that those show three bent legs—don't ask me for the proper terms, please, sir—instead of mere lines."

"The Isle of Man, you say? Most interesting. Manxmen have a distinctive way of speaking, do they not? Perhaps that is the accent Rhoodie and his comrades bear. It might form a useful basis from which to begin inquiries, at any rate."

"So it might." Gorgas smiled ruefully. "A pity to have to think about investigating men who are helping us so greatly, but they do seem rather too good to be true."

"You are not the first to use those very words about them, Colonel, and when something seems too good to be true, it is all too apt to be so. Well, now I have spent enough of your time this morning; with all my fretting about our benefactors, you will no doubt be thinking of me as Granny Lee—a nickname I assure you I was not sorry to lose after the first year of the war."

"I don't blame you for that, sir," Gorgas said, "nor for the other. Too many peculiar things hover about Rhoodie and his carbine for me to be easy with them, no matter how useful the gun may prove."

"That is exactly my view." Lee really stood this time. Through the window in Gorgas's office, he saw the white frame buildings of the Confederate laboratory on Brown's Island, separated from the mainland by a thin stretch of the James. Pointing across to them, he said, "I trust everyone at the cartridge loading works is busily engaged."

"Yes, sir," Gorgas said. "We have put last spring's misfortune behind us and go on, as we must. My wife fatigued herself very much, visiting and relieving the poor sufferers injured in the blast."

"How many died?" Lee asked.

"Ten women were killed at once; another twenty perished over the next several weeks. A considerable number more were burned but recovered."

"Terrible." Lee shook his head. "And as terrible that we must employ women and girls to produce the sinews of war for us. But with even our armies ever short of men, I suppose no good choice exists. You and your wife have your living quarters here in the armory, do you not?"

"Yes, sir, just a couple of doors down from here, as a matter of fact."

"You are fortunate, Colonel, in being able to honorably carry out your vital duty and yet remain in the bosom of your family."

"I often think so," Gorgas said.

"As you should; such circumstances are given to few, and ought not to be taken for granted. And now I will let you return to your duties. No, you need not see me out; I can find my way." Given that permission, Gorgas was already reaching for a pen as Lee shut the door behind him. The man was a glutton for work. Lee wished the Confederacy had more like him.

Piles of shells in the yard around the armory testified to the diligence of Gorgas and his crews. The muscular men loading some of those shells onto a wagon for transport to a railway station and thence to the field paused when Lee came out and walked over to his carriage. A couple of them lifted their caps to him. He nodded in return. They grinned as they went back to work.

Luke breathed whiskey fumes into Lee's face as Lee got in behind him. "You give 'em somethin' to brag on, Marse Robert, just because they see you." Lee glanced down, but the black man had his flask out of sight. He asked, "Where you want to go to now?"

Lee considered the question. He'd had no definite plans for the rest of the day. His first impulse was to rush headlong to the treasury, beard Secretary Memminger in his lair, and demand of him if he knew what an impossibly good bargain he was getting in Rhoodie's repeaters. But finance was not his own province. He said, "Take me back to the War Department."

"Yassuh, Marse Robert." Tight or sober, Luke could handle horses. He swung the team around another wagon coming into the armory to be loaded with shells, then drove back to Mechanic's Hall. Lee eyed with keen interest the building across the street from the War Department, a three-story, brown brick structure he'd gone by countless times before but scarcely noticed. His scrutiny was rewarded by the sight of a man in the mottled outfit that seemed the trademark costume of Andries Rhoodie and his comrades passing in through the building's marble-faced entranceway.

Officers with lace on their gray sleeves and civilians in black claw-hammer coats bustled in and out of Mechanic's Hall, as if the place were an ant's nest, with some workers going forth to forage and others returning with their spoils. Luke pulled up right in front of the building. A Confederate with the two stars of a lieutenant colonel on his collar shouted, "You damned stupid nigger, what do you think you're doing, blocking the—" The words stuck in his throat when Lee got out of the carriage. He pulled himself to attention and snapped off a salute that would have done credit to a cadet from the Virginia Military Institute.

Lee turned and said, "Thank you, Luke," before he returned it. The black man smiled a secret smile as he took the team around the corner to find a place to hitch it. The walk from the street into the foyer of Mechanic's Hall was only twenty or thirty feet, but in that short space Lee was saluted close to a dozen times.

He paused in the foyer to let his eyes adjust to the dimmer interior light.

Then he walked over to a desk where a clerk was industriously jotting in a ledger or notebook. After a glance at the enameled brass nameplate in front of the fellow, he said, "Excuse me, Mr. Jones, does Colonel Lee still maintain his office on the second floor?"

The clerk—John Beauchamp Jones his nameplate proclaimed him to be, as if by trumpeting his middle name he could make up for the utter plainness of those that flanked it—finished writing his sentence before he looked up. His thin, clean-shaven face bore a sour expression at the interruption. That quickly changed when he saw who stood before him. "Yes, General, he does. He's there now, I believe; I saw him go up this morning."

"Thank you, sir." Lee had not taken two steps toward the stairway before Jones returned to his writing.

He fielded more salutes on the second floor as he made his way down the hall to his son Custis's office. Custis was writing when he tapped on the open door, though with less zeal than John Jones had displayed. "Father! Sir!" he exclaimed, springing to his feet. He too saluted, then stuck out his hand.

Lee took it, swept his eldest son into an embrace. "Hello, my dear boy. You're looking very well. I see it is possible to find adequate victuals in Richmond after all."

Custis laughed. "I've always been heavier than you, Father. Here, sit down. Tell me what I can do for you. Is it—I hope it is—a post in the field?"

"I have none to give, son; I wish I did. I know how you chafe as President Davis's aide," Lee said.

Custis nodded, tugging at his beard in frustration. Though he was past thirty, it remained boyishly thin and silky on his upper cheeks. He said, "How am I ever to deserve command if I have not led men in the field?"

"Soon, I am sure, you will take the field in some capacity—everyone who has ability will be needed when spring comes. Do not think you have no value in your current post, either; you render the President and the nation important service."

"It is not the service I would give," Custis said stiffly.

"I know. I have been in that predicament myself, in western Virginia and then in the Carolinas. At the moment, however, your presence in Richmond may prove of considerable advantage to me."

"How so, sir?" The younger Lee still sounded dubious, as if he suspected his father of devising some make-work assignment to reconcile him to remaining in the Confederate capital.

But interest flowered on his face when Lee asked, "Do you remember the organization that calls itself America Will Break, of which I wrote you? The one which appears centered in the town of Rivington, North Carolina?"

"The people with those amazing repeaters?" Custis said. "Yes, of course I do. I shouldn't mind getting my hands on one of their carbines myself."

"That can be quite simply arranged, I think: you need only walk across the street, as the organization has established offices right opposite Mechanic's Hall. But I wish you would not."

Custis smiled. "You'd best have a good reason, Father, for if they are so close, I think I shall straightaway beat a path to their door."

"I believe I do have a good reason, Custis, or rather several of them."

Lee briefly outlined his conversations with Major Venable back at army headquarters and with Colonel Gorgas not an hour earlier. When he finished by telling Custis what the Rivington men were selling their repeaters for, his son stared and exclaimed, "You're joking!"

"No, my dear boy, I am not," Lee assured him. "And so you will grasp that I have cause to wonder about these people who call themselves America Will Break. They are on their way to becoming a power in the Confederacy, and I do not know whether they will prove a power for good or ill. There is a great deal I do not know about them, and I wish I did. That is where you come in."

"How?" Now Custis seemed eager, not doubtful. Before his father could answer, he went on, "Fifty dollars Confederate? Fifty dollars Confederate won't buy a pocket knife, let alone a repeating rifle."

"That is why I want you," his father said. "I cannot personally investigate these AWB establishments myself. Even if I had the time, I am too readily recognizable. For that matter, you may be as well; you favor your mother as much as me, but the name Lee draws attention to its bearer."

"Thanks to you, sir—what you have done makes me proud to bear it."

"You have made your own contributions to it, and will, I am confident, make more. You can aid your country now by recruiting a band of men— I care not whether soldiers or civilians—whose names and faces will certainly draw no notice, and by using them to keep watch on the men and offices of America Will Break. Report what you learn to me and, if it is of sufficient urgency, directly to President Davis. Your being his aide may well prove valuable in this task, for it gives you his ear."

Custis's face grew set and abstracted. Lee knew the look; his son was thinking through the task he had been given. It was not a formal order; he was not under his father's command. But he said, "Of course I'll take it on, sir. I see the need. Perhaps I ought to enlist some Negroes among my—

my spies, not to mince words. To a white man, no one is more invisible than a slave."

"That may be an excellent notion. If you make sure they are trustworthy and can be relied upon not to gossip, by all means make use of them. Do not stint in rewarding them, either, if they give you good service."

"I promise, Father, I shan't be niggardly."

"Good, for mostly being poor, they are—" Lee broke off and did his best to stare severely at his son, who was grinning to see his delayed reaction. "You young scamp!"

"I'm sorry, sir. I couldn't resist."

"You might have tried," Lee said. "I think I shall take myself away, before I find myself under further bombardments." He got up. So did Custis. They hugged again. "Take care of yourself, my dear son."

"And you, Father. Give my love to Rob when you get back to the army, and to Cousin Fitzhugh as well." One of Custis's brothers was in the artillery, his cousin a cavalry officer.

"I shall," Lee promised.

"Any word on Rooney?" Custis asked. His other brother, also a cavalry officer, had been wounded at Brandy Station the year before and captured while recuperating; for a time, he had been under threat of death.

Lee said, "The exchange talks seem to be moving forward at last. God willing, we'll have him back again next month."

"Thank heaven."

"Yes. I expect to be down here a few more days, doing this and that. Perhaps you and your wife will be able to stop by the house on Franklin Street before I have to return. If not, tell her I know I owe her a letter. And, Custis, I do attach much importance to this business of the Rivington men, believe me."

"I had not doubted it, sir. You are not in the habit of concerning yourself with trifles. I'll learn all I can of them."

"I'm sure you will. God bless you and keep you, Custis."

Lee walked out of his son's office and down the stairs. His way out to the street carried him past John Jones's desk. The clerk was turned away from him, talking to the man at the next desk: "My boy Custis's parrot happened to be loose from its cage. It swooped down on the meat as if it were a hawk, the miserable bird, and gulped it down before we could get it back again. Meat is too hard to come by in Richmond these days to waste on a parrot; we'll go without on account of it. I wish the damned talking feather duster would fly away for good."

Luke was waiting patiently outside Mechanic's Hall. He waved when he saw Lee, and called, "I'll get the carriage for you, Marse Robert." He hurried off to fetch it. Lee went down the marble stairs and stood to one side of them so he would not be in the way of people going in and out on War Department business.

"Good to see you smiling, General Lee, sir," a friendly passerby said, tipping his stovepipe hat. "Now I know things can't be bad." Without waiting for an answer, he went up the stairs two at a time and disappeared into Mechanic's Hall.

Lee's smile grew broader, though the stranger had been cheered by an amusement which had nothing to do with the prospective course of the war between Confederacy and Union. The thought uppermost in Lee's mind was that Custis Jones's parrot ought to make the acquaintance of Custis Morgan the squirrel.

⋆ IV ⋆

With his small, bald head, long nose, and long neck, Richard Ewell inevitably reminded everyone who met him of a stork. Having lost a leg at Groveton during Second Manassas, he could now also imitate the big white bird's one-footed stance. He was sitting at the moment, however, sitting and pounding one fist into the other palm to emphasize his words: "We smashed 'em, sir, smashed 'em, I tell you." His voice was high and thin, almost piping.

"I am very glad to hear it, General Ewell," Lee replied. "If those people send raiders down toward Richmond with the intention of seizing their prisoners there—and perhaps even the city itself—they must expect not to be welcomed with open arms."

"Oh, we met 'em with arms, all right," Jeb Stuart said with a grin, patting the AK-47 that leaned against his camp stool. The repeater's woodwork was not so perfectly varnished as it had been fresh out of the crate; it had seen use since then. Stuart patted it again. "And we sent Kilpatrick's riders back over the Rapidan with their tails between their legs."

Lee smiled. He'd liked Stuart for years, ever since the young cavalry corps commander's days at West Point with Custis. He said, "Excellent. But don't you think that leather might better have gone into shoes for the men?"

Ever flamboyant, Stuart wore crossed leather belts over his shoulders, each one with loops enough to hold a magazine's worth of brass AK-47 cartridges. The effect was piratical. But Stuart instantly became a contrite swashbuckler, saying, "I'm sorry, General Lee; it never crossed my mind."

"Let it go," Lee said. "I doubt the Confederacy will founder for want of a couple of feet of cowhide. But I take it I am to infer from your ornaments that you are pleased with the performance of the new repeaters in action."

"General Lee, yesterday I sold my LeMat," Stuart said. Lee blinked at that; Stuart had carried the fancy revolver with an extra charge of buckshot in a separate lower barrel ever since the war was young.

"The rifles are outstanding," General Ewell agreed. "So are the men who furnish them. If I had a drink in my hand, I'd toast them."

"I have some blackberry wine here in my tent, brought up from Richmond," Lee said. "If you truly feel the need, I should be glad to bring it out."

Ewell shook his head. "Thank you, but let it be. Still, had we not heard from those America Will Break fellows that Kilpatrick was on the move, who knows how much mischief he might have done before we beat him back?"

"As it was, I understand, some of their cavalry captured a train station on the line up from the capital not long after I passed through on the way back to the army," Lee said.

"Fugitives from the main band, after we scattered them," Stuart said. "I'm glad they got to the station too late to nab you. Otherwise, however badly the rest of their plan failed, they would have won a great victory."

"If a republic will stand or fall on the fate of any single man, it finds itself in grave danger indeed," Lee observed.

But Ewell said, "Our republic *is* in great danger, as well you know, sir. We would be in graver danger still, were it not for your Andries Rhoodie and his fellows. When Meade sent Sedgwick west with the VI Corps, when Custer went haring off toward Charlottesville, I would have shifted the entire army to meet them had Rhoodie not warned me of a possible cavalry thrust south from Ely's Ford."

"But Fitz Lee was sitting there waiting for the bold Kilpatrick," Stuart said with the smile of a cat who has caught his canary. "General Kill-Cavalry killed a good many of his Yankees by Spotsylvania Court House."

"I'm delighted Fitz Lee was there," Lee said, thinking kind thoughts about his nephew.

"So am I," Stuart said. "Also there was Rhoodie's friend Konrad de Buys. General Lee, that man is wilder in battle than any of Stand Watie's red Indians in the trans-Mississippi. He awed me, damn me if he didn't."

Any man about whom a warrior like Stuart would say such a thing had to be a man indeed. Lee said, "I wondered how the Rivington men would fare. But I wonder more how Rhoodie and de Buys knew Kilpatrick was coming. General Ewell, you say the Army of the Potomac feinted to the west to draw your attention to your left wing, and that the feint was competently executed?"

Ewell's pale eyes turned inward as he pondered that. "Very competently. Sedgwick's as good a corps commander as the Federals have, and Custer—what can I say about Custer, save that he wishes he were Jeb Stuart?" Stuart smiled again, a smile the brighter for peeping out through his forest of brown beard.

"Under normal circumstances, you might have been deceived, then, General Ewell, at least long enough for Kilpatrick to slip past you and make for Richmond?" Lee asked. Ewell nodded. "And you had picked up nothing from spies and agents to warn you Kilpatrick might be on the move?" Ewell nodded once more. Lee plucked at his beard. *"How did Rhoodie know?"*

"Why don't you ask him, sir?" Jeb Stuart said.

"I think I shall," Lee said.

Walter Taylor stuck his head into Lee's tent. "Mr. Rhoodie is here to see you, sir."

"Thank you, Major. Have him come in."

Rhoodie pushed his way through the tent flap. With his height and wide shoulders, he seemed to fill up the space the canvas enclosed. Lee rose to greet him and shake his hand. "Have a seat, Mr. Rhoodie. Will you take a little blackberry wine? The bottle is right there beside you."

"If you are having some, I wouldn't mind, thank you."

"I believe I set out two glasses. Would you be kind enough to pour, sir? Ah, thank you. Your very good health." Lee took a small sip. He was pleased to see Rhoodie toss off half his glass at a swallow; wine might help loosen the fellow's tongue. He said, "From what General Ewell tells me, the Confederacy finds itself in your debt once more. Without your timely warning, Kilpatrick's raiders might have done far worse than they actually succeeded in accomplishing."

"So they might." Rhoodie finished his wine. "I am pleased to help in any way I can. Can I fill you up again, General?"

"No, thank you, not yet, but by all means help yourself." Lee took another sip to indicate he was not far behind Rhoodie. He nodded imperceptibly to himself when the big man did pour again, as a fisherman will when his bait is taken. He said, "Interesting how you got wind of Kilpatrick's plans when the rest of the army would have been hoodwinked by Meade's motion toward our left."

Rhoodie looked smug. "We have our ways, General Lee."

"Marvelously good ones they must be, too. As with your rifles, they altogether outdistance that which anyone else may hope to accomplish. But how do you know what you know, Mr. Rhoodie? Be assured that I ask in the most friendly way imaginable; my chief concern is to be able to form a judgment of your reliability, so I may know how far I may count on it in the crises which surely lie ahead."

"As I think I told you once before, General, my friends and I can find out whatever we think important enough to know." Yes, Rhoodie was smug.

Lee said, "That hardly appears open to question, sir, not after your repeaters, your desiccated foods—though I wish you might find a way to provide us with more of the latter—and now your ability to ferret out the Federals' plans. But I did not ask what you could do; I asked how you did it. The difference is small, but I think it important."

"I—see." Suddenly Andries Rhoodie's face showed nothing at all, save a polite mask behind which any thoughts whatever might form. Seeing that mask, Lee knew he had been foolish to hope to loosen this man's tongue with a couple of glasses of homemade wine. After a small but noticeable pause, the big man with the odd accent said, "Even if I were to tell you, I fear you would not believe me—you would be more likely to take me for a madman or a liar."

"Madmen may babble of wonderful weapons, but they do not, as a rule, produce them—certainly not in carload lots," Lee said. "As for whether you speak the truth, well, say what you have to say, and let me be the judge of that."

Rhoodie's poker face hid whatever calculations were going on behind it. At last he said, "All right, General Lee, I will. My friends and I—everyone who belongs to America Will Break—come from a hundred and fifty years in your future." He folded his arms across his broad chest and waited to see what Lee would make of that.

Lee opened his mouth to reply, then closed it again while he did some thinking of his own. He did not know what he had expected Rhoodie to say, but the big man's calm assertion was nothing he had imagined. He studied Rhoodie, wondering if he had made a joke. If he had, his face did not show it. Lee said, "If that be so—note I say if—then why have you come?"

"I told you that the day I met you: to help the Confederacy win this war and gain its freedom."

"Have you any proof of what you allege?" Lee asked.

Now Rhoodie smiled, rather coldly: "General Lee, if you can match the AK-47 anywhere in the year 1864, then I am the greatest liar since Ananias."

Lee plucked at his beard. He himself had brought up the excellence of Rhoodie's equipment, but had not thought that very excellence might be evidence they were from out of time. Now he considered the notion. What would Napoleon have thought of locomotives to carry whole armies more than a hundred miles in the course of a day, of steam-powered ironclads, of rifled artillery, of rifle muskets with interchangeable parts, common enough for every soldier to carry one? And Napoleon was less than fifty years dead and had rampaged across Russia while Lee was a small boy. Who could say what progress another century and a half would bring? Andries Rhoodie might. To his own surprise, Lee realized he believed the big man. Rhoodie was simply too strange in too many ways to belong to the nineteenth century.

"If you intend to see the Confederate States independent, Mr. Rhoodie, you would have been of more aid had you chosen to visit us sooner," Lee said, tacitly acknowledging his acceptance of Rhoodie's claim.

"I know that, General Lee. I wish we could have come sooner, too, believe me. But our time machine travels back and forth exactly one hundred fifty years, no more, no less. We did not manage to obtain even the small one we have—steal it, not to mince words—until just a few months ago—just a few months ago up in 2013, that is. Still, all is not lost—far from it. Another year and a half and it would have been too late."

Those few sentences held so much meat that Lee needed a little time to take it in. By itself, the idea of travel through time was enough to bemuse him. He also had to come to grips with the notion of two stations in time— in his mind's eye, he saw them as train stations, with an overhang to keep passengers dry in the rain—each moving forward yet always separated from the other by so many years, just as Richmond and Orange Court House each moved as the Earth rotated on its axis, yet always remained separated from the other by so many miles.

Not content with those conceptions, Rhoodie had saved the most important for last. "You tell me," Lee said slowly, "that absent your intervention, the United States would succeed in conquering us."

"General Lee, I am afraid I do tell you that. Are you so startled to hear it?"

"No," Lee admitted with a sigh. "Saddened, yes, but not startled. The enemy has always put me in mind of a man with a strong body but a weak

head. Our Southern body is weak, but our head, sir, our head is filled with
fire. Still, they may find wisdom, while we have ever more difficulty maintaining what strength they have. They force themselves upon us, do they,
when all we ever wanted was to leave in peace and live in peace?"

"They do just that," Rhoodie said grimly. "They force you to free your
kaffirs—your niggers, I mean—at the point of a bayonet, then set them over
you, with the bayonet still there to make you bow down. The Southern
white man is ruined absolutely, and the Southern white woman—no, I won't
go on. That is why we had to steal our time machine, sir; the white man's
cause is so hated in times to come that we could obtain it by no other
means."

There was one question answered before Lee had the chance to ask it.
He sadly shook his head. "I had not looked for such, not even from those
people. President Lincoln always struck me as true to his principles, however much I may disagree with those."

"In his second term, he shows what he really is. He does not aim to
stand for election after that, so he need not mask himself any longer. And
Thaddeus Stevens, who comes after him, is even worse."

"That I believe." Lee wondered at Rhoodie's claims for Lincoln, but
Thaddeus Stevens had always been a passionate abolitionist; his mouth was
so thin and straight that, but for its bloodlessness, it reminded Lee of a
knife gash. Set a Stevens over the prostrate South and any horror was
conceivable. Lee went on, "Somewhere, though, in your world of 2013—
no, it would be 2014 now—sympathy for our lost cause must remain, or
you would not be here."

"So it does, I'm proud to say," Rhoodie answered, "even if it is not as
much as it should be. Niggers still lord it over white Southern men. Because
they have done it for so long, they think it is their right. The bloody kaffirs
lord it over South Africa, too, my own homeland—over the white men who
built the country up from nothing. There are even blacks in England,
millions of them, and blacks in Parliament, if you can believe it."

"How do I know I can believe any of what you say?" Lee asked. "I
have not been to the future to see it for myself; I have only your word that
it is as you assert."

"If you want them, General Lee, I can bring you documents and pictures
that make the slave revolt in Santo Domingo look like a Sunday picnic. I
will be happy to give you those. But, General, let me ask you this: Why
would my friends and I be here if these things were not as I say?"

"There you have me, Mr. Rhoodie," Lee admitted. Now he finished his
glass of wine and poured another. Though it warmed his body, it left his

heart cold. "Thaddeus Stevens, president? I had not thought the northerns hated us so much as that. They might as well have chosen John Brown, were he yet alive."

"Just so," Rhoodie said. "You captured John Brown, didn't you?"

"Yes. I was proud to be an officer of the United States Army then. I wish I had never found the need to leave that service, but I could not lead its soldiers against Virginia." He studied Rhoodie as if the man were a map to a country he had never seen but where he would soon have to campaign. Fair enough; the future was just such a country. Normally, no man had a map into it; everyone traveled blind. But now— "Mr. Rhoodie, you are saying, are you not, that you know the course this war will take?"

"I know the course the war *took*, General. We hope to change that course with our AK-47s. We have already changed it in a small way: Kilpatrick's raid would have penetrated much further into Virginia and caused much more damage and alarm had it not been for us—and for the valor of your troopers."

"I understand your Konrad de Buys showed uncommon valor of his own," Lee said.

Rhoodie nodded. "I've talked with him. He enjoyed himself. There's no room for cavalry in our time—too much artillery, too many armored machines."

"It is well that war is so terrible, or we should get too fond of it," Lee said. "I am glad to hear the horses, at least, are out of harm's way in time to come. They cannot choose to go into battle, as men do."

"True enough," Rhoodie said.

Lee thought for a while before he spoke again. "You say you think you have as yet affected the course of the war in only a small way."

"Yes." Rhoodie's poker face had disappeared. He was studying Lee as hard as Lee studied him, and not bothering to hide it. Lee felt as if he were back at West Point, not as superintendent, but as student. He had to assume Rhoodie knew everything about him that history recorded, while he knew—could know—only what Rhoodie chose to reveal of himself, his organization, and his purposes.

Picking words with great care, Lee said, "Then you will have knowledge of the opening events of the coming year's campaign, but your knowledge thereafter will decrease as our victories, should we have such, deflect events away from the path they would have taken without your intervention. Is my understanding accurate?"

"Yes, General Lee. You understand as well as any man could. My friends and I hope and expect that, with the Confederate States a bulwark of freedom and strength, the white man's cause all through the world will be stronger than in our own sorry history."

"As may be," Lee said with a shrug. "Bear with me a moment further, though, if you would. It follows from what you have said that our generals, including myself, will need to be informed as exactly as possible on the situation of the Federals in front of them at the moment the campaigning season resumes, that we may extract the maximum advantage from what you know."

"I will draft you an appreciation of what the Army of the Potomac plans to do," Rhoodie said. "One of our people will do the same for General Johnston in regard to the Army of the Tennessee. Other fronts will be less important."

"Yes, Johnston and I have our country's two chief field armies. I look forward to receiving your appreciation, Mr. Rhoodie. It may well give me an important edge as the year's campaign opens. Afterwards, I gather, things will have changed, and we shall have to rely on the valor of the men. The Army of Northern Virginia has never failed me there."

"You can rely on one other thing now," Rhoodie said. Lee looked a question at him. He said, "The AK-47."

"Oh, certainly," Lee said. "You see how I am already coming to take it for granted. Mr. Rhoodie, now I have answers to some of the matters which have perplexed me for a long while. Thank you for giving them to me."

"My pleasure, General." Rhoodie stood to go. Lee also rose. As he did so, the pain that sometimes clogged his chest struck him a stinging blow. He tried to bear up under it, but it must have shown on his face, for Rhoodie took a step toward him and asked, "Are you all right, General?"

"Yes," Lee said, though he needed an effort to force the word past his teeth. He gathered himself. "Yes, I am all right, Mr. Rhoodie; thank you. I ceased to be a young man some years ago. From time to time, my body insists on reminding me of the fact. I shall last as long as I am required, I assure you."

Rhoodie, he realized, must know the year—perhaps the day and hour— in which he was to die. That was a question he did not intend to put to the Rivington man; about some things, one was better ignorant. Then it occurred to him that if the course of battles and nations was mutable, so small a thing as a single lifespan must also be. The thought cheered him. He did not care to be only a figure in a dusty text, pinned down as immovably as a butterfly in a naturalist's collection.

"Is it your heart, General?" Rhoodie asked.

"My chest, at any rate. The doctors know no more than that, which I could tell them for myself."

"Doctors in my time can do quite a lot better, General Lee. I can bring you medicine that may really help you. I'll see to it as soon as I can. With the campaign coming up, we want you as well as you can be."

"You are too kind, sir." Yes, Rhoodie knew Lee's allotted number of days could change. He wanted to make sure they didn't unexpectedly shorten. Even that possibility made Lee feel freer. He thought of something else. "May I ask you an unrelated question, Mr. Rhoodie?"

"Of course." Rhoodie was the picture of polite attentiveness.

"These Negroes you mentioned who were elected to the British Parliament—what manner of legislators do they make? And how were they elected, if I may ask? By other Negroes voting?"

"Mostly, yes, but, to the shame of the English, some deluded whites sank low enough to vote for them as well. As for what sort of members they make, they're what you'd expect. They always push for more for the niggers, not that they don't have too much already."

"If they were elected to stand for their people, how are they to be blamed for carrying out that charge?" Storm clouds came over Andries Rhoodie's face. Lee said, "Well, Mr. Rhoodie, it's neither here nor there. Thank you once more for all of this. You've given me a great deal to think on further. And I do want to see that plan of what General Meade will attempt."

Once off the topic of Negroes, Rhoodie relaxed again. "It will be General Grant, sir," he said.

"Will it? So they will name him lieutenant general, then? Such has been rumored."

"Yes, they will, in just a week or so."

"And he will come east to fight in Virginia? Most interesting." Lee frowned, looked sharply at Rhoodie. "The day you first came to this camp, sir, you spoke of General Sherman as commanding in the west, and Major Taylor corrected you. You were thinking of the time when operations would commence, weren't you?"

"I remember that, General Lee. Yes, I was, and so I slipped." He nodded and ducked his way out of the tent.

After a couple of minutes, Lee stepped outside, too. Rhoodie was riding back to Orange Court House. Lee started to call his aides, then stopped to consider whether he wanted them to know the Rivington men were from out of time. He decided he didn't. The fewer ears that heard that secret, the better.

He went back inside, sat down once more at his work table. He reached out for that second glass of blackberry wine he had poured, finished it with two quick swallows. He seldom drank two glasses of wine, especially in the early afternoon, but he needed something to steady his nerves.

Men from the future! To say it was to find it laughable. To deal with Andries Rhoodie, with the new repeaters in almost everyone's hands now, with the small, square ammunition crates growing to tall pyramids by every regiment's munitions wagons, with the occasional shipments of desiccated food that helped keep hunger from turning to starvation, was to believe. The creaky machinery of the present-day Confederate States could not have produced such quantities of even ordinary arms and foodstuffs, let alone the wonders at Rhoodie's beck and call.

Lee thought about General Grant. In the west, he'd shown both straight-ahead slugging and no small skill. From what Rhoodie said, he would win here too, defeat the indomitable Army of Northern Virginia.

"We shall see about that," Lee said aloud, though no one was in the tent to hear him.

"Here you go, First Sergeant," Preston Kelly said. "They're 'most as good as new."

Nate Caudell tried on the shoes Kelly had repaired. He walked a few steps, smiled broadly. "Yup, that's licked it. The cold doesn't blow in between the soles and the uppers anymore. Thank you kindly. Pity you can't do more; a good many of us don't even have shoes to repair these days. Are you the only shoemaker in the regiment?"

"Heard tell there's another one 'mongst the Alamance Minute Men," Kelly answered. "Couldn't rightly swear to it, though. Them boys from Company K, they still stick close to themselves after all this time." Alamance County lay a fair ways west of Wake, Nash, Franklin, and Granville, which provided most of the manpower for the regiment's other nine companies.

"So they do," Caudell said. "Come to that, I wish you were in my company, Preston. The Invincibles would all be better shod if you were."

"Might could be, but then my boys from Company C'd be worse." Kelly spat a brown stream of tobacco juice onto the ground. "When you ain't noways got enough to go around, First Sergeant, some poor bastard always has to do without."

"Isn't that the sad and sorry truth?" Caudell said. "Well, thanks again for finding the time for me."

"Wasn't but a little repair, with more nailin' than new leather. You keep your gear in good shape, not like some folks as let things fall to pieces 'fore they fetch 'em in to be fixed. Hell, if I had more leather an' there was five of me, we'd be fine, far as shoes go."

That was one of the smaller ifs Caudell had heard through the long, hungry winter. He waved good-bye to the shoemaker and headed back to his own company's area. The parade ground was full of men watching two base ball nines go at each other. He decided to watch for a while himself.

The bat was hand-carved, and the ball, even seen from a distance, imperfectly round, but the players didn't mind. The pitcher underhanded his missile toward the batter, who took a lusty swing and missed. The catcher caught the ball on the first bounce and tossed it back to his battery mate. The pitcher delivered again. The batter connected this time, launching the ball high but not far.

"Mortar shot!" somebody yelled. "Y'all take cover!"

"Get out your bumbershoots—that one'll bring rain," somebody else said.

The shortstop circled under the ball. "Catch it, Iverson!" his teammates screamed. The shortstop did catch it. Everyone cheered except the batter, who had run to first base in the confident expectation he would be able to stay there. He kicked at the dirt as he left. Caudell didn't blame him. With a muddy, hole-strewn field to traverse, catching a ball barehanded was anything but easy.

Another batter came up. After taking a couple of pitches, he connected solidly. If the earlier pop had come from a mortar, this ball was blasted out of the brass muzzle of a twelve-pounder Napoleon. It also flew straight to the shortstop. He leaped high in the air and speared it. The watching soldiers went wild. The batter flipped his club away in disgust. The shortstop threw the ball to the pitcher, then rubbed his hands on the ragged seat of his trousers—that one had stung.

"Is that Iverson Longmire from Company G?" Caudell asked the man next to him. "He's something to watch."

"That's him," the private answered. "Yeah, he's a demon base baller, ain't he?"

After those two quick outs, four straight hits fell in, and two runs scored. Then another ball, this one on the ground, went to the intrepid Longmire. Caudell waited for him to gobble it up and throw it to first base. But at the last instant, it kicked up off a pebble and hit him right between the legs. He went down in a heap, clutching at himself. Two more runners crossed the plate—actually, a piece of wood from an AK-47 crate. The men who had cheered Longmire to the skies laughed until they had to hang on to each other to stay on their feet.

That was enough base ball for Caudell. He went past Captain Lewis's tent and the company banner. A few soldiers leaned against their huts. More than one was stripping an AK-47 and putting it back together again. The fascination with the new repeaters had not worn off in the month since they'd been issued.

"Hello, Melvin," Caudell said, seeing Mollie Bean outside her cabin. She was feeding rounds into a banana clip.

"Hello, First Sergeant," she answered. "Reckon we're gonna get ourselves some Yankees 'fore too long?"

Caudell took a step. He squelched in mud. Thanks to the work he'd just had done, it didn't soak his toes. All the same, he said, "My guess is, we won't move for a while yet unless the Yanks try something sneaky. Marching on muddy roads wears a man down too much for good fighting afterwards." Or even a woman, he thought, remembering to whom he was talking.

She said, "You're likely right. Comin' back from Gettysburg in the rain, wasn't nothin' but slog, slog, slog till a body wanted to fall down dead at the end of a day."

"Makes me tired just remembering," Caudell agreed. The 47th North Carolina had been part of the rear guard at Falling Rivers, Maryland, as the Army of Northern Virginia drew back into its home state, and had lost many men captured because they could not keep up.

All at once, Mollie Bean became intensely interested in the AK-47 magazine in her lap, bending her head down over it. "I need to see you, First Sergeant," someone said from behind Caudell.

He turned, lifted his hat. "Yes, sir. What it is, Captain Lewis?"

"Walk with me," Lewis said. Caudell obeyed, matching his pace to the captain's slow and halting strides. Lewis went by Mollie Bean without the least notice of her. With her head down, the brim of her cap hid her face from him. Caudell smiled to himself; she was expert at such small concealments. After a few steps, Lewis went on, "We have to get the most we can out of these new repeaters."

"Certainly, sir."

"I think that means thinning our firing lines," Lewis said. "With these rifles, we don't need to stand shoulder to shoulder to put out a large volume of fire. The more widely we space ourselves out, the more front we can cover and the smaller the target each individual man presents to the enemy."

"Sounds good to me, sir," Caudell said at once. "We were packed together so tight in the charge at Gettysburg, I still think it's a wonder all of us didn't get shot. The more space between us for the bullets to go by, the better."

"Space for the bullets to go by," Lewis echoed musingly. "I like that. You have a way with words, First Sergeant."

"Thank you, sir," Caudell said, thinking that if he did, it was because he wrote so many of them for other people. As with anything else, practice made them come easier.

Lewis said, "You hit on something important there. If a skirmish line will let us hold our position or advance as we might have before with a full firing line, that frees up the rest to move round the enemy's flank or probe his line for weaknesses. When we next go into the field, we'll have to maneuver accordingly. Some drill with more widely spaced lines would seem to be in order."

"I'll see to it, sir," Caudell said. George Lewis hadn't been a teacher before the war—he'd dabbled in politics—but two years as an officer had taught him full respect for drill and practice.

"Good," he said now. "Pass the word on to the sergeants and corporals. In battle, we'll often be maneuvering by squads, so they're the ones who will have to be able to put the men through the proper paces."

"I'll see to it," Caudell said again.

"I'm sure you will. Carry on, First Sergeant." Lewis limped away, a determined man who'd settled one piece of business but had many more to see to.

Nate Caudell lacked the captain's abrupt decisiveness. He stood scratching his chin for several seconds, wondering whether he should head straight back to his cabin and tell whichever of his messmates happened to be there what the captain had said. At last, he decided not to. He'd see them all together at supper, and tell them then. Tomorrow morning would be time for Corporals Lewis—who was no relation to the captain—and Massey.

Having made up his mind thus, he ran into Otis Massey not five minutes later. "Makes sense to me, First Sergeant," Massey said when Caudell was through relaying Captain Lewis's words. " 'Course, rememberin' it when them damnyankees is shootin' at us might could take a bit o' doin'."

"That's why we practice it beforehand," Caudell said patiently.

Massey shifted his chaw from one cheek to the other, which made him look for a moment like a sheep chewing its cud. "Yeah, reckon so." He'd always been a good soldier; that was how he'd got himself promoted. He was slower to grasp that, as corporal, he was responsible for his whole squad, not just himself.

Caudell walked down to his hut. He was about to go in when he saw a black man in Confederate gray going by with an AK-47 slung on his back. "How you doin', Georgie?" he called.

George Ballentine looked to see who was talking to him. "I's right well, First Sergeant, suh," he answered. "How you be?"

"I'm all right," Caudell answered. "So the boys in Company H let you have one of the new repeaters, did they?"

"Yassuh, they did. I's a regular No'th Carolina Tiger, I is," Ballentine said. "If'n I goes to the fightin' with food or some such, I gets to shoot back if the Yankees shoots at me."

"You've got a better rifle there than your master ever dreamed of. He'd have one too, if he hadn't run away on us," Caudell said. Ballentine had come to the regiment as bodyguard to Addison Holland of Company H. Holland was a deserter, six months gone now. Ballentine had stayed with the North Carolina Tigers as company cook, tailor, and general handyman. Caudell wondered about that. "Why didn't you take off too, Georgie? We haven't caught your master yet. Odds are we never would have got you."

Something changed in the black man's face; all at once it became a fortress to guard the thoughts behind it. Though he owned no slaves himself, Caudell had seen that guarded look on other men's Negroes many times. "Don' wanna be no runaway," Ballentine said. Caudell thought that would end the conversation; the black man had said what a black man had to say to get by in a white man's world. But Ballentine chose to elaborate: "I's just about like a free man now. The men, they treats me like one o' them. I don' belong to nobody in particular—jus' about as good as not belongin' t'nobody atall. Like you say, I even gots this here nice gun. How's I gonna do better'n that, runnin' away?"

Go north was the unspoken thought in Caudell's mind. It had to be in George Ballentine's, too. But risks went with it. If a Confederate picket spotted him trying to cross the Rapidan, he was dead. The other thing that struck Caudell was how much Ballentine's answer reminded him of Mollie Bean's. Neither had any prospects to speak of in the outside world; both had found in the army niches that suited them and people who cared about them.

"Company H is lucky to have you, Georgie," Caudell said. "They don't have to eat their own bad cooking."

Ballentine's dark face split in a grin. "Ki! That's a natural fact, First Sergeant, suh. Some o' them fellas, they burns water if they tries to cook it. I gots to go now—got me some chickens to stew up."

"Chickens?" Where Caudell had been mildly envious of the North Carolina Tigers before, now green-eyed jealousy woke to full clamor. "Where'd you come up with chickens, Georgie?"

"As' me no questions, I tells you no lies," the black man said smugly. He strutted on back toward his own company, visibly proud of his talent as a forager.

A horse came trotting off the road south from Orange Court House into the regimental encampment. Aboard it was Benny Lang. He pulled the animal up short in front of Caudell. His lean face was twisted with fury. He stabbed a forefinger in the direction of George Ballentine's back. "You, First Sergeant! What the bleeding hell is that fucking kaffir doing with an AK-47? Answer me, damn you!"

"He's not in my company, so I can't answer you exactly, Mr. Lang," Caudell said, speaking as carefully as if the Rivington man were an officer.

"Whose bloody company is he in, then?" Lang demanded.

"Company H, sir," Caudell said. He explained how Ballentine had come to be there, and how he had stayed with the company after Addison Holland abandoned it. "I'm sure it's all right."

"In a pig's arse it is. Teach a kaf—a nigger—to use a weapon, and next thing you know, he'll be aiming at you. Company H, you say? Who's captain there?"

"That would be Captain Mitchell, sir. Captain Sidney Mitchell."

"I am going to have a small chat with Captain Sidney fucking Mitchell, then, First Sergeant. We'll see if he lets a nigger touch a weapon after that, by God!" He jerked savagely on the reins to turn the horse, dug his heels into its sides. The animal let out an angry neigh and bounded off. Space showed between the saddle and Lang's backside at every stride; he was anything but a polished rider. But he clung to his seat with grim determination.

Rufus Daniel came out of the cabin. Along with Caudell, he watched Benny Lang's furious ride. "I take back what I told you a while ago, Nate," Daniel said. "Wouldn't want him for overseer after all—he purely hates niggers. That'd bring a farm nothin' but grief. Georgie Ballentine; I druther have him alongside me 'n half the white men in this company."

"Me, too." Caudell took off his hat so he could scratch his head. "Lang hates niggers as if they'd done something to him personally, not just—you know what I mean."

"Reckon I do," Daniel said. Hardly a white man in the South failed to look down on blacks. But the two races lived and worked side by side. They saw each other, dealt with each other, every day. Caudell could think of nothing likelier to spark a slave revolt than all whites displaying the ferocity Benny Lang showed.

"You know, I hope Captain Mitchell tells him where to get off," Caudell said. He had no great love for Negroes himself, but George Ballentine was part of the fabric of the regiment in a way Benny Lang could never be.

"Don't think he'll do it," Daniel said morosely. "Them Rivington fellers, they're where the repeaters 'n' cartridges come from. Ain't smart to rile 'em. Stacked against that, poor Georgie's a small fish."

Caudell sighed. "I'm afraid you're right, Rufus."

Laughter and shouts of fury, mixed with harsh coughs, came from behind him. He whirled around. When he saw a cabin with smoke billowing out its door and windows, his first thought was that it had caught on fire. Then he noticed the flat board placed over the top of the chimney. It wasn't a fire, it was a prank. To confirm that, the evident prankster stood a few feet away from his handiwork, laughing so hard he could barely stand up. That was unwise. Three men had been in the cabin, and they set on him with intent to maim. His laughter abruptly turned to cries of pain.

"Goddam fool," Rufus Daniel said.

"Yup. Well, we'd better get 'em apart." Caudell raised his voice to a shout: "You there, that's enough! Break it up!" He and Daniel ran toward the combatants. "Break it up, I tell you!"

The three turned loose the one. Now he could hardly stand because he'd been badly knocked around. Rufus Daniel put hands on hips, stared scornfully at the battered private. "Well, Gideon, looks to me like you got 'bout what you deserve."

Gideon Bass felt cautiously under his right eye. It was already purpling; he'd have a fine shiner tomorrow. But a grin quickly crept back onto his face. He was only nineteen, an age when a man is often willing to suffer for his art. "Oh, but weren't it a hell of a fine smudge, Sarge?" he said.

Caudell turned on the three men who had been smoked out. One had just taken the offending board off the chimney, and was sidling around toward the back of the cabin. Caudell's cough froze the would-be escapee in his tracks. "Nice try, John," he said. "Now come on back." As nonchalantly as he could, John Floyd rejoined David Leonard and Emelius Pullen. Caudell glared at all three of them. "You don't go beating on your mates."

"You seen what he done, First Sergeant," Floyd protested. His voice had an upcountry twang to it; he and Leonard were from Davidson County, a long way west of Caudell's home.

"I saw it," Caudell said. "You all should have just grabbed him and let Sergeant Daniel and me deal with him. We would have, I promise you that." He turned to Daniel. "What shall we do with 'em now?"

"Up to you, Nate, but I don't reckon tomfoolery's worth takin' to the captain," Daniel said. "These three done breathed smoke awhile, and this 'un's got a set o' lumps. You ask me, it's even."

"Fair enough," Caudell said after a pause intended to convey that he was going along with the suggestion only out of the goodness of his heart. When that pause had sunk in, he added, "This had better be the end of it. If there's a next time, you'll all be sorry. Understand?"

"Yes, First Sergeant," the miscreants intoned with unctuous sincerity.

"Why don't y'all go someplace else for a while, Gideon?" Rufus Daniel put in. "Someplace a good ways away, I mean, and stay there till suppertime."

Bass strode away. As he rounded a corner, Caudell heard him guffaw. He rolled his eyes. "What are we going to do with him?"

"Hope nobody wrings his fool neck till the fightin' starts. That oughta settle him down some, maybe," Daniel said. "Hope Dempsey don't hear about this, too, otherwise we 'uns is gonna get smudged one fine day."

"One fine day soon," Caudell said; Dempsey Eure loved mischief. "Other thing is, Dempsey's too smart to stand around waiting for us to come out and beat on him. He'd turn up an hour later looking all innocent, and we'd never be able to prove a thing."

Rufus Daniel grinned. "We'd git him anyways." He sounded as if he were looking forward to it.

When Sunday morning rolled around, Caudell joined most of the regiment at divine services. Chaplain William Lacy was a Presbyterian, while the majority of the men he served—Caudell among them—were Baptists, but he had proved himself a good and pious man, which counted for more than differences in creed.

"Let us bend our heads in prayer," he said. "May God remember our beloved Confederacy and keep it safe. May He lift up his hand and smite that of the oppressor, and may our true patriots in gray withstand their test with bravery."

"Amen," Caudell said. He added a silent prayer of his own for General Lee.

Lacy said, "I will take as my text today Romans 8:28: 'We know that all things work together for good to them that love God.' We see it illustrated in the events of the past few weeks. When our army came short of success at Gettysburg, many may have suffered a loss of faith that our cause would triumph. But now God has delivered into our hands these fine new repeaters with which to renew the fight, and through them He will deliver into our hands the Yankees who seek to subjugate us."

"You tell 'em, preacher!" a soldier called.

Lacy paced back and forth as he warmed to his sermon. He was a tall, lean man with a neat beard and clean-shaven upper lip. He wore a black coat of almost knee length, with green olive branches embroidered on each sleeve to show his calling.

"In times of peace, the coming of a new rifle could hardly be taken as a sign of God's love," he said. "But here and now, when we battle for the freedom which is more precious than life itself, how can we view the arrival of these AK-47s as anything save providential?"

"That's right!" a man said. Another shouted, "These here repeaters is gonna let us give the Yankees hell!"

The chaplain went on in that vein for a few more minutes, then called up soldiers who helped him pass out hymn books to the rest of the men. He didn't have enough to go around, but almost all the soldiers knew the hymns by heart anyhow. "We'll start today with 'Rock of Ages'—page forty-seven, for those of you with hymnals," he said. "I want to hear you put your hearts into it today—make a joyful noise unto the Lord!"

Caudell's voice rose with the rest. The men sang enthusiastically; there were enough of them that good voices and poor mostly blended together. As the last notes of the hymn died away, though, Caudell looked around in puzzlement. Something was missing, but he could not place what it was.

Lacy noticed nothing wrong. " 'Amazing Grace' now—page, ah, fifty-one in the *Army Hymn Book*."

"Amazing Grace" was harder to sing than "Rock of Ages," which required little more than vigor. Maybe that was why, halfway through the hymn, Caudell figured out what had bothered him before. His own singing faltered as he looked around again, this time for someone in particular. He did not see him.

The hymn ended. In the distance, another regiment—probably the 26th North Carolina, whose camp was closest to that of the 47th—was singing "The Old Rugged Cross." Caudell turned to the private next to him. "Where's Georgie Ballentine?"

"Huh? The nigger? Ain't he here?" the fellow said.

"No, he—" Caudell had to stop, for the regiment launched into "Praise God from Whom All Blessings Flow." He looked around once more while he sang. No, Ballentine wasn't here. His ears had already told him that— the black man's molasses-smooth baritone anchored the regiment's singing week in and week out, for he never missed a service.

Caudell spotted a corporal from the North Carolina Tigers close by. When the hymn was done, he caught his eye. "Where's Georgie, Henry? Is he sick?"

Henry Johnson shook his head, made a sour face. "Nope, he ain't sick. He done run off, day before yesterday."

"Run off? Georgie?" Caudell stared at him. "I don't believe it." He stopped and thought. "No, wait a minute, maybe I do. Did they take his rifle away from him?"

"You heard tell about that, did you?" Johnson said. "Cap'n Mitchell, he didn't want to, but that Benny Lang feller, he pitched a fit like you wouldn't believe. Said he'd go to Colonel Faribault, an' then to General Kirkland, and then to General Heth, an' all the way up to Jeff Davis till he got his way—maybe on up to the Holy Ghost, if ol' Jeff wouldn't give him what he wanted. Georgie, he took it right hard, but there weren't nothin' he could do. Weren't nothin' nobody could do. Afterwards, though, he seemed to settle on down some. But he wasn't there at roll call yesterday mornin', so he must've been shammin'. You know how niggers can do."

Just then, Chaplain Lacy called, "Page fifty-six, men—'Nearer My God to Thee.'" Caudell sang mechanically while he thought about what Johnson had said. Of course blacks grew adept at hiding their thoughts from whites. They had to, if they wanted to stay out of trouble. But George Ballentine had been so at home in Company H— Caudell shook his head. The joy had gone out of the service.

When "Nearer My God to Thee" was done, Henry Johnson said, "You know, I hope ol' Georgie makes it over the Rapidan to the Yankees, an' I don't give a damn who hears me say so. Even a nigger, he's got his pride."

"Yup," Caudell said. Instead of waiting for the next hymn, he drifted away from the open-air assembly. Johnson had hit the nail on the head. Not giving George Ballentine a repeater in the first place would have been one thing. But to give him one and then take it away—that was wrong. He hoped Ballentine made it over the Rapidan to freedom, too.

But the slave's luck as a runaway was no better than his luck with the AK-47 had been. Three days later, a wagon came squelching down the muddy highway from Orange Court House in the late afternoon. It wasn't a scheduled stop. "You have a load of those desiccated dinners for us?" Caudell called hopefully as the driver pulled off the main road.

"No, just a dead nigger—picket shot him up by the Rapidan Station. He was headin' for the river. Hear tell he likely belongs to this regiment." The driver jumped down and lowered the rear gate. "Want to see if it's him?"

Caudell hurried over, peered in. George Ballentine lay limp and dead on the planks, without even a cloth over his staring eyes. The lower part of his gray tunic was soaked with blood; he'd been shot in the belly, a hard, hard way to die. Caudell clicked his tongue between his teeth. "Yeah, that's Georgie."

"You gonna take charge of him?"

"Take him over to Company H, why don't you? He belonged to them." Caudell pointed the way. "I expect they'll want to give him a proper burial."

"What the hell for? He was a goddam runaway."

"Just do it," Caudell snapped. As if by accident, he brushed a hand against his sleeve to call attention to his chevrons. The driver spat in the roadway, but he obeyed.

Caudell's guess had been shrewd. The North Carolina Tigers even went so far as to ask Chaplain Lacy to officiate at the funeral, and he agreed. That told Caudell what the chaplain thought of the Negro's reasons for running away. Driven by guilt, Caudell went to the funeral too—had he not told Lang who Ballentine was and where he belonged, the black man would still be alive.

Lacy chose a verse from Psalm 19: "The judgments of the Lord are true and righteous altogether." Caudell wondered about that. He saw no evidence of divine wrath in Ballentine's death, only the wrath of Benny Lang. It did not seem an adequate substitute. He thought about talking things over with the chaplain, but ended up talking with Mollie Bean instead. However fine a man William Lacy was, he was also an official part of the 47th North Carolina. Caudell didn't feel comfortable discussing Georgie Ballentine's fate with anyone official. Mollie's place in the regiment was even less official than the Negro's had been.

"Ain't nothin' to be done about it now," she said, a self-evident truth.

"I know that. It gravels me all the same," he said. "It wasn't fair."

"Life ain't fair, Nate," she answered. "You was a woman, you'd know that. You ever work in a bawdyhouse, you'd sure as shit know that." Her face clouded, as if at memories she'd have sooner forgotten. Then that wry smile of hers tugged one corner of her mouth upwards. "Hell, First Sergeant Caudell, sir, you was a private, you'd know that."

"Maybe I would," he said, startled into brief laughter. But just as Mollie could not stay gloomy, he had trouble remaining cheerful. "I expect I'd know it if I were a nigger, too. Georgie sure found out."

"Niggers ain't the same as white folks, they say—they just go on from day to day, don't worry none about stuff like that."

"Sure, people say that. I've said it myself, plenty of times. But if it's true, why did Georgie run off when they took his repeater away?" Corporal Johnson's words came back to Caudell: *even a nigger, he's got his pride.*

"I know what you mean, Nate, but Georgie, he didn't seem like your regular nigger," Mollie said. "He just seemed like people—you know what I mean?"

"Yup," Caudell said. "I felt the same way about him. That's why he bothers me so much now." Ballentine had seemed like a person to Caudell, not just some nigger, because he'd got to know him. In the same way, Mollie seemed like a person to him, not just some whore—because he'd got to know her. He kept that part of his thought to himself, but went on in musing tones, "Maybe a lot of niggers seem like people to somebody who knows them."

"Maybe." But Mollie sounded dubious. "Some, though, you got to sell South, and that's the truth. They ain't nothin' but trouble to their own selves an' everybody around 'em."

"That's true enough. But you know what else?" Caudell waited for her to shake her head, then said, "If Billy Beddingfield was black, I'd sell him South in a minute, too."

She giggled. "And that Benny Lang, he knocked Billy sideways. So there's one up for him, to go with the one down for Georgie."

"I hadn't thought of that. It's not as big an up as Georgie is a down, not even close, but it's there. Reckon it goes to show nobody's all good or all bad."

"You got that right. He brung us the repeaters, too, to whup the Yankees with."

"So he did. That has to count for something, I suppose." Right then, Caudell did not care to give Benny Lang any points, but he was too just to find a way around it.

Mollie looked at him out of the corner of her eye. "Did you just fall by to chat, Nate, or did you have somethin' else on your mind?"

"I hadn't thought about anything else, but as long as I'm here—"

Robert E. Lee took off his reading glasses, slid them into his breast pocket. "So Lieutenant General Grant will go through the Wilderness, will he? I had rather expected him to try to duplicate McClellan's campaign up the James toward Richmond. It is the shortest route to the capital, given the Federals' regrettable control of the sea."

"He will send the Army of the Potomac through the Wilderness, General, at the beginning of May, as I've written there," Andries Rhoodie said positively. "His aim is not so much Richmond as your army. If Richmond falls while the Army of Northern Virginia lives, the Confederacy can stay alive. But if your army is beaten, Richmond will fall afterwards."

Lee thought about that, nodded in concession. "It is sound strategy, and accords with the way Grant fought in the west. Very well then, I shall deploy my forces so as to be waiting for him when he arrives."

"No, you mustn't, General Lee." Rhoodie sounded so alarmed, Lee stared at him in sharp surprise. "If he knows you've moved and are lying in wait for him, he can choose to attack by way of Fredericksburg instead, or up the James, or any other way he pleases. What I know only stays true if what leads up to it stays the same."

"I—see," Lee said slowly. After a few seconds, he laughed at himself. "Here I'd always imagined no general could have a greater advantage than knowing exactly what his opponent would do next. Now I know, and find myself unable to take full advantage of the knowledge for fear of his doing something else because I have prepared for this one thing. Thinking of what is to be as mutable comes hard to me."

"It comes hard to almost everyone," Rhoodie assured him.

Lee tapped with his forefinger the papers Rhoodie had given him. "By these, I am to have General Longstreet's corps returned to me from Tennessee before the campaign commences. I am glad to see that would have happened, for otherwise I should have been leery of requesting it, lest in so doing I disrupt the chain of events ahead. Yet were I without it, the Army of the Potomac would have overwhelming weight of numbers."

"May I suggest, General, that when it does come next month, you station it around Jackson's Shop or Orange Springs, rather than farther west at Gordonsville?" Rhoodie said. "As the fight developed, Longstreet's men nearly came too late because they had so far to travel."

"Will this change not make Grant change his plans in response?" Lee asked.

"The risk, I think, is small. Right now, Grant doesn't look at the Wilderness as a place to fight, only a place to get through as fast as possible so he can battle your army on open ground. He'll be wondering if you will choose to fight anywhere this side of Richmond."

"Is that a fact?" Lee meant the phrase as nothing but a polite conversational placeholder, but Rhoodie nodded all the same. Smiling a huntsman's smile, Lee said, "I expect we shan't keep him long in suspense as to that point, sir."

"The AK-47s should also be an unpleasant surprise for him," Rhoodie said.

"I should have attacked without them," Lee said. "Where better than the Wilderness? In the forest and undergrowth, the Federals' superiority in artillery is nullified—there are few places for it to deploy, and few good targets at which to aim. And my soldiers, farmers most of them, are better woodsmen than the Yankees. Yes, Mr. Rhoodie, if General Grant wishes to allow a fight there, I shall be happy to oblige him."

"I know that," Rhoodie said.

"Yes, you would, wouldn't you?" Lee looked down at those irresistibly fascinating papers. "Will you excuse me now, sir? I confess I feel the need to study these further."

"Certainly." Rhoodie stood to go. Then he said, "Oh, I almost forgot," and reached into a pants pocket. He handed Lee a bottle of small white tablets. "If your heart pains you, let one or two of these dissolve under your tongue. They should help. They may bring a spot of headache with them, but it shouldn't last long."

"Thank you, sir; you're most kind to have thought of it." Lee put his glasses back on so he could read the bottle's label. " 'Nitroglycerine.' Hmm. It sounds most forbiddingly medical; I can tell you that."

"Er—yes." Rhoodie's inscrutable expression made his face unreadable as he said, "It is, among other things, useful in stimulating the heart. And now, General, if you will excuse me—" He ducked out under the tent flap.

Lee stuck the jar in a coat pocket. He forgot it in moments, as he resumed his study of the information Andries Rhoodie had given him. Here, a month and more in advance, he read the ford by which each Federal division would cross the Rapidan and the road south it would take. Altogether without such intelligence, he had smashed the Yankees the year before at Chancellorsville, on the eastern fringes of the Wilderness. With it—

"If I cannot whip General Grant with what is in these papers," he said to no one in particular, "I am willing to go home."

A few minutes later, Perry brought in Lee's dinner, set it on the table in front of him, and hurried away. He did not notice the black man enter or leave; the food sat a long time untouched. Lee's eyes went back and forth from Rhoodie's documents to the map spread out on the cot beside him, but his mind did not see the names of units or the symbols that represented roads and hamlets. His mind saw marching men and flashing guns and patterns of collision . . .

Lee slid off Traveller. The horse's grassy, earthy smell mingled with the perfume of dogwoods at last in blossom. Spring had taken a long time coming, but was finally here in full force.

Sergeant B. L. Wynn came out of the hut that housed the Confederate signal station on Clark's Mountain. "Good morning to you, Sergeant," Lee said pleasantly.

"Morning, sir," Wynn answered, his voice casual—Lee was a frequent visitor to the station, to see for himself what the Federals across the Rapidan were up to. Then the young sergeant's eyes went wide. "Uh, sirs," he amended quickly.

Lee smiled. "Yes, Sergeant, I've brought rather more company than usual with me today." He paused to enjoy his own understatement. Not only were his young staff officers along, but also all three of the Army of Northern Virginia's corps commanders and a double handful of division heads. "I want them to get a view of the terrain from the mountaintop here."

"By western standards, this isn't much of a mountain," James Longstreet said. "How high are we, anyhow?"

"I don't quite know," Lee admitted. "Sergeant Wynn?"

"About eleven hundred feet, sir," Wynn said.

Longstreet's fleshy cheeks rippled in a snort. "Eleven hundred feet? In Tennessee or North Carolina"—his home state—"this wouldn't be a mountain. They might call it a knob. In the Rockies, they wouldn't notice it was there."

"It suffices for our purposes nonetheless," Lee said. "Standing here, we can see twenty counties spread out below us, as if on the map. Sergeant Wynn, may I trouble you for your spyglass?"

Wynn handed him the long brass tube. He raised it to his right eye, peered northward over the Rapidan. The winter encampment of Federal General Warren's V Corps, centered on Culpeper Court House, leaped toward him. Smoke floated up from chimneys; bright divisional flags bloomed like orderly rows of spring flowers. Grant had his headquarters by Culpeper Court House. A couple of miles further east, by Stevensburg, lay Winfield Scott Hancock's II Corps; the encampment of Sedgwick's VI Corps was beyond it, past Brandy Station—Lee thought for a moment of Rooney, returned at last to Confederate service. Farther north and east, past Rappahannock Station and Bealeton, were the cabins and tents of Ambrose Burnside's IX Corps, with the Army of the Potomac but not formally part of it. Colored troops made up a good part of that corps, Lee had heard.

He lowered the telescope. "All seems quiet still in the Federal camps. Soon enough, though, those people will move." He pointed east, toward the rank green growth of the Wilderness. "They will come by way of the fords there, Germanna and Ely's just east of it."

"You sound very sure," Longstreet said. Of all Lee's generals, he was most given to setting his own judgments against his commander's.

"I think I should have suspected it in any case, but I also have intelligence I regard as trustworthy on the matter from the Rivington men." Lee left it at that. Had he explained that Andries Rhoodie and his colleagues came from the future and thus could view Grant's plans through hindsight rather than guesswork, he was sure most of the assembled officers would have thought him mad. Maybe he was. But any other explanation seemed even more improbable than the one Rhoodie had given him.

"Ah, the Rivington men," Longstreet said. "If their ear for news is as good as their repeaters, then it must be very good indeed. One day before long, General Lee, at your convenience, I'd like to sit down with you and chat about the Rivington men. Had the I Corps not spent the winter in Tennessee, I'd have done it long since."

"Certainly, General," Lee said.

"I want to be part of that chat," A. P. Hill said. His thin, fierce face had an indrawn look to it; the past year or so, he'd had a bad way of taking sick when battle neared. Lee worried about him. Now he continued, "I'd like to speak to them over the way they treat our Negroes, sir. They show more care to the animals they ride. It is not right." The commander of III Corps was a Southern man through and through, but had even less use for slavery than did Lee.

"I have heard of this before, General Hill, and have hesitated to take them to task over what one might call a relatively small fault when the aid they have rendered us is so great," Lee said carefully. "Perhaps I am in error. Time permitting, we shall discuss the matter."

"May I borrow the telescope, sir?" Henry Heth said. Lee passed it to him. He turned the glass toward the Wilderness. With it still at his eye, he remarked, "The place is a bushwhacker's dream."

"Just so, Henry," Lee said, pleased the divisional commander saw the same thing he did. "The enemy are at their weakest in that kind of fight, and we are at our strongest."

Something hot and eager came into Heth's usually chilly gray-blue eyes. He fingered the tuft of light brown hair that grew just beneath his lower lip. "If we hurt them badly enough there, they may skedaddle back over the Rapidan and leave us alone for a while."

Longstreet shook his head. "I know Sam Grant. He's never been one to back away from a fight. He will come straight at us every day he leads the Army of the Potomac."

"We shall see what we shall see," Lee said. "If what the Rivington men say is to be believed, the enemy will begin their move on Wednesday, the fourth of May."

"Four days from now," Richard Ewell murmured to himself. "My men will be ready."

"And mine," A. P. Hill said. Longstreet simply nodded.

"I am confident we shall all meet the test," Lee said. Again he saw the upcoming battle in his mind's eye. So real, so convincing were the images he summoned up that his heart began to pound, as if he were truly in combat. And on the heels of that pounding came pain that squeezed his chest like a vise.

He set his jaw and did his best to ignore it. Then he remembered the medicine Andries Rhoodie had given him. He took the glass bottle from his pocket. He struggled with the lid before he got it open; he was not used to tops with screw threads. He removed a tuft of cotton wool, shook out one of the little pills, and slid it under his tongue as Rhoodie had told him to do.

The pill had no particular taste. That in itself separated it from the vast majority of the medicaments he knew, which displayed their virtue by being either sweet or aggressively vile.

Rhoodie had warned him the—he put on his glasses for a moment to read the name on the bottle again—nitroglycerine might bring on a headache. Sure enough, blood thundered in his temples. Still, he'd known far worse after a few goblets of red wine.

Blood also thundered in his chest. The grip of the vise eased. He took a deep breath. All at once, he seemed able to get plenty of air. He felt as if the weight of ten or twelve years had suddenly fallen from his shoulders.

He looked at the bottle of pills again. In its own way, it was as startling as the repeaters Rhoodie had furnished to his army. But then, a future without wonders would hardly be worth looking forward to. He returned the bottle to his pocket. "Four more days," he said.

★ V ★

The drums beat on and on, not just in the 47th North Carolina but all the III Corps's winter quarters. The hoarse, monotonous sound warned of battle to come.

Nate Caudell heard the long roll without surprise. For the past couple of days, couriers had galloped back and forth between Lee's headquarters and the encampment, a sure sign something was in the wind. Just the night before, Colonel Faribault had relayed the order that all men were to have three days' cooked rations at hand, which meant the army would move soon.

Caudell hurried to the cabin that had been his home for the past few months. A couple of his messmates were already there, frantically getting ready to move out. Dempsey Eure and Rufus Daniel came in hard on his heels. "Gonna feel funny, never seein' this place again," Daniel said as he started loading his meager personal property into his blanket.

"Sure is," Caudell said. "You want to pass me our frying pan there? I have room for it." With it in his blanket went the latest letter from his mother, a pocket Testament, a couple of reading primers, a second pair of socks, and his toothbrush. He tied the ends of the blanket together, covered it with an oilcloth, and draped it from left shoulder to right hip.

His marching rations consisted of a big chunk of corn bread, a smaller piece of salt pork, and several of the packaged desiccated meals that had lately started showing up in their supply shipments. He thought highly of those—they were better than what the cooks turned out almost any day and did not weigh down his mess bag.

He clicked a banana clip into his AK-47, made sure the change lever was in the safe position. Three more full magazines went into his pockets. He looked around to see if he had anything else to take. He didn't. He snaked through his comrades and went outside.

Only a few men had fallen in. More still ran here and there, shouting at each other, getting in one another's way. Captain Lewis and a corporal were loudly trying to bring some order to the confusion. Caudell added his voice to theirs. Then his fellow sergeants came up. The soldiers were used to obeying them. Inside half an hour, the company was fully formed on the parade ground along with the rest of the regiment. The blue CASTALIA INVINCIBLES banner fluttered in the sweet spring breeze in front of the captain.

Atlas Denton, the regimental color-bearer, carried the 47th's Southern Cross battle flag out in front of the assembled troops. Colonel Faribault followed the flag. "Company—attention!" Captain Lewis called. The other company commanders gave the same order. The whole regiment straightened in its ranks.

Without preamble, Faribault said, "The Yankees have crossed the Rapidan. They're moving south through the Wilderness. General Hill's corps will march east by the Orange Plank Road. We have the honor of being lead regiment in the lead brigade of the lead division."

Some of the men cheered. Caudell kept quiet, but a grin spread across his face. Being the lead regiment was privilege as well as honor—other soldiers would eat their dust, instead of their eating other men's.

Faribault went on, "We are to camp near Verdiersville tonight. As the morning is already well along, we have some smart marching to do. God willing, tomorrow we shall start to drive the Yankees out of our country."

The soldiers cheered again, this time with a baying eagerness in their voices. "By companies, form column of fours—and march!" Colonel Faribault called. With officers, sergeants, and corporals amplifying the simple command, the 47th North Carolina became a long gray serpent that wound its way out of the encampment, as if shedding a confining winter skin, and tramped north up the road toward Orange Court House.

The weather was fine and mild. A better day to march could hardly have been imagined. As Caudell had hoped, his new repeater seemed to weigh nothing. He looked back over his shoulder. That gray serpent seemed to have no end, as regiment after regiment followed the 47th North Carolina. But other, even longer, snakes, these clad in blue, surely lay ahead.

At Orange Court House, the 47th swung east onto the Orange Plank

Road. Despite its name, the road was imperfectly corduroyed. Much of it was just dirt. When Caudell looked back again, dust partially obscured the rear of Henry Heth's division and the lead brigades of that of Cadmus Wilcox, which took their place behind Heth's men.

More clouds of dust rose into the eastern sky ahead; General Ewell's corps was also on the move. Caudell looked south: sure enough, more dust still. Longstreet's men were heading east on the Pamunkey Road. The first sergeant nodded in satisfaction, warmed by the thought that the whole Army of Northern Virginia was back together again. He could not imagine any force of Federals beating these lean, tough soldiers. He felt proud to be part of such an army.

Before long, more than pride warmed him. Sweat trickled down from under the brim of his hat, darkened his tunic at the armpits. His feet began to complain; they hadn't worked so hard in months. The AK-47 on his shoulder did weigh something after all. What had been a pleasant outing turned into work.

The men had been singing since they set out. Some kept on; more, Caudell among them, began to find saving their breath the wiser course. After the fourth or fifth time, "The Battle Cry of Freedom," even the Southern version, wore thin.

Because the 47th North Carolina was at the head of the long Confederate column, parties of high-ranking officers often rode nearby. Caudell was used to seeing General Kirkland, the brigade commander, and General Heth. When A. P. Hill came by in his red battle shirt, he pointed him out to Allison High. "I don't know why you're raisin' such a fuss," the dour sergeant said. "When we get shot, it's on account o' the likes of him."

Not much later, the North Carolina regiment behind the 47th raised a cheer. Craning his neck to find out why, Caudell saw a gray-haired man aboard a gray horse with dark mane and tail; several younger soldiers rode with him. "It's General Lee!" he exclaimed.

His words were drowned out by a perfect torrent of cheers. Lee smiled and nodded; for a brief instant, his eyes locked with Caudell's. The first sergeant felt ten feet tall, able to conquer Washington City single-handed. When the cheers would not stop, Lee took off his hat and waved it. Someone called, "We'll whip 'em for you, Marse Bob!"

"Of course you will," Lee said. The soldier whooped with delight at having his beloved commander answer him. Caudell instantly felt jealous. He called to Lee too, but the commander of the Army of Northern Virginia chose that moment to swing Traveller's head around and ride back down the column. His aides followed. Caudell's shoulders slumped as he trudged along.

Everyone was dragging by the time twilight brought a halt to the day's march. Caudell wanted to throw himself full length on the ground. Instead, he went over to Captain Lewis, who looked even more worn than Caudell felt. "Sir, where's the nearest stream?"

Lewis pointed. "There's a creek over that way, about a quarter of a mile."

Caudell went back to the men of Company D, who were sprawled out as he wished he could be. "Fatigue detail," he said. A chorus of groans greeted the announcement. "Corporal Lewis, Privates Batts, Bean, Beard, Biggs, and Floyd, fall in with canteens to fetch water."

Now the groans came from the soldiers he had named. Mollie Bean took off a shoe and sock to display blisters the size of half-dollars. Ruffin Biggs pleaded that he had twisted an ankle. John Floyd alleged his Gettysburg wound was acting up.

Caudell would hear none of it. "Everyone else is as frazzled as you are, but it's your turn for the duty. We especially need the water for the des-iccated suppers a lot of us are toting."

Authority and logic were both on his side. Grumbling and letting out martyred sighs, the members of the fatigue detail slowly and sadly got to their feet. Their luckier comrades passed them canteens until each of them was carrying six or eight. Caudell aimed them toward the creek. They shambled away, complaining still.

Caudell told off another detail to gather wood for cook fires. Some men did not wait for hot food, but chewed on corn bread or wheatcakes. Others went without; a good many soldiers preferred eating their three days' ra-tions at the start of a march to carrying them.

A frying pan was not the ideal instrument for boiling water, but it was what Caudell had, and he managed. Then he opened one of the metallic ration packs and poured the water over it. A couple of minutes later, he was spooning up noodles and ground meat in tomato sauce. He'd had that supper before, and liked it. After a day on the march, he was hungry enough to lick the inside of the pack clean.

A few men carried shelter halves—spoil from the Federals. The ones who did joined together to put up their little tents and sleep inside them. More, Caudell among them, lay down on their oilcloths, spread their blan-kets over themselves, and slept under the stars, with hats for pillows.

Crickets chirped. Little frogs peeped; bigger frogs croaked. The sud-denly glowing periods that were fireflies punctuated the night. Caudell loved fireflies. When he was a boy, he'd snuck out of bed to press his nose against the window to watch them. He watched them now, but not for long. The snores from the men alongside fazed him not in the least. His own soon added to the chorus that threatened to drown out bugs and frogs alike.

When the drums woke him the next morning, he was convinced he could not march a step. His legs were one vast ache, his feet two sharper pains. The whole regiment moved like so many old men with rheumatism.

"Sign me up for the Invalid Corps," Dempsey Eure groaned. That corps took its members from men too badly wounded to stay in the regular army but still able to hold down a prison guard slot or other duty that required little in the way of activity.

"I can't move fast enough to get into the Invalid Corps," Edwin Powell said, neatly topping his fellow sergeant.

For all their complaints, the men moved out while the dew was still wet on the grass and the sun just coming up to shine in their faces. Caudell's feet still hurt, but before long he warmed up and limbered up and no longer felt elderly, just worn. When Lieutenant Winborne started singing "Maryland, My Maryland," he even joined in.

The 47th North Carolina led General Hill's corps past Verdiersville and New Verdiersville just south and east of it. About an hour after the soldiers passed New Verdiersville, they came to the massive earthworks Lee and Meade had dug by Mine Run the November before, each hoping the other would attack him. They were both disappointed, and the campaign had been a fizzle.

As he came up to the works, Caudell wondered if the army would be ordered into them. He could think of nowhere better to stand on the defensive. But Colonel Faribault rode up to the head of the column and shouted, "Forward!" They marched on, into the Wilderness.

"We're going to have ourselves a big fight today," Caudell said.

Nobody argued with him. Mollie Bean said, "Wonder where the Yankees are in there."

Caudell peered down the Orange Plank Road. Grant's whole army could have been within a quarter mile. As long as they kept quiet, the Confederates would never know until they stumbled over them. Trees and underbrush grew right up to the edge of the road, their branches interlacing overhead. The Wilderness was second-growth country, gullied and full of scrubby chinkapin and blackjack oaks, scraggy pines, hazel, and every kind of thorn- and bramble-bearing bush known to man. Get off the road and you were lost, maybe for good.

The occasional clearing seemed like a lamp going on in a gloomy room. Caudell blinked in the sudden strong sunlight as he marched past New

Hope Church on the south side of the road. "Place like this, 'No Hope Church' would be a better name for it," Dempsey Eure remarked.

Colonel Faribault rode up again. He had his sword out, which meant he thought action was near. No sooner had the thought run through Caudell's mind than the colonel said, "Skirmishers forward! We may come upon them any time now."

The picked men trotted east, their repeaters at the ready. Some hurried down the road; others crashed through the tangled undergrowth and headed into the woods. Caudell could trace their progress for a while by the way they swore when thorns and stickers gouged their flesh. But the skirmishers soon fell silent. Today, the Wilderness held more dangerous things than thorn bushes.

It was still midmorning when a brisk crackle of rifle fire started up, ahead of the main body of the regiment. The men looked at one another. Caudell saw pale, tense faces all around. He suspected his own was no ruddier, no calmer. However little they spoke of it, few men went into battle without fear. But the best way to overcome it, to avoid deserving comrades' scorn, was to pretend it did not exist. Without being ordered, the soldiers stepped up their pace.

A skirmisher, his tunic ripped, came pelting back. He gasped, "Bluebellies up ahead, cavalry fightin' on foot!"

"Company, load your rifles!" Captain Lewis ordered.

Caudell unslung his repeater, pulled back the charging handle. "Two clicks on your change levers, mind," he called. "Don't go shooting off all your rounds without good targets."

"Two clicks," the other sergeants echoed.

The regiment drew closer to the firing. Another skirmisher came back, this one staggering and cursing and dripping blood from his left forearm. "Where's Fowler?" he said. Several men pointed the way to the assistant surgeon's wagon. Still cursing, the wounded man went on toward the rear. Caudell's gut knotted. How many more would face chloroform and the knife—or the bone saw—before this day's work was through? And would he be one of them?

Then two more skirmishers appeared. They weren't hurt; they were grinning from ear to ear and prodding along a glum-looking Yankee whose buff chevrons said he was a cavalry corporal. Colonel Faribault came up to him, on foot now. "What's your unit?" he asked.

"Fifth New York Cavalry," the prisoner answered, readily enough. His voice held more than a bit of a brogue. He looked from his captors to the rest of the 47th North Carolina. "Faith, do the lot of yez have these funny-looking guns? I thought it was half a brigade we'd run into, not a wee skirmish line."

The Carolina men howled like wolves to hear that. "Take him back to General Heth for more questions," Faribault told the men who had captured the New Yorker. They led him away. The colonel went on, "Company I, forward to support the skirmishers. Other companies, form line of battle."

Behind their banner, the men of Company I hurried down the Orange Plank Road toward the fighting. Company by company, the rest of the regiment moved off the road into the Wilderness. The Castalia Invincibles were close to the center of the line, and so still close to the roadway. All the same, Caudell discovered at once that this was no place for fancy parade-ground maneuvering. Even keeping the line straight was next to impossible. "Forward!" he called to the handful of men he could see.

Forward meant vines wrapping around his ankles like snakes and branches hitting him in the face and pulling at his arms. He fell three times before he'd made a hundred yards. Then a bullet cracked past his head and slapped against a tree trunk not five feet away. He threw himself flat and crawled through the bushes on his belly.

Another shot rang out, and another. Bullets probed the underbrush, looking for him. The Federal cavalrymen had repeaters of their own. They might not have been AK-47s, but they were bad enough. Caudell peered through a screen of leaves, tried to spy the Yankee who was trying to kill him.

He saw no trace of uniform—the fellow was hidden as well as a red Indian. But he could not hide the black-powder smoke that rose every time he fired. It drifted up from behind a clump of blackberry bushes. Carefully, so as not to give away his own position, Caudell brought the rifle to his shoulder, squeezed off two rounds, one after the other.

He'd flushed his bird. The blackberry bushes stirred as the Federal trooper scrambled toward what he hoped was better cover. Just for a second, Caudell caught a glimpse of blue. He fired. The Yankee screamed. Caudell fired again. The scream stopped, as abruptly as if it had been cut off by a knife. Caudell dashed forward, past the bushes where the dead Yankee had been hiding.

The crash of gunfire resounded all around, louder by the minute as more and more Confederates got into the woods and collided with the Federals already there. As was their way, the dismounted cavalry had firepower out of proportion to their numbers, thanks to the seven-shot Spencer carbines they carried. But now the men of the 47th North Carolina could match them and more. It was a heady feeling. So was pushing the Yankees back.

They went unwillingly. In the tangled badlands of the Wilderness, a few determined men behind a log or hiding in a dry wash could knock a big piece of an assault back on its heels.

Caudell discovered one such knot of resistance by tripping over the corpse of a skirmisher who had been shot through the head. "Git down, dammit," a live Confederate growled at him. "They ain't playin' games up ahead there." He pointed over to a clump of oak saplings. "There's at least three of the bastards in there, and they won't move for hell."

Twigs cracked off to the right. Caudell swung his rifle that way, but the newcomers—almost invisible against the bushes in their gray and butternut clothes—were Confederates. "Yankees there," he called, pointing at the thicket. As if to underscore his words, a couple of Spencers barked, making all the rebels flatten out against the brambled ground.

He nudged the private next to him. "You and me, let's put some bullets through there, make them keep their heads down." When the fellow nodded, Caudell looked over to the soldiers who had just arrived. "You flank 'em while we keep 'em busy." The words were punctuated by a dive into better cover as the Federals fired at the sound of his voice.

He fired back. So did his companion. The other Confederates scrambled forward, from log to tree to bushes. Before they'd moved fifty feet, they disappeared from Caudell's sight. A few seconds later, though, their AK-47s snarled. As Caudell had noted on the practice range, the new repeaters had a shorter, sharper report than any rifle he'd known before. He could tell which was which without having to turn and look, an asset on a field like the Wilderness.

The oak thicket shook like a man with the ague. Caudell grinned savagely—the Yankees' cover from the side couldn't have been as good as it was from his direction. Four bluecoats ran for a stand of cedars. The private next to Caudell shot one of them. He went down in a thrashing heap, screaming and cursing at the same time. Dust puffed from the back of another Federal's jacket as one of the flankers scored a hit. That Yankee pitched forward onto his face and did not move again.

The other two cavalrymen stopped in their tracks. They threw down their carbines, thrust their hands into the air. "You got us, goddammit!" one of them shouted.

The private flicked a glance at Caudell. He nodded; he had no stomach for butchery. Cautiously, he made his way through the brush to the Federals. "Throw down your cartridge boxes and your mess bags," he told them. "Then pick up the wounded fellow there and head west. I reckon someone will take charge of you sooner or later."

"Thank you, Johnny Reb," one of the men in blue said as he shed ammunition and rations. He stooped beside his injured comrade. "Come on, Pete, we're going to pick you up now. It'll be all right."

"The hell it will," Pete gasped out between clenched teeth. He gasped again when the two unhurt cavalrymen hauled him to his feet and supported him between themselves. Seeing Caudell, he fixed him with a baleful stare and growled, "Where'd you bastards come by all these repeaters? I ain't been shot at so much in the last two years put together, and now one of you had to go and nail me."

"Don't anger him up, Pete," the cavalryman who had spoken before said. But his gaze kept flicking to Caudell's AK-47, too. "What kind of rifle is that, anyway, Johnny?"

"Never you mind." Caudell gestured with the barrel of the repeater. "Just get going." As the dispirited Federals obeyed, he scooped up their haversacks. He handed one of them to the private who had fought beside him. Both men grinned. "Good eating," Caudell said; even with the Rivington men's desiccated meals, belts had been tight all winter.

"Coffee and sugar too, likely," the private said dreamily. Not far away, a Spencer spoke. The private and Caudell dove for cover. A bullet could end all dreams in a hurry, or turn them to nightmares.

Caudell kept moving east, now quickly, now slowly. The Federal cavalrymen put up a stubborn fight, but more and more Confederates were coming into line against them. Caudell spotted men he did not recognize. "What regiment?" he called to them.

"Forty-Fourth North Carolina," one of them answered. "Who are you all?"

"Forty-Seventh."

"Let's go, Forty-Seventh!" A rebel yell ripped the air. "Let's flank these bluebellies out of their shoes again."

They drove the Federals past Parker's Store and the handful of houses that huddled in the clearing with it. The open space gave the Confederates a chance to dress their lines a little; victory had left them about as disorganized as defeat had the Yankees. Caudell almost stumbled over Captain Lewis. "What are we aiming to do now, sir?" he asked.

Lewis pointed east. "About three miles from here, I hear tell, the Orange Plank Road crosses the Brock Road. We want to grab that crossing. If we can do it, we cut the Yankees in half."

"Three miles?" Caudell gauged the sun, and was surprised to find how early it still was. "We can be there before noon."

"The sooner, the better," Lewis said.

Along with as many of the Castalia Invincibles as had reassembled around Parker's Store, Caudell plunged into the woods again. As he scrambled along, he munched on a hardtack from the Yankee cavalryman's haversack. The square, flat biscuit lived up to its name by the way it challenged his teeth. He choked it down, swigged from his canteen, and pushed on.

The Wilderness was like no battlefield on which he'd ever fought. At Gettysburg, the whole panorama of war had spread out before him. When the 47th North Carolina joined in the great charge against the center of the Federal position, Caudell had seen every rifle, every artillery piece that slaughtered his companions. Here, he could not even see more than a handful of those companions, let alone the Yankees they were doing their best to slay. All he knew was that the Confederates were still rolling east, which meant they were driving back the enemy.

By twos and threes, the Confederates dashed across a narrow roadway. Yankee bullets from the other side kicked up dust around their feet and knocked down more than one man, but before long the dismounted cavalry had to retreat again—they were not only outnumbered but outgunned. Caudell wondered if this was the Brock Road of which Captain Lewis had spoken. He didn't think he'd come three miles since Parker's Store, but in the tangle he couldn't be sure.

Evidently the Brock Road lay further on—he heard an officer yelling, "Come on, men, keep it moving! Give those damnyankees hell!" More rebel yells rang out. Caudell did his best to keep it moving. He reached up to settle his hat more firmly on his head, only to discover he'd lost it to a grasping branch or bush without ever noticing.

Somewhere to the north, he could hear a great crash of gunfire. Ewell's II Corps and the Federals were tearing at each other along the Orange Turnpike, then. He took a moment to wish his fellows well. A bullet crashed past his head and made him pay full attention to his own battle.

Cheers came from just ahead. Caudell wondered why; the fight seemed no different now from what it had been all along—confusing, exhilarating, and terrifying at the same time. Then, without warning, he found himself out of the underbrush and standing in the middle of a dirt road which had recently seen heavy traffic, a dirt road that, by the sun, ran north instead of east.

"It's the Brock Road!" a first lieutenant from some other regiment bawled in his ear. "We done beat the Federals to the crossroads and trapped the ones who've already gone by."

For a moment, that made Caudell want to yell, too. But when he said, "Holy Jesus," it came out in a whisper. He turned to the lieutenant. "Does

that mean they'll be coming at us from north and south at the same time?"
The lieutenant's eyes got wide. He nodded. Now Caudell shouted, as loud
as he could: "Let's get some branches, stumps, rocks, whatever the hell,
onto this road. We've got lots of Yankees heading this way, and we'd better
have something to shoot from."

The Confederates worked like men possessed. Attacking the Federals'
fixed positions at Gettysburg had taught them the value of field fortifications, no matter how quickly improvised. Caudell dragged fallen logs across
the roadway to help seal it off. On the other side of the junction with the
Orange Plank Road, more soldiers ran up breastworks facing south. Still
others started building barricades along the Orange Plank Road east from
the Brock Road.

The first lieutenant seemed to be the highest-ranking officer around.
"Run 'em back west, too," he said. "If the Yankees can't go through us,
they'll try to go around. They have to reconnect, or we chew 'em up in
detail." He grabbed two men by their jackets. "Go back and tell 'em to
fetch us all the cartridges they can. We're going to need 'em."

The privates sprinted off. In a way, Caudell envied them. He'd already
seen his share of fighting this morning. If he stayed here, he would see a
lot more than his share. He hunkered down behind the thickest log he
could find and settled himself to wait.

He did not wait long. A party of Yankee horsemen came trotting down
the Brock Road toward the breastworks. They pulled up in obvious dismay
as soon as they saw them.

The first lieutenant whooped. "Too late, Yankees! Too late!"

The horsemen—officers, some of them, by their fancy trappings—rode
forward again, more slowly now, to see just what sort of barrier the Confederates had built and how many of them crouched behind it. Caudell
took careful aim at the lead man, whose gray hair said he might be of high
rank. The range was long, close to a quarter mile, but worth a try. He
rested the barrel of the rifle on the log in front of him, took a deep breath,
let it out, pulled the trigger.

The Yankee tilted in the saddle, as if he'd had too much to drink before
he mounted. He slid off his horse and crashed to the dirt of the Brock
Road. "Good shot!" shouted one of the men by Caudell. He and several
others started firing at the men who had leaped down to help their stricken
comrade. The Federals heaved him over the back of the horse. They all
galloped away, though a couple of them reeled as if they were hit.

"Skirmishers forward!" the lieutenant said. "There'll be more where
those came from."

Men hurried up the road and north through the woods. An ammunition wagon reached the crossroads. Its horses were lathered and blowing. Caudell and several other soldiers helped the driver unload crate after crate of cartridges. The wagon also carried hatchets and shovels. The driver passed those out, too, so the men could strengthen the breastworks in whatever time was left before the enemy descended on them.

A corporal pried the lid off an ammunition crate. He started to reach down for a handful of cartridges, stopped and stared in disbelieving disgust. "What the hell goddam bucket-headed jackass sent us up a load of Minié balls?" The whole crate was full of paper cartridges for the rifle muskets the Army of Northern Virginia no longer carried.

By the howls of rage that rose from several other soldiers, they'd made the same unwelcome discovery. Caudell ground his teeth in fear and fury. A big part of the Army of the Potomac was bearing down on him. He and his comrades would need every possible round, and here were boxes and boxes of cartridges they couldn't use. "I just brung 'em up here," the wagon driver protested when the angry Confederates rounded on him. "I didn't load 'em in."

A few hundred yards to the north, the skirmishers began a brisk fire. A couple of them let go on full automatic. Caudell scowled and worked his jaws harder. Either they were overeager or a whole lot of Yankees were on the way, all packed together. He suspected he knew which.

"Here's the right ones!" somebody shouted, his voice rising in relief. Caudell hurried over, grabbed a couple of magazines, and stuffed them into his pockets. The firing was getting closer in a hurry, not just AK-47s but also the familiar deep roar of Springfields. Under the gunfire came the tramp of marching men.

The Confederate skirmishers dashed back toward the breastworks. Some turned to fire last shots. Others just scrambled over the barricade or off into the concealing woods.

"Yankees!" The shout came from a dozen throats at once, Caudell's among them. A thick blue column appeared on the Brock Road, a sword-swinging officer at its head. He pointed his sword at the Confederates' makeshift works. The Northern men, their bayonets gleaming even in the uncertain light, upped their pace to double-quick. They cheered as they charged, not the wild rebel yell but a more studied, rhythmic "Hurrah! Hurrah!"

Caudell thumbed his change lever to full automatic. His rifle spat flame. He used up what was left of his first banana clip in the twinkling of an eye. He rammed in another, fired it off at full automatic, too. He knew he would never find a better, more massed target.

When, a few seconds later, the second magazine was also gone, he stuck

on a third banana clip and glanced down to switch the change lever back
to single shots. He looked up over his sights at the head of the oncoming
Federal column. The lead ranks were all down, some writhing, some still
and obviously dead—he was far from the only rebel to have hosed the
Yankees with a stream of thirty bullets, or more than one.

The Northern officer, incredibly, still stood, still waved his men on. Even
as Caudell took aim at him, he spun backwards and fell, clutching at his
right side. But the Federals, stumbling over the wounded and slain men in
front of them, advanced without him. Through the unending rattle of gunfire came a bugle's high, thin cry, urging them forward.

The bluecoats in the lead fired at the Confederates who were slaughter-
ing them. Two men over from Caudell, a rebel sagged to the dirt, the back
of his head blown out. One or two others at the breastwork screamed as
they were hit. But then the Yankees had either to stop and reload or keep
on charging and trust they would live long enough to use bayonets or
clubbed rifles.

Even against a firing line of single-shot Springfields, both choices would
have been evil. Caudell had not been at the battle of Fredericksburg, where
Lee's men on Marye's Heights smashed wave after wave of attacking Yankees; the 47th North Carolina had not yet joined the Army of Northern
Virginia, but was further south in that state, on provost guard duty at
Petersburg. Now, though, he knew what the defenders must have felt then,
with men too brave to run away coming at them again and again, rushing
headlong toward annihilation.

The Federals on the Brock Road were brave men too, as brave as any
Caudell had ever seen. They kept trying to rush the long barricade. None
of them got within a hundred yards of it; no man in the open roadway
could push farther than that in the face of the withering fire the Confederate
repeaters put out. Wounded soldiers reached out and grabbed at the legs
of men pushing past, trying to hold them back from the deadly stutter of
the AK-47s. But the fresh troops shook off those hands and advanced—
until they were wounded or killed themselves.

At last even their courage could bear no more. The Federals stopped
hurrying forward into the meat grinder. Even then, they did not break and
run. They ducked into the woods and huddled behind the dead bodies of
their mates and kept up as strong a fire as they could.

Off the Brock Road to either side, the crackle of rifle muskets crept
closer to the Orange Plank Road. Caudell gnawed nervously on his lip.
The Yankees had cover in the thickets and tangles of the Wilderness. That
let their numbers count for more against the repeaters than was possible

on the road itself. If they forced their way around the crossroads, they might yet link up with the corps trapped to the south.

A whistling through the air, a crash—Caudell threw himself flat, all strategic considerations driven from his mind by pure and simple terror. The Wilderness was such a jungle that artillery could find few jobs. Firing straight down the Brock Road at the Confederate breastwork, unfortunately, was one of them.

The first shell landed short. A moment later, another one screamed overhead, to detonate about fifty yards beyond the barricade. Caudell's belly turned to ice. Split the difference between the two of them and . . . He'd been shelled at Gettysburg. He knew only too well what came after "and." The Federals started their hurrah again.

But the third shell was also safely long. If the Yankees had set up two guns in the roadway, perhaps the first one's crew had overcorrected. That kind of luck, though, could not last long.

It did not have to. Off to the left rose a great racket of AK-47 fire and rebel yells. The Northern hurrahs turned to shouts of dismay. Yankees began bursting out of the bushes and dashing across the Brock Road from west to east. For a moment, Caudell was too bemused even to shoot at them.

The first lieutenant, who still seemed to be the ranking officer at the crossroads, let out a whoop. "Here comes the rest of the corps, by God!"

Caudell whooped, too. If the Federals had formed their line in the woods to try to force the Confederates off the Orange Plank Road, then the rebels advancing from the west toward the junction with the Brock Road would have been ideally placed to take them in flank and roll them up—and, incidentally, to reach the Brock Road and drive away those field guns or put their crews out of action. Caudell had no idea which had happened. He did know no more shells landed close by, for which he was heartily glad.

Not all the Yankees had been smashed; firing continued in the woods as knots of soldiers refused to give ground. On a more open battlefield, that would have been impossible; in the Wilderness's thickets and tangles and clumps of bushes, men could find places to make a stand even after their comrades had given way. But the Confederates had gained a long stretch of the Brock Road.

Caudell sniffed. Along with the familiar tang of black-powder smoke and the sharper, thinner odor of the nonsmoking powder in AK-47 cartridges, he smelled burning weeds. All that shooting in the undergrowth had set the Wilderness ablaze. He shuddered at the thought of wounded and helpless men in there, watching the little flames lick closer . . .

The jingle of horses' trappings released him from his unpleasant reverie. He glanced back over his shoulder. Where the lowly lieutenant had led the Confederates through the heavy fighting at the crossroads, now Generals Kirkland and Heth were here to see how things stood. That was the way the world worked, Caudell thought.

"How clean the men look," William Kirkland said, a remark seldom made about the Army of Northern Virginia, especially after some hours of combat.

Henry Heth, quicker on the uptake, figured out why: "They haven't been biting cartridges all day, not with these new brass ones, so they've no need to look as though they were in a blackface minstrel show."

"That's true, by God," Kirkland said. "I hadn't thought about it." Caudell hadn't thought about it, either. After his struggle through the forest, he suspected he was quite grimy enough for any ordinary purpose.

He used the lull in the fighting to take some cartridges out of his pockets and refill the banana clips he'd emptied. Another horse came clopping down the Orange Plank Road, a dark-maned gray— Where Caudell had sat and tended to his business in the presence of his brigade and division commanders, he scrambled to his feet for General Lee. So did most of the other soldiers close by.

"As you were, gentlemen, please." Lee peered north up the Brock Road toward the blue-clad bodies that corduroyed it like so many planks. "Those people are paying dearly for every acre of Wilderness they hold," he remarked as he turned to look south. "Henry, push such forces as you can spare down along this road, if you please. General Hancock will be along shortly, unless I miss my guess."

"Yes, General Lee," Heth said. "We might have been in a bad way if he'd hit us from the south at the same time as Getty was coming down from the north."

"So we might have," Lee said, "but however brave its men may be, coordination of attacks has never been the Army of the Potomac's strong suit."

A good thing, too, Caudell thought. A dispatch rider galloped up to Lee. He held reins in one hand, an AK-47 in the other, and his message between his teeth. Lee read it, nodded, and rode off with him.

After reloading, Caudell lit up a cigar. He'd only taken a couple of drags on it when General Heth said, "I expect you heard what General Lee wants, boys. The sooner we get moving, the farther south we'll get, and the better the works we'll be able to set up before Hancock's men hit us."

The Confederates at the crossroads would have obeyed some commanders only slowly and reluctantly; they'd already seen their share and more of hard fighting for the day. But Heth and Kirkland and their staff officers rode down the road in front of the infantry, as if the idea that danger might lie ahead had never entered their minds. With that example before them, the foot soldiers followed readily enough. Fresh troops coming up the Orange Plank Road took their places at the breastwork they'd built.

A little more than a quarter of a mile south of the crossroads, the Brock Road narrowed and bent slightly to the east. Heth reined in. "This looks to be a good spot, boys," he said. "We'll stop 'em right here."

The soldiers attacked the timber on either side of the road for the field fortifications, mixed earth and stones in with the logs. Off in the woods, Caudell heard men making even ruder works to protect themselves from Yankee bullets.

Just as the skirmishers Heth had pushed out south of his main line began to fire, a couple of ammunition wagons brought fresh cartridges down the road. "Better not be them goddam Minié balls," several soldiers growled, using almost identical words. This time, they weren't. Caudell filled his pockets again, crouched behind the breastwork, and waited.

More and more single shots from Yankee Springfields mingled with the bark of the skirmishers' repeaters. The skirmishers crashed back through the undergrowth to Heth's main line. "We stung 'em," one called, off in the woods.

Federal skirmishers came first, trotting up the Brock Road to learn what lay ahead for their comrades. They stopped short when they spied the rebel breastwork that barred their path. One of the bluecoats raised his rifle musket to his shoulder, fired. The bullet kicked up dust a few yards short of the barricade. The Yankee dove into the bushes to reload. His companions turned and ran south to report what they'd seen.

A minute or so later, the head of the main Federal line came into view. Caudell's stomach churned. Lee might remark that the Yankees had trouble putting their attacks together, but every one they made was fierce. "Fire at will!" a Confederate officer shouted.

"Which one's Will?" some army wit shouted back. That stupid joke got made on every firing line, Yankee or rebel. Somehow it helped Caudell relax.

The front rank of Federals suddenly dropped to one knee. The second rank took aim over their heads. A couple of Yankees fell over or reeled back out of line—the Confederates had already begun to shoot. But then the Northerners' muskets, all in a row, belched flame and great curls of greasy black smoke.

Caudell thought the rebel beside him at the breastwork had tapped him on the left shoulder. He automatically glanced down. Neat as a tailor's scissors, a bullet had clipped his uniform without touching him. He shuddered. He could not help it. Lower by only a couple of fingers' breadth, and his precious arm would have ended on the slaughterhouse pile outside a surgeon's tent . . . if he'd managed to make it back to a surgeon's tent at all.

The fellow beside him, who he thought had tapped him, would never need a surgeon again. A Minié ball had clipped him, and clipped off the top of his head. Blood and shattered brains poured from the wound as he slowly toppled over backwards.

Caudell looked away, tried not to hear the cries of other men who had been wounded close by. Gettysburg had hardened him to horror. And if he did not help slay the Yankees rushing up the Brock Road toward the barricade behind which he crouched, he and all his fellows, hale and wounded alike, would surely perish.

The Yankees were reloading as they ran; most of them had to stop to use their ramrods. Caudell and everyone else on the breastwork who could still handle a rifle fired again and again and again. Men in blue coats began to drop and kept on falling, faster and faster. A few managed to fire again, but only a few. After that first volley, the rebels had it all their own way.

Miraculously, every bullet missed one Federal corporal. His face set and grim, he charged on alone toward the breastwork. "Don't kill him!"—the call ran up and down the line. The Confederates could still admire gallantry, even in a foe.

Firing slackened for a moment. "Go back, you damned fool!" Caudell shouted to the Yankee. "Look behind you!"

The corporal's double-quick faltered as the words reached him. Caudell could see him leave the exalted state in which he'd rushed toward certain death. He knew that state himself; it was all that had sustained him as he advanced on the Union guns up in Pennsylvania. Its ebbing came hard, hard. When it left a man, he felt more drained than after a week of forced marches, and rightly so for with it, he lost spirit as well as strength.

The Federal did look around. His shoulders sagged as he took in the carnage on the Brock Road, the ruin of his regiment. Some of his comrades were crawling or creeping or dragging themselves away from the dreadful fire of the Confederate repeaters. Others would not move again until the Last Trump sounded.

The corporal slowly turned back toward the barricade. "You rebs don't fight fair!" he shouted. Now his exaltation was gone, leaving only fear behind. He fled into a pine thicket off to one side of the road.

He was none too soon, for more Federals tramped up the Brock Road a few minutes later. The crossfire would have chewed him to pieces. The bluecoats came to a ragged halt when they saw what had happened to the first attacking party, but then moved ahead all the same. The South had gone into the war doubting Yankee courage. After three years of fighting, few in the Army of Northern Virginia doubted it anymore.

This group of Union men attacked more cleverly than had the previous one. Instead of forming a neat firing line—and a target that could not be missed—they advanced in rushes, a few men pausing to shoot while others moved up, then the men who had gained ground ducking into the bushes and providing covering fire for their companions to push ahead.

Caudell shot, missed, shot again, missed again. A Minié ball buzzed past his head. He involuntarily ducked—only men with no nerves whatever could keep from dodging when bullets zipped by. He fired again, at a Yankee less than two hundred yards away. The fellow threw down his Springfield and grabbed at his shoulder. He lurched away from the front line of fighting. A lot of Confederates were behind the breastwork. Even though Caudell had aimed at the Northerner, he couldn't be sure his was the round that had wounded him.

No matter how cleverly, no matter how boldly they attacked the rebel barricade, the Federals on the Brock Road could not drive the defenders from it. The fire from the Confederates' repeaters swept the roadway clean of life. Men fell, killed or wounded, but more replaced them. Teamsters and other soldiers fetched crates of cartridges to the breastwork. Ironic cheers rang out every time the crates proved to contain the proper ammunition. Once or twice they didn't, and the cartridge-bearers retreated, scorched by curses from the fighting men.

In the Wilderness proper, especially east of the Brock Road, the Federals were able to come to closer quarters with their foes. Their hurrahs and the boom of their Springfields crept ever nearer the line the Confederates held south of the Orange Plank Road.

Off to the north, a huge racket of riflery and cannons broke out. Lee had said the Federals had trouble putting their attacks together. They'd managed now. Had they done it sooner, the rebel lines between them would have been thin. The Confederates had won a critical couple of hours to bring more men forward and widen the stretch they held along either side of the Orange Plank Road. The Yankees were hitting them with everything they had now. They had more men. The Confederates had better rifles. Caudell hoped that would do the job.

Between assaults up the roadway, he filled banana clips, chewed on corn bread and salt pork, and drank from his canteen. The water was warm and turbid. It went down like champagne even so. He and his companions smoked and listened to the gunfire all around and tried to guess how the fighting was going away from their little piece of it.

"I think we got 'em," a beardless soldier declared.

"Didn't notice you come up, uh, Melvin," Caudell said. "Hope you're right, but I wouldn't bet on anything yet. They're putting a lot of their people into the fight this time. We're holding so far, but—"

Mollie Bean interrupted him: "Holy Jesus." She was looking over the breastwork; Caudell sprawled with his back against it. He whirled around. The Federals had given up on subtlety. A deep column of bluecoats, their bayonets fixed, stormed up the Brock Road at the double-quick. Officers trotted ahead of them, urging them on.

"All or nothin' this time, boys," somebody not far from Caudell said. "Them bluebellies is gonna run over us or die tryin'."

Caudell vastly preferred the second alternative. He aimed at a color-bearer in front of the first rank. As soon as the advancing Yankees reached the first men lying in the road—some of the wounded, as before to the north, tried to hold their fellows back, but others cheered them on—he started shooting. He did not know if his bullet struck home, but the color-bearer stumbled and fell. Another Yankee caught the regimental flag before it touched the ground, bore it forward a dozen paces more before he, too, was hit. Yet another Federal grabbed it and carried it on. Three more fell before the banner drew close enough for Caudell to read it: SIXTEENTH MASSACHUSETTS. Then still another color-bearer went down and the banner fell in the dust. No one picked it up.

No one was left to pick it up. Like the corporal before him, that last brave and lucky—at least lucky up to a point—color-bearer pushed far beyond his comrades. The Southerners' repeaters had worked a fearful slaughter. There was a limit beyond which flesh and blood could not be made to go. Caudell had met that limit on the third day at Gettysburg. Now he and the soldiers crouching to either side of him acquainted the Federals with it.

But another regiment came in right behind the slaughtered Sixteenth Massachusetts. The Federals leaned forward as they advanced, as if moving into a heavy rain. So they were, but the rain was of lead.

"This ain't war!" Mollie Bean yelled in Caudell's ear. "This here's murder."

"I reckon you're right," he answered, "but if we don't keep shooting them, they'll surely shoot us." She kept firing, so he supposed she agreed with him.

After that second Federal regiment wrecked itself assaulting the barricade, the rebels behind it had another brief respite. They used it to strengthen their protection. "If the Yankees are pushing this hard, they'll try us again before long," Caudell said as he set another log in place. By the way the rest of the soldiers worked alongside him, they thought as he did. More ammunition came up. He filled his pockets again. He wondered how many rounds he'd fired. He'd lost track. Far more than on any day with his old Enfield, he was certain. So had everyone else here. The drifts of Yankee corpses in front of the barricade, sometimes two and three men high, testified to that.

While he worked, Caudell kept an ear cocked to try to gauge how the rest of the battle was going. To the north, Federals and rebels still went at it hammer and tongs; by the sound of things, the line hadn't moved there, which was all to the good as far as he was concerned. The Yankees also kept trying to break through east of the Brock Road. A sudden flurry of hurrahs said they were close to doing it, too. Rebel yells and the wild snarl of AK-47s fired on full automatic answered them. The hurrahs ebbed.

"Knocked 'em back," Caudell guessed.

"They just keep comin'," a soldier said. "Dang fools don't know when they's licked." Remembering Pickett's charge, Caudell thought that a failing of which both sides were guilty. Just then, the soldier dropped the fence rail he was carrying and snatched up his repeater. "Oh, sweet Jesus, here they is again."

The new Federal attacking column marched up the Brock Road in perfect order, filling the roadway from edge to edge, each bluecoat a regulation thirteen inches from the man on either side of him. The Yankees hesitated when they saw ahead of them the ruins of the two regiments that had gone in before them; a few men in the first ranks took half steps instead of full marching paces. But shouts and curses from officers and sergeants quickly got their lines dressed once more, and they bore down on the breastwork with a hurrah.

The Confederates broke them. Mollie Bean had the right of it, Caudell thought as he fired again and again—using repeaters against such a bunched target *was* murder. But he had been right, too, for it was necessary murder if he was to live himself. The Northerners went down like ninepins. But more and more pushed forward to take their places until, at last, they would advance into the face of death no more, but turned and ran for the rear.

Caudell and his companions on the firing line raised a tired cheer to see them go. Dead and wounded men were thick on the ground behind the barricade, too, even if the Yankees had never come close to reaching it. The soldiers gave what rough first aid they could, and sent to the rear men who could walk. Hospital stewards, some wearing green sashes as their Federal counterparts did, came forward to haul off on stretchers men too badly hurt to travel on their own.

A small brushfire reached the roadway a couple of hundred yards south of the breastwork. It caught in the clothes of a Federal lying there. A few seconds later, his cartridges began exploding, *pop-pop-pop*, almost as if they were kernels from an ear of popping corn. Wounded men writhed frantically, trying to escape the flames.

Several Confederates started to scramble over their piled logs and rails and stones to go to rescue the Yankees from the fire. But they scrambled back a moment later, for yet another regiment of Federals appeared, battle flags flying, to hurl their bodies at the barricade.

Caudell's repeater was hot in his hands. He'd been shooting at bluecoats the whole day long—forever, it seemed. He glanced through leaves and drifting smoke at the sun. It was getting low in the west. Before too long, night would halt combat if nothing else did.

After three regiments had tried the barricade and failed, the Brock Road in front of it was clogged with bodies. More than one shot had come from behind them, as lightly wounded men used their comrades' corpses as barricades of their own. Now dead and wounded alike broke up the neat ranks of the oncoming Federals. They came on all the same. Caudell and his fellows began the grisly task of educating them about what repeaters could do.

The Federals had sufficient horrid examples right before their eyes. They did not rush with the same élan their predecessors had shown. When men at the head of the column began dropping, the bluecoats behind them hesitated. Through the cries of the wounded, Caudell heard officers screaming at their men, trying to get them to advance in spite of the scourging fire that lay ahead.

Then, drowning cries and screams alike, a great new eruption of gunfire broke out—to the south. The Federals on the Brock Road looked back over their shoulders in surprise and alarm. Even their officers stopped urging them forward for a moment.

Caudell frowned. As he tiredly wondered what the new fighting was about, Mollie Bean pounded him on the shoulder and yelled, "Longstreet!"

"Longstreet." He said the name once with no particular feeling. Then the lightning flashed inside his head. He yelled too; "Longstreet!" If Lee's war horse had pitched into this Federal corps from the south while A. P. Hill kept it from going north, the Yankees hereabouts were in more trouble than you could shake a stick at.

They knew it, too. They milled about, just out of good shooting range. But then they came on once more. Now the officers had no trouble with balky men. They knew they had to break through if their corps was to survive.

"Fire low!" Caudell shouted as the blue wave again surged toward the breastwork that dammed its progress. As the Confederates had three times before, they shredded the charge. No Yankee could come within fifty yards of that rude wall and live. The captains and lieutenants who headed the rush fell bravely, leading their men. Like most troops on both sides in the war, the common soldiers took heart from the example their officers set. Without that example, most of those who could made for the rear and at least temporary safety.

A couple of bluecoats stood where they were, their empty hands high in the air. "Don't shoot, you rebs!" one of them shouted, his northern accent sharp in Caudell's ears. "You done caught us."

Caudell looked around. "Where's that lieutenant?" he asked, seeing no one of higher rank than himself.

"He got shot," Mollie Bean answered laconically.

"Oh." Without showing more of himself than his head, Caudell called to the Federals, "Come ahead, Yanks. Make it pert, though—if we have to start shooting again, you all will be right in the middle."

The Northern men sprinted toward the barricade. More shouted directions from Caudell took them out of the roadway and through the edge of the Wilderness. Caudell listened to them scrabbling over the lower fieldworks there; they disappeared from sight until they came back out onto the Brock Road. The Confederates promptly relieved them of their haversacks and whatever money they had on them. "Shoes, too, Yanks," a barefoot private said. "One of you might could be my size, and if you ain't, I'll wear one pair anyways and pass the other on to somebody else."

The prisoners did not protest. "You just take what you want, rebs," one of them said as he pulled off his stout marching shoes. "I'm so glad you're not shooting at me anymore, I don't care about anything else. The way the bullets came at us, I figured you had a million men back here, maybe two."

The Confederates grinned at that. Caudell sent the two Federals to the rear. He stayed by the barricade, waiting to see if the Union men would mount yet another attack. The firing to the south was coming closer—that had to mean Longstreet was doing well. The firing to the north grew louder, too, or rather deeper; more artillery was mixing with the rifles there.

The sun sank, a blood-red ball looking down on blood through tangled branches and curls of smoke from gunpowder and brushfires. The fifth Yankee attack had not come. As darkness gathered, the sound of fighting to north and south began to slacken. It also eased in the woods east of the Brock Road, though it never died away altogether, and would flare up every so often in a brief spasm of ferocity.

Caudell looked up and down the breastwork. But for Mollie Bean, he saw no one he recognized. Any battle was liable to tear up a neat line of march; battle in country like the Wilderness made such disorder a sure thing. He asked, "Melvin, do you know where the rest of the boys from the 47th are?"

Mollie pointed east. "Some of 'em's over in the thickets yonder, maybe half a mile. I was with 'em for a while. Then I heard all the shootin' over here and figgered I'd come lend a hand."

"Things are dying down for the night, seems like," Caudell said. "Let's see if we can't bed down with our regiment." She nodded, and followed him as he headed into the undergrowth. Pushing through the rank second growth of the Wilderness was even worse in the evening twilight than it had been during the day. A red Indian would have laughed himself sick at Caudell's noisy, stumbling fight with thorn bushes and cedar saplings.

"Who's there?" a nervous voice called from up ahead.

"Two men from the 47th North Carolina," Caudell answered quickly, before the nervous owner of that nervous voice started shooting. Behind him, Mollie Bean chuckled softly. He ignored her; he had to think of her as a soldier now, not a woman. He called back, "Who are you?"

"Fifteenth North Carolina—Cooke's brigade," the still-invisible fellow answered. He sounded less nervous now. "Y'all are out o' Kirkland's brigade, right?"

"That's us," Caudell agreed gratefully. At least he was talking with someone from his own division.

"Keep goin' east. You'll find 'em."

Caudell kept going east. He never did see the man who'd given him directions. He and Mollie were challenged twice more in short order. He also challenged a couple of small groups of men himself: soldiers heading west, looking for their regiments. He was certain what they were before he opened his mouth. He challenged anyhow. In the Wilderness, certainty meant little.

That half mile took close to half an hour to cover. Then, to his disgust, Caudell learned he'd somehow gone right past his regiment and had to double back. Had Mollie scolded him for that, he would have sworn at her. But she said only, "The goin's rough hereabouts, Nate." Nodding a grateful nod she probably couldn't see, he pushed on.

He stumbled into a tiny clearing. Some soldiers were sitting around a campfire. One of them looked up. It was Dempsey Eure. "I will be damned," he said. "We reckoned you was buzzards' meat, Nate."

"I thought so myself, a couple of times." Caudell sank to the ground, footsore and weary. "You even managed to hang on to your plumed hat, Dempsey. I lost mine straight off."

"Wouldn't lose this beauty, Nate." Eure doffed it to Mollie. "Glad we didn't lose that there little beauty, either."

"You shut up, Dempsey, you hear?" she said. "Don't want no officers catchin' the wind from your big flappin' mouth."

"Sorry, uh, Melvin," Eure said contritely.

"Any water close by?" Caudell asked, shaking his empty canteen. "I'm bone dry."

Eure jerked his thumb to the north. "There's a little creek down that way, couple minutes' walk."

Hoping the couple of minutes would not stretch as the trip to find his regiment had, Caudell went off to look for the creek and to answer a call of nature which Mollie Bean's presence had forced him to suppress until now. Such modesty was a foolish thing, but it was his own; he sighed with relief as he buttoned his trousers.

He found the water by stepping into it. He took off his shoes and bathed his tired feet before he filled the canteen. Once he'd drunk, he felt better. He knew his comrades were only a few yards away, knew tens of thousands of Federals and Confederates were within a few miles, but for all he could see of them, he might as well have been alone in the Wilderness.

His ears told him otherwise. In spite of full darkness, firing went on between rival pickets. But the cries of the wounded were worse. In the tangle through which both armies had pushed their lines, a hurt man had a hard time getting to the rear, nor could his mates easily rescue him—or sometimes even find him. Wails, shrieks, moans turned the thickets to the haunt of tormented ghosts. Most of the sounds of pain came from the south, which meant they rose from Yankee throats. But Confederates also shouted out their hurt to the world.

Caudell shivered as he made his way back to the clearing, though the night was warm. What, save luck, had kept his tender flesh, rather than someone else's, from pouring out its blood in the unwelcome track of a bullet? Nothing of which he was aware. He patted himself, as if to prove he was still whole and unholed. How marvelous that each hand grasped, that each foot moved confidently in front of the other!

Once sitting again by the fire, he shared some of his food and the spoil from captured Yankee war bags with men who'd already gobbled the rations they were supposed to carry. A couple of soldiers went to sleep, their hats either over their eyes or under their heads as pillows. More, though, stayed up awhile to smoke and to hash over the battle and try to draw a bigger picture from the tiny pieces they'd seen.

Plainly, Lee had trapped a big chunk of the Federal army between Hill's corps and Longstreet's. Mollie Bean said, "Reckon we'll go on and try poundin' 'em to pieces come mornin'."

"That's clear enough," Otis Massey agreed. The corporal patted the AK-47 that lay on the ground beside him. "With these repeaters, might could be we'll even do it, too. Be a nasty butcher's bill to pay for certain if we was usin' muzzle-loaders instead."

"You've got that right, Otis," Caudell said as a general murmur of agreement rose from the soldiers. "A Yankee said we weren't fighting fair."

Dempsey Eure spat into the fire. "Fair didn't stop their cavalry from usin' their repeaters against single-shot muskets. Now they see what the shoe's like on t'other foot."

Talk about repeaters reminded Caudell he hadn't yet cleaned his. With more fighting ahead tomorrow, he wanted the rifle as ready as he could make it. He stripped the AK-47 and dug out a rag and the gun oil that had come with the weapon. The little black oil bottle said Break Free CLP. The sweet, almost fruity, smell of the oil mixed with the odors of coffee, food, and woodsmoke.

He was in the middle of putting the repeater back together when someone came crashing through the brush toward the clearing. Mollie Bean and a couple of other privates reached for their rifles, in case it was a Yankee who needed capturing. But it wasn't a Yankee—it was Colonel Faribault.

"Turn those aside, boys, if you please," he said when he saw he was looking down the barrels of several repeaters. "However much I admire Stonewall Jackson's memory, I have no desire to share his fate." The rifles were hastily lowered. But for accidents like that which had befallen Jackson, only a bad officer risked bullets from his own men. Faribault was a good one.

"What's the word, Colonel?" Caudell asked.

"Tomorrow morning, five o'clock, we go after Winfield Scott Hancock again," Faribault said. "God willing, we may put an end to the whole Federal II Corps. General Heth told General Lee we are driving them beautifully; I heard him say it myself."

The men round the campfire grinned and nodded to one another, pleased at the news and, as common soldiers have a way of being, proud they'd already figured out what their officers had planned for them. Caudell said, "How are we doing up by the Orange Turnpike?"

"We pushed them hard there, too, all the way back to the Germanna Ford Road—they don't care for our repeaters, not a bit of it," Faribault answered, and a couple of soldiers yowled with glee. But the colonel held up a hand. "I think the Yankees have all the artillery in the world set up in the clearing around Wilderness Tavern. General Ewell tried mounting an assault on it, but the Federal guns knocked his men back into the woods."

Soldiers' talk is sometimes curiously bloodless. Caudell did not need any sanguinary speech to picture the storm of shells and cannon balls, case shot and grapeshot, that must have greeted the onrushing Confederates— or the torn and broken bodies that bombardment must have produced. He'd heard the big guns start to roar late in the afternoon. Now he knew why.

"What're they going to do up there, Colonel?" Otis Massey asked.

"That I can't tell you, Otis, for I don't know," Faribault said. "I shouldn't worry, though; I expect General Lee will come up with something."

"Reckon you're right about that, Colonel," Massey said. Caudell thought so, too. Lee had a way of coming up with something. The 47th North Carolina had joined the Army of Northern Virginia after Chancellorsville, but he knew how Lee had divided his outnumbered army and then divided it again, to fall on Joe Hooker's flanks and drive him back over the Rapidan in dismay and defeat. Not even all the artillery in the world could long contain a man with the nerve to devise a scheme like that. Caudell was sure of it.

"Want to sleep here tonight, Colonel?" he asked. "It isn't fancy hospitality, but it's what we have."

Faribault's laugh sounded more tired than amused. "I thank you, First Sergeant, but I've a ways to go before I think of sleep. If I'm to lead the regiment tomorrow, tonight I must learn where this day's fighting scattered the men and let them know what is required of them. Thus far I've found less than a quarter part. I expect I shall be busy well into the evening."

"Yes, sir," Caudell said. He expected that Faribault wouldn't sleep at all tonight, not if he intended to track down the whole 47th in the jungle of the Wilderness. He also saw Faribault knew that. It was part of what went with being a colonel if one aimed to make a proper job of it, as Faribault plainly did.

"May we succeed tomorrow as we did today, and may God keep all of you safe through the fighting to come," Faribault said. He limped off into the woods. Before long, the occasional spatters of picket firing and the never-ending groans from the wounded swallowed the sounds of his footsteps.

"He's a good colonel," Mollie Bean remarked.

"I was just thinking the same thing," Caudell said as he clicked the receiver plate back into place on his rifle. "He sees to his men before he worries about himself." He spoke as if he were giving a lesson back in the classroom; he wanted Otis Massey to listen to him. Though a corporal had fewer men in his charge than a colonel, he needed to look out for them, too. But if Massey was paying attention, he showed no sign of it.

Caudell's sigh turned into a yawn. He undid his blanket roll, wrapped himself up, and fell asleep by the fire.

The long roll woke him early the next morning, or so he thought until he realized where he was. The rattle was not drumsticks on snares; it was gunfire, the reports bunched tighter together than the fastest drummer could hurry his sticks. The fighting had begun again, even if sunrise still lay ahead.

No time to boil water for a desiccated meal. Caudell choked down a couple of Yankee hardtack biscuits. He clicked off the AK-47's safety, clicked again to fire single shots. The private who'd been on watch in the clearing woke the men too worn to rouse even for the racket of battle close by.

"We don't have an officer with us," Caudell said. That was nothing new; after the third day's fighting at Gettysburg, three of the 47th's ten companies had been commanded by sergeants. He went on, "Remember, though, the Yankees are likely in worse shape than we are, because we whipped their tails yesterday. Let's go get 'em."

One by one, the Confederates climbed over the rude barricade of branches and earth and stones behind which they'd fought the day before. They spread out into a firing line, though not one of the parade-ground sort, not in half-light in rugged, overgrown country.

A rifle fired, not far ahead. It was a Springfield. Caudell burrowed deep into the brush he'd been cursing till that moment. He crawled forward. Twigs and thorns grabbed at his clothes like children's hands.

The Springfield boomed again. He peered through bushes, waited. Something moved—something blue. He fired. An instant later, a bullet buzzed past his head, so close he felt the wind of its passage on his ear. It had not come from the man at whom he'd shot—a couple of Yankees were working an ambush, and he'd stumbled right into it.

He scuttled backwards toward a fallen log he'd seen a few yards away. Another bullet zipped by him before he got there, and no sooner had he taken cover than another flew by, just over his head. He buried his face in the musty dirt. A twig the last Minié ball had clipped fell on the back of his neck. It tickled. He did not brush it away.

After half a minute or so, he slid sideways toward the far end of the log. He still could not see the Federals who were shooting at him, but the smoke that lingered in the cool air under the trees told him where they might be. He fired several times in quick succession, blessing his repeater all the while. He didn't know whether he'd scored any hits, but a thrashing in the bushes ahead said the Yankees were getting out of there.

Or he thought it said that. These Yankees were sneaky customers. He advanced with infinite caution. Only when he'd gone past the clump of oak saplings where they'd hidden did he dare believe he'd really driven them off.

He pushed farther south. Once or twice, Federals shot at him. He shot back. Again, he had no idea whether he hit anyone. That was hard enough to tell on a battlefield where the foe stood right in front of you. In the Wilderness, it was impossible.

He rejoined Otis Massey and several other soldiers with whom he'd spent the night. The firing ahead grew ever more intense. A few minutes later, he discovered why: the bluecoats were fighting from behind a breastwork of their own. Hereabouts, it stood at the far edge of a cleared space. Even with the AK-47 in his hands, his mouth went dry at the prospect of charging those blazing rifles.

"Form your line here in the woods, men," an officer said. Most of the Confederates stayed low, on their knees or their bellies. The officer walked up and down as if on a Sunday promenade. Minié balls made branches dance all around him, but he affected not to notice them.

As he strode past the stump behind which Caudell crouched, the first sergeant recognized Captain John Thorp of Company A. Thorp was a slim, little fellow with nondescript features. He wore a thin line of mustache that tried to give him the air of a riverboat gambler but couldn't quite bring it off. However he looked, though, his courage was beyond reproach.

"Make sure your banana clips are full, men," he said, and paused to let the soldiers stuff in as many bullets as they could. "At my word, we'll give them a good shout and go for their works. Ready? . . . Now!"

Yelling like fiends, the rebels burst from cover and dashed toward the barricade. Half—more than half—of Caudell's yell was raw fear. He wondered if that was true of the men to either side of him, or if, like Thorp, they were immune to the disease. No sooner had the thought crossed his mind than the private on his right spun sideways and crashed to the grass, blood spurting from his thigh.

Caudell squeezed the trigger again and again and again. His aim was poor, but he put a lot of bullets in the air. With the AK-47, he could shoot and move at the same time. No more stopping to reload under remorseless enemy fire, no more ramrod slipping through sweaty fingers, no more jabbing it against the ground or hitting it with a rock—if you could find a rock.

More Confederates fell, but so did Yankees in back of the breastwork.

Just in front of Caudell, a bluecoat's head exploded into red ruin. He yowled like a catamount and started scrambling over the logs.

A bayonet almost pinned his arm to the untrimmed branch he was holding. With a four-foot rifle and eighteen inches of steel on the end, the snarling Federal who stabbed at him had all the advantage in that kind of fight. The fellow raised his Springfield for another thrust. Caudell shot him at a range of perhaps a yard. The Federal folded up like a man punched in the belly. Unlike a man punched in the belly, he wouldn't unfold later.

Then Caudell stood on the south side of the barricade, another Confederate beside him. One of them turned east, the other west. They both shot rapidly down the crumbling Yankee line—repeaters were made for enfilade fire. Federals went down one after another. More and more men in gray reached the breastwork.

Caudell suddenly realized the AK-47 wasn't kicking against his shoulder. He threw himself flat while he clicked in a fresh clip. With his old Enfield, loading while prone had been next to impossible, leaving a man not only without a bullet but a perfect target for any foe who had one. Still prone, Caudell started firing again.

A few Yankees kept shooting back at the rebels. More fled into the woods, some with their rifles, some throwing them away to run the faster. More yet threw down Springfields but did not flee. They threw their hands into the air and shouted, "Don't kill us, Johnny! We give up!"

Captain Thorp sent the bluecoats who had surrendered north over the barricade and into captivity. "Just keep your hands high, and you'll be all right till someone takes charge of you," he told them before giving his attention back to his own men. "Come on! We've broken them. One more good push and they'll fall to bits."

South and south again—Caudell's clothes were tatters by afternoon, but he did not care. Thorp had been right: once the Yankees' field fortifications cracked, some of the dogged fight went out of them at last. When repeater fire broke out near them, they started to yield instead of shooting back. Or some of them did; here and there, stubborn bands of bluecoats gave no quarter and asked for none.

A bullet hissed malignantly past Caudell. He dove for cover. Bullets whistled through the brush where he lay. He rolled frantically. The fusillade continued. Either that was a couple of squads of Yankees up ahead or—
"Lee!" he shouted. "Hurrah for General Lee!"

The shooting stopped. "Who are y'all?" a suspicious voice called.

"Forty-Seventh North Carolina, Hill's corps," he answered. "Who are *you*?"

"Third Arkansas, Longstreet's corps," the unseen stranger answered. "What kind of rifle you carryin' there, No'th Carolina?"

No Yankee was likely to know the right answer to that yet. "An AK-47," Caudell said.

By way of answer, the fellow who'd shot at him let loose with an unmistakable rebel yell. Caudell cautiously stood. Another man in gray came out of the thicket ahead. They clasped hands, pounded each other on the back. The soldier from Arkansas said, "Goddam good to see you, No'th Carolina."

"You, too," Caudell said. More than half to himself, he added wonderingly, "We really have broken them." He still had trouble believing it, but if he and his comrades coming down from the north were meeting Longstreet's men coming up from the south, the Federals caught between them had to be in a bad way.

The private from the 3d Arkansas might have picked the thought right out of his mind. "Damn straight we've broke 'em," he said happily. "Now we pick up the pieces."

★ VI ★

General Lee sat easily on Traveller, watching his soldiers splash up out of the Rapidan at Raccoon Ford. Once on the north side of the river, the men paused to put their trousers back on before they formed ranks again. Many of them had no drawers. That bothered Lee more than it seemed to bother them. They grinned and cheered and waved their hats as they marched past.

Lee waved back every so often, letting the men know he saw them and was pleased with them. He turned to Walter Taylor. "Tell me the truth, Major: did you ever expect to see us moving to the attack again?"

"Of course I did, sir," his aide answered stoutly. Startlement filled his eyes as the possible import of the question sank in. "Didn't you?"

"I always had the hope of it," Lee said, and let it go at that. A new regiment was fording the river, its battle flag fluttering proudly as the color-bearer carried it in front of the troops. Lee had trouble reading a printed page without his spectacles, but he easily made out the unit name on the flag forty feet away. He called, "You fought splendidly in the Wilderness, 47th North Carolina."

The soldiers he'd praised cheered wildly. "You've made them proud, sir," Walter Taylor said.

"They make me proud; any officer would reckon his career made to command such men," Lee said. "How can I help but admire their stead-fastness, their constancy and devotion? I stand in awe of them."

"Yes, sir." Taylor looked back over the Rapidan, toward the winter encampments of General Ewell's corps. "Only a few regiments still waiting on the road. Then all of General Hill's corps will have crossed, along with Ewell's."

"I wish Longstreet's men could be with us as well, but for the time being I must leave them behind to guard the fords further east, lest General Grant, rather than shifting in response to my movement, should try to cross the Rapidan again and march on Richmond. I think that unlikely, but neglecting the possibility would be ill-advised."

"Strange to think of one corps, and that made up of but two divisions, holding back the whole Army of the Potomac," Taylor observed.

"Even with our repeaters, I am uncertain whether Longstreet could do that, Major. But he can certainly delay those people and give us the chance to return and perhaps pitch into their flanks." Just for a moment, Lee's smile turned savage. "And let me remind you, the whole Army of the Potomac no longer exists, at least not as it did before the fighting in the Wilderness began. Hancock's corps is for all intents and purposes *hors de combat*, and the rest of the Federal force received rough handling as well. I doubt anything less than that would have persuaded General Grant to retreat."

"He had little choice, unless he aimed to stay where he was and have his whole army chewed up," Taylor said. "Another day of fighting at close quarters and he'd not have had left an army with which to retreat."

"The maneuver was well executed; Grant made skillful use of his superiority in cannon to hold off our infantry while he pulled back his own." Lee stroked his beard as he thought. "He handles his men better than any previous commander of the Army of the Potomac, save perhaps General Meade, I believe, and he is more aggressive than Meade by far."

Taylor grinned. "One of the prisoners we took said he had the air of a man who had made up his mind to ram his head through a stone wall. He ran up against one in the Wilderness, but he didn't go through."

"No, but now we shall have to go through him, and that after he has made the acquaintance of our repeaters. Any man may be taken by surprise once, but only a fool will be surprised twice, and General Grant, I fear, is not a fool."

"What then, sir? Shall we try to outmarch him and approach Washington from the north and west, as we did last year?"

"I have been considering precisely that." Lee said no more. His mind was not fully made up, and might change again. But if he moved straight up the line of the Orange and Alexandria Railroad toward Washington, Grant would have to try to block his path. Without the new repeaters, assaulting a bigger army that stood on the defensive would have been suicidally foolhardy. Lee had made it work even so, against Hooker at Chancellorsville. But the Wilderness had shown him Grant was no Hooker. Grant could be beaten; he could not be made to paralyze himself.

Lee made his decision. He pulled out pen and pad, wrote rapidly, then turned to a courier. "Take this to General Stuart at once, if you please." The young man set spurs to his horse, rode off at a trot that he upped to a gallop as soon as he could. Lee felt Walter Taylor's eyes on him. He said, "I have ordered General Stuart to use his cavalry to secure the Rappahannock crossing at Rappahannock Station and to hold that crossing until our infantry joins them."

"*Have* you?" One of Taylor's eyebrows lifted slightly. "You'll go straight for Grant, then?"

"Straight for Washington City, at least for the time being," Lee corrected. "I expect General Grant will interpose himself between his capital and me. When he does, I shall strike him the hardest blow I can, and see what comes of it."

"Yes, sir." By Taylor's tone, he had no doubt what would come of it. Lee wished he had no doubts himself. His aide asked, "How soon do you think we could reach Washington City?"

"We *could* reach it in four or five days," Lee said. Taylor stared at him. Deadpan, he went on, "Of course, that is only if General Grant becomes a party to the agreement. Without his cooperation, we shall probably require rather more time."

Taylor laughed. Lee allowed himself a smile. He had slept perhaps four hours a night since the campaign started, rising at three every morning to go see how his men fared. He felt fine. His chest had pained him a couple of times, but one or two of the tablets the Rivington men had given him never failed to bring relief. He was not used to medicines that never failed.

With reins and feet, he urged Traveller forward. His aides rode after him. He scarcely noticed them; he was thinking hard. He'd beaten Grant once, and badly. But simply beating the Army of the Potomac did not suffice. He'd beaten the Federals again and again, at Chancellorsville, at Fredericksburg, at Second Manassas, in the Seven Days' Campaign. They kept returning to the fray, and, like the mythical Hydra, seemed stronger every time they were cast to the ground. They were as determined in their insistence that the South return to the Union as the Confederate States were in their desire to depart from it.

"I must *suppress* them," Lee said aloud. But how? The new repeaters had caught Grant by surprise in the Wilderness. There Lee had also been able to use the detailed knowledge of Grant's movements the Rivington men had brought him from 2014. They'd wanted to change the world of here and now, and they'd succeeded, but that meant they were no longer a move ahead of the game.

As for Grant, he'd handled his army about as well as could be expected, given the trouble in which he'd found himself. In a defensive fight, with his powerful artillery to back up his numbers, he might yet be very rough indeed.

And, Lee wondered, how long before some clever Northern gunsmith works out a way to make his own AK-47? Colonel Gorgas had been unsure it was possible. Gorgas was gifted, but for every man like him in the Confederacy, the North had three or five or ten, and the factories to assemble what those gifted men devised. If the Federals suddenly blossomed forth with repeaters of their own, the situation would return to what it had been before the men from out of time arrived.

"Not only must I suppress those people, I must do it quickly," Lee said. Every minute's delay hurt him and helped Grant. He brought Traveller up to a trot. The exact moment he got to Rappahannock Station almost certainly would not matter, but all at once any delay seemed intolerable.

In the middle of the afternoon, a courier on a blowing horse rode up to him, held out a folded sheet of paper. "From General Stuart, sir."

"Thank you." Lee unfolded the paper, read: *"We hold Rappahannock Station. Federal pickets withdrew northeast past Bealeton. We pursued, and discovered more Federals approaching the town from the southeast, their cavalry leading. We shall endeavor to hold the place unless your orders are to the contrary. Your most ob't. servant, J. E. B. Stuart, Commanding, Cavalry."*

Bealeton. Another sleepy hamlet was about to have its name written down in history in letters of blood. Lee wrote: *"General Stuart: Hold your position at all hazards. Infantry is advancing in your support. R. E. Lee, General Commanding."* He gave the message to the courier, who booted his tired mount into a trot and then forced a gallop from it.

Lee turned to Walter Taylor. "Major, I should like to confer with my corps commanders. We have driven the enemy's pickets past Bealeton, General Stuart informs me, but the main force of the Army of the Potomac is now approaching that town with a view to contesting our possession of it."

"I'll fetch the generals, sir," Taylor said. He rode away.

Dick Ewell came back to Lee first, his peg leg sticking out from the saddle at an odd angle as he reined in his horse. Having fought farther to the north in the Wilderness than Hill's men, his corps headed the line of march today. He cocked his bald head and listened intently as Lee explained the report from Stuart. When Lee was done, he asked, "Can the troopers hold back the whole Federal army long enough to permit us to deploy?"

"That is the question," Lee admitted. "With their repeaters, I hope they may."

"We'd best hurry, all the same." Ewell glanced at one of his aides. "Order the men up to quickstep."

As the aide rode off, A. P. Hill rode up. Always gaunt and hollow-eyed, he no longer seemed on the edge of breaking down, as he had before the campaign began. *Victory*, Lee thought, *agrees with him.* As he had with Ewell, he told Hill of the new situation.

Hill's jaws worked as he listened. Finally he said, "I don't care for the prospect of fighting with the river close in our rear. We almost paid for that at Sharpsburg."

"I remember," Lee said.

"Grant isn't such a slowcoach as McClellan was, either," Hill persisted. "He wasn't what you'd call smooth in the Wilderness, but he got more of the Army of the Potomac into the fight than we've seen before."

"I want him to put his men into the fight, if that means they are advancing straight into the fire of our new rifles," Lee said. "Not even the resources of the North will stand such bloodlettings indefinitely repeated . . . which reminds me, have we enough ammunition for another large fight?"

"Two trains full of cartridges came into Orange Court House from Rivington this morning," Walter Taylor said.

"That should be all right, then," Lee said, relieved. Thanks to the Rivington men, his soldiers had won a smashing victory in the Wilderness. Thanks to them, the Army of Northern Virginia would have the wherewithal to pursue another one. But without a continued flow of munitions from the Rivington men, his army would soon be, if it was not already, unable to fight at all. Lee reminded himself to write once more to Colonel Rains in Augusta to see if he had succeeded in producing loads suitable for the AK-47.

"How would you have us deploy?" Ewell asked.

Lee had been working on that with most of his mind ever since the message came back from the cavalry. He saw battlefields as a chess player looked over his board, save that for him no two matches were played on the same squares and both players moved at the same time. "Post your men in the most advantageous line south from Bealeton toward the Rappahannock, General, using General Johnson's division as your reserve," he answered. "General Hill, you will form the left. Move behind the line General Ewell will establish and into position. Be prepared to attack or defend, as shall seem most advantageous."

The corps commanders nodded. Walter Taylor drew out a map from a saddlebag, unfolded it. Lee traced with his finger the dispositions he had in mind. The generals looked, nodded again, and rode off, Hill all business in the saddle, Ewell instantly recognizable because of his outthrust wooden leg.

"Send also to General Longstreet, Major," Lee said as Taylor put away the map. "Tell him he must be ready to move at a moment's notice, either to pitch into General Grant's rear or to come to the support of the rest of this army. Send the order by telegraph; he must have it as soon as possible."

"Yes, sir." Taylor noted down Lee's instructions, summoned a courier to take them to the army's field telegraphy wagon. "I'll also send a copy by messenger," he said.

"Very good," Lee said. Like the Confederacy's railroads, Southern wires were imperfectly efficient. He envied the Federal army its far more elaborate system. But he could have headed that Federal army, sent messages along that system as he chose. Having declined, he was content to make do with what his chosen country could provide.

Dempsey Eure let out a loud, unmusical bray. "If I was a mule, they'd shoot me after a march like this, on account of I wouldn't be of no more use nohow."

"You're a damn jackass, Dempsey, and you're marchin' to give some Yankee the chance to shoot you," Allison High answered. A few men who heard the exchange had the breath left to chuckle. Most simply plodded on, too busy putting one foot in front of the other to have room for anything else.

Mulus Marianus, Nate Caudell thought in the small part of his mind not emptied by fatigue. He wished Captain Lewis were close by; of all the Castalia Invincibles, Lewis was the only other man who had any Latin and might have appreciated the allusion. But the captain's bad foot was giving him trouble on the march, and he'd fallen back to the rear of the company.

Caudell coughed. The 47th North Carolina was not in the lead today. The men tramped through a gray-brown cloud of dust that left their hides and uniforms the same color. Every time Caudell blinked, the grit under his eyelids stung. When he spat, his saliva came forth as brown as if he were chewing tobacco.

He'd already forded both the Rapidan and the Rappahannock, but the memory of splashing through cool water was only that, a memory. Reality was muggy heat and sweat and dust and tired feet and the distant thunder of gunfire to the east. The Federals were not going to leave Virginia without more fighting, and were not of the mind to let the Army of Northern Virginia get free of its home state again, either.

Then shots came from the right front, not heavy rolling volleys mixed with artillery where General Ewell's men were already hotly engaged with the Federals, but a spattering of skirmisher fire. "Grant's looking to flank us," Allison High guessed. "He's got men and to spare to try it."

"If he didn't lose three for our one in the Wilderness, I'll eat my shoes," Caudell said.

"And if he did, he still has more men than we do," High answered, which was so manifestly true that Caudell could only click tongue between teeth by way of response. He tasted wet dust when he did.

The regimental musicians beat a brisk tattoo on their drums. "By the right of companies into line!" Captain Lewis echoed, shouting as loud as he could so the whole company could hear him. With a certain relief, Caudell strode off the dust-filled roadway into the field to one side of it. The air would be fresher, at least for a while.

General Kirkland's whole brigade was shifting into battle formation, 44th, 47th, and 26th North Carolina forward, with the 11th and 52d going into line behind them. Regimental and company flags took the lead as color-bearers stepped out in front of their units. Caudell looked leftward for the banner of Company E of the 44th North Carolina; it was his favorite in the whole brigade. He grinned when he spied it, though it was too far away to seem more than a tiny green square. He knew its device—a snapper with mouth agape—and the company nickname, TURTLE PAWS, spelled out below.

"Skirmishers forward!" Colonel Faribault yelled. Men from every company trotted ahead of the main line.

"Get a move on, Nate," Rufus Daniel called when Caudell failed to advance with the rest of the skirmishers. "Lieutenant Winborne done got hisself shot, so they're your boys."

Caudell was glad for the thick coat of dust on his face; no one could see him turn red. He'd completely forgotten that, with the third lieutenant wounded, the skirmishers fell to him. A couple of them laughed as he dashed up to join them. "Make sure your pieces are loaded and ready," he growled. The skirmishers paused to check, which took their attention off him for a moment.

They hurried forward, each man a couple of yards from his neighbors to either side. "Do we aim to go straight toward the shooting?" somebody called. Caudell didn't know the answer.

Third Lieutenant Will Dunn of Company E did. "No, we're to move to the left of it," he answered. "If there's a hole there, we'll plug it till the rest of the brigade comes up."

A few minutes later, three people sang out "Yankee skirmishers!" at the same time. Wishing for his lost hat, Caudell raised a hand to shade his eyes. Sure enough, a thin line of bluecoats, tiny as insects in the distance, was approaching the thin gray-clad line of which he was a part. Behind them, a cloud of dust masked more Federal soldiers.

The Yankees were still too far away to make worthwhile targets. They spotted the rebels at about the same time they were seen. Caudell watched them adjust their line. He admired the way they shifted; they might have been on the parade ground, exercising for an inspector general rather than maneuvering on the field of battle. Polished rifle barrels and bayonets revealed the men who kicked up so much dust to their rear.

Lieutenant Dunn carried a pair of field glasses on a leather strap around his neck. He lifted them to his face for a better look at the foe ahead. When he let go with a cry of outrage, Caudell and all the Confederates in earshot stared at him. The field glasses had already fallen to his chest again. Pointing ahead, he shouted, "You know what those are up ahead, boys? Those are nigger troops!"

A couple of rebels started shooting the second they heard that. At a range still close to half a mile, they did no harm Caudell could see. Whatever color they were, the Federal skirmishers had the discipline to hold their fire. Caudell's jaw tightened. Escaped slaves and free Negroes—they would have no reason to love Southern men any better than he and his comrades loved them.

The bayonets on AK-47s were permanently secured under the barrel by a bolt. Caudell hadn't brought his forward at any time during the Wilderness fighting. Neither had any other Confederates he remembered seeing. Now several men paused to deploy them. With black men ahead, bullets were not enough for them. Seeing black men in uniform made it literally war to the knife.

As far as Caudell was concerned, any man with a rifle musket in his hands, be he white, black, or green, was a deadly enemy so long as he wore a blue coat. Still as if on parade, half the Yankee skirmishers—now they were close enough for Caudell to tell they were Negroes with his unaided eye—brought their Springfields to their shoulders in smooth unison and fired a volley at Caudell and his comrades.

The range was still long; had Caudell been leading that Federal skirmish line, he would not have had his men shoot so soon. Even so, a couple of men from the skirmish line fell, groaning and cursing at the same time. The Negroes who had fired began to reload; those who had not raised their weapons to volley again.

"Give it to 'em!" Caudell shouted. All the other company skirmish leaders yelled orders that meant the same thing.

Caudell raised his own rifle and started firing while he advanced on the Negro skirmishers. They began to drop as the Confederates' repeaters filled the air in their neighborhood with bullets. The blacks still on their feet, though, kept loading and firing as coolly as any veterans. A couple of white men with swords—officers, Caudell supposed—shouted commands to them. Those officers soon fell. They would have been natural targets on any skirmish line and were all the more so here because of whom they led. But even after they went down, their black soldiers continued to fight steadily.

"Jesus God almighty!" shouted a private named Ransom Bailey, a few feet away from Caudell. He pointed toward the oncoming line of battle behind the colored skirmishers. "They's all niggers! Looks like a division of 'em!"

"Worry about them later," Caudell told him. "These ones up front are enough trouble for now."

Skirmish lines seldom came to grips with each other. One would usually retreat because of the other's superior firepower. The Confederates badly outgunned the black Union troops, but the Negroes would not retreat. They made charge after charge against the Southerners' merciless rifles. Only when just a handful of them were still on their feet did they stubbornly withdraw.

By then, they did not have far to go; the regiments of which they were a part had almost caught up with them. The black troops' line was wide and deep. Because their regiments were new and untried, they had far more men in them than units which had already seen hard fighting. They deployed with the same almost fussy neatness the skirmishers had shown.

Behind Caudell, behind the whole brigade, cannon went off with a crash. Round shot and shells began landing among the Negro soldiers. A cannon ball knocked down a whole file of men. The Negroes did not break. Their front rank went to one knee; the second rank raised rifle muskets above their comrades' heads. They volleyed as smartly as had the Federals rushing up the Brock Road to attack the breastworks there.

The 47th North Carolina was not behind a breastwork now. It had been hurrying forward to get round the Federals' right; Grant had sent these blacks to stop Lee's advance. Where they collided, they would fight. Officers shouted, "Advance!" Bugles echoed the command. After that blast of fire from the Negroes, though, some Confederates would never advance again.

Yankee artillery was on the field, too. A shell shrieked past Caudell, exploded just in front of the main rebel battle line. The blast and the fragments blew a hole in it. The men on either side who had not been hit closed ranks and came on.

The third and fourth ranks of black soldiers stepped forward, while the first and second reloaded. Their volley was not as neat as the first one had been; fire from the Confederate repeaters tore at their line. Officers went down one after another. In most units, North and South alike, officers commonly wore outfits like those of their men, but for insignia of rank, the better to avoid drawing the enemy's eye to them. But the men who commanded the black troops stood out not only because of the color of their skin but also for their fancy dress. "Shoot the nigger-lovers before the nigs!" a private not far from Caudell shouted. Many of his comrades seemed to be taking his advice.

After that second volley, the Negroes raised a cheer—a wild shout much closer to a rebel yell than to the Northern white soldiers' usual hurrah— and advanced on Kirkland's brigade at the double-quick. Caudell and his fellow skirmishers fell back into their own front ranks, to keep the main body of Confederates from shooting them in the back.

Between shells and rifle fire, the battle din was deafening. A near miss from a shell knocked the man beside Caudell into him. He fell over. Somehow he hung on to his repeater. Two men stepped on him before he managed to get to his feet. He looked down at himself, hardly daring to believe he was still intact. Muttering a prayer of thanks, he started shooting again.

The black soldiers were frighteningly close. They'd taken dreadful casualties, but still they came on. Even as he did his best to kill them, Caudell admired the courage they showed. It occurred to him that George Ballentine might have fought well, if anyone had given him the chance—and if Benny Lang hadn't made him want to run away instead.

Because their regiments started so large, the colored troops greatly outnumbered the rebels at the start of the engagement. That meant they still had men left when their battered line and that of the Confederates crashed together. They threw themselves on the Southerners with bayonets and clubbed muskets.

The Confederates wavered. Their AK-47s were not made to double as spears. But they could still shoot. Black men fell, clutching at chest or belly or legs. Screams and curses almost overwhelmed the thunder of gunfire.

Right beside Caudell, a colored soldier drove a bayonet into a Southerner's belly. The Confederate shrieked. Blood dribbled from his mouth. He crumpled to the ground as the Negro ripped out the bayonet. Caudell fired at the black man. His rifle clicked harmlessly. He'd fired the last round in his clip without noticing. Grin flashing whitely in the middle of a black face made blacker by gunpowder stains from Minié ball cartridges, the Negro spun toward Caudell, ready to spit him, too.

Before he could thrust with the bayonet, a rebel landed on his back. The two men went down in a thrashing heap. The Confederate tore the Springfield from the colored man's hands. He heaved himself up onto his knees, rammed home the length of edged steel that tipped the musket. The Negro screamed like a lost soul. The Southerner stabbed him again and again and again, a dozen times, a score, long after he was dead. Then, grinning like a devil that seizes lost souls, he got to his feet.

"Thanks, Billy," Caudell gasped. "That was bravely done."

"Shitfire, Caudell, you don't got to thank me none for killin' niggers," Billy Beddingfield said. "I do that for my own self."

Hand-to-hand fighting seldom lasted long. One side or the other soon found the punishment too much to bear. So it was with the black Federal troops now. They broke away from their foes and retreated to the north. The Confederates raked them with heavy fire from their repeaters. That was finally enough to make the Negroes run, though even then some turned back to shoot at the Southerners.

A fresh magazine in his AK-47, Caudell took his own pot shots at the colored soldiers. Rescuing him like that was the sort of thing that could earn Billy Beddingfield his corporal's chevrons again. As long as the regiment was in active combat, he was as good a soldier as any officer could want. Trouble was, he'd already shown he couldn't hold his temper in camp.

Kirkland's brigade—Heth's whole division—pushed ahead, trampling down early wheat and corn as they advanced. The very precision of the blacks who opposed them cost those Negroes dearly. Their officers still handled them as if they were in a review rather than a battle, and used extra time to make every maneuver perfect. Meanwhile, the ragged Confederates took a heavy toll with their repeaters.

A few Negroes tried to surrender when the rebels overran them. Caudell brusquely jerked the muzzle of his AK-47 southward; two frightened blacks babbled thanks as they shambled away. A few seconds later, a rifle barked behind him. He whirled. The colored men lay twisted on the ground. Their blood spilled over cornstalks and soaked into the dirt. Billy Beddingfield stood above them, that devilish grin on his face once more.

"They'd given up," Caudell said angrily.

"A nigger with a rifle in his hands *cain't* give up," Beddingfield retorted. Before Caudell could answer, Captain Lewis tapped him on the shoulder. "An ammunition wagon just came up," Lewis said, pointing. "Pull out as many of your skirmishers as you can find, then have each man draw two or three clips' worth of cartridges. Make for that stand of plum trees up there." He pointed again. "From there, you ought to have a fair shot at that Yankee battery that's been tearing us up." Even as he spoke, another shell whistled overhead, to land with a crash an instant later.

Caudell looked from the plums to the distant battery. The Federal artillerymen were busy at their pieces, working together with drilled precision. "Even that's long range," he said dubiously.

"I know it is," Lewis said. "I wouldn't send you out there if we still carried our old muzzle-loaders. But these repeaters let us send enough bullets their way that some are likely to hit."

"All right, sir." Caudell rounded up four men who'd been on the skirmish line with him. They got their extra ammunition and made for the plums. One was wounded before he got there. He staggered back to the rebel line. Caudell and the other three reached the little grove.

Up ahead, the artillerymen were still at their trade. One soldier set ball and powder inside a Napoleon's muzzle. Another rammed them down to the bottom of the barrel. A third jabbed a wire pick through the vent to pierce the bag that contained the powder. Still another attached primer and lanyard. That same man yanked on the lanyard and fired the piece. The fellow with the rammer swabbed it down. Back at the limber that held the ammunition chest, two more soldiers handed another bag of powder and a ball to a third, who carried them at a run to the man who loaded them into the smoothbore. The process began again.

Caudell and his comrades began to interrupt them and the other five gun crews that made up the battery. "Take your best shots," he told the skirmishers. He and they stood behind stout tree trunks, not so much for protection as to give themselves cover. "We aren't going to hit all the time, but we'll do them some harm."

A gunner went down, then another. Caudell kept firing steadily. Still another man reeled away from his cannon. A few seconds later, a rammer was hit as he ran up to the muzzle of his piece with a soaked sponge. Replacements took over for men wounded or killed. They began to fall, too.

Although the Confederates were shooting from cover, the muzzle flashes of their rifles quickly gave them away. Someone pointed toward the plums. Artillerymen leaped to a Napoleon's handspike, began swinging the twelve-pounder toward the stand of trees. Even from half a mile, the gun's bore, though only a bit more than four and a half inches wide, seemed a huge and deadly cavern to Caudell.

"Take out that crew!" he shouted—needlessly, for the skirmishers had already started shooting at the gunners. The corporal or sergeant who stood behind the Napoleon to gauge the range clapped a hand to his face and toppled. A rammer fell, grabbing at his leg. Another man snatched up the swab-ended pole and carried on.

The brass cannon belched flame and a great cloud of thick white smoke. A round shot smashed a tree not twenty feet from Caudell with a noise like a giant clapping hands. The artillerymen began their drill once more. Two more of them went down before they could fire again. This time they chose a bursting shell. "My arm!" a skirmisher wailed. The Federal artillerymen stolidly resumed their appointed tasks. When yet another man was hurt, one of the drivers from the limber crew replaced him.

Another shell exploded in the grove. Fragments thumped against the trunk which sheltered Caudell. He fed bullets into a banana clip and hoped the next shell would be a dud. Federal gunners, unfortunately, used better fuses than their Southern counterparts.

But the next shell did not come. The depleted gun crews fired a last couple of shots, then rushed to attach their cannons to the limbers. Some of them snatched out pistols and began to fire them. The drivers urged teams into motion.

Four of the guns in the battery made good their escape. Caudell shouted with delight as rebels advancing from the southeast swarmed over the other two. One of those was the Napoleon that had been trying to blast his comrades and him out of the grove. "We did something worthwhile, boys!" he yelled to the other skirmishers. "We kept 'em too busy to run till it was too late for 'em anyhow."

The Yankee infantry was pulling back too, north and east along the line of the Orange and Alexandria Railroad. The black foot soldiers did not run like a frightened mob, but they did not show the same extraordinary stubbornness they had displayed earlier in the day, either; against the Confederates' repeaters, that had only gotten more of them killed.

Caudell sent a fatigue party out to a stream not far away. He waited to eat until they came back; he wanted to boil water for a desiccated meal. Most of the Castalia Invincibles did not bother to wait. After plundering the haversacks of the black troops they'd fought, they had plenty of hardtack and salt pork. The rich smell of brewing coffee soon filled the night air around the campfires. More than a few Confederates sported new blue trousers or new shoes—more spoil from the battlefield.

"They sent them niggers out carrying' everything but bake ovens on their backs," Rufus Daniel said. He had a new pair of pants himself.

"Niggers." Otis Massey spat as he said the word. "Niggers with guns. That's what the Yankees want to do with us—goddam niggers with guns, all over the South."

A general mutter of agreement rose from the soldiers who heard him. Dempsey Eure said, "Heard tell the Yankees'd given 'em guns. But you give a man a gun, that don't mean he can fight with it. Never reckoned in all my born days that if you give a nigger a gun, he'd fight the way them fellers did."

"They's too stupid to know they's gettin' whipped," said a private named William Winstead.

More people nodded at that, but Caudell said, "You weren't with us at Gettysburg, Bill. They'd seen what we did to their skirmish line, so they had to know they were going into the meat grinder. But they kept coming, the same way we did then. Anybody here going to tell me they didn't fight like soldiers?"

"Only thing niggers is good for is slaves," Winstead said positively. Again, a good many soldiers nodded along with him.

Caudell wanted to argue more. Despite questions about Georgie Ballentine, he'd always thought pretty much as Winstead did. So did most people in the South; so, for that matter, did most people in the North. But as a teacher, he'd urged his students—especially the bright ones—to test what people said about the world against the world itself. Here, what they said and what he'd seen didn't add up the same way. The Negroes had fought as well as anyone could expect.

One of the other things he'd seen in the world, though, was that most people didn't really want to look at it straight on. Going with what they said—whoever *they* were—was easier and more comfortable than trying to figure out how things truly worked.

So instead of directly challenging Winstead, Caudell shifted the argument: "I saw Billy Beddingfield kill a couple of niggers who'd surrendered. I didn't reckon that was right—I sure as hell wouldn't want them to kill us if we had to give up to them."

"Any nigger comes at me with a gun, that's a dead nigger," Winstead said. "An' I wouldn't surrender to 'em anyways, no matter what, on account of what they'd do to me if I done it."

"Some truth in that," Caudell had to admit. "But if they can learn to fight like soldiers, they might be able to learn to act like soldiers other ways."

"They better," Dempsey Eure added. "Otherwise this here war's gonna turn even uglier'n it is already."

"You've got that right, Dempsey," Caudell said. This time, nobody disagreed. Who could deny that black men and what to do about them lay at the heart of the war between the states? The North was convinced it had the right to dictate to the South how to treat them; the South was equally convinced it already knew. Caudell wanted no part of having someone hundreds of miles away telling him what he could or couldn't do. On the other hand, if Negroes really could fight like white men, the South's answers didn't look so good, either.

Caudell reflected that America would have been a much simpler place were the black man not around to vex it. Unfortunately, however, the black man was here. One way or another, North and South would have to come to terms with that.

"Major Marshall, I should like you to draft a general order to the Army of Northern Virginia, to be published as soon as it is completed," Lee said.

"Yes, sir." Charles Marshall took out notepad and pen. "The subject of the order?"

"As you must be aware, Major, the enemy has begun to employ against us large numbers of colored soldiers. I aim to order our men that, if these colored troops be captured, their treatment at our hands is to differ in no particular from that accorded to any other soldiers we take prisoner."

"Yes, sir." Behind Marshall's spectacles, his eyes were expressionless. He bent his head and began to write.

"You do not approve, Major?" Lee said.

The younger man looked up from the folding table on which he was working. "Since you ask, sir, in no way do I approve of arming Negroes. The very concept is repugnant to me."

Lee wondered what his aide would have thought of General Cleburne's proposal that the Confederacy recruit and use Negro troops in pursuit of its independence. But President Davis had ordered him to keep silent about that. Instead, he said, "Major, not least of my concerns in issuing this order is fear for the safety of the thousands of our own captives in Northern hands. Last summer Lincoln issued an order promising to kill a Confederate soldier for each Union man slain in violation of the articles of war, and to put at hard labor one man for every black captive returned to slavery. By all means make that point explicit in the language of the order, to help the men understand its promulgation is, among other things, a matter of practical necessity."

"You've thought a step farther ahead than I did," Marshall admitted. "Put that way, I see the need for what you have asked of me." He bent to his task again, this time with a better will. A few minutes later, he offered Lee the draft.

The general skimmed through it. "This is very fine, Major, but could you not insert, perhaps after 'the valor of your arms and your patient endurance of hardships,' something to the effect of 'your patriotic devotion to justice and liberty'? You might also end by appealing to the men's sense of duty, than which no soldierly virtue is of greater importance."

Marshall noted the changes, handed the paper back to Lee. "Now we have it," Lee said. "Have the order distributed at once; I want it read in every regiment by this evening, or tomorrow at the latest."

"I'll see to it, sir," the aide promised.

"Good. Now on to other business." Lee unfolded several newspapers. "These have been sent on to me by those behind Federal lines who are in sympathy with our cause. Not only does the government in Washington City often inadvertently reveal its intentions in the press, but through it we can gauge Northern sentiment toward the war."

"And?" Marshall asked eagerly. "What is the Northern sentiment toward the war, now that we have beaten back yet another 'Forward to Richmond!' drive?"

"I shall be delighted to provide you with a representative sampling, Major." Lee held a newspaper close to his face; even with his spectacles, the small, cramped letters were hard to read. "This is the *New York Times*: 'Disaster! Grant's army overthrown in the Wilderness. Forced to retreat above the Rappahannock, and there defeated once more.' Below these headlines, the story continues as follows: 'Unhappily, like many of our engagements, the late fighting, though serving to illustrate the splendid valor of our troops, has failed to accomplish the object sought. The result thus far leaves us with a loss of upwards of 40,000 men in the two battles'—useful information there—'and absolutely nothing gained. Not only did the rebels hold their lines, but they are advancing behind the impetus of their new breech-loading repeaters, against which the vaunted Springfield is of scarcely greater effect than the red man's bows and arrows.' "

"I wish that were true," Marshall said.

"It would make the task before us rather easier, would it not?" Lee chose another paper. "Here is a statement from Stanton, the Federal Secretary of War, as reported in the *Washington Evening Star*: 'A noble enthusiasm must reanimate our gallant army, who have been battling so long for the preservation of the Union. We have, it is true, recently met with serious disasters. We have suffered much, and must be prepared to suffer more, in the cause for which we are struggling. Let us, then, fellow-countrymen, tread the plain path of duty. Let us show the fortitude, endurance, and courage of our race, and not permit the brute force of the enemy's arms to extinguish the life of this Republic.' "

Marshall smiled the special smile of a man contemplating his foe's discomfiture. "That, sir, is a cry of pain."

"So it is. Secretary Stanton is notorious for them," Lee said. He shook his head. "It is also almost perfectly foolish. So far as I am concerned, so far as anyone in Richmond is concerned, the United States may proceed exactly as they care to, provided only that they extend to us the same privilege."

"Does Stanton go on?"

"Oh, at some length." Lee put the newspaper aside. "None of it, however, is much more to the point than that which I just read you."

Charles Venable came into Lee's tent. "Dispatches from Richmond, sir, and a copy of yesterday's *Daily Dispatch*." He glanced over at the Northern papers on the folding table. "I suspect its tone is rather more cheerful than theirs."

"I suspect you are correct, Major," Lee said. "Business before pleasure, however. The dispatches, if you please."

Venable handed them to him. As he read the first, he felt a great load of worry lift from his shoulders. "General Johnston has held General Sherman at Rocky Face Ridge, with heavy losses on the Federal side, and then again at Resaca and Snake Creek Gap, when he tried to use his superior numbers to outflank us. Sherman's forces are now halted; prisoners report he dares not seek to outflank us again for fear of the casualties he would sustain from our rifles."

"Business and pleasure together," Venable exclaimed.

"True enough, Major." Lee had feared that only his own army would derive full benefit from the repeaters the Rivington men had provided. He'd never been so glad to be proved wrong. True, Johnston had given up a little ground to the enemy instead of advancing as the Army of Northern Virginia was doing, but the enemy in Georgia had more room to maneuver than was true here. And Johnston was a counterpuncher in any case, a master of the defensive. Lee would not have wanted to be a Federal general assaulting a position he chose to hold, the more so when his men were armed with AK-47s.

"What is the other dispatch, sir?"

"We shall know in a moment." Lee opened the envelope. He read the paper inside, refolded it, and put it back in its place before he lifted his head to face his aides, both of whom were fidgeting in an effort to contain their curiosity. Lee said, "In southwestern Virginia, General Jenkins with twenty-four hundred men was engaged by Federal General George Crook with between six and seven thousand on the ninth of this month just south of Cloyd's Mountain."

"Yes, sir," the two men said together. They both sounded anxious; close to three-to-one was long odds against any army.

Lee lifted their suspense: "Our troops succeeded in holding their position; the Federals withdrew to the north and west up the Dublin-Pearisburg Turnpike. Among their dead were General Crook and Colonel Rutherford Hayes, who commanded a brigade of Ohioans. I regret to have to add that General Jenkins was also wounded in the action and had his right arm amputated. But as General McCausland—who replaced him—adds, the victory has preserved our control of the Virginia and Tennessee Railroad, without which rail connection between the two states would have been broken."

"That's excellent news, sir!" Charles Marshall said. "Perhaps the tide has turned at last."

"Perhaps it has," Lee said. The words seemed to hang in the air, as if only now, when he spoke them aloud, did he acknowledge their truth in his heart. He'd grown so accustomed to fighting at long odds that the edge the Rivington men's repeaters gave remained difficult to believe in completely. He read on in the dispatch: "General McCausland reports that a prisoner declared the fire from our repeaters made the battlefield appear one living, flashing sheet of flame."

"The *Daily Dispatch* certainly thinks the war as good as won." Charles Venable began to read from the newspaper he'd brought: " 'Our information is such as to give encouragement to the hope that the sacred soil of Virginia will soon be rescued from the hands, and divested of the polluting tread, of the Yankee invader. The great battles of the week just past, fought in the Wilderness and in and around the hamlet of Bealeton, resulted in the overthrow of the army of the Federal Government, with a loss that is perhaps unequalled in the annals of the present war. General Lee has utterly routed the force under Meade and Grant. There are no grounds upon which to question the glorious success of our arms.' "

"Were wars fought in the newspapers, they would be won by both sides in the first days after they were declared," Lee observed. "In one way, that would be as well, for it would spare a great part of the effusion of blood which accompanies warfare as it actually is. In another sense, though, newspaper chatter can be dangerous. If those responsible for actually prosecuting a war take seriously the contempt for the foe which is typical newspaper fare, they leave themselves open to a defeat for which they would have only themselves to blame."

"But we actually *do* have the Federals on the run," Venable protested.

"No one could be gladder than I to see those people in retreat, Major," Lee said. "But if we only drive them into the fortifications across the Potomac from Washington City, then we have gained nothing but time, and these people can make better use of time than we. They have come back from too many defeats. I want to give them a lesson sharp enough to impress itself upon even the most stolid and stubborn of their leaders."

"What do you intend, sir?" Charles Marshall asked.

Slamming his way straight up the line of the Orange and Alexandria no longer seemed as attractive to Lee as it had before. He traced on the map the plan that had come to slow fruition in his mind. "This will require General Stuart's cavalry to more effectively screen our forces from the enemy than was achieved in last year's campaign, but I trust and believe he has learned that lesson by heart—and once more, the repeaters his troopers carry will aid their efforts. As for General Longstreet's part in keeping the enemy off balance, no one, I think, could play it better. Major Marshall, if you would be so kind—?"

Marshall took out the pad on which he had drafted Lee's general order. The leader of the Army of Northern Virginia began to frame the specific commands that would set his men in motion once more.

Andries Rhoodie's horse came trotting up to Lee as he rode alongside the head of a long column of gray-clad troops. The Rivington man politely stayed a few feet outside the group of generals and officers with Lee and waited to be recognized. "Good morning, Mr. Rhoodie," Lee said. He studied the way Rhoodie handled his bay gelding. "Your horsemanship has improved, sir, since I first had the pleasure of your acquaintance."

"I've had a good deal of practice since then, General Lee," Rhoodie answered. "Before I came to join your army, I'd spent little time on horseback."

The officers with Lee concealed scornful expressions, some well, some not so well. A man who habitually rode in a buggy was hardly a man at all—and what other reason could there be for eschewing horses? Lee thought he knew the answer to that question, which to the others must have been purely rhetorical: by the distant year 2014, men must have discovered better means of transport than either horses or buggies. Lee wondered whether railroads ran down the center of every street in every city in the almost unimaginable time from which the Rivington man had sprung.

One day, he might ask Rhoodie about such things. The priceless knowledge that man had to hold in his head! No time now, though; no time, all too likely, until the war was done. No time for anything save the immediate till the war was done. To the immediate, then: "How may I help you today, Mr. Rhoodie?"

"I'd like to speak with you in private, General Lee, if I could," Rhoodie said.

"Wait until I finish my business with these gentlemen, sir; then I am at your disposal," Lee said. The staff officers took his ready acquiescence without blinking, but some of his commanders raised eyebrows. Rhoodie wore no uniform save the mottled clothing the Rivington men habitually used—who was he to deserve their chief's sole attention? Lee gave them no chance to dwell on it: "Now, gentlemen, let's make certain of our dispositions as we approach Middleburg . . ."

The division commanders and brigadiers rode off to make sure their forces conformed to the line of march Lee had spelled out. He glanced at his aides. They fell back fifteen or twenty yards. Lee nodded to Andries Rhoodie. He brought his bay up shoulder to shoulder with Traveller.

"And what can I do for you, sir?" Lee asked.

Rhoodie's answer took him by surprise: "You can rescind your general order for treating captured kaffirs—niggers—like white prisoners of war. Not only that, General Lee, you can do it immediately."

"I shall not, nor, let me remind you, have you the right to take a tone of command to me, sir," Lee said coldly. "Common humanity forbids it, not only in regard to our treatment of the Federals' colored troops, but also in that the Federals have promised to mistreat the prisoners they hold to the same degree to which we maliciously harm their men."

"You go about giving the nigger equality in any one way, General Lee, and you set foot on the path to making him equal in all ways." Rhoodie sounded less peremptory than he had a moment before, but no less serious. "That is not what America Will Break stands for, General. If you don't care to bear that in mind, we don't care to keep providing you with ammunition."

Lee swung his head around to stare at the Rivington man. Rhoodie's smile was less than pleasant. Lee nodded slowly. Having wondered if this moment would ever come, he was the more ready for it now that it was here. He said, "If President Davis ordered me to do such a thing, sir, I should present him with my resignation on the spot. To you, I shall merely repeat what I said a moment before: no." He urged Traveller up to a trot to leave Rhoodie behind.

Rhoodie stayed with him; he *was* a better rider than he had been. He said, "Think carefully about your decision, General. Remember what will happen to the Confederacy without our repeaters."

"I remember what you said," Lee answered with a shrug. "I have no way of verifying it for myself, save by living up to the day. I bid you remember that, if our cause should fail, yours fails as well. You must act as your conscience dictates, Mr. Rhoodie, as shall I."

Now it was Rhoodie's turn to stare at Lee. "You would sacrifice your precious Virginia for the sake of kaffirs who were doing their best to kill your own men?"

"As General Forrest has said upon occasion, war means fighting, and fighting means killing. But there is a distinction to be drawn between killing on the battlefield, where foes face one another man against man and army against army, and killing helpless prisoners after the fighting is done. It is the distinction between man and beast, sir, and if it is a distinction you find yourself incapable of drawing, I shall pray to God for the salvation of your soul."

"I believe in my heart, General Lee, that God has established that white men are to rule over blacks," Rhoodie said, and Lee, no mean judge of character, discerned nothing but sincerity in his voice. The Rivington man went on, "As for General Forrest, his men didn't take any high moral tone when they captured Fort Pillow last month. They found kaffirs in arms there, and they disposed of them."

Lee's mouth twisted in a grimace of distaste; the report of the Fort Pillow massacre had come to his notice. For a moment, he wondered how Rhoodie had heard of it. Then he shook his head, annoyed at himself. In one sense, Rhoodie had known about Fort Pillow for a century and a half. Lee said, "General Forrest is not under my command. I would never deny his abilities as a soldier. Of his other qualities, I am less well qualified to speak."

In point of fact, most of what he'd heard about Nathan Bedford Forrest was unsavory. Much of the fortune the man had amassed before the war came from slave trading. Less than a year ago, he'd been shot by a disgruntled subordinate, whom he'd proceeded to stab to death with a penknife. He would never have fit in among the Virginia aristocrats from whose numbers Lee sprang. But only Jeb Stuart deserved to be mentioned in the same breath as a Confederate cavalry commander.

Rhoodie said, "America Will Break is happier with Forrest's performance than with yours, General Lee. I tell you again, if you do not rescind that general order, we will be forced to cut off your supply of cartridges."

Lee thought about swooping down on Rivington with a couple of brigades. That would assure the Confederacy of however many cartridges were there. But how many was that? As Secretary of War Seddon had said, the place seemed more a transshipment point than a factory town. And for all Lee knew, the Rivington men could disappear into the future and never come back. He rather wished they would, though what point to a raid on them then?

He said, "As I told you, Mr. Rhoodie, do as you feel you must, and I shall do likewise. For now, I wish you a good morning."

"You will regret this, General Lee," Rhoodie said. Though he held his voice low and steady, he could not keep angry blood from mounting to his cheeks. He jerked his horse's head around, hard enough to draw an angry snort from the animal. He rode off at a fast trot, looking neither right nor left.

The staff officers rejoined Lee as soon as Rhoodie had gone. Charles Marshall looked after the Rivington man. "Am I to construe that he did not gain of you that which he had hoped for?" he asked with lawyerly curiosity.

"You may construe it if you like, Major," Lee said drily. "Before too long, the whole army may well construe it. Nevertheless, we shall proceed."

All his aides looked curiously at him when he said that. He said no more. If Rhoodie did indeed cut off the flow of AK-47 ammunition, it would soon become obvious—perhaps not so soon as it might have under other circumstances, for the retreating Federals had wrecked the railroad between Catlett's Station and Manassas Junction, which left the Army of Northern Virginia dependent upon horse-drawn wagons for supply, but pretty soon just the same.

The aides had learned better than to push Lee when he did not care to be pushed. Everyone in the army knew better than to push him, save occasionally James Longstreet. That made Rhoodie's blunt demand all the more startling, and all the more annoying. Lee angrily tossed his head to one side, as if snapping at his own ear. No matter how sweetly the Rivington man framed that demand, he would have refused it.

What if no more cartridges were forthcoming? Lee thought about that. He did not care for any of the conclusions he reached. Reequipping his army with repeaters had taken a couple of months. If he required that much time to go back to rifle muskets, the Army of Northern Virginia was done for. The Army of the Potomac would never leave it alone long enough to make the changeover, not in spring.

He reproached himself for not having had his men pick up the precious brass cartridges they'd expended in the fighting thus far. Even if Colonel Gorgas and Colonel Rains had to load them with ordinary black powder and unjacketed lead bullets, they'd keep the AK-47s in action a while longer. He thought about sending men back to Bealeton to glean such cartridges as they could—in the miserable tangles of the Wilderness, the brass was likely gone forever.

He decided to hold off. He had succeeded in imposing his will upon Federal generals throughout the war; even the capable, aggressive, and determined Grant now moved to his tune—thanks in no small measure to Andries Rhoodie's repeaters. Now to learn whether he could outlast Rhoodie, a man nominally an ally, in strength of purpose.

The army continued past the dormered cottages of Middleburg, on toward Leesburg and Waterford. Stuart's cavalry slashed up to seize a stretch of the Alexandria, Loudon and Hampshire Railroad and keep Grant's men from using the train to get to Leesburg first. Lee ordered the troopers to hold the Federal infantry as long as they could. He would never have given such a command to soldiers with single-shot rifles. But one man with an AK-47 was worth a fair number with Springfields . . . and by now, the Federals knew that as well as Lee did.

The lead elements of the Army of Northern Virginia went through Leesburg the next day, tramping past the elms and oaks that shaded the white-pillared buildings of the courthouse square. Lee rode back to check on the ammunition supply and learned a new wagon train had just come in, up from the end of the Warrenton railroad spur.

"Excellent," he said softly. "Excellent." A few minutes later, he saw Andries Rhoodie riding along beside the long gray files of Confederates. He gave no sign he'd noticed the Rivington man, but affectionately patted the side of Traveller's neck with a gloved hand. He'd called Rhoodie's bluff, and got away with it. Rhoodie needed him as much as he needed Rhoodie.

Rain in his face, rain turning the roadway to muddy soup. Nate Caudell slogged on. When the weather was fine, he'd wished for rain to cut the dust. Now that he had it, he wished for dust again. Mud was worse.

The road, already chewed up by countless feet, disappeared into water ahead. White's Ford had steep banks; two years earlier, Stonewall Jackson had had to dig them down before wagons and artillery could cross. Caudell held his repeater and haversack over his head as he splashed into the Potomac. The river was waist-high. He did not mind. He was already soaked. He knew only relief that the rain hadn't made the water at the ford rise any higher.

Regimental bands played on the northern—here, actually the eastern—bank of the Potomac. The downpour did nothing to improve their musicianship, but Caudell recognized "Maryland, My Maryland." As it had the previous two summers, the Army of Northern Virginia stood once more on Northern soil.

Thanks to the rain, that soil clung to Caudell in abundance. Similarly bedraggled, Dempsey Eure observed, "If this really was my Maryland, I'm damned if I'd go boasting about it."

"Doesn't look like much, does it?" Caudell agreed. The wet weather kept him from seeing a great deal in any case; even the long, low bulk of South Mountain to the west lay shrouded in mist and rain. But he remembered Maryland as distinctly poorer country than the fat farms and houses farther north in Pennsylvania.

And, though Maryland was a slave state, its citizenry did not gather at White's Ford to greet the Army of Northern Virginia. Not a civilian was in sight. Somewhere out there, Caudell was sure, Federals scouts and pickets waited to catch their first glimpse of the men in gray. That could not be helped. Caudell knew more fighting lay on this side of the Potomac.

"Come on, you Invincibles!" First Lieutenant Willie Blount shouted. "Keep it moving! Plenty more behind us, by God."

Caudell and the other sergeants echoed the command. They and their men crossed the Chesapeake and Ohio Canal—which ran parallel to the Potomac—on a makeshift bridge the army engineers had thrown across at a lock. A cavalryman sat his horse at a crossroads not far past the canal. Rain dripped from his horse's mane and tail, from the brim of his hat, from the end of his nose. He used his saber to wave everyone south.

After a couple of miles, the road branched again. This time, several horsemen waited at the fork. "Whose division?" one of them called.

"General Heth's," Caudell answered, along with several other men.

The rider held out a gloved hand to shield a list from the downpour. After he checked it, he pointed southeast rather than due south. "Y'all are on the road to Rockville—fifteen miles, maybe a tad more. Give it all you can. You're supposed to be there by sundown."

The fellow was too obviously an officer to make laughing in his face a good idea, but Caudell felt like it. Nor was he the only one; snorts and half-stifled guffaws rose from the throats of a good many safely anonymous privates trudging along in line. The 47th North Carolina had crossed the Potomac a little before noon; it had to be after that hour now. Fifteen miles by sunset was forced-march speed, but might have been possible on a dry road. In mud, it was not going to happen.

"We'll do our best," Caudell said. The horseman waved an acknowledgment. He didn't repeat the order, so he probably knew it couldn't be carried out.

Caudell marched on. While Maryland was not flowing with milk and honey, it also hadn't been a continual battleground. The foraging looked good. General Lee's orders required any requisitioned goods to be paid for with Confederate money. With the Confederate dollar worth only a few cents in gold, Caudell did not mind throwing away some paper if that meant he could take what he needed.

The regiment did not make Rockville by the time darkness fell. Instead of marching on through the night, Colonel Faribault pulled his men off the road to camp in a wheat field. "I'll be glad for a little sleep," Caudell said, relief in his voice, as he struggled to get a campfire going with damp fuel, and water still drizzling down from the sky. "Fancy-pants officers with their suede gloves can order you to march to hell and gone, but they don't know anything about what it's like to fight once you've got there."

"Y'all got that one right, Nate," Allison High said. "Here, you want to take a burnin' branch from me? I got this here fire goin' pretty good, even if it is smoky enough for a smudge."

"Thanks, Allison." With the help of the branch, Caudell's fire finally caught. It too put out a great cloud of greasy black smoke. "If this were daylight, I reckon the Yankees in Washington City would figure we were burning Rockville, from all the smoke we're making."

"Hell with Rockville." Tall and lean, the firelight reflecting redly from his eyes, High resembled nothing so much as a leading wolf in a pack closing in on prey. "If I'm to do some burnin', let me do it *in* Washington City. That'd be a burnin' to remember, an' a foragin' we'd never forget. What do you want to bet Marse Robert's right now cypherin' out how to do it?"

"No bet, Allison. He can't be doing anything else, not with us in Maryland." The mere thought of foraging in the vast Federal supply depots by Washington made Caudell breathe hard. But taking the Northern capital would mean more than that. "If we take Washington, the war's as good as won."

"Wouldn't that be somethin'?" Allison High said dreamily. He looked south and east, as if he could pierce rain and night and close to twenty miles' distance to see the White House and Abraham Lincoln cowering inside it.

Caudell feared that Lincoln wasn't cowering. "There's forts all around the place, they say." Attacking the field works on Cemetery Ridge left him leery of moving against positions prepared years in advance and filled with guns bigger than any that could keep up with an army on the move.

But High, so often gloomy like the current weather, was for once nothing but sunshine. "Yeah, there's forts, but where's old Abe gonna find the men to put in 'em? Only Federals in the whole world can fight a little bit is in the Army of the Potomac, an' that's on account of they learned from us. Longstreet's givin' Grant hell down the other side of the Potomac, an' we'll surely whip any greenhorns the Yankees stick in those works o' theirs."

"Hope you're right, Allison." Caudell glanced fondly at his AK-47. Without the repeaters, how could Lee have dared to attack Grant's whole army with one undersized corps? Even with them, the first sergeant could not imagine Longstreet defeating the immense Army of the Potomac. But if he could keep the Federals in play, offer threat enough to prevent them from filling the trenches in front of Lee's men elbow to elbow with men in blue coats . . . if he could do that, Nate Caudell had some hope of going home to Nash County once the war ended. If Longstreet failed, Caudell would be lucky if his name was written in pencil on a piece of board above the shallow grave that would hold him.

He wrapped his rubber blanket around himself to hold mud and rain at bay. His worries were not enough to keep him awake, not after the marching and fighting he'd been through. He slept like a stone.

When he awoke before dawn the next morning, shots were coming from Rockville, the thunder of field artillery every so often braying through crackling rifle fire. He gnawed on corn bread. A weevil crunched between his teeth. He ignored it and finished the small square loaf. He was still chewing when the 47th North Carolina moved out.

As he drew closer to the fighting, he recognized the reports of the Federal rifles ahead; he'd heard their like in the first hours of fighting in the Wilderness. "Sounds like dismounted Yankee cavalry with those seven-shot Spencers of theirs," he said. "That could be trouble. Those are about the best rifles they have."

"There ain't enough dismounted cavalry in the whole goddam United States Army to slow us down," Rufus Daniel said, "not with these here guns in our hands."

He was right. The Federals fought briskly, but by the time the 47th North Carolina came up to Rockville, they had already been driven out of town. Confederate cannon had knocked down some of the houses; a couple of them were burning as Caudell marched past. A dead bluecoat lay in the street. Another one hung limply from a window of the Hungerford Tavern. His blood ran down the wall, collected in a puddle under him. Not far away sprawled a rebel in butternut, equally dead.

Yankee field artillery was still in business south of Rockville, throwing shells into the town to slow the Confederate advance. Caudell ducked involuntarily as a projectile screamed by overhead and landed with a crash behind him. A moment later, human screams joined the shell's mindless shrieks; that one had struck home.

But the Federal field guns could not hold their positions, not after the dismounted cavalrymen who protected them had been driven out of Rockville. They limbered up and rolled off. As Caudell watched, two horses in one team went down. The drivers cut them out of harness. The bronze Napoleon limped away, hauled by the four animals left to the team.

The dismounted Federals kept up a stubborn rearguard action, fighting from behind boulders, apple trees, and farmhouses to let the cannon make good their escape. Nor were the guns alone in their flight from the Army of Northern Virginia. Wagons and carriages of every description filled the road that led to Washington.

"Doesn't seem like Yankee civilians much care to take what their army's been dishing out in Virginia," Caudell said, pointing to the swarm of refugees ahead.

"Reckon they figure we owe 'em somewhat for that," Rufus Daniel said. He shifted his pipe to one corner of his mouth, spat out of the other. "Might could even be they're right."

"Maybe." Caudell looked southeast. Nothing lay between Lee's soldiers and Washington City but its ring of forts. It was a big *but*. He suspected Marse Robert would keep the army too busy for it to do much wrecking for wrecking's sake.

★ VII ★

The spyglass showed Lee a small, bright circle in the middle of blackness. It made the heart of Washington City seem close enough to reach out and touch. There was the White House, flanked on the right by the three-story brick building with columned entranceway that housed the Federal War Department, on the left by the Greek Revival columns of the huge Treasury Department building, with the smaller State Department headquarters in front of it. South of the White House, across a lot empty but for temporary barracks, he could make out the tall but unfinished obelisk intended to honor George Washington, to the east the Capitol, its great dome done at last.

Lee admired Lincoln for continuing work on the dome in the midst of war; it showed the Northern President thought about more than the immediate present. Lee frowned a little. How to reconcile such thoughtfulness with the vicious tyrant Andries Rhoodie had described?

He dismissed the irrelevant problem as he lowered the glass, sweeping in an instant across the city to the works that held him away from it. Those works were formidable. The Federals had cut down all the trees within two miles in front of them, to rob advancing rebels of cover from the big guns in their forts. A network of trenches in front of the forts protected them and the field artillery positions between them.

"If it were done when 'tis done, then 'twere well it were done quickly," Lee murmured.

"Macbeth," Charles Venable said beside him.

"In this instance, Major, we would be wise to heed the Bard's tactical advice." Lee passed the long brass tube to his aide. "Examine the trenches carefully, if you would. They are not yet full, and the men in them, I hear, are garrison troops, not the veterans of the Army of the Potomac. We may break through tonight; tomorrow will be far more difficult, and the day after surely impossible."

"Tonight?" Venable echoed.

Lee glanced at him with amusement. "Are you so careful of your words that you expend them only as single shots? Yes, tonight. The worst mistake I've made in all this war, and the one that cost us dearest, was the assault on Cemetery Ridge that third day at Gettysburg. The position ahead is stronger, and the cannon in it bigger. Were we to make a daylight attack, they would slaughter us before we drew close enough for our repeaters to rescue us. In the darkness, they will have more difficulty finding proper targets."

"But a night battle?" Venable had more than one word at a time in him after all. "How do you propose to control a night battle, sir?"

"I don't propose to," Lee answered. He almost laughed at the shocked look on Venable's face. "Can we but come to close quarters with the enemy, I think we shall break through somewhere along the line. Once we do, the advantage will be ours—and with it, I hope, Washington City."

"Yes, sir." Venable did not sound convinced. Lee was not altogether convinced himself. He was convinced, however, that the Army of Northern Virginia would never have a better chance to take Washington. And if the Federal capital fell into Southern hands, how could Britain and France and the rest of the world continue to deny the Confederate States of America were as true and genuine a nation as the United States? The stakes made the risk worthwhile.

He dictated orders, sent them to his corps commanders. The army began to shift into a line that centered on the Seventh Street Road, from the earthworks of Fort Slocum in the east past Fort Stevens to Fort de Russy in the southwest. The sun slipped down the western sky. Lee watched the Federal lines and waited. He did his best to appear impassive, but his heart thudded in his chest, and with the thudding came pain. Absently, he slid one of the little white pills from Andries Rhoodie under his tongue. The pain went away.

Twilight was deepening when Walter Taylor came up and said, "Sir, Rhoodie requests permission to speak to you."

The Rivington man had not been so formal before Lee defied him. At first Lee intended to say he was too busy. Then, remembering the nitro-glycerine tablet, he softened. "Tell him he may, but to be quick."

Taylor led Rhoodie up to Lee. "General," Rhoodie said, politely dipping his head. Lee returned the gesture. Taking Lee's warning literally, Rhoodie plunged ahead: "General Lee, if you intend to attack the Federal forts tomorrow, my men and I can help."

"I intend to attack tonight, sir," Lee answered, and had the somber satisfaction of watching Rhoodie's jaw drop. The Rivington man muttered something in his own guttural language.

But he quickly recovered. "You're as bold as you are said to be, that's certain. We can still help you, maybe even more. Whatever the differences you and I have had, America Will Break aims for the South to win this war."

That was the gamble Lee had made when he defied the big man from the future. Now he said, "Thank you, Mr. Rhoodie, but you've already furnished us plenty of repeaters." He pointed to the AK-47 slung on Rhoodie's back. "The handful you and your comrades might add will make scant difference in the outcome of the fight."

"But we have something you do not." The Rivington man took from his knapsack a green-painted spheroid a little bigger than a base ball. A metal shaft stuck out from it. "This is a rifle grenade, General. The AK-47 can shoot one about three hundred yards. They should do nicely for spreading confusion in the Federal trenches and forts, wouldn't you say?"

"A rifle grenade?" The Federals sometimes used hand grenades fused with percussion caps. They were, however, limited by the strength of a man's arm. Shot from rifles . . . "It would almost be as if we were shelling them without employing artillery, wouldn't it?"

"Exactly," Rhoodie said.

"Any surprise we can effect will surely accrue to our advantage. Very well, Mr. Rhoodie, you and your men may proceed. I aim to move forward at ten tonight. You will, I presume, wish to obtain your firing positions somewhat before that time."

"Yes, General. Let us move out a bit ahead of your forces so we can soften the way for them."

"I sincerely appreciate your joining in our fight, sir." Though he did not say so, Lee was also curious to see how the Rivington men would fare in combat. Konrad de Buys fought well enough on horseback to satisfy as exacting a critic of courage as Jeb Stuart. So far as Lee knew, though, none of the other men from America Will Break had gone into action. He thought of them more as military engineers than frontline troops. Of course, his own career had also begun in the engineers . . . "Good luck to you, Mr. Rhoodie."

"Thank you, General. May we meet again tomorrow, inside Washington." Rhoodie touched a finger to the brim of his mottled cap and hurried away. Lee watched till he was out of sight. However brutal some of the principles he espoused, he knew the right wish to make.

"Pin that on there good for me, Nate," Alsie Hopkins said. Caudell made sure the scrap of paper was securely attached to the back of Hopkins's shirt. As he stepped away, the private went on, "Thanks for writin' it for me, too."

"I hope you don't need it, that's all, Alsie," Caudell said. He'd written names and home towns or counties for several soldies already tonight. If they died assaulting the fortifications ahead—which seemed only too likely— their loved ones might eventually learn they had fallen. For that matter, he'd had Edwin Powell pin his own name on the back of his shirt.

He saw Mollie Bean checking her rifle by firelight. He knew she had trouble with her letters; he'd taught her a little out of a primer every so often. But when he asked her if she wanted him to write her name for her, she shook her head. "Only people who care a damn whether I live or die are right here in the company with me."

Captain Lewis strode from fire to fire. "Into formation," he said quietly. "It's time." No drums or bugles announced the rebels' assembly, the better to keep the Federals from learning what Lee intended.

The sky was gray and overcast as Caudell came to the edge of the strip the Yankees had denuded of standing trees. The Federal forts and trenches that lay on the high ground ahead were deeper darknesses against the night. Caudell was grateful no moonlight betrayed his comrades to the bluecoats with field glasses and telescopes who were surely peering out at their foes.

"We advance in skirmisher order," Captain Lewis said. "They'll hurt us less with their artillery that way, and the repeaters should let us fight through their trenches once we get up to them. God bless every one of you, and may you all come through safe."

"You too, Cap'n," several soldiers called to him. Caudell said nothing aloud, but the thought was in his mind.

Lewis held his watch close to his face, waited, swung his arm forward. Caudell and the company's other proper skirmishers moved out ahead of the rest of the men. He felt horribly exposed to the Yankee guns, as if he were going into battle naked. He quivered every time he stepped on a dry leaf or broke a twig with his foot.

Like flowing shadows, the Confederates moved forward all along the line. It seemed impossible the Federals could not see them, could not hear the beat of their feet against the soil, the jingle of cartridges in their pockets. But stride after cautious stride brought Caudell closer to the enemy works without the slightest sign the men inside them guessed he and his fellows were coming.

The ground was so bad a tight battle line could not have held together in any case, not even in daylight. The Federals had left on the ground most of the trees they'd felled. Caudell was constantly on the dodge and fell several times when branches he hadn't seen tripped him.

He'd advanced perhaps a third of the way when the Federals woke up. Drums began to pound within their lines, beating out the same long roll that called the Confederates to action. A flash of light from an opening in the embrasure of Fort Stevens, a boom—a louder, deeper boom than any he'd heard from a cannon before—and a shell screamed through the night to crash down somewhere behind Caudell. Men screamed back there. Another blast came, and another, and another, as all the fort's eight-inch howitzers and thirty-pounder Parrott rifles opened up.

Sparks of light blinked on and off in the rifle pits in front of the main Federal trench. They reminded Caudell of the fireflies he'd always loved. He would not think of fireflies in the same way again. Still, pickets shooting into the night at the range of a mile could hit someone only by luck.

More explosions came from Fort Stevens. Not all of them, though, seemed to accompany shots from the big siege guns—some sounded more like shells landing than cannon going off. But Lee's field artillery was only now starting to go into action. It had had to move up with the infantry so its guns could reach the forts.

Whatever the explosions were, they disrupted the smooth firing Caudell had seen from the Federal artillerymen outside Bealeton. That was a blessing—every Northern shell not fired meant Southern men not dead.

Some of the flashes from the Yankee rifle pits were not aimed at the oncoming Confederates, but at each other, or perhaps at a space between two of them. No sooner had Caudell made that guess than a chatter of AK-47 fire confirmed it. Somehow, Lee had snuck somebody up close to the Federal line before the main attack got rolling. Caudell wondered if those advance scouts were somehow responsible for the troubles the Federal cannoneers were having. He hoped so.

He tramped on toward the waiting Federals. Here and there, soldiers in the rebels' leading ranks began to shoot. He knew those bullets were probably wasted, but sometimes a man had to answer the enemies who were trying to lay him low.

He was within a couple of hundred yards of the abatis of downed trees that protected the trenches ahead when one of the guns from Fort Stevens let go with a blast of canister. He threw himself flat when he heard the deadly hiss of the lead balls. Canister fire from a Napoleon was dreadful enough. Canister fire from an eight-inch gun . . . When he turned his head, he saw that a gap had been blown in the line to his right, as neatly and thoroughly as if the men had been swept away by a broom.

By then the Yankees were shooting from their main line. Caudell stayed low, trying to find a swell of ground behind which to shelter before he scuttled forward again. The abatis loomed ahead. Already rebels were pulling saplings out of the way to make paths for their comrades to reach the trenches. The bluecoats shot them down as they worked. More men took their places.

Others answered the Federal fire. Had they had only rifle muskets, their task would have been hopeless, for they were exposed while their enemies enjoyed good shelter. But the AK-47s fired enough faster than Springfields to redress the balance. As more and more Confederates got up to and through the abatis, they began to beat down the defenders' fire.

Sharp branches tore at Caudell's clothes as he pushed toward the trench line. For a moment, he thought he was back in the Wilderness; some of the undergrowth there had been about as thick as this deliberately made obstruction. The Federal fire was worse here, though. He saw the glint of a rifle barrel as it swung to point straight at him. He fired first, then ducked low—the muzzle flash would have drawn Yankees' notice to him. Sure enough, two bullets cracked through the space where he had been standing a moment before.

He crawled forward. There was already fighting in the trenches, Confederates and Federals shooting and shouting and cursing as hard and fast as they could. He recognized Springfields by their reports and by the clouds of smoke that rose like swirling fog when they were fired. He shot into the fogbank once, twice, heard a man cry out. He thought the cry carried a Northern accent. He hoped it did. He slid down into the trench on his backside.

"Keep moving!" a Southern voice cried, authority behind it. "We don't want to stay stuck in these damned trenches. It's the city we want, Washington City. Keep moving!"

That was easier said than done. The Federals fought desperately. Their numbers made their single-shot muzzle-loaders almost a match for the rebels' repeaters. Every new corner in the earthworks brought deadly danger. In hand-to-hand combat, the bayonets that tipped Yankee Springfields were actually of use.

A shell landed in a Federal-held section of trench. Caudell yowled like a catamount. Then another shell exploded, and another, and another, the blasts spaced much too close together to come from even the quickest-firing gun. "What the hell is that?" somebody shouted.

"I don't rightly know, but I think it's on our side," Caudell shouted back. Anything less than a shout went unnoticed in the din. He howled out a rebel yell, as much to tell himself he was still alive and fighting as for any other reason.

Yet another of those mysterious shells crashed down among the Yankees. Behind Caudell, somebody yelled, "Go on, you lazy buggers. I've put the fear of God in them for you." The shouter did not sound like a Southern man, but Caudell recognized his voice all the same: it was Benny Lang.

He turned around. For a moment, he thought the Rivington man had the trick of invisibility. Not only were his clothes splotchy, but he'd also painted his face in dark, jagged stripes. Only his fierce grin told where he was. Instead of his usual cap, he wore on his head what looked like a mottled pot. "What the devil's that?" Caudell asked, pointing.

"A helmet," Lang answered. "You bloody bastards can do just as you please, but I don't fancy getting shot in the head—or anywhere else, come to that." He had an AK-47 in his hands and another on his back. He stuffed something fair-sized and roundish into the muzzle of the rifle he was holding. When he fired, the report sounded strange, almost metallic. An instant later, another crash went up from the trenches. Lang must have seen Caudell's flabbergasted expression. His voice was smug: "Rifle grenade."

"Whatever you say." Without thinking, Caudell grabbed the Rivington man by the arm and yanked him toward the fighting. "Come on. Let's take 'em out." Only later did he remember that Lang could have thrown him through the air if he didn't care to come along. But Lang just shrugged and followed.

The grenade bombardment cleared a long stretch of trench; Caudell stepped on and over bodies, some still, others thrashing in torment. Not only that, the rain of explosives seemingly from nowhere had set a good many unhurt Yankees running. Not all, though. A bluecoat raised himself up on one knee, fired from the hip. The bullet caught Benny Lang in the belly. "Oof!" he said.

Caudell cut the Federal down with a short burst of fire. Then he turned to see how Lang was. Actually, he was already sure. Belly wounds always killed, if not from loss of blood, then from fever.

But Lang was not down and screaming, was not, in fact, down at all. He hurried past Caudell, calling back over his shoulder, "Come on, damn it. They're wavering. We can break them."

"Wait a minute." Caudell reached out and took Lang's shoulder, this time to hold him back. "I saw you shot," he shouted in the Rivington man's face. "Why aren't you dead?" Put that way, the question sounded stupid, but Caudell didn't care. He didn't think he believed in ghosts, either, but he would hardly have been surprised to feel his fingers sink straight through what should have been Benny Lang's flesh.

But Lang remained solid. Under the brim of his helmet, his thin face bore a smirk. "Yes, I was shot. My belly'll have a bruise tomorrow, too, I should expect. As for why I'm not dead—" He took Caudell's hand, set it where the Minié ball had struck. Under his tunic, he wore something with flat, hard scales. "Flak jacket."

"What's a flapjack?" Caudell asked, wondering if he'd heard straight.

"It's body armor. Now get moving, damn you. We've wasted too bloody much time here already."

Caudell got moving, his mind awhirl. No one wore armor—armor thick enough to stop a rifle bullet would have put enough steel on a soldier to double his weight. But there went Benny Lang, moving lightly down the length of trench he'd cleared, the trench where his guts and his life hadn't spilled into the dirt. Caudell wanted to shake the Rivington man like a terrier shaking a rat, to shake from him the secret of where he'd found that impossible armor.

The same place he found his rifle grenades, the first sergeant thought, and then, a moment later, *the same place the Rivington men found these AK-47s.* The only trouble was, Caudell could not imagine where in the world that place might be.

He did not dwell on it for long. The Federals tried to counterattack, but by then enough rebels had come forward to chew their assault to bloody rags. And then, without warning, a blast like the end of the world came from Fort Stevens. Caudell staggered. He dropped his rifle to clap both hands to his ears. Bursting shells filled the sky, a thousand Fourths of July all boiled down into an instant. Night turned to noon.

He saw Benny Lang's lips move as that unnatural light faded, but his hearing was still stunned. He shook his head. As he stooped to recover his repeater, Lang put his mouth against his ear and screamed, "The magazine's gone up!"

He heard the Rivington man as if from many miles away, but he heard him. Maybe he wouldn't be deaf forever after all. And certainly, he thought as the ability to think slowly returned, Fort Stevens wouldn't work any more murder against the men in gray.

A little later another magazine, this one from a fort farther away, also blew up. "Fort de Russy," Lang shouted—he didn't quite have to scream anymore for Caudell to hear him. "Or maybe that was Battery Sill, between Stevens and de Russy." Caudell didn't care which magazine it was. He was just glad it was gone.

He heard a roar ahead. That he heard it meant it was loud. Wondering what had gone wrong, he hurried toward the noise, his AK-47 at the ready. By the fickle light of explosions behind him, he scrambled up onto high ground. A good many Confederates were already there, all of them yelling like madmen. He stared, wondering what had taken possession of them. Then he started yelling himself. He and his comrades had fought their way through the Federal trenches. Now no set defenses remained between them and Washington City.

Which did not mean the untaken Yankee forts had quit fighting. He threw himself flat when a big shell came down far too close for comfort. "Keep moving!" an officer cried—a sensible command which Caudell had grown thoroughly tired of tonight. The officer went on, "The farther inside their lines we get, the fewer of those cannon will bear on us." Suddenly given a good, sensible reason to move, Caudell scrambled to his feet and ran south as fast as he could go.

More shells shrieked by, these from the field guns of a battery east of the junction of the Seventh Street Road and the Milkhouse Front Road. The officer told off a detachment to take that battery in the rear. Most of the soldiers, Caudell among them, he sent south down the Seventh Street Road toward Washington. "Form by regiments if you can, by brigade if that's the best you can do," he said. "This won't be just a parade—we'll have more fighting to do."

"Forty-Seventh North Carolina," Caudell called obediently. "Kirkland's brigade. Forty-Seventh North Carolina . . ."

Before long, he found himself with a solid band of North Carolinians, close to half of them from his own regiment. Benny Lang stayed with them. That pleased Caudell: you never could tell when more of those rifle grenades might come in handy, or, for that matter, what other tricks the Rivington man had up his sleeve. Caudell still wondered why he called his wonderful armor a flapjack.

Then from ahead came the roar of a volley of Minié balls and, hard on their heels, shouts and oaths. Word came back quickly: the Federals had thrown a makeshift barricade of logs across the road and were firing from behind it. "Flank 'em out!" someone a few feet ahead of Caudell said. "Two squads to the left of the roadway, two to the right."

"Who are you, to be giving orders?" Caudell demanded.

The man turned. Even in the darkness, his plump features, neat chin beard, and sweeping mustaches were unmistakable. So were the wreathed stars on his collar. "I'm General Kirkland, by God! Who are *you*, sir?"

"First Sergeant Nate Caudell, sir—47th North Carolina," Caudell said, gulping.

"Well, First Sergeant, get up there and take one of those flanking squads," Kirkland thundered.

Cursing his own big mouth, Caudell hurried forward toward the fighting. He passed Benny Lang. "You come, too," he said. "One of those grenades of yours ought to startle the Yankees enough to make our job easier." Lang nodded and came.

The Federals had not had time to extend the barricade far off the roadway itself. They had a few men posted in the bushes, but, thanks to their repeaters, the rebels pushed past them and circled around behind the improvised breastwork.

Benny Lang loaded and fired a rifle grenade. Several Federals started to turn at the odd report. The grenade landed among them. They all shouted in alarm when it went off, and a couple of men its fragments had wounded went on crying from pain. The others, though, fired out into the night in the direction from which the little shell had come; one Minié ball snarled past Caudell's head.

By then, though, he and his comrades were shooting at the muzzle flashes from the Federals' Springfields. A Northerner started screaming and would not stop. Others shouted for their lives: "You got us surrounded, rebs! Don't shoot no more! We give up!"

General Kirland's booming, authoritative voice came out of the night: "You Yanks put that barricade up there. You can get to work and help tear it down." Caudell heard timbers shift, heard men swear mildly, as they often did when a physical task went slightly wrong. Northern and Southern accents mingled as Lee's troops and their prisoners worked side by side. Even before the logs were all removed, Kirkland said, "Forward, boys, forward. You won't let 'em stop us now, will you?"

The sky began to grow light in the east not long after Caudell marched past the junction of the Seventh Street Road and another dirt track that was marked Taylor's Lane Road to the southwest and Rock Creek Church Road to the northeast. Now Washington City was less than two miles away. Caudell had trouble believing he'd fought all night; only a couple of hours seemed to have gone by. The Yankees still kept up a sullen fire to the front and flanks of the advancing Confederate column, but nowhere sharp enough to do more than harass it.

As dawn progressed, Caudell could see farther and farther. Washington lay spread out before him like a painted panorama. He was surprised at the mixed feelings the Federal capital evoked in him. Excitement, anticipation, the almost hectic flush of triumph—he had expected all those.

But seeing the White House for the first time in his life, seeing the Capitol . . . up until three years before, those had been national shrines for him as much as for any Northern man. He found they still had the power to raise a lump in his throat. Nor was he the only one for whom that held true. The Confederate advance slowed as men gaped at what they'd come to capture.

"Go on, God damn you all," General Kirkland shouted. "D'you want to wait until Grant brings the rest of his army over the Potomac on the Long Bridge and makes you fight for the city house by house?"

That got the rebels moving again. Then someone said, "They ain't comin' over no Long Bridge, if that's it straight ahead there. It's burnin'." Sure enough, a column of smoke rose from the middle of the Potomac.

Kirkland must have had a telescope, for a moment later he said, "Not only is it burning, by God, but it's broken as well. The artilleryman who did that deserves a general's wreath, and I don't care a jot whether he's but a private soldier. He's sealed the victory for us."

"He's sealed all the ants in the nest, too, and they don't much fancy it," Caudell said to a soldier nearby. He pointed toward the city ahead. At this distance, the people in the streets did seems small as ants. But ants did not drive carriages, and ants generally moved with greater purpose than the throngs who jammed the avenues ahead. All they knew was that they wanted to flee the oncoming Confederates. Any person who got in their way was as much an obstacle as a tree or a post.

The soldier by Caudell spat in the dusty road. "What you want to bet we don't catch us one single congressman at the Capitol?"

"I don't care about Yankee congressmen," Caudell said. "What I'd like to do is catch Abe Lincoln. That'd be about the only way my name would ever go down in history."

By the look of him, the ragged soldier had never worried about going down in history. But his eyes lit up at the prospect of capturing Lincoln. "Let's try it, by God! Somebody's got to be first to the White House." Then he shook his head. "Naah—even if we are, reckon he'll've run off too, along with everybody else."

"Worth a shot at it." Caudell hurried over to General Kirkland; he thought well of commanders who stayed up with their troops. He wondered where Colonel Faribault and Captain Lewis were—maybe dead back in the trenches, maybe just a few hundred yards away in the confused aftermath of victory. Gaining the brigadier's ear might be worth more now anyway. "Sir, may we head for the White House?"

The ear Caudell had gained was a keen one. "You're that mouthy sergeant from the fight in the dark, aren't you?" Kirkland fixed Caudell with an icy blue stare. But his expression warmed as he thought about the suggestion—what Southerner could resist going after the man for fear of whom his state had seceded?

Kirkland looked around, gauging how far other Confederate units had come. "I have no orders to the contrary, and we might get there first, mightn't we? Let's see if we can—why the hell not?" He waved his sword, pointed southwest, and shouted new orders. The soldiers cheered.

Into Washington City! The rebels tramped down Vermont Avenue in loose skirmish order, repeaters at the ready. Civilians peered from houses. Some came outside to gape at the spectacle they had never imagined. A few people cheered—Washington had its share of Southern sympathizers.

Caudell coughed loudly as he passed a pretty girl. So did a good many other men; the soldiers sounded as if they'd all caught cold at once. Overwhelmed by such vigorous public praise, the girl flushed and fled indoors.

About a hundred yards farther on, a company of Federal soldiers turned onto Vermont Avenue. They must not have realized Lee's men were already in the city. The first couple of ranks never knew it; the Confederates cut them down as soon as they came into sight. A few men returned fire. Others dashed for cover. Shrieking noncombatants ran every which way, including right between the rival forces.

"Get out of there, you damned fools!" Caudell shouted, appalled at the idea of having to fight a battle in a crowd of civilians. When the Federals kept shooting, he found himself without any choice. He dove behind a hedge and looked for targets.

Benny Lang did not seem to care who got stuck in the middle of a fight. He sent a grenade through the window of a house from which Yankees were shooting. A moment later, the blast blew out every pane in that window and the one next to it. Three bluecoats dashed out of the house, as terrified as any ordinary Washingtonian. They would have done better to stay where they were. The Confederates stretched them lifeless before they'd run ten paces.

Rebels darted down side streets to get around the Federals. The fight did not last long. Outnumbered and outgunned, the Northern men died or fled. "Keep going!" Kirkland shouted. "Don't let 'em stop you now!"

Caudell and his comrades kept going. Neither he nor any of them had slept for a full day; neither he nor any of them cared. He could see the White House ahead. With that for a target, rest could wait.

He felt like crying when a lieutenant waved him onto Fifteenth Street instead of letting him keep on going straight down Vermont Avenue. The lieutenant saw his disappointment. Grinning, he said, "Don't feel too bad, soldier. Once upon a time, General McClellan lived down this way. His house ought to be worth seeing."

Caudell thought the house, near the corner of Fifteenth and H streets, a mean hovel, though it was three stories high, with shuttered windows and a railed porch under them from which to receive well-wishers. Who cared where a discredited Federal general had lived when the President's house was so close?

But he and the men with him had been sent only a little out of their way. Blue-coated officers were hurrying in and out of a brown brick building on the north side of Pennsylvania Avenue. Caudell fired a quick burst that sent them tumbling back inside. "Guard this place!" he told some of the other rebels on the avenue. He spent the next few minutes arguing them into it; they wanted the White House as much as he did. That afternoon, he learned he'd helped capture the headquarters of the Federal defenses for Washington.

That was later, though. As soon as he had men with repeaters posted all around the building, he hurried west along Pennsylvania Avenue to the big white mansion that had housed his Presidents until 1861 and now was home to the leader of another country.

The White House drew Confederates like a lodestone. Caudell's delays had let General Kirkland, portly though he was, get there before him. Kirkland was shouting, "You men keep your order, do you hear me? Think about what General Lee will do to anyone who lets harm come to this building or anyone inside it."

Lee's name was a talisman to conjure with. It calmed men who, without it, might gleefully have rampaged with torches. Across the lawn, under the front colonnade, stood Federal sentries. They carried rifles, but made no move to raise them to the firing position. They just kept staring at the ever-growing numbers of ragged men in gray and homespun butternut who filled the broad cobblestoned street and now hesitantly advanced over the grass toward them. They did not seem to believe this hour could ever have come.

Remembering Gettysburg, remembering the botched fight at Bristoe Station, remembering the long, cold, hungry winter south of the Rapidan before the repeaters came, Caudell marveled at the hour, too. As he pressed

toward the White House with his comrades, his feeling that the world had
turned upside down deepened further, for out among the bluecoats came
a tall, thin figure dressed in funereal black. Caudell looked around for the
private who'd guessed the Federal President would run. By happy chance,
the fellow was standing not ten feet from him. He pointed. "See? We've
bagged Old Abe after all."

Lincoln's name ran through the rebels. A few cheers rang out, and a
few jeers, but not many of either. The force of the moment seized most
men with almost religious awe. Still slowly, they came forward across the
White House lawn to the base of the steps. There they halted, staring in
wonder at the edifice and Lincoln both. Caudell was in the fourth or fifth
row of tight-packed troops.

As they hesitated, Lincoln came down the steps toward them. One of
the Federal sentries tried to block his path. He said, "What does it matter
now, son? What does anything matter now?" Beneath his frontier twang,
he sounded tired past all endurance. The young sentry, beard still downy
on his cheeks, stepped back in confusion.

Caudell frankly stared at the President of the United States. Southern
papers and cartoonists made Lincoln out to be either a backcountry buffoon
or a fiend in human shape. In the flesh, he did not seem either. He was
just a tall, homely man whose deep-set eyes had already seen all the griefs
in the world and now this crowning one piled atop the rest.

He coughed and turned his head to one side. When he somehow found
the resolution to face the crowd of Confederate soldiers again, those eyes
glistened with the tears he would not shed. Caudell thought they were tears
of sorrow, not weakness; it was the expression a father would wear, watching his beloved son die of a sickness he could not cure.

Not all the rebels stayed solemn. A short, broad-shouldered corporal in
front of Caudell and to his left spoke up brashly: "Well, Uncle Abe, you
gonna try and take our niggers away from us now?" It was Billy Beddingfield; Caudell hadn't realized he'd been promoted again. He was also certain Beddingfield, like most Southern soldiers, had not a single Negro to
his name.

Beddingfield brayed laughter at his own wit. A good many men joined
him. Lincoln stood on the White House steps, waiting to see whether the
rebels would quiet down. When they did, he said, "I did not become
President with the intention of interfering with the institutions of any state
in the Union. I said that repeatedly, at every forum available; the great
regret of my life is that you Southerners would not credit it."

"What about the Emancipation Proclamation, then?" half a dozen soldiers shouted at once. Some of them profanely embellished the question.

Lincoln did not quail. "Everything I have done, I have done for the purpose of holding the Union together and of restoring it once it was torn asunder. Had I thought that meant freeing all the slaves, I should have freed them all; had I thought it meant leaving them in chains, in chains they would have stayed. As it chanced, I thought the wisest course was to free some and leave others alone—note that even now I have hesitated to touch the institution in those states which remained loyal. The proclamation was a weapon to hand in the war against your rebellion, and I seized it. Make what you will of that."

"Damn little good it did you," Billy Beddingfield said. Again, some of the rebels laughed. But Caudell gave his beard a thoughtful tug. He hadn't known the Emancipation Proclamation was selective; the papers had painted it as a desperate effort to incite blacks to rise up against their masters. So it was, to some degree. But if it was a blow against the Confederate government rather than against slavery *per se*, that made it more or less what Lincoln claimed it was—an unpleasant ploy, but a ploy nonetheless.

The Federal President said, "Personally, I hate slavery and all it stands for." That took courage, in front of the audience he faced. He let the rebels' boos and hisses wash over him. When they slackened, he went on, "It is too late now, I think, to rescind the proclamation I issued. Too much has happened since. But if only the Southern states were to return to the Union, the Federal government would fully compensate former masters for their bondsmen's liberty—"

The rebels laughed, loud and long. Lincoln hung his head. Caudell, strangely, found himself respecting the man. Anyone who clung to his principles strongly enough to refuse to abandon them even in complete defeat owned more sincerity than he had credited Lincoln with possessing.

Lincoln drew himself up to his full and impressive height. His black suit conformed perfectly to the motion; it was far from new and had been worn so often that it molded itself to its owner's shape. "If my death would restore the seceded states, I would beg for your bullets," he said. "If the Union fails, I have no wish to live."

From most politicians, that would have been just talk. Looking at the sorrow that masked Lincoln's rough-hewn features, Caudell was convinced he meant every word of it. But if he thought the Federal government had the right to tell states they had to stay in a Union they no longer desired, then he might be sincere, but to Caudell's way of thinking he was sincerely wrong.

Some of the Confederates were willing to find him most literally sincere, too. Billy Beddingfield started to raise his AK-47. Caudell grabbed the repeater and pushed it back down. "No, Billy, damn it," he said. "This isn't like shooting a couple of nigger prisoners." Nobody had ever assassinated a President of the United States. Caudell could imagine nothing surer to bring on lasting enmity between U.S.A. and C.S.A.

Beddingfield turned on him, scowling. "He don't deserve no better, all the trouble he brung on us." He started to swing the rifle back toward Lincoln. Caudell ground his teeth. Benny Lang had handled Beddingfield easily enough, but he knew he couldn't match the Rivington man. And how strange to think of fighting a man from his own regiment to save the President whose troops he'd been battling these past two and a half years!

Before Beddingfield could shoot, before the fight could start, a murmur ran from back to front through the crowd of soldiers in gray: "Marse Robert! Marse Robert's here!" Caudell looked around. Sure enough, Lee sat aboard Traveller. The crowd parted before him like the waters of the Red Sea. He rode up to the base of the White House steps.

Lincoln waited for him, infinitely alone. One of the Federal sentries began to lift his Springfield. Another man slapped it down, as Caudell had with Beddingfield.

Lee took off his broad-brimmed gray felt, bowed in the saddle to Lincoln. "Mr. President," he said, as respectfully as if Lincoln were his own chosen leader.

"See?" Caudell whispered to Billy Beddingfield.

"Shut up," Beddingfield hissed back.

"General Lee," Lincoln said with a stiff nod. He looked from the Confederate commander to the men of the Army of Northern Virginia, back again. His lips quirked in what Caudell first thought a grimace of pain. Then he saw it was a grin, however wry. Lincoln half-turned, waved toward the imposing bulk of the White House behind him. "General, do you want to step into my parlor with me? Seems we have a bit of talking to do."

He'd been eloquent when talking to the soldiers. With Lee, he sounded like a storekeeper inviting a customer in to haggle over the price of potatoes. Caudell was instantly suspicious of such a chameleonlike shift of style. But Lee said, "Of course, Mr. President. I'm sure one of my men will hold Traveller's head." As he dismounted, three dozen men sprang forward for the privilege.

A colored servant brought in a pot of coffee and two cups on a silver tray. "Sit down, General, do sit down," Lincoln said.

"Thank you, Mr. President." Robert E. Lee took the chair to which Lincoln had waved him. Lincoln poured the coffee with his own hands. "Thank you, sir," Lee said again.

Lincoln's chuckle held a bitter edge. "A fair number of generals have sat in that chair, General Lee, but I'll be switched if you're not the politest one of the lot." Still standing himself, he peered down at Lee. "I think this country would be a good deal better off if you'd sat down in it some years sooner."

"You honored me by offering me that command," Lee said. "Having to decline it tore my heart in two."

"When you declined it, I think you tore the United States in two," Lincoln answered. "Set against that, your heart's a small thing."

"I am in the end a Virginian first, Mr. President," Lee said.

"You come out with that so coolly, as if it explained everything," Lincoln said. Lee looked at him in some surprise; he thought it did. Lincoln went on, "I take the view—I have always taken the view—that the interest of the several states should count for more than the interest of any one of them."

"There we disagree, sir," Lee said quietly.

"So we do." Rather to Lee's relief, Lincoln sat down. A good-sized man himself, Lee did not care to be towered over, and Lincoln was as tall as any of Andries Rhoodie's friends. He reached out a long arm to tap Lee on the knee. "Something I want you to think on, General: You've taken Washington for the moment, but can you keep it? There are many more Union soldiers around the city than Confederates in it. Can you stand siege here?"

Lee smiled, admiring Lincoln's audacity. "I'll take the chance, Mr. President. The beef depot and slaughterhouse by the Washington Monument could alone subsist my army for some time, and it is far from the only such source of supply in the city. To us, sir, having come here, we feel we are entered into the land flowing with milk and honey. We've made do with very little in the past."

"Yes, you can find milk and honey here, I expect, though you'd better watch out that the sutlers and commissary officers don't adulterate 'em before they ever get to your men." Lincoln studied Lee. "But where will you get more cartridges for those newfangled repeaters your men carry?"

"We have a sufficiency," Lee said, more calmly than he felt. That one sharp question was plenty to dispel any lingering doubts about Lincoln's ability. The man understood what war required. Lee wondered if the Army of Northern Virginia did have enough ammunition for another big fight. The men had spent it like a drunken sailor throwing away money after six months at sea.

Lincoln's eyes bored into him. He remembered that the Federal President had been a lawyer before he took up politics. He was practiced at sniffing out falsehood hiding behind a mask of rectitude.

Lee said, "Let me ask you something in turn, Mr. President, if I may:

Are you prepared to destroy Washington City to drive us out of it? That is what you would have to do, you know; already we are looking to our own defense here. Would your countrymen support you in such an action, especially at a time when Confederate arms are gaining successes against other Federal forces besides the Army of the Potomac?"

"My countrymen elected me to hold the Union together, General Lee, and that I shall undertake to do by whatever means necessary so long as there is any hope of this war's success," Lincoln said. Lee felt a slight chill as he gauged the big man in the velvet-upholstered chair. Here, even more than with General Grant, he at last encountered a Northern man with strength of purpose to match his own and President Davis's. Lincoln continued, "If the only hope of saving the Union is to make this city into a funeral pyre and then immolate myself upon it, that I shall do, and let the voters judge come November whether I did right or wrong."

If he was bluffing, Lee was glad never to have met him at a poker table. And yet the game they were playing now was poker on a grander scale, with the fate of two nations pushed onto the table for stakes. This time, though, Lee knew he was holding aces. He turned a new one face up, drawing a telegram from his pocket and handing it to Lincoln. "Mr. President, you say you will carry on so long as you feel you can win the war. Here is a dispatch I received this morning which may shed some light on your chances of doing so."

To read the telegram, Lincoln slipped on a pair of gold-framed spectacles much like Lee's own. That was hardly surprising; the two leaders were only two years apart in age, and a man's sight grew long in the middle years, regardless of whether he was born in mansion or log cabin.

The Federal president peered over the rims of his glasses at Lee. "This paper is genuine"—he pronounced it *genuwine*—"General?"

"You have my oath on it, Mr. President." Lee had not thought of offering Lincoln a false telegram. Had it occurred to him, the stratagem would have been a good one. But Lincoln was more ready to counter deception than he was to offer it.

"Your oath I will accept, General, though those of few others—in gray or blue—under these circumstances," Lincoln said heavily. "So Bedford Forrest with thirty-five hundred men has beaten our General Sturgis with over eight thousand north of Corinth, Mississippi, has he?"

"Not only beaten him but wrecked him, Mr. President. His men are in full flight toward Memphis, with Forrest in pursuit. From his report, he has captured two hundred fifty wagons and ambulances and five thousand stands of small arms, not that those latter are of much concern to us. Do you suppose you can keep his cavalry off General Sherman's supply line much longer? Do you suppose Sherman can long survive with the railroads wrecked as Forrest's men are in the habit of wrecking them?"

Lincoln bent his head, covered his face with his large, bony hands. "It is the end," he said, his voice muffled. "I wish one of your rebels had shot me out there, so I should never have to live past this black day."

"Don't think of it so, Mr. President. Call it rather a new beginning," Lee said. "The Confederate States never wanted more than to go their own way in peace and to live in peace with the United States."

"No right cause impelled you to dissolve the Union, only fear—misguided fear, I might add—that I would act precipitately against slavery. I was willing to let it remain in place where it was and slowly to wither there."

"Mr. President, I hold no brief for slavery, as you may know. But I do believe the rights of a state to be of higher importance than those of the Federal—or Confederate—government."

"This war has undermined the powers of the separate states, North and South alike," Lincoln said. "Both Washington and Richmond levy direct taxes and directly conscript men, no matter how the governors moan and bellow like branded calves. Can any separate state hope to resist their power? You know the answer as well as I."

Lee stroked his beard. Lincoln had a point. Even his precious Virginia, by far the greatest of the Confederate states, followed first the will of the national government, then its own. He said, "I am but a soldier; let those wiser in such matters settle them as seems best."

"If you were 'but a soldier,' General Lee, we wouldn't be sitting here talking with each other right now." Lincoln's mouth twisted in that melancholy grin of his. "And I wish to thunder that we weren't!" His gaze sharpened again. "Weren't for those repeaters you've broken out with like a dog's new spring fleas, I don't think we would be, either. If I knew where you were getting 'em, I'd buy a batch for my own side, I tell you that."

"I believe you, Mr. President." Lee meant it. Lincoln was an inventor of sorts; he'd once patented a device for getting riverboats across stretches of low water. Anyone in the North who came up with a new rifle or cartridge made a beeline for the White House, hoping to impress him with it. Lee went on carefully, "As for our new rifles, we do not import them from overseas. They come from within the Confederacy."

"So say the rebels we've captured," Lincoln answered. "I own I find it hard to credit. The rifles are better than any we make, and you Southerners haven't a tithe of our factories. So how did you turn out so many so fast?"

"The how of it is not important, Mr. President." Lee could not discuss the Rivington men and their secret with his nation's chiefest enemy—with the man, indeed, who was his nation's chiefest reason for existing. Oddly, though, he found he wanted to. Of all the men he'd met, Lincoln seemed least likely to call him a lunatic; the Federal President had a breadth of vision that might be wide enough to take in the notion of men coming back from 2014. Lee's brows came together. Again, how could the man before him be capable of the outrages Andries Rhoodie ascribed to him? Lee shrugged. That how was not important, either. "What is important is that my men and I are here. As I said before, I believe we can stay here, and that other Confederate armies are likely to continue to win victories. Your war to subjugate the South has failed."

"I will not give it up," Lincoln said, stubborn still.

"Then the United States will give up on you," Lee predicted. "But the choice is not altogether in your hands, sir. When I leave the White House, my next call will be at the British ministry, to pay my respects to Lord Lyons. Since I shall be in the position to do that, how can he fail to recognize the Confederate States as a nation which has succeeded in winning its independence?"

He did not say—he did not need to say—that if Great Britain recognized the Confederacy, France and the other European powers would surely follow her lead . . . and not even the stubbornest U.S. President could continue war on the Southern states in the face of that recognition.

Lincoln's long, sad face grew longer and sadder. Even now, though, he refused to yield, saying, "Lord Lyons hates slavery. So do the British people."

"Britain recognizes the Empire of Brazil, does she not, despite its being a slaveholding land? For that matter, Britain recognized the United States before the start of our unfortunate war, and does still, in spite of your continuing to hold slaves—last year's Emancipation Proclamation was remarkably silent on the subject of Northern Negroes in bondage."

Always sallow, Lincoln turned a couple of shades darker. "They are being attended to. Come victory, all in the United States would have been free." He cocked his head at Lee. "And you have just claimed to be no great friend of slavery yourself, General."

Lee lowered his eyes, acknowledging the hit. "The most I will say for it is that, controlled by humane laws and influenced by Christianity and an enlightened public sentiment, it may be the most practicable means for blacks and whites harmoniously to live together in this land."

"It is an evil, sir, an unmitigated evil," Lincoln said. "I shall never forget the group of chained Negroes I saw going down the river to be sold close to a quarter of a century ago. Never was there so much misery, all in one place. If your secession triumphs, the South will be a pariah among nations."

"We shall be recognized as what we are, a nation among nations," Lee returned. "And, let me repeat, my being here is a sign secession *has* triumphed. What I would seek to do now, subject to the ratification of my superiors, is suggest terms to halt the war between the United States and Confederate States." Lincoln refused to call Lee's country by its proper name. As a small measure of revenge, Lee put extra weight on that name.

Lincoln sighed. This was the moment he had tried to evade, but there was no evading it, not with the commander of the Army of Northern Virginia in his parlor. "Name your terms, General," he said in a voice full of ashes.

"They are very simple, Mr. President: that Federal troops withdraw from such parts of the territory of the Confederate States as they now occupy. As soon as that is done—perhaps even while it is being done—we shall depart from Washington City, and U.S.A. and C.S.A. will be at peace."

"Simple, eh?" Lincoln leaned forward in his chair, the picture of a man determined not to be cheated in a horse trade. "What about West Virginia?"

"That is a delicate area," Lee admitted. When Virginia left the Union, its northern and western counties refused to go along; Federal guns had protected them in their secession from secession. Now the area was one of the United States in its own right. Lee could not doubt that was what the bulk of its people wanted, even if Virginia still claimed the territory. He countered, "What of Missouri and Kentucky?"

Both states sent representatives to the Confederate Congress as well as to Washington. Kentucky was the birth state of Lincoln and of Jefferson Davis, too, while Missouri's civil war was as much neighbor against neighbor as North against South. Lincoln was right. Deciding borders wouldn't be simple.

"Well, what about Missouri and Kentucky?" the Federal President said. "Asking me to leave the valley of the Mississippi, where we as yet remain supreme, is hard enough. But if you expect us to pull off our own soil so you can walk in, you can think again, sir. Emancipation is already far along there as well—you may not want those states, for you will have to fight a new war to restore their colored folk to servitude."

It was Lee's turn to sigh. That might be true wherever the Federal armies had gone. But it was a worry for politicians, and for the future. Now— "This sort of talk gets us nowhere, Mr. President, save to the spilling of more blood, which is what I now seek to prevent. Will you undertake to remove your soldiers from all disputed territory but those two states and what you people call West Virginia, with the status of those areas to be settled by negotiation at a later date?"

"Have you the authority to offer such terms?" Lincoln asked.

"No, sir," Lee admitted at once. "As I said before, I shall have to submit them to Richmond for my President's approval. I was speaking informally, in an effort to bring the fighting to a close as quickly as possible. If you could arrange to reconnect the telegraph lines between here and Richmond, you would be able to treat directly with President Davis, without my serving as intermediary."

Lincoln waved a hand. "Reconnecting the telegraph'd be simple enough." Lee knew that was so only for a nation with the abundant resources the United States enjoyed, but held his peace. Lincoln continued, "Still and all, I think I'd sooner talk with you. You have sense enough for a whole raft of Presidents, seems to me." If he noticed he'd included himself there, he gave no sign of it.

"As you wish, Mr. President," Lee said. "My feeling is, if the bloodshed once stops, we can then sit down across from one another at a table and settle these remaining issues. They may bulk large in your vision now, but they are of small importance when set beside the main question of the war, which is whether the South should be free and independent."

"They look plenty big from over here, but then, what you rightly call the main question has been answered the wrong way." Lincoln shook his head. "And now I have to make the best of it for my country. Very well, General Lee, if we cannot bring you back—and it seems we can't—we shall have to learn to live alongside you. I'd sooner do that talking than shooting."

"So would I, sir," Lee said eagerly. "So would every soldier in the Confederate army, and, if I might make so bold as to speak for them, very likely the soldiers in your army as well."

"You're very likely right, General. How is it that soldiers are always so much more willing to pack in a war than civilians?"

"Because only soldiers actually fight," Lee answered. "They understand how much of what is afterwards called glory is but memory trying to put a good face on terror and torment."

"General Lee, I wish to heaven you'd chosen the Northern side," Lincoln burst out. "You see clear enough to have won this war for us before the South ever started turning out these cursed repeating rifles that have sent so many of our lads to their graves too young."

"Too many on both sides have gone to their graves too young," Lee said. Lincoln nodded; at last the two men had found a point upon which they agreed without reservation. Lee stood to go. Lincoln rose from his chair in sections, like a carpenter's fancy ruler unfolding. Looking up at him, Lee added, "It is decided, then? You will order an armistice and withdrawal on the terms I outlined?"

"I will." Lincoln's mouth twisted on the words as if they were pickled in vinegar. "Would you be so kind as to put them in writing, to prevent any misunderstanding?"

Lee reached into his waistcoat pocket. "I have pen and paper, at least an order pad. May I trouble you for ink?" Lincoln waved him to a desk against the wall. He bent to use the inkwell, wrote rapidly. When he was done, he handed the pad to the President of the United States.

Lincoln read rapidly through the couple of paragraphs. "They are as you said, General. Will you be kind enough to lend me your pen?" He set his signature beside Lee's. "Now let me have that second copy, if you please."

Lee tore off the original, gave Lincoln the sheet below it. The Federal president folded it and put it away without looking at it, as if he had already seen more of the words on it than he cared to. Lee dipped his head to Lincoln. "If you will excuse me—?"

"You don't need to wait on my leave," Lincoln said with more than a little bitterness. "Conquerors, after all, do as they please."

"History has never recorded any man less anxious to be noted as a conqueror than I."

"Maybe so, but history will also note you are one."

Lee and Lincoln walked together to the door of the reception room. Lincoln opened it, gestured for Lee to precede him through. In the ante-chamber outside, Lee's staff officers stood chatting amicably enough with a couple of bright-looking young men in civilian clothes. All heads turned toward the general and the President. No one spoke, but a single question was visible in the eyes of all. Lee answered it: "We shall have peace, gentlemen."

His aides shouted and clapped their hands. The two men in civilian suits also smiled, but more hesitantly. Their gaze swung to Lincoln. "I see no good prospects remaining for the continuation of this war," he said. Where to Lee that was a matter for rejoicing, Lincoln sounded funereal. Lee imagined what he would have felt, presenting his sword to General Grant in a conquered Richmond. In deliberately lighter tones, Lincoln continued, "General Lee, let me present my secretaries, Mr. John Hay and Mr. John Nicolay. They're good lads; they should enjoy the privilege of meeting the latest hero."

"Hardly that," Lee protested. He shook each secretary's hand. "I am pleased to make your acquaintance, gentlemen."

"Pleased to meet you, too, General Lee, but I'd sooner have done it under different circumstances," Hay said boldly.

"Now see here, sir—" Walter Taylor began.

Lee held up a hand to head off his aide's anger. "Let him speak as he will, Major. Would you wish otherwise, were your cause overthrown?"

"I suppose not," Taylor said grudgingly.

"There you are, then." Lee turned back to Lincoln. "Mr. President, if you will excuse me, I should like to give the good news of our"—he searched for the least wounding way to put it—"our agreement that there should be an armistice to the brave men who have borne so much these past three years."

"I'll come with you, if you don't mind," Lincoln said. "If this thing must be, we ought to put the best face we can on it and let them see us in accord." Surprised but pleased, Lee nodded.

The crowd of ragged Confederates on the White House lawn had doubled and more since he went in to confer with Lincoln. The trees were full of men who had climbed up so they could see over their comrades. Off in the distance, cannon still occasionally thundered; rifles popped like firecrackers. Lee quietly said to Lincoln, "Will you send out your sentries under flag of truce to bring word of the armistice to those Federal positions still firing upon my men?"

"I'll see to it," Lincoln promised. He pointed to the soldiers in gray, who had quieted expectantly when Lee came out. "Looks like you've given me sentries enough, even if their coats are the wrong color."

Few men could have joked so with their cause in ruins around them. Respecting the Federal President for his composure, Lee raised his voice: "Soldiers of the Army of Northern Virginia, after three years of arduous service, we have achieved that for which we took up arms—"

He got no farther. With one voice, the men before him screamed out their joy and relief. The unending waves of noise beat at him like surf from a stormy sea. Battered forage caps and slouch hats flew through the air. Soldiers jumped up and down, pounded on one another's shoulders, danced in clumsy rings, kissed each other's bearded, filthy faces. Lee felt his own eyes grow moist. At last the magnitude of what he had won began to sink in.

Abraham Lincoln turned away from the celebrating rebels. Lee saw that his hollow cheeks were also wet. He set a hand on Lincoln's arm. "I'm sorry, Mr. President. Perhaps you should not have come out after all."

"You don't suppose I'd've heard them in there?" Lincoln asked.

Lee sought a reply, found none. He looked to the bottom of the steps, where Traveller remained calm in the midst of chaos. With a last nod to Lincoln, he went down the stairway to his horse. As he'd told the U.S. President, he had another call to make in Washington.

Neither the Stars and Stripes nor the Confederacy's Stainless Banner flew over the building up to which Lee rode. No soldiers crowded in front of it to gape and point save the few who had followed him through the streets of the city, and they were gaping and pointing at him rather than his destination. Nevertheless, after the White House, this nondescript, two-story structure with the Union Jack on the roof was the most important place in the city for the South.

He walked up the slate pathway to the front door, rapped once on the polished brass knocker, and waited. Over the British ministry, he had not even the rights of a conqueror. His staff officers dismounted from their horses but did not presume to follow him, not here.

The door opened. An elderly, very bald man in formal attire peered out at him. "You would be General Lee?" he asked. His accent was soft in a way different from Lee's Virginia speech.

"I am he," Lee said, bowing. "I should like to pay my respects to Lord Lyons, if I may."

"He has been expecting you, sir," the elderly man said. "If you will come with me—?"

He led Lee down a long hall, past several chambers where clerks' heads came up from their papers so they could stare at him, then into a sitting room. "Your excellency, the famous Confederate general, Robert E. Lee. General, Lord Richard Lyons."

"Thank you, Hignett. You may go." The British Minister to the United States got up from his overstuffed armchair.

Lee already had his hand out. "I am delighted to meet you at last, your excellency," he said sincerely. The South had been struggling to win British recognition since before the war with the Union began.

"General Lee," Lord Lyons murmured. He was in his late forties, with a round, very red face, dark hair and side whiskers, and almost equally dark circles under his eyes. An elegantly tailored suit came close to disguising his plumpness. "Please make yourself comfortable, General. You are indeed the man of the moment."

"Thank you, your excellency." Lee sat in a chair not far from the one from which Lord Lyons had risen. "As I have, ah, come to Washington City, I thought it fitting that I pay my respects to you, since your government has no present minister in Richmond."

Lord Lyons steepled his fingertips. "A state of affairs you hope will change."

"I do, your excellency. Either the Confederate States of America are an independent nation, or they are but a dependency of the United States. No other earthly power claims the right to govern us, and my presence here argues against the second interpretation of our status that I mentioned."

"Argues powerfully, you are too discreet to say. Am I correctly informed that you visited President Lincoln before you came here?"

"Yes, your excellency." Lee concealed his surprise, and after a moment realized surprise was foolish. It was the business of the British minister to be well informed.

"May I enquire as to the results of that meeting?" Lord Lyons said. Lee briefly sketched the terms of the armistice agreement with Lincoln. Lord Lyons listened intently. When Lee was done, the minister gave a slow nod. "He has in effect, then, conceded the independence of the Confederacy."

"In effect, yes. What choice had he, sir? Our armies have in the current campaigning season been uniformly victorious—"

"This due in no small measure to the new repeaters with which you have equipped yourselves," Lord Lyons interrupted. He could not hide the keen interest in his voice. Behind a calm exterior, Lee smiled. Everyone was keen to find out where those repeaters came from. He wondered what Lord Lyons would have made of the true answer. He remained unsure just what to make of it himself.

But that was by the way. "Yes, your excellency, with the aid of our new rifles, we have halted or driven back the Federals on all fronts—else I should not be here conversing with you. President Lincoln rightly recognized"—he chose the word with deliberation—"that it would be only a matter of time before we freed our territory and wisely chose to spare his soldiers the suffering they would have to undergo in struggles bound to be futile."

"With these victories to which you refer, the Confederate States do seem to have retrieved their falling fortunes," Lord Lyons said. "I have no reason to doubt that Her Majesty's government will before long recognize that fact."

"Thank you, your excellency," Lee said quietly. Even had Lincoln refused to give up the war—not impossible, with the Mississippi valley and many coastal pockets held by virtue of Northern naval power and hence relatively secure from rebel AK-47s—recognition by the greatest empire on earth would have assured Confederate independence.

Lord Lyons held up a hand. "Many among our upper classes will be glad enough to welcome you to the family of nations, both as a result of your successful fight for self-government and because you have given a black eye to the often vulgar democracy of the United States. Others, however, will judge your republic a sham, with its freedom for white men based upon Negro slavery, a notion loathsome to the civilized world. I should be less than candid if I failed to number myself among the latter group."

"Slavery was not the reason the Southern states chose to leave the Union," Lee said. He was aware he sounded uncomfortable, but went on, "We sought only to enjoy the sovereignty guaranteed us under the Constitution, a right the North wrongly denied us. Our watchword all along has been, *we wish but to be left alone.*"

"And what sort of country shall you build upon that watchword, General?" Lord Lyons asked. "You cannot be left entirely alone; you are become, as I said, a member of the family of nations. Further, this war has been hard on you. Much of your land has been ravaged or overrun, and, in those places where the Federal army has been, slavery lies dying. Shall you restore it there at the point of a bayonet? Gladstone said October before last, perhaps a bit prematurely, that your Jefferson Davis had made an army, the beginnings of a navy, and, more important than either, a nation. You Southerners may have made the Confederacy into a nation, General Lee, but what sort of nation shall it be?"

Lee did not answer for most of a minute. This pudgy little man in his comfortable chair had put into a nutshell all of his own worries and fears. He'd had scant time to dwell on them, not with the war always uppermost in his thoughts. But the war had not invalidated any of the British minister's questions—some of which Lincoln had also asked—only put off the time at which they would have to be answered. Now that time drew near. Now that the Confederacy was a nation, what sort of nation would it be?

At last he said, "Your excellency, at this precise instant I cannot fully answer you, save to say that, whatever sort of nation we become, it shall be one of our own choosing."

It was a good answer. Lord Lyons nodded, as if in thoughtful approval. Then Lee remembered the Rivington men. They too had their ideas on what the Confederate States of America should become.

★ VIII ★

Mollie Bean's eyes flashed when she saw Caudell. "You hear the latest of what that rascal Forrest done?"

"No. Tell me," he said eagerly. Nathan Bedford Forrest's exploits were usually worth hearing, and Mollie, being who she was, usually—as now—found out about them before most people.

She said, "When the telegraph for the armistice got to him, he made like it never did, and took his boys hell-for-leather up into Tennessee—wrecked a big long stretch of the railroad that was feedin' General Sherman's army. Some o' them bluecoats is nearly starvin', I hear tell."

"After this past winter, I know more about starving than those Yankees are ever likely to," Caudell said. "But what did Lincoln and the other Federal bigwigs have to say about him breaking the armistice that way?"

"Reckon they carried on some, but with us here where we are, what can they do but carry on?"

Mollie waved a hand. Along with a good part of the rest of A. P. Hill's corps, the 47th North Carolina was encamped in the White Lot, the big empty space between the White House and the stump of the Washington Monument. The barracks they occupied had been intended for Pennsylvania regiments on the way south; now the shoe was on the other foot. What with those fine barracks and rations from the bottomless Federal depots, Caudell hadn't lived so well since he joined the army, and seldom before.

Mollie went on, "They're callin' him Hit-'em-Again Forrest, 'cause they say he wanted to hit the Yankees one more lick, to remind 'em they was whipped."

"Hit-'em-Again Forrest." Caudell said it slowly, savoring the taste. "Yup, that does sound like him. And that's about the best nickname I've heard this side of Stonewall Jackson." With some dignity, he added, "Not that Nathan's a bad name."

"That's right, it's just about the same as yours." Mollie laughed. "Too bad it ain't your bankrolls that's just about the same."

Caudell laughed too, ruefully. "Too bad is right. But if he made his money dealing niggers the way I've heard, well, it's not anything I'd feel easy about doing for myself." He knew that was hypocritical. The Confederate constitution enshrined the right to own slaves and trade them within the nation's borders. The Southern economy rested on the backs of its black labor force. But a lot of people who could never have stomached the butcher's trade ate meat.

Mollie waved again. "Isn't this grand? Here I am, a nobody from a nowhere town in North Carolina, and now I've seen Richmond and Washington City both. Who'd've figured I'd travel so far? Must be close to two hundred miles down to Rivington."

Caudell nodded. The army had expanded his life. Before the war, outside of a couple of trips to Raleigh, he'd spent his whole life inside Nash County. Now he'd been in several different states and even—though recalling it still came hard sometimes—a foreign country: the United States.

Whether in a foreign country or not, Washington was still the source of traditions he held dear, as London once might have been to an early Carolina colonist. He'd spent most of his off-duty time wandering through the city rubbernecking, and was far from the only soldier in gray to go off and see what he could see. The White House secretaries had had to set up a regular tour, taking Confederates through the Presidential mansion in company-sized groups.

He'd also walked over to the Capitol. Federal senators and congressmen were beginning to return to Washington, though a fair number of the important-looking men he'd seen flinched from him and his comrades as if they were Satan's spawn set loose on earth.

The ordinary folk of Washington City did better at taking their occupiers in stride. Their principal complaint against the rebels was that they had too little money, and that in Confederate currency. Lee had issued an order that made the locals take Southern money in exchange for goods and services, but he could not make them like it.

Caudell had bought himself a drink at Willard's, a couple of blocks east

of the White House, on the corner of Fourteenth Street and Pennsylvania
Avenue. Lincoln and Grant had each spent his first night in Washington
City at Willard's. Everyone who was anyone in Federal Washington fre-
quented the hotel; its bars, sitting and dining rooms, and corridors had
probably seen more war business done than any other place in the city,
the White House not excepted. That was why Caudell went there; Willard's
fame—or notoriety—had spread south as well as north.

He found his shot overpriced and the whiskey villainous. "Is this what
you served General Grant?" he asked indignantly.

The bartender, an Irishman of impressive size, glared down at him. "The
very same, Johnny Reb, and I found himself not so particular as you."
Caudell shut up. From some of the stories he'd heard about Grant's drinking, the fellow might even have been telling the truth.

Fighting Joe Hooker had also drunk at Willard's, and given his name to
the blocks south and east of it. Caudell stayed away from what the natives
called Hooker's Division. Confederates who did go in to visit such establishments as Mme. Russell's Bake Oven, Headquarters U.S.A., and Gentle
Annie Lyle's place quickly learned to travel in pairs. Gamblers, pickpock-
ets, flimflam men, and the girls themselves preyed on soldiers in gray as
readily as they had on soldiers in blue. Plenty of men came back without
a cent; a few did not come back at all.

Outside of the monuments, Washington City left Claudell disappointed.
So had Richmond, outside of Capitol Square. They both seemed just towns
intent on their own concerns. For the leading cities of great nations, somehow that was not enough. Rocky Mount and Nashville back in Nash County
were towns intent on their own concerns. One day, maybe, he'd get back
to Nash County and to his own concerns. Soon, he hoped.

The Confederate bands on the White House lawn struck up "The Star-
Spangled Banner." General Lee saluted the color-bearer, who marched
before the party of high-ranking Federal officers coming to reclaim Washington from the Army of Northern Virginia. The flag of the United States
had been his, not long ago, and still commanded his respect.

The Federals also had a band with them. It returned the compliment by
playing "Dixie"—not the South's official anthem, but the tune most closely
associated with it. A short, slim man with a close-trimmed, light brown
beard and three stars on each shoulder strap stepped out from among his
comrades, strode briskly up to the waiting Confederate officers. He saluted.
"General Lee?" His voice was quiet, his accent western.

Lee returned the salute. "General Grant," he acknowledged formally,
then went on, "We met once in Mexico, I believe, sir, though I confess to

my embarrassment that your face does not seem perfectly familiar to me. Doubtless it is the beard."

"I remember the day," Grant said. "I recognized you at once, beard or no."

"You're too kind, when I've also gone all gray while you remain so brightly fledged," Lee said. "Let me commend you on your excellent band."

Grant shrugged. His long cigar waggled at one corner of his mouth. "I care nothing for music, I'm afraid. I know only two tunes: one's 'Yankee Doodle' and the other isn't." He brought the small joke out pat, as if he'd used it many times before.

Lee laughed politely, then turned serious once more. "Please believe me when I express my sincere compliments on the skill with which you handled the Army of the Potomac, General Grant. Never in the course of the war did I face an abler opponent, nor one who put more of his men into the battle."

Grant's pale blue eyes met and held his. All at once, he realized how much the Federal commander still ached to fight. "Had it not been for your repeaters, General Lee, I maintain we should have been treating on the streets of Richmond rather than here."

"That may be so, General," Lee said. From what Andries Rhoodie had told him, it *was* so. But Ulysses Grant did not need to know that. And the South did have those repeaters.

Having Rhoodie pop up in his thoughts made Lee glance over to the Rivington men, who stood in a small group of their own on the White House lawn, a few paces from the assembled officers of the Army of Northern Virginia. Not all the men from out of time were there. Two had died in the fighting outside Washington, and another three were wounded. Confederate soldiers had carried one of them back to the surgeons, who amputated his shattered leg.

The Rivington men got their other two wounded fighters back to a physician of their own. From what Lee had heard, Confederate soldiers who saw their wounds thought they would lose limbs, too. Yet here both of them stood with their comrades, bandaged but whole. Their eyes were clear of fever, too, and fever killed more men than bullets. The Rivington men had also reclaimed the man upon whom the Confederates had operated. Fever had already seized him; the surgeons were sure he could not last long. The doctor from out of time broke the septic fever, though. That Rivington man was not here, but by all accounts he would live.

All the Confederate surgeons were still scratching their heads; a few had already begged the Rivington physician for lessons. Lee's hand went for a moment to the vial of white pills in his waistcoat pocket. In 2014, medicines did what they claimed to do.

Lee's thoughts returned to the ceremony. "Shall we proceed, sir?"

But Grant still had the recent battle on his mind. "If your gunners hadn't wrecked the Long Bridge, we would have driven you out of Washington City even after you penetrated our fortifications outside of town."

"Your men crossing in large numbers from Virginia certainly would have made our task more difficult," Lee said. "You have Brigadier General Alexander to blame for their inability to do so." He gestured toward the artillery commander of Longstreet's corps.

E. Porter Alexander was an enthusiastic-looking officer of about thirty, with sharp gray eyes and a full, rather pointed brown beard. He said, "Blame my pair of rifled Whitworth cannon, General Grant. Those two English guns were the only pieces I had with the range and accuracy to hit the bridge from my position."

"Shall we proceed, sir?" Lee asked Grant again. This time the Federal commander gave a brusque nod. Lee turned to the Confederate musicians. "Gentlemen, if you please."

The bandsmen struck up a brisk tattoo. The Confederate sentries who had patrolled the White House grounds since the Army of Northern Virginia seized Washington now formed themselves in two neat ranks. Their leader, a lieutenant in a clean, well-pressed uniform, borrowed specially for the occasion, saluted Lee.

Lee returned the courtesy, then spoke formally to Grant: "In recognition of the armistice between our countries, and in recognition of the cooperation United States forces have shown in removing themselves from the territory of the Confederate States, it is my honor to return custody of the White House, and through it of all Washington, to the U.S.A."

"I accept them back, General Lee, on behalf of the United States of America," Grant said—hardly a fancy speech, but well done in a plain sort of way. The Southern musicians fell silent. After a moment, Grant remembered to signal to his own band. They took up the same tattoo the Confederates had abandoned; Lee wondered if Grant noticed it was the same. Federal sentries in blue marched onto the White House lawn to replace the sentries in gray who had come away from the mansion.

"May our two nations long enjoy peace and amicable dealings with each other," Lee said.

"I also hope peace is maintained between us, General Lee," Grant said.

Lee fought down a touch of pique. Even now, the Federal leaders remained reluctant to acknowledge the Confederacy as a country in its own right. Back to basics, then: "We shall return to Virginia tomorrow. My thanks to your engineers for having so quickly and competently repaired the Long Bridge."

"We shan't be sorry to see the Army of Virginia go immediately"— Grant said the word as if it were spelled *immejetly*—"and that is the truth, sir. We would have had you on your way sooner, but—"

"But you were busy wrecking the fortifications on the Virginia side of the Potomac and removing your guns from them so we should have no opportunity to turn them against you," Lee finished when the commander of the Army of the Potomac ran down in the middle of his sentence. Grant nodded. Lee went on, "In your situation, I should have done the same."

Lee glanced back toward the White House, wondering if President Lincoln would come out to take part in the ceremony. But Lincoln, as he'd done since the day when Washington fell, remained inside.

Rumor said his melancholia was at such a pitch that he spoke to no one, but stayed alone all day in a darkened room. Lee knew rumor lied. Federal messengers went in and out of the White House at all hours of the day and night. That was as well. No less than the Confederacy, the United States would need a strong hand to guide them through the aftermath of war. But for now, the pain of loss was simply too much to let Lincoln show himself in the Southern-held Federal capital.

"Good day to you, General Grant." Lee held out his hand. Grant shook it. His grip was hard and firm; though small, he seemed strong. Lee nodded to the Confederate band. It began to play "Dixie." Grant turned toward the Confederate flag a color-bearer carried. He removed his black felt hat. "Thank you, sir," Lee said, glad Grant at least would publicly salute the Stainless Banner.

"If it's to be done, it should be done properly," Grant said, echoing Lincoln. "I wish it weren't being done."

The Federal band swung into "The Star-Spangled Banner." Lee immediately removed his own hat in salute to the flag that had once been his. Those Confederate officers who wore hats imitated their leader. Almost all of them had served in the old army under that flag. Many had fought in Mexico and against Indians alongside the Federal officers behind Grant. Those bonds were sundered forever now.

The music ended. Lee and Grant exchanged one last salute. The Confederate officers left the White House grounds to return to their quarters; many of them were staying at Willard's. Lee and his aides still slept in their tents, which they'd set up near the State Department building. But even Lee did not deny himself Willard's table. The oysters were monstrous good.

He turned to Walter Taylor. "We shall go home now. Let the tents be struck."

The Yankees had built a fort to cover the southern end of the Long Bridge. Lee stood on the earthen walls and watched the soldiers of the Army of Northern Virginia file past, bands playing, flags fluttering in the breeze, men singing and cheering the end of the war. Some of the soldiers tramped south to Alexandria, to take the Orange and Alexandria Railroad—or that portion of it still intact—toward Richmond. Others marched northwest along the road that paralleled the Potomac, headed for Fort Haggery across from Georgetown. Though armistice had come, Confederates and Federals still felt the need to take precautions against each other.

Lee walked over to the post to which Traveller was hitched. He let Walter Taylor untie the horse, then mounted. He rode northwest himself. His staff officers followed. They kept a careful distance—ahead, hardly more than a mile away, stood Arlington on its commanding hill. Arlington, the mansion in which he'd been married; Arlington, the great house in which his wife had lived, and he too, when duty brought him close to Washington; Arlington, from which Mary Custis Lee had fled a week before Virginia formally seceded . . . Arlington, which the Federals had captured and used as their own for the three years since.

Every minute brought Lee closer, every minute showed him more clearly how harsh the Federals had been. Earthern forts scarred the grounds he had labored so hard to restore in the years just before the war. Endless stables for Federal cavalry had gone up between the mansion and the Potomac. The horses were out of them now, but the memory of their presence lingered still. Lee wished for Hercules to cleanse the row on row of wooden sheds, but even the demigod might have found it beyond his powers.

Also deserted were the cabins and huts south of the stables. No, not quite deserted: a black face peered out at Lee from behind a wall, then vanished again. But most of the free Negroes had fled their shantytown when Washington fell for fear of being reenslaved in the aftermath of Confederate victory. Irony there, Lee thought; he had manumitted all the estate's nearly two hundred bondsmen on his father-in-law's death.

The west wind blew the stables' stench away from him. But a new miasma came from Arlington itself, a miasma compounded of sweat and filth and pus and suffering: the Federals had made his home into a hospital. Dwarfed by the heavy Doric columns of the porch, doctors in blue still hurried back and forth. Lee had exempted the place from the general

Federal evacuation of Southern soil until the last wounded man could be moved without suffering.

Arlington's lawns had been sadly neglected under the Northern occupation; they were uncut, unwatered, and unkempt. Here and there, not far from the mansion, fresh, raw upturnings of red Virginia earth further marred what had once been a smooth and lovely expanse. Under that freshly turned soil lay Federal soldiers slain in the Wilderness, at Bealeton, and, he supposed, in the fighting in and around Washington City. The Confederate repeaters had filled all Washington's proper cemeteries to overflowing. Injured men who died here stayed here.

One of the hurrying Federal doctors at last caught sight of Lee. When the man recognized him, he stopped so short he almost stumbled. Then he came down the hill toward him at a trot. He saluted as if Lee commanded his own army. "Sir, I am Henry Brown, surgeon of the 1st New Jersey." He wore captain's bars and a haggard expression. "How may I help you? May I show you through—your home?"

"Wounded men yet remain inside, sir?" Lee asked.

"Yes, General, perhaps to the number of a hundred. The rest have either recovered sufficiently to be taken elsewhere or—" Brown jerked a thumb in the direction of the new graves.

"I cannot imagine your soldiers would wish to see me, when I am the author of their pain," Lee said. "I would not inflict myself upon them."

"Many of them, I think, would be pleased if you visited." One of Brown's eyebrows quirked upward. "As you may be aware, sir, you are held in considerable respect by the Army of the Potomac." Lee shook his head. The surgeon persisted: "It truly would help restore their spirits, I believe."

"Only if you are certain, sir," Lee said, doubtful still. Brown nodded vigorously. Lee said, "Very well, then. I am relying upon your good judgment."

He swung down from Traveller. When his staff officers saw him head for the mansion, they exclaimed and dismounted, too. They rushed after him. Charles Marshall drew his sword; Venable and Taylor took out pistols instead. "You mustn't go alone into that nest of Yankees, sir," Taylor protested.

"I thank you for taking thought of my safety, gentlemen, but I doubt I am thrusting myself into a desperadoes' lair," Lee said.

"No, indeed," Henry Brown said indignantly.

Flanked by his aides and the surgeon, Lee strode between the two central columns up onto the porch of his old home. A startled Federal sentry at the door presented arms to him. He politely dipped his head to the man.

Not long ago, the fellow would have been overjoyed to kill him. Now he remained on Confederate soil only because Lee declined to evict his wounded comrades.

The sickroom smell, almost palpable outside, grew thicker still when the sentry opened the door to let Lee go through. A surgeon probing a wound looked up in surprise. "Get on with it, goddam you," his patient gasped. Then he too saw who stood in the doorway. "No. Wait."

Lee looked at the thin men who lay on cots in what had been his front room. They stared back, many of them with fever-bright eyes. His name ran in a whisper from bed to bed. A young blond soldier, his right arm gone at the shoulder, heaved himself up to a sitting position. "You come to gloat?" he demanded.

Lee almost turned on his heel to walk out of Arlington then and there. But before he could move, another Federal, this one with only half a left leg, said, "Come on, Joe, you know he ain't that way."

"I came to see brave men," Lee said quietly, "and to honor them for their bravery. The war is over now. We are countrymen no longer. But we need be enemies no longer, either. I would hope one day for us to be friends again, and hope that day comes speedily."

He walked from bed to bed, chatting briefly with each man. Joe and a couple of others turned their heads away. But as Henry Brown had predicted, most of the men seemed eager to meet him, eager to talk with him. The question he heard oftenest was "Where'd you rebs get those damned repeaters?" Several men added, as Ulysses Grant had, "Wouldn't've been for them, we'd've licked you."

"The rifles come from North Carolina," he said over and over, his usual answer, true but incomplete. As usual, the Federals found it hard to believe. As usual, they would have found the truth even harder.

One big, high-ceilinged room after another. Lee gave all his attention to the broken men on their canvas cots. They deserved it; they had fought as gallantly as any Southerner and kept up the fight as long as they could in the face of the AK-47s' overwhelming firepower. Concentrating on the soldiers also kept him from noticing how Arlington itself had suffered. But the brutal fact struck home, no matter how he tried to avoid it. He'd never been good at self-deception.

The mansion—his mansion—had till recently held far more wounded Federals than now inhabited it. Their blood and other, less noble, bodily fluids stained rugs, floors, walls. Those floors and walls were also scarred and chipped from the rough use they'd taken since 1861. He'd expected nothing better.

He'd also expected much of the old furniture to be missing. Rich goods in the house of an enemy were fair game for soldiers. But he had not expected the vandalism of what remained, the destruction for destruction's sake. Yankees had carved their initials into those bureaus and chests that were too heavy to carry off and had escaped being chopped up for firewood. Scrawls, some of them filthy, decorated the walls.

The sole relief Lee knew was that Mary was not at his side. Arlington had been her home before it was his; seeing it now would bring her only grief. The war had been cruel to her: forced from Arlington, then from White House, the family plantation on the Pamunkey—the plantation had ended up as McClellan's base for his assault on Richmond, and White House itself burned to the ground. Now the South had victory, but at what price?

Only now did he think that he could have avenged the burning of one White House with the burning of another. He shook his head, rejecting the idea. Bandits and guerrillas made war that way; civilized nations did not.

"We must have a just and lasting peace, gentlemen," he told the wounded Federals lying in the room where he and Mary had so often slept together. "We *must*."

Maybe the vehemence in his usually gentle voice touched the soldiers. One of them said, "I expect we will, General Lee, with men like you around to help make it."

Moved in spite of himself, Lee said, "God bless you, young man."

"Out this door here," Henry Brown said, pointing.

"I do know my way, doctor, I assure you," Lee replied. Brown stammered in embarrassed confusion. Lee was embarrassed, too, at his own sarcasm. "Never mind, sir. Lead on."

At last the ordeal was over. Lee and his staff officers walked out of Arlington to their horses, which were cropping the grass they could reach. The Federal surgeon said, "Thank you for your gracious kindness, General. The men will remember your visit for the rest of their lives, as shall I."

"Thank you, doctor. I hope that, by your aid and that of your colleagues, those lives are long and healthy. A good afternoon to you, sir."

Henry Brown hurried back into Arlington to resume his duties. Lee stood by Traveller for several minutes without mounting, his eyes never moving from the mansion. At last, Charles Venable asked hesitantly, "Are you all right, sir?"

Recalled to himself, Lee started slightly. His fist came down on Traveller's saddle, hard enough that the horse let out a startled snort. His eyes were still on Arlington. "Too bad," he said. "Too bad! *Oh, too bad!*"

He climbed aboard Traveller and rode away. He supposed his staff officers followed, for they were there when he needed them again. But he did not look back.

The train puffed into Manassas Junction, jerked to a noisy stop. The thick black smoke that blew back into every car smelled strange, wrong to Nate Caudell: the engine was a big, coal-burning brute, newly captured from the Yankees, not wood-fueled like the locomotives the Confederacy had been using.

"All out, boys," Captain Lewis called. "We've got more marching to do." The men of Company D rose, and part of Company E with them. After the fighting from the Wilderness to Washington City, a single passenger coach was more than enough to hold a company.

As she stepped down from the train, Mollie Bean said, "Smoothest railroading trip I ever took."

"No wonder," Caudell said, crunching down onto gravel beside her. "This stretch of the Orange and Alexandria stayed in Federal hands up till the very end of the war. They didn't have to make their trains run on patches and prayers the way we did." He stretched till something crackled in his back. His seat had been too hard and too upright. He supposed he should count himself lucky all the same. Some Confederates were coming south on freight cars.

"Don't just stand there," Captain Lewis said sharply. "Form by squads. I want you to look smart."

The company lined up behind the Castalia Invincibles banner, which now more nearly resembled a lace doily than a proper flag, so many bullets and shell fragments having pierced it in the late campaign. Its polished mahogany staff was new, however, as was the gilded eagle atop that staff. The men had clubbed together to buy them in Washington. A Minié ball had snapped the old staff in the fighting near Fort Stevens.

Two squad leaders were also new. Edwin Powell had taken a fourth wound outside Washington City. From this one, unlike the others, he would not rejoin Confederate service; it cost him his left arm. And Otis Massey went into the trenches around the Federal capital, but he never came out again. Two veteran privates, Bill Griffin and Burton Winstead, took their places. For that matter, Captain Thorp of the Chicora Guards headed the regiment; a leg wound had laid up Colonel Faribault.

Bill Smith and Marcellus Joyner, the surviving regimental musicians, got the 47th North Carolina moving. Some people cheered as they marched through Manassas Junction. Some just stood and watched, their faces expressionless. The Yankees had held the town for most of the war; by the look of them, a good many local shopkeepers hadn't let that stop them from getting fat. Almost everyone seemed better fed than the victorious soldiers of the Army of Northern Virginia.

The men tramped southwest down the line of the railroad. They'd gone less than a mile before Caudell whistled softly. "When the Yankees set out to tear up a train track, they didn't fool around, did they?" he said softly.

"Nope," Dempsey Eure agreed, surveying the line with a critical eye. "That there's what I call wreckin' with a vengeance."

Railroads were prime targets for soldiers North and South all through the war. Locomotives hauled more men and supplies faster than they could move any other way. Wrecking the enemy's tracks was one of the best ways to keep him from doing what he wanted to do. Here the Federals had torn up a ten-mile stretch of their own track to keep the Confederates from using the line against them after the battle of Bealeton.

Burning ties, uprooting rails, heating them in the flames, and then bending them—that was all part of the game. But the Yankees had gone a step farther. Somehow they'd not just bent the rails they'd taken up, but twisted them into corkscrews that lay in the tall grass and shrubs as if discarded there by giants.

When Caudell spoke that conceit aloud, Dempsey Eure said, "Wish I had me the bottle them giants was openin' with corkscrews that size. Reckon I could put walls inside an' live like it was a plantation house. There'd be room and to spare, that's certain."

"I just wonder how long it'll be till this stretch gets rebuilt," Caudell said. "But for Tredegar Iron Works, the South doesn't have any place that rolls track, and a godawful lot of it's been ruined."

Dempsey Eure worried less over the state of the Confederacy's railroads than that Caudell hadn't cared for his joke. Snapping his fingers in annoyance, he said, "Your frettin' over things bigger'n you ain't gonna change 'em none."

Since that was true, Caudell didn't answer. Neither did he stop worrying. Night was falling by the time the 47th North Carolina reached Catlett's Station, where the railroad became functional once more. The regiment camped outside the little town.

Not everything flammable had been burned. A tumbledown barn furnished wood for campfires. Caudell reflected that one day soon the army would have to give over its free and easy ways of destruction; that barn had undoubtedly belonged to a citizen of Virginia. Caudell hoped he was a Union man, but whether or no, his property was going up in flames.

Soldiers gathered round the fires, boiling coffee, toasting hardtacks, cooking up stews with salt pork and desiccated vegetables. Caudell ate till he was full, filled his tin coffee cup three times. He'd started getting used to a full belly again, after so long living on less. He suspected the vast supply dumps in and around Washington City could have fed the entire Confederate nation, not just the Army of Northern Virginia. The soldiers were still enjoying captured Yankee rations.

He stuck a twig into the flames, used its lighted end to get a cigar going. He held the flavorful smoke in his mouth a long time, savoring it; it went so well with real coffee. He tried to blow a smoke ring when he let it out, but it emerged in a ragged cloud. He lay back on his elbows with a smile. Failing usually annoyed him, but not tonight.

"Get you somethin' more to eat, Nate?" Mollie Bean said, standing. "I could use a bit more myself."

"No thanks . . . Melvin. I've had plenty. There was so much of everything up in Washington that I sometimes wonder why the North ever wanted us back. Seems they had a-plenty just by themselves."

That drew mutters of agreement from everyone who heard it. Allison High said, "Without our new rifles, reckon the Yankees might've wore us down in the end. Like Nate says, they had them a heap more of everything else."

"You always were a gloomy cuss, Allison," William Winstead said. "We'd've licked 'em no matter what kind of guns we was totin'. We's tougher'n they are."

"They were plenty tough enough, Bill," Caudell put in, and again no one said no. "And there were always an awful lot more of them than there were of us. I'm just awfully happy I had myself a repeater."

"That's so, Nate; can't argue it," Winstead said. "I'm going to see if I can't sneak mine back with me down to the farm. It'd make a better huntin' gun than the one I got, so long as I can keep it in cartridges."

"You got that straight, Bill," said Kennel Tant, another farmer. "Ain't lookin' forward to a one-shot muzzle-loader again, no indeed."

"The guns and cartridges come out of Rivington, for heaven's sake," Caudell said. "That's not a long trip for any of us. I expect we'll be able to buy more ammunition there."

"That'll take gettin' used to, havin' to buy cartridges again," Allison High said. He paused, his long, gloomy features visibly souring further. "Wonder what them Rivington men'll charge for 'em."

Silence—unhappy silence—reigned around the campfire. Prices all through the Confederacy had spiraled dizzily high. In the army, that did not matter so much: food, a little; shelter, of a sort; and clothing, sometimes, were provided. But when a man had to pay for them again . . . Caudell thought about laying down fifty or seventy-five dollars for a hat, when that was several months' pay for a teacher. The farmers who made

up the vast majority of the Castalia Invincibles were lucky. At least they
would be able to feed themselves once they got home. He wondered how
he would manage.

Someone else was thinking along with him: Dempsey Eure said, "Might
could be I'll stay in the army."

"I only hope they'll want to keep you," Caudell said. That brought on
another break in the talk. With peace at hand, the army would shrink
drastically. Still, he doubted it would shrink to the tiny force the United
States had had before the war—how could it, with such a long border to
defend against those same United States? Men without prospects, men
without families would want to stay in, and some might be able to.

"Wouldn't mind another stretch myself," Mollie Bean said. "Still and
all, wouldn't be so easy—" She let her voice trail away. Caudell understood
her hesitation. Soldiering now would be garrison duty, most of it, and how
could she hope to keep up her masquerade under such circumstances? On
the other hand, having known the true comradeship of men, how could she
go back to serving as a mere receptacle for their lusts? If she couldn't stand
that any longer, though, what could she do? All good questions, and he
had answers for none of them.

Or was that so? "You know, Melvin," he said, careful to respect her
public façade of masculinity, "the better you read and cipher, the more
choices you have with your life, the more different things you could do if
you wanted to."

"That's so," Alsie Hopkins said. "Me, I don't know my letters from next
week, so I can't do much but farm. 'Course, I never wanted to do much
but farm, neither."

Mollie looked thoughtful. "You've taught me some, Nate. I reckon I
could do with more. You still carry a primer in your knapsack?"

"Two of 'em, and a Testament, too," he answered.

"Whip 'em out," she told him. Caudell dug in his knapsack, came out
with a good Confederate primer: "If one Southern man can lick seven
Yankees, how many Yankees can three Southern men lick?" was one of
its arithmetic lessons.

"What'd she ask him to whip out?" Dempsey Eure asked. But he spoke
softly, so Mollie would not hear and be hurt. Everyone in the Castalia
Invincibles was fond of her. She walked over, sat down beside Caudell,
and bent her head to the book.

The Orange and Alexandria Railroad was broken again north of Bealeton;
the regiment had to detrain and march over the recent field of battle. The
furrows plowed by shell and solid shot still tore the ground, though sprout-

ing grass and wildflowers were beginning to repair those gashes on the green body of the earth.

"It's like a different place now," Rufus Daniel said. "A sight more peaceful without Yankees all over it, too."

So many Yankees and Confederates would never leave Bealeton again. Humped-up dirt marked shallow common graves. Some of them had been dug too shallow; from one a fleshless arm protruded, the clawlike hand at the end of it reaching toward the sky. Dempsey Eure pointed. "Look at the old soldier, beggin' for his pay!"

Caudell snorted. "And you want to stay in the army, Dempsey, so you can end up just like him?"

"We'll all end up like him sooner or later, Nate," Eure answered, unwontedly sober.

"There you are right, Sergeant," Chaplain William Lacy said. "The questions that remain are the path one takes to reach that end and one's fate thereafter."

Eure could not stay serious long. "Preacher, if it's all the same to you—I'd sooner take the railroad."

A lot of chaplains would have swelled up in righteous wrath and thundered damnation at him for his flippancy. Lacy made as if to grab the AK-47 off a nearby soldier's back and aim it at the sergeant. Laughing, Caudell said, "Go easy there, Chaplain, you're a noncombatant."

"A good thing you reminded me." But Lacy was laughing, too. Laughing came easy on a bright summer's day with the war well and truly won. No one had laughed around Bealeton back in May, no one at all.

The regiment boarded another train south of the little town. The wheezing locomotive that pulled it had served all through the war without much in the way of servicing. Nor had the rails seen enough repairs. Before the train got to Orange Court House, it went off those rails twice, dumping soldiers in wild confusion. In the second spill, one man broke an arm, another an ankle. "Hell of a thing, takin' casualties after the fightin's over," Allison High said glumly.

"Could have been worse, as rickety as this line's gotten," Caudell answered. Both men were panting. Along with everyone else, they had shoved their car back onto the tracks by main force. Caudell contrasted this stretch of the Orange and Alexandria to the formerly Federal track and engine north of Manassas Junction. He shook his head: just another sign of the abundance of Northern resources. He wondered how long the Confederacy would need to rebuild and recover after three years of hard fighting.

The train rattled past Orange Court House, then past the 47th North Carolina's winter quarters. Some of the huts had been burned; most of the others were torn down for their timber. Caudell watched the camp disappear behind him without regret. That had been the hungriest winter of his life.

At Gordonsville, the train swung onto the Virginia Central line for the trip down to Richmond. The roadbed was so rough that here and there Caudell's teeth would click together as if winter's cold had suddenly returned. "Anybody want to put some money down on how often we derail before we finally get there?" Rufus Daniel asked. The pool drew some lively action. Caudell bet on three times, and shared the pot for winning. An extra ten dollars Confederate didn't hurt, though he would sooner have had a two-dollar Yankee greenback or, better still, two dollars in silver. He hadn't heard the sweet jingle of coins in his pocket for a long time.

The train stopped for the night just past Atlee's Station, a few miles north of the Confederate capital. Captain Lewis announced, "We'll lay over for a day here, to let the whole Army of Northern Virginia gather. Before all the regiments head for their home states again, they'll hold a grand review—we'll all march through the streets and let the people cheer us."

"I like that," Allison High said. "Let 'em have a good long look at the poor skinny devils who did the fightin' for 'em. Give 'em somethin' to remember, not that they will."

Caudell waved his hand. "They may not remember us, but I expect they'll remember our campfires glowing against the sky." As far as the eye could see, fires flickered every few feet, thousands of fires. Caudell blinked, a bit bemused. Artists would paint this moment one day: the last bivouac of the Army of Northern Virginia.

"They should just be glad it's our fires they're seeing, 'stead of the Yankees'," Rufus Daniel said. Derisively, he hummed a few bars from the Northern "Battle Hymn of the Republic"—"I have seen Him in the watchfires of a hundred circling camps." Daniel spat into the campfire. "And that for John Brown's goddamned body, too."

Again, the talk ran far into the night. The officers did not try to make the men go to bed. They were going home soon, too, and instead of captains and lieutenants would soon become farmers and clerks, friends and neighbors once more. No more battles lay ahead, only a triumphal parade. The discipline of the field was fading fast.

The next morning, the army woke, not to the bugle's blare or the rattle of the snare, but to the wild bellow of steam whistles, calling the soldiers to their trains. Company by company, regiment by regiment, they filed aboard. One by one, the trains puffed off toward Richmond. The one in which 47th North Carolina rode made the trip without incident, which cost Caudell the banknote he had won the day before.

Shouting officers in impossibly clean uniforms did their best to maintain order as the troops disembarked at the wooden shed which served as the Virginia Central depot. They pointed northwest up Broad Street: "Go on, go on! No, not *you*, sir! Wait your turn, if you please. *Now* go!"

"Come on, boys," Captain Lewis yelled. "Just like we were back at old Camp Mangum—let's show these Richmond ladies how we can march." There was a stratagem nicely calculated to get the best from the Castalia Invincibles, Caudell thought—but then, Lewis had always had that knack.

Bands blared as the assembled soldiers marched up Broad Street, blasting out tunes like "The Battle Cry of Freedom," "When Johnny Comes Marching Home," and "Tramp, Tramp, Tramp! The Boys Are Marching." The sidewalks were packed with people wearing their holiday best, ladies in hoop skirts and bonnets and lace, men with stovepipe hats that interfered with the view of those behind them. Some waved small flags: the Stainless Banner, the earlier Stars and Bars, and Confederate battle flags of every description. Red, white, and blue bunting decorated every building, as did garlands of bright summer flowers.

The railroad tracks that ran down the center of Broad Street made Caudell careful about where he put his feet; the last thing he wanted was to stumble in front of such an enormous audience. A man who fell here might not live it down for the rest of his life, not with so many witnesses from his own county to keep bringing it up and reminding him about it.

Because he worried more about his marching than where he was, Caudell hardly looked up for the first several blocks of the grand review. When he did, the 47th North Carolina was tramping past the First African Baptist Church, at the northeast corner of Broad and College. The large, sprawling building had a slate roof, no spire, and a low iron fence and gate all around it.

Despite the church's name, Caudell saw no Africans in front of it. The thought made him pay more attention to the crowd. Richmond had a good-sized Negro population, most slave, a few free, but he spied hardly any colored faces. A few grinning pickaninnies gaped at the parade; that was all. The black folk of Richmond, he suspected, would sooner have come out for a parade of bluecoats through their city's streets.

Across the street from the African Baptist Church was the Old Monumental Church, a two-story building in the classic style, surmounted by a low dome and fenced with stone below and iron bars above. Streamers ran from tree to tree in front of the fence; small boys perched in the trees and cheered the passing soldiers. Caudell reached up to wave his hat to them, then jerked down his hand, feeling foolish—he still hadn't replaced that old felt he'd lost in the Wilderness.

Capitol Square was just a short block south of Broad Street, but the bulk first of the Powhatan Hotel and then of Richmond's city hall kept Caudell from seeing as much of it as he would have liked. Across the street from the hotel stood the almost equally massive Greek Revival pile of the First Baptist Church.

"Eyes—left!" Captain Lewis said. Caudell's head twisted as if on clockwork. Just past the city hall—a building as severely Hellenic as the church—was a reviewing stand. On it stood President Davis, tall and supremely erect. Beside him, in a coat much too large for his slim frame, was his Vice President, Alexander Stephens. Stephens, hardly bigger than a boy of fourteen, looked pale and unhealthy, and seemed to be holding himself upright by main force of will.

Other civilian dignitaries—congressmen, judges, Cabinet members, what have you—crowded the reviewing stand, but Caudell had eyes only for two gray suits in the midst of the black. Just below Jefferson Davis stood General Lee, his hat off in salute to the soldiers marching past. Another, older man in fancy uniform, a man with a high forehead, rather foxy features, side whiskers, and an elegant imperial of mixed brown and gray, was a couple of people away from Lee.

"That's Joe Johnston," Caudell exclaimed, pointing.

"By God, you're right," Rufus Daniel said. "Is the Army of Tennessee here, too, then?"

"Damned if I know," Caudell answered. "There was so much confusion at the train station that the Army of the Potomac might be marching along behind us, and we'd never know it." All he could see of the parade was the couple of companies ahead of the Castalia Invincibles and, twisting his neck, the company right behind.

Rufus Daniel barked out a couple of syllables of laughter. "Reckon we'd find out right quick if there was bluebellies back there." Just for a moment, his left hand slid to the sling of his AK-47. Caudell grinned and nodded. He was home from Washington City; the only Federal soldiers to have reached Richmond arrived as prisoners of war.

The 47th North Carolina passed the reviewing stand and the Broad Street Methodist Church with its immensely tall spire. On down Broad Street they marched. As Captain Lewis had asked of them, they did the memory of their Camp Mangum days proud, keeping their alignment and distance from one another with an ease that bespoke their two years of practice in the field. Their step was smooth and elastic, the swinging of their arms as steady as the beat of a pendulum.

A middle-aged woman threw a bunch of purple daisies. Caudell caught it out of the air. If he'd had a hat, he would have put it in the band;

Dempsey Eure wore bright buttercups along with his turkey feather. Since he was bareheaded, Caudell reached over his shoulder and stuck the stems into the barrel of his rifle. The woman clapped her hands.

Thus ornamented, Caudell made his way past the depot of the Richmond, Fredericksburg and Potomac Railroad and, a block farther on, the new and impressive Richmond Theater, with its pilasters reaching from the second floor almost to the top of the building. The railroad tracks continued down the middle of the street for close to another twenty blocks before they swung north toward the destinations the train line's name promised.

The crowds began to thin out by the time the tracks left Broad Street: that was at the very edge of town. Provost marshals waved the men on. "Out to Camp Lee!" they shouted, pointing north and west. Caudell marched with a fresh will: where better to end the grand review than a camp named for the South's grandest soldier?

The broad green expanse of Camp Lee lay about a mile beyond the point where Richmond's buildings stopped. Another tall reviewing stand, its boards still white and new, stood at the western edge of the lawn. A big Confederate flag on an even taller pole flew beside it. In front of it were other banners mostly of red, white, and blue: captured Federal battle flags. Caudell puffed up with pride when he saw how many there were.

"Hill's corps, Heth's division?" a provost marshal said. "Y'all go *this* way." Along with the other units in Henry Heth's division, the 47th North Carolina went *this* way. Caudell found himself off to the left of the reviewing stand, but close enough to the front that he might be able to hear at least some of what a speaker on that stand had to say.

Before any speaker spoke, though, the grounds had to fill. Turning his head this way and that, Caudell saw the whole Army of Northern Virginia arrayed to the left of the reviewing stand, Hill's corps, Ewell's, and Longstreet's, too. Then a provost marshal bellowed, "Bishop Polk's corps? Over *here*." Sure enough, the Army of Tennessee had also come to Richmond to join the review.

"Who cares?" Allison High said. "Just means we have to stand here twice as long while they get wherever they're supposed to go."

It wasn't quite twice as long, for only part of the Army of Tennessee seemed to be here after all. The rest of it, Caudell supposed, was likely to be *in* Tennessee, reclaiming land that had been under the Federal thumb for most of the war. Even so, the sun had sunk low in the northwest—and, from where Caudell stood, almost directly behind the reviewing stand— when Jefferson Davis, Robert E. Lee, and Joe Johnston rode down the aisle between the Army of Northern Virginia and the Army of Tennessee. The two armies shouted themselves hoarse, each trying to outcheer the

other. The Army of Northern Virginia outnumbered its rival and so had
the better of that contest. The President and his generals waved from
horseback, acknowledging the salute. The three men ascended the reviewing stand together.

Quiet came slowly and incompletely. The lean, hard soldiers who had
done so much, endured so much behind their tattered battle flags, were
not the sort from whom to expect perfect discipline or perfect courtesy.
Lee and Johnston understood that. They had stopped a couple of steps
below President Davis. Now they bowed, first to each other and then up to
him. His answering bow, deeper than theirs, went not to them, but straight
out to the soldiers they had led. The men raised another cheer. Their high,
shrill war cries split the air.

"We shall hear the rebel yell no more," Davis said, which brought fresh
outcries and shouts of *No!* He held up a hand. "We shall hear the rebel
yell no more, for we are not rebels, nor have we ever been. We are free
and independent Southern men, with our native Southern yell—"

The President could not go on after that for some time. Caudell yelled
at the top of his lungs but could not hear his own shout, for the cries of
the two great Confederate armies rolled through his head, loud as the noise
of the battlefield. His ears rang when the cheering finally faded away, and
fresh yips and yowls kept breaking out somewhere in the assembled hosts
every few minutes.

As a result, he heard Davis's speech not as a complete and polished
oration, but as a series of disjointed phrases, a sentence here, a paragraph
there: "We showed ourselves worthy of the inheritance bequeathed us by
the patriots of the Revolution; we emulated that heroic devotion which made
reverse to them but the crucible in which their patriotism was refined."
"—our high-spirited and gallant soldiers—" "I congratulate you on the series
of brilliant victories which, under the favor of Divine Providence, you have
won, and, as the President of the Confederate States, do heartily tender to
you the thanks of the country whose just cause you have so skillfully and
heroically served." "—driven the invader from your soil and wrung from an
unscrupulous foe the recognition of your birthright, community independence. You have given assurance to the friends of constitutional liberty of
our final triumph in the struggle against despotic usurpation."

Repeated cheers rose as long as President Davis praised the soldiers
before him. He did not content himself with that, however, but went on to
speak of the Confederacy in the abstract: "After the war of the Revolution,
the several states were each by name recognized to be independent. But
the North willfully broke the compact between the independent states and
claimed its government to be, not such a compact, but set up over and

above the states, perverting it into a machine for their control in domestic affairs. The creature was exalted above its creators, the principals made subordinate to the agent appointed by themselves. Thus our states dissolved their connections with the others, and thus our glorious Confederacy was born."

Caudell heard that part clearly, for the men stood quiet through it. It was an appeal to the intellect, not to the passions; had he been standing in that place on this occasion, he thought he would have left it out. Every word of it was true, but it was not what the soldiers needed to hear now: Davis thought too much, felt too little.

He seemed to sense that himself, and why not?—he had been a soldier before he turned to politics. He did his best to reach a strong conclusion: "No one may successfully undertake the gigantic task of conquering a free people. This truth, always so patent to us, has now been forced upon the reluctant Northern mind. Mr. Lincoln discovered that no peace was attainable unless based upon the recognition of our indefeasible rights. For that, I have to thank the indomitable valor of our troops and the unquenchable spirit of our people. God bless you all."

Again, Caudell cheered as loudly as anyone. Realizing the independence of the Confederate States was a heady moment, one he still sometimes had trouble believing had truly come. But in thanking soldiers and people, Jefferson Davis had omitted one factor that also played a major part in freeing the South: the Rivington men and their repeaters. Caudell wondered if they resented remaining unmentioned and unpraised.

The applause faded, died. The men of the armies of Northern Virginia and Tennessee stood in the deepening twilight, talking with their friends and comrades of what they'd done today. "Well, Nate, it's all over now," Mollie Bean said. "What the hell comes next?"

"I wish I knew," he answered. For himself, he had a pretty fair idea: he would go home and do his best to put his life back together the way it had been before the war came. For Mollie, though, that choice looked grimmer.

Captain Lewis answered the question for the short term: "We'll stay here at Camp Lee tonight. Rations are supposed to come tomorrow morning, and then they'll start mustering us out."

The captain, Caudell noticed, hadn't said anything about rations for tonight. That failed to surprise him; once the Army of Northern Virginia got down below Bealeton again, it had returned to the care of the creaky Confederate commissary department. He shrugged. He wouldn't go hungry, as he still had his last three or four hardtacks from Washington. They were stale by now, but he'd eaten much worse—and much less. Going back to worrying over how fresh his food was—as opposed to whether he'd have any—would be strange.

Mollie said, "When we get a fire goin', Nate, will you spend some time with me by it with them books of yours?"

"Sure I will, Melvin," he answered. "You've learned a lot since you took up your studies in earnest." He meant every word of that. He wished his students who were half Mollie's age showed half the intensity she displayed.

Her lips curled back in something that was not a smile. It pulled the skin tight against her bones, let him see for a moment how she would look when she was an old woman. She said, "I should've done more sooner. Now it's about too late."

"It's never too late," he said. She shook her head, apparently determined to be gloomy. He persisted: "You have the trick of reading now. To hold it, all you need to do is keep on reading and not let it lie fallow. It's just like"—he groped for a comparison that would make sense to her—"like stripping and cleaning your AK-47. That was hard at first, but you kept practicing till you got the knack. Now you don't even have to think about it anymore."

"Maybe," she said, anything but convinced.

"You'll see." Instead of a primer, he got out his pocket Testament that evening. Mollie protested, but he said, "Try it. See if I'm not right." He opened the little book, pointed to a place. "Start right here."

"I can't do it." But Mollie bent her head close to the tiny print of the Testament and began to read: " 'Jesus took bread, and blessed it, and brake'—why don't it say *broke*?—'it, and gave it to the . . . the disciples, and said, Take, eat; this is my body. And he took the cup, and gave thanks, and gave it to them, saying, Drink ye all of it; For this is my blood of the new testament, which is shed for many for the re . . . uh . . . remission of sins.' " Her face lit up in that special way she had; just for a moment, she outshone the campfire. "Goddam, I did it!"

"Yup," Caudell said smugly, almost as pleased as she was. "You stumbled a couple of times on the harder words, but that can happen to anybody. It doesn't matter anyhow. What matters is that you read it and you understood. You did, didn't you?"

"I surely did," she answered. "I *surely* did." Caudell had been reading since he was a little boy; he took literacy for granted. Not for the first time since he'd joined the army, he saw how much it meant to someone who came to it late.

Once started now, Mollie did not want to stop, not even when the campfire died into red embers and Caudell yawned until he thought his jaw would break. Almost everyone else was asleep by then, some men wrapped in blankets, more simply lying on the grass under the stars. That was no hardship, not on a fair, warm night. Caudell thanked heaven the war had not lasted into another winter. The men would have been without blankets then, too.

Finally, he could hold his eyes open no more. "Melvin," he said, "why don't you just keep that little Testament? That way, you'll always have something to read."

"A book of my own? A Testament of my own? To keep?" In the faint firelight, Mollie's eyes were enormous. She glanced this way and that. When she saw no one close by was paying any attention, she leaned over and gave Caudell a quick kiss. Her voice sank to a throaty whisper: "We weren't right out here in the open, Nate, I'd do better'n that."

Instead of rising to the occasion, he yawned again, even more gigantically than before. "Right about now, I think I'm too worn to do any woman any good, or myself either," he said, whispering too.

Mollie laughed. "Not one man in ten'd admit as much, no matter how true it was. Most'd sooner try, and then blame you when it turned out they couldn't." She shook her head, as if at a bad memory, then kissed him again. "Might could be we'll find us another chance before too long, Nate. I hope so. You sleep good now, you hear?"

"I will, Me—Mollie." He risked her real name. "Thanks." As he rolled himself in his blanket, he wondered if they would find another chance. They wouldn't be thrown together anymore, not with the 47th North Carolina mustering out. He would go back to teaching, and she—he didn't know what she'd do. He hoped it would be better than what she'd come from and that the letters he'd taught her would help make it so.

He wriggled to get comfortable. The grass was soft against his cheek, but his long-lost hat would have made a better pillow. He twisted again, turned his head back toward the fire. There sat Mollie Bean, stubbornly reading the Bible.

Just as troops had filled Broad Street in the grand review the day before, so now they filled Franklin Street. Then, marching out of Richmond, they had moved briskly. Now, coming back into the city, they advanced at a snail's pace.

Nate Caudell's stomach growled. The promised morning rations had never arrived at Camp Lee. Somehow that seemed fitting. The Army of Northern Virginia had always been able to fight. Staying fed was another matter altogether. *Well, no matter,* he thought. When his point on this long, slow line reached Mechanic's Hall at last, some War Department clerk would officially sever his connection with the Confederate army.

"Maybe," he said dreamily, "they'll even pay us off as they let us out."

Allison High snorted. "This here's just getting-out day, Nate, not the Judgment Day. They ain't paid us in so long, reckon they forgot they're supposed to."

"Besides, way prices are, what they owe us ain't worth worryin' over, anyhow," Dempsey Eure added.

"They owe us more than money," Caudell said.

"They won't remember that either, not longer'n a few months," High answered. Caudell wanted to contradict the cynical sergeant, but found he couldn't. The guess seemed only too likely.

Slowly, slowly they inched toward Capitol Square. Some people came out to look at them, but only a handful compared to the day before. A teamster driving an immense wagon from the back of the near wheeler of his six-mule team had to pull to a stop when the soldiers blocked his path down Fifth Street. He swore loudly at them.

Allison High let out a grim chuckle. "Some of them bastards won't remember longer'n a few minutes, let alone months."

Rufus Daniel dealt with the foul-mouthed teamster more directly. He unslung his AK-47 and pointed it at the man. "You just want to be a little more careful who you're cussin' around, don't you, friend?" he asked in a pleasant voice.

The teamster suddenly seemed to realize Daniel was far from the only man there with a rifle. He opened his mouth, closed it again. "S-s-sorry," he managed at last. When the soldiers finally cleared the way, he snapped his whip over the mules' backs, jerked the reins with unnecessary ferocity. The wagon rattled through. The Castalia Invincibles bayed laughter after it.

They crawled past Sixth Street, past Seventh. The sun climbed ever higher into the sky. Sweat poured down Caudell's face. When he wiped his forehead with his sleeve, the wool turned a darker shade of gray. "I might not shoot a wagon-driver," he said, "but I do believe I'd kill a man for a tall glass of beer."

As if in answer to that irregular prayer, four ladies came out of one of the fine houses between Seventh and Eighth. A black woman pushed the oldest lady in a wheeled chair. That lady had on her lap, and the other white women carried, trays filled with glasses of water. They all came up to the cast-iron fence in front of their house. "You must be hot and thirsty, young men," the woman in the wheeled chair said. "Come help your-selves."

Soldiers crowded against the fence in the blink of an eye. Caudell was close enough and quick enough to get a glass. He downed it in three blissful swallows. "Thank you very kindly, ma'am," he said to the woman from whose tray he'd taken it. She was not far from his own age, attractive if rather stern-featured, and wore a maroon satin dress that, like the house from which she'd come, said she was a person of consequence. Emboldened because he was sure he'd never see her again, Caudell plunged: "Do you mind if I ask whose kindness I'm thanking?"

The woman hesitated, then said, "My name is Mary Lee, First Sergeant."

Caudell's first thought was mild surprise that she'd read his chevrons. His second, when he really heard her name, was hardly a thought at all: he automatically stiffened to attention. Nor was he the only one; every man whose ears caught the name *Lee* straightened up at the mere sound of it. "Ma'am, thank you, ma'am," he stammered.

"There, now you've gone and frightened them," said the youngest Lee daughter—actually, she was hardly more than a girl.

"Oh, hush, Mildred," Mary Lee said, sounding like every elder sister in the world. She turned back to Caudell. "After you brave men have done so much for your country, helping you now is our privilege, and the least return we can make."

The woman in the wheeled chair nodded vigorously. "My husband never fails to marvel at the spirit the soldiers under his command showed all through the war, even when things looked blackest." She turned her head so she could look up at the servant behind her. "Julia, fetch the tray of cakes now, if you please."

"Yes, mist'iss," the black woman said. She walked back to the house, vanished inside.

By then, the soldiers ahead of the Castalia Invincibles had advanced several yards. The men shouted for them to move up too. Where before Caudell had cursed the line for moving too slowly, now he cursed it for moving too fast. He had to go on. Company E enjoyed the Lee ladies' cakes. Caudell tried to stay philosophical. He hadn't expected to meet Marse Robert's daughters, and did his best to be satisfied with that.

The line froze up again between Eighth and Ninth streets. Philosophy had trouble competing with an empty stomach; Caudell wished he'd gotten to eat one of those cakes. At last, though, he and his comrades snaked into Mechanic's Hall, advanced toward the desks in the foyer. Signs above those desks read A-B, C-D, E-F, G-H, and I-K. Caudell got into the appropriate line.

"Name and company?" asked the clerk behind the C-D desk.

"Nathaniel Caudell, Mr., uh—" Caudell read the man's nameplate. "—Jones."

"Caudell, Nathaniel." John Beauchamp Jones meticulously lined through his name. He reached over to a pile of paper, handed a sheet from it to Caudell. "This is your railroad pass home, to be used within five days' time. You will be required to turn in your rifle and ammunition at the station before boarding your train." He glanced at Caudell's sleeve. "First sergeant, eh?" He took a paper from another stack, wrote a number on a blank line. "Here is a warrant for two months' back pay, which will be honored at any bank in the Confederate States of America. Your nation is grateful for your service." Unlike Mary Lee, Jones sounded as if he were parroting a memorized phrase. Even before Caudell turned to go, he called out, "Next!"

Caudell looked at the sum for which his pay warrant had been issued. Forty dollars Confederate wouldn't go far. And he'd been owed four or five months' pay (he couldn't remember which), not two. Still, he supposed he was lucky to get any money (or even the promise of money) at all. He stuck the warrant in a trouser pocket, went back out onto Franklin Street.

The line of waiting men in gray still stretched northwest up the street as far as the eye could see. A couple of fellows in another uniform, the mottled green-brown of the Rivington men, sat on the steps of the building across from Mechanic's Hall and watched the thick, slowly advancing column. Their red and white banner with its spiky black symbol flew atop that building alongside the Confederate flag. As Caudell started down the stairs of Mechanic's Hall, the Rivington men solemnly shook hands.

⋆ IX ⋆

Robert E. Lee rode Traveller up Twelfth Street toward President Davis's residence: *up* in the most literal sense of the word, for the Greek Revival mansion stood on the tip of Shockoe Hill, north and east of Capitol Square.

Jefferson Davis met him in front of the gray building that, despite its color, had come to be known as the Confederate White House. Lee dismounted. Traveller swung his head down and began to crop the grass beside the walkway.

"Good morning. Good to see you, General," Davis said as the two men shook hands. The President turned his head, called, "Jim! Come and see to General Lee's horse." All at once, he looked nonplused, an unfamiliar expression for that stern countenance to bear. "That's twice I've done that this month alone, and it was January when Jim ran off, and Mrs. Davis's maid with him." He raised his voice again: "Moses!" A plump black man came out of the mansion, took competent charge of Traveller.

Lee followed Davis to the porch. The black-painted iron banister was rough under the palm of his right hand as he climbed the stairs. "Come into the parlor," the President urged, standing aside so Lee could precede him.

Another slave brought in a tray of coffee, rolls, and butter. Lee broke a roll, but sniffed at the butter before he began to spread it. He set down the knife. "I believe I shall have it plain today," he said.

Davis also sniffed at the butter dish. He made a sour face. "I'm sorry, General. Impossible to keep it fresh in this climate."

"I know; I've found that, too. It's of no consequence, I assure you." Lee ate the roll, drank a cup of coffee. By the taste, the brew had some of the real bean in it; with the armistice, commerce was beginning to revive. But he also noted the sharp flavor of roasted chicory root. Times were still far from easy. He leaned forward in his seat. "How can I help you today, Mr. President?"

Davis fiddled with the black silk cravat under his wing collar. He leaned forward too, set his half-empty coffee cup on his knee. "Despite the armistice between ourselves and the United States, General, many points of disagreement obviously remain, the most urgent of them being precisely where our northern boundary shall rest."

"Yes, that is a pressing concern," Lee said.

"Indeed." Davis smiled thinly at the understatement. "Mr. Lincoln and I have agreed to appoint commissioners to settle the matter amicably, if that proves at all possible." The smile disappeared. "I sent commissioners to Washington from Montgomery before the war began, to settle our points of difference with the Federal government. Not only did he then refuse formally to treat with them, he and Secretary of State Seward led them to believe all would be peacefully resolved, when in fact they were planning the resupply and reinforcement of Fort Sumter. This time, I expect no such games."

"I should hope not," Lee said.

"And that is why I bade you join me here today," Davis went on: "to ask if you would be kind enough to serve as one of my commissioners. Your colleagues would be Mr. Stephens and Mr. Benjamin. I want to have one military man as a member of the commission, and a man in whose judgment I may implicitly rely."

"I am honored by the trust you repose in me, Mr. President, and pleased to serve in any capacity in which you think I might be of assistance to the nation," Lee said. "Has President Lincoln also appointed commissioners?"

"He has," Davis said. His mouth tightened, and he did not seem pleased about going on.

Finally Lee had to prompt him: "Who are they?"

"Mr. Seward; Mr. Stanton, the Secretary of War." Davis stopped again. He got the last name out from between clenched teeth: "For his third commissioner, Lincoln has had the infernal gall to propose Ben Butler."

"Has he?" Lee said, dismayed. "It is an insult."

"It is indeed," Davis said. Butler, an accomplished lawyer and Democratic politician before the war, had turned into the worst sort of political general once fighting broke out. In Virginia, he had started the practice of treating escaped Southern slaves as contraband of war. As Federal proconsul of New Orleans, he had insulted the city's women and made himself so loathed that the Confederacy vowed to hang him without trial if he was captured. Sighing, the President went on, "I wish we'd caught him as he was retreating from Bermuda Hundred. Then, if we'd found enough rope to go round his fat neck, we'd have been rid of him for good. But with the war ended, Lincoln has conferred diplomatic immunity upon him, and molesting him would only rouse fresh hostilities—with the onus of guilt for them upon us."

Lee sighed, too. "Your reasoning is cogent, as always. Very well, Ben Butler it shall be. Are we to go to Washington, or will the Federal commissioners come here?"

"The latter," Davis answered. "As we were the victors, theirs is the obligation to acknowledge that victory by visiting us. The telegraph will keep them adequately connected to Mr. Lincoln. Moreover, I entertain the hope that Butler will lack the courage to reenter a nation he has done so much to defile, thereby removing from us the requirement of treating with him." By the doleful tone in his voice, he found that unlikely.

So did Lee. Though uncertain how much courage Butler possessed, he knew the man was long on effrontery. He asked, "When will the two gentlemen and Mr. Butler arrive?"

Davis smiled at his choice of words. "In three days' time. I've arranged for them to stay at the Powhatan House and for an armed guard to ensure nothing unfortunate befalls Mr. Butler: the forms must be observed, after all. Your discussions themselves will take place in the Cabinet room, which, being but one floor below my own offices, will enable me to quickly form a judgment as to any disputed points."

"Very good, Mr. President," Lee said, nodding. Davis was a man to keep a close eye on everything that was done in his administration. Lee went on, "Mr. Benjamin must be pleased to have more activity in his sphere these days than was formerly the case."

"Oh, indeed," Davis said. "Along with the European powers, the Emperor Maximilian has sent a minister from the city of Mexico, and Dom Pedro of Brazil has also extended to us his nation's recognition. As our social institutions are so like those of Brazil, I find that last recognition long overdue, but I shall take no public notice of the delay."

"Have you specific instructions for the adjustments we are to seek from the United States?" Lee asked.

"I did not object to the armistice terms you proposed to Lincoln—as a starting point for our discussions. As to how much more than that starting point the Federals prove willing to yield, well, General, on that we shall have to await events. The Rivington men, who have always been uncommonly well informed, seem to be under the impression that they may well surrender both Kentucky and Missouri, as well as specie payments to serve as an indemnity for what they worked upon our country, which, after all, bore the brunt of the recent fighting."

"Kentucky *and* Missouri? That was not the impression Mr. Lincoln created in me. Quite the opposite, in fact." Lee frowned. He wondered how much—he wondered just what—the Rivington men had told Jefferson Davis. Though dealing with his own President, he felt the need to be circumspect in finding out. He said, "The Rivington men know a great many things, Mr. President, but they do not know everything there is to know."

"I sometimes wonder." Davis fell silent. He cocked his head slightly to one side, as if studying Lee. Then he murmured four words: "Two oh one four."

Lee grinned in genuine admiration; it was all he could do to keep from clapping his hands. Had he not learned the secret of America Will Break, the numbers would have been meaningless to him. As it was . . . "So, Mr. President, they have also told you they're from a time yet to come and given proofs you find convincing?"

"They have." Jefferson Davis's features were too stern, too disciplined, to be very expressive, but a tiny widening of his eyes, an easing of the tension that pulled, as if with purse strings, at the corners of his mouth, showed his relief. "I wondered if I was the only one to whom they'd entrusted their secret."

"So did I," Lee admitted. "I am glad to learn otherwise. But did they not tell you, sir, that while they came from the future, it was a future wherein the Federals overcame us, a future they traveled back here to prevent?"

Davis nodded; his wide, thin mouth narrowed again. "Yes, and of many evils that would arise there. Thaddeus Stevens." He spoke the abolitionist's name as if it were a curse. "If nothing else, they have kept that evil from overfalling us, for which alone we should be in their debt."

"All true, Mr. President. They helped me greatly by their foreknowledge of the course Grant's thrust into the Wilderness would take. But once I and others began to act upon that foreknowledge and change what would have been, the world grew apart from what they knew. Andries Rhoodie said as much to me; they now see through a glass, darkly, even as other men. They cannot *know*, then, it seems to me, upon what terms Mr. Lincoln's commissioners will settle with us."

Davis reached up to stroke the graying tuft of hair under his chin. "I see the point you are making, General. It is well taken. Nevertheless, they remain astute men, and their considered judgments worthy of our closest attention."

"Certainly, sir." Again choosing his words carefully, Lee added, "Any group within our confederation which found itself possessed of such power as the Rivington men enjoy would be worthy of our closest attention."

"Lest they seek to dominate it, you mean?" Davis said. Lee nodded. So did the President, rather grimly. "That thought has crossed my mind, often in the small hours when I would be better off asleep. When the North remained our chiefest foe, it was a little worry. Now it is a larger one. I am glad to find that a man of your quality shares it. I gain confidence that, at need, I shall be able to pass on the burden to someone already familiar with it."

"Sir?" Lee said, not quite catching the President's drift.

Davis's eyes bored into his. "You know that under the terms of the Constitution of the Confederate States, I am limited to a single six-year term. After the 1867 elections, our nation must have at its head someone able to rise above faction and lead us all. I can think of no one more likely than you to meet that requirement and, additionally, to meet whatever challenge the Rivington men may present. I chose you as a commissioner not only for your undoubted and unmatched abilities, but also to help keep you in the public eye between now and our election day. One thing I have learned is that the people forget too soon."

"You are serious," Lee said slowly. He had not been so startled since the day when General McClellan, relying on a captured set of Confederate orders, abandoned his usual indolence and broke through the South Mountain gap to force the battle of Sharpsburg. This surprise was almost as disagreeable as the other had been. "I have never taken an interest in politics, Mr. President, nor ever cared to."

"I was trained as a soldier myself, as you know perfectly well. I would ten—a hundred—times rather have commanded troops in the field than spent my days wrangling with a recalcitrant Congress over the minutiae of legislation whose urgency in the situation in which we found ourselves should have been apparent to anyone this side of raving idiocy, a state to which I frequently thought Congress was striving to reduce me. But I remained where fate and duty placed me, and I entertain no doubt that, come the time, you will do the same."

"May that cup pass from me," Lee said.

"You know what passed with Him who first made that prayer, and how, when the hour came, He drank the cup to the dregs." The President smiled his thin, wintry smile. "We've known each other better than half our lives, since the West Point days when we were youths learning to be soldiers—and to be men. Now that we are become what once we aspired to be, how may we fail to recognize that which is required of us?"

"Give me battle, any day," Lee said.

"Battle you shall have, even if it be battle without flags or cannon. That, if nothing else, this office holds."

Lee still shook his head. Davis did not press him further. The President was not always an adroit politician; his own passionately clear view of affairs made him have trouble compromising with those who held differing opinions. But Lee knew Davis had hooked him as neatly as if he were a crappie in a gravel-bottomed stream. Just as a crappie would go for a worm, so Lee leaped high when his duty was invoked. Oh, but the hook was barbed, barbed. "I think I should sooner face the frying pan than the Presidency," he muttered.

"Of course," Davis said, taking the privilege of the last word, "for the Presidency is the fire."

With a screech of iron against iron, a deep-throated bellow from the steam whistle, and a series of jerks as cars came together as closely as their couplings would allow, the southbound train pulled to a halt. Nate Caudell wiped his face with his sleeve. With the windows shut, the passenger car was a stinking sweatbox. With them open, so much smoke poured in that all the soldiers would have taken on the look of a traveling blackface minstrel show.

A brakeman stuck his head into the compartment, shouted, "Rivington! All out for Rivington! Half an hour layover."

Mollie Bean got to her feet. "This here's where I leave."

"Good luck to you, Melvin." "Y'all take care now, you hear?" "We uns will miss you." Whether she was called Melvin or not, her disguise could not have held up much longer, not from the way the Castalia Invincibles hugged her as she walked to the front of the car.

Caudell got off at Rivington too, though he intended to board again, for he was traveling through to Rocky Mount. He told himself he just wanted to stretch his legs and to get a look at the town from which the marvelous Confederate repeaters had sprung, but somehow he was not surprised to end up walking beside Mollie.

"I'm sorry you chose to stop here," he said after a little while.

"On account of what I'm likely to be doin', you mean?" she asked. He felt himself reddening, but had to nod. Mollie sighed. "Readin' and cipherin' or no, I couldn't set on anything else that seemed promisin', if you know what I mean." She looked up at him. "Or was you maybe thinkin' of takin' me along with you?"

Caudell had thought of it, more than once. Being with Mollie as a soldier, as a companion, made him think differently about her—and in many ways more of her—than any other woman he'd known. But . . . she was still a whore. He could not make himself forget that. "Mollie, I—" he said, and could not go on.

"Never mind, Nate." She set a hand on his arm. "I shouldn't've asked you. I know how things are. I just hoped— Oh, shit*fire*." The more she sounded like a soldier, the harder the time he had remembering she was anything else. She forced animation into her voice: "Will you look at this place? Don't hardly seem like the same town I left two years ago."

Caudell looked. The train tracks ran down the middle of what passed for Rivington's main street. The train station was of familiar Southern type, with clapboard walls, an eight-foot roof overhang on either side to keep off the rain, and unloading doors for freight and passengers. But everything was freshly painted and almost preternaturally clean; two Negroes with long-handled mops went around swabbing off soot as Caudell watched. Several others picked up trash and tossed it into sheet-metal bins. He'd never seen anything like that before anywhere.

Just west of the station stood a row of warehouses that were plainly new: the pine boards from which they'd been built were a bright, unweathered straw color. Sentries wearing the motley green-brown that was the uniform of the Rivington men and carrying AK-47s walked a beat around the warehouses. They looked alert and dangerous, and measured Caudell with their eyes when he glanced their way. They did not seem much impressed, which irritated him. What sort of action had *they* been through?

"Never seen them before," Mollie said; Caudell wondered if she meant the warehouses or their arrogant guards. She pointed to the corduroyed road that ran west from the new buildings until it disappeared into the pine woods that grew almost to the edge of town. "That there's new, too. Wonder where it goes? Never knew anybody to live out that way."

"Fancy road to go nowhere," Caudell said; corduroying was expensive.

"Have to ask at the Excelsior." Mollie nodded toward a rather shabby hotel a few doors down from the station. It hadn't been repainted any time recently. Neither had the general store, the Baptist church, or the black-smith's shop nearby. They seemed reassuringly normal. But beyond them was another hotel that dwarfed the old Excelsior. It was smaller than the Powhatan in Richmond, but not much. In bold red letters above the door-way, its sign said NOTAHILTON. "What's a Notahilton?" Mollie said, her eyes wide. "That's new since I left. So are the bank and the church by it."

"Damned if I know what a Notahilton is," Caudell answered. "Shall we wander over and find out?"

"Wouldn't want you to miss your train, Nate. Fellow said half an hour."

"Just because he said it doesn't make it so. Half an hour train time is usually an hour and a half if you're not railroading." Despite his confident words, Caudell glanced back toward the train. The local Negroes certainly seemed more diligent than the ordinary run of slaves. He supposed he oughtn't to have been surprised; if the Rivington men worked niggers hard in the army, they would hardly let them slack at home.

But his eyes opened wide at the vim with which a crew of four black men hauled wood from a covered rick and tossed it into the tender, at the care with which another slave, this one hardly more than a boy, oiled the trucks under each car. In his experience, most niggers would not have bothered to lift the oil can as they went from one car to the next: they would let a stream of oil spill onto the ground, though it had cost a dollar and a half a gallon even before the war. This Negro wasted not a drop; few white mechanics would have been so fussy.

Caudell stuck his hands in his trouser pockets. One hand closed on his pay warrant. He took it out. "I know what I can do fast, though: turn this into money. Let's try your new bank instead of the Notahilton."

"I got one of them, too," Mollie said. "Let's go."

FIRST RIVINGTON BANK proclaimed the gilded sign above the entrance. Three clerks waited behind a high counter. A guard stood inside. He nodded politely to Caudell and Mollie. Caudell nodded back, also politely: the guard carried a repeater with the safety off and wore green-brown. He looked like a combat soldier.

"How can I help you gentlemen?" asked the clerk whom Caudell and Mollie approached. He had an accent like Benny Lang's. Caudell passed him the warrant. "Forty dollars? Yes, sir, with pleasure." He opened a drawer on his side of the counter, took out two big gold coins, a tiny gold dollar, two silver dimes, and a large copper cent, then passed them across the polished marble. "Here you are."

Caudell gaped at the coins. "Gold?" he said, his voice a startled croak.

"Yes, sir, of course," the clerk said patiently. "Forty dollars is 990 grains, or two ounces thirty grains. These are one ounce apiece." He picked up the big coins, let them ring sweetly against the counter. They were like no coins Caudell had seen before, with the profile of a bearded man on one side and an antelope on the other, but below the antelope were magic words: 1 OZ. GOLD, .999 FINE. The clerk went on, "Thirty grains of gold comes to $1.21, which is your balance here."

"I—never expected gold at all," Caudell said. "Just banknotes." No matter how big a lie that .999 FINE was, he had to come out ahead on this deal. He also abruptly understood why the First Rivington Bank needed a guard with an AK-47.

The clerk frowned at him. "This is Rivington, sir. We deal properly here, especially to soldiers." His eyes dared Caudell to challenge him. All at once, Caudell was convinced his gold was the real thing. He scooped it up.

"Pay me, too." Mollie passed the Rivington man her warrant.

"Twenty-six dollars, Private, makes 643-½ grains, which is . . ." The clerk thought for a moment. "A trifle more than an ounce and a third." He took out another of those one-ounce coins, another one smaller but otherwise identical—"Here is a quarter-ounce piece."—a gold dollar, three quarters, and, after another pause for thought, a one-cent piece. "That should do it."

Mollie and Caudell both shook their heads in disbelief as they left the bank. "Gold," Mollie whispered. "I got me a bit of a stake."

"Me, too," Caudell said. Rivington men might trade gold dollars for Confederate dollars one for one, but no one else did. Forty dollars in gold would take him a long way. "Let's go spend some of it, and have ourselves a drink at that Notahilton."

"That sounds right good to me," Mollie said. But just then, the steam whistle let go with a blast that rang through the town. "Oh, *god*dam." She kicked at the dirt, began to turn away.

"I guess they mean that half an hour after all," Caudell said regretfully. Then he had an inspiration: "Tell you what, Mollie: one of these days soon, you go on into that Notahilton, find out what it's like. Then you write me a letter and tell me about it. I'll write back; I promise I will. That way we can stay friends, even if we're far apart."

"Write a letter?" Mollie looked more frightened than she ever had, marching into battle. "Nate, you learned me some readin', but writin'—"

"You can do it. I know you can. In fact, I'll write you first, so you'll know where I am; I'm not sure whether I'm going to stay in Nashville or head on up to Castalia. And I expect to hear back from you, do you understand?" He did his best to sound like a first sergeant.

"I don't know, Nate. Well, maybe if you do write first, I can try and answer you back. If you do." *If you don't want to forget you ever knew me the minute that train rolls out of here*, he read in her eyes. He wondered how many lies she had heard over the years, and from how many men.

"I'll write," he promised. The train whistle wailed a second warning. Caudell scowled. "They did mean it." He hugged Mollie hard. It would not have seemed out of place to an onlooker even had she been only a fellow soldier. Through her shirt, though, her small firm breasts pressed against him. She hugged him, too. "Good luck to you," he said.

"To you, too, Nate." The whistle wailed again. Mollie pushed him away. "Go on. You don't want to miss it."

He knew she was right. He turned and trotted toward the train. He didn't look back until just before he climbed aboard. Mollie was walking, not to the Notahilton, but into the old Excelsior. He shook his head, stared down at the dirty parquet floor of the passenger car. The train jerked, began to roll. Very soon, the bulk of the station hid the hotel from sight—very soon, but not soon enough.

"Rocky Mount!" the brakeman yelled as the train wheezed to a stop. "One-hour layover. Rocky Mount!"

Caudell climbed to his feet. Allison High stood too, held out his hand. "I wish you well, Nate, and that's a fact," he said.

"Thank you, Allison, and the same to you." Caudell walked to the front of the car, shaking a few more hands as he went. Allison High sat back down; he wouldn't get off until Wilson, down in the next county.

Caudell jumped down. Leaving the train for the last time made leaving the army seem real. He looked around. Save for the sign that told what town it belonged to, the station might have been cut from the same mold as Rivington's: cut from that mold, and then left out in the rain for eighty or a hundred years. It was weather-beaten; two of the windows had empty panes; the decorative wooden latticework that edged the roof was broken in half a dozen places.

He looked north toward the mound on the far side of the falls of the Tar River, where Rocky Mount had first begun to grow. He had a clearer view than he really wanted; the year before, Federal raiders had burnt most of the cotton mills and cotton and tobacco warehouses that stood between the train station and the older part of town. Here a wall stood, there a few charred timbers. The odor of burnt tobacco still hung in the air.

Off to one side lay the fine house that belonged to Benjamin Battle, who owned the mills. Somehow, it had escaped the flames. Seeing that, Caudell clicked his tongue between his teeth. "Them as has, gits," he muttered to himself. He seldom let such uncouth Southernisms pass his lips, but nothing more refined seemed appropriate.

He walked over to the station. The stationmaster, a tall, thin, dour fellow in his sixties, peered out at him through one of the glassless panes. They had a few seconds' staring contest before the stationmaster unwillingly said, "He'p you, so'jer?"

"When's the next stage for Nashville?" Caudell asked.

Now the stationmaster smiled, exposing pink gums and a few yellowed stubs of teeth. "Just set out an hour or so ago," he said with malicious satisfaction. "Ain't gonna be another one fo' two days, might could be three."

"Damnation," Caudell said. The stationmaster's smile got wider. Caudell wanted to knock out the teeth he had left. He'd done some huge number of dozen-mile hikes in the army, and plenty worse than that, but the thought of returning to civilian life with one was less than appetizing. He turned away from the window. The stationmaster chuckled till he started to cough. Caudell hoped he'd choke.

Another train, this one coming up from the south, let its whistle squeal as it pulled into Rocky Mount. Caudell walked over to the east side of the station to have a look at who was coming in. A few small boys and old men joined him. Idlers, he thought. For the moment, he was an idler himself.

He gaped at the skeletal faces pressed against coach windows, at the rags and tatters that covered those emaciated bodies. Who were these victims of disaster, and how could his fellow spectators take the sight of them so calmly? Then an old man remarked, "Mo' Yankee prisoners headin' home," and Caudell noticed that most of the train passengers' rags were, or might once have been, blue.

He shook his head in mute, horrified sympathy. The men of the Army of Northern Virginia had gone hungry. The memory of that hunger would stay with him all his life. But these men had starved. Now he understood the difference. He also felt ashamed that his country could have let them suffer so. But with everything scarce, was it any wonder the Confederacy had seen to its own first?

Only a couple of men got off the train to stretch their legs; perhaps only a couple of men had the strength to do so. One of them spied Caudell. The man looked in better shape than most of his comrades; even his uniform was hardly more ragged than the first sergeant's. "Hello, Johnny Reb," he said with a nod and a grin. "How're they hangin'?"

"Hello," Caudell answered, rather more hesitantly. Casting about for something more to add to that, he asked, "Where'd they catch you, Yank?"

"Bealeton, just this past spring," the Federal said. He jerked a thumb back toward the train. "Otherwise I'd look more like these poor devils."

"Bealeton?" Caudell exclaimed. "I was there, in Hill's corps."

"Were you? We fought some of Hill's men. Matter of fact, I was leading the 48th Pennsylvania there, in the IX Corps. I'm Henry Pleasants. I am—

I used to be, I guess I mean—a lieutenant colonel." Pleasants tapped the silver oak leaf on his left shoulder strap; the right strap was missing. He stuck out his hand.

Caudell shook it, gave his own name. He said, "We went up against IX Corps troops, but they were niggers. They fought better than I thought they might, but we chewed 'em up pretty good."

"That would have been Ferrero's division," Pleasants said. "They were all colored troops. I was under Brigadier General Potter." He shook his head ruefully. He was somewhere not far from Caudell's age, with dark hair, very fair, pale skin, and a scraggly beard that looked new. He went on, "Worse luck for the country, you chewed up the whole Army of the Potomac pretty good, you and those damned repeaters of yours."

"*I* wouldn't say it's worse luck for the country," Caudell retorted.

"No, I don't suppose you would." Pleasants chuckled. He seemed a man well able to take care of himself under any circumstances. "And since your side won, the history books won't say that, either. But I do. It's too damn bad. So there."

Caudell laughed. He found himself liking this cheerfully defiant Northerner. "Tell you what, Yank—suppose I buy you a drink and we can argue about what's good and what's bad?"

"For a drink, Mr. First Sergeant Nate Caudell, sir, I'll argue or not, just as you please. Where shall we go?"

Caudell thought about asking the sour stationmaster, decided not to bother. "We'll find a place." His confidence was soon rewarded. Of the three or four rebuilt buildings by the station, two proved to be taverns. He waved his new friend toward the cleaner-looking one.

Pleasants glanced back toward the train, which did not seem likely to go anywhere any time soon. He ran a hand through his hair. "Damned if I see how you people ever managed to get from here to there. I've been on three different gauges of track since I set out from Andersonville, your locomotives are all fixing to die, and your tracks and beds are wearing out even though they're on flat, easy ground. Disgraceful, if you ask me."

"We manage," Caudell said shortly. He eyed the Northern man. "You sound like you know what you're talking about."

"Damn well ought to." It was amazing how well Pleasants could preen in such a shabby uniform. "I was a railroad engineer for years before I went into mining instead. But to hell with that. Are we going to stand out here gabbing all afternoon, or will you buy me that drink?"

When Caudell set his two silver dimes in front of the taverner, they bought him a quart jug. One drink turned into several. The whiskey hit Caudell hard; he'd stayed mostly sober in the army. He stared owlishly across the rickety table at Pleasants. "Why the devil do you want to go back North at all, Henry? You Yankees, you have engineers of this and engineers of that coming out of your ears. You stay down here, you could write your own ticket. Not much mining in this part of the state, but the railroads are crying for somebody who knows what he's doing."

Pleasants stared back for a little while before he answered; he was feeling his load, too. "You know, Nate, that's tempting, it truly is. But I have me a train to catch." He got up and wobbled toward the door. Caudell followed. They took a couple of steps in the direction of the station before they noticed the train was gone—possibly long gone, by the way the sun had become a sullen red ball just above the horizon. "It's an omen, that's what it is," Pleasants declared. "Here I'm meant to be." He struck a pose, staggered, and reeled into Caudell. They both laughed, then went back to the tavern.

The fellow who ran the place admitted he had rooms above the bar. For a gold dollar, Caudell got use of one of those rooms, a promise of breakfast, his two dimes back, and ten dollars in Confederate paper. He also got a thin tallow candle, hardly more than a taper, in a pewter holder to light his way up the stairs.

The room had only one bed, and that none too wide. Neither man cared. Caudell set the candle on the window while they undressed, then blew it out. Straw hissed and whispered as he and Pleasants lay down. Next thing he knew, it was morning.

He used the chamber pot, splashed water from the nightstand pitcher on his face and hands. Pleasants, who was still in bed, looked up at him accusingly. "You, sir, snore."

"Sorry." Caudell splashed himself again. The water was pleasantly cool, and took the edge off the ache behind his eyes. If Pleasants was similarly afflicted, a night spent with a bed companion who snored must have been grim. "Sorry," he repeated, more sincerely this time.

A big plate of ham and grits and corn bread and honey further eased their pain. Pleasants was whistling as he went outside. He pointed back to the train station. "This miserable excuse for a railroad is the Wilmington and Weldon, am I right?" By his tone, he knew perfectly well he was right.

Caudell started to be offended. The Wilmington and Weldon, and its continuation up to Petersburg, had been a Confederate lifeline, carrying supplies from the blockade-runners at the port up to the Army of Northern Virginia—and sending rifles, ammunition, and desiccated meals from Rivington as well. From necessity, it had received such care as the South could give. Then he remembered his one short trip down to Manassas

Junction on a line recently Northern. By Pleasants's standards, this was a miserable excuse for a railroad.

Pleasants went on, "Then I suppose I have to make my way to Wilmington to hire on. That would be—hmm—a hundred miles, maybe a hundred ten." He seemed to have consulted a map he kept in his head.

"Here." Caudell gave him the change from the night before. "This will help you get there, Henry. The South needs more men like you than it has."

Pleasants took the money. "The South needs more men like you, too, Nate," he said soberly. "I'll pay you back every cent of this, I promise." He clapped him on the shoulder.

"Don't fret over it," Caudell said, his voice gruff with embarrassment.

"I shall fret over it. By what you said, you'll be in these parts for a while, in Nashville or—what was the name of the other town?—Castalia, that was it. I expect the postmaster will be able to track you down. You'll hear from me, sir." He started for the station.

Caudell went with him. Not long after Pleasants bought his ticket, a southbound train chugged into the station. More discharged Confederate soldiers got off, but none from Caudell's company. Some stared at the warm good-bye one of their kind gave an obvious Yankee, but no one said anything about it.

Caudell decided to walk to Nashville after all. He had only the pair of one-ounce gold coins from Rivington in his pockets, and doubted a stage driver would be able to make change for his passage. *Almost easier*, he thought, *to be honestly poor.*

The walk, at his own speed instead of to the tap of a drum, was pleasant enough. Tobacco alternated with corn in the fields by the side of the road, along with forests of pine and maple. Squirrels wearing Confederate gray chattered in the branches of the trees. Caudell closed his eyes, stopped in the middle of the road. He had gone far away, done things dark and terrible, things he'd never imagined when he set out for Raleigh to be a soldier; seen the marvels—and behind the marvels—of two nations' capitals. Now he was home, and safe. The realization soaked into him, warm as the sun that beat down on his head. He never wanted to leave Nash County again.

He walked on. After another mile or so, he passed a gang of blacks weeding in a tobacco field. They did not notice him. Their heads were down, intent on the work. Hoes rose and fell, rose and fell, not quickly but at a steady pace that would finish the job soon enough to keep the overseer contented—the eternal pace of the slave.

He'd grown used to faster rhythms. He also remembered, from his dealings with the Rivington men and from what he'd seen in Rivington itself,
that slaves could be made to work to those rhythms. But why bother?
Things got done, either way. Slowing down was part of coming home, too.

And as for slowing down, he would have screamed at the Castalia Invincibles for ambling along as he was doing. He did not get to Nashville
until late afternoon. Maples and myrtles lined and shaded the road, which
took the name First Street for its short journey through the town. Though
born and raised in Castalia, Caudell had spent most of his adult life here:
the county seat and the surrounding farms boasted enough children to keep
a teacher busy.

But how small the place looked, now that he was seeing it with his
traveled eyes! A well-thrown stone would fly from one end of Nashville to
the other. Not even a hotel: what point to one, since the railroad had passed
the town by. Old Raeford Liles ran the post office as part of his general
store on the corner of First and Washington. The post office . . . Caudell
remembered a promise he had made. He walked in. A bell above the door
jingled.

The grocer looked up over the rims of his half-glasses. A grin split his
whiskery, wrinkled face. "Good to have ye back with us, Nate! Tell me
what the war was like."

Filthy, boring, hungry, terrifying past any nightmare. How to explain all
that to the eagerly waiting old man, to show him the stuff from which his
imagined glory was distilled? At his first bump against it, Caudell saw the
problem was as impossible as squaring the circle. "Another time, Mr.
Liles," he said gently. "For now, have you any writing paper?"

"Matter of fact, I do," the storekeeper answered. "Got in some a few
months back, and it don't move what you'd call quick. Even got envelopes,
if you need one." He looked over his glasses at Caudell again, this time
slyly. "You find yourself a sweetheart up in Virginny?"

"No." Caudell shook his head at the very idea, no matter how many
times he'd bedded Mollie Bean. Comrade, friend, bed partner—all that,
certainly. But sweetheart? If she'd been his sweetheart, he told himself,
he'd have brought her to Nashville. He borrowed a pencil to write her a
note that said where he was.

"Got money to pay, or we gonna have to do some kind of swap?" By
his tone, Raeford Liles expected the latter. His reading glasses magnified
his eyes. They got bigger still when Caudell took out one of his one-ounce
gold coins. He rang it on the counter, bit it, weighed it in an apothecary's
balance. "Goddam, it's real," he remarked when he was satisfied at last.

"Gonna have to dig some to change it. It'd be, hmm, close on twenty gold dollars, eh? Call it nineteen and three bits, if that's all right with you."

Caudell had already made the calculation. "Square enough, Mr. Liles."

"All right. Don't you go away. I got to retreat to the plunder room." The grocer shuffled into the back of the store, where he remained for some time. He emerged at last with a gold eagle and enough silver to make up the other nine dollars and change. "Wouldn't give this for them ass-wipes the gov'ment calls money, but you give me straight goods, you get straight goods back."

"Thanks." Caudell shoved two silver half-dimes back toward him. "I'll have a postage stamp, too, if you please." While Liles got it, he wrote Mollie Bean's name on the envelope, sealed the note inside. Lilies smiled knowingly when he saw the addressee. Caudell had been sure he would, but somehow it annoyed him less than he'd expected.

"Gentlemen." Robert E. Lee bowed as he entered the Cabinet room on the second floor of the former U.S. customhouse.

"General Lee." His fellow Southern commissioners both rose from their seats to return the compliment. Lee was struck by how odd they looked, standing side by side. Vice President Stephens was short, gaunt, gray, and sober-looking, Secretary of State Benjamin tall, portly, dark-haired, though a year older than Stephens and only four years younger than Lee, and wearing his usual bland smile, a smile that claimed he knew more about matters of state than any other three people living.

He said, "Join us, General. Our Federal counterparts, as you see, are not yet arrived." Lee took a seat, leaned back against green baize. Note paper, pen, and inkwell waited his use, but he wished he'd thought to ask that a map be brought to the Cabinet room.

A Confederate captain, commander of the armed guard assigned to the Federal peace commissioners, strode into the Cabinet room. "The honorable William H. Seward, U.S. Secretary of State," he announced. "The honorable Edwin M. Stanton, U.S. Secretary of War." Polite neutrality left his voice; scorn replaced it. "Major General Benjamin F. Butler."

The three Northern men came in. Lee, Benjamin, and Stephens rose to greet them. As they had decided beforehand, the Confederate commissioners bowed to Lincoln's emissaries, then sat down again, thus avoiding the issue of whether or not to shake hands with Ben Butler.

One of Seward's eyebrows rose slightly as he bowed in return, but he made no comment. Though a New Yorker, he looked hewn from New England granite—most especially the majestic promontory of his nose, which dominated his long, thin, clean-shaven face. Stanton was younger, shorter, stouter, with a thick, curly beard and a look of driving energy. He made Lee think more of the high-priced lawyer he had been than the Cabinet member he was now.

Ben Butler came last, the uniform of a Union major general still stretched over his short, corpulent frame. With his mustache curling down over each corner of his lips, he reminded Lee of nothing so much as a sagging walrus. His wattled jowls sagged, the sacks under his eyes—sacks as big and dark as carpetbags—sagged onto his cheeks, which also sagged themselves; the fringe of hair that wreathed his bald crown sagged greasily onto his neck. Even his eyelids sagged. But the eyes they half-concealed were sharp and dark and full of calculation. He was no soldier—he'd proved that in several fights—but he was not the buffoon he looked, either. Before the war, he'd been an even fancier lawyer than Stanton.

The Federal commissioners sat down across the mahogany table from their Southern hosts. After a couple of minutes of chitchat meant to be polite—but during which the three Confederates managed to avoid speaking directly to Butler—Seward said, "Gentlemen, shall we attempt to repair the unpleasantness that lies between our two governments?"

"Had you acknowledged from the outset that this land contained two governments, sir, all the unpleasantness, as you call it, would have been avoided," Alexander Stephens pointed out. Like his body, his voice was light and thin.

"That may be true, but it's moot now," Stanton said. "Let's deal with the situation as we have it, shall we? Otherwise useless recriminations will take up all our time and lead us nowhere. It was, if I may say so, useless recrimination on both sides which led to the breach between North and South."

"You speak sensibly, Mr. Stanton," Lee said. Stephens and Benjamin nodded. So did the other two Federals down from Washington City. He went on, "Our chief difficulty will be to keep the bitterness engendered by our Second American Revolution from poisoning further relations between the two countries which now comprise the territory formerly held by the United States of America."

Butler said, "We have recognized your Confederacy's independence, General Lee—recognized it at rifle point, I concede, but recognized it nonetheless." He paused to draw in a wheezy breath. "Further, in exchange for your withdrawal only from our capital, we have removed our forces from the entire broad reach of territory under our control this past June, withdrawing to the line you yourself proposed, sir. I question the propriety of entering into these further negotiations for any purpose whatsoever."

Judah Benjamin turned to Lee. "If I may, sir?" Lee raised one finger of his right hand as a sign for the Secretary of State to continue. Benjamin did, in the deep, rich tones of a trained orator: "Mr. Butler will surely be aware that, in a republic, soldiers have not the authority to set down final terms of peace. Nor did General Lee presume to do so. He merely arranged a halt to hostilities so that peace might afterwards be established: thus we are met here today."

"So we find out how much you rebs can jew out of us, you mean," Butler said coarsely.

A slow flush mounted to Benjamin's cheeks. Lee was, outside of his profession, a peaceful man, but he knew that, had anyone touched his own honor so, he would have continued the conversation only through seconds. But Benjamin had risen to prominence despite a lifetime of such abuse. His voice was calm as he replied, "Mr. Butler will please remember that when his half-civilized ancestors were hunting the wild boar in the forests of Saxony, mine were the princes of the earth."

"Oh, bravo, Mr. Benjamin," Stephens said softly. Edwin Stanton coughed and spluttered and looked away from Ben Butler. Even Seward's craggy features found room for a small smile.

As for Butler, his countenance changed not a jot. It was as if he'd tried to anger Benjamin not out of hatred for his race, but solely to gain an edge in these talks. Studying him, Lee concluded that was exactly why he'd done it. *No, not a buffoon,* he decided. *A dangerous man, the more so for being in complete control of himself.*

"Shall we continue?" Seward said after a moment. "Perhaps the simplest way would be to set forth the points remaining at issue between us, and then to seek to settle them one by one, not letting failure over any one deter us from reaching agreement on such others as lend themselves to it."

"A reasonable plan," Alexander Stephens said. Where Butler had been personally inflammatory, the Confederate Vice President was politically so: "There is, to begin with, the matter of Maryland—"

Edwin Stanton jerked as if stuck by a pin. His face turned red. "No, by God!" he shouted, pounding the table with his fist. "Maryland belongs to the Union, and we will fight again sooner than yield it. For one thing, with it goes Washington City."

"We *had* Washington, sir," Judah Benjamin interjected.

Stanton ignored him. "For another, despite any troubles we may have had there at the outset of the war, the people of Maryland stand foursquare behind the United States. They shall not willingly submit to your rule."

Lee suspected that was true. "Maryland, My Maryland" notwithstanding, the Army of Northern Virginia had received scant aid or comfort from that state's inhabitants in either the Sharpsburg campaign or the more recent

invasion that had led to the capture of Washington. Despite some thousands
of slaveowners, Maryland was in essence a Northern state. He said, "Let
us set Maryland aside for the time being, merely noting now that its status
has been questioned. Perhaps it may be included in some larger agreement
solving the status of all disputed border states."

"Very well, General. I did but raise the question," Stephens said. "As
Secretary Seward so wisely stated, we should proceed to settle what we
can. There are, for example, the thirty-eight northwestern counties of Virginia which have been illegally included among the United States under
the name West Virginia."

"Illegally?" Seward raised a tufted eyebrow. "How can a nation founded
on the principle of secession fail to acknowledge the applicability of the
principle when employed against it? Surely you would not be branded
hypocrites before the world?"

"Successful hypocrites seem to bear up under the opprobrium remarkably well," Benjamin said, his habitual smile perhaps a hairsbreadth
broader. "But let us continue to lay out the territories whose possession
remains at issue, or rather the states: we have not yet mentioned Kentucky
or Missouri."

Both sets of commissioners leaned forward. Both nations had strong
claims to both states, though Federal forces were currently in possession
of them. Ben Butler said, "Given the pleasant time your armies are having
farther south in the valley of the Mississippi, it will be a long time before
you see Missouri, Mr. Benjamin." Now he addressed the Confederate Secretary of State as if completely indifferent to his religion.

He managed to be unpleasant nonetheless. Not all the Negro regiments
the Federals had raised while occupying Louisiana, Mississippi, Arkansas,
and Tennessee had gone north with their white comrades upon the armistice. Some stayed to carry on the fight. *Lincoln predicted as much*, Lee
remembered; *he said it would take a war to return slavery to those parts.*

"Bedford Forrest has beaten the niggers at Sardis and Grenada," Stephens said. "He is advancing on Grand Gulf now. I expect he will manage
to hit 'em again, as people say." His laugh sounded like the wind ruffling
dry grass.

But he did not ruffle Butler. "He may well defeat them in the field,
orphaned as they be," the fat political general admitted. "What then? Did
you not recently call the territory north of the Rapidan 'Mosby's Confederacy'? You shall presently face the prospect of subduing a 'Nigger Union'
down there, and may you have the same joy of putting it down as we did
with Mosby."

Obnoxious as Butler was, Lee began to see why, aside from his political connections, Lincoln had chosen him as a peace commissioner. Born with an eye toward his own advantage, he sought advantage for his country with a like single-mindedness.

Lee said, "Thus far, we appear to have more problems than solutions for them. Shall we continue to set them forth, so they all lay on the table at once?"

"We may as well," Seward said, "though I hope we shan't provoke ourselves into a new round of fighting because our difficulties appear insuperable."

"The state of Texas borders both the Indian Territory and New Mexico Territory," Alexander Stephens said significantly.

"Good luck sending another expedition to New Mexico," Stanton replied. "We can bring men down from Colorado faster than you can get them across the West Texas desert. We showed you that two years ago."

"You are likely to be right there, sir," Lee said. Stanton, he noted, made no such claim for the Indian Territory north of Texas. The war there had not ended with the armistice, for the Indian tribes roused to battle by the Union and Confederacy could not be checked so easily by the Great White Fathers' commands. Only chaos ruled the Territory now.

"Are there any other territorial questions at issue between us?" Judah Benjamin asked.

Stanton said, "There had better not be, for we've gone from the Atlantic to the Rio Grande. Wherever we touch, we disagree."

"So it would appear." The Confederate Secretary of State's smile never wavered. "That leaves the question of the amount of indemnity owed to us for the destruction U.S. forces wreaked upon our land. I would say"— which meant, as everyone at the table knew, that Jefferson Davis would say—"two hundred million dollars seems an equitable sum."

"You may say it if you like," Seward replied. "I gather that your constitution, derived as it is from our own, guarantees freedom of speech. Collecting what you claim is another matter altogether."

"Hell will freeze over before you rebs see two hundred million dollars," Stanton agreed. "A quarter of that sum would be extravagant."

"We may not have to wait for the devil to get chilblains, nor anywhere near so long," Benjamin said silkily. "Today is September 5, after all. In two months, you Northerners will hold your Presidential election. Would Mr. Lincoln not like to have a treaty of peace to present to the people before November 8?"

The three Federal commissioners looked glumly across the table at him. Defeat had turned Northern politics even more chaotic than they had been in the then–United States during the four-cornered Presidential race of

1860. Lee's seizure of Washington had delayed the Republican convention in Baltimore, but when it finally convened, it renominated Lincoln and Hannibal Hamlin . . . whereupon the radical Republicans seceded—both Northern papers and the *Richmond Dispatch* used the word, with perhaps different flavors of irony attached to it—from the party and put forward as their candidate John C. Frémont, who as general in Missouri had tried to emancipate that state's slaves in 1861, only to see his order overruled by Lincoln. They chose Senator Andrew Johnson of Tennessee to run with him; Johnson still stubbornly refused to admit that his state no longer acknowledged the authority of Washington, D.C.

The Democrats were in no better condition. Meeting in Chicago, they had just finished choosing Governor Horatio Seymour of New York as their Presidential candidate, with Clement Vallandigham of Ohio for a running mate. And General McClellan, disappointed at failing to gain the nomination, was vowing that he, like Frémont, would mount an independent campaign. That second split gave Lincoln a ray of hope, but only a faint one.

Judah Benjamin rubbed it in: "Perhaps we should wait to see how your patron fares come November, gentlemen. A Democratic administration might well prove more reasonable." Any administration with Vallandigham in it was likely to be reasonable from a Southern point of view; he had favored accommodation with the Confederacy even when its prospects looked blackest.

But Ben Butler said, "No matter what happens in the election, I remind you that Abraham Lincoln shall remain President of the United States until March 4 proximo."

"A point well taken," Lee said. Though reluctant to agree with Butler on anything, he found a half-year's delay unconscionable. "The sooner peace comes, the better for all, North and South alike."

"A man bolder than I would be required to presume to disagree with General Lee," Alexander Stephens said. "Let us continue, then." Lee could not tell what went on behind Judah Benjamin's smiling mask. But Benjamin did not say no.

Secretary of State Seward said, "Having set forth the areas where we disagree, I think we would be hard-pressed to do much more today. In any case, I should like to telegraph a statement of your position to President Lincoln, and to receive his instructions before proceeding further. May I propose that we adjourn, to meet again on Wednesday the seventh?"

Lee found both Stephens and Benjamin looking at him. It should not have been that way; the other two commissioners outranked him by virtue of their places in the civil government. But they were looking at him. He would not show annoyance in front of the men from the United States.

"That seems satisfactory to me," he said, adding, "We shall also have to consult with our President as to our future course."

"Simple enough for you," Stanton said. "We, though, are like dogs tethered by a wire leash." His voice had a rumble in it that made it sound like a growl. Lee smiled at the conceit.

Butler said, "Better dogs tethered by a wire leash than a dog running loose from a wire leash, as Forrest did last June."

"I trust the gentlemen in this room will not permit General Butler's opinion to go beyond it," Lee said quickly. Butler was no gentleman; he'd made that plain by his every action during the war, and again by his slur aimed at Judah P. Benjamin. But Nathan Bedford Forrest, by all accounts, was no gentleman either. If he heard what Butler had called him, he would not bother with the niceties of a formal challenge. He would simply shoot Butler down . . . like a dog.

The Federal commissioners rose, bowed their way out. When they were gone, Alexander Stephens said, "If you will forgive me, General, Mr. Secretary, I shall leave the consultation in your no doubt capable hands. The President and I, while always preserving our respect for each other, have not been in agreement often enough of late for us to find it easy to speak together without friction. Good day to you both; I shall see you on Wednesday." Getting out of his chair took a struggle, but he managed, and walked out of the Cabinet room.

Benjamin and Lee walked up the flight of stairs to Jefferson Davis's office. "Ironic, is it not," the Secretary of State said, "that four years ago Benjamin Butler did everything in his power to gain Davis the Democratic nomination for the Presidency. I wonder where we should all be today had he succeeded."

"Somewhere other than here, is my guess," Lee answered, admiring the dispassionate way in which Benjamin spoke of the man who had insulted him. He also wondered if Benjamin knew the true origins of the Rivington men; his own thoughts, since the day when Andries Rhoodie set forth those origins to him, had frequently dwelt on the mutability of history. Before he could find a way to ask that would cover him if the answer was no, he and the Secretary of State reached the President's door.

Davis listened to their report, then said, "About as I expected. Maryland would cost us another war to win, and would make the United States our eternal enemy even if we took it. Likewise Virginia's departed counties." He did not mention the troubles Lee had had in what was now West Virginia early in the war. Every Confederate general there had come to grief.

"I think we will win the Indian Territory in the end, for whatever it may prove to be worth," Benjamin said.

"As to what, who can say? Kentucky was worth little when I was born there." Davis frowned. "I should like to gain possession of New Mexico, and Arizona and California with it. A railroad across the continent will surely come soon, and I would have it come on a southern route. But again, that will prove difficult. The Federals currently hold the land, and we should be hard-pressed either to conquer it or, given the present unfortunate state of the Treasury, to buy it from them even if they were willing to sell. Perhaps we shall be able to make arrangements with the Emperor Maximilian for a route from Texas to the Pacific coast of Mexico."

"Better that a transcontinental railroad should lie entire within our own territory," Benjamin said.

"Not if we have to fight to make a thousand-mile stretch of that territory our own," Lee replied. "Stanton had the right of it earlier today; our logistics are poor, and we have as yet few repeaters in the Trans-Mississippi. Besides which, no war with the United States would remain confined to the western frontier."

Jefferson Davis sighed. "I fear you are probably right, sir. And even with the repeaters, we desperately need to restore ourselves before we contemplate further combat. Very well; if we cannot talk the Federals out of New Mexico and Arizona, we shall have to go on without them. The same cannot be said of Kentucky and Missouri."

"The United States will not yield them," Lee warned. "Lincoln said as much when I was in Washington City, and his commissioners were not only firm but also vehement on the subject this afternoon."

"I shall not tamely yield them to the North, either," Davis said. "With them, we should be a match for and independent of the United States in all respects. Without them, the balance of power would tilt the other way. We should find especially valuable the manufactories which have sprung up in Louisville and elsewhere along the Ohio. I reluctantly infer from the war that we may not remain a nation made up solely of agriculturalists, lest in a future conflict the United States overwhelm us with their numbers and their industries."

"We have the Rivington men to set against their factories," Benjamin said. "But for the Rivington men, I gather we should have been overwhelmed." *He does know, then,* Lee thought.

Davis said, "The Rivington men are with us but not of us. Against the day when their purposes and ours might diverge, I would have the Confederate States capable of proving a match for and independent of them, as well as of the North."

"That seems a wise precaution," Benjamin agreed.

Davis was not really interested in the Rivington men at the moment; the talks with the United States were his principal concern. He pulled the conversation back toward those talks: "How did the Federals take the demand for two hundred million?"

"Noisily," Benjamin answered, which made the President laugh. The Secretary of State went on, "Stanton claimed a fourth of that would be—extravagant was the word he used."

"Which means the United States might pay that fourth, or more," Davis said. "Even fifty million in specie would be more backing than our paper now enjoys, and would greatly boost confidence in that paper's value, which in turn would help bring prices down to a more realistic level. Gentlemen, I rely on you to wring as large a sum from the Northern coffers as you may."

"We shall, Mr. President," Lee said.

"I have perfect faith in your abilities—and also in those of Mr. Stephens, though we are often at odds with each other," Jefferson Davis said: almost a mirror image of the words the Vice President had used to describe their relationship. Davis continued, "Now I must needs return to these other matters of state, particularly this latest note from the British minister regarding our prospective participation in the naval patrol off the African coast to interdict the slave trade. You have seen it, Mr. Benjamin?"

"Yes, sir," Benjamin said.

"I do not care for its tone. Having recognized us, the British ought to use us with the politeness they grant to any other nation. Our Constitution forbids the importation of slaves from Africa, which should suffice to satisfy them but evidently does not. In any case, we, unlike the United States, have not the naval force to permit us to comply with the Ashburton treaty, a fact of which the minister cannot be unaware, but with which he chooses to bait us." Davis's lip curled in scorn.

Judah Benjamin said, "The nations of Europe continue to abhor our policy, try as we will to convince them we cannot do otherwise. Mr. Mason has written from London that Her Majesty's government might well have been willing to extend us recognition two years ago, were it not for the continuation of slavery among us: so Lord Russell assured him, at any rate. M. Thouvenel, the French foreign minister, has expressed similar sentiments to Mr. Slidell in Paris."

Slavery, Lee thought. In the end, the outside world's view of the Confederate States of America was colored almost exclusively by its response to the South's peculiar institution. Never mind that the U.S. Constitution was a revocable compact between independent states, never mind that the

North had consistently used its numerical majority to force through Congress tariffs that worked only to ruin the South. So long as black men were bought and sold, all the high ideals of the Confederacy would be ignored.

President Davis said, "The 'free' factory worker in Manchester or Paris—yes, in Boston as well—is free only to starve. As Mr. Hammond of South Carolina put it so pungently in the chambers of the U.S. Senate a few years ago, every society rests upon a mudsill of brute labor, from which the edifice of civilization arises. We are but more open and honest about the nature of our mudsill than other nations, which gladly exploit a worker's labor but, when he can no longer provide it, cast him aside like a used sheet of foolscap."

Nothing but the truth there, Lee thought—but also nothing that would convince anyone who already opposed slavery, as did the vast majority of countries and individual men and women outside the Confederate States. Diffidently, he said, "Mr. President, now that we are no longer at war with the United States, would it not be possible to fit out a single naval vessel for duty off the African coast? The symbolic value of such a gesture would, it seems to me, far outweigh the cost it would entail."

Davis's eyes flashed. Lee read *Et tu, Brute?* in them. Then calculation replaced anger. Judah Benjamin said, "If that be feasible, Mr. President, it would go some way toward accommodating us to the usages of the leading powers."

"And how far did those powers go toward accommodating us before we assured our own independence?" Davis said, his voice bitter with remembered slight. "Not a single step, as I recall: confident in their strength, they despised us, Britain chief among them. And now they expect us to forget? Not likely, sir, by God!"

"In no way do I advise you to forget, sir," Benjamin said. "I merely concur with General Lee in suggesting that we demonstrate acquiescence where we may, against a time when we are in a position to be able to give concrete evidence of our displeasure."

Davis drummed the fingers of his right hand on his desk. "Very well, sir. Enquire of Mr. Mallory at the Navy Department as to the practicability of doing as General Lee suggested, then prepare a memorandum detailing for me his response. If the thing can be done, I shall communicate to the British our willingness to do it. There are times, I confess, when I believe our lives would have been simpler had no Negroes ever been imported to these shores. But then we should only have required some other mudsill upon which to build our society."

"Futile to pretend now that the black man is no part of our Confederacy," Lee said. "And as he is such a part, we shall have to define his place in our nation."

"One reason we fought the late war was to define the black man's place in our nation, or rather to preserve our previous definition of his place," Benjamin said. "Do you now feel that definition to be inadequate?"

"Preserving it may yet prove more expensive than we can afford," Lee said. "Thanks to the Federals, the Negroes of parts of Virginia, the Carolina coast, Tennessee, and the Mississippi valley have had a year, two, three, to accustom themselves to the idea of being free men and women. General Forrest may—General Forrest had better—defeat their armed bands in the field. But can he at the point of a bayonet restore their previous habit of servility?"

For some time, none of the three men in President Davis's office spoke. Davis scowled at Lee's words; even Benjamin's customary smile slipped. Lee himself felt rather surprised, for what he'd said took him farther than he'd consciously intended to go. But a smoldering slave insurrection, no doubt aided and abetted from the United States, was every Southern man's worst nightmare.

He glanced toward Jefferson Davis. "Tell me, sir: If, earlier in the war, you found us forced to the choice between returning to the United States with all our institutions guaranteed by law and carrying on as an independent nation at the cost of freeing our Negroes, which would you have done?"

"When the delegates of the Southern states met in Montgomery, General, we made a nation," Davis said firmly; Lee gave him credit for not hesitating. "To preserve that nation, I would at need have taken any steps required, up to and including carrying on a guerrilla war in the mountains and valleys of the interior against Federals occupying all our settled places. Any steps required, sir, any at all."

Lee nodded thoughtfully; no one who once met President Davis could doubt that, when he said a thing, he meant it. "I am relieved it did not come to that, Mr. President." He stroked his gray beard. "I fear I am too old to have taken up the bushwhacker's trade."

"As am I, but at need I should have learned it," Davis said.

"Where now?" Judah Benjamin asked. "Shall Forrest continue unchecked with fire and the sword, or will you offer the Negroes in arms against us an amnesty during which they may peacefully return to our fold?"

"As what? As free men?" Davis shook his head. "That would create more troubles than it solves, by offering our Negroes incentive to rise up against us and, once risen, to continue their insurrection in the hope of so impressing us by their spirit that we yield them what they seek. No, let them first see that fire and the sword remain our exclusive province and that they may not hope to stand against us. Once they grow convinced of that, a show of leniency is likelier to produce the results we desire."

"As you think best, Mr. President," Benjamin replied.

Jefferson Davis turned to Lee. "How say you, sir?"

"I say that the prospect of armed Negroes stubbornly resisting so able an officer as General Forrest, and the performance of the colored regiments which confronted the Army of Northern Virginia, trouble me profoundly," Lee answered. "That the one group shall be defeated, as the other was, is hardly open to doubt. But if the Negro makes a proper soldier, can he continue to make a proper slave?"

Davis tried to make light of what he'd said: "Don't tell me you are turning abolitionist, sir?"

"That is not a word to use lightly to a Southern man, Mr. President," Lee said, biting his lip. Thinking of General Cleburne's memorial that had urged the arming and emancipation of certain black men, and also of General Hill's loathing of the institution of slavery, he felt he had to add, "If I were, I should hardly be the only Confederate officer to hold such sentiments." Davis's mouth twisted, but after a few seconds he had to nod.

Judah Benjamin sighed loudly. "We left the United States not least in the hope that the Negro problem would vex us no further once we were free and independent. And yet we have it with us still, and now no one to blame for it but ourselves—and the Negro, of course." That gnomic observation effectively ended the meeting.

★ X ★

When Lee returned to the rented house on Franklin Street that evening, he was in a dark and thoughtful mood. The sight of the black serving woman, Julia, who opened the door for him, did nothing to ease his mind. "Evenin', Marse Robert," she said, "Yo' wife and daughters, they already eat—they don' expec' you be so late. Plenty o' chicken 'n' dumplings left over, though."

"Thank you, Julia." He stepped into the front hall, took off his hat, hung it on the hat rack. Then, after taking a couple of steps toward the dining room, he paused and turned back.

"Somethin' wrong, Marse Robert?" Julia asked. The candle she held highlighted the frown lines on her face. She said quickly, "Hope I ain't done nothin' to displease you."

He hastened to reassure her: "No, Julia, not at all." But he still did not go in to have supper. When he spoke again, he was as cautious as he had been while addressing President Davis: "Julia, have you ever thought you would like to be free?"

The candlelight, with its exaggerated shadows, played up her shift of expression, or rather her shift to the lack of expression slaves used to conceal themselves from their masters. "Reckon everybody—everybody colored, I mean—think about that now and again, suh." Her voice likewise yielded him nothing.

He persisted: "What would you do if you were free?"

"Don't rightly know what I could do, Marse Robert. Don't have much book learnin'. Much? Don't have none." Julia kept studying Lee from behind the cautious mask her face wore. She must have decided he meant what he said, for after a moment she went on, "Wouldn't mind findin' out what free was like, I tell you that, suh."

"I thought as much." It was the answer Lee would have given, were he in Julia's shoes; it was, he thought, the answer anyone with spirit, black or white, man or woman, would give. "If you were free, would you be willing to stay on here with my family and work for wages?"

"That's what I got to do to be free, that's what I do," Julia answered at once.

Lee saw he had made a mistake. "No, no, Julia, you misunderstand. I aim to free you, and will whether you say yes or no. But as you have no other situation, I wanted you to know you could continue to find employment in this house."

"God bless you, Marse Robert." The candle flame reflected from the tears in Julia's eyes. Then, as the reality of what he'd promised sank in, she began to think aloud: "If I be free soon, maybe I learn to read. Who *knows* what I do, if I be free?"

Learning their letters was against the law for blacks in Virginia, as it was in most of the Confederate States. Lee forbore to mention that. For one thing, the law was observed less rigidly for free Negroes than for slaves. For another, Julia's desire to learn bespoke the sort of drive she would need as a freedwoman. What he did say was a commonplace: "I gather my ladies are still in the dining room?"

"Yes, suh, Marse Robert. I go tell them you here." Julia turned and fairly raced toward the back part of the house, her shoes clattering against the oak floorboards. Lee followed more slowly.

His wife and daughters were chatting around the dining room table when he came in. Julia had already hurried in and then out past him once more. Mischief in her voice, his youngest daughter Mildred said, "Good heavens, Father, what did you tell her: that you'd sell her South if she didn't move quicker?" His daughter Mary and his wife smiled. Agnes did not, but then Agnes seldom smiled.

Normally, Lee would also have smiled; he had trouble imagining the enormity Julia would have to commit to make him even imagine selling her South. Good servants who worked for good masters—which, without false modesty, he knew himself to be—did not have to worry about such things. But that the joke could be made at all spoke volumes about the institution of slavery.

Now he answered seriously, "Precious life, I told her I intended to free her."

Like her daughters, Mary Custis Lee stared at him. "Did you?" she said. Her voice was sharp, and with some reason. The money to buy Julia had been hers, income from the estates currently in such disarray. Before the war, that income had been vastly more than his own. Moreover, in her invalid state she required near constant care.

"Why on earth did you decide to do that, Father?" Mary Lee echoed her mother.

"What shall I do without her?" Mary Custis Lee added.

Lee chose to respond to his daughter's question first: "Because, my dear, I have seen that, try as we may, we cannot escape the conclusion that the day for slavery is past. We fought our great war for independence just completed so that our states could govern themselves as they thought best. And we have won it, and so brook no interference in our institutions from the North or Washington City. Well enough. But the world beyond our borders has not ceased to be, nor to despise us, despite that independence." He mentioned Lord Russell's remark to James Mason.

His eldest daughter bristled. "If Washington has no business meddling in our affairs, still less does England."

"That may be so. Yet when virtually all the world abhors one's practices, one has to wonder at the propriety of those practices. And the bravery the Northern colored troops displayed made me wonder at the justice of continuing to hold their race in bondage. But the final straw for me is the struggle the former Yankee Negro regiments of Louisiana and the other states of the Mississippi valley continue to wage against General Forrest."

"But Father, so many people think Forrest a hero for putting those black men down," Agnes said.

"Let them think so who will. But the Negroes still under arms in Mississippi and Louisiana must surely know their cause is doomed: General Forrest is a most able commander and has behind him the full weight of the Confederacy. Yet the Negroes continue to fight—as would I, in their place. To show such spirit, they must be men like any others, from which it can only follow that enslaving whites were as proper as doing so to blacks."

"No one would uphold that proposition," Mary Lee said.

"This is all very pretty and all very logical, Robert, but who shall care for me if Julia is set at liberty?" Mary Custis Lee said.

"I expect she will, but for wages," he answered. "Perry has served me so for years."

His wife sniffed, but said, "If your mind is quite made up—"

"It is," he said firmly. "I do not presume to judge others, but I find I cannot in good conscience continue to own human beings who, I am become convinced, are inferior to me by circumstance alone, rather than by birth."

"Very well." Mary Custis Lee surprised him with a smile. "My father would have approved."

"I suppose he would." Lee reflected that his father-in-law had enjoyed the services of a couple of hundred slaves while alive and emancipated them only in his will, when he could make use of them no more. It was magnanimity of a sort, but to Lee's mind not enough.

He also thought of Jefferson Davis's remark that he would have pursued Southern independence even if that meant going into the hills and fighting for years, and of his own reply that he was too old to make a bushwhacker. Plenty of desperate ex-Union Negroes were of a proper age to learn that trade, and plenty more blacks who might not themselves fight would quietly support those who did. Before the war, slave revolts in the South had been few and small and soon stamped out. Those days were gone. The Confederate States had won one civil war. No matter how fiercely Forrest fought, another was just beginning.

He laughed at himself. He had never imagined taking up arms against the United States of America. And now, having done so, he saw no better way to serve the new country he had helped create than to become an abolitionist.

Talks with the Federal commissioners dragged on. The smaller issues resolved themselves: in exchange for the Confederates' abandoning claims to New Mexico, the United States yielded the Indian Territory. Judah Benjamin had predicted as much after the first meeting. Lee wondered why what seemed so obvious took so long to decide.

"You will never make a diplomat, General Lee, despite your many accomplishments and virtues," Benjamin said; his constant smile widened slightly to show real amusement. "Had the United States quickly conceded the Indian Territory to us, we should have been emboldened to press harder on the issue of Missouri. By the same token, had we given up New Mexico without a struggle, the Federals might well have perceived that as weakness, and so been less inclined to see reason over the Indian Territory."

Put that way, the negotiations reminded Lee of a campaign of attrition, the sort Grant seemed to have had in mind against him in the spring of 1864. Attrition was not his style. Whether he faced an enemy in the field or a difficulty in his life, he always aimed to overcome it with one bold stroke.

Though it had failed Grant, attrition worked, at least to a point, for Seward, Stanton, and Butler. By making it clear that the United States were willing to fight over Maryland and West Virginia, they convinced Jefferson Davis to yield them. Lee concurred in that decision; having fought in both states, he'd seen that their people favored the Union.

Kentucky and Missouri were something else again. The United States were willing to fight to keep them, but the Confederacy was equally willing to fight to acquire them. Tempers on both sides ran high. Lee looked for the bold stroke that might cut through the knotty problem. At length, the idea for such a stroke came to him. He set it before President Davis. Davis generally preferred directness himself and, after some initial hesitation, gave his assent. Then Lee waited for the proper moment to let it loose.

That moment came in late September, after a series of fiery speeches by Frémont seemed to put Lincoln on the defensive, even among Republicans. All three of the Federal commissioners came to a negotiating session looking worn. Butler, who had begun the war as a Democrat, these days had one foot and a couple of toes of the other in Frémont's camp. Stanton, a Lincoln loyalist, was gloomy to find so hard a road ahead of his patron. And Seward, who had first sought the Presidency himself and then tried to dominate Lincoln while Secretary of State, had the appearance of a man who wondered yet again how fate could have allowed that gangling bumpkin to overcome him.

Seeing the men across the table from him in the Cabinet room thus distracted, Lee said, "My friends, I think I have found a way to simply settle our difficulties concerning the disputed states of Kentucky and Missouri. Surely you will agree that our two great republics ought to be able to resolve our problems in a spirit that accords with the principles we both espouse."

"Which principles are those?" Stanton asked. "The ones which proclaim that one man ought to be able to buy and sell another? *We* do not espouse such principles, General Lee."

Lee did not show the frown he felt. That he privately agreed with Stanton only made more difficult the public position he was required to maintain. He answered, "The principle that government is based upon the consent of the governed."

"And so?" Ben Butler's voice was filled with a lawyer's professional scorn. "I presume the Negroes of your dominions have consented to your domination of them?"

"They have the same franchise among us as in most of the Northern states," Judah P. Benjamin replied. He gave Lee a courteous nod. "Pray continue, sir."

"Thank you, Mr. Secretary." Lee looked across the table at the commissioners from the United States. "Gentlemen, here is what I propose: Let the citizens of the two states in question decide the matter for themselves in a fair vote, not to be influenced by force or the presence of troops of either the United or Confederate states. President Davis will pledge the Confederate States to abide by the result of such an election. It is his sincere hope that President Lincoln will also concur with what is, after all, the most equitable solution possible to the dilemma confronting us."

"Equitable?" William H. Seward accomplished more with a slightly raised eyebrow than Butler had with ostentatious scorn. "How do you presume to speak of equity, sir, when you call for the withdrawal only of Federal forces and of none of your own?"

"How do you presume to speak of equity when, by holding down these states through force of arms, you prevent them from exercising their sovereign rights?" Lee returned.

Ben Butler sniffed, "Just another of the worthless schemes you Confederates keep inventing and advancing."

"No, sir," Judah Benjamin said. "My predecessor as Secretary of State, Mr. R. M. T. Hunter, set forth a similar proposal in letters of February 1862 to Messrs. Mason and Slidell in London and Paris respectively. We have been willing—indeed, eager—to put our faith in the will of the people most directly affected by the choice involved. The United States continually proclaim their adherence to democracy. Have they less affection for it when it might bring a result contrary to their desires?"

"Certainly we do," Stanton said. "So do you, or you'd not have bolted the Union when the last election went against you."

That shot had some truth to it. Vice President Stephens showed as much by ignoring it in his reply: "Gentlemen of the United States, in simple justice's name, we request that you transmit to President Lincoln the proposal General Lee advanced, and at your earliest convenience return to us his response."

"As you are aware, he has empowered us to act as his plenipotentiaries in this matter," Seward said.

Lee sensed that the Federal Secretary of State was unwilling to do as Stephens had asked. Throughout the war, Lincoln had, despite his determination to return the South to the United States, occasionally shown flexibility as to how that return might come about. He had also continued to believe, against all evidence, that considerable pro-Union sentiment remained in the seceded states. If he also exaggerated the two border states' affection for rule from Washington, Lee's was a notion to which he might be inclined to listen. Lee had counted on that when he put it forward.

Prodding, he said, "Surely you gentlemen cannot fear your President would overrule you?"

That earned him a glare from Stanton, a basilisklike gaze from Butler, and Seward's usual imperturbability. Seward said, "Since this appears to be a condition upon which you insist, we shall do as you require." He got to his feet. "Accordingly, there seems little point in continuing today's discussions. Would you be so kind as to prepare your formulation in writing, in order to eliminate the risk of misapprehension on our part of what you have in mind?"

Lee drew from an inside coat pocket a folded sheet of paper which he presented to Seward. "I have taken the liberty of doing so in advance of your gracious acceptance."

"Er—yes. Of course." Seeming faintly nonplused, Seward skimmed the paper to make sure it was what Lee had said it was, then nodded and leaned sideways to store it in the carpetbag that sat to the left of his chair.

As he did so, Alexander Stephens put in, "General Lee is too courteous a gentleman to ask you to consider whether you find this proposition of his preferable to the prospect of renewed conflict against repeating rifles, but I would have you remember that possibility and the, from your perspective, unfortunate results of the last such series of meetings."

"Those results are seldom far from our thoughts, I assure you," Seward said icily. Stanton ground his teeth. The sound was quite audible. Lee had heard of such a thing, but never before actually heard the thing itself: yet another surprise, if but a tiny one, in a year filled with marvels.

But Ben Butler said, "If you Southerners were so hot to return to the fray, Mr. Vice President, you would have dispensed with these polite conversations and fired your terms at us from the barrel of a gun. As you choose to do otherwise, I will thank you to follow the example of your courteous general and refrain from such threats henceforward."

Butler was so distinctly homely as to be a caricaturist's dream; so, in an utterly different way, was his master, Abraham Lincoln. Lee found him thoroughly repulsive. To say he was corrupt weakened the word, though somehow he'd kept anyone from proving he had sticky palms. He made a laughable soldier. But in a battle of wits, he was far from unarmed. And he visibly heartened his fellow commissioners as they took their leave of Benjamin, Stephens, and Lee.

"Now we wait," Lee said. Having waited for the precise instant so often in the field, having waited for the right day on which to present his pro-

244 ★ THE GUNS OF THE SOUTH

posal, he remained prepared once more to quench his iron will in the tempering bath of patience.

Judah Benjamin said, "With the Federals all factions, Lincoln may find himself too distracted to give us a sensible reply any time soon. Last I heard, McClellan was calling for an invasion of the Canadas, presumably to acquire for the United States territory to recompense them for that which they lost on our achieving independence."

"The invasion might well succeed, too, with any general save McClellan at its head," Stephens said.

The three Confederate commissioners laughed, none too kindly. Benjamin said, "Better than any soldier since Quintus Fabius Maximus, he deserves the title Cunctator, but Fabius' delaying tactics served his own state, while those of McClellan aided only us."

Lee was by nature charitable. Here his charity stretched no farther than silence, for Benjamin spoke manifest truth. A vigorously conducted campaign up the Peninsula might well have resulted in the fall of Richmond two years before the Rivington men arrived with their AK-47s. For that matter, a vigorously conducted Union assault at Sharpsburg later in 1862 almost surely would have destoyed the Army of Northern Virginia. But in matters military, the words *vigorous* and *McClellan* did not belong in the same sentence.

"Curious how he's still a hero to so many Northern soldiers," Stephens remarked.

"Well, why not?" Benjamin said. "Their war failed to give them a true hero. We were more fortunate." He was looking straight at Lee.

For his part, Lee looked down at the elaborate floral pattern of the carpet. He had always known respect from within the military community and in the late war had done his best to continue to earn that respect. He had never anticipated the wider admiration that had come his way, admiration which led Jefferson Davis to urge him to run for President, admiration which made a worldly sophisticate like Judah P. Benjamin call him hero without apparent irony. He still did not know what to make of such admiration. The mention of Fabius reminded him of the practice, during a Roman triumph, of having a man stand beside the officer being honored and whisper, "Remember, you are mortal." The Romans had been a solidly practical people.

He needed no outside reminders of his own mortality. The pain in his chest that sometimes came when he exerted himself too strenuously told him all he needed to know. The white pills from the Rivington men helped keep him in the field, but against the years everyone campaigned in vain.

He rose, bade his colleagues farewell, went downstairs and out into the street. To his relief, the constant steambath heat of summer was beginning to ease. A colored attendant, seeing him emerge, dashed away to the nearby stables and soon returned with Traveller. "Here you is, Marse Robert."

"Thank you, Lysander," Lee said. The slave grinned widely at having his name recalled; he, of course, had no way to know such recall was but one of the thousand small tricks by which an officer won his men to him. It was, Lee had heard, also a politician's trick. The thought vaguely disturbed him. He did not care to become a politician. Yet if that became his duty . . . Swinging up onto Traveller swept away such profitless musing. He rode west, toward the rented house in which he was living.

Traffic remained busy, but without its wartime urgency. Fewer soldiers, fewer rumbling supply wagons crowded the streets. Ladies had room to stroll without putting their hoop skirts in danger of being crumpled. Gentlemen had the leisure to stop and admire the ladies and to tip hats to them as they passed. Lee smiled, both at the byplay he watched and at the way of life a Confederate victory had preserved. Something precious would have gone out of the world had the South lost.

Angry shouts, the pound of running feet, a yell with words to it: "Get the filthy nigger!" A shabbily dressed black man dashed across Franklin from Eighth Street, almost in front of Traveller's nose. The horse snorted and reared. Lee had hardly begun to fight him back under control when at least a dozen whites, many waving clubs, came pounding after the Negro.

Nothing will anger a professional soldier faster than the sight of a mob, raw force turned loose on the world without discipline. "Halt!" Lee shouted, tossing his head in a perfect fury of rage. Two of the white men at the head of the baying pack wore pieces of Confederate uniform. The abrupt command and the tone in which it was given brought them up short. Others tumbled into them. But at the very front, a fellow in the overalls and leather apron of a blacksmith brought down the Negro with a flying tackle. Even he, though, did not hit the black man with the hammer he carried in his right hand.

"What–in–God's–name–is–going–on–here?" Lee demanded, biting off the words one by one. He glared at the men before him. Now they looked sheepish rather than vicious. Several, like the one who had tackled the Negro, were smiths; others, by their clothes, day laborers who hadn't labored many days lately. But one was a policeman and another, Lee saw with a touch of disquiet, wore the mottled tunic and trousers of the Rivington men. That fellow set hands on hips and insolently stared back at Lee.

Ignoring him for the moment, Lee asked the policeman, "You, sir, were you seeking to quell this unseemly disturbance?"

From the ground, the Negro answered before the policeman could: "He weren't doin' no such thing, suh! He leadin' 'em on."

"You deserve everything you'll get, you—" The white man sitting on the black raised his hammer, as if to strike. Then he met Lee's eyes. The sword Lee carried was a purely ceremonial side arm, part of his dress uniform; one blow from that hammer would have snapped it in two. In any case, the sword stayed in its sheath. But Lee's presence was a stronger weapon than any sword. The smith lowered the hammer as carefully as if it were a fused shell.

"Perhaps you will do me the honor of explaining why you have chosen to run wild through the streets of Richmond," Lee said with ironic courtesy.

The smith flushed, but answered readily enough: "To teach this here nigger a lesson, that's why. He works so cheap, he takes my customers away. How's a white man supposed to make a living if he has to work alongside niggers?"

Two or three other blacksmiths growled agreement. So did the day laborers, the policeman, and several members of the crowd that was rapidly gathering to watch the proceedings. The only black face to be seen was that of the fellow the smith was sitting on. "Let him up," Lee said impatiently. When the smith did, Lee asked the Negro, "What have you to say for yourself?"

"I'se a free man, suh. I done bought myself out jus' befo' the war start, spend all my time since down to the Tredegar Iron Works, doin' what smifs do. Since the shootin' stop, things get right slow there, an' they don' give me 'nough work to keep busy, so I set up fo' my own self. Jus' tryin' to git along, suh, that's all I do."

"Are you willing to work for less than these men here?" Lee asked.

The Negro smith shrugged. "Don' need much—jus' tryin' to git along, like I said." He showed a flash of spirit: " 'Sides, if'n I charge as much as they do, they call me an uppity nigger, say I's actin' like I's as good as they is. That's how things be, suh."

Lee knew that was how things were. He turned to the smiths who had tackled the Negro. "Is what this man says true? He's done you no harm, he aided his country—and yours—all through the war, and you seek to take the law into your own hands against him?"

"Reckon what he says is true enough." The white man looked down at his feet so he would not have to face Lee's wrath. But he stubbornly went on, "Who says he's done me no harm? He's stealing my livelihood, goddam it. I got my own family to feed. Am I supposed to drop down to nigger wages myself to stay even with this black bastard? Don't seem right nor fair to me."

"When has General Lee ever had to worry about what's fair or right for ordinary whites?" The Rivington man's half-British, half-harsh accent was as out of place on the Richmond street as his mottled clothes, but he seemed to speak for many in the crowd: "He has more houses, has more land, than he knows what to do with. Not for the likes of him to worry about a kaff—nigger—taking his work away. So where does he get the right to stand up on the mountaintop and tell us we can do nothing about it?"

"That's the truth, by God," someone said. "So it is," somebody else echoed.

What Lee had were more debts and obligations than he knew what to do with. Nobody here would care to listen to that, though, or believe it if he heard it. The Rivington man knew how to swing folk his way, and went about it ruthlessly—no one native to Richmond would have attacked Lee head-on as he did.

Lee knew he had to reply at once, or lose the authority his position brought him: this would be closer to the rough and tumble of the battlefield than to his polite if sometimes savage exchanges with the Federal commissioners. He said, "Poor men have more to fear when the laws go down than the rich, for they are less able to protect themselves without law. You had all better shiver when you see a policeman rioting rather than putting down a riot, for he may well come after you next, or stand aside when someone else does."

The policeman, a great many eyes suddenly upon him, did his best to sink into the dirt of Franklin Street. Lee continued, "No one, not even the men pursuing him, claims this Negro broke any law or, in fact, did anything wrong. Will they come after *you* next, sir, if they don't care for your prices?" He startled a man in the crowd by pointing at him. "Or you? Or you?" He pointed twice more, got no reply.

The Rivington man started to say something. Lee interrupted him, glaring at the men in Confederate gray: "Your comrades gave their lives, and gave them gladly, so we could live under laws of our own choosing. Do you choose now to live without law altogether? I should sooner have surrendered to Abraham Lincoln and lived under Washington City's rule than subject myself to no rule at all. You make me ashamed to call myself a Virginian and a Southerner."

His troops had always feared his displeasure more than any Minié ball. One of the former soldiers choked out, "Sorry, Marse Robert." Another simply turned on his heel and walked away, which seemed to be a signal for the whole crowd to start dispersing.

The Rivington man, still uncowed, said, "I never thought anyone who called himself a Virginian and a Southerner would take the black man's part over the white's. People will hear of this, General Lee."

I shall make sure people hear of this, was what he meant. "Say what you will, sir," Lee answered. "Being without ambition for any post other than the one I presently hold"—which was true and more than true, no matter what Jefferson Davis had in mind for him—"I fear no lies, while the truth will only do me credit."

The Rivington man stamped away without replying. The soles of his heavy boots left chevroned patterns in the street. Lee had noticed that before. Absently, he wondered how such gripping soles were made; they were plainly superior to smooth leather or wood. *One more trick from the future,* he thought. He rather wished the future had been content to take care of itself and leave his own time alone. Wishing did no good. He flicked Traveller's reins and rode on.

Custis Lee tossed a copy of the *Richmond Sentinel* on his father's desk. "What's all this in aid of?" he asked, pointing to a story most of the way down the right-hand column of the front page. "By the way it reads, you rode with John Brown instead of bringing him to justice."

"Let me see, my dear boy." Lee bent close to read the small, sometimes smeared type. When he was finished, he broke out laughing. "From this alone, any man would think me worse than a radical Republican, wouldn't he? But since people know perfectly well that I am no such creature, I trust they shall not judge me by this alone."

"I would hope not," Custis agreed. "But what gave rise to such a—curiosity, shall I say?—in the first place? Something must have, I suppose, besides a reporter's malice."

"Malice there was, but not a reporter's." Lee briefly explained the germ of truth behind the *Sentinel* story.

"I didn't *think* you'd say Lincoln would have made the Southern Confederacy a better president than Jeff Davis," his son remarked. "It doesn't sound like you, somehow." He laughed too, at the size of his own understatement.

"It doesn't much, does it? The Rivington man who gave the *Sentinel* the story laid things on far too thick for anyone of sense to take the piece seriously." But Lee's laughter soon dried up. "Had the Rivington man not been present, the affair would have gone unreported, as indeed it should have. For that matter, I wonder if he did not instigate the whole affair. He tried his utmost to incite the crowd against the free nigger, and against me for taking the poor wretch's part. It is not the first disagreement on the subject I have had with the men of America Will Break."

Custis Lee also grew serious. His features, fleshier than his father's, were well suited to sober consideration. He said, "They are dangerous enemies to have. I've watched them ever more closely since you set me the task this past February. For one thing, they spend gold freely, and in a nation as strapped for specie as is ours, that alone grants them influence disproportionate to their numbers."

"So I have heard," Lee said. " 'For one thing' implies 'for another.' What else have you heard?"

"As will not surprise you, they line up behind those hardest on the Negro question." Custis shook his head. "Try as we will to escape it, it remains with us, doesn't it, Father? A bill was recently introduced in the House of Representatives calling for the reenslavement or expulsion of all free Negroes in the Confederate States. Congressman Oldham of Texas, who wrote the bill, bought a fine house hereabouts—not far from yours, as a matter of fact—and paid gold for it. And Senator Walker of Alabama, who was thought certain to oppose the legislation, has been unwontedly quiet about it. I had to undertake some little digging to find out why, but I managed."

"Enlighten me, please," Lee said when Custis fell silent.

"It seems," Custis said, raising one eyebrow, "the Rivington men somehow obtained a daguerreotype of Senator Walker enjoying the, ah, intimate embraces of a woman not his wife. Their threat to reproduce the photograph and spread it broadside through Montgomery was plenty to gain his silence."

"Not what one would call a gentlemanly tactic," Lee observed.

"No, but damned effective." Custis chuckled. "It must have been a damned languorous embrace, too, for them to have held still long enough for the camera to capture them. And how could they have failed to notice that camera and the man behind it?"

"The Rivington men brought us something new in the line of rifles. Why should they not also have cameras better than ours?"

Lee spoke casually, but the words seemed to hang in the air after they left his lips. The repeaters, the desiccated foods, the medicines the Rivington men brought from 2014 were marvels here and now, for he and his fellows saw them apart from their proper context. But in 2014, they had to be ordinary. Of what else might that be true? *Of almost anything*, was the only answer that came to Lee. The thought worried him. If the Rivington men could pull wonders out from under their hats whenever they needed one, how could anybody keep them from doing whatever they wanted? He came up with no good answer to the question.

"You see, Father, they can be dangerous," Custis persisted.

"I never doubted it, my dear boy." Lee wondered if some man in mottled clothing had followed him around with an impossibly small camera. He'd always had an eye for pretty women, and with his wife both ill and no longer young, he might well have been thought likely to commit an indiscretion. But duty ruled his personal life as sternly as his public one. His hypothetical photographic spy would have gone home disappointed.

"What now, Father?" Custis asked.

"Pass on what you've learned about Congressman Oldham and Senator Walker to the President," Lee said. "That is something he needs to know, and you may not have uncovered all of it."

"I shall inform him directly," Custis promised. He reached across the desk, set a hand on his father's arm. A little surprised and more than a little touched, the elder Lee looked into his son's eyes. Concern in his voice, Custis said, "You take thought for yourself as well. The Rivington men are unkind to those who choose to stand against them. They may choose means more direct than this." He tapped the copy of the *Richmond Sentinel*.

"In any case, they are but a handful among us, and not worth my worry," Lee said. "If I allow them to turn me aside from my own purpose, they shall have beaten me."

Custis nodded, reassured. Lee, however, found himself less easy of mind, not more, after his bold words. The Rivington men might be a handful, but they were a handful with powers the more dangerous for being so largely unknown. He would not walk soft on their account, but he would not close his eyes to them, either.

"Sit down, my friends," Judah Benjamin said as the Federal peace commissioners came into the Cabinet chamber. He, Vice President Stephens, and General Lee waited for Lincoln's representatives to take chairs before they seated themselves. Then Benjamin went on, "Am I to understand you have at last a reply to our proposal for elections in Kentucky and Missouri?"

"We do," William H. Seward said.

"Took you, or rather Mr. Lincoln, long enough," Alexander Stephens observed acidly. "Your election is less than three weeks away."

"You and Mr. Benjamin both served as U.S. Senators," Seward said. "You understand that reaching a decision of such importance cannot be hurried." Lee—and no doubt his colleagues with him—also understood the decision, whatever it was, had been timed to furnish Lincoln the greatest possible political advantage. No one, however, was crass enough to say so straight out.

"And what conclusion has your principal reached, sir?" Benjamin asked when Seward showed no sign of announcing that conclusion without being urged to do so.

The U.S. Secretary of State said, "Regretfully, I must inform you that the President declines your suggestion. He still maintains the position that the Federal Union is indivisible, and cannot in good conscience acquiesce to any plan which involves its further disruption. That is his final word on the subject."

Lee sat very still to keep from showing how disappointed he was. He saw war clouds rising over the two states still in dispute. He saw trains setting out from Rivington, trains full of AK-47s and metal cartridges. He saw the men of America Will Break further cementing their influence over the Confederate States: in battle, their aid would be a *sine qua non* against the richer North.

"I wish Mr. Lincoln would reconsider," he said.

Seward shook his head. "As I told you, General, I have given you his final word. Have you any further propositions to set before him?" When none of the Confederate commissioners replied, he got to his feet. "A very good day to you, then, gentlemen." With Stanton and Butler in his train, he swept out of the chamber.

"How can our nation bear another war so soon?" Lee groaned.

"It may not come to that, General Lee." Judah Benjamin's perennial smile grew broader. "Having lost the war, Lincoln must show as much strength now as he can. His 'final' word may seem much less so after the eighth proximo. If he wins the election, he will no longer need to posture before the voters, and so may be more inclined to see reason. And if he loses, he may consent for fear the Democrats will offer us greater concessions come March."

Lee stroked his beard as he considered that. After a few seconds, he bowed in his seat to the Confederate Secretary of State. "Were my hat on, sir, I would take it off to you. I see yet again that in matters political, I am but a babe in the woods. Deception is an essential element of the art of war, yes, but in your sphere it seems not only essential but predominant."

"You manage nicely, General, despite your disturbing tincture of honesty," Benjamin assured him. "The proposition the Federals are considering came from you, after all."

"Honesty is not always a fatal defect in a politician," Alexander Stephens added. "Sometimes it even becomes attractive, no doubt by virtue of its novelty."

The two veterans of the political arena chuckled together, Benjamin deeply from his comfortable belly, Stephens with a few thin, dry rasps. The Vice President's eyes flicked over Lee, who wondered if Stephens knew of Jefferson Davis's plans for him and, if so, what he thought. Stephens might well have wanted the Presidency for himself and resented Lee as a rival.

If he did, he gave no sign. All he said was, "As no further progress seems likely before the United States hold their elections, we may as well recess until those results are known. Unless one of you gentlemen objects, I shall so communicate to the Federal commissioners."

Judah Benjamin nodded. So did Lee, saying, "By all means. Nor will I be sorry to gain a further respite. After so long in the field, I find being in the bosom of my family exceedingly pleasant. Indeed, if you will be kind enough to excuse me, I shall head for my house this very moment."

Again, no one objected.

Nate Caudell hurried into the Nashville general store. Raeford Liles looked up at the tinkle of the doorbell. "Oh, mornin', Nate. What can I do for you today?"

"You can sell me a hat, by God." Caudell ran his hands through his hair and beard. Already wet, they came away wetter. Rain drummed on the roof, the door, the windows. "I lost my last one up in the Wilderness and I've been without ever since."

"What d'you have in mind?" Liles pointed to a row of hats on hooks up near the ceiling. "A straw, maybe? Or a silk stovepipe, to get duded up in?"

"No thanks to both of those, Mr. Liles. All I want is a plain black felt, same as the one I lost. Say that one here, if it fits me, and you don't want half my next year's pay for it."

They haggled amiably for a while. Caudell ended up buying the hat for thirteen dollars in banknotes. Confederate paper had gone up now that the South was no longer at war. He knew he could have had the hat for a silver dollar and a little change, but like most people he spent specie only when he had to.

He jammed the hat down low on his head, braced himself to brave the rain again. "Don't go yet," Liles said. "Almost forgot—I got a couple of letters for you here." He reached under the counter, handed Caudell two envelopes. Then he cocked his head and grinned. "This here Mollie Bean up in Rivington, you courtin' her? Pretty gal, I bet."

"She's a friend, Mr. Liles. How many times do I have to tell you?" Caudell's cheeks heated. His flush must have been visible even in the dim store, for Raeford Liles laughed at him. That only made him blush harder. To give himself a moment in which to recover, he looked at the other envelope.

It was from Henry Pleasants, down in Wilmington. Caudell grinned when he saw the engineer's name. Pleasants had indeed been snapped up by the Wilmington and Weldon Railroad, at a salary a good many times the one Caudell made for teaching school. He opened the letter, quickly read through it. Sure enough, everything was still going well for Henry: "I expect to escape my rented room here before long, and buy myself a proper house." Caudell could not evade a pang of jealousy at that. *He* was living in a rented room on Joyner Street, and had no prospect of escaping it.

Pleasants went on: "I do wonder that you Carolinians ever built a railroad at all, or kept it running once built, with your dearth of men trained not only in the mechanic arts but also in any sort of skilled labor. I have written to several miners in Pennsylvania, some of whom I knew before the war, others who served in my regiment, urging them to come hither. I hope they take me up on this soon, while travel arrangements between U.S.A. and C.S.A. remain pleasantly informal."

Caudell hoped so, too. As Pleasants said, the South needed every sort of skilled workman. The engineer's last phrase brought him up short. Proud as he was of belonging to an independent nation, he kept encountering implications of that independence which hadn't occurred to him. One of these days, and probably one day soon, he would need a passport if he wanted to visit Pennsylvania. The last time he'd gone into that state, his only passport had been a rifle.

He folded Pleasants's letter, returned it to its envelope, and put that envelope and the one with Mollie Bean's letter in a trouser pocket. Raeford Liles chuckled knowingly. "You ain't gonna read that there one where anybody else's eyes might light on it, is you? Must be from your sweetheart, I says."

"Oh, shut up, Mr. Liles," Caudell said, which only made the storekeeper laugh harder. Giving up, Caudell went out onto muddy Washington Street. He ran a block to Collins Street, almost fell as he turned right, ran two more blocks and turned left onto Virginia, then right onto Joyner. The widow Bissett's house was the third one on the left.

Barbara Bissett's husband, Jackson, had died in camp the winter before. Now she rented out a room to bring in some money. Her brother and his family shared the house with her and her boarder, so everything was perfectly proper and above reproach, but Caudell would have had no interest in her even had the two of them been alone there together. She was large and plump and inclined to burst into crying fits for any reason or none. He would have sympathized if he thought she was mourning her lost Jackson, but she'd been like that before the war, too.

Once inside his own upstairs room, he took both letters from his pocket.

The rainwater had blurred Henry Pleasants's fine round script on the envelope, but the paper inside remained dry. And Pleasants's letter had shielded Mollie's from the wet. Her hand was anything but fine and round, but this was the fifth or sixth letter she'd sent, and with each her writing grew more legible.

He opened the envelope and drew out the single sheet of the letter; Pleasants had gone on for three pages. "Dear Nate," he read, "I hope you is wel sinse I last rote. Got this hear paper at the Notahilton, wich sels like it was a ginral stor. But Rivington is a cawshun al ways, as you seen for your ownself. I bin out to Benny Langs hous wich is one of the ones out in the woods like we saw when you was there. He dident reckonize me on a count of I was warin a dres in sted of my old youniform."

Caudell clicked his tonguc between his teeth and made a sour face. Mollie didn't say why she'd gone out to Benny Lang's place, but he could paint his own mental pictures. He didn't care for them. Scowling still, he read on:

"The hous is poorly"—after a moment, he realized Mollie meant *purely*—"remarkabul. Benny Lang he dont us lanterns or even gas lights. He has a thing ware you pres a nob on the side of the wal and a light coms on up top. I ast him how do you do that and he laffs and tels me eleksity or som thing like that wat ever it may be. Wat ever it may be it is the best light for night time you cood think of ever in yor born dayes. Its more remarkabul than the AK47 if you ask me."

Caudell whistled softly. After those repeaters, desiccated meals, and gold paid, dollar for dollar, for Confederate paper, he supposed he shouldn't have been surprised by anything that came from Rivington, but a fine light that went on *here* if you pushed a knob *there*? He wondered how electricity—if that was what Mollie was trying to write—could do that; so far as he knew, it had no use past the telegraph.

Her letter continued: "May be on a count of this light making night into day wich sounds like Good Book tauk and giving him time to read Benny Lang he has hole cases ful of books. May be one of them tauks about eleksity. If I get the chans I wil try to find out on a count of it sounds like a thing worth noing. Yor true frend al ways, M. Bean, 47NC."

A reliable light by which to read at night . . . The notion roused pure, sea-green envy in Caudell. Even on a gloomy, rainy day like today, reading in front of a window was less than comfortable. Reading at night, with one's head jammed down close to both book and a dim, flickering, smoky candle, brought on eyestrain and headaches in short order. Though he had scant use for Abraham Lincoln, the stories of how the U.S. President studied law by firelight raised nothing but admiration in him. To sit down with a law book in front of a fire night after night after night, after a hard day's work each day, took special dedication—and perhaps special eyes as well. He wondered how Lincoln could see at all these days.

He also wondered whether Lincoln could possibly be reelected after leading the United States into a losing war. With both Democrats and Republicans split, the North was growing more parties than it knew what to do with. Caudell read newspaper reports of their bickering with detached amusement, as if they were accounts of the unsavory doings of an ex-wife's kin. Not for the first time, he thought the Confederacy well free of such chaos. Where the North had too many parties, the South had none. The war had been too all-consumingly important to let such organized factions develop. He hoped they would not emerge now that peace had taken the strain off his country.

Writing in bad light was no easier than reading, but he sat down on his bed to compose replies to Pleasants and to Mollie Bean. He knew no better way to spend a Saturday afternoon, and also knew that if he did not answer now, he probably would not get another chance until next Saturday. He would be at church tomorrow and teaching school from sunup to sundown the rest of the week.

"I hope you are well," he wrote to Mollie. "I hope you are happy in Rivington with all its wonders." In his mind's eye, he saw her on a bed with Benny Lang, maybe under the sunlike glare of one of the lights she'd described. He shook his head; even imagining anything so shameless embarrassed him . . . and left him wishing he were there instead of the Rivington man.

Thinking about the light helped him pull his pen back toward the impersonal: "If you learn more about eleksity and how it burns in the lamps there, let me know. If the Rivington men will sell it outside their town, it sounds better than whale oil or even gas. And tell me more about these books you mentioned. Are they just print on paper like our own, or are they filled with colored plates to go along with the words?" If even the lights in a Rivington man's house were something special, what would his books be like? Caudell chose the fanciest thing he could think of, and smiled at the power of his own imagination.

He went on, "Your letters keep getting longer and more interesting. I hope to have many more of them, and hope that you now and then remember the wide world outside Rivington." He hesitated, then added, "I also hope to see you again one day. Your friend always, Nathaniel N. Caudell." He looked down at that last line, wondering whether he ought to strike it out. Mollie might think he meant only that he wanted to have her again. Or she might show up on the doorstep of the widow Bissett's house, either in tart's finery or in her old Confederate uniform. He wondered which would stir up the greater scandal.

But in the end, he decided to leave the sentence alone. It was true, and Mollie had sense enough not to read too much or too little into it. He waited until the ink dried, then folded the letter and put it in an envelope. He thought about going back to Raeford Liles's store to post that letter and the one to Henry Pleasants, but only for a moment. Monday would do well enough, if the rain had let up by then.

Lightning cracked. While it lasted, it lit his room with a hot, purple glare and turned every shadow black as pitch. He blinked, afterimages dancing inside his eyes, and wondered if the eleksity lights were that bright. He hoped not. Too much light could be as bad as too little. Thunder boomed overhead.

He set the letters on top of the chest of drawers by the wall opposite the bed, then went back and lay down. The rain kept coming. Another bolt of lightning lit up everything in harsh relief, then died. Thunder growled again. Children—not a few grown men and women, too—were afraid of it. He'd had his own anxieties, until Gettysburg and the Wilderness and the ring of forts around Washington. After a few cannonadings, thunder was nothing to worry about.

He pulled his new hat down over his eyes so the lightning would not bother him anymore. Inside of five minutes, he was snoring.

Boys and a few girls, their ages ranging from five up toward full adulthood, crowded the benches of the Nashville, North Carolina, schoolhouse. The building, on Alston Street several blocks south of Washington, was near the edge of town and hardly deserved to be called a schoolhouse at all—schoolshed would have been a better word for it. The walls were timber, the roof leaked—though the rain was done, wet, muddy spots remained on the floor as reminders of its recent appearance. "Get away from there, Rufus!" Caudell shouted at a small boy who was about to jump in one of the wet places.

Rufus sulkily sat back on his bench. Sighing, Caudell stood between two of his older students, who had a geometry problem chalked on their slates. "If these two angles are equal, the triangles have to be congruent," one said.

"*Are* the angles equal?" Caudell asked. The youth nodded. "How do you know?"

"Because they're—what's the name for them? Vertical angles, that's what they are."

"That's right," Caudell said approvingly. "So you see that—"

Before he could point out what the budding Euclid was supposed to see, a girl gave a piercing shriek. Bored with sitting on his bench, Rufus had yanked her braids. Caudell hurried over. He habitually carried a long, thin stick; he'd been using it to point to the figures in the geometry lesson. Now he whacked Rufus on the wrist with it. Rufus howled. He probably made more noise than the girl whose hair he'd pulled, but it was noise of a sort the students were used to ignoring.

Without breaking stride, Caudell went back and finished the interrupted lesson. Then he walked over to three or four nine-year-olds. "You have your spelling words all written down?" he asked. "Take out your Old Blue Backs and we'll find out how you did." The children opened their *Webster*'s *Elementary Spellers*, checked the scrawls on their slates against the right answers. "Write the proper spelling of each word you missed ten times," Caudell said; that would keep the nine-year-olds busy while he taught arithmetic to their older brothers and sisters. He also thought fleetingly that Mollie Bean could have done with some more work in the *Elementary Speller*.

From arithmetic, he went on to geography and history, both of which came from the *North Carolina Reader* of Calvin H. Wiley, a former state school superintendent. Had everyone in the state been as heroic and virtuous as Wiley made its people out to be, North Carolina would have been the earthly paradise. The discrepancy between text and real world did not bother Caudell; school books were supposed to inculcate virtue in their readers.

He went over to his youngest students, said, "Let me hear the alphabet again."

The familiar chant rang out: "*A, B, C, D, E, F, G—*"

"Mr. Caudell, I got to pee," Rufus interrupted.

"Go on outside," Caudell said, sighing again. "You come back quick now, mind, or I'll give you another taste of the switch." Rufus left hastily. Caudell knew the odds of his return were less than even money. And by tomorrow morning, he would have forgotten all about being told to come back. Well, that was what the switch was for: to exercise his memory until it could carry the load for itself.

For a wonder, Rufus did return. For a bigger wonder, he recited the whole alphabet without a miss. Knowing he wasn't likely to get a bigger surprise that day, Caudell announced a dinner break. Some children ate where they sat; others—though not as many as in spring—went out to sit on the grass. The youths to whom he'd taught geometry came up to him while he was eating his sowbelly and hoecakes. "Tell us more about how you all got into Washington City, Mr. Caudell," one of them said.

The down was beginning to darken on their cheeks and upper lips. They wondered what they'd missed by staying home from the war. Had it gone on another year or two, they would have found out. Having seen the elephant, Caudell would willingly have traded what he knew for ignorance.

"Jesse, William, it was dark and it was dirty and everybody was firing as fast as he could, us and the Yankees both," he said. "Finally we fought our way through their works and then into the city. I tell you, pieces of it I don't remember to this day. You're just doing things in a fight; you don't have time to think about them."

The two boys stared at him in admiration. The smaller children listened too, some of them trying not very well to pretend they weren't doing any such thing. "But you weren't afraid, were you, Mr. Caudell?" Jesse asked, obviously confident of the answer. "They made you first sergeant, so they must've known you'd never be afraid."

One of the reasons Caudell had been made first sergeant was that the man in that position did much of his company's record-keeping and so needed to have neat handwriting. He wondered what Jesse and William would say to that. Their idea of war did not include such mundane details. He answered, "Anybody who isn't scared when people shoot at him, well, he's a fool, if you ask me."

The youths laughed, as if he'd said something funny. They thought he was being modest. He knew he wasn't. As with Raeford Liles, he faced a chasm of incomprehension he could not bridge. He finished his last hoe-cake, wiped his hands on his pants, went out behind a tree himself, then walked back into the schoolroom and resumed lessons.

He sometimes thought that, if he ever quit teaching, he could join a circus as a juggler. With a roomful of children of all different ages, he needed to keep busy the ones he wasn't actually instructing at any given moment. When the eight-year-olds were doing addition in *Davies' Primary Arithmetic*, the twelve-year-olds were parsing sentences from *Bullion's English Grammar*. Meanwhile, Jesse and William practiced their elocution, William putting fire into Patrick Henry's "Give me liberty or give me death," Jesse giving William Yancey's tribute to Jefferson Davis on Davis's becoming provisional president at Montgomery less than four years before: "The man and the hour have met," William declared loudly. Some of the younger children clapped.

Caudell dismissed his clutch of scholars about half an hour before sunset, to let the ones who did not live in town—the vast majority—find their way home to their farms before it got dark. A few local children—Colonel Faribault's sons, the daughter of the justice of the peace—did not attend his school because they were off at fancy expensive private academies. Far more stayed away because they worked in the fields all day long, all year long.

That saddened him. Many of those children would still be living when the twentieth century rolled around, and would have not a letter to their names. Of course, if they came to school instead of working in the fields, they might be less likely to be living still in that distant day, for small farms needed every hand they could get, just to make ends meet.

After his students were gone, he straightened up benches and cleared away trash. He shut the door behind him, a door whose lock had long since rusted into uselessness. Little inside was worth stealing, anyhow. The school boasted neither blackboard, globe, charts, nor much of anything else in the way of equipment.

Caudell looked back over his shoulder as he walked up Alston Street. "Yup, I'm about it," he said to no one in particular. He kept on walking.

The bell jingled as Caudell went into the general store. "Today, Mr. Liles?" he demanded. "Are we ever going to find out who won up North?" A week and a half after the election, its results remained in doubt.

Finally, though, finally, Raeford Liles grinned at him. "Got me a couple copies of Thursday's *Raleigh North Carolina Evening Standard*, one o' the *Raleigh Constitution*, an' even one o' the *Wilmington Journal*. You jus' go ahead an' take your pick—they all tell what you want to know."

"About time," Caudell said. "Give me an *Evening Standard*, then." He slapped seven cents down on the counter. The storekeeper gave him his paper. The headline leaped out at him:

HORATIO SEYMOUR ELECTED PRESIDENT OF UNITED STATES!

In slightly smaller letters, a subhead proclaimed,

Black Republicans Repudiated at Polls.

Caudell took a deep breath. "So they turned him out, did they?"

"Looks that way," Liles agreed cheerfully.

The more of the story Caudell read, the more misleading that subhead looked. He'd already known the election was very tight; with most of the results in at last, it looked close as a Minié ball cracking by one's head. Lincoln, in fact, had taken twelve states to Seymour's ten; McClellan won tiny, conservative Delaware and his home state of New Jersey, while Frémont prevailed only in radical Kansas. But Seymour won the states that counted: among them, New York, Ohio, and Pennsylvania gave him 80 of his 138 electoral votes, while Lincoln garnered 83, McClellan 10, and Frémont but 3. Out of more than four million votes cast, Seymour led Lincoln by only thirty-three thousand.

Liles had been reading the papers, too. He remarked, "Can't see how even the damnfool Yankees came so close to electing that stinking Republican twice. Wasn't oncet enough for 'em? He'd just go an' start a war with somebody else."

"I don't know, Mr. Liles." Caudell thought back to that mad morning when he'd ended up on the White House lawn. Like almost all North Carolina, he'd despised Lincoln, who'd won not a single vote in the state in 1860. But the man who came out to talk to the army that had defeated his own deserved more respect than the South had given him. "I don't know," Caudell repeated. "There was something about him—"

"Bosh," the storekeeper said positively. "Now this here Seymour, might could be he'll keep the niggers in line, much as a Yankee can, anyways. If'n he manages that, reckon we'll get on with him all right. Hope so, I truly do."

"So do I, Mr. Liles." Caudell looked down to the newspaper again. Accounts of the Northern elections took up most of the front page. In the lower right-hand corner, though, was a story about Nathan Bedford Forrest's continuing war against the remnants of the colored Union regiments in the Mississippi valley. Of late, they'd been reduced to guerrilla raids rather than stand-up battles, but Forrest had bagged a whole band near Catahoula, Louisiana, and hanged all thirty-one men. Caudell showed Raeford Liles the article. "We're having enough trouble keeping our own niggers in line."

"I seen that story." Liles took off his glasses, polished them on his apron, set them back in place. "You ask me, that's just what niggers in arms is askin' for, an' I ain't sorry to see 'em get it. An' if Hit-'em-Again Forrest hits 'em a few more licks like that one there, God damn me if'n I wouldn't be right pleased to see him President oncet Jefferson Davis steps down."

"I hadn't even thought about that," Caudell said slowly. The Confederate Presidential elections were still almost three years away. That seemed like a very long time, but really wasn't, not when Caudell had been thinking only a few weeks before about the onset of the twentieth century. After a pause, he went on, "First man I'd care to see in Richmond, if he wants the job, is General Lee."

"He wouldn't be bad either, I suppose," Liles admitted.

"Not bad?" To any man who had served in the Army of Northern Virginia, faint praise for Robert E. Lee was not nearly praise enough. "There's not a man in the Confederate States who'd be better, and that's counting Hit-'em-Again Forrest, too."

"Mmm . . . might could be you're right, Nate. But I do hear tell he's too soft on niggers."

"I don't think so," Caudell said. Though he'd settled back as best he could into his prewar way of life, some of the things he'd seen while on active duty refused to go away: Georgie Ballentine, running off because the Rivington men wouldn't trust him with a rifle; the colored troops at Bealeton, holding their ground under murderous fire until flesh would stand no more . . . "This whole business of niggers isn't as simple as it looks."

"Bosh!" Raeford Liles said. "Only thing wrong with niggers, aside from they's lazy, is they costs too much. I was thinkin' maybe I'd buy me a buck one o' these days, help around this place some. But Lord Jesus, the money it takes! Now that cotton's movin' again, the cost of prime hands done went through the roof—planters is biddin' against each other so as they can harvest the most crops. Poor storekeeper like me can't stay with 'em."

"Everything is dear these days." Caudell's smile went from sympathetic to wicked. "That goes for things in this store, too, you know."

"Will you listen to the whippersnapper!" Liles raised aggrieved eyes to heaven. "Do I look like a man doin' any more'n just scrapin' by?"

"Now that you mention it, yes. You want to talk about just scraping by, you try living on a schoolteacher's salary for a while."

"No, thank you," the storekeeper said at once. "My pa, he learned me to read and write and cipher back before you were born. I got nothin' against you in particular, Nate, you know that, but that's the way it ought to be, you ask me. I'm not nearly sure it's the state's business to go schoolin' folks. It's liable to set all sort o' silly ideas loose."

"Times are more complicated than they used to be," Caudell said, "and more ideas are running around loose than there used to be: what with the telegraph and the railroad and the steamship, it sort of has to be that way. People ought to know enough to be able to deal with them."

"Maybe so, maybe so." Raeford Liles sighed. "Things were sure enough simpler when I was a boy, and that's a fact."

Caudell suspected every generation ever born had said that, and also suspected that, when he was old and gray, he would look back fondly on the days before the Confederate States gained their freedom. But Raeford Liles's lifetime had seen an uncommon amount of change, and the next years would see more. And one in four adult white men in North Carolina could not read or write. "Not everybody has a father willing to work as hard as yours, Mr. Liles. We ought to give some of the others a hand."

"The hand's in my pocket, takin' out taxes," Liles complained. Then he brightened. "Could be worse, I reckon. If them damn Yankees had won, likely they'd try taxin' me to school niggers." He laughed at the very idea. So did Nate Caudell.

⋆ XI ⋆

The three Federal peace commissioners filed glumly into the Confederate Cabinet room. Lee, Judah Benjamin, and Alexander Stephens rose to greet them. Lee kept his expression sober as he sat, to avoid even the appearance of gloating.

"The people of the North have spoken," Benjamin observed. His voice was suave, but that served only to plant the barb more deeply.

"Oh, go to the devil," Edwin Stanton snarled. The Secretary of War looked tired and drained and sounded bitter.

"I admired President Lincoln's statement of concession," Lee said, trying still to soften the moment. "He was wise to urge your country to unite behind the new leaders the citizens chose: 'with malice toward none, with charity for all.' The phrase deserves to live."

"Lincoln deserved to win," Stanton retorted. "I'd sooner see Horatio Seymour making phrases for the ages."

"So he may," Alexander Stephens said. "Come next March 4, he will have his chance. I wonder whom he will name as his representatives in these discussions."

"Perhaps no one," William H. Seward said. The Confederate commissioners leaned forward in their chairs as the U.S. Secretary of State continued, "Perhaps we shall succeed in resolving all outstanding issues between us before President Seymour is inaugurated."

"Lincoln could have resolved them at any time up to this point," Lee said. "Indeed, his dilatory approach to these negotiations has upon occasion disappointed me."

"It also cost him twenty-two electoral votes, as both Kentucky and Missouri favored Seymour," Judah Benjamin added.

"Even if they'd both gone Confederate, it wouldn't have been enough to turn the election, worse luck," Ben Butler said after a quick calculation.

"As may be." Seward waved a hand to put an end to side issues. "President Lincoln has directed me to inform you gentlemen that he is now willing to abide by the results of elections in the two disputed states, upon the model advanced by General Lee, and suggests as the date for said elections Tuesday, June 6, 1865. He also suggests that we fix ninety million in specie as the amount of composition due the Confederate States, half of said amount to be paid before March 4, the other half within thirty days after the elections in Kentucky and Missouri."

"Well," Judah P. Benjamin said. Lee glanced over at the Confederate Secretary of State with considerable respect—again, he had guessed which way events would go. "Well," Benjamin said again, as if gathering himself. Finally he managed something more coherent: "Most constructive, gentlemen. I hope you will forgive us if we request an adjournment until tomorrow so that we may consult with President Davis."

"He won't get more from us," Stanton said gruffly. By his tightly clenched jaw, he regretted Richmond's getting so much.

"No, not from you, certainly." By stopping there, Alexander Stephens let the Federal commissioners worry about just how much Horatio Seymour might surrender to the South.

Lee broke in: "As Secretary Benjamin has said, this is a matter that requires the President's decision. Shall we meet here again tomorrow at our usual hour?"

The men from the United States left the Confederate Cabinet room. Their feet dragged across the carpet. To Lee, they seemed more like beaten men now than when they had first begun these negotiations: even their own countrymen had repudiated their policies.

The Confederate commissioners went up to Jefferson Davis's office. This time, Alexander Stephens accompanied his colleagues. Davis looked up from the papers on his desk. "Something of importance has occurred for you to be here so soon," he said. When he saw Stephens, his eyes widened. "Something of importance has occurred for *you* to be here at all, sir."

"Something has indeed, Mr. President." Stephens told of Seward's concession.

"Ninety million?" Davis plucked at the hair under his chin, as he did when thinking hard. "We have no hope of wringing more from Lincoln; of that I am sure. But from Seymour, who knows what we might get? Both border states, perhaps, without the necessity of military action or the risks of the ballot box."

"I think that highly likely, Mr. President," Stephens said. "Vallandigham might as well speak our counsel straight into Seymour's ear." Judah Benjamin nodded.

Davis turned to Lee, who stood in silence. "May I hear your opinion, General?"

"Yes, Mr. President." Lee paused for a moment to marshal his thoughts. "Whether or not we may hope for more from President-elect Seymour than from President Lincoln strikes me as moot. The United States have accepted a proposal we ourselves advanced. How can we honorably impose further conditions upon them now? Let us have peace, sir; let us accept the composition they offer; let the voters of the two states at issue choose under which flag they would sooner live."

"You feel strongly about this," Davis said.

"I do, sir; as the proposal involved was originally mine, I feel it touched upon my own honor as well as that of the nation." Lee took a deep breath. "If you seek to impose further conditions upon the United States, I shall have no choice but to tender my resignation from the Army of the Confederate States of America."

Almost, he hoped Jefferson Davis would force him to resign. When he'd left the U.S. Army in 1861, he'd wanted nothing more than to go home and plant corn. And he had had enough of war, war on a scale beyond any he'd imagined, in the Second American Revolution to last him the rest of his life.

Judah Benjamin essayed a chuckle. "You cannot be serious, sir."

"Try me," Lee said. Benjamin's habitual smile contracted.

"We could squeeze the Federals for more," Davis said. But he was talking to himself rather than to Lee; having known Lee for upwards of thirty-five years, he knew also that Lee would keep his promise. Still to himself, the President continued, "But that would make the next war inevitable, a prospect I confess I do not relish." He looked to Benjamin and Alexander Stephens. "Does General Lee's resolve impress you as it does me?"

"General Lee's resolve has always impressed me," Stephens said.

"Let us accept the terms offered, then, and may almighty God grant that they prove best for our country," Davis said.

Lee, Benjamin, and Stephens spoke together: "Amen."

"I have the honor to inform you that President Davis accepts in all its particulars the proposal you put forward yesterday," Lee said when the

U.S. commissioners returned to the Confederate Cabinet room the next morning.

"In all its particulars?" Edwin Stanton stared. "As simple as that? You're not going to try and squeeze more out of us?" Unwittingly, he used the same word as had Jefferson Davis.

"As simple as that." Lee repeated what he had said to the Confederate President the day before: "Let us have peace, sir."

"President Lincoln predicted you would say as much," William Seward said. "To my embarrassment, I must confess I disagreed with him. Sometimes, however, one is happier to be proved wrong than right."

"I also find myself surprised," Ben Butler said. Lee believed that; Butler was not the sort to settle for less than the most he could get. The politician-turned-general went on, "Even with acceptance of these terms by both sides, certain practical details remain to be settled."

"Ah?" Alexander Stephens made a small interrogative noise. Lee tensed in his chair. If the "practical details" Butler set forth proved impractical, peace between United States and Confederate States might yet fall through.

Butler said, "As the United States shall have to withdraw their troops from the two states contested between us, President Lincoln requests that Confederate forces simultaneously withdraw to a distance of at least twenty miles from the northern borders of Tennessee and Arkansas, so as to ensure that you do not attempt to seize the disputed territory by a *coup de main*."

Stephens and Judah Benjamin looked to Lee. This time it did not bother him, as the issue was a military one. He said, "I see no objection, so long as the Federal withdrawal continues as agreed. If it should falter, we shall do as seems best to us."

Butler nodded impatiently, as if that went without saying. To him, it probably did; he always looked out for his own interest first. He went on, "The President proposes leaving behind one thousand soldiers, five hundred in each state, to serve to guarantee the fairness of the election and the count." He held up a hand to forestall objections. "He will undertake to furnish in advance a list of their names to whomever you may designate, and will accept a like number of Southern troops in Kentucky and Missouri for the same purpose, their names to be similarly provided to our designee."

The three Confederate commissioners leaned close to one another, murmured among themselves. At length, Alexander Stephens said, "Subject to the concurrence of President Davis, we agree. Is there more?"

"Yes, one thing," Butler said. "He proposes that each side send into the disputed states a single high-ranking official to serve as election commissioner, and to be fully empowered to act for his government in all matters pertaining to the elections. Such a person, obviously, must be acceptable to both sides." Butler smiled, displaying for a moment yellowed teeth beneath his mustache. "I gather, therefore, that I am not to be considered as the Federal representative. President Lincoln directs me to say he would raise no objections were your government to name General Lee to this position."

"Me?" To his annoyance, Lee's voice broke with surprise. "Why me? I am no politician, to properly oversee an election."

"That may be exactly why." Stephens sent a suspicious look toward Ben Butler. "Perhaps Mr. Lincoln has in mind machinations which a man who is more—seasoned, shall we say?—in politics might easily note and forestall, but which, because of General Lee's probity, he might fail to detect?"

Ben Butler threw back his head and laughed raucously. "If I were the one choosing the election commissioners, that's just why I'd pick someone like Lee." Lee bristled; to select someone for the express purpose of taking advantage of his honesty would be a Butler trick through and through. The fat lawyer continued, "It is not, however, President Lincoln's intention, as witness his suggestion for General Lee's Federal counterpart: he advances for your consideration the name of General U. S. Grant, whose political naïveté will be no secret to you."

Lee knew nothing of General Grant's politics, whether naive or otherwise; his only concern for Grant had been as a soldier. He turned to Stephens and Benjamin, whose expertise lay in matters political. "He is certainly no radical Republican," Judah Benjamin admitted, pursing his plump lips. "He might well be a shrewd choice, in fact, for Seymour, when he takes office, would be unlikely to replace him."

"As an opponent, he struck me as direct and forceful," Lee said, "nor do I know of anything in his personal life which might disqualify him." Actually, he had heard Grant drank to excess on occasion, but that was Lincoln's worry, not his.

"You are, then, willing to adhere to these conditions for the vote in Kentucky and Missouri?" Seward said.

"We shall lay them before President Davis," Lee said; after a glance at his colleagues, he continued, "adding as our opinion that he should look upon them favorably." He looked at Benjamin and Stephens again; they nodded. They kept looking back at him, too. He needed a moment to figure out why. When he did, he sighed and said, "If the President is of the opinion that I am the proper man to represent the Confederacy in the two disputed states, I shall of course undertake that duty."

"Oh, capital," Edwin Stanton said. Butler smiled his oleaginous smile. Seward unbent enough to dip his head in approval. Butler passed to the Confederate negotiators a written-out draft of Lincoln's proposal. However murky his thoughts, his script was flowing and clear.

Lee, Stephens, and Benjamin made the by-now-familiar trip to Jefferson Davis's office once more. The President heard them out, read through the paper, then turned it sideways, as if scrutinizing it from a new angle might reveal some hidden pitfall. Not seeming to turn one up, he asked his commissioners, "You gentlemen are inclined to agree to these terms?"

"We are," Lee said firmly. The Vice President and Secretary of State echoed him.

"Let it be so, then," Davis said. He looked down at the paper again, set a hand over his eyes. His fingers were long and thin and pale, the fingers of a violinist or a concert pianist. "I never dreamt, when I first ascended to this position, that the road to peace would be so long or require so many sacrifices. But I thank God we have successfully traversed that road to its promised end."

Lee also briefly bent his head in a thankful prayer. When he raised it again, he asked, "Will you also post me to the disputed states as Lincoln suggests, Mr. President?"

Davis pursed his thin lips. "My only concern there is that Lincoln has, throughout his administration, demonstrated himself to be a politician with few scruples when it comes to reaching his ends. Our interests in Kentucky and Missouri might be better served by someone of, ah, similarly elastic principle."

"If he intended chicanery, he would have proposed as his own nominee there someone other than General Grant, who is not himself a political man," Lee said. "Nor would he have set the date for the election three months after the end of his own term. And finally, a bold man indeed would be required to plot deceit when the White House now lies within range of Confederate artillery."

"All cogent points, especially the last," Davis admitted. "I am to infer, then, that you desire the position?"

"Yes, so long as you believe I can properly fill it," Lee said. "The proposal, after all, was mine; I should like to help bring it to fruition."

The President leaned forward, extended his hand to Lee. "On to Kentucky, then, and to Missouri."

"Kentucky?" Mary Custis Lee's voice betrayed her dismay. "Missouri?"

"You need not say them as if they were the ends of the earth, my dear

Mary." Lee essayed a small joke. "Texas, now, Texas is the end of the earth."

The joke fell flat. "With the war over, I had hoped you would be able to stay here in Richmond with me and with the rest of your family," his wife said.

You'd hoped, in other words, that I'd be able to carry on my soldiering from behind a desk, Lee thought. But the thought brought no anger with it. How could Mary be blamed for wishing they might stay together? Gently, he said, "True, the war is over, but I still wear my country's uniform." He touched the sleeve of his gray coat. "You knew that when you married me, all those years ago; you've always managed very well."

"Oh, indeed, very well," she said bitterly. Where he had touched his coat, she set her hand on the arm of the wheeled chair that confined her.

Lee flinched, as he would not have under enemy fire. Mary had not been a cripple during earlier separations; the war had cost her what was left of her health. He offered what comfort he could: "I am not going into battle, only to oversee peaceful elections. And I shall be back in Richmond for the summer."

"Another half a year, gone forever."

He pulled a dining room chair close, sat in it so he could talk without looking down at her. "For better or worse, my dear, I *am* a soldier, as you have known these many years; the idea is not one to which you must suddenly accustom yourself. And I have my duty and shall not turn aside from it."

"Not even for those who love you," his wife said. He bent his head and did not answer; it was, after all, the truth. Mary Lee sighed. "As you say, Robert, I know I am a soldier's wife. Sometimes, though, as in these past few months' peace, it is pleasant to try to forget."

"Dear Mary, we have no peace, only an armistice which may be broken at any time, should the United States—or ourselves—find that advantageous. If heaven grant, I hope to help forge a true peace, a lasting peace. Were anything less in my mind, I assure you that I should not have accepted this posting."

"So you say. So you may even believe." His wife's voice remained sharp, but the anger had gone from her face, leaving behind only resignation. "I am still of the opinion that, if Jefferson Davis commanded you to campaign in hell to fetch a coal to light his cookstove, you would make your good-byes to me as you always do and set off without any thought past the fact that you had been ordered."

"Maybe I would." Lee thought about it. He started to laugh. "Likely I would, I suppose. I trust I would return with that coal, though, or at least give Old Nick a fight for it worth his remembering."

That at last won him a smile from Mary. "I'm certain you would." One of the lamps in the dining room flickered and went out, filling the chamber with shadows and the odor of cooling oil. Mary asked, "How late has it gotten to be?"

"Half past ten," Lee answered after a look at his pocket watch.

"Late enough," she declared. "Will you assist me upstairs?"

"Of course. Let me go up with a light first." He rooted through a sideboard drawer until he found a candle, which he lit at a lamp that still burned. He took it up to their bedroom, where he lit two more with it, then quickly went downstairs again. The house was very still; his daughters and Julia had already gone to bed. The wheels of Mary's chair rumbled over the floorboards as he pushed her to the stairway.

Leaning some on the banister and more on him, she made her way to the second floor. He steered her to the bedroom. She sat down on the bed while he took out a nightdress, held it up for her approval. "Yes, that will do," she said. He helped her out of the confining, tight-waisted dress and petticoats she wore during the day. From long practice, he dealt with her clothes as readily as with his own. "Thank you," she told him. "I'll miss your touch when you're gone."

"Will you?" he said. At that moment, as much by chance as anything else, his hand happened to lie on her left breast. It was not, in the abstract, a breast to kindle passions; the years and a succession of hungry babes had had their way with it. But his wife's flesh remained dear to him. Their long separations made each return seem like a new honeymoon. Of itself, something in his voice changed. "Shall I blow out the candles?"

She understood him; after thirty-three years of marriage, she generally understood him. "If you think you will be able to get that nightdress onto me into the dark," she answered.

"I expect I shall," he said. He got up and blew out two of the three candles, then paused thoughtfully, took a nightshirt from its drawer, and set it on his bed. The room plunged into blackness as he blew out the last light.

Afterwards, he felt the sharp twinge in his chest that came with exertion. He reached over to the nightstand for the bottle of little pills from the Rivington men. He put one under his tongue. The pain faded. The bottle did not rattle as he put it back; he remembered it had been all but empty. As sleep took him, he reminded himself to get more nitroglycerine from them before he set out on his travels. Their arrogance was disagreeable, but their abilities helped justify it.

*   *   *

As the crow flies, Louisville is about 460 miles from Richmond. Lee was no crow. He had to take the railroad, which made his journey almost twice as long. The Virginia and Tennessee train squealed and skidded along tracks slick with winter ice as it fought its way down to Chattanooga. That journey alone was as long as the crow's flight to Louisville. In the bad weather, it took three days. Lee was glad to lay over for a couple of days and recover his strength.

"I wish some ingenious Southerner—or even Yankee, come to that— would invent a railroad car in which it was possible to lie down and get some decent sleep," he said to Charles Marshall. Sitting bolt upright all the way from Richmond had left him sorer than he would have been from the same amount of time in the saddle.

Major Marshall was younger and sprier, but the journey had taken its toll on him, too. He nodded as vigorously as the crick in his neck would allow. "We have smoking cars and dining cars and cars with washrooms. Why not sleeping cars? They'd let a man ride the rails as the rails could be ridden, rather than his being forced to pause every few hundred miles or perish."

A white man drove Lee and Marshall from the railway station to a hotel. Their locomotive chugged off to the train shed, a long stone and brick building with a curious curved roof and a half-story lengthwise arcade, mostly devoted to windows, poised atop that.

Two more whites at the hotel manhandled the luggage into the lobby. Lee watched them with more than a little curiosity; in a Southern town, he would have expected slaves to do the hauling. The driver noticed his repeated glances. "Ain't many niggers left hereabouts," he said. "Most of 'em went north with the Yankees when they pulled out, and the ones that's left, they're still actin' like they was free—*eee*mancipated, they calls it, an' they won't work less'n you pay 'em. A lot of folks, they'd sooner give cash money to whites."

"You haven't tried forcing them back into bondage?" Marshall asked. He'd accompanied Lee because, being a lawyer, he was the most politically astute of the general's aides.

"A couple men what tried that, they ended up dead, and their niggers run off to join the bandits in the hills," the driver answered morosely. "Makes some folks reckon it's more trouble'n it's worth, less'n Hit-'em-Again Forrest's got his army in town."

"Once a man has been some while free, it's hard to take that from him again, even with an army at one's back," Lee said. The driver gave him an odd look but finally decided to nod.

From Chattanooga, the railroad crossed the Tennessee River at Bridge-port and swung down briefly into Alabama. At Stevenson, Lee and Marshall switched to a Nashville and Chattanooga Railroad train for the trip north-west to the capital of Tennessee. The farther north and west they got, the longer the land had lain under Federal hands . . . and the fewer Negroes they saw. Lee wondered how many lurked in the bare-branched forests, clutching Springfields and wondering if this particular train was worth at-tacking.

Sometimes, when the train would stop at a town, Lee got off and walked about for a few minutes. Whenever he did, men in worn coats of gray or butternut came up to shake his hand or just to stare at him. It made him uneasy. He wondered how politicians so easily went out to press their constituents' flesh. Then he wondered how, if the Confederate Presidency came his way, he would manage himself.

From Nashville's station and train shed—which, by contrast to Chatta-nooga's, were solid and square, with crenelated walls and with towers at each corner—he rode north into Kentucky. The Stars and Stripes still flew there, not the Stainless Banner. Kentucky's own blue flag was also promi-nently displayed, as if to show that the people there thought of their own homes first, ahead of both nations competing for their allegiance. To Lee, who had chosen Virginia over the United States, that was as it should be.

Men in pieces of Confederate uniform still came to see him at every stop. But so did men who wore blue coats: Kentucky's sons had fought on both sides in the war, more of them, in fact, for the Union than the Confederacy (the North, after all, had held the state through almost the whole of the war). The Federals seemed as curious about him as did their brothers and cousins who had fought for the South.

"You rebs gonna invade us again if we vote to stay in the U.S. of A?" a fellow wearing corporal's stripes on a blue coat asked at Bowling Green, where Confederate general Albert Sidney Johnston had made his head-quarters back in the days when the war was young.

Lee shook his head; he tried to put Albert Sidney Johnston, killed at Shiloh, out of his mind. "No, sir, we shall not: we intend to abide by the results of that vote, whatever it may be, so long as it be free and fair."

"Reckon you can't say plainer'n that," the ex-corporal remarked. "I heard tell you was a devil of a fightin' man, but I never heard you was a liar."

At Munfordsville, another thirty or forty miles up the Louisville and Nashville Railroad, two groups of former soldiers, one in gray, the other wearing blue, approached Lee at the same time. They glared at each other. Some of them carried pistols on their belts; they all wore knives. Lee was about to turn and go back into his coach, in the hope that that would end the confrontation. Then one of the bluecoats surprised him by starting to laugh.

"Tell us all what amuses you, sir," Lee said cordially, including himself, the veterans in gray, and the other ex-Federals with a broad wave.

The Union man carried himself like a young officer. He spoke like one, too: "I just happened to remember our lovely state's motto, General Lee."

"Which is?" Lee asked, wondering what a motto could have to do with anything.

Then, with relish, the bluecoat quoted it: " 'United we stand, divided we fall.' " He waved too, encompassing the rival groups at the train station and, by extension, all the disunited groups in a most disunited state.

Lee laughed, loud and long. The ex-Confederates followed his lead, as he'd thought they might. Then the men who had fought for the North laughed, too. After that, whatever trouble there might have been evaporated. He chatted with both groups until it was time for the train to pull out. Then, as he turned to leave, he said, "See, here you are, my friends—fraternizing again."

The men chuckled. One of them, a lean, muscular fellow in ragged butternut, said, "You officers wasn't supposed to know about that."

"Oh, we did," said the former Federal who'd known about Kentucky's motto, thus confirming Lee's impression of him. He added, "Sometimes we knew when to look the other way, too," which drew more chuckles.

"If we fraternized even in the midst of war, as we did, surely we shall contrive to get along with one another now that peace is here," Lee said. Without waiting for an answer, he returned to the train. As it jerked into motion, he looked out the window at the men who had so recently fought each other. They went on talking together, amiably enough. Lee took that to be a good omen.

Louisville, on the southern bank of the Ohio, was a big city. Before the war, it had held 68,000 people to Richmond's 38,000, though becoming a national capital was swelling the latter town these days. As Lee got down from the train, a man jumped in front of him, pencil and notebook poised. "Fred Darby, *Louisville Journal*, General Lee," the fellow said rapidly. "How does it feel, sir, to enter a town Confederate armies never succeeded in reaching?"

"I am not here as a conqueror," Lee said. "That the United States and Confederate States went to war once was disastrous; a second conflict would be catastrophic. Rather than fight again, the two nations have agreed the justest course is to let the citizens of Kentucky and Missouri choose which nation they prefer. My role here, like General Grant's, is to serve as an arbiter of that process, to ensure that it takes place without coercion of any sort."

"What do you think Kentucky ought to do with its niggers, General?" Darby said.

That question again, Lee thought. Wherever he went, it went with him. "That is for your people to decide," he answered. "Negroes may be either slave or free in both the U.S.A. and the C.S.A."

"We'd have to be a slave state if we voted for the South, wouldn't we?"

"So the Confederate Constitution states, yes," Lee admitted reluctantly.

"Does that mean the niggers who were freed here during the war—and there were a lot of 'em—would have to go back to being slaves?" the reporter asked.

"By no means," Lee said, firmly this time. "Again, barring legislation from Richmond"—he thought of Congressman Oldham—"that would be a matter for your own legislature. As I am sure you are aware"—though sure of no such thing, he was unfailingly polite—"there are free Negroes in every state of the Confederacy, many thousands of them in some states."

Darby scribbled in his notebook. "General Lee, let me also ask you—"

"If you please, sir, not now," Lee said, holding up a hand. "Having just arrived after some days of travel, I would prefer not to be interviewed here in the train station. I expect to remain in Kentucky and Missouri until June. Surely we shall speak again." The reporter started to ask his question anyhow; Lee shook his head. Charles Marshall came up beside him, his face stern. Darby finally seemed to get the message. With a half-disappointed, half-angry scowl, he hurried away.

"The nerve of the damned Yankee," Marshall grumbled. "President Davis would have no business interrogating you so, let alone some brash reporter."

"He is but doing his job, Major, as we do ours." Lee grinned wryly. "I will admit to not being sorry he is now doing it somewhere else."

In the ride to the Galt House on the corner of Second and Main, Louisville seemed very much a northern city, in that the vast majority of the people on the streets were white. Of the few Negroes Lee saw, several wore the remnants of Union uniforms. A couple of them turned to stare—and to glare—at his gray coat, and Charles Marshall's.

General Grant was standing in the hotel lobby when Lee came in. He walked over to shake Lee's hand. "One glance at the map and I knew I would beat you here, sir," he said. "The railroad line from Washington to Louisville is much more direct than that from Richmond. I would have arrived sooner still if all the line of the Baltimore and Ohio ran north of the Potomac. But even so, I got in day before yesterday."

"As you say, General, you enjoyed the shorter route." Lee hesitated, then added, "I must say, sir, that I am happier to be meeting you again in this fashion than I was during the late war."

"I'm a great deal happier to see you like this, that's certain," Grant said, puffing smoke from his cigar, "and ever so much better here than in the melancholy circumstances that surrounded us at Washington. Shall we dine together? Lieutenant Colonel Porter, my aide, is here with me. I hope he might join us."

"Of course, if I may bring Major Marshall here," Lee answered. He waited for Grant to nod, then continued, "Perhaps you will give us an hour in which to freshen ourselves? If it suits you, we shall meet you here at"— he glanced at a clock on the wall; its pendulum swung away the seconds— "half past seven."

"Very good, sir," Grant said. They shook hands and went their separate ways.

Grant's aide, Horace Porter, was a tough-looking fellow in his late twenties, with dark, wavy hair, stern eyes set in a forward-thrusting face, and a sweeping mustache set above a narrow strip of chin beard. "Pleased to make your acquaintance, gentlemen," he said when Lee and Marshall came down from their second-floor rooms. "As we are on neutral ground here, shall we proceed to the dining room together?"

"An admirable suggestion," Lee said with a smile.

Once seated, Grant said, "I have often stayed at the Galt House; my wife and I both have relatives in and close by Louisville. In summer, the terrapins from the Ohio are very fine here, but at this time of year we'd best stick to beef and potatoes." His dinner companions accepted the suggestion. When the roast arrived, Grant cut a piece for himself but sent it back to the kitchen for more thorough cooking. "I can't abide bloody meat," he explained, "or blood of any sort, come to that."

"An odd quirk for a general," Lee said.

Grant chuckled in self-deprecation. "So it is, but I expect we all have our crotchets." The colored waiter brought back his beef. It was black on the outside and gray on the inside. It had to be as tough as shoe leather, and taste like it, too, but he ate it with every sign of enjoyment.

Porter drank two glasses of whiskey; Lee and Marshall shared a bottle of wine. Despite rumors about Grant's tippling, he stuck to coffee. Once the main course and the plum pudding that followed had been cleared away, Lee said, "General, if I may make so bold as to enquire, how do you view your role and that of your men here?"

Grant paused for thought before he answered. He had a poker-player's face, one that revealed nothing unintended. "More that of policeman than soldier, I believe: to keep either side from doing too much in the way of smuggling rifles, to keep this a political fight and not a new outbreak of civil war, and to keep the election as honest as may be. And you, sir?"

Lee's glass still held a little wine. He raised it in salute to Grant. "We shall get on capitally, sir. I could not have hoped to combine accuracy and succinctness so."

"We would do well to cooperate if we hope to maintain the fragile peace here and especially in Missouri," Porter said; his flat Pennsylvania accent—his father was a former governor of the state—contrasted with both Grant's western speech and the soft Virginia tones of the Confederate officers. "Both states already hold enough rifles, and to spare, to break out in fresh fighting even were no new weapons smuggled across any borders."

"Quite true," Lee said, remembering blue coats and gray at Munfordsville. "Having spent so much time at war, we soldiers deserve a spell as peacemakers and peacekeepers, would you not agree?"

"I'd toast you, sir, if I had strong drink before me," Grant said.

"I am pleased to accept the spirit of the toast without the spirits," Lee said. Charles Marshall raised an eyebrow, Horace Porter snorted and then tried to pretend he hadn't, and Grant chuckled, just as if, less than a year earlier, the four men hadn't done their best to slaughter one another's armies. It was, in fact, a most convivial evening.

A sunbeam stealing through the window woke Lee up. He left his nightcap on when he got out of bed; the fire in the fireplace had died during the night, and the room was almost as cold as his tent outside Orange Court House had been the winter before. After a good, satisfying stretch, he walked over to the sideboard where his uniform hung.

Everything happened at once then. A rifle roared. The window by which he was standing blew in, showering him with splinters of glass. A bullet buzzed past his head and smacked into the opposite wall.

He instinctively ducked, though even as he did so, he knew the motion was useless. He made himself straighten, ran the two steps to the window. By the sound, the rifle had been a Springfield; whoever was firing would need time to reload, time in which he could duck. Only later did he think two gunmen might have waited outside.

The outer air was even colder than that in his room. He stuck out his head, looked up and down the street. A man was running away, fast as he could go. A couple of other people pursued him, but only a couple—the hour was too early for many people to be out and about. A rifle lay against the front wall of the bakery that lay opposite the Galt House on Second Street.

Charles Marshall pounded on the door. "General Lee! Are you all right?"

"Yes, thank you, Major." Lee let his aide in to prove it. On his way back to the bed, he started to hop. "No, not quite, I fear; I seem to have cut my foot on some of this glass. A maid will have to sweep it up."

"You have some in your beard, too," Marshall said. Lee ran his fingers through it. Sure enough, glittering shards fell down the front of his nightshirt. Marshall's voice rose with outrage as the full import of the situation sank in: "Someone tried to kill you, sir!"

"So it would appear," Lee said. By then, the hall outside his door was full of staring, chattering people, among them a pop-eyed Horace Porter. He spoke to them: "I am grateful for your concern, my friends, but, as you see, I remain uninjured. Major, would you be so kind as to shut that, so I can get properly dressed?"

Marshall obeyed, although, to Lee's secret annoyance, he stayed inside himself. "Who could want to harm you, sir?" he asked as Lee buttoned his trousers.

"There are undoubtedly a goodly number of Northern men who have little cause to love me," Lee replied. As he pulled on his boots, he reflected that some men from the South also failed to look on him with affection. But no. An assassin from the Rivington men would have used an AK-47 at close range, not a Springfield—and with the automatic fire from an AK-47 would have been far more likely to accomplish what he'd set out to do.

Charles Marshall put his head out the window. He whistled softly. "At that range, you were very lucky, sir." He paused, looked out toward where the rifle lay. His tone turned musing. "Or perhaps, from the position this murderer took, the reflection of the sun against the glass here helped throw off his aim."

"Let me see." Lee also gauged the angle. "Yes, it could well be so— but that is also luck of a sort, is it not?" Shouts came from the direction in which his assailant had fled. He turned his head that way. Of themselves, his eyebrows shot up. "Good heavens, Major, they seem to have caught him. Quick work there." He drew back so his aide could have a look.

Behind his spectacles, Marshall's eyebrows also rose. "It's a nigger, by God!" he exclaimed.

"Is it?" Lee displaced Marshall again. Sure enough, the man being dragged along in the middle of the crowd was black. He saw Lee looking at him, started to shout something. One of his captors hit him just then, so his words were lost.

Lee left the window and went out into the hall, which was still crowded with people but not the mad crush it had been a few minutes before. General Grant caught his eye. "I hear you were shot at," Grant said. Lee nodded. Grant's mouth shaped a thin smile. "Not how I'd care to be awakened for breakfast. As long as you're up, though, shall we go have some?"

"An excellent suggestion," Lee said, liking the way the Federal general made no undue fuss about the incident—but then, Grant had earned a reputation for coolness under fire.

Breakfast, however, proved next to impossible. Lacking Grant's sang-froid, a stream of local dignitaries—mayor, sheriff, lieutenant governor of Kentucky, along with a couple of others whose names and titles Lee failed to catch—came up to him and expostulated over the horror of what had just happened, how he should not deem it in any way an expression of how true and honest Kentuckians felt about him or the Confederacy, and on and on. The excited locals all but rent their garments. Lee answered as patiently as he could. Meanwhile, his ham and eggs sat on the plate in front of him, untouched and getting colder by the minute.

The officials ignored Grant, who drank cup after cup of black coffee, sliced up a cucumber, dipped the slices into vinegar, and ate them one after another, methodically, until they were all gone. It was not the sort of breakfast for which Lee would have cared, but at least Grant got to eat it.

When what seemed like the seven-hundredth uninvited guest approached the table, even Lee's glacial patience started to slip. His hand tightened on the fork he had finally managed to pick up, as if he intended to stick it into this importunate fellow instead of his ham. But the man proved to have news worth hearing: "Found out why that crazy nigger took a shot at you, General."

"Ah?" Lee's grip on the fork relaxed. "Tell me, sir." Interest also sparked in Grant's eyes.

"He was yellin' an' cussin' and carryin' on about how if you hadn't gone and took Washington City, the Federals would've won the war and set all the niggers down South free."

"I suspect there may be some truth in that," Lee said. "No doubt General Grant will concur."

"No doubt at all," Grant said promptly, and Lee remembered first how much the Federal commander had wanted to go on fighting and then what the outcome of that fight would have been without the intervention of the Rivington men. Grant continued, "That does not give that Negro or anyone else the right to go shooting at General Lee now, though. For better or worse, the war is over."

"What will they do with him?" Lee asked.

"Try him and hang him, I expect," the Kentuckian answered with a shrug. "Oh, he said one other thing, General Lee: he said you must own a rabbit's foot off a rabbit caught in a graveyard at midnight, or else he never would have missed you."

"Morning sun is a likelier reason than anything from the black of night," said Lee, who had no such charm. He explained how the would-be assassin had picked a poor spot from which to fire.

The Kentuckian laughed. "Ain't that just like a fool nigger?" He made as if to clap Lee on the back for his escape, but thought better of it; Lee was not a man to inspire casual familiarity from strangers. Leaving his gesture awkwardly half-completed, the fellow departed. Lee's breakfast was ruined, but he ate it anyhow. A bad breakfast was far preferable to the prospect of no breakfast at all, ever again.

During the next few months, Lee traveled all through Kentucky and Missouri. He ran up more miles, faster, than he ever had on campaign, but then, but for that one Negro, no one was shooting at him now.

Grant traveled even farther, especially in Missouri. Missouri had no direct train connections with Kentucky, Tennessee, or Arkansas—Lee had to travel by coach from Columbus, Kentucky, to Ironton, Missouri, where the St. Louis and Iron Mountain Railroad reconnected him with the rail network. Grant, on the other hand, could reach St. Louis—where he had once lived—quickly and easily by way of the Ohio and Mississippi across Indiana and Illinois, and made several trips there.

Lee was pleased at how well both sides held to their pledges of keeping soldiers out of the disputed states. That did not mean no one invaded Kentucky and Missouri, however. Every politician, Northern and Southern, who could stand on a stump and put one word after another, or ten thousand after another ten, flooded into the two states to tell their people just why they should choose the United States or the Confederacy.

Listening to a pro-Confederate orator thunder abuse at the North at a torchlight rally one night in Frankfort, Charles Marshall made a sour face and said, "Anyone can tell he spent the war safely far away from the firing lines. Had he ever faced the Yankees in battle, he would own far more respect for their manhood than he currently displays."

"How right you are," Lee replied, as appalled as his aide at the oratory: the speaker had just called the Northerners cold-blooded, fat-faced, nigger-loving moneygrubbers. Lee went on, "I confess to a certain amount of embarrassment at representing the same nation as does this eloquent fellow." To emphasize his distaste, he turned half away from the shouting, gesticulating man up on the platform.

"I know what you mean, sir." But Marshall, as if drawn by some horrid fascination, kept watching the orator. Red light from the torches flickered off his spectacle lenses. "Even if he wins votes, he also sows hatred."

"Just so," Lee said. "For example, have you seen this?" He took out a pamphlet and handed it to Marshall.

His aide held it close to his face so he could read it in the torchlight. " 'What Miscegenation Is! And What You May Expect if Kentucky Votes Union,' " he quoted. He gave the pamphlet a bemused look. "The cover is—striking."

"That is one word which may truthfully apply to it," Lee admitted. The pamphlet showed a black man, his nose and lips grotesquely exaggerated, embracing a white woman and tilting her face up for a kiss. "We are, fortunately, not responsible for this document: you will note the learned lawyer Mr. Seaman had it printed in New York."

"By the look of the thing, the learned Mr. Seaman, merely by existing, besmirches the legal profession." Marshall held the pamphlet between thumb and forefinger, as if to minimize his contact with it. "Are the contents as lurid as the cover?"

"Easily," Lee said. "And many of our speakers, though it did not originate with us, distribute it broadside, as a warning against what may come should the Republicans gain the upper hand again. It may perhaps be effective, but I find it repugnant."

"The Yankees have hardly been kind in what they say about us," Marshall said. "Can we afford to indulge such scruples?"

Lee merely looked at him until he hung his head. "I am disappointed in you, Major. Can we afford not to indulge them? Regardless of whether we ultimately find ourselves in possession of Kentucky and Missouri, we shall have to live with ourselves—and with the United States—afterwards. Poisoning the air with lies will not make matters easier."

"You view these matters from a higher plane than I have reached," Marshall said, still sounding ashamed. "You truly would not mind if the disputed states chose the Union over us, would you, sir?"

"I hope they see the Confederacy's merits, as I have," Lee replied after some thought. "But I would sooner see them go willingly with those people than unwillingly with us. That, after all, is the principle upon which we formed our nation, and for which we fought so long and hard. That—not this." He took the pamphlet from Charles Marshall, let it fall, and ground it beneath his boot heel.

Major Marshall thrust a telegram into Lee's hands. "You must see this directly, sir."

"Thank you, Major." Lee unfolded the flimsy paper. The words on it leaped out at him:

14 MARCH 1865. U.S. LIEUTENANT ADAM SLEMMER CAPTURED TWO MEN WITH A HORSE TRAIN OF AK-47S AND CARTRIDGES THIS DATE TOMPKINS-VILLE KENTUCKY. PLEASE ADVISE. RICHARD INGOM, CAPTAIN, C.S.A. ELEC-TION OBSERVERS.

Lee wadded up the telegram and flung it against the wall. "Those god-damned fools," he ground out—who else would be running repeaters but the men from Rivington? His head tossed like an angry stallion's. "Do they think they are lords of the earth, to arrogate to themselves the authority for such an action? Where the devil is Tompkinsville, Major?"

"Just north of the Tennessee border, sir, southeast of Bowling Green. It's not on any railroad line." Marshall must have expected and prepared for the question, for he answered as quickly and certainly as if Lee had enquired about the location of Richmond.

"We can get to Bowling Green quickly, then. We'll hire horses there and ride for Tompkinsville. Telegraph ahead to Captain Ingom that we are on our way, and on no account to allow rifles or prisoners to proceed until we arrive."

"I'll head directly for the telegraph office, sir." Marshall hurried away.

Two days later, the two gray-clad men reined in their blowing horses in front of Tompkinsville's only hotel. Lee felt his years as he dismounted; he hadn't ridden so hard for so long since his Indian-fighting days in the west. He was not surprised to see General Grant leaning against one of the columns of the hotel's false front. Touching the brim of his hat to Grant, he said, "The stableman at Bowling Green told me you'd got there before us, sir."

"I wish I could have done as well at Bealeton, sir," Grant replied; by the sound of his voice, he would be mentally refighting his battles against Lee the rest of his life. He went on, "I've not been here long myself—no more than a couple of hours."

"Then you will already have spoken to your Lieutenant Slemmer."

"So I have. Seems he and his companion, Lieutenant James Porter, were riding a bit south of here when they came upon two men leading several heavily loaded horses. Becoming suspicious, they got the drop on the men and forced them to reveal what the loads were: your pestiferous repeaters and ammunition for same. They brought the men and horses here to Tomp-kinsville, where your Captain Ingom, who happened to be in town, was fully acquainted with the situation."

"Generous of you," Lee said; had Ingom not seen the Northern men bringing in their prisoners, he suspected he would never have heard of the incident. But that was what the observers were for: to make sure both sides played by the rules to which they'd agreed—rules that frowned on gun running. Lee asked, "Have you yet questioned these men?"

"No, sir. When Captain Ingom told me he had notified you and you were on your way, I decided to wait until you got here. The men and horses are under guard at the livery stable down the street. Will you join me?"

Lee inclined his head. "By all means. And let me express my thanks for your scrupulous observance of the proprieties obtaining in this matter."

"Anything else would only cause more trouble, I thought," Grant said.

In the stable, a Federal lieutenant held an army Colt revolver on two men sitting glumly in the hay. Sure enough, they both wore the mottled caps, coats, and trousers of the Rivington men. "On your feet, you," the lieutenant barked. His captives made no move to obey until they saw Lee and Grant. Then they stood, slowly, as if to show they would have done the same thing without being ordered.

One of them swept off his plain, ugly cap in a gesture that made it seem a cavalier's plumed chapeau. "General Lee," he said, bowing. "Allow me to present my comrade, Willem van Pelt."

"Mr. de Buys." That smooth bow, so like Jeb Stuart's, brought the Rivington man's name back to Lee.

"You know this fellow?" Grant's voice was suddenly hard and suspicious.

"To my mortification, I do." Ignoring the proffered introduction, Lee growled, "What the devil are you doing here, Mr. de Buys?"

Konrad de Buys's eyes were wide and innocent. A catamount's eyes were innocent, too, just before it sprang. Lee wondered how the Northern soldiers had got the drop on a warrior of his quality. The Rivington man said, "We were just coming up to sell a few guns, General, sporting guns, you might say. Is anything wrong with that?"

"Is anything wrong with pouring oil on a fire?" Lee retorted. De Buys still looked innocent. His comrade, Willem van Pelt, was big and stolid and seemed stupid; Lee would have bet that was as much a façade as de Buys's innocence.

"To whom were you going to sell these rifles?" Grant asked.

"Oh, there are always buyers," de Buys said airily.

"No doubt," Lee said. He could picture the sort of men de Buys had in mind—raiders to sweep down on little towns before the election, or on the day, and to make sure the folk there voted the right way. He turned to

Grant. "Will you step outside with me for a moment, sir?" They stayed outside longer than a moment. When they returned, Lee said, "Mr. de Buys, General Grant here has graciously agreed to buy every one of your repeaters, and their accompanying cartridges."

That got through the fronts both Rivington men held up as shields against the world. Willem van Pelt spoke for the first time: "No way we'll sell to his bloody sort."

"Oh, but gentlemen, he will give you a finer price than you could hope to receive from anyone else," Lee said.

Grant nodded. "That's right." He reached into a trouser pocket, took out a silver dollar, and tossed it at Konrad de Buys's feet. "There you go, for the lot of 'em."

An angry flush mounted de Buys's cheeks. "Be damned to your dollar, and to you, too."

"You'd best take it," Grant told him. "With it, you and your friend there can ride back to Tennessee. Without it, you go North under guard for more questions—a lot more."

Willem van Pelt worked his jaw and tensed, as if to make some sort of move. The Federal lieutenant, an alert young man, swung his revolver toward the Rivington man. "Easy, Willem," Konrad de Buys said, setting a hand on van Pelt's arm. He swung his hunting cat's gaze toward Lee. "So you'd sooner work with the Yankees than with us, eh, General? We'll remember that, I promise you."

"The United States have business in Kentucky and Missouri till June, and have handsomely kept their agreements with us. You, sir, do not belong here, not if you are running guns. Now get your horses and go, and count yourselves lucky to have that opportunity." Lee turned to Grant. "Perhaps your lieutenants will ride with them a ways, to ensure that they do cross the border." Then, to de Buys, in tones of palpable warning: "You personally and your colleagues shall be held responsible for the safety of the two Federals."

Grant chuckled: "It seems you needn't fret over that, General, not when my lads captured these fellows in the first place."

"They never would have, if they hadn't come on us when I was in the bushes with my pants around my ankles," Konrad de Buys growled. Grant's chuckle turned into a laugh.

Lee laughed, too, but was inclined to believe the Rivington man. With or without their marvelous repeaters, his kind were uncommonly dangerous, and de Buys himself more so than most. "Remember what I told you," Lee said sternly, and was relieved to see both Rivington men give grudging nods.

They and the Federals rode south from Tompkinsville that afternoon. Grant stayed in town to await the lieutenants' return, so he and they could start the repeaters on their journey northwards. Lee and Marshall set off for Bowling Green. As they rode out of Tompkinsville, Marshall said, "Are you sure it is expedient, sir, just to give some dozens of repeaters to the Yankees like that?"

"Did I believe they had none, Major, I assure you I should never have done so," Lee answered. "But they surely possess samples a-plenty, whether seized from prisoners or taken from beside corpses, as our men used to take Springfields to replace the smoothbore muskets they'd been issued. And by ceding the guns, I kept the Rivington men out of Northern hands. As they know about a good many things besides AK-47s, I count them as more important than the rifles."

"Ah. Put that way, I see your point." Marshall ran a hand through his wavy blond hair. "They do sometimes seem all but omniscient, don't they?"

"Yes," Lee said shortly. That was what worried him about the men of America Will Break. After a moment, he added, "Omniscient they are not, however, for I can think of one thing they surely do not know."

"What's that, sir?" Marshall sounded genuinely curious.

"Not to meddle in our politics." Lee booted his hired horse into a trot. Marshall matched him to keep up. They rode some time in silence.

People argued even as they filed into the Louisville park. It was Good Friday. Under other circumstances, many of them would have been in church. But church would be there Easter Sunday, and the Sunday after that, and the year after that. They might never hear a President—or rather, a recent ex-President—of the United States again.

U.S. flags flew at all four corners of the speakers' platform. They still displayed thirty-six stars, though eleven states had left the Union for good and two more were wavering. Some of the people in the crowd waved the old banner, too. But others carried one of the several versions of the Confederate flag. Already the rival factionalists were beginning to push and shove each other.

Charles Marshall's spectacles lent him a supercilious air as he stood at the edge of the swelling throng. Perhaps that was no accident, for his voice held a definite sniff: "Considering where he took his country, Lincoln has considerable nerve to show his face in Kentucky and urge it to follow his lead."

"Lincoln *has* considerable nerve," Lee said, "and this is, after all, his birth state. But I question his political wisdom in coming here—Seymour and McClellan both outpolled him in this state, Seymour by an enormous margin, so how can he hope to sway any substantial number of voters?"

A year before, he would never have thought to make such political calculations. His life had been simpler then, his only problem the straightforward one of beating back the Army of the Potomac when it began to move. With all his soul, he longed for those simpler days, but he knew it would take another war to bring them back, and that was too high a price to pay.

Marshall started to say something, but his words were lost in the peculiar roar, half cheer and half hiss, that went up from the crowd. It reminded Lee of a locomotive with a bad boiler. The man who produced that frightening mixture of hate and adulation stood on the platform, unmistakably tall and unmistakably lean, and waited for the tumult to ebb. At last, it did.

"Americans!" Lincoln said, and with a single word drew all attention to himself, for no one, whether staunch Union man or backer of the Confederacy, denied himself that proud title. Lincoln used it again: "Americans, surely you know I should rather have given up all my life's blood sooner than see my beloved nation torn in two."

"We can fix that for you, by God!" a heckler yelled, and a savage chorus of jeers arose.

Lincoln spoke through them: "Both sides in the late conflict spoke the same tongue, prayed to the same God. That He chose to grant victory to the South is a fact I can but strive to accept, understand it though I do not, for the judgments of the Lord are true and righteous altogether. I bear no animus against the men I still believe my brethren, nor have I ever."

"It don't work both ways!" the leather-lunged heckler shouted. Lee thought the fellow wrong, though during the simpler days of the war he would have agreed with him. Lincoln truly saw one nation rather than a federation of sovereign states, and acted on that belief, misguided and mistaken though Lee believed he was.

Now he continued, "You have rejected me, as well you might have, seeing how I failed to preserve the Union I swore to protect and defend. But I am only one small man. Do with me as you see fit; it will be no less than I deserve. But I pray you, men of Kentucky, with all my heart and all my soul and all my mind—do not reject the United States of America."

More catcalls rang out, along with scattered cheers. Lincoln ignored both; Lee had the odd feeling that he was talking to himself up there on the platform, talking to himself yet at the same time desperately hoping others would hear: "Important principles may—and *must*—be inflexible. We all declare for liberty, but we do not always mean the same thing by it. In the United States, liberty means each man may do as he pleases with himself and his labor; in the South, the same word means some would do as they please with other men and that which they produce. To the fox, stealing chickens from the farmer looks like liberty, but do you think the fowl agree?"

"Just like honest, backwoods Abe to talk about foxes and hencoops," Charles Marshall said, a sneer in his voice. Lee started to nod, but thought better of it. Yes, the image was not one he could imagine hearing from Jefferson Davis's lips, but it illuminated the point Lincoln had made just before more vividly than might many a polished phrase. And that point was far from a bad one. Lee had the uncomfortable feeling of being more in sympathy with his country's foes than with such friends as the men of America Will Break.

Lincoln said, "Men of Kentucky, men of America, if you vote to go South, you vote to forget Washington and Patrick Henry, Jefferson and Nathan Hale, Jackson and John Paul Jones. Remember the nation your fathers joined, remember the nation so many of you fought so bravely to defend. God bless the United States of America!"

Some cheered; more, Lee thought, booed. He found no small irony in the fact that three of Lincoln's "American" heroes, Washington, Patrick Henry, and Jefferson, had been slaveholding Virginians; Martha Washington's blood ran in the veins of his own wife. And the South revered the Founding Fathers no less than the North; he remembered coming into Richmond on Washington's birthday and finding the War Department closed. And for that matter, Washington on horseback appeared on the Great Seal of the Confederate States. This time, he had no sympathy for Lincoln's claims.

The former U.S. President descended from the platform. Here and there, instead of dispersing, men held their ground and argued with one another, standing nose to nose while they shouted and waved their arms. But no riot followed Lincoln's speech. Given the volatility of Louisville—of all Kentucky, and Missouri, too—Lee knew only relief over that.

Marshall in his wake, he strode through the thinning crowd toward Lincoln. He was a tall man himself, and Lincoln, especially after resuming the stovepipe hat he had shed while speaking, possibly the tallest man in the park. The ex-President was easy to keep in sight.

Lincoln soon spotted Lee. He waited for him to come up. "Mr. President," Lee said, inclining his head.

"Not anymore," Lincoln said. "And we both know whose fault that is, don't we?"

The Rivington men's, Lee thought. Without them, from what they'd said, Lincoln would still be President, and President of a nation intent on taking vengeance on the unsuccessfully seceded Southern states. Yet he did not sound bitter; he seemed wryly amused, as if talking of the world's vagaries with a friend. Try as he would, Lee could not see in this elongated, homely man the ogre Andries Rhoodie had described.

But all that was by the way. Lincoln dwelt in the White House no more, and the nightmare future would not come to pass. Lee asked, "What do you plan to do now, sir?"

"Till the election, I aim to go through Kentucky and Missouri like Satan going up and down in the world, and do everything I can to hold 'em in the Union," Lincoln said, and poked more fun at himself by adding, "Not that some of the people in both states don't already figure me for the devil, I expect. After that . . ." His voice trailed away. "After that, I suppose I'll go home to Springfield, practice law, and get old. When I was younger, I never thought I'd escape obscurity, so going back to it should be easy enough. Maybe one day, when all this fuss has died down, I'll write a book about how everything would have turned out for the best if it hadn't been for Bobbie Lee."

"You will, I hope, forgive me, sir, for holding the opinion that these matters *have* turned out for the best," Lee said.

"You don't need my forgiveness, General, though you're polite to ask for it. Even under your Southern constitution, every man may hold what opinions he likes, eh? Candide believed to the end that this was the best of all possible worlds." Lincoln let out a wry laugh. "What does what I think matter, anyhow? I'm going back into the shadows. But you, General, your future stretches out ahead lit with torches and paved with gold."

"Hardly that, sir," Lee said.

"No? Where else for the noblest Virginian of them all but at the head of—of his country?" Lincoln's mouth twisted. Even now, going on a year after the South had won its independence, acknowledging the Confederacy pained him.

Lee also wondered whether he meant the crib from Shakespeare as compliment or sarcasm. He answered, "I am proud to serve my state and my nation in whatever capacity they choose for me."

Lincoln looked down at him. As always, he found that disconcerting; he was used to holding the high ground in conversation. "Serving a country is all very well, General, but when the time comes, will you be able to lead it in the direction you know it must go?" He did not wait for a reply, but touched a finger to the brim of his hat and departed.

Charles Marshall stared after him. "How could the North have been so misguided as to elect that man its President?" He mimed a couple of steps' worth of Lincoln's loose-jointed gait.

"He *is* peculiar-looking, to himself, I understand, not least. But he knows the proper questions to ask." Lee also watched Lincoln until he disappeared behind some willows with their full skirts of new spring leaves. The proper question indeed: if he said slavery might possibly have to end one day, who in the South would listen to him?

"Sorry to disturb your supper, General Lee, sir," a messenger boy said, dumping a tall pile of telegrams onto Lee's table in the Galt House dining room.

"It's all right, son." Lee raised an eyebrow in humorous resignation. Already telegrams leaned in drunken profusion against a platter of stuffed duck, against a bowl of peas, a gravy boat, wineglasses; already they covered the bread and hid the relish trays from sight. Lee went on, "It's plain I'll be reading more than eating for yet another night."

The messenger boy probably did not hear that last sentence; he was hurrying back to the telegraph office for a new load of messages. General Grant said, "When you're done with those, sir, if you'd be kind enough to pass them my way—"

"Certainly." Lee went through the sheaf one by one, occasionally pausing to cut another bite from the slice of saddle of mutton in front of him. Behind him, a small colored boy with a large peacock fan stirred the still, muggy air that went with June evenings in Louisville. "Not too hard, there," Lee warned him as the papers on the table shifted. "You don't want to blow them into the soup, now do you?" The little slave giggled and shook his head.

Lee finished the pile. "No great irregularities here," he told Grant.

The Federal general was also going through a stack. "Nor in mine, it seems." He reached bottom just after Lee did. "Shall we exchange prisoners?"

In return for the reports the Federal election inspectors had sent to Grant, Lee gave him the latest set of messages he himself had received from the Confederate inspectors. As Grant said, the vote had on the whole proceeded smoothly. Some precincts from the south and west of Missouri had yet to report. Lee suspected no one in those parts had voted; regardless of armistices, regardless of Federal occupation troops, the civil war there went on. But the area was thinly populated anyhow. Even had all its votes gone for the Confederacy, the state as a whole would have remained in the Union.

Kentucky was another matter. Grant acknowledged as much when he said, "In the coming week, General Lee, I shall shift my headquarters to St. Louis, so as to maintain them within the territory of the United States."

"You may even find it more congenial than Louisville, from your previous acquaintance with the city," Lee said.

"I doubt it." Grant's face never gave away much, but his voice turned bleak. "I was out of the army—on the beach, you might say—while I was there, so my memories are not entirely happy ones. And, as you may understand, sir, I cannot rejoice at Kentucky's having voted itself out of the Union to which I owe everything I have in this world."

"I respect the sincerity of your sentiments; no, further—I admire it. I hope you will understand that the people of Kentucky are equally sincere in theirs." By close to four to three, Kentucky's voters had chosen to cast their lot with the South.

Grant said, "I recognize it, but I own to having a great deal of difficulty admiring it. To speak frankly, I believe the Southern cause one of the worst for which people ever took up arms, and one for which there was not the least excuse. That you fought so long and valiantly for such a patently bad cause has always been a wonder to me."

"We in turn were perpetually amazed at the United States' determination to expend so much in treasure and lives to try to restore by force the allegiance the people of the South were no longer willing to give voluntarily."

"That's over now, it appears, for better or for worse. If you visit me in St. Louis under flag of truce, General, be sure I shall gladly receive you." Grant rose. "Now I hope you will excuse me. I find I haven't the stomach for supper, not when I am forced to watch yet another state wrenched away from the Union."

Lee also stood, shook hands with Grant. He said, "Kentucky was not 'wrenched'; it went of its own free will."

"Small consolation," Grant said, and left the table. Instead of going upstairs to his room, he walked over to the bar and began to drink. Though he had stayed sober until the day of the election, he was still on his bar stool when Lee went upstairs, and still on it, drunk, asleep, when Lee came down for breakfast the next morning.

"Shall I wake him?" Charles Marshall asked, eyeing Grant's slumped form with distaste.

"Let him be, Major," Lee said. Marshall gave him a curious look. He almost added, *There but for the grace of God go I*, but at the last moment kept silent. Not for the first time, he wondered how his life would have gone after a surrender at Richmond. Not well, he suspected: who would care about the high general of the losing side?

George McClellan should have considered that before he ran his bootless race for President, Lee thought. But then, McClellan's timing was generally bad. His own humor quite restored by that snide thought, Lee sat down to wait for a breakfast menu.

⋆ XII ⋆

The summer sun beat down on Nashville's main square. The maples that grew along Washington and Alston streets gave some shade, but could do nothing to cut the heat or the oppressive humidity. When a buggy rattled west down Washington, it kicked up so much dust that it reminded Nate Caudell of his marching days in the army. But despite the beastly weather, a good-sized crowd had assembled in front of the Nash County courthouse.

"What's going on?" Caudell asked a man who looked about to melt in frock coat, vest, cravat, and stovepipe.

"The nigger auction starts at noon," the fellow answered.

"Is that today?" Caudell, who could no more afford a slave than he could a private railroad coach and a locomotive to haul it, skirted the edges of the gathering and started into Raeford Liles's general store. The front door was locked. Caudell scratched his head—but for Sunday, Liles never closed the place. Then he saw the storekeeper among the men waiting for the auction to start. Liles was serious about wanting a servant, then.

Caudell recognized several other potential buyers, among them George Lewis; his former captain had been elected to the state legislature, and lately spent more time down in Raleigh than in Nash County. Lewis saw Caudell, too, and waved to him. Caudell waved back. He had to check himself from coming to attention and saluting.

But the crowd held a good many strangers, too. Caudell heard the soft accents of Alabama and Mississippi, while a couple of men spoke with a

Texas twang he remembered from the army. His ears also caught another accent, one that made his head whip around. Sure enough, there stood three Rivington men, talking among themselves. Despite the coming of peace, they still preferred the splotched, muddy-looking clothes they'd worn in camp and into battle. They looked more comfortable in them than most of the Southern gentlemen did in their more formal attire.

The courthouse clock struck twelve. Men with watches took them out to check them against the clock. A minute or so later, the bells of the Baptist church announced the coming of noon. After another brief delay, the bells of the Methodist church, which was farther down Alston Street, also declared the hour. Caudell wondered which clock was right, and whether any one of them was. It didn't really matter, not to him; who but a railroad man like Henry Pleasants needed to know the time exact to the minute?

Despite its announced starting time, the slave auction showed no sign of getting under way. By the way they chatted and smoked and dipped snuff, few of the would-be buyers had expected that it would. But the Rivington men began to fidget. One of them pointedly looked at his wrist—Caudell saw he wore a tiny watch there, held on with a leather strap. A few minutes later, the Rivington man looked at his wristwatch again. When nothing happened after a third such irritated glance, the man shouted, "What the bleeding hell are we waiting for?"

His impatience set off the crowd like a percussion cap igniting the charge of a Springfield cartridge. In an instant, a dozen men were yelling for things to get moving. If he'd kept quiet, they likely would have stood around another hour without complaining.

A man in a suit of exaggeratedly dandyish cut hurried out of the courthouse and sprang up onto the platform that had been hastily built in front of it. Pausing only to spit tobacco juice into the dust, he said, "We'll commence shortly, gentlemen, I promise. And when you see the fine niggers Josiah A. Beard has to sell"—he preened slightly, to show one and all he was the Josiah A. Beard in question—"you'll be glad you waited, I promise you will." His broad, beaming face radiated candor. Caudell distrusted him on sight.

He kept up a bright stream of talk for another few minutes. The Rivington men quickly started looking impatient again. Before they started a new round of shouts, though, a black man came out of the courthouse and up to stand beside Josiah Beard. The auctioneer said, "Here we are, gentlemen, the first on the list, a fine field hand and laborer, a Negro named Columbus, aged thirty-two years."

"Let's see him," one of the Texas men called.

Beard turned to Columbus. "Strip off," he said curtly. The black man pulled his coarse cotton shirt over his head, stepped out of his trousers. "Turn around," the auctioneer told him. Columbus obeyed. Beard raised his voice, spoke to the audience: "Now you see him. Not a mark on his back, as you'll note for yourselves. He's tractable as well as willing. He's a genuine cotton nigger, by God! Look at his toes, at his fingers. Look at those legs! If you have got the right soil, buy him and put your trust in Providence, my friends. He's as good for ten bales as I am for a julep at eleven o'clock. So what am I bid for this fine buck nigger?"

The bidding started at five hundred dollars and rose rapidly. The Texas man who'd asked to see all of Columbus ended up buying him for $1,450. Even with prices still high, that was a goodly sum, but he seemed unperturbed. "I could sell him in Houston tomorrow and make four hundred back," he declared to anyone who cared to listen. "Niggers is still mighty dear anywheres in the trans-Mississippi."

Another black mounted to the stand. "Second on the list," Beard said. "An excellent field hand and laborer, gentlemen, named Dock, a Negro aged twenty-six years." Without waiting for a customer's request, he added, "Strip off, Dock."

"Yassuh." Dock's Negro patois was thick as molasses. He shed his shirt and trousers, turned before he was told to do so. His back, like Columbus's, had never known the lash, but an ugly scar seamed the inside of his left thigh, about six inches below his genitals.

Josiah Beard once more started to extol the slave's docility. Before he was well begun, George Lewis called, "Hold on, there! You, boy! Where did you get that bullet wound?"

Dock's head lifted. He looked straight at Lewis. "Got this heah outside o' Water Proof, *Louz*iana, las' yeah, f'um dat Bedford Forrest. He done cotched me, but my three frens, they gits away."

The auctioneer did his best to pretend Dock had never been a soldier in arms against the Confederacy. Bidding was slow all the same, and petered out just past eight hundred dollars. One of the Rivington men bought the slave. He paid gold, which did a little to restore Josiah Beard's spirits.

As Dock came down from the platform toward him, the Rivington man told him, "You do your work and we'll get on fine, boy. Just don't put on airs because you used to carry a rifle. I can lick you any way you name: bare hands, axes, whips, guns, any way at all. Any time you want to try, you tell me, but you have your grave picked out beforehand. Do you understand me?"

"You don't need to lick me none, masser—you gots de law wid you," Dock said. But before he answered, he measured his new owner with his eyes, saw that the Rivington man meant exactly what he said and could back it up without the law. He nodded, more man to man than slave to master, but respectfully nonetheless.

Caudell thought the Negro sensible to submit—if he was submitting and not shamming. If he was shamming, he'd likely regret it. Caudell had seen that the Rivington men were uncommon fighters.

More slaves went up on the block. Some did have scarred backs. A couple of them showed the marks of bullets. One black, when questioned, said he'd belonged to the 30th Connecticut and had taken his wound at Bealeton. That made Caudell frown, for Lee had ordered captured Negroes treated like any other prisoners. Someone had seen a profit in disobeying.

The Rivington men bought most of the slaves with bullet wounds, and got them cheap. The ones they didn't buy, the Texans did. Caudell suspected they would try to unload their purchases on fellow westerners who were desperate for labor and who might not recognize a bullet scar when they saw one.

"Seventeenth on the list," Josiah Beard said presently. "A fine tanner and bricklayer, named Westly, a griffe aged twenty-four years." Westly, who stood beside him, was slightly lighter of skin than most who had preceded him; griffes carried one part white blood to three black.

The bidding was brisk. Raeford Liles raised his hand again and again. Caudell understood why: a slave with two such desirable skills as tanning and bricklaying would quickly be able to learn what he needed to help out at a general store, and would make Liles extra money when he rented him out around town.

But when the griffe's price edged toward two thousand dollars, Liles dropped out with a frustrated snarl of disgust. A Rivington man and a fellow from Alabama or Mississippi bid against each other like a couple of men holding flushes in a poker game. Finally the man from the deep South gave up. "Sold for $1,950," Josiah Beard shouted.

"Masser, you lets me keep some o' my pay when you rents me, I works extra hard for you," Westly said as his new owner came up to take him off the block.

The Rivington man laughed at him. "Who said anything about renting you, kaffir? You are going to work for me and for nobody else." The griffe's face fell, but he had no choice save going with the man who had bought him.

More field hands were sold, and then a prime bricklayer and mason, a black man named Anderson. The auctioneer beamed like the rising sun as the Negro's price soared up and up. Again Raeford Liles bid, again he had to drop out. The fellow from the deep South who had bid on Westly ended up buying Anderson for $2,700 when the Rivington man who had been bidding against him abruptly quit. He did not look altogether happy as he went up to pay Josiah Beard. Caudell did not blame him. As someone in the crowd remarked, "Hellfire, you can buy yourself a Congressman for cheaper'n $2,700."

After Beard disposed of all the male slaves on his list, he sold several women, some field hands like the men, others cooks and seamstresses. "Here's a Negro named Louisa," he called as yet another wench climbed up beside him. "She's twenty-one years old, a number-one cook, and a prime breeder. Tell the gentlemen how many little niggers you've already had, Louisa."

"I's had fo', suh," she answered.

"She's good for many more, too," the auctioneer declared, "and every one pure profit to her owner. And she's a good-tempered wench, too." He turned her around, pulled down the top of her dress to display her clear back. She fetched Josiah Beard almost as much as Anderson had, and looked smug when the Texan who had bought her led her away. Some Negroes, Caudell knew, took pride in the high prices they brought. It made more than a little sense: an owner with a large investment in his animate property was likely to treat it better.

The slave trader looked out at his audience. A smile stole across his face. "Now, gentlemen, as the *pièce de résistance*, I have to display for you a mulatto wench named Josephine, nineteen years old, and a fine hand with a needle."

Caudell caught his breath as Josephine climbed up onto the platform beside Beard. He let it out again in a sudden, sharp cough. So did most of the men who saw her. She was worth every bit of that vocal admiration, and more. She might have had a trace of Indian blood as well as white and Negro; her cheekbones, her slightly slanted eyes, and the piquant arch of her nose argued for it. Her skin, perfectly smooth, was the precise color of coffee with cream.

"I'd like a piece o' that, resistance or no resistance," a man close by Caudell said hoarsely. The schoolteacher found himself nodding. The slave girl was simply stunning.

Instead of simply showing Josephine's back, as he had with the other wenches, the auctioneer unbuttoned her dress and let it fall to the boards. She was bare under it. The coughs from the crowd doubled and doubled again. Her breasts, Caudell thought, would just fill a man's hand; their small nipples made him think of sweet chocolate. Josiah Beard turned her around. She was as perfect from behind as from the front.

"Put your dress back on," the auctioneer told her. As she stooped to obey, he called out, "Now, gentlemen, what am I bid?"

To Caudell's surprise, the auction started slowly. After a moment, he understood: everyone knew how expensive she would be, and everyone was hesitant about risking his money. But Josephine's price climbed steadily, past $1,500, past $2,000, past $2,500, past the $2,700 that had bought the skilled bricklayer and mason, past $3,000. Bidders dropped out one by one, with groans of regret.

"Three thousand one hundred and fifty," Josiah Beard said at length. "Do I hear $3,200?" He looked to the Alabama man who had stayed in the auction all the way. The man from the deep South stared hungrily at Josephine, but in the end he shook his head. The slave trader puffed out his lips in a small sigh. "Anyone else for $3,200?" No one spoke. "Thirty-one fifty once." A pause. "Thirty-one fifty twice." Beard clapped his hands together. "Sold for $3,150. Come forward, sir, come forward."

"Oh, I'm coming, never fear," said the Rivington man who had just bought Josephine. The crowd parted like the Red Sea to show respect for someone who would pay so much for a chattel. The Rivington man reached into his knapsack, pulled out a paper-wrapped roll of gold coins, then another and another. "There's a hundred and fifty ounces of gold," he said, then opened yet another roll and counted out thirteen more. He passed the money to Beard, roll by roll and then coin by coin. When at last he was done, the slave trader had more than thirteen pounds of gold and a slightly sandbagged expression. Still matter-of-fact, the Rivington man said, "Along with the wench, you owe me eleven dollars."

"Yes, sir," Josiah Beard said, not even questioning the calculation. He peeled the money from the fat roll of bills he had collected over the course of the afternoon. "Let me have your name, sir, if you please, for the bill of sale."

"I'm Piet Hardie. P-i-e-t H-a-r-d-i-e. Spell it right."

"Let me have it again, sir, to make sure I do." Beard wrote, then straightened and turned to Josephine. "Go on, girl, go to him. He bought you—you're his."

Moving with a grace that matched her beauty, Josephine descended from the auction block. Piet Hardie slipped an arm around her waist. She stood very straight, neither pulling away nor pressing herself against him. A collective sigh of envy went up from the crowd. The fellow from Alabama who had been the next-to-last bidder said, "Tell me, sir, what are you going to do with her now that you got her?"

Hardie threw back his head and laughed uproariously. "What the bleeding hell do you think I'm going to do with her, sir? The same thing you'd have done if you'd bought her."

The Alabama man laughed, too, ruefully. Caudell happened to be watching Josephine's face. It congealed like cooling fat. She must have hoped the Rivington man would differ from others in more ways than his dress. Finding out so harshly that he did not could only be a cruel disappointment.

"For a very reasonable price, gentlemen, I can supply shackles, to ensure that your animate property doesn't become more animated than you'd care for." Josiah Beard chortled at his own wit. Several men came up to purchase restraints.

Caudell drifted away from the town square. For him, the slave auction had been nothing more than a way to pass part of a long Saturday afternoon. He could not even dream of owning a slave, especially in summer with his school closed. Tutoring, writing letters for illiterate townsfolk, and neatly transcribing county records gave him income sufficient to keep from starving, but not much more.

George Lewis fell into step beside him. "How are you today, Nate?"

"Well enough, thank you, sir." Though captain no longer, Lewis was a big enough man in Nash County for Caudell to keep on giving him the title of respect. "I see you didn't buy any niggers today."

"Didn't plan to; I have enough for the tobacco acreage I grow—maybe even too many. More than anything else, I came to see what prices were like, in case I decide to sell a couple."

"Oh." Caudell had known for a good many years now that he would never be a wealthy man. The knowledge no longer bothered him. Sometimes, as now, he derived a certain amusement from listening to the things wealthy men had to worry about. *Do I have too many slaves for my land? Should I sell a few?* No, that was a problem which would never trouble him.

Some of his thoughts must have shown on his face. George Lewis clapped him on the back and said, "If you're having trouble, Nate, you just let me know. I don't aim to let anybody who served in my company do without so long as I can help it."

With stubborn pride, Caudell answered: "That's right kind of you, but I'm doing well enough, sir." Lewis raised a politely dubious eyebrow. "There's plenty worse off than I am," Caudell insisted.

"Most of 'em have farms, though, to keep food on their tables," Lewis said. On the edge of anger now, Caudell shook his head. Lewis shrugged. "All right, Nate, if that's how you want it, that's how it'll be. You ever change your mind, all you ever need do is let me know about it."

"I will," Caudell said, knowing he wouldn't. Lewis's concern touched him all the same. The captain's children did not attend his school; Lewis could afford better. But he looked out for rich and poor in the country. Caudell had voted for him without hesitation last fall and was ready to do it again if he stood for reelection.

Lewis made his good-byes and went off. Caudell was about to head back to his room when Raeford Liles called after him, "Got a letter for you, Nate. Let me open up again." Caudell trotted back to the general store. Liles worked the key, threw the front door wide. He went behind the counter. "Here y'are: from that gal o' yours up Rivington way."

"She's not my gal," Caudell said, as he still did whenever he got a letter from Mollie Bean or sent her one.

"Too bad for her if she's not, on account of I wish everything and everybody in Rivington'd get blown to hell and gone, and if she was your gal I'd leave her out of that there wishin'."

"I wish you would do that, Mr. Liles," Caudell said.

"Only since it's you as asks me, Nate." Liles proceeded to curse the town of Rivington and its inhabitants with vigor and inventive wit whose like Caudell had not heard since an army mule driver tried to flay the hides off his beasts with his tongue one afternoon when they bogged down in a road a week of rain had converted into a true bog. "An' the worst of it is, they all got money fallin' out their backsides like it was turds. Three thousand one hundred fifty mortal dollars for that there mulatto wench? The devil fry me for bacon in the mornin', Nate, what the hell's he gonna get from her he couldn't go down to the whorehouse an' have for a few beans? It don't feel no better on account of it's expensive, now does it?"

"I don't suppose so," Caudell said, after a small hesitation brought on by thinking of Mollie and of the trade she plied in Rivington.

The storekeeper never noticed that his answer came a beat late. Liles was in full spate, like the Mississippi in flood season. He was also getting to what really bothered him: "Or that griffe Westly or that nigger Anderson, almost two thousand for the one and twenty-seven hundred for the other, by Jesus! I been to other auctions, too, and had the same thing happen to me. How's a man supposed to get the help he needs when he can't noways afford to buy it? Niggers is gettin' so dear, it's damn near cheaper to do without 'em. An' them Rivington men is a big part o' runnin' the prices up, 'cause they just don't give a damn how much they spend. What's an honest man supposed to do?"

"Go on as best you can the way you are—what else can you do?" Caudell said. Liles was not a wealthy man like George Lewis, but he was a long way from poor. Caudell had trouble sympathizing with his complaints, not when his own chief worry was figuring out how to stretch his summer money so he could pay the widow Bissett for his room and eat anything better than corn bread and beans.

But Liles glared at him over the tops of his half-glasses. "Younger folks these days hasn't got no respect for their elders."

Caudell glared back. At thirty-four, he hardly felt himself still wet behind the ears. And Raeford Liles, with his store full of good things and getting fuller every day now that the war and the blockade no longer pinched him, might have spoken a little more kindly to someone who'd fought to keep him in the storekeeping business. Allison High had been right—with the war over, memories of what it meant were short. He wondered how Allison was getting along, down in Wilson County, and realized guiltily that he hadn't thought about him in weeks. Memories were short, all right.

He said, "Never mind, Mr. Liles—we all have to go on as best we can the way we are, I expect." Without waiting for an answer, he went back out into the baking sunshine of the town square. The bell over the front door jingled when he shut it.

He walked slowly back to the widow Bissett's house; moving any way but slowly would have invited heatstroke. He took off his black felt hat and fanned himself with it. The moving air briefly cooled the sweat that ran down his face and trickled through his beard, but the sun smote the top of his head with savage heat. He hastily replaced the hat.

He'd baked outdoors, but found himself poaching instead when he went into his upstairs room. He did not stay long enough even to open Mollie's letter. Grabbing a length of line and a couple of hooks, he headed for Stony Creek, north of town. Sitting on the bank under a tree—maybe taking off his shoes and letting his feet trail in the water—was the best way he could think of to fight the heat of a summer day. He might even catch his own supper, too, which would save him some money.

He used his clasp knife to dig worms out of the soft soil, baited the hooks, and tossed them into the water. Then he lit a cigar, blew a ragged smoke ring, and, as near content as he could be in such weather, pulled the letter from his pocket once more and used the knife again, this time to do a neat job of slitting the envelope.

Mollie went on for most of two pages. After nearly a year of correspondence with him, her handwriting was better than that of some of the twelve-year-olds he taught. Her spelling remained wildly erratic, but most of those twelve-year-olds had that problem too, Old Blue Back notwithstanding.

Much of the letter was chatter about her day-to-day life: a dress she'd made, a cake one of her friends had baked, a complaint about the high price of shoes. Smiling, he thought she and Raeford Liles could have commiserated together. As usual, she said little about the way she spent her nights. She knew he knew what she did, and doubtless did not care to remind him of it unnecessarily.

Living as she did in Rivington, though, even her day-to-day life was out of the ordinary. One passage leaped from the page at Caudell: "Last weak I come down with dyareaer worsen I ever got it in the army. Benny Lang he comes to see me and wen he sees how sick I am he gos off and wen he comes back he gives me sum pils to take and I takem and next day I am rite as rain. I wish we wood of nowed a bout it wen we was to gether on a count of a lot of good men who dyareared them selvs to deth could of been saved."

Caudell nodded, just as if Mollie were there to see him. Diarrhea had killed as many men, North and South, as bullets. With soldiers packed tightly together, eating food and water that were often bad—and the water frequently made worse by their own sinks nearby, or by men ignoring the sinks and doing their business straight into a stream—how could it be otherwise? Doctors could sometimes slow the illness, but they boasted no magical pills to cure it overnight—not outside of Rivington, they didn't. Even the mention of Benny Lang, whose name showed up fairly often in Mollie's letters, failed to annoy Caudell as it usually did: wonder overcame what he still refused to admit to himself was jealousy.

And wonder and jealousy both surged in him when, toward the end of her letter, Mollie wrote, "One thing I may not have tole you a bout is that wen I went to a Rivington mans hous I mean one of the ones out in the woods last week I went in side and it was as cool as spring in ther you may be leev me or not just as you like. And it was not cool atall out side likely it weren't in Nashvil too. That if you ast me is as big a thing as the lites that burn elextristy or what ever the Rivington men cal it. The thing the cool air comes out of is a box on the wall with a nob on it like the ones that makes the elextristy lites burn. I wish for it al the time on a count of hear in my room it aint cool atall. Dont you wish you was in Rivington to? Yor true frend al ways, M. Bean, 47NC."

Caudell wished with all his heart and sweaty soul he were in Rivington, or at least in that house. If any of Mollie's letters had given him the slightest hint the town held enough children to support a school, he would have moved without a second thought. Rivington had to be the boomingest town in the state, the place where everything happened first, even ahead of Wilmington and Raleigh.

The railroad, the telegraph, and the camera had all come to North Carolina since his own boyhood. Now Rivington boasted these wonderful electricity-burning lights and cool air in summer. Both those things sounded as interesting as the camera any day. He wondered when they would appear outside of Rivington and why he hadn't heard about them in the newspapers. The railroad had been ballyhooed for years before it finally arrived.

Just then, he got a bite. He tossed aside Mollie's letter and his speculations, and pulled a bullhead out of the creek. The fish flopped on the bank; he had to grab it to keep it from wriggling back into the muddy water. It had swallowed the worm. He dug up another one, impaled it on the hook, and tossed in the line again to see what else he could catch.

He waited with an angler's patience for a fish or fat turtle to go for the bait. By the sun, he had an hour or so of daylight left. Maybe, he thought, he would make a little fire right here, cook his supper, and sleep out on the grass. The mosquitoes would eat him alive, but that might be better than tossing and turning in his hot bed. He plucked at his beard as he tried to make up his mind. If he didn't hook anything more than one little bullhead, it wouldn't matter anyhow. That wasn't much of a supper.

Something stirred in the clump of jasmine on the far side of the creek. He looked up, got a glimpse of brown hide through the leaves. Deer, he thought, and then, with a tinge of alarm, or maybe cougar. He sat very still. The big cats rarely attacked man unless provoked. With his sole weapon a clasp knife, he had no intention of doing anything provoking.

The leaves parted. His breath went out in a startled grunt, as if he'd been kicked in the belly. Peering out at him, her lovely face frightened as any hunted wild thing's, was the mulatto wench Josephine.

Before either of them could say anything, before the girl could turn and bolt into the woods, hounds belled back in the direction of town. Josephine's eyes, already wide and staring, showed white all around the iris. Her lips skinned back from her teeth. "Hide me!" she hissed at Caudell. "I do anything you wants, massuh, *anything*, long as I don't gots to go back to that feller bought me. He a *devil*, he is. Hide me!"

Caudell had seen her up on the auction block, naked as the day she was born and ever so much more tempting. The thought of her doing *anything* he wanted raised a dark excitement in him. But hiding a runaway slave was against every law in the Confederacy—and where could he hide her, anyway? More daunting than mere lawbreaking, too, was imagining the revenge Piet Hardie would take on him if he tried and failed.

The hounds cried again, louder and closer. Josephine moaned. She plunged away through the bushes, leaving Caudell just as well pleased he had not had to tell her yes or no. He quickly got up, pulled in his line, picked up the bullhead he'd caught, and started back to town. That way he would not have to tell the Rivington man yes or no, either. He wondered what the fellow had done to Josephine to make her run so, then shook his head. Better not to know.

When the hounds chorused again, they were only a few hundred yards away, and plainly on the scent. Caudell heard Piet Hardie shout, too, at the men who ran with the dogs: "Keep them on the leash. If they mark her, by God, I'll pay you in paper instead of gold!"

Barbara Bissett fried the bullhead crisp and golden brown on the outside and firm and flaky and white in the center. It was as fine a fish as Caudell could have wanted and, with hot corn bread, turned into a pretty fair supper after all. Even so, he hardly tasted it.

The Georgia Railroad engine wheezed to a halt. The conductor came into the car in which Lee was riding. "Augusta!" he bawled. He hurried along, left the car, went into the next one. Faintly, through two doors, Lee heard him announce the stop again.

He got to his feet. "Major, you may send me to a lunatic asylum if, having once returned to Richmond, I voluntarily board a train again at any time within the next ten years," he said to Charles Marshall. "I am heartily sick of traveling from hither to yon inside a box"—he waved to show he meant the passenger coach—"as if I were a parcel to be delivered by the postman."

"For the good of the country, sir, I may find myself constrained to act as if I have not heard you," his aide answered. "I beg you, however, not to take this as implying I fail to sympathize with your point of view."

Lee looked around as he got off the train. "The city is larger than I had thought it to be."

"About fifteen thousand inhabitants, I am given to understand," Marshall said. He looked about, too. "Seems a pleasant enough place."

Among the gaggle of people greeting new arrivals and wishing Godspeed to departing loved ones was a rather corpulent middle-aged man who wore Confederate gray and a colonel's three stars on his collar. He pushed his way through the crowd Lee always seemed to draw, as if he were a lodestone attracting iron filings. With a salute, the fellow said, "George W. Rains, sir, at your service."

Lee returned the courtesy, then extended his hand. "Delighted to see you, Colonel. Allow me to present to you my aide, Major Marshall."

When the formalities were complete, Rains said, "I have my carriage here. May I drive you to the hotel? I've arranged rooms for you and Major Marshall at the Planters', which is by far the finest establishment in the city. Even English travelers, men with wide experience of the world, think well of the Planters'—with the exception, I fear, of the tea, which, one of them complained, was so weak he did not see how it got out of the spout."

"I should find that no great hardship, Colonel, preferring coffee as I do," Lee said. "I am confident you will have done everything necessary for our comfort. Your exemplary management of the powder mills here throughout the course of the war makes me certain of your ability to tend to such trifles."

A bare-chested slave attached to the train station carried the newcomers' bags to the carriage. Lee gave him a dime; having come from Kentucky, he still had on his person a fair sum of U.S. specie. The slave grinned, displaying uneven yellow teeth. Colonel Rains raised a quizzical eyebrow but said nothing. He flicked the reins to set the carriage in motion.

"Your shops are busy here," Charles Marshall observed.

"They were even busier during the war," Rains answered. "A large portion of the goods that came into Charleston and Wilmington through the blockade were sold here at auction, for dispersal all over the interior of Georgia and South Carolina."

"Is that a book store there?" Lee asked, pointing. "Perhaps I shall buy a novel, to commemorate my stay here. It's been a good many years since I've had the leisure to enjoy a novel, but I just may indulge myself."

"They're first-rate on a train," Rains said.

"As I was telling Major Marshall, Colonel, I feel at the moment a certain—sufficiency—in respect to trains," Lee said. "On the off chance, however, that I may be forced to ride them more than I would wish, I shall have to investigate that shop. Merely an off chance, of course, as I say." Lee admired Rains for keeping his face so straight. He wondered how many more thousands of miles he would put in rattling along over the iron rails before his career was done.

They pulled up in front of the Planters' Hotel. Slaves strolled out to take charge of Lee's luggage. He and Marshall got down from the carriage. "I will leave you gentlemen here, to recover from the rigors of your journey," Rains said. "If it pleases you, I shall return for breakfast tomorrow, then drive you over to the powder mill."

"You are very kind, Colonel," Lee said. "That sounds most satisfactory. I'll see you, then, at eight o'clock tomorrow morning, if that be not too early."

"Eight o'clock will be fine." Rains saluted again. "Good day to you, sir, Major." The carriage rolled away. Lee and Marshall went into the hotel. Spurred on by shouts from the white manager and clerks, the serving staff did everything but carry them to their rooms. Yet the shouts were good-natured, and Lee got the impression an ordinary guest would have received treatment no different from his own. He thought better of the Planters' for that impression.

Supper did nothing to disappoint him, and over chicory-laced coffee the next morning he told Rains, "Your establishment here compares quite favorably to the Galt House in Louisville, Colonel. Smaller, certainly, but very fine."

"I've heard of the Galt House, though I never stayed in it. I think, sir, if you were to say that to Mr. Jenkins behind the front desk, you would have to stand back quickly to keep from getting hit by the buttons that flew off his waistcoat as he swelled up with pride."

Lee smiled. "I'd sooner risk buttons than a good many other things that have flown through the air in my direction." He drained his cup, got to his feet. "Perhaps this evening, when we return, I shall brave Mr. Jenkins's waistcoat. Meanwhile, though—"

The powder mill lay by the Augusta Canal, a couple of furlongs west of the Savannah River. The road ran past underground powder magazines, each separated from its neighbors by thick brick traverses. "Is that tin sheathing on the roofs of the magazines?" Lee asked.

"Zinc," Rains answered. "It happened to be more readily available at the time. Sooner than wait for tin to appear, I went ahead with what I had. That was what I had to do all through the war, if I wanted to accomplish anything. Pharaoh made the Israelites make bricks without straw. Looking back on all my contrivances here, I sometimes think I could have made bricks without clay."

Young Georgia soldiers had stood sentry around the magazines. More guarded the big wooden shed that housed the powder mill. They stared and pointed and lost almost any semblance of military discipline when they saw Robert E. Lee. Colonel Rains coughed drily. "They all wish they'd been bold in battle like you, General. The life of a soldier far from the cannon's roar has little glamour to it."

Lee thought Rains was speaking for himself as well as for his men. Raising his voice so the Georgia lads could hear along with their commander, he said, "Without your labor, Colonel, and that of your garrison, the cannon never could have roared. How much gunpowder did you produce for the Confederacy here at Augusta?"

"Just over two million pounds," Rains answered. "Of that total, about three fourths was sent north to Richmond for use by the Army of Northern Virginia. The balance went to the big guns in the fortifications around Charleston, Wilmington, and Mobile. Still more would have gone north to you had the infantry and cavalry not suddenly reequipped themselves with these newfangled AK-47s."

"Indeed," Lee said. "That reequipment and its consequences are the reason I have come to Augusta."

"So you intimated in your telegram from Louisville." A horse with a uniformed rider came trotting up to the powder mill. "Ah, good," Rains said. "Here is Captain Bob Finney, who is superintendent of the arsenal a couple of miles outside of town and thus responsible for the production of small-arms ammunition, percussion caps, and other such military materiel. Between the two of us, we should display a truly staggering amount of ignorance for you."

Finney arrived in time to hear that last remark. He was a cheerful-looking, round-faced man in his middle twenties who wore a close-trimmed reddish beard like that of the Federal general Sherman. "Yes, indeed, General Lee, if it's ignorance you want, you've come to the proper place," he said gaily as he dismounted. "We turn out more of it than munitions these days, as a matter of fact."

Rains smiled, plainly used to the captain's forward tongue. "If you gentlemen will step into my office"—a small hut next to the powder mill—"we shall see how much ignorance we can produce today."

One of the chairs in the ramshackle office did not match the other three, which made Lee suspect Rains had borrowed it for the occasion. Charles Marshall said, "Colonel, does not the thought of working so close beside a place where so much gunpowder is produced ever weigh on your mind?"

"Not a bit, Major," Rains answered at once. "In a fifteen-hour day, we can manufacture close to ten thousand pounds. If by unhappy accident such an amount went up, I should be translated to my heavenly reward before I had the chance to notice the explosion. Under those circumstances, what point to worrying?"

"Put that way, none, I suppose," Marshall admitted. Even so, he could not help sneaking a glance out the window toward the powder mill.

"To business, then," Rains said. "General, I gather from your telegram and from the correspondence I have had with Colonel Gorgas in Richmond that you are aware the powder which propels the bullet from the cartridge of an AK-47 is not, properly speaking, gunpowder at all."

"Yes, I am aware of that," Lee said, remembering the tiny cylindrical grains of powder Gorgas had shown him at the Confederate Armory more than a year before. "I decided to come here before returning to the capital for two reasons: first, to learn what progress if any you have made toward duplicating that powder, and, second, if your progress has been small, to find out whether these cartridges may be reloaded with powder and bullets of our own manufacture."

"Captain Finney and I have pursued these investigations on parallel tracks," Rains said. "If I may, I would prefer that he speak to your second question first, as his results have been less problematical than mine."

"However would prove most convenient for you, of course." Lee turned to Finney. "Captain?"

"I've never been handed a more interesting problem, sir," the arsenal superintendent said. He sounded enthusiastic at facing such a challenge, which made Lee nod in approval. Enthusiastic still, Finney continued, "I can't tell you how much I admire the Rivington men, either. They must have forgotten more about gunsmithing than any twelve gunsmiths know."

That might be nothing but literal truth, Lee thought. Aloud, he said, "I also admire their ability with firearms, Captain." What he thought of them in other respects was irrelevant to the issue at hand. "Please carry on."

"Yes, sir. I gather you know these AK-47 cartridges have their percussion primers on the inside, not in separate caps the way, say, Minié balls do." Finney waited for Lee to nod again. "You may not know that all the primers have the same shape, to ignite the powder in just the same way every time—really marvelously clever."

"I did not know that," Lee admitted.

"I've not been able to duplicate the effect, either," Finney said. "By replacing the expended primer with a dab of the mixture of fulminate of mercury and the other substances used in percussion caps, then inserting rather less gunpowder into the case than the powder previously found there, I have achieved by trial and error a load that will fire from the AK-47."

"Excellent, Captain," Lee breathed.

Colonel Rains said, "He makes light of the danger he underwent in what he so casually calls 'trial and error,' General. He would allow no one but himself to test the loads; only the sturdiness of the AK-47 more than once prevented serious injury when a load proved too heavy. Two of the repeaters did in fact burst in the early days of his experiments, both, fortunately, while being fired from a rest by means of a cord."

Finney dismissed Rains's praise with a shrug. "It's not as if I were fighting, or anything of the sort. In any event, my loads are still makeshifts compared to the originals. Our gunpowder fouls the barrel much worse than that which is proper for the repeaters, which is an especially significant difficulty because some of the gas provides the force used to draw each successive round into the chamber. One rifle fired repeatedly with my loads became so foul it would no longer do so; the charging handle had to be employed to clear the chamber after each shot."

"That would make the weapons, at worst, the equivalent, say, of a Henry repeater," Lee said musingly. "Still highly useful, in other words. You have done well, Captain. I presume you are also producing your own bullets?"

"Yes, sir, and they're not as good as the originals, either—Colonel Rains tells me Colonel Gorgas explained to you about the fouling problem from good old plain lead without any fancy copper nightshirt."

"So he did, though not in quite those terms." Lee let amusement show in his voice. "Your loads will shoot, though. That is the important concern."

Charles Marshall said, "You can load spent cartridges, Captain, and you can reproduce the bullets that go into them. Can you also manufacture new cartridge cases?" Lee leaned forward in his seat to hear Finney's reply. If the Confederacy could produce its own ammunition, that would be a long step forward on the road to independence from the Rivington men.

"I've not been able to do it yet," Finney said, and Lee knew his face fell. But the captain went on, "I've not given up, either. Before we got to know the AK-47, we Southerners didn't have much to do with repeaters or with turning out any kind of brass cartridges. Now that we're at peace with the U.S.A. again, I expect we'll be able to license a setup from the people who make ammunition for the Henry or one of the other Northern repeaters. Once I have the tools, maybe I'll be able to jigger 'em to turn out these cartridge cases instead. I aim to try, anyway."

"Thank you, Captain, for your courage and your energy," Lee said sincerely. "If you've not made all the progress for which you might have hoped, you have made a good deal. Only in novels is the hero commonly fortunate enough to discover everything he requires to save the day at the precise instant he requires it."

"That's the truth, by God!" George Rains said. "I hope, General, that you'll grant me the same forbearance you've given Captain Finney, not least because I stand more in need of it."

"Tell me what you have learned," Lee said. "Let me judge, though I am already confident you have done your utmost."

"I sometimes wonder," Rains said. "I was proud of my knowledge of chemistry until I began investigating the powder the AK-47 uses as propellant. Now my feelings are closely similar to those expressed by Captain Finney: I have been shown how much I do not know. The realization is galling."

"This is a remark I have heard repeatedly in connection with the Rivington men and their products," Lee said, adding to himself, *and I know why, too.* "Suppose you tell me now what you have found out, and leave the enigmas for another time."

"Thank you, sir," Rains said gratefully. "Almost twenty years ago, a German named Schönbein produced an explosive by steeping cotton fibers in strong nitric acid."

Lee raised an eyebrow. "You don't say. There is a use for cotton I had not imagined. Some in our country have called it king, but none dreamed it could be a munition of war. Were you exploring that possibility here before you began receiving AK-47 cartridges?"

"No, sir," Rains answered at once, and in emphatic tones. "The stuff has always been too temperamental for any sane man to want to use—till now. One of the constituents of AK-47 powder is a nitrocellulose. I have confirmed this both by chemical means and by examination of the powder under a glass; the appearance of the cotton remains almost unaltered despite exposure to the acid. But somehow, perhaps in the purification process, its explosive properties have been rendered far more reliably consistent than those of the product with which I—and the world—was previously familiar."

"This appears to be considerable progress, Colonel," Lee said. "My congratulations."

"I don't feel I merit them, sir." Rains made a sour face. "I have some idea of what the powder does and of its ingredients, but none at present as to how I might duplicate the effect for myself. Nor is this treated cotton its sole constituent part: more than half of it is another nitrogenous compound, one which I believe to have a chemical affinity to glycerine."

"A—nitroglycerine, you might say?" Of itself, Lee's hand went to the waistcoat pocket which held the vial of small white pills from the Rivington men.

Rains beamed at him. "Exactly, General! I had not thought you so chemically astute, if you will forgive my saying so."

"Of course," Lee said abstractedly. He wondered if his pills were liable to blow a hole in his jacket when he least expected it, and wondered also whether the men from America Will Break hoped they would. It seemed a clumsy way to try to get rid of a man. Besides, the little pills really did relieve the pains in his chest. He decided that, since they had resided in his pocket for more than a year without detonating of their own accord, they could probably be relied upon to remain intact. Gathering his wits, he said, "Have you sought to manufacture any of this, ah, nitroglycerine for yourself?"

"Yes, most cautiously," Rains said. "I have nitric acid, and glycerine proved available from a soap works in town. I mixed minute quantities of them; the resulting compound is so explosive that it promptly proceeded to shatter the flask in which it was produced when that flask was accidentally bumped against the edge of a table. Fortunately, the fragments of glass did me no serious damage."

"Very fortunately," Lee echoed. Not so long before, in Louisville, he'd also been lucky with glass fragments.

Rains said, "There are other ingredients in the AK-47 powder which I am having more difficulty analyzing. I have to hope they are the secret to controlling the force of that powder: soldiers would, I suspect, suffer a loss of morale if, for instance, their cartridges exploded upon being carelessly dropped."

"You are likely to be right," Lee said. Being a man inclined to understatement himself, he knew a good one when he heard it.

Captain Finney's temperament ran the other way: "If that happened, you wouldn't find a regimental ordnance sergeant who would dare poke his head out of his tent, for fear of meeting up with a bunch of privates carrying a noose."

That was probably also true, but a commanding general's dignity did not permit acknowledging it. Lee said, "By all means continue your investigations, Colonel Rains. The Confederacy is fortunate to have you. If any man now living can uncover the secrets of this powder, I am confident you are he."

"Thank you, sir." Rains paused thoughtfully. " 'Any man now living'? An interesting phrase." Lee sat in silence, not elaborating one bit; he realized he had carelessly said too much already. At last, seeing he would get no more out of him, Rains shrugged and said, "I shall go on with my researches, and promptly communicate to you in Richmond any new results. With peace here, I am able to devote more time to this project than was heretofore possible."

"That's the truth," Bob Finney agreed. "Before, with the powder mill and the cannon foundry and these new cartridges and everything else, I don't think you ever slept—you just went turn and turn about and relieved yourself." He grinned mischievously. "Sometimes, I expect, you were even too busy to do that."

"I should have told you to stay back at the arsenal," Rains growled in mock anger. He gave an exaggerated shudder and turned back to Lee. "Is there anything more, sir?"

"I think not, Colonel; thank you," Lee answered. "May I trouble you for a ride back to the hotel, however? I should like to start arranging my return to Richmond; having been away so long, I begrudge every further unnecessary minute."

"I quite understand that sentiment," Rains said. "Take my carriage back, if you care to; I can ride in and pick it up at any time, and our conversation has made me eager to go back to investigating this remarkable powder." By the way he stirred in his chair, he seemed eager to be at it that very moment.

"Are you certain?" Lee asked. Rains nodded vigorously—sure enough, he did not care to waste time as a driver. Lee inclined his head. "Most generous of you, sir; I am in your debt."

Rains waved that away, too. When Charles Marshall took the reins of the carriage, the colonel hardly waited for the horses to start moving before he hurried back to get to work again. "He reminds me of a hound on a scent," Marshall said.

"An apt comparison," Lee agreed, though he wondered how many Northern hounds were following that same trail.

The carriage rolled along, raising a small cloud of dust behind it. Men in the street waved to Lee; more than one woman dropped him a curtsy. He gravely raised his hat to return each salutation. When Marshall drove past the book shop he had seen before, he said, "Let me out, Major, if you would. I think I *shall* buy a novel. The Planters' is only a few blocks off; I'll walk it from here."

"Yes, sir." His aide pulled back on the reins. The team slowed, stopped. As Lee got down, Marshall said, "While you browse, sir, I'll go over to the train station and arrange our return passage to Richmond."

"That would be excellent." Lee walked into the shop. The carriage rattled away. The bookseller looked up. When he saw who his new customer was, his eyes widened. He started to speak, then thought better of it as Lee headed straight for a shelf, making it plain he did not care to be interrupted right then. After some frowning thought, he pulled out *Ivanhoe* and carried it over to the man who ran the shop. Its heft promised it would keep him amused through a long, slow train ride.

The bookseller looked unhappy, an expression that fit his long, thin face well. "I'm afraid I can't let you have that, sir."

Lee stared at him. "What? Why ever not, Mr."—what had the name on the sign outside been?—"Mr. Arnold?"

"It's my last copy," Arnold said, as if that explained everything. To him it must have, for he went on, "If I sell it to you, sir, I won't have another, and heaven only knows when I'll see more again."

"But—" Lee gave up when he saw how determined the bookseller looked. Trying not to laugh, he turned and replaced *Ivanhoe* on its shelf, picked up a copy of *Quentin Durward* instead. "You have several of these, Mr. Arnold," he said, deadpan.

"Yes, sir," Arnold said, now seeming as happy as his doleful physiognomy permitted. "That will be three dollars paper or seventy-five cents cash money." He bobbed his head up and down when Lee gravely handed him three U.S. quarters.

Back at the hotel, Lee told Marshall about "Arnold's book." His aide snorted and said, "It's soldiers who are supposed to husband their ammunition, not booksellers."

"Well put," Lee said. "Are our arrangements completed for returning to Richmond?"

"Yes, sir. We depart tomorrow on the nine o'clock train and go by way of Columbia, Charlotte, Greensboro, and Danville."

"I see," Lee said.

"Is something wrong, sir?"

"Not—wrong, precisely, Major. I was wondering if we would pass through Rivington, that's all. It might have been interesting to see."

"I'm sorry, General; by your remarks to Colonel Rains, I assumed you would wish to travel by the most direct route. Going over to Wilmington and then up through eastern North Carolina would be like traversing the two legs of a right triangle rather than its hypotenuse. If you like, however, I'll go back to the train station and have our tickets revised."

Lee thought about it. "No, never mind, Major. As you say, fastest is best. And perhaps I would do better to stay as far away from Rivington as I can." Marshall gave him a curious look, but he declined to elaborate.

Summer gave way to fall. School started again. As usual, the children, especially the younger ones, had forgotten much of what Caudell had taught them the spring before. He was resigned to that and spent the first couple of weeks of classes getting them back to where they'd been. That also let him start his handful of new five- and six-year-olds on their *ABCs* and numbers. Some of them stared at slates and chalk as if they'd never seen such things before. Likely they hadn't.

Establishing discipline was also dicey as usual. The first time he switched a five-year-old for kicking one of his little classmates, the boy just looked at him scornfully and said, "My pa, he licks me a lot harder'n that."

"Do you want me to try again?" Caudell asked, raising the switch. He would have sworn the boy thought it over before finally shaking his head.

Whenever he let them go at the close of a day, the children would scatter in all directions, shouting as joyfully as if they'd just been released from a Yankee prison camp—or, for that matter, a Southern one; he remembered the skeletons in rags going back to the United States from Andersonville. He wished he could work up that much excitement over school's getting out. Most days, he just felt tired.

One afternoon when the black gum and maple trees were beginning to change color, he got back to the widow Bissett's house to find Henry Pleasants sitting on the front porch waiting for him. Grinning, he charged up the steps to shake his friend's hand. "How did you manage to get the time off to come up and see me?" he asked.

"I have all the time I need," Pleasants answered. When Caudell looked puzzled, he amplified: "The railroad let me go."

"They did what?" Caudell said indignantly. "Why would they go and do a damnfool thing like that? Where are they going to find anyone half as good as you?"

"That I don't know. They don't either, I'm sure. They let me go anyhow," Pleasants said. "As for why . . . shall we go for a walk?" His eyes slid to the house. Caudell heard Barbara Bissett moving around in the parlor. He caught Pleasants's drift, nodded, and started down the street. Pleasants came with him. A backwards glance showed Caudell the widow disappointedly standing by a front window.

"Tell me," Caudell said after they'd got out of earshot. He kept his voice low.

So did Pleasants. "It was the way I treated the Negroes, they said."

"What?" Caudell gaped. Memories of Josephine's terrified face—and of her sweet, ripe body—surged through him. "You were too rough on them?" He could not imagine Pleasants, whose disposition lived up to his name, producing that kind of fear in anyone.

"Too rough?" His friend stared, too, then started to laugh, rather bitterly. "No, no, no. The railroad let me go because I treated them too much like men."

"Is *that* what happened?" Caudell said. He'd heard of other Northerners dismissed from positions for just the same reason.

"That's what happened, by God." Pleasants searched for a way to explain himself: "Nate, you're a teacher. You must know the difference between people who are stupid and people who are only ignorant."

"Of course I do." Before he went on, Caudell looked around. They'd walked south from the widow Bissett's house. A couple of minutes were plenty to get them to the edge of town. No one was around to overhear. "Too many of the people in this county are ignorant. Plenty in my company couldn't write their names, or read them if they were written out. But I don't reckon there are more stupid people here than anywhere else. I taught more than one man his letters while we were in the army." *And Mollie Bean, too*, he added to himself. "They learned fine, when I gave them the chance they hadn't had before."

"I've had the same experience, with the Cornishmen and Irish and Germans who work the Pennsylvania mines. They don't know much, but they're not idiots or children—show them what they need to do, explain why, and they'll go on from there. You don't need to stand over them with a whip. The ones who won't work, you turn loose."

"You can't turn niggers loose," Caudell pointed out.

"That's true, but I didn't want to stand over them with a whip, either. I was afraid I'd have to: you people have kept them pig-ignorant, much worse than the white men who used to work for me up North. But I decided I'd do the same as I did there—I broke the gangs in half, setting 'em against each other, and I gave half a dollar to each man on the crew that put down the most ties or hauled the most gravel for the roadbed each day. I gave them work quotas they had to meet, or else neither half got paid. I wanted 'em to have a reason to work besides my say-so, if you see what I mean. And after I gave 'em that reason, I just stood back and let 'em go to it."

"How did all that work? I know some white men who'd swing a hammer for half a dollar a day." In summer, Caudell thought, he might have been one of those men himself.

"Don't forget they only got the money if they did the most work. That went the same as it would in the mines—they got the idea real quick. And inside of a week, somebody in one half-gang figured out a faster way to get the gravel from the freight car to the roadway. The day after that, both half-gangs were doing it the new way. Be damned if I know whether niggers are as smart as white folks, Nate, but they aren't as stupid as people down here think, and that's a fact."

"If you got the work out of them, how could the railroad people complain?" Caudell asked.

"I guess the trouble is, if you treat a Negro like a man, he's going to act like a man. My gangs started bragging and strutting in front of other laborers, and getting in fights with them, and even talking back to whites who showed they didn't know what the hell they were doing."

"Uh-oh," Caudell said.

"Uh-oh is right," Pleasants agreed. "You ask me, that's a stupid thing for a Negro to try in this country, no matter how right he is—maybe especially if he's right. But somebody who feels like a man doesn't take kindly to orders from a fool. The whole thing was partly my fault, too. My crews were used to telling me when they thought they had good ideas, or if they thought I had a bad one. I'd listen. Why not? Sometimes they were right. Down here, though, if you're black, you're wrong."

"You talk like an abolitionist," Caudell said.

Pleasants shrugged. "If niggers really are a lot less than whites—if they're stupid by nature, I mean—I might see some justice in slavery. If they're backwards just because they're ignorant, why not enslave ignorant white men, too?"

Caudell pondered that. In his mind, he saw Georgie Ballentine again; and black men in blue uniforms standing up under the fire of AK-47s; and Josephine, lovely flesh to be sold and abused because it came in a dark wrapping. Was that justice? Before the war, he'd taken it for granted. He'd taken a lot of things for granted before the war. He wondered what would have happened had the North won and forced the South to free its slaves. How would they live? Where would they work? "You couldn't just go and turn them loose all at once," he said.

"Mmm—maybe not," Pleasants said, though he didn't sound convinced. Then he laughed. "I suppose you'd lynch anybody who tried, after you're just through fighting a war to keep them slaves."

"The war wasn't about slaves," Caudell said. "At least, it wasn't about slaves till Lincoln made it that way. He lost the war, and he's not U.S. President anymore, either. And the niggers the Yankees freed while they were holding our land are just going to complicate our lives for the next twenty years."

"Not if Nathan Bedford Forrest has his way," Pleasants said. When Caudell looked a question at him, he went on, "By the papers, Forrest would just as soon kill the Negroes he catches as make slaves out of them again."

"He's a hard man, by all accounts," Caudell admitted. "Some folks like to take that line." As vividly as if it had happened the day before, he heard the bark of an AK-47, saw a grinning Billie Beddingfield standing over the corpses of two Negro soldiers who had tried to surrender at Bealeton.

Pleasants watched the line between his eyes deepen, the corners of his mouth turn down. "You don't have the stomach for massacre yourself, do you?"

"I guess not." Caudell felt that in some obscure way he betrayed the Confederacy by admitting his doubts to this man from the North, who happened to be his friend. To keep from having to do it again, he changed the subject: "What will you do now? Head back to Pennsylvania?"

"That's the first thing I thought of, I tell you frankly. Then I had a better idea." Pleasants smiled foxily. "You know the old saying, 'Living well is the best revenge'? The railroad paid me good money, and I never did get around to buying that house down in Wilmington, so I have a tidy sum in a bank there. I was thinking of moving up here to Nash County, buying myself a farm, and working it with free labor, white and black both. How does that strike you?"

"Your new neighbors may not like it—"

"Along with the farm, I'll buy a rifle," Pleasants said, looking very much like a man who had commanded a Union regiment.

"—but if anybody can make a go of it, I expect you're the fellow," Caudell finished. He meant it. If ever he'd met an all-around competent man, Henry Pleasants was the one. "Come to think about it, folks hereabouts will likely give you more leeway than they would somebody who was born in North Carolina. They'll reckon you're a damnfool crazy Yankee who doesn't know any better."

"I love you too, Nate." Pleasants snorted in suppressed mirth. "Maybe I *am* a damnfool crazy Yankee. If I had any sense, I would go back to the United States, you know? But letting a bunch of rich peckerheads in embroidered waistcoats run me out of here just sticks in my craw. So I figure I'll stay around and show 'em."

"You're stubborn enough to make a Southern man, that's certain." Caudell cocked his head to one side. "You aim to buy a farm up here, you say? Why not down around Wilmington? The land is better there. You could raise rice or indigo, make more than you would here at tobacco and corn."

"The delta land is richer, but it costs more, too. And besides—" Pleasants paused to clap Caudell on the back. "I thought I'd sooner live close by a friend."

"Thank you, Henry." They walked along in companionable silence for several steps. Caudell tried to remember if he'd ever had a finer compliment. He couldn't think of one. A few stars poked through the clouds that drifted by overhead. The evening, he realized, was getting chilly. It had a habit of doing that in fall, even if one tended to forget about such things during the seemingly endless days of summer. Which reminded him—"Do you have a place to stay in town?"

"Yes, I've hired a room over the Liberty Bell tavern, thanks—the same as we did in Rocky Mount, that first day we met."

"Ah." The neutral noise covered a certain amount of relief. Caudell would gladly have shared his room with his friend, but he was far from sure Barbara Bissett would have been glad about having an unexpected guest. And while Pleasants would have to endure her gimlet gaze for only one day, he himself might never hear the end of her complaints.

Pleasants said, "Do you remember what else we did in Rocky Mount that day?"

"Pieces of it, anyhow," Caudell said, smiling reminiscently.

"Shall we go and do it again?"

"Don't know if I want to get that drunk. I have to teach tomorrow, and

I'd sort of like to be able to know who I am and what I'm doing. But I wouldn't say no to a drink or three." Caudell and Pleasants both turned around in the road. The not-so-bright lights of the not-so-big city lay ahead. They hurried toward them.

Raeford Liles was putting boxes of cloves and peppercorns on a shelf in a back corner of his general store when Nate Caudell came in. Behind the counter, a gray-haired Negro made change for a woman buying a thimble. She put money and thimble into her handbag, nodded to Caudell as she headed for the door.

"Morning, Mrs. Moye," he told her. She nodded again. The bell jingled to signal her departure. Caudell said, "I didn't know you'd finally bought yourself a nigger, Mr. Liles."

"Who, Israel there?" Liles turned around, shook his head. "Didn't buy him, Nate—ain't you seen niggers too high for the likes of me? He's a free nigger, new in town just a couple days and lookin' for work, so I done hired him. He's right sharp, Israel is. Israel, this here's Nate Caudell, the schoolteacher."

"I's pleased to make your 'quaintance, suh," Israel said.

"Where'd you come from, Israel?" Caudell asked.

"Las' few years, suh, I been livin' ovah in New Berne, an' in the Hayti—the colored folks' town—across the Trent from it."

"Have you?" Caudell eyed the black man with new curiosity. New Berne had been in Federal hands from early 1862 to the end of the war, and served as a mecca for escaped slaves from all over North Carolina. Colored regiments recruited there had raided the northeastern part of the state, and more blacks in the area labored to support the Union war effort. Some of them had left with the withdrawing Yankees, but not all. Caudell wondered if Israel's freedom papers were genuine—and if Raeford Liles had bothered asking to see them.

The Negro reached under the counter. "If you Nate Caudell, suh, you gots a letter here."

He gave Caudell an envelope which, sure enough, was addressed to him. He recognized Mollie Bean's handwriting. For a moment, that was all he noticed. Then he blurted, "You can read!"

"Yes, suh, so I can," Israel admitted. He sounded anxious; teaching blacks their letters was against the law in North Carolina. Defensively, he went on, "The Yankees, they had schools there, an' they learned lots of us to read. Now they showed me, don' reckon I can jus' go an' forget it again."

"I hired him on account of he reads," Raeford Liles said. "You're one who's always been talkin' about changin' times, Nate, an' I reckon maybe you're right, at least partways—like Israel said, he ain't gonna forget what he learned. The damnyankees messed with niggers for years at New Berne, an' at Beaufort an' Carolina City an' Washington an' Plymouth, too. There's probably thousands and thousands o' niggers in the state with their letters now, goddamn it. Shootin' 'em'd be purely a waste; might as well get the most use we can out of 'em.''

Israel waited to hear how Caudell would answer. More than a few North Carolinians, Caudell thought, would cheerfully have shot thousands of black men. But as Henry Pleasants had said, he couldn't stomach a massacre. "I think you've done well, Mr. Liles,'' he said. "No matter how much we wish they could, things aren't going back to just like they were before the war. Wars tear things up; that's what they're all about. One way or another, though, I expect we'll get along.''

"You got pretty good sense, Nate,'' Liles said.

"Yes, suh,'' Israel agreed softly. "Tha's all I try to do, is git along.''

Caudell shrugged. "If I'm so all-fired smart, why aren't I rich?'' He took the letter and walked out into the street. Once out there, he used his free hand to jam his hat as far down over his ears as he could. The trees that lined Washington and Alston were bare-branched now; snow had fallen once or twice. This Saturday afternoon was clear enough, but Caudell's breath puffed out in a smoky cloud.

He opened the envelope as he walked back to the widow Bissett's house. "Dear Nate,'' he read, "the big thing hear in Rivington to day is skandul. A nigger went name of Josefeen wich belonged to one of the Rivington men called Peet Hardy has gon and hung her self. I seen her oncet or twice in town and its a shaym on a count of she was a bout the purttiest gal black or wite I ever seen. But I reckon I aynt serprized on a count of I went to Peet Hardys hous oncet and I aynt never going back a gain not for all the gold in the woreld he is that crool. The Rivington men is hard on there niggers weve noed that sins we was in the army to gether but even the rest of them has bad things to say a bout Peet Hardy. Non of the girls wil go to him no more Im not the onely one. I no you dont like me to tawk a bout wat I am and wat I do but Nate to day I cant help it I feel so bad for that Josefeen. If you are my true frend I no you will understand. Yor true frend al ways, M. Bean, 47NC.''

Caudell stared down Alston Street without really seeing it. Instead, with frightening vividness, he saw Josephine's dress fall from her shoulders, saw her dark charms exposed for buyers to admire, saw the frustrated lust on the Alabama man's face when Piet Hardie—a schoolmaster even in his own thoughts, he spelled the Rivington man's name correctly in his mind—

outbid him. He also saw her face peering through the jasmine by Stony Creek, heard the terror in her voice, heard the nigger hounds baying on her trail. He wondered what Hardie had done to her, to make her first try to flee and then take her own life. *Mollie would know*, he thought, and then shivered in a way that had nothing to do with the cold. Some knowledge, he decided, he could live without.

He read the letter again, then slowly and deliberately tore it into tiny pieces. He hurled them down to the dirt of the street. The chilly wind whirled them away, as if it were snowing again after all.

⋆ XIII ⋆

Robert E. Lee glanced over at a map of Kentucky, then noted a last couple of corrections to an order changing the size of the garrisons in the new Confederate fortifications along the Ohio River. With a satisfied nod, he fixed his signature to the bottom of the paper. Then he got up, stretched, and set his hat on his head. The sky was beginning to go more purple than blue—enough for one day. In peacetime, he could think that and keep his conscience clear.

The lobby of Mechanic's Hall was all but deserted when he went downstairs. Even John Beauchamp Jones's proud brass nameplate presided over a bare desk and an empty chair. A sentry came to attention as Lee walked past him into the gathering twilight.

Another man in Confederate gray was coming down the steps of the building across the street from the War Department, the building that was the Richmond headquarters of America Will Break. Lee's mouth tightened, ever so slightly; he wished soldiers would stay away from the Rivington men, especially since the war was more than a year and a half over. He had contemplated a general order to that effect, but set the notion aside as being unjust and without foundation in fact: the Rivington men troubled him, but on balance had done his country far more good than harm.

As he and the other man approached each other, he noticed the fellow's tunic buttons were grouped in three groups of three. His frown deepened.

What was a general doing, consorting with the Rivington men? He peered through the gathering darkness, but did not recognize the officer.

The other man appeared to have no such doubts about him, but then his face was arguably the most widely known in the Confederacy. The man saluted, then held out a hand and said, "General Lee, sir, I'm delighted to meet you at last. I am Nathan Bedford Forrest."

"The pleasure is mine, General Forrest. Forgive me, I beg, for not knowing you at once." As he spoke, Lee studied the famous cavalry commander. Forrest was a big man, a couple of inches taller than he, with wide shoulders but otherwise whipcord lean. He bore himself almost as erectly as Jefferson Davis. His hair receded at the temples; gray streaked it and his chin beard. Deep shadows dwelt in the hollows of his cheeks.

His eyes—as soon as Lee saw those gray-blue eyes, he understood how Forrest had earned his reputation, for good and ill. They were the hooded eyes of a bird of prey, utterly intent on whatever lay before them. Of all the officers Lee had known, he could think of only two whose visages bore the stamp of implacable purpose that marked Nathan Bedford Forrest: Jackson, whom he would mourn forever, and John Bell Hood. What this man set out to do, he would do, or die trying.

Lee said, "I was just heading home, sir. Will you take supper with me?"

"I wouldn't want to put you to any trouble, General," Forrest said doubtfully. His voice was soft and pleasant, with a st.ong flavor of backwoods Tennessee.

"Nonsense," Lee declared. "There will be plenty. In any case, I may keep you too busy to eat, as I intend to talk your ears off."

Forrest's smile enlivened his brooding features remarkably. "I am at your service, then, General Lee, and I will make sure I keep my hands on my ears at all times."

"My house is only a few blocks away," Lee said. "Do come along. I've wanted to meet you for some time, to discuss with you your extraordinary campaigns in the west, but circumstances have kept you in the field even while the rest of us enjoyed the fruits of peace."

"Blame the Yankees, for trifling with our niggers," Forrest said.

"I am sick to death of blame, General Forrest, and of endless recriminations on both sides, let me say," Lee added hastily. "The United States are here, as are we; our two nations have a common border which stretches for two thousand miles, more or less. Either we learn not to be distracted by our differences or we fight a war every generation, as the nations of Europe are in the habit of doing. I would not care to see such folly come to our shores."

"Spoken like the true Christian you are, sir," Forrest said. "Still and all, knowing I can lick the Yankees whenever I need to will make me sleep better of nights. As for the nigger soldiers they left behind, we'll be years gettin' 'em all to remember who their masters are. And for that, I wish God would send all the Yankees straight to hell."

"Do you think it can be done, even given years?" Lee asked.

"Kill enough of 'em, General Lee, sir, and the rest of 'em will get the notion," Forrest said with brutal pragmatism.

The cavalry general and Negro fighter seemed very sure of himself, but Lee still wondered if simple savagery could produce even a Tacitean peace. The promise of force had always had its place in maintaining slavery and keeping revolts from breaking out, yet that promise rarely had to be kept in the days before the war. He wondered how—and whether—the Confederacy could withstand a constantly simmering rebellion.

Hoping to change the subject, he asked Forrest, "What brings you to Richmond at last?"

"I think I wrecked the last nigger robber band that halfway deserved to be called a regiment, so I had the leisure to present my report in person," Forrest answered. "I gave it to a clerk this afternoon, so I dare say you'll see it tomorrow. I thought I'd look at the slave markets, too; plenty of prime niggers here, since this is the capital."

"I see." Lee could not keep a certain chill from his voice. He knew Forrest had made his fortune trading slaves, but he had not expected him to refer to it so openly. No Virginia gentleman would have done so, that was certain.

Forrest might have picked the thought from his mind. "I hope I've not offended you, sir. My father was a blacksmith who neither read nor wrote. He died when I was sixteen, leaving me the oldest of eight brothers and three sisters, so I've had to come up as I can. My son will be a gentleman, but I've not had the leisure to learn that way of life myself." He drew himself up straighter than ever in touchy pride.

"You've done well for yourself, General Forrest, and for your family, and for the Confederate States," Lee said, which had the virtue of being both true and polite—gentlemanly, as a matter of fact. Nevertheless, he could not quite suppress a touch of pique at Forrest's implied criticism of his own upbringing and social class.

By then the two men had reached Lee's house. Lee knocked on the front door, took off his coat as he waited for Julia to open it. Forrest followed his example; now that spring was here, an uncovered moment at night was no longer uncomfortable. Crickets chirped here and there in the grass.

The door swung open. Julia's smile of greeting for Lee turned to a questioning look when she saw he had a companion. As he handed her his coat, he said, "I've brought a guest home, as you see. This is Lieutenant General Forrest, of the Confederate cavalry."

Julia had been reaching out to take Forrest's coat and hang it on the tree by Lee's. The motion froze. So did Julia's face. For the first time since Lee had manumitted her, he saw her features go blank in the special way Negroes used to hide all feelings from their masters. After a long pause, she did hang up Forrest's coat. Then she turned and hurried away, long skirts rustling about her.

"You're too easy on your staff, sir," Forrest remarked with a tone of professional expertise. "Slaves need to have in mind who the masters are."

"She's a freedwoman," Lee said. "I no longer own any slaves."

"Oh." Now Forrest hid whatever his true feelings were behind a mask as impenetrable as Julia's. Lee remembered he had been a gambler as well as a slave dealer.

Julia returned, followed closely by Lee's wife and daughters. In an instant, Forrest became, if not a gentleman, then at least a polished simulacrum of one, bowing over the younger women's hands and bowing even lower over and kissing that of Mary Custis Lee. "We are delighted to welcome such a famous commander," Lee's wife said.

"Thinking on the commander who lives here, you are much too kind to my own poor self," Forrest said, bowing yet again. Then he grinned an impish grin. "I'll take all the flattery I can get, though."

He proved a lively guest at the supper table, using silverware, a gravy boat, and a heel of bread to show how he had won his victory north of Corinth, Mississippi. "You use your horses, then, merely to transport your troopers, but have them fight dismounted?" Lee said.

"That is my rule," Forrest agreed. "A horse has use in getting a man from here to there faster than he can march, but what good is it in a fight but to give a choicer target than a man on foot? That was true before; what with the coming of the repeater, it's doubly so these days."

"Many others did likewise, both among the enemy and our own horse soldiers," Lee said, thinking of Jeb Stuart. "How do you account for your greater success with the tactic?"

"From what I've seen, sir, most of 'em did it because circumstances forced it on 'em. Me, I aimed to fight my men so from the start. I drove 'em hard, too, and always stayed up at the very front of the pack. With all the guns my own escort party carried, I used it to plug any holes or to break through when I saw the chance." Forrest grinned again. "Worked right well, too."

"There I cannot disagree," Lee said thoughtfully. "Should we style your men dragoons, then?"

"General Lee, I don't care what you call them, and they don't care what you call them. But when you do call them, they fight like wildcats with rattlesnake fangs, and that I do care about. Will you pass me the sweet potatoes, sir?"

Lee watched the way Julia acted around Forrest. She was a good enough servant not to ignore him altogether, but she plainly wanted to. Yet even when she was busy at the opposite end of the table, her eyes, big and fearful, kept sliding toward him. He must have seemed the bogeyman incarnate to her; Negroes had been using his name to frighten their children ever since the Fort Pillow massacre, and his campaigns against the black soldiers left behind in the Mississippi valley when Union forces abandoned Confederate soil only made his reputation the more fearsome.

He knew it, too. Every so often, when he spied Julia watching him, he would raise an eyebrow or bare his teeth for a moment. He never did anything overt enough for Lee to call him on it, but Julia finally dropped a silver ladle, picked it up, and fled as ignominiously as the luckless Federal general Sturgis, whom Forrest had smashed though outnumbered better than two to one. Chuckling, Forrest said, "Sturgis moaned to one of his colonels, 'For God's sake, if Mr. Forrest will let me alone, I will let him alone.' But I wouldn't let him alone; I aimed to whip him out of his boots, and I did it."

Mildred Lee rose from her chair. "If you men are going to fight your battles across the tablecloth, I will leave you to your sport."

"If you stay, we won't fight them," Forrest said quickly. Hard-bitten as he was, he could also be charming, especially to women.

But Mildred shook her head. "No, I should only spoil your fun, for you know you'd still wish to, and Father did not bring you home so he could listen to me. He can do that any night, after all."

"He can do that any night, after all, *when* he is in Richmond," Mary Custis Lee said, an edge to her voice. Lee sighed silently. Even after nine months without straying from the capital, his wife had not forgiven him his long trip to Kentucky and Missouri. Mildred turned and left the room, followed by Agnes and Mary; Lee's eldest daughter wheeled Mary Custis Lee ahead of her.

"Well." Lee rose, took a cigar case off a cabinet shelf, offered Forrest a smoke.

Forrest shook his head. "I never got the habit, but you go on yourself."

"I don't use them, either; I keep them for guests." Lee put the case away, then asked, "Did you also come to Richmond to see the men from America Will Break?"

"What if I did?" Forrest said. "Those repeaters of theirs made my men five times the fighters they would have been without them." He gave Lee a measuring stare. "By all accounts, we'd have lost the war without their aid."

"By all accounts indeed." Lee studied Nathan Bedford Forrest in return. Cautiously, he said, "Am I to infer that the accounts you mentioned include the one given by the Rivington men themselves?"

"Just so. I gather you've also heard this account?" Forrest waited for Lee to nod, then said softly, almost to himself, "I wondered if I was the only one they'd told. Well, no matter." He gathered himself. "Do you believe what they say, sir?"

"Or do I find it fantastic, you mean? I can imagine nothing more fantastic than men traveling in time as if by railroad." Forrest started to say something; Lee held up a hand. "But I believe nonetheless. Any madman may claim to come from the future, but madmen do not commonly carry proof for their assertions. Their artifacts convince more strongly than their words."

"My thought exactly, General Lee." Forrest drew in a long, relieved breath. "But with the artifacts comes the tale, and the tale they tell of the history ahead makes me believe more what I already thought: that the South is the last and brightest hope of the white race, and if we ever turn loose of the niggers here, they'll ruin everything everywhere."

"If all the Rivington men say is true, that may be a justifiable conclusion," Lee said. Maybe that belief explained some of Forrest's savage conduct in his war against the blacks, although, as he'd said himself, he'd had no use for Negroes—save as a source of income—even before the Rivington men came to help the Confederacy win its independence. Lee went on, "Yet all the trend of the nineteenth century makes me wonder. The nations of Europe almost unanimously find chattel slavery abhorrent, and us on account of it; most of the South American republics have abandoned it; even brutal Russia has freed its serfs. The trend in history seems to be ever toward more liberty, not less."

"Are you saying you believe the Negroes ought to be freed, sir, after the war we fit to keep them slaves?" Forrest's voice remained low and polite, but took on an unmistakable note of warning; his rather sallow complexion turned a shade redder.

"We fought the war, as you say, to ensure we would be the only ones with the right to either preserve our institutions or change them, and we have won that right," Lee answered. "Not only the opinions of the outside world but also the course of the war and of your own gallant efforts after our armistice with the United States have compelled me to alter somewhat my view of the black man."

"Not me mine, by God," Forrest growled. "At Fort Pillow, we killed five hundred niggers for a loss of twenty of our own; the Mississippi ran red for two hundred yards with their blood. That ought to show Negro soldiers cannot cope with Southerners—in other words, that they deserve to be just what and where they are."

"They fought well enough at Bealeton, and elsewhere against the Army of Northern Virginia in our advance on Washington City," Lee said: "no worse than their equally inexperienced white counterparts, at any rate. And in your campaigns in the lands formerly under Federal occupation, have you found them such easy prey as you did at Fort Pillow?"

He purposely did not mention the stories that said most of the Negroes at Fort Pillow had been slain after they surrendered. Forrest bristled even so. "Even a rat will fight, if you push him into a corner," he said contemptuously.

"But if you don't, he will not," Lee replied. "The Negroes could quietly have returned to their bonds, at no danger to themselves. That they chose what most of them must have known to be a futile fight—all the more so, as your men were armed with repeaters—must, I believe, provoke the contemplation of any thoughtful man."

"Their grandfathers fit when they were in Africa, too, I expect," Forrest said with a shrug: "fit and lost, or they'd not have been caught and shipped over here. The ones I fit after the armistice? They were better than those worthless, hapless niggers at Fort Pillow, that I grant you. But that they fit 'well enough'? I deny it, sir, or I'd not have licked them over and over again."

"There our opinions differ," Lee said. Forrest inclined his head to show he agreed with that much, if with nothing else Lee had said. Lee persisted, "I do not feel the views of the rest of the world may be ignored with safety for our state, nor do I think we can take the Negro's lack of manliness as much for granted as before. Sooner than see the Confederacy eternally plagued with revolt and insurrection, should we not begin a program of—"

"Just one damned minute, sir," Forrest broke in. Lee blinked; he was not used to being interrupted, let alone so rudely. Forrest sprang up from his chair and thrust his face, now quite red, up against Lee's. "General Lee, you're high-born, you're high-minded, you might as well be a saint carved out of marble, and everybody says you'll be President as soon as Jeff Davis steps down. But if you are talking in any way, shape, or size about making people free niggers, sir, I will fight you with every ounce of strength in my body. And I won't be alone, sir, I promise you that. I won't be alone."

Lee rose, too. He wondered if Forrest would lay hands on him. The cavalry officer was some years his junior, but Lee promised him a nasty surprise if he struck first. He also wondered if Forrest would challenge him. He did not consider Forrest a gentleman, but the Tennesseean no doubt thought of himself as one . . . and was no doubt very quick with a pistol. But he had offered Forrest no personal insult: if anything, the reverse was true.

The two men glared at each other at closer than arm's length for some little while. Lee battled down his own rage, said tightly, "General Forrest, I no longer find you an agreeable guest here, nor will you be welcome at my home again."

Forrest snapped his fingers—left-handed; he had also eaten that way. "See how much I'd care to come back. I'd just as soon eat at Thaddeus Stevens's house. The men of America Will Break may have saved the South from his tender mercies, but I see we can grow our own crop of Judases." He spun on his heel and stomped away, his boots crashing on the wood floor, then slammed the door so violently that the flame in every lamp and candle in the dining room jumped. Lee listened to his furious footsteps receding down the walk. He slammed the iron gate that gave onto the street with a loud metallic clang.

Several women exclaimed upstairs. Lee walked to the bottom of the stairway and called, "It's perfectly all right, my dears. General Forrest chose to leave a bit sooner than he thought he might, that's all."

But it wasn't all right, and he knew it. Till now, his only enemies had been men his professional duty called him to oppose: Mexicans, western Indians, John Brown, soldiers and officers of the United States. Now he had a personal foe, and a dangerous one. He blew a long breath out through his mustache. He could feel the difference. He did not care for it.

Nate Caudell wiped sweat from his forehead, paused to rest a moment in the shade of a willow tree. His chuckle was half amused, half chagrined. Henry Pleasants's new farm was only five miles or so up the road from Nashville toward Castalia, and here he'd started breathing hard before it came into sight. In the army, a five-mile march wouldn't have been worth complaining about. "I'm getting lazy and soft," he said out loud.

He pushed on. Before long, he came to a split-rail fence. As soon as he turned into the lane that led to the farmhouse, a white man who was hoeing a vegetable garden enclosed by another fence turned and let out a loud halloo to announce his arrival. The fellow's voice had an Irish lilt to it; when he turned back toward Caudell, his pale, freckled face looked vaguely familiar.

"Good day," Caudell said, lifting his hat. "Have I seen you somewhere before?"

"Faith, sir, I don't think so. John Moring I am, and I've spent most of me time till now down by Raleigh—saving a spell in the army, that is."

"That's where—" Caudell began, and then stopped. Moring hadn't been in his company, and had disappeared from the Forty-Seventh North Carolina not long after Gettysburg. But that was almost three years ago now, and no one these days was making any effort to track down deserters. Caudell shrugged. "Never mind. Is Mr. Pleasants at home?"

"You're Nate Caudell, are ye not? Aye, he's here, sir. Where else would he be?"

Caudell lifted his hat again, walked on down the lane. He passed a stable with a cattle pen beside it, jumped over a tiny stream, then went by a corncrib and a woodpile. He wrinkled his nose at the smell of the pigpen by the corncrib, but beyond it stood the farmhouse, in the middle of a large, irregular yard where chickens and turkeys scratched.

Henry Pleasants came out onto the house's covered porch just as Caudell got to the end of the yard. He waved to his friend and hurried over to greet him. Barnyard fowl scattered, clucking and gobbling indignantly. "Hello, Nate," he said, pumping Caudell's hand. He waved out to the fields that stretched back from the house. "Crop should be all right, God willing, though we've had less rain than I'd hoped for."

"Good." Caudell looked at the fields, too, and back at the cow barn and pigpen, then at the farmhouse itself, a two-story whitewashed clapboard building with a timbered roof and a tall brick chimney—no planter's mansion this, but no hovel, either. "It all looks very fine, Henry. I'm happy for you."

"I still need a man with a good head for figures, Nate, to keep me from having to do my own bookkeeping," Pleasants said. "You know I'd pay you better than your schoolteaching does."

He'd made that offer the last time Caudell came to the farm, too. As he had then, Caudell shook his head. "I like teaching school, Henry. It's not a line of work you get into for the money. And besides, I'd sooner be your friend than your hired man."

"The one wouldn't leave out the other, Nate. You know that."

"All right, but no thank you all the same." Caudell knew nothing of the sort. As a teacher, he worked for wages but was largely free in what he did and how he did it. That suited his independent nature far better than sitting at a ledger with Henry Pleasants looking over his shoulder ever could.

A black man carrying a jar of whiskey and two glasses came out of the farmhouse. "Thank you, Israel," Pleasants said.

"I knew I hadn't seen you around the general store lately, Israel," Caudell said. "When did you start working for Henry here?"

"Two—three weeks ago, suh," the Negro answered. "Mistuh Pleasants, he pay as good as Mistuh Liles, an' he got mo' books to read, too. Now I learned how, I surely do love to read, suh, that I do. Mistuh Liles, he fuss some when I go, but it weren't like he own me."

"Only trouble I have with Israel is getting his nose out of a book when I need him for something," Pleasants said. "If I can teach him ciphering, maybe I'll make him my bookkeeper, Nate, since you don't want the job." He spoke jocularly, but then turned and gave Israel a careful once-over. "Maybe I will at that, by God. I wonder if he could learn? Israel, do you want to try to learn arithmetic? If you can do it, it would mean more money for you."

"I likes to learn, suh, an' I likes money might well. You want to show me, reckon I try."

"You're a hard worker, Israel. Maybe you *will* learn. If you do, you can keep books for a lot of people in town, too, you know, not just for me," Pleasants said. "Keep at it and you'll end up with a fine house of your own one day."

Caudell almost smiled at that, but at the last minute kept his face straight. It could happen. Thanks to the war, things were looser these days than they ever had been. A free Negro sensible enough to stay out of trouble might come a long way without a lot of people noticing.

"You want to show me, suh, reckon I try," Israel repeated. "I got no place better to go than here, looks like. I's jus' glad I didn't head No'th when the bluecoats sail away. By what the papers say, it's rougher bein' a nigger up there than down here—they hangs you to a lamp post jus' fo' walkin' down the street."

"You might be right, Israel, though I'm embarrassed to admit it," Pleasants said.

Caudell nodded. "White men up North blame Negroes for the war, seems like." Savage antiblack riots had convulsed New York and Philadelphia within days of each other, as if word of one triggered the next. In Washington, Confederate pickets across the Potomac watched Federal troops battle arsonists intent on burning down the colored part of town. And along the Ohio River, white men with guns turned away slaves fleeing across from Kentucky, saying, "This ain't your country"—and opened fire if the Negroes would not go back. Southern papers reported every atrocity, every upheaval in the United States in loving detail, as if to warn blacks they could expect no warm reception if they ran away.

Israel heaved a long sigh. "Ain't easy bein' a nigger, no matter where you is."

That, Caudell thought, was no doubt true. Israel set down the whiskey jar and went back into the house. Caudell swigged from his glass. He coughed, got it down. The fire in his throat turned to warmth in his belly, warmth that spread through him. Pleasants raised his glass. "Here's to a free-labor farm."

"A free-labor farm," Caudell echoed. He drank again; the warmth intensified. He looked around. The impression he'd had as he walked up to the farmhouse persisted. "A free-labor farm that's doing right well for itself."

"If the weather stays close to decent and prices hold up, I'll get by," Pleasants answered. He was new to farming, but seemed to have already picked up the man of the land's ingrained aversion to sounding too optimistic. He went on, "By what the papers say, weather's even worse farther south and west. I hate to see anyone else hurt, but it may help me."

"How many hands do you have working for you?"

"Seven men—three free blacks, two Irishmen—"

"I saw one of them in your vegetable patch." Caudell lowered his voice. "Maybe you ought to know he ran off from my regiment."

"Who, John? Did he?" Pleasants frowned. "I'll keep a close eye on him, then, though he's given me no trouble so far. Anyway, I also have a couple of local white men here, and Tom—he's one of the blacks—bought his wife Hattie free a couple of years ago, and she does the cooking for us." As if the words were a cue, a long, unmelodious horn blast sounded from the back of the house. Pleasants grinned. "There's dinner now. Come on, Nate."

Dinner—fried ham, sweet potatoes, and corn bread—was served outdoors, in back of the house behind the kitchen. Hattie, a very large, very brown woman, seemed personally offended unless everyone who ate from her table stuffed himself until incapable of moving. Caudell was more than willing to oblige her. Happily replete, he leaned back on his bench and joined in the byplay between Pleasants and the farm hands.

Besides John Moring, Caudell also knew Bill Wells, who had joined his company not long before the last year's campaign started. Wells had been only eighteen then; twenty now, he still looked years younger. "You better not send me out to fill canteens, Mr. First Sergeant, sir," he said with a grin.

"I'll let Henry here give you your fatigues now," Caudell retorted, which made Wells duck as if a bullet had cracked past him.

Hattie's husband Tom, Israel, and the other colored man, whose name was Joseph, sat together. They were quieter than the whites, and took little part in the banter that flew around the rest of the table—though at liberty, free Negroes had to be leery about taking liberties. But when Israel started boasting about how he was going to learn arithmetic, Tom raised an eyebrow and said, "If you de man who do my pay, Israel, I gwine count it *twice* when I gits it, an' that a fac'."

"You couldn't even count it oncet, nigger," Israel said loftily.

"Marse Henry, I know he pay me right," Tom said. "You—" His pause carried a world of meaning.

After a while, Henry Pleasants looked at his pocket watch and said, "Time to get back to it." The workers got up and headed past the old overseer's cabin toward the fields. Joseph reached out and snagged a sweet potato so he would have something to munch on if—unlikely as the notion seemed to Caudell—he got hungry in the middle of the afternoon.

"This is very fine, Henry," Caudell said as Hattie cleared away the plates. "You've done well for yourself, as usual."

Instead of cheering Pleasants, the praise made him melancholy. He sighed, looked down at the planks of the table, ran a hand through his dark, wavy hair. In a low voice, he said, "If only Sallie could see this farm."

"Sallie?" Caudell peered at his friend. In all the time he'd known Pleasants, he'd never heard him mention a woman's name. He tried to figure out why, picked the most likely reason he could think of: "Didn't she want to come South with you, Henry?"

Pleasants turned to stare at him; the pain in his eyes told Caudell at once that he'd made a mistake. "She would have come anywhere with me. But—oh, hell." Pleasants shook his head. "Even now, how hard this is! We were married, Sallie and I, just at the start of 1860; I would take oath we were the happiest couple in Pottsville. Around Christmas, she would have borne my child."

"Would have?" Caudell knew a sinking sensation. Gently, he asked, "Did you lose her in childbed, Henry?"

"I didn't even have her so long." Unshed tears glistened in Pleasants's eyes. "She started to moan—God, such dreadful moans may I never hear again!—before dawn one October morning. She blazed with fever. The doctor lived only a couple of blocks away. I ran through the darkness to his house, fetched him back still in his nightshirt. He did all he could, I know that, but Sallie . . . Sallie died the same day."

"May she have gone to a better world, as I'm sure she has." The words felt flat and empty to Caudell, but he had none better to offer. Doctors could do so little—but he wondered, just for a futile moment, if a Rivington man could have saved her.

Pleasants said, "She was a finer Christian than I can ever hope to be, so I am sure of it as well. But it took four big strong miners to keep me from leaping into the grave after her. Without her, the world was cold and empty and not worth living in. After Fort Sumter, my aunt Emily asked if I'd ever thought of enlisting in the army. I took her up on it: she must have thought it would help me forget. That was partly my reason, I suppose."

Caudell knew he had not finished. "What was the rest?"

"If you must know, Nate, I hoped I would be killed. What better way to be set free from my sorrow and pain and uselessness? I lived, as you see, but you seemed a gift from God that day in Rocky Mount. I seized on any excuse not to go back to Pottsville, as you may imagine."

"Whatever your reasons were for staying here in North Carolina, I'm glad you did. Life goes on. It's the oldest thing in the world to say, but it's true. If nothing else can, going through a war the size of ours will teach you that. At camp the last night after Gettysburg—" It was Caudell's turn to have trouble continuing. So many friends had fallen in that futile charge, but he and his fellow survivors had to carry on as best they could.

Henry Pleasants nodded. "I do know that, but I know also that the words are easier to speak than to live. Moving on toward six years now that Sallie's gone, yet the memory of her pierces me still. I would have spoken of her to you before, but—" He tightened his lips, blew air out through them. "It still hurts. I'm sorry."

"I don't blame you." As Pleasants had before, Caudell waved to the fields and the fine farmhouse. "She'd be proud of what you have here." Caudell hesitated, wondering if he should say what had sprung into his mind. He decided to: "And if she was like a lot of Northern women, I reckon she'd be proud of the way you're running this farm with free labor, too."

"I thank you for that, truly I do. It can't have come easy, not from a North Carolina man. But you're right—Sallie was strong for abolition, likely stronger than I was then. I don't think I could have hoped to meet her in the world to come if I'd bought Negroes to work this place."

Caudell only grunted. He reached for the whiskey jug. More and more these days, he leaned against slavery himself. But he would not say that out loud, not yet, not even to a close friend who sprang from the North. If word he had such notions ever got around, he might be lucky to lose only his job. He finished his drink, then said, "Show me the inside of the house, why don't you?"

"I'd be glad to." Pleasants also emptied his glass, then led Caudell in through the open kitchen door. Hattie looked over her shoulder at him from the little tin tub in which she was washing the dishes. The furniture in the big sitting room was country-made, and therefore cheap, but looked comfortable: low chairs and a sofa, all with the seats of undressed calfskin. Hand-hewn shelves full of books lined one wall.

A washroom with a tin tub on feet and several storage rooms took up the rest of the ground floor. "Bedrooms are upstairs," Caudell said: "one for me; one for Israel, who works more around the house than in the fields; one for my Irishmen; and one for the two local boys. Hattie and Tom and Joshua sleep in the overseer's cabin out back. I think they find that very funny and very satisfying; I know I would, in their shoes. There used to be a row of slave huts out there, too. I've knocked down every one of them."

"It's your farm, Henry. Do you get the work out of your people that an overseer could with a slave gang?"

"I certainly believe so, given what some of my neighbors tell me they expect from their Negroes. The two Irishmen are capital workers and the free blacks good enough. The ones with whom I've had the greatest diffi-culty are the local white men, if I may tell you that without causing offense. I've had to let several of them go; they will not work steadily for hire, and think the very idea smacks of turning them into niggers, as one of them said."

"A lot of white folks in the South are like that," Caudell said. "If they have to work at tasks slaves normally do, they feel as if they are slaves themselves."

"But that's wrong, don't you see?" Pleasants said earnestly. "Keeping slaves degrades all labor, free and slave alike, and there's nothing wrong with labor in itself. But when even a good many of your artisans are slaves, where's the prod for a white man to learn a skill? Your rich planters here are very rich indeed; I'll not deny that for a moment. But your poor are poorer than they are in the United States, and have fewer choices open to them to improve their lot. Where is this country of yours—country of mine now, too—going?"

"I don't think we worry so much about *going somewhere* as folks do up North," Caudell said. "Most of us are just content to stay where we are." Throughout the war, *All we want is to be left alone* had served as a Con-federate rallying cry.

"But the world keeps changing, whether you do or not," Pleasants pointed out. "You can't keep walls up forever—look at Admiral Perry's trip to Japan."

Caudell made a wry face and held up his hand. He suspected—he was virtually certain—his friend was right. That didn't mean he wanted to admit it, or even to talk about it very much. "Let us finish getting back on our feet after the war and we'll do pretty well for ourselves," he insisted.

"All right," Pleasants said pacifically, seeing he had irked his friend. Still, he did not abandon the argument: "The war's been over for a couple of years now, Nate, and the world's not in the habit of waiting."

Josiah Gorgas's round face beamed like the sun. "I am truly delighted you could visit the armory on such short notice, General Lee."

"When you sent word yesterday that you had something worthy of my consideration, Colonel, I naturally made it a point to come investigate at once," Lee answered. "Your performance, both in the war and since, gives me every confidence in your judgment. Your note, however, I found mysterious. *What* precisely am I here to consider?"

The Confederate ordnance chief walked out of his office, returned a moment later with a pair of repeating rifles. "These," he said proudly.

He held one of them out to Lee, who took it and said, "I have become moderately familiar with the AK-47 over the past couple of years, and this—" His voice trailed away as he examined the weapon more closely. When he spoke again, it was without sarcasm. "This rifle appears different in certain small ways from those to which I have become accustomed. What have we here, Colonel?"

"A copy of the AK-47 manufactured here at the armory, sir. Two copies, as a matter of fact."

"Oh, how excellent," Lee said softly. He worked the charging handle of the rifle Gorgas had given him. The smooth, well-oiled *sniick!* took him back to the tents northwest of Orange Court House and to the day he first heard that sound. He looked along the barrel. The Confederate gunsmiths had substituted a simpler sight for the calibrated one which normally graced an AK-47. "Have you tested these weapons as yet, Colonel?"

"Yes, sir," Gorgas said. "We have successfully duplicated the repeating action of their models. When fired with cartridges furnished by the Rivington men, they also shoot about as accurately and with recoil similar to those models. Though trials have as yet been limited, they appear sturdy enough." His eyes flicked away from Lee as he said that. He remembered the cavalry carbines which had proven as dangerous to their users as to the enemy, then.

"Have you tried firing them with the loads prepared down in Augusta?" Lee asked.

Gorgas nodded. "Again, they served. The flight path of the bullet is considerably higher with those loads, and the recoil considerably increased." The ordnance chief winced reminiscently and rubbed his right shoulder. "As a matter of fact, when loaded with ordinary gunpowder, the rifle kicks like a mule."

"A minor defect," Lee said. "You've done marvelously well, Colonel Gorgas."

"Not as well as I'd like to," Gorgas answered, displaying the resolute perfectionism that suited him so well to his position. "For one thing, try as I might, I've not come close to matching the metal that goes into the barrel of the originals. So far as I can tell, it is as nearly indestructible as makes no difference. The ones we turn out both foul more and are more difficult to clean than their prototypes. For another, both the rifles you see here are almost entirely handmade. Not only is production very slow on account of that, but parts from one weapon are not interchangeable with those of the other."

"I presume you are working toward remedying this difficulty?"

"Working *toward* it is the appropriate phrase, sir. I am endeavoring to tool up to produce AK-47s as we did Springfields, but the going is slow. We were aided immeasurably in turning out Springfields by capturing the arsenal at Harper's Ferry and the tools it contained. Here I can gain no such advantage. Much as I love our country, sir, we have not been a manufacturing nation. Much of our industry, such as it is, was called into being by the exigencies of the late war." Gorgas's face assumed the mournful expression of a bloodhound on a difficult track. "Moreover, the AK-47 is a considerably more complex weapon, requiring many more steps in its production, than the rifles we are used to making. By this time next year, I expect to be producing it in some quantity. How much earlier than that I can hope to turn it out remains to be seen."

Lee considered what the ordnance chief had said. It was not all he might have wished to hear. The United States emphatically *was* a manufacturing nation, second in the world after only Great Britain. He had visions of huge factories in Massachusetts or New York—or Massachusetts *and* New York—making repeaters in carload lots. But as Gorgas said, the South had been proudly agricultural until war and Federal blockade forced it to try to make some of the things it could no longer buy with cotton and tobacco. He supposed he should have been pleased with its progress, not worried about how backward it remained. He willed himself to be pleased, since he had no other choice.

"You've done splendidly, Colonel," he said, as enthusiastically as he could. "By all means convey my congratulations to your clever artisans. I am glad to know we may one day be able to declare our independence from the men of America Will Break, just as we have from the United States." He wished that day would come at once, but even seeing it ahead gave him no small relief.

Given the reported deployment of the Federal troops who have entered New Mexico from Colorado, Mr. President, I am convinced those troops are intended to lend moral support to the rebels in conflict with the Mexican Emperor Maximilian, as President Seymour has publicly declared. Nevertheless, I hope I might take the liberty of urging upon you the westward extension of railroads in Texas so that we become more readily able to meet dangers which may arise from that quarter. Now that the Tredegar Iron Works are producing track once more, the prospect of such a line appears to me to be deserving of your most serious consideration. You may perhaps recall Secretary Stanton's contemptuous reference to our lack of any such means of transportation throughout the vast expanse of west Texas. I—

He looked up from the passage to gather his thoughts . . . and discovered Andries Rhoodie standing across the desk from him. The big Rivington man had come into his office so quietly that he'd failed to notice him. "Do please be seated, Mr. Rhoodie," he said, embarrassed. "I hope I've not ignored you long?"

"No, not long," Rhoodie said as he sat. A man of lighter spirit might have eased the moment with a joke, but Rhoodie, serious to the core, made no such effort. He paused only to rub at his reddish mustache for a moment before bulling ahead: "We of the AWB are not pleased with you, General Lee."

"This is not the first time such a misfortune has occurred, Mr. Rhoodie," Lee observed. He watched Rhoodie frown, as if unsure whether he was being made sport of. Like General Grant, the Rivington man had trouble going in any direction but straight on. "What have I done to raise your hackles this time?"

"You favor freeing the blacks here," Rhoodie said, blunt still.

"I was not aware my private opinions were your concern, sir, nor do I believe them to be so," Lee replied. As against Grant, he essayed a flanking maneuver. "In any case, how have you become privy to my opinions on the subject? I have kept them private, and certainly have not communicated them to you."

"You have spoken of these opinions to patriotic officers who disagree with them as strongly as we do."

To Nathan Bedford Forrest, he meant: Lee worked that out with hardly a pause for thought. The rough Tennesseean had as much as said he was hand in glove with the Rivington men. Lee wondered if he'd said too much to Forrest. He decided he had not: keeping his thoughts secret would have implied he was ashamed of them, which he was not. He said, "I repeat, sir, that my private opinions are not your concern."

"If they stayed private, I might agree with you," Rhoodie answered. "But everyone says you will be the one to succeed Jeff Davis, and then your private opinions will be all too public. They go square against everything we stand for. My opinion—my *private* opinion, General Lee—is that they go square against everything the Confederacy stands for."

"There, obviously, we disagree. In a republic like the Confederate States, the people and their representatives will eventually be responsible for choosing between us."

Rhoodie breathed hard through his nose. "So you do aim to run for President, do you?"

As he'd told Jefferson Davis, Lee had no knowledge of politics, no interest in politics. But he also had no intention of permitting Andries Rhoodie to dictate to him. He thought he'd taught that to the Rivington man in the aftermath of Bealeton. Rhoodie, though, seemed hard to convince. Lee said, "And what if I do?"

"If you do, General Lee, you will certainly never see another vial of nitroglycerine tables as long as you live—I promise you that," Rhoodie said.

This man would sooner see me dead than President, Lee thought with a slow surge of wonder. *He truly would. But more even than that, he wants to bend me to his will.* He looked steadily at Andries Rhoodie. "I have known for some years now that I am no longer a young man. I am also a soldier. No doubt I should be lying if I said death held no terror for me, but I assure you most earnestly that whatever terrors it does hold are insufficient to make me deviate from my chosen course for the sake of your white pills."

"I beg your pardon, sir," Rhoodie said, and startled Lee by sounding completely sincere. He went on, "Of course I do not question your courage. I took altogether the wrong tack to persuade you that your views are mistaken, and I apologize for it."

"Very well." Lee still eyed Rhoodie with suspicion, but no more handsome apology could have been demanded on pain of meeting with pistols.

"Let me suggest something else," the Rivington man said after a short pause for thought. Now he made his blunt-featured face as affable as he could, and sweetened his voice: "Your charming wife has long suffered from ailments beyond the power of the medicine of these times to cure. That does not mean, though, that those ailments will stay incurable forever . . ."

He was a good fisherman. Having dangled the bait in front of Lee, he fell silent and let him paint his own mental pictures: Mary free of pain; Mary hurrying toward him, upright and happy and out of the prison of her wheeled chair; Mary whirling with him as an orchestra played a sprightly waltz. Had Rhoodie spoken of Mary before he crassly threatened with the nitroglycerine pills, Lee knew he would have been tempted as, perhaps, never before in his life. He was more vulnerable through his family than through any danger aimed at himself, for their well-being was more impor-tant to him than his own.

Now he waited until his words were properly deployed before he com-mitted them to battle: "You had better go, Mr. Rhoodie."

He felt fury like a fire inside him. Most men quailed from him when he let that anger show. Andries Rhoodie, however, was an ironclad himself. He scowled back at Lee. "You think America Will Break will let you get by with your insolence forever, because we tolerated you more than we should have, back when the Confederate States still had the North to beat. We needed you then. But now the Confederacy is well established. If you try to twist it out of its proper course, America Will Break will break you."

"And what, in your doubtlessly ominiscient opinion, is our proper course, pray tell?"

The Rivington man ignored the heavy sarcasm. He answered as if the question were seriously meant: "The one for which you left the useless Union, of course: to preserve the South as a place where the white man can enjoy his natural superiority over the nigger, to show the world the truth of that superiority, and, at need, to act in the future in concert with other nations to preserve it."

"Ah, now we come down to it," Lee said. "You are saying that unless we serve as your obedient cat's-paws in some time to come, we fail of our purpose—our purpose to you, that is. Mr. Rhoodie, our reasons for leaving the United States were more complex than those you name, and if we fought to gain our independence from them, we shall do likewise as nec-essary against you and yours. And I warn you, sir, that if you speak to me of this matter again, I shall not be responsible for my actions. Now get out of my sight."

Andries Rhoodie stood up, dug in his pocket, and tossed an old, worn half cent on the desk in front of Lee. "This is how much I care for whether you'll be responsible for your actions." He tramped out of the office, slammed the door behind him.

Lee glared in shocked outrage. Had he been Bedford Forrest, Rhoodie never would have got out of Mechanic's Hall alive. But Forrest and Rhoodie were allies. Lee's heart thudded heavily in his chest. As had become his habit, he reached for his pills. He had the vial in his hand before he consciously noticed from whom it had come. With an angry growl, he put it back in his waistcoat pocket. His first thought was *Better to die without the Rivington men than live with their cures.*

He wondered if that also held true for the Confederacy as a whole. He thought about it seriously, then shook his head. His nation deserved to be free. For that matter, how could a good and effective medicine be morally wrong, no matter where it came from? He took out the pills again, let one melt under his tongue. While he had them, he would use them. When they were gone, he would do without, as he had until the Rivington men found their way into his life.

There, that was one decision made, he thought with some satisfaction as he replaced the nitroglycerine tablets once more. "One?" he said aloud. Then he realized that, as in the heat of battle, he had made up his mind without understanding how or even when he'd done so.

He *would* seek the Presidency next year. That the men of America Will Break did not want him to have it was reason enough, and more.

"How are you tonight, dear Mary?" he asked in the quiet of their bedroom after he'd helped her upstairs that evening. Down below, Mildred was playing the piano and singing with her sisters. Most nights, he would have stayed down there and sung with them, but his mind remained full of Andries Rhoodie.

"I am as I am—none too well, but very much here. And how are *you,* Robert?" Few people could have followed Lee's thoughts, but after more than a third of a century, his wife was one of them. She went on, "Something new is troubling you, or I miss my guess, while I have only my usual collection of aches and pains."

"Troubling me indeed." As exactly as he could, Lee recounted the confrontation with Rhoodie.

Mary Custis Lee bristled indignantly when he told how the Rivington man had promised to cut off his supply of pills. Lee could almost see her hair rise under her ruffled nightcap. Then he had to tell her Rhoodie had offered to restore her health. Candlelight filled the lines of her face with deep shadows as she cocked her head to one side to study him. Slowly, she asked, "Could he have—cured me, Robert?"

"I do not know," he answered. After a moment, he reluctantly added,

"I confess I have not known the Rivington men to make false claims. However big their brags, they have a way of backing them up."

"What . . . what did you tell him?"

"I told him to get out of my office and never come back," Lee said. "Can you find it in your heart to forgive me for that?"

His wife did not reply, not right away. Instead, she looked down at herself, at the shrunken, twisted legs that had once been so lively, at the pain-filled flesh that had imprisoned her spirit for so many years. At last she said, "I am not surprised at it. I've known all our lives together that you place your country ahead of everything else. I understand that; I am used it it; I have taken it as an article of faith since the day you set the ring on my finger, and I dare say before that."

"Then you do forgive me?" he said in glad relief.

"I do *not*," she answered sharply. "I understand. I can even accept; you would not be the man you are, had you said yes to Rhoodie. I would no more have expected you to say yes than that the sun would shine green tomorrow. But sometimes I wish you had even an ounce of bend in you."

"Do you want me to visit Rhoodie in his headquarters? He would receive me, I think, despite the harsh words that lie between us."

"You say now that you would go to him." Her hands brushed the notion aside with a quick, scornful gesture. "Surely your precious duty would find some way of coming between the words and the deed."

He wanted to be angry at her for that cynical gibe, but could not: she was too likely right. Already he regretted his rash offer: how could he sell the Confederacy for the sake of one person's comfort, even if that person was his wife? He knew he could not, and knew she would pay the price for his not doing so. Sighing, he said, "I unfortunately belong to a profession that debars all hope of domestic enjoyment."

"You have been wed to that profession, and to your country, longer and more deeply than ever to me," Mary Custis Lee said, which was also true.

He said, "I am not necessarily wed to that profession forever." His wife, taking a wifely privilege, laughed at him.

Richmond, Virginia
June 27, 1866

Sir:
I have the honour to tender the resignation of my commission as general in the army of the Confederate States of America.

Very resply your obt servt,
R. E. Lee
General, C.S.A.

Lee sanded the letter dry, looked down at the words he had written. Even in black ink on creamy white paper, they did not yet seem real to him, just as there was a moment of quiet shock before the pain of a wound struck home. Yet this resignation came easier than the one he had made six years before, from the colonelcy of the 1st U.S. Cavalry. Then he had been cruelly divided in his own spirit, wishing he could remain with the United States but knowing Virginia in the end meant more to him. Now the Confederacy was at peace; its armies could carry on without him. His course lay elsewhere.

He wished he could show the letter to his wife first, to see her expression once she'd read it. After their go-round of the night before, her expression ought to be worth seeing. But that was a diversion he would have to forgo. He picked up the paper, carried it down the hall.

Secretary of War Seddon looked up from the papers that crowded his own desk. Despite those papers, he looked stronger and healthier than he had during the war, when his labors all but consumed him. Even his smile was less cadaverous these days. "A good morning to you, General. What can I do for you?"

"I have here a letter which requires your attention, sir."

"Give it to me, then." James Seddon read the two-line note, then raised his large head to stare at Lee. "What has occasioned this?"

"If I am to meet my full responsibility to the Confederate States of America, Mr. Secretary, I must necessarily do so in and from a civilian capacity. Proceeding directly from the ranks of the military to any civil office strikes me as more appropriate to ancient Rome than to our present republic."

"Civil office, you say?" Seddon studied Lee, then slowly nodded. "You will understand, General, that rumors pertaining to your possible plans for the future have been in wide circulation for some time now."

"As with paper money, so with rumors: the wider the circulation, the less value they retain," Lee said.

The Secretary of War smiled his rather unnerving smile. "No doubt, no doubt. I certainly did not care to presume on our acquaintance to enquire of you your plans, the more so as they may well have been unclear even to you. I hope you will permit me to say, however, that I should be confident of our nation's future in your hands."

"You are gracious, sir, and place more trust in me than I deserve," Lee said. Seddon shook his head, no doubt taking Lee's words for a commonplace of polite speech. Lee wished it were so. The—disorderly—quality of civilian life, and especially of civilian administration, worried him. The Rivington men worried him more. In war and peace, he had tested himself against the ablest of his own time, and had prevailed. But how could he know all the resources the men from a distant time held in reserve?

He could not know . . . and he had made the men of America Will Break his enemies, past hope of reconciliation. As best he could tell, he had earned the right to worry.

Jefferson Davis held a fortnightly levee at the Confederate White House. As Lee rode Traveller up Twelfth Street toward the Presidential mansion, he reflected that one day the place would need a name not derived from one in Washington City. The Confederacy could not go on forever as a mere copy of the United States and its institutions; the South would develop institutions of its own.

His lip quirked. The South had one institution all its own, and he hoped to begin the job of laying that one to rest.

Lamps and candles blazed bright through the broad windows and open door of the Presidential residence, casting a warm golden glow on the walkway outside. Lee dismounted from Traveller, tied the horse to the iron fence outside the mansion, gave him a nose bag full of hay. Traveller snorted appreciatively and began to eat. "I wish some people were so easily pleased," Lee murmured and went up the stairs and into the house.

Varina Davis met him near the door. "How good of you to join us this evening," she said with a smile. "You are quite as handsome as ever in your dark civilian suit."

He bowed over her hand. "You are too kind to me, Mrs. Davis." She was a pretty, dark-haired woman, some years younger than her husband— and also a good deal more outgoing. Without her, the President's levees would have been too austere to be worth visiting. As it was, the gatherings, if not the most intellectual in the city—that distinction surely belonged to Mrs. Stanard's salon—were the most variegated, with congressmen, judges, soldiers, and officials of the administration mingled promiscuously with merchants, preachers, and simple citizens anxious to conduct business with Jefferson Davis or simply to see him, and with ladies corresponding to all those types.

Lee ran a hand down the sleeve of his black wool formal coat. Being out of military gray still seemed strange and unnatural, as if he were parading through Richmond in his underclothes. He added, "I am also most pleased at how lovely you look out of black."

Varina Davis's eyes were shadowed for a moment. "As you will know, what with the sad loss of your Annie, the passing of a child is hard to bear." A little more than two years before, her little son Joe had fallen from some scaffolding and died the same day. She and Lee shared a few seconds of sad remembrance. Then she went on, "But life also calls to us, and we must continue as best we can. Do come in; I know my husband will be glad to see you."

The President stood by a table crowded with punch bowls and plates of fried chicken and ham, baked potatoes, and tall cakes with yellow icing. Standing with him, a chicken leg in one hand and a glass in the other, was Stephen R. Mallory, the Secretary of the Navy, a tall, heavily built man who resembled nothing so much as an Anglo-Saxon version of Judah P. Benjamin, save that his jowly, beard-fringed face more usually bore frown than smile.

Jefferson Davis beckoned Lee to him. As Lee approached, the President said loudly, "I am confident that when my term expires, sir, I shall leave the nation in your capable hands."

Silence spread outward as everyone present turned to stare at Lee. After his resignation, Richmond had buzzed with political rumors. Now, all at once, the gossip acquired solid flesh—a figure of speech almost inevitable when looking toward the rotund frame of Secretary Mallory. Lee knew his answer would gain similar weight. He said, "If that be the will of the people, I shall humbly accept it, though conscious as always of my own shortcomings."

Still in that public voice, Davis replied, "I am equally confident that the people, observing your manifold virtues, will think as highly of them as do I, and as they assuredly merit." By then Lee was close by. As he dipped out a glass of lemonade, Davis, reverting to normal tones, said to Mallory, "You see how it is done, Mr. Secretary—no vulgar party politics, such as first forced us to abandon the United States and then left that unhappy nation divided against itself, will mar our republic's smooth transition from one chief magistrate to the next."

"Our states do seem more united in purpose than those which claim that title." Mallory had a big bass voice; Lee, in a moment of irrelevant irreverence, wondered if it was because he was shaped like a big bass fiddle. The Secretary of the Navy went on, "I can see no issue which would divide our happy confederation." He tossed aside the gnawed chicken bone, piled ham and potatoes onto a plate, and poured gravy over both.

"I see one," Lee said.

Jefferson Davis's features, always thin and dyspeptic, pinched further, as if at some sudden new gastric pang. "It will not be an issue if you do not choose to make it one," he said.

"It will," Lee answered. "Sooner or later, it will return to haunt us; how could it do otherwise? I would sooner engage the problem at a time of my own choosing than let it grow to crisis strength and overwhelm us."

"You may wear a simple suit, sir, but you still speak like a soldier," Mallory said. Though pompous, he was also keen: "You have grown dissatisfied with our treatment of our Negroes, have you not? I recall it was at your urging that we sent the *Alabama* to join the antislavery patrol off the west African coast."

"Many of the South's best men have long been dissatisfied with slavery; too many have chosen to keep that dissatisfaction to themselves," Lee said. "I do not believe we can afford to do so any longer. As for the *Alabama*, I am glad we had it to send."

"So, no doubt, is Captain Semmes," Mallory replied. The *Alabama* had been in Cherbourg harbor with the *U.S.S. Kearsarge*, a much more formidable vessel, waiting just outside French territorial waters for it to emerge when word came of the fall of Washington and the armistice.

"They might well disagree with you about slavery even in the United States, General Lee," Jefferson Davis said. "Their constitutional amendment to abolish it just went down to defeat in the Illinois legislature, despite the vociferous protests of Mr. Lincoln." His voice took on a certain satisfaction at his wartime rival's discomfiture. "Only two U.S. states outside New England have ratified that amendment, and only one since Seymour became President."

"But slavery is now legal in only two of their states, Maryland and Delaware, and is moribund in the latter," Lee said. "Further, the Negro constitutes but a tiny fraction of their population, which is emphatically not the case with us. Thus he presents them a smaller problem and allows them to confront it more nearly at their leisure."

"You know we disagree on this question. Still, I shall not lose sleep over it," Davis said. "For one thing, I may be wrong; the Negroes in the Union army and the guerrillas who remained on our soil after the Federal withdrawal proved themselves capable of deeds more manly than I would have expected from their race." For Davis to admit he might be wrong was very nearly a prodigy. His mouth thinned as he weakened that admission by continuing, "For another, believe as you may, you will have your hands full in getting Congress to accede to your wishes. You will have your hands full in getting Congress to do anything at all." His own battles with the legislative branch, though milder now than during the crises of the Second American Revolution, left him with a permanently jaundiced perspective on its utility.

Lee frowned as he contemplated that aspect of government in action— or perhaps of government inaction. As a commanding general, he could give orders and feel sure they would be obeyed—and if they were not, he had the power to punish those who failed in their duty. But the President of a republic like the Confederate States of America could not rule by fiat. If Congress refused to go along with him, he was stymied.

As if reading his thoughts, Jefferson Davis reached up to put a hand on his shoulder. "Take heart, sir, take heart. While we have as yet no political parties in the Confederacy, our Congress was and is most definitely divided into factions favoring and in opposition to myself; but, so far as I know, no faction opposed to Robert E. Lee exists within the bounds of our nation, not after the extraordinary services he has rendered to it."

"If he speaks in any way against the continued servitude of the black man, such a faction will spring to life soon enough—he is right about that," Stephen Mallory said.

"True," Lee said, thinking that an anti-Lee faction, in the persons of Nathan Bedford Forrest and the men of America Will Break, was already very much alive. "Well, if I fail of election on that account, I shall return to the bosom of my family without any great anguish. I wasted too large a part of my life away from them. I shall not dissemble for the sake of votes— I leave such ploys, as you said, Mr. President, to politicians in the North."

Davis raised his glass in salute. "Long may those ploys remain there." Lee and Mallory drank with him.

Julia came up to Lee in the study. " 'Scuse me, Marse Robert, but there's a soldier here to see you."

"A soldier?" Lee said. Julia nodded. Lee gave a whimsical shrug. "Having resigned from the army, I thought I would henceforth be free of soldiers." The black freedwoman looked back in incomprehension. Lee got up from his chair. "Thank you, Julia. Of course I shall see him."

The "soldier" proved to be a pink-cheeked second lieutenant who looked so young that Lee wondered if he could possibly have seen service in the late war. When he saw Lee, he went into a brace so stiff that Lee feared for the integrity of his backbone. "General Lee, sir, I have a letter here, sir, which the Secretary of War directed me to deliver into your hands. Sir."

"Thank you very much, Lieutenant," Lee said, accepting the envelope the youngster in gray proffered. After extending his hand to give it to Lee, the lieutenant returned to attention. "You may go," Lee told him.

"No, sir. I am directed to wait and bring your reply, if any, to the Secretary."

"I see. Very well." Lee broke the seal on the envelope. It held not one but two letters, the first folded around the second. The outer sheet was in James Seddon's copperplate script: *My dear General Lee: In view of the political developments centering on your name which have of late occasioned so much gossip and so many wildly speculative stories in the Richmond papers, and in view of the rumored estrangement between yourself and General Forrest on the one hand and between yourself and America Will Break on the other, I send you the enclosed so you may act upon it as you see fit and as the times demand. I have the honor to remain, your most ob't &c., James A. Seddon.*"

Lee opened the inner sheet. The handwriting and spelling on that one both left something to be desired; Nathan Bedford Forrest's formal schooling had lasted only a few months. But the import of the letter was clear enough: Forrest was resigning his commission in the Confederate army. His last sentence explained why: "If Genl Lee thinks he will be come the Presedent with the job handed him on a silver platter," he wrote, "Genl Lee can think again."

Lee read Forrest's letter several times, shook his head. As far as he could see, the South had just acquired political parties. Jefferson Davis would not be pleased. He was not pleased himself.

The young lieutenant asked, "Shall I take any message back to the Secretary of War, sir?"

"Eh? Lieutenant, you may convey to Mr. Seddon my gratitude, but past that, no, I have no message."

⋆ XIV ⋆

Raeford Liles bustled about inside his general store, straightening a bolt of cloth here, scratching out a price and writing in a new one there. He muttered under his breath as he worked. Some of the mutters were sulfurous; since Israel went off to work for Henry Pleasants, he hadn't found anyone who suited him as an employee.

Nate Caudell slapped a wooden pocket comb on the counter. He glanced at the low stack of three-day-old *Raleigh Constitution*s there. "Looks as though you were right, Mr. Liles," he said.

Liles's head poked up between a couple of woven straw fans. "Right about what?" he asked. When he saw Caudell looking down at the newspapers, he scowled. "This ain't a library, you know. You want to read that, you can buy it."

"All right, I will." Caudell lifted the top paper, set it by the comb. "You were right about having General Forrest to vote for—it says here he *is* going to run for President."

"Good for him," Liles said. "He'll keep the niggers in line if anybody can. Way things seem sometimes nowadays, the North might as well have won the war."

"I don't know." Caudell read further. "Anybody who calls Robert E. Lee 'a traitor to the ideals that form the basis of our republic' is crazy and nothing else but. Without Robert E. Lee, the North *would* have won the war, and we wouldn't be here arguing now."

"You know I never had a bad thing to say about Robert E. Lee," Liles answered, and Caudell had to nod, for that was true. The storekeeper continued, "But from what I hear, Lee is makin' noises about lettin' all the niggers go free, an' if the war wasn't about slavery, then just what the hell was it about?"

"Slavery was a big part of it, sure enough," Caudell admitted, "but it wasn't the whole reason for the war. Besides, from all I've read, Lee's not talking about freeing all the slaves at once. I agree with you, anybody who did that would be out of his mind. But the Yankees turned too many niggers loose for us ever to get 'em all back. You've said as much yourself. It makes me think we can't keep 'em all in bonds forever."

Raeford Liles grunted. "You been listenin' to that damnfool Yankee friend o' yours too much. Might could be you ought to go North your own self."

"Don't you call me a Yankee," Caudell said hotly. "You'd better not call Henry a damnfool, either, not when you look at the crop his farm brought in." What with too little water and then too much, 1866 had been a hard year all through the South. But Pleasants, with his engineering knowledge, got his crops enough water in the dry times and not too much in the wet, and sent enough tobacco and corn to market to make himself the envy of his neighbors.

Liles grunted again. "Well, all right, maybe he ain't a damnfool. But I ain't fond o' no smart Yankees, neither—what business does he have down here, anyways?"

"Making a living, same as you or me." Caudell could not quite keep from remembering that Henry Pleasants was making a much better living than he was, and a better living than Raeford Liles, too. But Pleasants was his friend, so he went on stoutly, "He could have gone back to Pennsylvania after the war was over, but he chose to stay down here and become part of our new country instead."

"If he was as fine as you make him out to be, Nate, he'd walk across Stony Creek outen gettin' his feet wet."

"Oh, horseshit. He's no more the Second Coming than he is a devil with a pointy tail, the way you paint him." Caudell tossed coins, some Federal, some Confederate, down on the counter, stuck the comb in his pocket, and walked out of the general store with the newspaper. The closing door cut off Liles's reply in midword.

He suspected Henry Pleasants would remain a Yankee in the eyes of Nash County until the sexton shoveled dirt down onto his coffin; if he ever married again, whatever offspring he had would likely be labeled "the Yankee's brats." *Their* children might escape the taint of Northern origin, or might not. Nash County was a clannish place.

One column of the *Raleigh Constitution* was labeled "events of interest from foreign parts." He read a report from Montevideo dated October 29 (six weeks old now, he thought) on the South American war between Paraguay and all its neighbors. Closer to home, the Mexican forces of the Emperor Maximilian, stiffened by a couple of brigades of French troops, had inflicted another defeat on the republican army led by Juarez. Caudell nodded in some satisfaction at that—Maximilian's government remained friendly to the Confederacy.

The next foreign item came from Washington. That still sometimes struck him as odd. He half expected it to be a protest from President Seymour against the aid the French were giving Maximilian, but it was just the opposite: the report said that most of the U.S. troops in the New Mexico and Arizona territories were being withdrawn. Seymour had in fact issued a protest, but to the government of Great Britain for increasing its garrisons in the Canadas. Adding those two items together, Caudell smelled war brewing. He wondered when it would boil over. From his own experience against the Yankees, he thought England was about to get a nasty surprise.

A drop of rain smacked the dirt street in front of him, then another one. Still another hit the brim of his black felt hat. He hurried back toward the widow Bissett's, glad the rain wasn't snow. His head turned at a colorful broadside, freshly pasted—it hadn't been there when he went to the general store—on a fence along Alston Street. SAVE THE CONFEDERACY— VOTE FOR FORREST! the poster exclaimed in big letters. Below that legend was a picture of the stalwart cavalry leader.

Rain or no, he paused to stare at the broadside. The election was eleven months away. He'd never heard of starting a campaign so early. He trotted on, scratching his head. A couple of houses farther down the street, he discovered another political poster. This one, besides Forrest's picture, bore a four-word slogan: FORREST—HIT 'EM AGAIN!

He passed several more such sheets by the time he got to his room. He wondered how many he had not seen, how many had been stuck up all over town to make sure everybody saw at least one. He wondered how many towns like Nashville the Confederacy held, and how many of those had been similarly broadsided. He wondered how much all that had cost. Nathan Bedford Forrest was supposed to be rich. If he campaigned on this scale till November, he would need to be richer than Caudell thought he was.

When he passed a broadside partly protected by an overhanging roof, he paused for a closer look. Under Forrest's hard but handsome features appeared a line of small type: *Prepared by van Pelt Printers, Rivington,*

North Carolina. Caudell studied that for a couple of minutes before he went on. If the Rivington men were working with Forrest, he would have all the money he needed.

From an upstairs window in Arlington, Lee looked across the Potomac toward Washington, D.C. Smoke curled up from hundreds, from thousands of chimneys, rising to the true clouds and also turning to a dirty gray the smoke that blanketed the city.

Lee's mood was a dirty gray, too. "Bedford Forrest is a very devil," he said, throwing a copy of the *Richmond Examiner* down onto a tabletop. "He makes political hay merely by noting where this place is." He picked up the paper again, read, "No wonder General Lee chooses to reside only a stone's throw from the heart of Yankeedom. His ideas show him to be a Yankee himself, in gray clothing."

"Let him say whatever he wants," Mary Custis Lee answered. "Now that my dear home has been made habitable once more, I would live nowhere else. I always felt myself an uprooted plant in Richmond."

"I know that, my dear, nor did I protest when you wanted to remove here," Lee answered. For one thing, he knew such protest would have done no good; with her mind once made up, his wife was harder to drive from a position than any Federal general. For another, he had not imagined Nathan Bedford Forrest could turn his choice of residence against him.

Union commanders had underestimated Forrest throughout the war, and paid for it again and again. Lee was beginning to wonder if he and all of official Richmond had not made the same mistake. Who would have thought a rough-and-ready planter, with no education to speak of, would prove so effective on the stump? And who would have imagined he would prove as energetic in political campaigning as in military? He fairly flew from town to town, made his speeches, and was gone on the next train to make another one seventy-five miles down the track. Lee thought of the shock Andrew Jackson had created in Washington after almost half a century of well-bred Presidents from Virginia and Massachusetts. The frontier might seize the Confederate capital much sooner.

Mary Lee said, "Help me up, please, Robert." He got her to her feet. On his arm, she went over to the window, too. She, however, looked not across the Potomac toward Washington but down at the grounds of Arlington. She nodded, as if pleased with herself. "The snow hides them, and it is not all."

"Them?" Lee asked.

"The graves of the Yankees who died here. Grass and flowers in the summertime, snow in the winter, and I can begin to forget those cursed Northerners who lie on our grounds. That is not easy, not after they did everything in their power to debase and desecrate Arlington."

"The ones who lie here were not those who hurt this place," Lee said. "The thieves, the mutilators, are most of them safe in the United States." He still did not feel easy about letting her replant the sloping lawns and the gardens around Arlington to erase all remembrance of the Union graves, but in the end had let her have her way. She cherished the mansion as if it were part of her family, which in a way it was.

She said, "I wish they could be made to answer for their crimes. The garden my father laid out all ruined and changed; the splendid little forest leveled to the ground; the graves— The graves, at least, I have attended to."

"Many crimes committed in time of war go unanswered," Lee said. "And as for their perpetrators, they now live in another country, which was, after all, the point of the war. Nor are we guiltless of crimes of our own." Thinking of Forrest made the affair at Fort Pillow spring to mind. He shook his head. That had been a bad business, with soldiers black and white (mostly black) shot down as they tried to surrender and after they had surrendered. The only thing Forrest had to say about it now was his familiar dictum: *War means fighting, and fighting means killing.*

Mary Lee's comment was, "I think it is shameful for you to speak of our gallant men and the thieving Yankees in the same breath."

"Through a good part of the war, our gallant men kept themselves supplied by thieving *from* the Yankees," he said.

She waved that aside, as if it were of no account. She, of course, had never been in the field, never known firsthand the desperate want under which the Southern fighting man had suffered till the last days of the war. She went on, "I think it is shameful, too, for General Forrest to try to tar you with the Yankee brush. You did so much more than he to make our nation free, and now he calls you abolitionist."

"To be just, it is what I seem to have become." He felt Mary take a deep breath, decided to forestall her: "Oh, not in the sense he means, surely, the sense of imposing emancipation by force if necessary, and without compensation, as those people did in the lands they occupied. But we must find a means through which the Negro may be gradually brought toward freedom, or face trouble unbounded in the future."

His wife sniffed. "How do you propose to gradually free the Negroes? Either they are slaves, as they have been, or they are *not*. I see no middle ground."

"I shall have to define one," Lee said. Normally, the middle ground was as dangerous politically as in war, for it left one vulnerable to fire from both sides. Here, though, he would at least be safe from that. Out-and-out abolitionists, in the Northern, radical, sense of the word, were so thin on the ground in the Confederacy that he could probably count them on his fingers and toes. All the fire his way would come from a single direction, from those who thought owning blacks only right and proper. But fire from a single direction could be deadly, too. He'd seen that in defeat and victory, at Malvern Hill, Fredericksburg, Gettysburg, Bealeton . . .

"I wish we could have simply lived out our days here, without worry about either war or politics," Mary said. "You have given so much, Robert; can there never be an end to it?"

"I wish there could." He meant it; he'd never known how much he truly missed his family until, for the first time in his life, he saw them every day. The life of a gentleman farmer at Arlington would have suited him very well. But— "I fear I cannot so easily abandon my duty."

"That word." Mary Lee made a sour face. "Help me back to my chair now, if you please. I would not want you to try your strength too long by the necessity of supporting me and your duty both."

He did as she asked, then returned to the window. A moving black dot in the snow became a horseman and, a moment later, a horseman he recognized. "Here's Custis, up from Richmond," he said, deliberately trying to sound cheerful and hoping the arrival of their eldest son would help lift Mary out of her bitter mood.

She was at least willing to change the subject. "Take me downstairs," she said.

He pushed the chair to the stairs, then helped her down them. Another chair waited at the bottom on the stairway: procuring a second had proved easier and more convenient than manhandling a single one up and down several times a day, and Mary was almost helpless by herself now. The offer Andries Rhoodie had given Lee was seldom far from his thoughts. If only it had come from somewhere, anywhere other than America Will Break . . .

Custis's three sisters were already greeting him by the time Lee and Mary came to the front hall. Between hugs, Custis stamped snow onto the rug. "Sisterly embraces aren't warm enough to thaw me out," he said, whereupon Mildred poked him in the ribs and made him jump. "Let me sit by the fire and warm up; then I'll tell my news."

"And what *is* that news, dear boy?" Lee asked a few minutes later, after Custis was comfortably ensconced in a cane-back chair in front of the crackling fireplace.

His son waited to reply until he took a cup of coffee from the tray Julia brought in. "That's the real bean," he said once he'd sipped. "I'd grown so used to chicory during the war and afterwards that sometimes I find myself missing it." He drank again, set the cup down on a small, square table ornamented around the edges with polished brass tack heads. At last he said, "General Forrest has settled on a running-mate."

"Has he?" Lee leaned forward in his own chair. "Who is the individual so honored?"

"Another western man—Senator Wigfall of Texas."

"I see." After a few seconds' consideration, Lee said musingly, "It is as well, then, that the election is not to be settled by pistols at ten paces. Both Forrest and Wigfall are accomplished duelists. While I would not hesitate to face either gentleman, my skill in such matters has never been tested, and I would not lightly hazard a Vice-Presidential candidate in such an affair."

Custis chuckled, but quickly sobered. "You ought to get about the business of choosing a Vice-Presidential candidate, Father. When Forrest announced his candidacy against you, I took it for little more than a joke. But the man is in deadly earnest, sir, and is campaigning as hard as he drove his own troops, which is to say, very hard indeed."

"From everything I have ever heard and from everything I have ever seen, anyone who underestimates General Forrest's energy or resolve is but preparing himself to be dreadfully surprised," Lee said. "Had he the education to accompany them, he might well have been the greatest of us all. That is by the way, however. I do now admit to regretting the absence of political parties among us; having such structures in place would have facilitated my selection of a colleague. I intend to deal with the matter soon, dear boy, and your telling me that Forrest had done so but fortifies my resolve."

"He has a party as well," Custis answered. "He and his henchmen are styling themselves Patriots and working to enlist other office seekers to run under their banner. You will also no doubt have learned by now that he has the monetary support of America Will Break for his campaign; the building across the street from the War Department doubles as his Richmond headquarters."

"Were I a man to shoot a messenger for the news he brought, son, you would do well to run for your life," Lee said. "I have always shunned politics; soldiers in a republic can properly pursue no other course. When I agreed—reluctantly—to run for the Presidency, I expected the election to be a matter of form. But I never undertook a campaign in which I did not expect to prevail, nor do I aim to make this one the exception."

His son nodded approvingly. That pleased him, but only in an abstracted way; his mind was full of what he would have to do to win. Up until a few minutes before, he had been doing his best to think like a politician. As that was not his forte, no wonder he'd had little luck. Now he resolved to do what he did best: think like a soldier, and treat Forrest as an adversary like McClellan or Grant.

His hand went up to the collar of his jacket. It was a plain civilian coat of black wool, but he imagined he felt the familiar wreathed stars of a general once more. He got up from his chair. "Back to Richmond," he said. "I have work to do."

Early fireflies winked on and off, like shooting stars brought down to earth. Nate Caudell tried to recapture his childhood glee at seeing them. He did his best, but could not quite manage it. The little bugs reminded him too much of muzzle flashes in the dark.

In any case, the fireflies were not the only beacons in the night. Caudell stood on Washington Street, watching the torchlight parade stream into the Nashville town square. Decked out in gray hoods, the paraders sang the "Bedford Forrest Quickstep" as loud as they could: "He chased the niggers and they did run; He chased the niggers and he gave 'em the gun! Hit 'em again, hit 'em again, hit 'em again—Forrest!"

Henry Pleasants stood beside Caudell. He said, "You know what these Trees of Forrest remind me of, Nate?"

"What's that?"

"You won't like it," Pleasants warned. Caudell gestured impatiently. Pleasants said, "They remind me of Lincoln's Wide-Awakes in 1860: all dressed up in what's almost a uniform, all full of piss and vinegar for their man, and all ready to stomp on anyone who doesn't like him. And because they're excited, they make other people excited, too."

"We didn't have any of those Wide-Awakes down here," Caudell said. "Come to that, Lincoln wasn't even on the ballot down here."

"Maybe not, but somebody in the Patriot camp must have been paying attention to the way he ran his campaign. Remember, he won that race, too, even if he wasn't on the ballot anywhere in the South."

"Are you saying that means Forrest will win, too? It'd take more than a fancy parade to get me to vote for anybody but Robert E. Lee, and that goes for anybody who served in the Army of Northern Virginia."

"But not everybody in the country did serve in the Army of Northern Virginia. Me, I'd sooner vote for Lee than Forrest any day, but what do I know? I'm just a damnyankee—ask my neighbors."

At the tail end of the parade marched a big man thumping a bigger drum. The watching crowd spilled into the street and followed him into the square. In front of the courthouse, the same platform that had served for the slave auction was up again. Three or four of Forrest's Trees stood atop it, torches held on high. More crowded close, so the platform was far and away the brightest place in the square.

One of the hooded Trees shouted, "Here's his honor the mayor!" The rest of the group hollered and clapped as Isaac Cockrell clambered to the top of the platform. He was not an old man; he was, in fact, several years younger than Caudell. But he was short and fat and rather wheezy. Among the stalwart Trees, he cut an unprepossessing figure.

"My friends," he said, and then again, louder: "My friends!" The crowd kept right on chattering.

Caudell cupped hands to his mouth, yelled, "Hire a substitute, Cockrell!" The mayor had bought his way out of the 47th North Carolina a couple of months before Gettysburg, and stayed prosperously at home while the regiment did its desperate work. Caudell was not the only man who remembered. Several other veterans whooped in gleeful derision at his cry.

Isaac Cockrell flinched but quickly gathered himself. "My friends," he said yet again, and this time was able to go on from there: "My friends, we're here tonight to show we all want Nathan Bedford Forrest to be the next President of our Confederate States of America."

Forrest's Trees raised a cheer. So did a good many men and women in the crowd; the women, of course, could not vote, but they enjoyed a rousing political spectacle no less than their husbands and brothers, fathers and sons. But Caudell's was not the only voice that shouted "No!"—far from it. To drown out their opponents, the Trees started singing the "Bedford Forrest Quickstep" again.

Henry Pleasants knew the answer to that. "Lee!" he boomed, making his voice as deep as he could. "Lee! Lee! Lee!" Caudell joined the one-word chant. So did the other Lee men—most of them veterans like him. Their cry rose to rival the bawled-out "Quickstep."

Raeford Liles was singing Forrest's anthem at the top of his lungs. He saw that Caudell belonged to the other camp. "You look like nothin' but a stupid damn tree frog, Nate, hunchin' up your shoulders every time you chirp out 'Lee!'"

"I'd sooner look like a tree frog than have the brains of one," Caudell retorted. Liles stuck out his tongue. Caudell said, "Who looks froggy now?"

Having launched into his speech, Mayor Cockrell kept on with it through the hubbub, though for some time no one except perhaps the Trees up on the platform with him could hear a word he was saying. *Just as well,* Caudell thought. But gradually, backers of Forrest and Lee both quieted down enough to get bits of the mayor's speech: "Do you want your niggers taken away from you? If you do, vote for Lee, sure enough. Vote for Forrest, though, and your children'll still keep 'em, and your grandchildren, too."

"What niggers?" a heckler yelled from the back of the crowd. "I ain't got no niggers. Most of us ain't got no niggers—ain't got the money for it. How many niggers *you* got, Cockrell?"

That hit home hard enough to make the mayor draw back a pace. He owned about half a dozen Negroes, which, while it did not make him a planter, certainly established him as well-to-do. He rallied gamely, though: "Even if you don't own any niggers, do you want them free to work for low wages, lower than a white man would take?"

The heckler—Caudell suddenly grinned, recognizing Dempsey Eure's voice—would not be stilled: "Can't hardly work for less'n I make, farmin' the place I farm."

Cockrell's argument might have carried more force in a bigger town, a place where more people did in fact work for wages. But Nash County was overwhelmingly rural, even by the standards of North Carolina. Tied to the soil as they were, its people had scant experience with wages of any sort, high or low.

Seeing their speaker falter, Forrest's Trees started singing again. By then their torches were guttering out, letting the square return to night. Caudell and the other Lee backers answered the "Quickstep" with their own call. Both groups, though, were running out of steam. By ones and twos, people began drifting away. Sometimes, in low voices, they carried on their arguments. Sometimes, away from the heat of the rally, they found themselves able to laugh at how stirred they'd gotten.

Caudell said, "It's still early spring. We'll all be done to a turn if this kind of thing keeps up till November."

"Keeps life from getting dull, doesn't it?" Pleasants answered as he walked back toward the stable to get his horse.

"I suppose so." Caudell walked on another few steps with his friend, then added wistfully, "I remember when life was dull, or I thought it was, anyway. You know what? Looking back, it doesn't seem so bad."

Lee had been waiting for the knock on the door of the suite at the Powhatan House. He got up and opened the door. "Senator Brown!" he said, extending his hand. "Thank you for doing me the honor of coming here."

"The honor is mine, sir." Albert Gallatin Brown of Mississippi was a strikingly handsome man in his early fifties, with dark wavy hair worn rather long, and bushy side-whiskers that reached down to the line of his jaw. His suit was of the most stylish cut (a good deal more so than Lee's); his patent leather shoes gleamed in the gaslight.

"Do please sit down," Lee said, waving him to a chair. Brown sank back into the soft cushions, crossed his legs, lay one arm on the velvet arm of the seat. He seemed the picture of ease; Lee envied him his ability to relax so completely. "You are perhaps curious as to why I asked if you would see me today."

"Call me—intrigued." Brown's dark eyes, shadowed in their sockets, revealed very little. He was a veteran politician, having served in the Mississippi state legislature, in the U.S. Congress, and as a U.S. senator alongside Jefferson Davis until his state left the Union. He'd also fought as a Confederate captain before he was chosen for the new nation's Senate.

Lee said, "My purpose is not to keep you in suspense, sir. I want to ask if you will serve as my Vice-Presidential candidate for the forthcoming elections."

Brown's relaxation dropped from him like a cloak. He leaned forward in his seat, said softly, "I thought it might be so. Even to be considered as your running mate does me more credit than I deserve—"

"Not at all, sir."

But Brown had not finished. "—Yet before I say yea or nay, there are certain matters concerning which I must satisfy myself." He waited to see how Lee would take that.

Lee was delighted. "If my views are in any way unclear to you, I would not have you blindly embrace them. Ask what you will."

"Thank you, sir." Brown dipped his head. "In one way, your invitation to me is surprising, for I perceived you as being President Davis's chosen successor and, as you may know, the President and I have not always been in complete accord." That was an understatement. While willing to do whatever proved necessary to win the war, Brown had consistently maintained war powers resided with the Confederate Congress, not with the President. He obviously remembered the angry exchanges he'd had with Davis.

"Had it not been for the President's urging, I should not have sought the Presidency; that I admit," Lee said. "I could hardly deny it—I was never struck with political ambition, nor do I feel it now to any great degree. But if you doubt I am my own man, then I thank you for your time here today and apologize for having inconvenienced you. I will discuss the position with someone else."

"No need," Brown said quickly, holding up a hand; he had political ambition. "You are quite clear; indeed, the fact that you have asked me says a great deal for your independence from Davis in and of itself. But the next question cuts to the bone: what precisely *is* your stand on the Negro and his place in our society?"

"I do not believe we can successfully keep him in bonds forever, and so I feel we must begin the process of lifting those bonds as quickly as is practicable, lest he tear them off himself and, in so doing, work far more harm upon us. If you find that position untenable, sir, the door is but a few steps away."

Brown did not get up and leave. But he did not sing hosannas in praise of Lee's generosity, either. He said, "Let me quote for you article one, section nine, clause four of the Constitution of the Confederate States: 'No bill of attainder, *ex post facto* law, or law denying or impairing the right of property in Negro slaves shall be passed.' "

"I am familiar with the clause," Lee said. "That it is an impediment to what I propose, I cannot deny. Let me ask you a question in return, if I may." He waited for Brown to nod before continuing: "Suppose the war, instead of turning in our favor in 1864, had taken a downhill course, as it might well have done without our troops' being newly armed with repeaters. Would you then have favored giving weapons to and emancipating certain of our slaves in order to preserve our republic, the Constitution notwithstanding?"

"In such a crisis, I would," Brown said after only a brief pause for thought. "Saving the nation is to me more important than any temporary damage to the Constitution, which can be made good later if the nation survives."

"Fair enough. I submit to you, then, that the Negro as slave presents us with a continuing crisis, even if one less imminent than the prospect of forfeiting the Second American Revolution. The time to deal with it is before it becomes imminent, lest we be forced to act in haste and perhaps desperation."

Brown pondered that, then startled Lee by throwing back his head and laughing. At Lee's quizzical look, he explained rather sheepishly, "I marvel that I am sitting here listening to you at all, let alone carefully considering your ideas, when in the U.S. Congress I called for opening California to slavery, by force of arms if necessary, and for the annexation to the United States of Cuba and the Mexican states of Tamaulipas and Potosí to serve for the planting and spreading of slavery."

"Yet here you sit," Lee said. From Brown's words and votes in the Confederate Senate, he had gathered that the man was moderate on the question of the Negro. He had not thought to go back and learn what Brown had said as a U.S. congressman and senator. That, evidently, had been an oversight on his part. He wondered why the man did not rise up on his hind legs and storm out, as Nathan Bedford Forrest and Andries Rhoodie had before him in like circumstances.

"Here I sit," Brown agreed. He laughed again. "Circumstances alter cases. When we were part of the United States, we had to seek to extend slavery wherever we might to balance the corresponding expansion of the Northern States and our consequent loss of power within the U.S. But now we are no longer within the U.S. and may act as we deem best, without fear it will weaken us before our political foes."

"That is most sensibly spoken, sir," Lee said with admiration. "Then you are with me?"

"I have not said so," Brown answered sharply. "I concede there may be circumstances under which some fort of emancipation is justified. We must, however, offer the voters a program they can stomach, or all this fine talk is so much moonshine. How do you propose to go about setting the niggers free?"

"In a word, gradually," Lee said. "I have, I hope you will believe, given this a good deal of thought. I do not and shall not propose confiscatory legislation. I understand that would be politically impracticable."

"I hope you do," Brown said. "If you don't get elected, nothing else matters."

Again Lee longed for the clean, well-defined world of the soldier, where compromise had to be made only with weather and terrain and what the enemy would allow, not with one's own principles. But the politician who could bring home half a loaf counted himself ahead of the game.

"I do not wish slavery to become the sole issue in this campaign," Lee said. "Many others are of no small urgency: our relations with the United States, the still deplorable state of our finances, and our posture relative to Maximilian and the Mexican insurgents, to name just a few. We have yet even to establish a Supreme Court. On none of these matters has Forrest expressed a position; he owns but one drum to beat."

"A good point, and one we can tax him with. But none of those, save maybe what we do about the United States, will make people *sweat*. They'll get up in arms over the nigger question. You still need to answer me about that."

"So I do," Lee said. "As I see it, as a beginning we need to encourage emancipation in every way possible and to prepare freedmen to learn useful trades. During the war, several of our states relaxed their laws against slaves' learning to read and write. I would extend that relaxation throughout the Confederacy. For the next step, I would propose a law allowing a slave, or anyone else on behalf of that slave, to pay for his release at the price for which he had been sold or was valued by a competent appraiser, the owner not having the privilege of refusing said price."

Albert Gallatin Brown pursed his lips. "You might get by with that, not least because it is so much less radical than what hotheads on the other side say you want."

"I have not finished," Lee warned. Brown sat back and composed himself to listen further. "If a slave or someone who wished to buy his freedom could not pay the whole price at once, I would let them pay one sixth, the master again being compelled to accept, to give the slave one day to work for himself each week, another free day being added for each sixth paid, until the slave's labor is entirely his own."

"That goes farther, but is again reasonable, and certainly not confiscatory," Brown said.

"The plan is modeled after one proposed but unfortunately not accepted some years ago in the Empire of Brazil," Lee said. "Since I became convinced of the necessity of this change, I have sought intently for ways to facilitate it. My former aide Charles Marshall, whose training is in the law, recently brought the Brazilian proposal to my notice. To it I would add a couple of additional features."

"Which are?" Brown asked.

"First, I would take a small percentage of the property tax paid into the Treasury on slaves each year and use it to establish an emancipation fund to free or begin freeing as many Negroes as this revenue would permit. And second, I would propose a law to the effect that all Negroes born after a certain date should be reckoned freeborn, though owing service to their mothers' masters for the first twenty-one years of their lives, in which time they should also be prepared to live free. I have in mind, you see, not to murder slavery, but to let it peacefully die of old age."

"Ten years ago, in Charleston or Mobile or Vicksburg, they'd have hanged you from a lamp post for putting forward a scheme like that," Brown remarked. He ran a finger along the bottom edge of a side-whisker as he thought. Finally he said, "We've all seen a great many surprising things these past ten years, haven't we? All right, General Lee, I'm with you."

"Splendid!" Lee stuck out his hand. "Sir, we are confederates."

Brown's gaze suddenly turned inward. "Not just confederates," he said quietly, "but Confederates." Lee could hear the capital letter falling into place. Brown went on, "I think you've just named our party."

"Confederates." Lee tasted the word on his tongue. He said it again, firmly, and nodded. "Confederates we are."

*   *   *

The fiddler and banjo player swung from "Ye Cavaliers of Dixie" to "Stonewall Jackson's Way" to "Mister, Here's Your Mule." Hearing the old war songs again took Nate Caudell back to campfires and sore feet and the smell of powder. Nothing made a man feel so intensely alive as knowing he might not be alive much longer.

When the musicians played "Dixie," that remembered intensity— cherished all the more now that it was gone—filled him too full to let him keep on singing as he had been doing. From somewhere deep inside him, a rebel yell clawed its way up his throat and out between his teeth. It was not a sound that properly belonged in the sleepy, peaceful Nashville town square, but he did not care. He had to let it loose or burst.

Nor was his the only yell that ripped through the afternoon. Most of the men in the crowd—almost all the men under forty-five in the crowd—were veterans of the Second American Revolution, and most of them, by their faces, by their shouts, were as caught up in their memories as he was. A hat sailed through the air, then another.

The last sweet notes of "Dixie" died away. The banjo man and fiddler got down from the flag-draped platform. George Lewis climbed up onto it. Caudell found himself coming to attention and had to fight back a sudden, sharp order to the people around him to straighten their ranks. Then he saw a good many other men, especially those who had fought in the Castalia Invincibles under Captain Lewis, were also squaring their shoulders and bringing their feet together.

But Lewis was not wearing a captain's three bars these days, only the wing collar and cravat that befit a prosperous civilian and legislator. The collar fit snugly, too; he had to have gained twenty or thirty pounds in his time down in Raleigh. Noticing that made Caudell smile; anyone who hadn't put on weight since his army days wasn't half trying.

Lewis said, "My friends, I don't even know that we needed to get together here today. So many of us marched under Marse Robert, fought under Marse Robert—we all know what he's like. Is there anybody here from the Army of Northern Virginia who's such a big fool that he doesn't aim to vote for Robert E. Lee come November?"

"No!" Caudell shouted. So did most of the men around him. Carried away by the moment, several women called "No!" too.

But most was not all. Just as Caudell had heckled Isaac Cockrell at the Forrest rally, so now someone bellowed, "I ain't gonna vote for nobody who wants to take my niggers away!"

Cockrell had tried to go on as if no one were harassing him. George Lewis met his challenger head-on. Peering into the crowd to see who had shouted at him, he said, "Jonas Perry, you *are* a big fool." That raised a laugh. Lewis went on, "For one thing, everybody here knows those three niggers of yours don't do a lick of work anyway, so they'd be no great loss to you." The laugh got louder; whenever he was in town, Perry spent most of his time complaining about how lazy his slaves were. Lewis grew serious: "Anyhow, Lee doesn't aim to take away anybody's niggers. That's a damned lie."

"He don't want us to keep 'em no more, neither," Jonas Perry yelled back. "How we gonna get our crops in without 'em? You, Mr. Big Assemblyman George Lewis, sir, you got a lot more niggers'n me. How *you* aim to get your crops in without 'em?"

Lewis hesitated. The crowd muttered. Caudell started to worry. If a rally went wrong, a lot of votes could go wrong, too. He looked around. Like him, a lot of people stood tensely, waiting to hear what George Lewis would say. Along with the whites, he also saw several colored men and women in the square. They were not part of the rally; they had work to do. But whatever they were doing, they had their heads turned toward the platform on which some of them had been sold. All at once, Caudell realized the election in which they could not take part mattered more to them than to him or George Lewis or any white man. He would merely be dissatisfied with the results if Lee lost, while they would have any hope of liberty dashed for at least six years.

Almost too late, Lewis answered Jonas Perry: "Jonas, if I said I liked the whole of Lee's plan, I'd be a liar. But the way I look at it is this: Sometimes holding on to a thing just for the sake of holding on to it gets to be more trouble than it's worth. Bedford Forrest did everything he could to whip the niggers in arms and make them stop fighting, but you still read about bushwhackings and murders in Louisiana and Arkansas and Mississippi in the papers all the time. And Tennessee—the Yankees sat on Tennessee for two years and turned every nigger in the state loose, near enough. There's not a prayer of getting them all back with their proper masters there. Hell's bells, man, you know half the free niggers, and then some right here in North Carolina were slaves before the Yankees came down on the coast. I'm not asking you to like it. I'm asking you if it's true. Is it?"

"Yes, but—" Perry said.

This time, Lewis interrupted him. "But me no buts. The niggers who are uppity can't run North anymore, either; now that we're free of the United States, they don't want our riffraff. We always said we hated niggers running off, but it was a kind of safety valve for us. Now we're stuck with all of 'em, and the valve's tied down. Do you want it to blow? Do you want to see Santo Domingos all through the South?"

"You think I'm crazy?" Perry said hoarsely. Caudell understood the catch in his voice; to a Southerner, *Santo Domingo* carried the same *frisson* of horror as *violation* did to a delicately reared woman. Slave uprisings, slave massacres, had always been rare and tiny in the South. But all whites knew, admit it or no, that a great rebellion could always happen . . . and tens of thousands of black men had learned to handle firearms in the course of the Second American Revolution.

"No, I don't think you're crazy, Jonas; I just think you haven't thought the thing through, and I think Marse Robert has," Lewis said. "Lee's plan doesn't hurt anybody in the pocketbook, and it gives us back our safety valve again. It gives us lots of years to figure out what the hell to do with the niggers. Vote for Forrest, and things stay just the way they are now— till they blow sky high."

Perry didn't answer, though the crowd had grown so quiet a whisper could have been heard. Caudell had his doubts that Lewis had convinced the burly farmer, but he'd made him thoughtful.

Into that silence, Lewis said, "Here's one more thing: This is *Lee* we're talking about. If somebody else had put this notion forward, I'd fret about it a lot more than I do. If I trust the judgment of any man on the face of the earth, it's Robert E. Lee."

Heads bobbed solemnly up and down, Caudell's among them. Lee was human; he could make mistakes. Any man who'd charged up toward Cemetery Ridge wearing gray knew that—for too many, it was the last thing they ever knew. But Lee had held off the Federals in Virginia, though constantly outnumbered, and beat them and taken Washington City when the repeaters gave him a chance, had helped arrange the peace with the U.S.A. and presided over Kentucky's joining the Confederacy. If all that was not enough to deserve support, what was?

"I had a whole big speech all ready to roll out, but I don't think I'm going to bother with it now," Lewis said. "The only reason I can see that anyone would want to vote for Forrest instead of Lee is over slavery, and I've covered that as well as I know how, talking with Jonas here. When we're talking about anything else—dealing with the United States and other foreign countries, making paper money worth what it says it is, all that sort of thing—Lee has it over him, and I think everybody knows it. A vote for Lee and Brown moves the Confederacy forward. A vote for Forrest and Wigfall holds us back. Thank you for listening to me, my friends. I'm through."

The crowd cheered lustily, and began the chant of "Lee! Lee! Lee!" that Henry Pleasants had begun at the Forrest rally. The banjo picker and fiddler struck up "Dixie" again. Voices lifted in song. Caudell raised his with the rest. Only when he was walking back to his room did he think to wonder how fitting the tune was at a rally for a man who wanted to move, however gradually, on slavery.

Chattering like magpies, Caudell's students hurried out of the run-down schoolhouse and scattered for their homes. It had been a long day for them; summer was almost here, and the sun rose early and set late. The only thing that helped them—and their teacher—endure was knowing that with summer came an end to lessons.

When Caudell, slower and tireder than the children, went outside, he found a black man waiting for him. "Hello, Israel," he said. "Can I do something for you?"

"Yes, suh, you can. I wants you to help me with my 'rithmetic, suh. I pays you to do it." He reached into his pocket, took out a tan-and-brown Confederate five-dollar bill.

"Wait, wait, wait." Caudell put his hands in the air. "You don't need me, not when you work for Henry Pleasants. He's a real engineer—he knows more about mathematics than I'll ever learn."

"Yes, suh, he knows it. But he knows it so good, he cain't teach it to me: seem like he done forgot how he ever learn in the fust place, if you know what I mean," Israel said. Caudell had to nod; he'd known people like that. The Negro went on, "But you, suh, you a *school*teacher. You *used* to showin' folk what don't know nothin' how to do things jus' a step at a time, like them Yankee teachers they had at the Hayti 'cross the Trent from New Berne. An' these here fractions, they drivin' me to distraction. I gots to know 'em, if I's ever goin' to keep Marse Henry's books for him. Please teach me, suh." Israel displayed the banknote again.

Nothing—not even poor dead Josephine, with her promises of sensual delights—could have been better calculated to tempt Caudell than someone standing in front of him and begging to be taught. That Israel was black worried him less than it would have before the war. For one thing, Israel was free; for another, he was already literate and had not gotten into any trouble on account of it.

That did not mean Caudell had no qualms. "If I do agree to teach you, Israel, when will you be able to come into town? Will Henry let you take time off from your work?"

Sadly, Israel shook his head. "No, suh, he sho' won't. I gots to work fo' my keep. I finish all my cho's early today so as I can get here an' ask you. But if you wants to help me learn, I come in soon as I'm done, an' walk back in the dark. That don't matter none to me."

"How many days a week would you want to do that?" Caudell asked.

"Many as you want," Israel answered at once.

Caudell studied him. If he meant what he said, he had more hunger for knowledge than any of the regular students in the school. A full day's work, five miles on foot into Nashville, a lesson, another five miles back to the farm, with one of those hikes, at least, and maybe both, made in the night and cutting into his sleep . . .

"If you really want to try, I guess we could manage three evenings a week and see how that goes," Caudell said. His own curiosity was piqued. He wondered just how much the Negro could do.

"Thank you, suh, thank you!" Israel's big happy grin seemed almost to split his face in two. Then he sobered. "How much you want me to pay you?"

Could he have afforded to, Caudell would have done it for nothing. He could not afford to, and he knew it, especially with the lean months of summer staring him in the face. "How does five dollars every other week sound?"

"Like a lot o' money," Israel said mournfully. "Reckon I gots to pay, though, if I wants to learn."

"How much would that work out to per week?" Caudell asked, wanting to see what his new pupil already knew.

"Two dollars an' fifty cents," Israel answered without hesitation. "You ask me about cash money, I can cipher just fine. But when it's two an' a half barrels o' this an' three an' a quarter pounds o' that, I goes all to pieces."

"It won't be so bad." Caudell did his best to sound reassuring. "Come on back to the widow Bissett's with me. As long as you're here, you might as well start your lessons—soonest begun, soonest done." *And,* the resolutely practical part of him added, *the sooner I start getting paid.*

He did not take Israel up to his room. They worked on the front porch till it got too dark to see, and then for a while after that by candlelight, their heads close together. But the candles also lured bugs, until they were doing more slapping than studying. Finally Israel got up. "I better get on back, 'fore I's eaten up altogether."

"All right, Israel. I'll see you Wednesday, then. You've made a fair start, I think." Actually, Caudell was more than a little impressed. By his own account, Israel had had no schooling at all until he ran off to Federally held territory during the war. But he learned readily enough, and his mere presence here was proof of his willingness—even his eagerness—to work.

Caudell blew out the candles. Night closed down on the porch, hot and close and sticky and completely dark except for the faint glow of a single lamp in the parlor inside. Israel stumbled going down the stairs, and again on the short path that led out to Joyner Street. "See you Wednesday, suh," he called. Then, but for the sound of his footsteps, he might have vanished from the face of the earth.

Barbara Bissett sat waiting for Caudell to come in, her plump face set in disapproving lines. Without preamble, she snapped, "I don't want that nigger coming round here again, do you understand me?"

"What? Why not?" Caudell said, taken by surprise.

"On account of he's a nigger, of course." His landlady sounded surprised, too, but for a different reason. "What will the neighbors say if they see a nigger coming round my house all the time? I ain't white trash that's sunk so low as to have to make friends with slaves."

"He's free," Caudell said. That had no effect on the widow Bissett; she took one of the deep breaths she used to inflate before she went on her crying jags. Anxious to head that off, Caudell added, "He's just studying arithmetic with me."

"I don't care what he's doing, do you hear me?" Barbara Bissett could write her own name, read a little, and handle money. Past that, her knowledge stopped, nor had she ever shown any inclination to learn more. But she held the whip hand now: "He comes round here again, Mr. Nate Caudell, you can just go and find yourself another place to live, do you understand me? You better understand me."

"I understand you," Caudell said resignedly. Though he did not own much in the way of worldly goods, he had had to pack up everything and move out on a moment's notice so often during his time in the army that he'd developed a permanent aversion to the very idea. "We'll find somewhere else."

Wednesday, he met Israel well away from the widow Bissett's house, took him back to the school, and drilled him there. That was where the lessons continued. Adding and subtracting fractions went well enough, so long as they had the same denominator. But when he showed Israel that a half times a half was a quarter, the Negro shook his head in bewilderment. "It was always a two under the line befo'. How come it be a fo' now?"

"Because you multiplied it," Caudell said patiently. "How much is two times two if they're not under the line?"

"Fo'," Israel admitted. But no light went on in his eyes; he couldn't make the stretch from whole numbers to those peculiar-looking entities called fractions.

"Let's try it another way," Caudell said. "You know money. Suppose you have fifty cents. What's another name for that?"

"Half a dollar," Israel said.

"All right, what's half of half a dollar?"

"A quarter." Israel did know money. Suddenly, he stared at the slate where Caudell had chalked the problem. "Half times a half is—a quarter," he said slowly. Now his face lit up; though he was about fifteen years older than Caudell, he looked like a little boy discovering that, if you put the sounds *c* and *a* and *t* together, they turned into a word. "Half times a half *is* a quarter, an' it don' matter whether it's money or not."

"That's right," Caudell said, grinning his own grin: moments like these were what made his low salary worthwhile. "So what would half times a quarter be?" He tensed as he waited for the black man's reply. Did Israel truly grasp the principle, or had he just figured out one special case?

Israel frowned in fierce concentration, but not for long. "Half times a quarter—that'd be an eighth, wouldn't it, Marse Nate?"

"Yup!" Caudell all but shouted it. Now both men grinned, the one in relief, the other in excitement. "You have it, Israel."

"I got it," Israel said. "I sho' 'nough do, an' ain't nobody can take it away from me, neither. What else you goin' to learn me 'bout this multiplyin' fractions?"

He raced through the rest of that topic, doing his drills as fast as Caudell could give them to him. But he ran headlong into another wall when, a couple of days later, the time came for him to divide fractions instead of multiplying them. Caudell taught him the same technique he used with his regular students: invert the divisor and then multiply.

"We already done multiplyin'," Israel protested. "This here's supposed to be dividin'."

"It is," Caudell said. "Dividing and multiplying are the inverse—the opposite—of each other, the same way adding and subtracting are. Dividing by a fraction, or by any number, is the same as multiplying by its inverse. They're just separate parts of the whole thing that makes up arithmetic, you know."

To his amazement, he found that Israel knew no such thing. He'd learned the rules for each operation without thinking about whether it was related to any other. His jaw fell and his eyes went wide as he took in the concept and made it part of himself. "Ain't that somethin' grand?" he said at last. "Five times two is ten, so *of course* ten divided by five is two. It ain't no accident. It all fits together."

"Yup, it sure does," Caudell said.

"You say 'sho',' Marse Nate, but you the first person ever show that to me. Nobody else ever bother showin' me it fit together. It's like a puzzle, ain't it, where all the pieces go just so an' make up a whole big picture you couldn't never guess from lookin' at 'em apart. I had the pieces, but

I never seen the whole picture till now. Show me this trick o' yours again, will you? I bet I understands it this time aroun'.''

He did, too. At the next session, Caudell showed him how to find common denominators for fractions. He was slow to see the point of that until Caudell said, "It's what you do when you get twenty-five and a half bushels of corn from this field and thirty-seven and a third from that one and you need to know how much you have in all."

Israel's face took on the intent look with which Caudell had become familiar. "I got you, suh." He proved himself right in short order. As he started back toward Henry Pleasants's farm, he asked, "What's the next lesson?"

Caudell spread his hands. "There is no next lesson, Israel. Far as I can see, you've learned everything you need—you should do fine from here on out." And, as far as he could see, Israel had learned as well and as fast as a pretty bright white man. He was less surprised at that than he thought he ought to be, and a lot less surprised than he would have been before the war.

"Thank you, suh. Thank you from the bottom of this heart o' mine." Israel knew better than to shake hands uninvited with a white. He dipped his head and headed north toward the farm.

"It was my pleasure," Caudell called after him.

Israel didn't answer. Caudell started back to the widow Bissett's house. He knew she couldn't have done as well as the black man had, not if her life depended on it. But she would not have Israel in her house. Before he got free, she could have bought him, assuming she scraped up the money— an unlikely assumption. Caudell tugged on his beard, then kicked at a rock. "If there's any justice in that, damned if I can see it," he said out loud. Nashville was already sleeping. No one heard him.

The buggy clattered down the road. Raeford Liles spat a brown stream of tobacco juice into the dust. Then he scowled at his horse's hindquarters. "*Git* up," he snapped, flicking the reins. The horse twitched one ear. Other than that, it ignored him.

Nate Caudell laughed. "Just another old soldier."

"Miserable, lazy, good-for-nothing creature." Liles flicked the reins again, harder this time. Maybe the horse moved a little faster, but Caudell wouldn't have bet more than a dime on it.

He said, "Thanks for giving me the ride into Rocky Mount."

"That's all right, Nate. I was going to hear Bedford Forrest give his speech come hell or high water. Since you wanted to listen to him, too, I'm pleased to bring you along."

"He's giving a lot of speeches, isn't he?" Caudell said.

"Goin' all round the country. If your precious Mr. Robert E. Lee wants to sit up in Virginia and let his people do his work for him, he's liable to lose this here election." As if to emphasize his words, the storekeeper spat again, then wiped his chin with his sleeve.

"I don't know," Caudell said, frowning. "It doesn't seem dignified, somehow, for a man to do his own campaigning for President. Only one I can remember, back in the U.S. days, was Douglas in 1860, and look what it got him."

"Douglas!" Liles spat again, to show what he thought of Stephen A. Douglas. "All he was good for was splittin' his party. But Forrest now, Forrest is different. He don't say 'Go on up there'—he says 'Follow me.' If something needs doin', he does it his own self."

Caudell didn't feel like yet another argument with Liles, so he let the conversation lag. Fields and forests flowed slowly past. He'd come up this road three years before, after seeing the wonders of Virginia, Maryland, Pennsylvania, and Washington City. Since then, he hadn't been as far from Nashville as Rocky Mount. Away from the railroads, travel stayed as slow as it had always been. Listening to a speech a dozen miles distant meant a whole day away.

Rocky Mount had spread itself to welcome the Presidential candidate. Confederate flags flew everywhere; bunting decorated the buildings in the center of town—most of them new since the war. A platoon of Forrest's Trees in their Confederate-gray capes ushered spectators toward the platform from which their man would speak. Beside the platform, a band thumped away on the "Bedford Forrest Quickstep," over and over and over again. In front stood a platform loaded with food and drink. "Y'all help yourselves," a Tree said expansively.

As Liles poured himself a drink of whiskey, he said, "All this must cost a pretty penny, if Forrest does it every stop he makes."

"Look around," Caudell suggested.

Liles did. The whiskey glass stopped halfway to his lips. "Rivington men," he said in disgust.

Several of them, wearing their usual muddy green, prowled the edges of the Rocky Mount town square, AK-47s in their hands and serious expressions on their faces. Caudell couldn't figure out what they were up to until he remembered the Federal sentries at the White House after the rebel army broke into Washington. *Bodyguards, that's what they are,* he thought.

"If they're for Forrest, that's the best reason I can think of to vote for Lee," Liles said.

"They are." Caudell pointed to the flagpoles that sprouted from the corners of the platform. "Look, those are their flags flying under the Stainless Banner." He'd seen the AWB's three-spiked insignia on Benny Lang's jacket and again in Richmond across from Mechanic's Hall.

"They got their own *flag*? What the hell business they got, havin' their own flag?" Liles demanded. "They ain't a country, nor a state neither. I just figured them things was there for decoration." And indeed, the red and white banners with their black central emblems fit in well enough in the sea of red, white, and blue that had washed over Rocky Mount.

"No," Caudell said. The storekeeper answered him, but he didn't hear what Liles said. He'd just recognized one of the Rivington men—Piet Hardie. He wanted to go up to him, grab him by the front of the shirt, and snarl, *What did you do to the mulatto wench that made her hang herself? What did you do to frighten Mollie Bean, who wasn't frightened at Gettysburg?* That seemed unwise; not only was Hardie half again his size, he was also carrying a repeater. But if Piet Hardie backed Nathan Bedford Forrest, it was, as Liles had said, another reason to favor Robert E. Lee.

The town square filled rapidly. Most of the people there took no special notice of the Rivington men; some, mostly men of an age to be veterans, came up and talked with them in a friendly way about the AK-47s. Caudell knew the South might have lost the war without them. He couldn't make himself like the Rivington men even so.

To the bang of a drum, the Trees called out, "Hit 'em again! Hit 'em again! Forrest! Forrest!" A couple of men went up to the platform and sat down on the front edge, rifles across their knees. A plump man whose name had escaped Caudell went up there too, and launched into a speech of his own. Finally one of the Rivington men turned around and glared at him. After a few seconds, the glare got through. The plump man said, "And now, my friends, without further ado, the man you've been waiting for"—"And waiting for," Liles put in sourly—"the next President of the Confederate States of America, Nathan Bedford Forrest!"

The Trees redoubled their chant, but the shouts of the crowd all but drowned them out. Forrest bounded up onto the platform. He stood there for a moment, letting the cheers wash over him. He was a bigger man than Caudell had expected, and had more presence. Like Lee, he was impossible to ignore, or to take lightly.

He raised both hands, lowered them again. The noise in the square went down with them. Into the quiet he had caused, Forrest said, "Thank you all, for coming here to listen to me today." His accent was unpolished, but his voice was smoother than Caudell would have guessed. Smooth or not, though, it carried.

He went on, "In Richmond, they think they can pass on the Presidency like it was a farm going from father to son. In Richmond, they think it's a matter betwixt gentlemen." He loaded the word with scorn. "Are they right, the *gentlemen* up in Richmond?"

"No!" people shouted back. Caudell kept silent. So did Raeford Liles, but they were in the minority.

Forrest stalked back and forth across the platform. He was by no means a classic speaker, but he was effective all the same. The farther into his speech he went, the louder and more booming his voice became. Soon it was easy to imagine him roaring out orders through the din of battle, and easy to imagine men jumping to obey.

"Up in Richmond," Forrest cried, "Mr. Robert E. Lee says he knows better'n you what to do with your property. Hear me now, people, it's not for me to say freein' slaves is always a bad thing. I freed plenty o' my own, and they went through the war with me as my teamsters."

His bodyguards from Rivington did not care to hear that. Rivington men, Caudell knew, generally didn't care to hear anything about easing restrictions on blacks. The one who had glared down the plump functionary turned his stare on Forrest. But the former cavalry general was made of sterner stuff and ignored that warning gaze.

In any case, he did not keep the Rivington men worrying long: "If you want to free your niggers, that your business. But if the government goes an' tells you you've *got* to free your niggers—hell's bells, gentlemen, am I right or am I wrong, but didn't we fight a war with a government that wanted to tell us that?"

This time, the roar from the crowd was "Yes!" and this time, Raeford Liles roared along with the rest. Caudell did not roar "Yes!" He was not inclined to heckle, though, either, as he'd heckled Isaac Cockrell. That had nothing to do with the men with rifles who sat on the platform; the thought that rifles might be turned on a heckler simply never entered his mind. But Forrest, unlike Cockrell, had to be taken seriously.

As seemed to be his way no matter what he did, he returned to the relentless attack: "My friends, I give you that Robert E. Lee helped the Confederate States get free of the Yankees, and I tip my hat to him on account of it. But before Robert E. Lee ever fit for the Confederacy, the Yankees wanted to make him their commander—and he almost took on the job. When he did decide to stick with his state, Virginia made him a general straight off. That's a rugged way to fight a war, by God, isn't it?"

The men in the crowd laughed appreciatively. Warming to his subject, Forrest went on, "Me, I started the fight as a private. I wanted to get right in—couldn't wait to get right in. My friend Senator Wigfall, our next Vice President"—he paused for applause—"helped fix up the surrender of Fort

Sumter back when Robert E. Lee, that *gentleman* up in Richmond, was still a colonel in the army of the U.S. of A. If you all want some Bobbie-come-lately, I reckon you can vote for Lee. But if you want men who were with the Confederate States of America from the git-go, you'll stick with Wigfall and me. I thank you kindly for listening to me today." He bowed and got down from the platform.

The drum began to beat again. Forrest's Trees chanted, "Hit 'em again! Hit 'em again!" One of the Rivington men raised his AK-47 to his shoulder and fired a short burst into the air. Caudell saw the muzzle flash, but hardly heard the report through the thunderous cheers of the people around him.

The band struck up the "Bedford Forrest Quickstep," and then a minstrel tune, one Caudell didn't know. He turned to Raeford Liles, asked, "What's that?"

"It's called, 'I'm Coming to My Dixie Home.' It's a nigger talkin' about life up North," Liles answered. He sang a few bars: "I'd rather work de cotton patch, And die on corn and bacon, Dan lib up Norf on good white bread, Ob Abolition makin'.' I got the sheet music back at the store, if you ever want to take a look at it."

"That's all right," Caudell said quickly: trust Liles not to miss a chance to try to sell him something. Just then, the noise around them redoubled. Nathan Bedford Forrest was plunging into the crowd, shaking men's hands and bowing over those that belonged to ladies. People surged toward him from all over the square. Caudell didn't particularly care to meet him, but was swept along by the tide.

Forrest's big hand almost swallowed up his. "Will you vote for me, sir?"

Looking up at that strong, determined face, Caudell had to work to make himself shake his head. "No, sir, don't reckon so now. I fought under General Lee, and I'll stick by him."

Behind Forrest, a bodyguard who had plunged after him—and whom he was ignoring—scowled at Caudell. Caudell waited for the famous Forrest temper to explode. But the ex-general only nodded and said, "Good to find a man who's loyal and not ashamed to say so. You might"—as a rustic would, he pronounced it *mought*—"change your mind. I hope you do." He turned to Raeford Liles. "What about you, sir?"

"I might could vote your way," the storekeeper allowed. "I was leanin' that way, but I'd care for you more if the Rivington men cared for you less."

Now Forrest showed anger. "Any man who wants to keep the right of property in niggers is a Patriot, by God. If that's you, you're with me, same as they are. And if it ain't, be damned to you." He spun away as if Liles had ceased to exist.

"He doesn't leave much room for doubt, does he?" Caudell said after they had finally got free of the crowd and headed back toward the buggy.

"No." Liles still looked like a man who'd bitten into something sour. "That'll hurt him, too."

"Good," Caudell said. He waited for the storekeeper to argue with him, but Liles just kept walking.

⋆ XV ⋆

No sooner had Robert E. Lee ventured outside the Powhatan House to enjoy the brisk fall air than reporters swooped down on him like stooping hawks. He nodded to them, unsurprised; they had become familiar over the past few months. By unspoken agreement, they let him alone as long as he was within the hotel, but he became fair game the moment his foot hit the sidewalk.

"Mr. Quincy, you were here half a step ahead of the rest, I believe," Lee said to the man from the *Richmond Whig.*

"Thank you, General." Virgil Quincy poised pencil over pad. "If I may ask, why have you chosen to remain here in Virginia while Bedford Forrest travels all over the country, speaking, it seems, at every town big enough to boast a railroad station?"

"General Forrest is, of course, free to conduct his campaign in any fashion that suits him." Lee had learned to speak slowly enough to let the reporters take down his words. "I might add a point which sometimes seems in danger of being forgotten: that is to say, I also enjoy the same freedom. The entire Confederacy surely knows where I stand on the issues of the day; perhaps General Forrest still feels the need to make his ideas more widely accessible to the voters."

Quincy twirled a waxed mustache between thumb and forefinger as he considered his next question. "How do you feel about Forrest's questioning your initial loyalty to the Confederate cause?"

"I prefer to allow my contributions to that cause to speak for themselves. If they do not make it plain where my loyalty lay, nothing I can say will do so." For public consumption, Lee kept his fury tightly bottled. He was used to newspapers sniping at him from time to time. But to have his loyalty impugned by a man he had admired until their differing views created a chasm between them, and for no better purpose than political advantage— that was hard to bear. He had not imagined Forrest would stoop so low, which, if anything, but served to illuminate his own political naïveté.

Virgil Quincy took a step back; Lee's rule was to allow each reporter two questions. Edwin Helper of the *Richmond Dispatch* approached in Quincy's place. "To change the subject, if I may, sir, what do you think of the war just begun by the United States against England over the Canadas?"

"I deprecate war in general," Lee replied. "As to this war in particular, I would be less than truthful if I said I was sorry to see so many U.S. troops drawn hundreds of miles to the north of our frontier." He smiled; several reporters chuckled. He added, "Even with the accession of Kentucky to the Confederacy, the United States are a larger, more populous nation than the C.S.A. The implications to be drawn from that should be clear to the observer."

"They're not quite clear to me," Helper said. "What do you think our course ought to be?"

"To continue the scrupulous neutrality President Davis has proclaimed and is observing," Lee answered at once. "Any other course involves us in risks which should not be run." Senator Wigfall was shouting for a Southern invasion to seize the slave states remaining in the U.S.A. while that country was otherwise engaged. Some fire-eaters shouted right along with him. Others, though, remembering how England's not-so-scrupulous neutrality had almost ruined the Confederacy during the war, were all for allying with the United States against her.

"Should we not at least demand concessions from the U.S.A. as the price of our neutrality?" asked Rex Van Lew of the *Richmond Examiner*.

Lee shook his head. "They are our brothers. Though we no longer live in the same house with them, having grown up to enjoy one of our own, putting demands upon brothers strikes me as a bad business, and one which cannot fail to bring resentment."

"He's right about that, by God," Virgil Quincy said. "I've yet to hear the end of the time I asked my brother for fifty dollars, and it was back before the war."

The reporters laughed. Lee walked down Broad Street with the newpapermen trailing along behind him. Van Lew said, "What is your opinion of General Forrest's actively campaigning for a whole year in his quest to defeat you?"

"I admire his energy without wishing to employ mine to similar purpose," Lee said. "I also doubt the benefit, either to the nation or to the electorate, of repeating oneself so often. Now, gentlemen, if you will excuse me, I should like to get in something of a constitutional." He increased his pace. The reporters were decades younger than he—he would be sixty-one come January—but several of them began puffing as they hurried to keep up.

Rex Van Lew had used up his allotted questions, but asked another one anyhow: "How will you feel when the election is over, sir?"

"Relieved," Lee answered promptly.

"Win or lose?" three reporters asked at the same time.

"Win or lose," he said. "Relieved at least of suspense if I win, relieved of responsibility if I lose. While I hope and expect to win, the prospect of quiet retirement is by no means altogether unattractive, I assure you."

He walked on. Three years before, the Army of Northern Virginia had paraded in triumph down this very street. Now most of those soldiers were long since back at their peacetime trades. That, he thought, was as it should be. He blinked, then smiled—he even had a peacetime trade of his own, though he'd never expected to turn politician.

"What's funny, General?" Edwin Helper asked.

"Life; or, if you'd like, the fortunes of war," Lee said. In Capitol Square, George Washington in bronze pointed ahead, urging on invisible followers, or perhaps the country as a whole. Lee gravely tipped his hat to his wife's adoptive ancestor, then went on with his constitutional.

Nate Caudell gauged the creeping shadows in the classroom. He put down his chalk. "That's enough for now. We'll pick it up again after dinner." Several students let out barely suppressed cheers and grabbed for the bags and old newspapers in which they'd brought their noontime meals. For that matter, his stomach was growling, too.

He wolfed his ham and corn bread, gulped from a canteen full of cold coffee. Then he hurried over to the town square. Extra flags flew above the courthouse; a long line of men snaked in through the front door. Unfamiliar buggies and wagons, horses and mules, were hitched everywhere—farmers from half the county were in town to vote today.

A lot of them were men he'd known in the army but seldom saw these days. He waved to Dempsey Eure, who was just tying his horse in a narrow space between two buggies. They got into line together. "Patriot or Confederate?" Caudell asked. Since Eure had heckled Mayor Cockrell at the Forrest rally, he thought he knew what answer to expect.

Sure enough, the ex-sergeant said, "I'm voting Confederate. I followed Marse Robert into Washington City, so I don't reckon I'll run away from him now. How about you, Nate?"

"The same," Caudell said. "He ought to have an easy time of it here and in Virginia, where so many served under him. Out farther west, though, they know *about* him but they don't really know *him*, if you know what I mean. And they do know Forrest out there."

"That's why they vote—to see what happens," Eure said.

"Yup." Caudell looked his friend over, smiled as he saw something familiar. "You still wear a feather in your hat, do you? How are you getting along?"

"I get by," Dempsey Eure said with a shrug. "Married Lemon Strickland's sister Lucy not long after I got home, you know. We got ourselves a boy two years old, an' she's in the family way again. How times does get on—before too long, suppose I'll be sendin' Wiley to that school of yours. You fix him so he knows more'n his old man, you hear?"

"If he's anything like his old man, he'll do fine," Caudell said. He noticed Eure hadn't really said anything about his fortunes except *I get by*. He didn't push for more; come to that, he couldn't have said more himself.

The line advanced. Caudell blinked as he went from sunshine into the gloom inside the courthouse. Mayor Cockrell and Cornelius Joyner, the justice of the peace, sat behind a stout wooden table. "Here's the roll, Nate," Joyner said when Caudell came up to him. "Sign your name on the line." He pointed to show where.

Caudell signed. Quite a lot of men had already voted. Most had signed their names, but for a depressingly large number of voters, only an X, witnessed by mayor and justice of the peace, appeared in the signature column of the register. Isaac Cockrell handed Caudell a ballot and a much-sharpened stub of pencil.

He voted for Lee and for Albert Gallatin Brown without hesitation, then went on through the rest of his choices. Sion Rogers, he saw, was running for Congress and billing himself a Confederate. Caudell voted for him. He might have done so even if Rogers ran as a Patriot, for he'd been the 47th North Carolina's first colonel until he resigned his commission early in 1863 to become Attorney General of North Carolina.

When Caudell was done, he folded his ballot and returned it to Cornelius Joyner, who slid it through the slot of a wooden box with an impressively stout padlock. "Nathaniel N. Caudell has voted," the justice of the peace intoned, his voice loud and deep enough to make Caudell proud of having done his civic duty.

"Wait a minute," Mayor Cockrell exclaimed when Caudell started to walk out with the pencil. "You bring that back right now, you hear? We're startin' to run low on 'em." Red-faced, Caudell returned the little stub.

Meanwhile, Judge Joyner announced to the world that Dempsey Eure had exercised his franchise. Eure's eyes were twinkling as he left the courthouse with Caudell. "You should've told him to buy a substitute for his damn pencil, Nate," he said. "That *was* you back this spring, wasn't it? Sure sounded like you if it wasn't."

"It was me, all right," Caudell said. "Good thing his honor's ears aren't as good as yours." The clock above the courthouse chimed one. "I've got to get back to the schoolhouse, Dempsey, before they burn it down. By God, it's good to see you."

"And you." Dempsey Eure thumped him on the back. "I wondered if they'd have to get us back into butternut before we met up again."

"It would take a good deal to get me back into uniform, and that's a fact," Caudell said. His friend laughed and nodded. He went on, "I really do have to get back." He hurried on down Alston Street while Dempsey Eure went to reclaim his horse.

When he walked into the schoolroom again, one of the little boys there called, "Who won the election, teacher?"

Through the snorts and giggles of the older pupils, Caudell—who had to smile himself—gravely answered, "We won't know for a few days yet, Willie. They have to count all the votes and send the count to Richmond, which takes a while. Now, class, who can tell me all twelve Confederate states and their capitals?" Hands shot into the air.

As he had in the Galt House in Louisville, so Lee now sat in the dining room of the Powhatan House in Richmond with telegrams piled so high on the table in front of him that he could hardly get to, let alone enjoy, his plate of smothered chicken. He knew now that he'd been foolish to order his favorite dish on a night when he couldn't give it his full attention.

A boy brought in a new set of returns. Since Lee had knife in one hand and fork in the other—he did manage a distracted bite every now and then—Albert Gallatin Brown took the telegrams. As he read them, his face fell. "Forrest and Wigfall remain ahead of us in Louisiana."

"That is unfortunate," Lee said—blurrily, as his mouth was full. He chewed, swallowed, and resumed, sounding like himself again: "I had hoped to carry Louisiana, as its white voters have greater and longer familiarity with free Negroes, especially in and around New Orleans, than is the case elsewhere in the Confederacy."

"The election is more closely contested than I thought it would be," Brown agreed. He sounded gloomy, and with reason: he and Lee were also trailing in Mississippi, his home state.

Lee looked at the map tacked up on an easel beside the table. Having it there made him feel more as if this were a military campaign; it was, in fact, borrowed from the War Department, and would have to go back to Mechanic's Hall once all the results were in. He was leading handily here in Virginia and in North Carolina, by rather less in Georgia and lightly settled Florida, and by a fair margin in Kentucky, which he had helped bring into the Confederacy and which was now voting for the first time for the President of the country it had freely chosen.

South Carolina had already come down against him: the Palmetto State, alone in the South, still chose its Electoral College representatives by vote of the legislature rather than of the people. Thus its choice had quickly, and painfully, become known.

He was losing Alabama, too, along with Louisiana and Mississippi. The cotton states, the ones whose livelihoods most depended on plantations and their slave labor, were unwilling to vote for anyone who questioned Negro servitude in any way.

That left Arkansas, Texas, and Tennessee. Votes from the two western states were slow coming in. Those from Tennessee had arrived in large numbers, but every new telegram changed the leader there. At the moment, Forrest was ahead by nearly a thousand votes; an hour before, Lee had led by almost exactly as many.

Albert Gallatin Brown was studying the map, too. "We badly need Tennessee," he said. The deliberate lack of emphasis in his voice highlighted his words as effectively as a shout.

"You have no confidence in the results from the other two?" Lee asked.

"Have you?"

"Possibly some hope for Arkansas," Lee said. Only after he had spoken did he realize he had in effect written off Texas. It, too, was a cotton state, and also one that had boomed since the war, with Negroes in great demand and fetching high prices. Were Texans likely to vote against prosperity? It went against human nature.

Brown had been doing sums on the back of a telegram. "If Forrest takes Tennesee—and Arkansas," he added in deference to Lee's hope, which he did not seem to share, "that will give him sixty-four electoral votes."

"And sixty are required for election," Lee said heavily. Only once before had he felt as he did now: watching his men swarm up the slope toward the Union lines on the third day at Gettysburg. He had been confident they could carry everything before them, as he had been confident his own campaign would convince the people he offered the nation the wisest course. Was he to be proven as disastrously wrong now as he had been then?

A new messenger boy—the other had presumably gone home for the evening—arrived with more telegrams. Lee took them, unfolded the first few. He read them, set them down on the table. "Well?" Brown asked.

"Arkansas, or the first considerable returns therefrom." Again Lee declined to continue. This time, his running mate did not press him: he could figure out what silence meant. Lee made himself get the words out: "The trend is against us."

"So it all rides on Tennessee, does it?"

"It would appear that way, yes—or do you think results in any of the other states likely to change?"

Albert Gallatin Brown shook his head. He surprised Lee by starting to laugh. At Lee's raised eyebrow, he explained, "Even if I fail of election, I remain in the Senate, and shall continue to serve my state as best I can."

Again, Lee found himself envying Brown's quick adaptability. If he was not elected, he would go back to Arlington, put in a crop on the sloping fields, and no doubt be more contented living the life of a semiretired gentleman farmer than as President of the Confederate States of America. Yet the idea of losing the election was intolerable to him; he would carry the weight of that rejection for the rest of his days.

The night dragged on. A colored waiter took away the dishes. Fresh stacks of telegrams replaced them. Before long, the whole big table was flooded. In Louisville, Lee had been getting returns from only two states. Now six times that many were voting.

"I have more election results here," someone said. This was a man's voice, not the treble of previous boys from the telegraph office. Lee looked up to find Jefferson Davis holding a handful of telegrams. The president said, "I waylaid the messenger at the dining room door." He pulled out his watch. "It's already past two. How long do you aim to stay up?"

"Until we know, or until we fall asleep in our chairs—whichever comes first," Lee answered. The outgoing President smiled. Lee said, "From where are your telegrams, sir?"

"I beg your pardon, but I have yet to look at them." Davis did so, then said, "These first several are from Tennessee: from Chattanooga and its environs, mostly."

"Let me hear them," Lee said, suddenly alert.

The President read off the returns. As he did, Brown scrawled figures
and, lips moving, rapidly added them up. Finally he said, "That cuts Forrest's lead there in half, more or less." He glanced over at a pile of telegrams off to one side. "We gain when reports come in from the eastern
part of the state, but fall behind when they're out of the west."

"The plantations in Tennessee are in the south and west. The planters
there, I would infer, want their slaves back," Davis said. One eyebrow
quirked as he turned toward Lee. "Whereas you, sir, are winning the votes
of folk who, during the war, I feared would go over to the United States
en masse, as did those of what must now be known as West Virginia. How
can you call yourself a good Confederate, sir, if those who half wanted to
be Yankees give you the election?"

But for that eyebrow, Lee would have thought the President in earnest.
As it was, he hoped Davis was making one of his wintry jokes. He gave
back another one: "If Forrest had seen the result there before the rest of
the country voted, no doubt he would have taxed me with the same charge."

"He did anyhow," Brown pointed out.

"He succeeded all too well," Lee said. "I don't know whether you have
kept track of how things stand, Mr. President, but—" He used a forefinger
to point out on the map which states were going to whom.

Jefferson Davis gnawed on his lower lip as he pondered the shape of the
election. "Sectionalism appears to remain alive and well among us," he
said, shaking his head. "That is dangerous; if we cannot cure it, it will
cause us grief down the road: the United States, after all, tore asunder
from a surfeit of sectionalism."

"The Constitution of the Confederate States does not provide for secession," Albert Gallatin Brown said.

"Neither did the Constitution of the United States," Davis replied. "But
if the western states have the gall to seek to abandon our confederacy as
a result of this election, we shall—" He stopped; for once his façade
cracked, leaving him quite humanly confused. "If they seek to abandon
our confederacy, at the moment I have no idea what we shall do. In any
event, the decision will be yours, not mine, General Lee."

"Very possibly not," Lee replied. "If the returns from Tennessee continue to favor Forrest, the decision will be his. And in that event, the states
which favor him, and which favor the indefinite continuation of Negro servitude, shall have no cause for complaint as a result of this election."

Jefferson Davis let out an audible sniff. Though his background was more
like Forrest's than Lee's, he had enjoyed the education denied to Forrest,
and had come to identify himself completely with the old, landed aristoc-

racy of the South. He said, "I cannot imagine that—that brawler at the head of our nation."

"The voters, unfortunately, seem to have suffered no similar failure of imagination," Lee said.

"That is not so," Brown said stoutly. "The aggregate total of the popular vote continues to favor us, regardless of what the Electoral College may say."

"By the Constitution, however, the Electoral College is the final arbiter of the election. I shall not dispute its results, whatever they prove to be," Lee said. "If we set aside the Constitution for our convenience, what point in having it?" No sooner were the words out of his mouth than he realized others would apply them to his own views on slavery. *It is not the same thing*, he told himself, not quite comfortably.

The messenger boy whose function President Davis had usurped now returned with a fresh set of results, which he placed in front of Lee. Brown asked, "Where are these from?"

Lee unfolded the top one, read it. "Texas," he answered. His tone of voice said all that needed saying about the way the votes there were going. He did his best to find a silver lining to the cloud. "We had no great hope for Texas in any event." He opened another telegram. "Ah, now this one from North Carolina is more like it: we have carried Nash County by three to two."

"Good," Brown said. "What are the numbers?" Lee read them off. As Brown wrote them down, he grinned the grim grin of a fighter who has landed a telling blow. Jefferson Davis's smile held something of the same quality. Lee's own initial burst of enthusiasm quickly faded. The news from North Carolina was no more cause for jubilation than that from Texas was cause for despair: the two sets of returns merely confirmed and extended trends that were already there. Results that went against those trends would have been more interesting.

"Anothuh cup of coffee, suh?" the waiter asked.

"No, thank you," Lee said. "I am sufficiently awash as is. My elder brother Sydney has always been the naval officer of the family, but at the moment I am certain I am shipping more water than he."

As the waiter left, Lee put a hand to his mouth to cover a yawn. Altogether without intending to, he fell asleep in his chair. A few minutes later, more telegrams arrived. Jefferson Davis took them and read the results to Brown, who asked, "Shall we wake the general?"

"No," Davis said. "They make no significant changes. When more word from Tennessee arrives, that will be time enough."

"By the feel of things, the only definitive word from Tennessee will be the last word. It will be days before we have the final count."

"Then we needs must compose ourselves to wait," Davis answered. "And all the less point to waking him now, would you not agree?"

Nate Caudell stared at the empty space on the counter where newspapers should have lain. "Confound it, Mr. Liles, when are they going to come in?"

"They've been in," the storekeeper said. "Went right back out again today, too—I done sold every copy I had. Went faster'n I ever seen 'em before, matter of fact." Caudell stared at him in blank dismay. Grinning, he went on, "You ask me pretty enough, might could be I'll tell you who won Tennessee."

"Why, you—" Caudell swore as he hadn't sworn since his army days. Raeford Liles laughed at him. When he finally ran down, he said, "You'd better tell me, before I start tearing this place apart." He sounded as menacing as he could.

It was, he knew, a poor best. Liles didn't quiver in his shoes; in fact, he didn't stop laughing. When he'd let Caudell hang long enough, though, he said, "Vote from Knoxville came in at last. That nails it down tight—Lee carried the state by twenty-five hundred votes."

"That's first rate," Caudell said, letting out a long sigh of relief. The results had hung in the balance for more than a week. Usually, even if one or two states' returns remained in doubt, the shape of a national election grew clear soon enough. This time, everything rode on the one closest state. Caudell asked, "How big an edge in the popular vote did Lee end up with?"

"Just under thirty thousand votes, out of almost a million cast: sixty-nine to fifty in the Electoral College," Liles said. "But if a couple thousand people in Tennessee had gone the other way, well, we'd be talkin' about President Forrest now, no matter what the popular vote had to say."

"I know." For as long as Caudell could remember, people had complained about the Electoral College of the United States; the only reason they didn't complain more was that it normally did a good job of reflecting what the people decided. For whatever their reasons, the Confederate founding fathers had included an Electoral College in the new nation's Constitution; and in its first real test—Jefferson Davis having run unopposed—it had almost thrown the Confederacy into turmoil by its mere existence. He said, "What are they saying about the election in the west and southwest?"

"The states Forrest won, you mean?" Liles said. Caudell nodded. The storekeeper told him: "They're still bawlin' like pigs that burned their noses on hot swill. From what the papers say, Senator Wigfall's makin' noises like they ought to up and pull out of the Confederacy, set up a new one of their own to suit them."

"What? That's crazy," Caudell said. After a moment, he wondered why. The South had left the United States after an election it could not stomach. "What does Forrest have to say about that?"

"Hasn't said anything yet," Liles answered, which struck Caudell as ominous.

He also noticed something else. "You don't seem to be up on your hind legs on account of Forrest has lost."

"I ain't," Liles admitted. "Oh, I voted for him, spite of the Rivington men and everything else. I ain't easy about lettin' all the niggers loose. But I reckon we won't go far wrong with Bobbie Lee in Richmond. God willin', a few o' them hotheads in South Carolina and Mississippi'll see it the same way once they settle down a bit an' stop listenin' to nothin' but their own speeches over and over."

"I do hope you're right," Caudell said. "Fighting one civil war was plenty for me—I've seen the elephant now, and I don't care to see it ever again, thank you very much."

"I can't believe they'd try anything so stupid—just can't believe it," Liles said. "Damnation, Nate, might could be they'd have to fight us an' the United States at the same time."

"Wouldn't that be a fine mess?" Caudell said. The very idea of three-cornered civil strife made him want to pull his hat down over his eyes. But after he thought about it, he shook his head. "I reckon the United States have enough on their hands with England up in the Canadas. Did you read what the papers had to say about the war there?"

"Sure did. We—the Yankees, I mean," Liles amended with a shame-faced chuckle, "whipped 'em again on land, up near a place called Ottawa, I think it was. But their navy shelled Boston harbor, an' New York, too—started a big fire there, the paper said. Hell of a thing, ain't it?"

"It is indeed," Caudell said. Like the storekeeper, he almost instinctively sided with the U.S.A. in a quarrel against Great Britain. His enmity with the North was new, and fading now that the Confederacy had gained its freedom. Britain, though—Britain had been the bogeyman since his school-boy days. "That's a war I'm just as glad we're no part of."

"Amen," Liles said. "Next time I'll save you a paper no matter what, Nate, I promise."

"You'd better," Caudell said, mock-fiercely. As he left the general store, he found himself half-delighted Lee had won the election, half-worried because even that victory looked to be bringing trouble in its wake. He clicked his tongue between his teeth. The older he got, the more he wondered if there was such a thing as an unmixed blessing.

Robert E. Lee's heels made a reassuringly solid sound as he walked down the stairs from the great columned porch of Arlington and onto the lawn. Even the boards of those stairs were new since the war; the old timber, uncared for while the Federals occupied the mansion, had grown dangerously rotten. The lawn, at the moment, was patchy and yellow, but spring would restore its lushness for him.

Someone rode up the path toward Arlington. At first Lee thought it might be one of his sons, but he soon saw it was not. After another few seconds, when he did recognize the rider, his brows contracted in a frown. It was Nathan Bedford Forrest.

He stood stiffly, waiting for the former cavalry general to approach. After their hot words in Richmond, after the bitter campaign, he wondered that Forrest had the nerve to visit him here. He would have liked nothing better than sending his adversary away unheard. Had he been merely Robert E. Lee rather than President-elect of the Confederate States of America, he would have done just that. The good of the country, though, demanded that he give Forrest a hearing.

He even made himself take a few steps toward Forrest, who reined in and dismounted. His horse began cropping the sere grass. Forrest began to raise his right hand, then stopped, as if unsure whether Lee would take it and unwilling to give him cause to refuse. He dipped his head instead, a sharp, abrupt gesture. "General Lee, sir," he said, then added after a tiny pause, "Mr. President-elect."

"General Forrest," Lee said, with the same wary politeness Forrest had used. He was not ready to shake hands with his recent rival, not yet. Seeking neutral ground on which to begin the conversation, he nodded toward Forrest's horse. "That is a handsome animal, sir."

"King Philip? Thank you, sir." Forrest's eyes lit up, partly, perhaps, in relief, partly with a horseman's enthusiasm. "I rode him in a good many fights. He's old now, as you'll note, but he still carries me well."

"So I saw." Lee nodded again. Then, because he found no other polite but meaningless questions to ask, he said, "How may I serve you today, sir?"

"I came—" Forrest had to start twice before he could get it out: "I came to congratulate you for winning the election, General Lee." Now he did hold out his hand, and Lee took it.

"Thank you, General Forrest—thank you," Lee said with no small relief of his own.

"I'll do anything I can to make things easy for you as you take over," Forrest said.

"Will you?" Lee said, all at once suspicious as well as relieved. "After the—unpleasantness which marked the campaign, that is good to hear, but—" He let his voice trail away. Forrest was notoriously touchy; if he was in earnest, no point to stirring him.

But he would not be stirred, not today. He waved his hand. "All that was just business, just trying to put a scare"—he pronounced it *skeer*—"on you and on the people out there who did the voting, same as I would have on a Yankee general, to get him runnin'." He waved again, this time encompassing the whole of the Confederacy. "I came close."

"That you did, sir," Lee said. "And having come so close, you are most generous to come here now with your support."

"When it comes to niggers, General Lee, I don't agree with you still, and I don't reckon I ever shall," Forrest said. "But I lost. The whys of it don't matter. That I got beat is a self-evident fact, sir. If I carried on now, it would be nothin' but folly and rashness. I wanted to meet you like a man and say that to you straight out."

Lee saw he meant it. This time, he held out his hand to Forrest, who squeezed hard. Lee said, "The nation owes you a debt of gratitude for taking that view. I hope you will forgive me for saying that I wish more of those who followed you would do likewise. The talk of new secession out of the southwest is deeply troubling to me, and Senator Wigfall has produced more than his share of it."

"He does go on, don't he?" Forrest grinned, then sobered. "I tell you what, General Lee. If those damn fools try and leave the Confederacy, I'll put my uniform back on and whip 'em into line inside of six weeks. I mean it, sir. Tell it to the papers, or if you'd rather, I'll tell it to 'em my own self."

"If you would do that, General Forrest, I think it would have a very happy effect on all concerned."

"Then I will," Forrest said.

"Would you care to come inside and take some coffee with me?" Lee asked. In Richmond, he had ordered Forrest out of his house; now he tacitly apologized.

But Forrest shook his head; he remembered the quarrel, too. "No, sir. I do this for the country's sake, not yours. I will abide by the vote of the people, but they—and you—have not the power to make me like it. I aim to keep on working against you in every way I lawfully can."

"That is your right, as it is the right of every citizen. Congress will have to ratify my proposals in order for them to take effect, of course; I anticipate considerable disputation before that comes to pass." Lee and Albert Gallatin Brown had been going over the list of congressmen and senators returned to office, trying to work out the odds of their favoring the commencement of even gradual, compensated emancipation. He thought his program had a chance of passage; he knew it was far from assured.

Forrest bowed to Lee. "We *have been* rivals; I reckon we'll stay rivals. But we've both fought for this country. We *can* work together to keep it whole. That's what I came to say, General Lee, and now I've said it. A good morning to you, sir." He bowed again, swung up onto King Philip, and rode away.

Lee plucked at his beard as he watched Forrest go. He felt as if a weight had come off his shoulders. Nathan Bedford Forrest was still a political foe, but seemed not to want to remain a personal enemy after all. That suited Lee; political foes, he was learning, could be dealt with. The casual thought brought him up short—was he in fact turning into a politician in his old age? He stopped to consider the idea carefully. At last he shook his head. His inevitable slide into decay hadn't yet progressed so far.

Dressed in his Sunday best—which, save for being the newest of his four shirts and three pairs of trousers, was no different from what he wore the other six days of the week—Nate Caudell hurried into the Nashville Baptist church. Once inside, he took off his hat and slid into a place on one of the hard wooden pews. Several people—including the preacher, Ben Drake—sent disapproving looks his way; the service was about to begin. He avoided Drake's eye as he sat.

Yancey Glover strode importantly to the front of the hall, nodded to the preacher, and waited a few seconds to let everyone notice him standing there. Then the precentor launched into "A Mighty Fortress Is Our God." The congregation joined in. They had no hymnals; Glover's big bass voice pulled them through the song. That voice was one of the reasons the church elder had the precentor's job.

"Rock of Ages" came next, with several more hymns right behind. The congregation warmed up, both physically—a chilly, nasty rain was falling outside—and spiritually. Yancey Glover marched back to his seat. Ben Drake pounded a fist down on the pulpit, once, twice, three times. The preacher was an impressive-looking man of about forty-five, with a full head of wavy gray hair; he'd served a few months as a lieutenant in the Castalia Invincibles, till chronic dysentery forced him to resign his commission.

" 'I know thy works,' " says the Book of Revelation," Drake began, " 'that thou art neither cold nor hot: I would thou wert cold or hot. So then *because* thou art lukewarm, and neither cold nor hot, I will spew thee out of my mouth.' That's what God says, my friends—you cannot, you dare not, be lukewarm. Again, in the Book of Deuteronomy, 'Thou shalt love the Lord thy God with all thine heart, with all thy soul, and with all thy might.'

"Not 'with some of thy might,' friends, not 'with a little of thy might, when thou hast the time.' 'With all thy might,' as hard as you can, all the time, while you're eating or working or bathing or reading. You can't be lukewarm, or the Lord will spew you out of His mouth, and you don't want that, no indeed you don't, for if the Lord spews you out of His mouth, who's going to suck you right on in? You know who, my friends—Satan, that's who. Paul says in his epistle to the Philippians, 'Whose end is destruction, whose God is their belly, and whose glory is in their shame, who mind earthly things.' So what do you want to do? Do you want to fret yourselves about the things of this world, or about God, Who endures forever?"

"God!" the congregation shouted with a single voice. Nate was as loud as anyone. He'd been sorry when Drake had to leave the regiment; people listened to him. He might have become captain instead of George Lewis when John Harrison resigned in October 1862. If he'd led on the battlefield half as well as he did from the pulpit, the Castalia Invincibles would have been in good hands.

He went on glorifying God and casting scorn on Satan and the things of this world for the next couple of hours. By the time he was done, he had his congregation up on their feet, urging him on. He made Caudell ashamed of the way he drank and swore and even of the way he smoked. As he had more than once before, he vowed to abandon his wicked habits. He'd never managed to keep any of those vows. That shamed him, too.

Another round of hymns closed the service. Some people went up to the pulpit to talk with the preacher about his sermon. Others hung around in small groups inside the church. Some of them talked about the sermon, too; for others, tobacco or horses were of more pressing interest, even on Sunday. Young men took the chance to eye young ladies, and even, if they were bold enough, to say hello. Church was a town social center, a place where everyone gathered.

Caudell, more social caterpillar than butterfly, was about to head out into the rain when a woman called, "Don't go, Nate." He turned around. The woman smiled at him. She was fairly tall, with gray eyes, black curls that fell past her shoulders, and a mouth that was too wide for perfect beauty—her smile emphasized that. He'd noticed her earlier, partly for her own sake but mostly because he hadn't seen her in church before. She smiled again and repeated, "Don't go."

She still didn't look familiar, but that voice— "Mollie!" he exclaimed. "What are you doing here?" No wonder he hadn't recognized her—he'd never seen her dressed as a woman till this instant.

Raeford Liles, who was standing nearby, cackled like a laying hen. "So this here's your sweetheart, eh, Nate? Let me meet her, why don't you?"

Caudell introduced them. He didn't bother contradicting the store-keeper, not anymore. Liles fussed over Mollie Bean as if he were a planter and she a fine lady, not least to embarrass Nate. He was embarrassed, but not on account of that. Several other Castalia Invincibles, men who knew Mollie was no lady, were among those who stood around chatting in the church. Most of them, though, were with their wives; whatever they thought, they had to be discreet.

He said, "What brings you to Nashville, Mollie?"

Her smile blew out. "I got a problem, Nate." Caudell gulped. Raeford Liles started to cackle again. Mollie fixed him with a gaze that would not have looked out of place over the sights of an AK-47. "I ain't in a family way, mister, so you can just drag your mind out of the ditch," she said quietly. Liles blushed all the way up to the top of his head, started coughing and couldn't stop, and retired in disorder.

"What's the matter?" Caudell asked. He was relieved for a couple of reasons: first that she wasn't pregnant—even if he'd had nothing to do with it—and second that she hadn't noticed him worrying that she was.

"It ain't somethin' I can explain in just words," she said. "You got to see it, an' even then it don't make sense—or I ain't been able to make it make sense, anyways. You know a whole lot more'n me; it's on account of you I'm able to read and write at all. So I reckoned if anybody I knew could cipher this out, it was you, an' I brang it to you. I had to get out of Rivington anyhow."

Those few sentences raised enough questions in Caudell's mind for any six school quizzes, but he contented himself with one that might lead to answers for the rest: "Where are you staying?"

"In one of the rooms up above the Liberty Bell." Mollie's lip curled. "This town don't have a proper hotel, let alone anything like the Notahilton. Come on over with me; I got the book you need to see there."

"Let's go," Caudell said. Wren Tisdale, who ran the saloon, had fought in the Chicora Guards, not the Castalia Invincibles. Even if Mollie had given him her whole proper name, it probably meant nothing to him. Caudell put his hat back on. Mollie opened the small, long-handled umbrella she was carrying.

They splashed over to the Liberty Bell; Mollie used her free hand to hold her skirts out of the mud. Wren Tisdale nodded to them as they came in; he was a dark, dour man whose looks belied his name. This being Sunday, the bar was quiet and deserted. The saloonkeeper's eyebrows rose slightly when they climbed the stairs together, but he kept his mouth shut. Caudell's ears heated just the same.

Mollie's room was small and none too clean. It held only a bed, a stool, a pitcher, and a chamber pot. On the bed lay a couple of carpet bags. Mollie dug in one. Caudell averted his eyes as lacy feminine undergarments flew this way and that; being easy with her came harder now that she was so unequivocally a woman. Finally she said, "Here, Nate, this here's what you got to see."

As she'd said, it was a book. The paper cover, somewhat crinkled from rough treatment, showed a U.S. flag crossed with a Confederate battle flag. *"The American Heritage Picture History of the Civil War,"* Caudell read aloud.

"Open it up anywheres," Mollie said. "Here, come on, sit down beside me."

He sat, though at a greater distance than he'd used to back in the days when she wore uniform tunic and trousers. Then, as she'd suggested, he opened the big, heavy book at random. He found himself looking at a discussion of the Vicksburg campaign, at a woodcut from *Leslie's Illustrated Newspaper*, and at photographs of Generals Grant and Van Dorn. "I've never seen photographs just put into a book like that before, instead of being made into engravings first," he breathed. "And look at that painting above the picture of Grant there."

"Once upon a time, you wrote me for a joke, asking if the Rivington men had books with colored pictures all through 'em," Mollie said. "Now you can see 'em for yourself."

Caudell only half heard her; he had just read the caption under that colored picture. "It says this here is a photograph, too. But there's no such thing as colored photographs. Everybody knows that." Without his willing it, his voice rose in protest. He flipped through several pages, found color on about every other one: on maps, on reproductions of paintings, and on what, by their clarity, seemed to be more photographs. Scratching his head in befuddlement, he turned to Mollie. "Where did you get this?"

"Rivington—I stole it from Benny Lang," she answered matter-of-factly. "Sometimes, after we was done—well, hell, you know done with what—

he'd go off an' do other things, his own business, I mean, until he was ready for his second round. One of them times, I pulled this here book out of a case he kept by—by the bed. With that fine light he had in there, readin' was easy. But this here book, it purely perplexed me. What year is it, Nate?"

"What *year*?" He stared at her. "It's 1868, of course—January 18, if you want to get picky."

She gestured impatiently. "I know that, I really do. But look in the front of the book."

He did. The date of printing did not appear on the title page, as it did in most books he knew. He turned the page. Sure enough, there was the information he needed, next to the table of contents. "Copyright—1960?" he said slowly. "And this edition was printed in—1996?" His voice trailed away, then firmed again. "That's impossible."

"Is it? Look here." She pointed to a section he hadn't yet noticed, something called "Library of Congress Cataloging in Publication Data." The author, someone named Bruce Catton, was listed as having been born in 1899. Richard M. Ketchum, who was called editor at the top of the page, seemed to have been born in 1922. And the book itself fell under "United States—History—Civil War, 1861–1865."

"But the war ended in 1864," Caudell said, as much to the book as to Mollie. If he'd been bewildered before, now he was completely at sea.

Mollie went to the next page. "That ain't what it says here, is it?"

Caudell's eyes grew wide as he read the first two sentences of the introduction, which talked about the South surrendering. Of themselves, his eyes kept reading. By the time he got through that two-page introduction, he was ready to question his own sanity. Every calm, rational word spoke of a long-ago war the United States had won. If this Richard Ketchum was either a maniac or a prankster, he didn't let on once.

Caudell started reading in earnest. Before long, he realized going through the whole book in detail would take too long. He skimmed over the astonishing pictures and maps, read their captions. After a while, he asked, "Does Benny Lang know this book is gone?"

"Don't reckon so," Mollie answered. "I moved a skinny book from the shelf on top so as to fill up part of the space this one took, and fiddled with both shelves so the holes didn't show. Then I hid this one with the, ah, dainties I used to fetch over to Benny's place sometimes, and got it back to my room without him bein' the wiser. Read it there some more, times I was by myself, an' the more I read, the more I got confused, till I figured I had to come to you."

Till today, Caudell had seen Mollie only in ragged gray and butternut.

Picturing her in "dainties" distracted him from the book for a little while. But soon the story of the war engrossed him again. The farther he got, the less he understood, and the more he came to wonder whether this Bruce Catton really was writing in some distant future time. He kept referring to what he called the Civil War as having happened well in the past.

And he kept assuming the United States had won and the Confederate States lost. That was clear very early on, when he talked about the overwhelming material advantages the North enjoyed, and about the trouble the South had in creating a navy out of nothing, and about the Confederacy's two-pronged offensive into Kentucky and Maryland in 1862 as a chance to win the war which failed.

Catton also talked about slavery as something dead and long departed; the feeling underlying his words seemed to be revulsion that it had ever existed. Lincoln's Emancipation Proclamation, which the results of the war had rendered meaningless and which all the South heartily loathed in any case, was to Catton a harbinger of great things ahead. Not even the staunchest Yankee should have been able to consider it as having any great effect.

Gettysburg . . . Caudell studied the paintings of the third day's fight, then turned to a calm photograph of the battlefield after the fight was done. The weathered granite and bronze monument there looked as if it had stood for decades if not centuries, yet the fight was only four and a half years in the past. He looked up at Mollie. "Does your scar still pain you?"

"The one from Gettysburg, you mean? It twinges right smart sometimes." She looked at the colored photograph, too; she understood what he was driving at. "Don't reckon it'd trouble me a-tall if I waited till that was took."

He raised an eyebrow. Somewhere down deep, she believed those impossible dates of 1960 and 1996. He shivered, and not just because the room was chilly; he was starting to believe them himself. When he looked down to the *Picture History of the Civil War* once more, he discovered it was almost too dark to see. Evening had snuck up on him like a dismounted Yankee cavalryman in the Wilderness.

He went downstairs, asked Wren Tisdale for some candles. Leering, the saloonkeeper supplied them. "You can go straight to hell, you and your filthy mind," Caudell growled. "We're up there reading a book, and if you don't believe me, you come on up and watch us." He lit one of the candles at the fireplace, hurried back to Mollie's room.

A few minutes later, he heard someone coming partway upstairs and then hastily going back down. He laughed, said to Mollie, "Tisdale, checking up on us." She giggled, too.

His awareness of the world around him diminished once more as he bent close to read by candlelight. After a while, he raised his head in complete mystification. "Everything from the Wilderness on is wrong," he said. "Grant didn't go south—we went north. And Johnston stopped Sherman." A picture of one of the fierce, jaunty "bummers" who, the book claimed, had looted their way across Georgia, stared mutely up at him.

"It don't talk none about our repeaters, neither," Mollie said.

"By God, you're right. It doesn't." Caudell flipped to the back of the book; he already discovered it had an excellent index. Nothing was listed about repeaters, nothing about AK-47s. "But they won the war for us. Without them—"

"We'd maybe have lost," Mollie put in. She pointed to the *Picture History of the Civil War*. "Like in there."

Caudell kept going through the book. He found a picture of the Tredegar Iron Works, said to have been taken after Richmond fell. He found the story of Lincoln's reelection over George McClellan, who, he knew, had actually run fourth in the election of 1864, and no mention whatever of U.S. President Seymour's participation in the race. He found photographs of Richmond in ruins, and a painting of Lincoln going through the city in a carriage.

His eyes filled with foolish tears (foolish, for why should he be moved at what had never happened?) as he found word of the surrender of the Army of Northern Virginia to overwhelming Federal forces and a final photograph of a grim-faced Robert E. Lee, said to have been made just after that surrender. At the very end of the book, he found a painting from 1890—a year that, to him, still felt far in the future—of Union veterans parading in Boston. Seeing the white beards of the officers marching in the first rank made gooseflesh prickle up on his arms.

He found himself altogether confused. Either Bruce Catton had never heard of the world in which he lived, or the man was the most inspired hoaxer of all time—even 1960. After some hard thought, Caudell found he could not believe the *Picture History of the Civil War* a hoax. For one thing, it was too perfect, too detailed. For another, even if an obsessed man somehow spent a lifetime assembling everything that went into this book—*a lifetime when?* Caudell wondered; no printer in 1868 could have produced anything like it—why would anyone else have cared to view the product of his obsession?

"What do you think, Nate?" Mollie asked when he finally closed the covers.

"I think—" Caudell stopped, as if saying what he thought somehow made it more real. But no help for it: "I think this may truly be a book from—from the twentieth century."

She threw her arms around him and kissed him on the cheek. "Oh, sweet Jesus, thank you! I was thinkin' the same thing, and thinkin' I had to be out of my head."

"Believe me, I feel the same way." But when he looked down at the volume that should have been impossible, his resolve firmed. "All the other choices seem even crazier, though."

"Seems like that to me, too. But if it's real, Nate, it's important. What are we going to do about it?"

That brought him up short. "You've had more time to think about this than I have." Not wanting to sound as if he was accusing her, he quickly added, "But you're dead right. If this comes out of Rivington, it ought to shed some kind of light on all the other peculiar things the Rivington men have." Not just AK-47s went through his mind, but also desiccated meals, Benny Lang's helmet and bullet-stopping flapjack (he still wondered if he'd heard that straight), and the marvelous lights and artificial coolness about which Mollie had written. He'd never before thought of all those things together. Now that he had, he saw what a mountain of strangeness they made, a mountain beside which the *Picture History of the Civil War* was by itself but a foothill.

He knew he was not a man cut out to handle mountains. He thought of bringing the book to George Lewis, shook his head the moment the idea occurred to him. Taken as a whole, the mystery of Rivington was far too big for Lewis, too. With that realization came an answer to Mollie's question: "Robert E. Lee needs to see this book."

Mollie stared at him. "Robert E. Lee? Marse Robert?" Her voice rose to a squeak. "The *President*?"

"He's not the king," Caudell said. "He's not even President yet, and won't be for more than a month. Remember how it was in Richmond? Jeff Davis had his house open every other week, just so he could meet people. Captain Lewis went there once, to shake his hand."

"I ain't no captain." Mollie vehemently shook her head. "I'm just a— hell and damnation, Nate, you know what I am." She set a hand on the book in his lap. "You go, Nate. You can tell Marse Robert what it's all about, better'n I ever could."

"Me?" Caudell was tempted—anyone who brought something this important to Richmond would become important himself, if only by association. But then, regretfully, he said, "No, it wouldn't be right. For one thing, you got the book, so you should be the one who takes it. For another, you've lived at Rivington, so you can tell Marse Robert all about it. He'll want to know that; the Rivington men were strong for Forrest in the election."

"Oh, were they ever," Mollie said. "You never heard such cussin' and fussin' and carryin' on as when Tennessee went for Lee."

"There, you see? And besides, Mollie, you're already traveling. Me, I have to teach school tomorrow and the next day and the day after that, or else throw away a job I like and that I'm good at." He took a deep breath. "I'll do it if I have to, I guess, but you're a better choice."

"But I'm nothin' but a no-'count whore," Mollie wailed. "Marse Robert, he won't want nothin' to do with the likes of me."

"I don't know. He has an eye for pretty ladies, they say," Caudell said. But that made matters worse, not better. He tugged at his beard, then suddenly grinned and asked, "Do you still have your old uniform?"

"Yeah, I do," she replied, sounding puzzled at the change of subject. "What about it?"

"If you won't go as Mollie, go as Melvin," he said. "You know Marse Robert would do whatever needed doing for one of his old soldiers—and you soldiered as hard as anybody."

She had to nod. Slowly, she said, "Might could be that'd work." Her laugh came shaky, but it was a laugh. "Always kept it in case I had to get out of somewhere quiet and sneakylike. Never reckoned I'd want to get into someplace that way." A hand flew up to her hair. "Hate to chop this short again after it's been growin' since the war. But if it needs doin', it needs doin'. I got me a little scissors right here." She rummaged in one of the carpetbags, found what she was looking for, handed Caudell the scissors. "You cut it, Nate. You can see what you're doin'."

Caudell hadn't cut hair since the war ended. A Negro barber would have laughed scornfully at the job he did, but when he was through, Mollie looked more like a man, or at least a beardless youth, than a woman. But the dress she still wore, and the feel of her thick, curly hair running through his fingers as he worked, the occasional moments when his hands brushed against the smooth, warm skin of her cheek, her ear, her neck, reminded him she was no man, even if she could put on the outer seeming of one.

Her hands checked what he had accomplished. She smiled. With her hair short, all at once it was the saucy smile of the Mollie beside whom he'd marched and fought—and lain. "That's good, Nate. Thank you. You want to shut the door there, so as I can change?" He did as she asked; after a moment's hesitation, he stood outside in the hallway. Through the thin wood panel, he heard her chuckle, and felt himself blush. She opened the door a couple of minutes later. "How do I look?"

Shabby was the first word that came to mind. No one could look anything but shabby in trousers, tunic, and forage cap that had gone through the war, even if those clothes were cleaned and mended, as Mollie's were. But seeing her in uniform somehow excited him in a way her hoop skirt and petticoats had not—this was the way she'd looked when he went to her cabin.

She was used to reading men's eyes. "You want to come back inside, Nate?" she asked softly. "Handy thing about this outfit is, it goes off a sight easier than the one I had on before." Not trusting himself to speak, he nodded, stepped in, and closed the door again.

They lay side by side afterwards on the narrow, clothes-strewn bed. The next to last candle Nate had got from Wren Tisdale still burned. Had the saloonkeeper known, he could have leered with impunity. Mollie stroked Caudell's cheek, just above the line where his beard started. She said, "I always remembered you were sweet about it. You treat me like I'm some-body, not just—a place to stick it in."

"Funny," he said, sitting up. "I always thought the same about you—that you weren't just going through the motions, I mean."

"Not with you. Other times—oh, the hell with other times. I wish—" Grimacing, she broke off without saying what she wished. Caudell thought he could make a fair guess. He rather wished she had no other times to come between them, too.

Mollie got off the bed and started to dress. So did Caudell; the room was cold. As he pulled up his trousers, he said, "I have some money saved up that I can give you for train fare, if you need it." He did not have much, but for this he was ready to use it.

"Don't fret yourself." Mollie finished buttoning her private's tunic, then slid over her head a small velvet bag on a thong. She tucked it under the tunic; it clinked slightly as it settled between her breasts. "I hear tell gold's still right scarce most places, but not in Rivington. You seen that for your-self. I got plenty."

"All right," Caudell said, not altogether unhappily. He thought of some-thing else. "When you go to Richmond, don't go back through Rivington, in case Benny Lang has noticed his book is missing after all. The Rivington men might be watching the Wilmington and Weldon Railroad. Go south to Goldsboro from Rocky Mount, then over to Raleigh or Greensboro, so you can head north on the Raleigh and Gaston or the North Carolina Railroad up to the Richmond and Danville."

"That's right smart, Nate. I'll do it," Mollie promised. "I'll hire me a wagon first thing tomorrow to take me to the Rocky Mount train station." She grinned a grin that took him back to their days round campfires to-gether. "Won't Mr. Wren Tisdale be confused when I go downstairs in the mornin'?"

"Not unless you go barefoot," he said, noticing a gap in her disguise.

He kicked one of his shoes over to her. "Here—take these. I have another pair in my room. My feet won't freeze on the way back. Reckon my shoes'll fit you like socks on a chicken, but if you have to, you can get yourself some proper ones on your way north."

"Oh, Nate, not your shoes!" But she saw the need for what he'd said as clearly as he did. She stooped, started to put them on, then stopped and stuffed the toes with wadded-up clothes from a carpet bag. "Just like I'd've done in the war, taking big ones off a dead Yankee." She got up and hugged him. "Thanks for not thinkin' I'm crazy on account of all this. Thanks for—" She hugged him again, hard. "For bein' a friend, and more than a friend."

He hugged her, too, felt the womanly shape of her through the uniform that masked it from the eye. *More than a friend indeed,* he thought. "Come back here when you can, if you care to," he said. It was not any sort of promise, but it was as close to one as he could make himself come. Had she pressed for more, he might well have fought shy of the little he'd said. But she only nodded; maybe she'd not expected even so much.

Freezing mud squelched between his toes as he walked out of the Liberty Bell. His head, though, his head was in the clouds, and not just because he'd broken a long spell of abstinence. Not only had he held a willing woman in his arms, he'd somehow held a bit of the future in his hands.

Lee walked out of St. Paul's Episcopal Church. The shadow cast by George Washington's equestrian statue, across Ninth Street in Capitol Square, shielded his eyes from the low, wan winter sun. Beside him, Jefferson Davis said, "A fine sermon, do you not agree?"

"Yes, as usual," Lee said. "Mr. President, let me tell you again how grateful I am that you have agreed to serve as my Secretary of War. I hesitated to ask it of you, lest you should feel it beneath your dignity to assume a Cabinet position after having held the Presidency."

Davis snorted. "Nonsense, sir. I am ineligible under the Constitution to continue as President; if I am to remain in public life, it must necessarily be at some lower level. The post you offered suits me well, and I am glad to have it."

Lee was about to reply when a light, hesitant voice said, "Beggin' your pardon, General Lee, sir—"

Frowning, he turned to deal with whoever had presumed to interrupt his conversation with President Davis. He saw a smooth-faced private in a worn uniform, clutching a parcel wrapped in coarse brown paper and twine to his chest. "Yes, Private—?" he asked, voice polite but frosty.

The soldier, who at second glance looked not quite young enough to be so free of beard, came to attention but held on to the parcel. "M-Melvin Bean, sir, 47th North Carolina. I got here a book you ought to see, sir."

"Never mind that now, young man," Jefferson Davis said impatiently. He walked on, looking back to see if Lee was following.

Lee was about to when the private said something that made him stop in his tracks: "It's a book from Rivington, sir."

"Is it?" Lee said. Davis had gone too far to hear the half-dozen soft, nervous words, but, seeing that the ordinary soldier had somehow gained Lee's attention, he shrugged and headed off toward the Presidential mansion.

"Yes, sir, it surely is," Melvin Bean said. The private gulped, licked his lips, and then went on in a ragged whisper, "Other thing you ought to know, sir, is that inside this here book, it says it was printed in nineteen hundred and sixty, sir."

"By God," Lee said softly. Private Bean looked ready to bolt and run. Lee did not blame him in the least. He himself knew the secret of the Rivington men. But if this common soldier had somehow stumbled across it, not only would he have trouble believing it, he would have even more trouble believing anyone else would believe it. Quickly, Lee set out to ease his mind: "Private, you had better come back to the Powhatan House with me. This is most assuredly something I must see. Have you a horse?"

"No, sir—came up by train." Melvin Bean gaped at him, blurted, "You— you mean you believe me, sir? Just like that?"

"Just like that," Lee agreed gravely. "Wait here a moment, if you please." He ducked back inside the church, spoke with a vestryman, then returned to Private Bean. "There—now Traveller will be seen to. Walk up Capitol Square and then to the hotel with me, if you would be so kind, and tell me how this book—"

"It's called the *Picture History of the Civil War*, sir," Bean said.

"The *Picture History of the Civil War*? From—1960, you said?" A shiver of wonder ran up Lee's spine. How would the Second American Revolution look, from a distance of a hundred years? He and Melvin Bean turned right from Ninth onto Broad Street. "Tell me at once how it came into your possession."

The story was less than clear, and left him imperfectly edified. He gathered a woman friend of Bean's had actually gotten the book away from the stronghold of America Will Break, but a couple of times the private said "I" when he meant "she." Lee did not press him. For the sake of a volume from Rivington—and from 1960!—he was willing to overlook a discrepancy or three.

Private Bean, by his accent, was a country boy. Lee expected him to gape at the red velvet and gold-leaf splendor of the Powhatan House's lobby, but he took it in stride, merely muttering something Lee did not quite catch: to him, it sounded like "It's not a not a hilton." Lee led him to his own suite and closed the door after them. He turned on the gaslight, sat by it, and pulled up another chair for Melvin Bean. "Now, if I may, the *Picture History of the Civil War*." In anticipation, he slipped on his spectacles.

Bean handed him the parcel. He cut the twine with a pen knife, undid the paper wrapper, and stared at the book for a long moment before he opened it. The unusual quality of the printing struck him at once. His lips shaped a silent whistle when he saw the copyright and publication dates. He turned the page, came to the introduction. For a moment, he was confused and jolted when he read of the war's ending with the South's surrender. Then he understood, and said quietly, "So this is how it would have been, had the Rivington men not come back to us."

"Sir?" Melvin Bean said. He was at the very edge of his seat, and still looked ready to flee at any moment. He also looked hungry: Lee had seen that expression too many times in the war ever to mistake it.

He stood up. Melvin Bean bounced to his feet, too. Lee took some bills out of a trouser pocket, handed twenty dollars to the private soldier. "Why don't you buy yourself some dinner, young man? The cooks here are quite fine. Ask for my usual table in the dining room, and tell them to send a boy back here to me if they doubt your right to sit there. Later, perhaps, I shall have questions for you, but first I want to read awhile."

Bean stared at the money without reaching for it. "I couldn't take that from you, General Lee, sir."

Lee pressed it into the private's hand. "You can, and you shall."

"I got money o' my own," Melvin Bean said, drawing himself up with prickly pride.

"As may be. Use this anyhow, please, if for no other reason than as a token of my thanks for having brought this volume to my notice." He took Bean by the elbow, steered the private to the door, and pointed in the direction of the dining room. "Go ahead, please, as a favor to me." Still shaking his head, Melvin Bean walked slowly down the hall.

Lee went back to his chair, picked up the *Picture History of the Civil War*, and plunged in. He was not normally an enthusiastic reader; when he'd come back to Richmond from Augusta, Georgia, he'd had half a dozen chapters to go in *Quentin Durward*, and those six chapters remained unread to this day. But he held in his hands a volume he had never imagined he would be able to examine. He eagerly seized the chance.

This Bruce Catton's style was less Latinate, less ornate, more down-to-earth than Lee would have expected from a serious work of history. He soon ceased to notice; he was after information, and the smooth, flowing text and astonishing pictures made it easy to acquire. He had to remind himself that Catton was writing long after the war ended and that, to the historian, it had not gone as he himself remembered.

But the odd tone ran deeper than that. Catton plainly saw chattel slavery as an outmoded institution which deserved to perish; to him, the Emancipation Proclamation gave the United States the moral high ground for the rest of the war. Lee had trouble squaring that with what Andries Rhoodie had said about the hatred between black and white which was to come.

The sun sank; the only light left in Lee's room was the yellow pool beneath the gas lamp. He never noticed—he had reached 1864, and all at once the world he knew turned sideways. He studied Grant's campaign against him, and Sherman's against Joseph Johnston, and nodded most soberly. That relentless hammering used Northern resources simply to club the Confederacy into submission. It was the sort of attack he had feared most, and one which only the Rivington men's AK-47s could have disrupted.

He winced when he read of John Bell Hood taking Johnston's command in front of Atlanta. Hood had the fierce visage of a lion and boldness to match. At the head of a division, he was a nonpareil. But for boldness, though, he lacked all qualification for army command. He would attack whether attack was called for or not . . . Over the next few pages, Lee read what had come—*what would have come*, he made himself remember—of that.

He also took far more careful note of the political maneuvering in this other version of the war than he would have before his own not-altogether-voluntary entry into politics. He was unsurprised to discover Lincoln re-elected; Andries Rhoodie had told him of that. But Rhoodie had also spoken of Lincoln treating the Confederate States as conquered provinces after their defeat, and that proved nothing but a lie: even with the war all but won, Lincoln had tried to get the Federal Congress to compensate Southern slaveholders for the animate property they were losing. Past reunion and emancipation, Lincoln had intended to impose no harsh terms upon the states which had lost their war for independence.

Absurdly, rage filled Lee at Rhoodie's untruth. *A man who knew the future might at least have the courtesy to report it correctly*, he thought. That Rhoodie had lied argued he and America Will Break had their own political agenda, one which they aimed to impose on the Confederacy. Given their support for Nathan Bedford Forrest and all their efforts against the Negro, the nature of that agenda was easy enough to deduce: the permanent dominance of the white man. But by the tone of the *Picture History of the Civil War*, white supremacy was an outmoded idea in their own day, just as the course of history would have led Lee to believe. Did that make them maverick heroes, or simply mavericks?

The question being unanswerable for the time being, Lee put it aside and kept reading. He pursed his lips and tightly clenched his jaw when he came upon a picture of a wrecked locomotive in the burned-out ruins of the Richmond and Petersburg Railroad depot. A few pages farther on, he encountered himself, old, grim, and defeated, standing on the back porch of the rented house in which he and his wife had lived in Richmond. It was uncanny, seeing himself in a photograph for which he'd never posed. As eerie was the photograph on the facing page of his farewell order to the Army of Northern Virginia, unmistakably in the handwriting of Charles Marshall, and as unmistakably nothing Marshall had been compelled by fate to write.

He read of Lincoln's second inaugural address and of the broad peace Lincoln hoped to gain, and, a page later, he read of the bullet that had slain Lincoln on Good Friday evening in 1865. He clicked his tongue between his teeth at the thought of a President dying at an assassin's hands. Then, all at once, he shivered as if suddenly seized by an ague. He had seen Lincoln in Louisville that Good Friday, had listened to him plead without avail for Kentucky to stay in the Union, had even spoken with him. He shivered again. In defeat in the world he knew, Lincoln had wanted to martyr himself for the United States. In the other world, where there was no need for it, he had been made a martyr in the hour of his greatest triumph.

At last, Lee closed the *Picture History of the Civil War*. His joints creaked and protested when he got up from his chair: how long had he been sitting, rapt? He took out his watch. He blinked—it was after midnight.

"Dear God, I've entirely forgotten Melvin Bean!" he exclaimed. He hoped the young soldier had bought supper as well as dinner with his money, hoped even more that he was still here—perhaps stretched out asleep on a couch in the hotel lobby—to be questioned. Lee opened the door, hurried down the hall to find out.

To his dismay, he found no gray-clad soldier taking his ease in the lobby, or at the bar. No waiter recalled serving supper to any such person. Scowling, Lee headed for the front desk. Bean had said he had money; maybe, just maybe, he'd taken a room here.

The desk clerk regretfully spread his hands. "No, sir, nobody by that name has checked in today." He spun the registration book on its revolving stand so Lee could see for himself. Then he turned to the bank of pigeon-holes behind him. "This came in for you this afternoon, though, sir."

Sure enough, the envelope he held out bore Lee's name in a sprawling scrawl. Lee accepted it with a word of thanks, slit it open. When he saw what was inside, his breath went out in a surprised hiss.

"Something wrong, sir?" the clerk asked anxiously.

After a moment, Lee said, "No, nothing wrong." He took the twenty dollars out of the envelope, returned the bills to his pocket, and slowly walked back to his room.

"What can I do for you today, General Lee?" Andries Rhoodie asked, more than ordinary curiosity in his deep, rough voice. "I tell you straight out, I'd not expected you to ask me for a meeting."

"Nor had I expected the need for my doing so to arise," Lee answered. "I find, however, that you and your colleagues have been less than completely candid with me and with others in the Confederacy concerning the course events would have taken had America Will Break not intervened on our behalf—or perhaps on your own behalf would phrase it more accurately."

"Haw!" Rhoodie fleered laughter. "You find that, do you? I tell you now, what I have said before is the truth. And even if it weren't, how the devil would you know?"

Lee sat beside a small marble-topped table, covered at the moment with an antimacassar borrowed from the couch. He pulled the cloth aside to reveal the *Picture History of the Civil War*. "By this means, sir."

Rhoodie's air of disdainful arrogance crashed in ruins; for the first time since he'd known the Rivington man, Lee saw him altogether at a loss. Rhoodie lost color, gave back a pace, sank heavily into a chair. His mouth opened, but no sound came forth. After a few seconds of gathering himself, he tried again: "How did you come by that book?"

"That is none of your affair," Lee said.

Though he had no intention of revealing it to Rhoodie, the question still bothered him. As far as he could tell, Melvin Bean had disappeared from Richmond, nor had discreet questions at the railway depots revealed anyone who had seen a person of his description boarding a southbound train, whether in uniform or other men's clothing. Lee had also had the military records examined: sure enough, a Melvin Bean had been mustered out along with the rest of the 47th North Carolina in 1864, but there the trail ended. It was a puzzle, but one that was not relevant here and now.

He went on, "In any event, no matter how I obtained the volume, it speaks for itself."

"So it does," Rhoodie said, rallying. He was neither weakling nor fool, and not a man to be cast down long. "It tells you how the United States would have crushed your country and your dreams to dust without us. You've not been any too bloody grateful for our help, either."

"I freely acknowledge it," Lee said. "As for gratitude, I should feel more were I surer your aid was disinterested, intended to further our ends rather than your own."

"Some of us died in the taking of Washington," Rhoodie growled.

"I know, but for what cause?" Lee reached out to lay a hand on the *Picture History of the Civil War.* "As you can imagine, I have read this work repeatedly, and with the closest attention. Yes, our struggle for freedom would have failed without you; in so much you told the truth. But in other regards—you spoke of Lincoln's tyranny over us, of ceaseless strife between black and white, of other evils whereof your book here makes no mention. What it does mention is a continuing search for justice and equality between the races, one incomplete even in that distant future day, but nonetheless of vital import to both North and South. This seems to me to be in accord with a continuation of the trends that have grown here in my own century, and dead against your account of what lies ahead."

"Nonsense." A wave of Rhoodie's hand brushed aside Lee's words. "Or would you care for one of your daughters to marry a kaffir and submit to his loving embrace?"

Lee did not particularly care for the idea of his daughters marrying at all. He answered, "No, to be frank, I should not care for that. But it is neither here nor there. The discrepancy between your words and the tone of this history makes me wonder whether you and American Will Break are in accord with the spirit of the future, as you claim, or whether you are in fact as misplaced and out of step with your own time as John Brown was with his."

Andries Rhoodie had gone white before. Now he turned red. One big fist clenched. His guttural accent came thicker than Lee had ever heard it as he ground out, "Since you aim on taking the Confederacy to the devil, General Lee, we will show you what we are. That I vow."

"Do not think to threaten me, sir."

"I do not threaten," Rhoodie said. "I promise."

⋆ XVI ⋆

"You jus' leave it all to me, Marse Robert," John Dabney said. "I promise I take care of everythin' for you, make your inauguration day special."

Robert E. Lee liked that kind of talk, whether from a junior officer during the war or, as now, from a caterer. Smiling, he said, "I place myself entirely in your hands, John."

The rotund Negro beamed. "Make me a raft o' mint juleps for drinks. The Prince of Wales, he like my mint juleps, you know that, sir?"

"So I've heard, yes." Now Lee kept a damper on his smile: Dabney told that story at any excuse, or none. But it was true; when the prince visited Richmond in 1860, he'd praised the colored man's juleps to the skies. The renown that won Dabney helped him gain so many cooking and bartending jobs that he'd been able to buy himself and his wife their freedom. Before the end of the war, he'd started his own restaurant and catering service. Since then, no one who was anyone in Richmond would think of holding a large entertainment without his supervision.

Dabney's eyes got a faraway look as he added some detail to the feast that would follow Lee's installation as President. The Negro could neither read nor write; he had to carry in his head all the preparations for each of the banquets he had in progress. Nobody had ever known him to slip up on that account.

Lee went into the bedroom of his Powhatan House suite. There Julia and his daughters were helping Mary Custis Lee into her gown. "You look

404 ★ THE GUNS OF THE SOUTH

lovely, my dear," he said. "That shade of creamy yellow is particularly becoming to you."

"I wish I'd had the seamstress make a jacket to go with the dress," his wife answered. "It's a raw day out there."

"Early March is apt to be," Lee admitted. "Still, the sun is shining. If I'd chosen to be sworn in on Washington's birthday, as President Davis did, rather than waiting until March 4, we should have displayed ourselves in Capitol Square in the midst of a snowstorm: hardly an edifying spectacle for the people."

"Why did you decide to wait?" his daughter Mary asked. "With the family's connection to Washington, I'd expected you to follow Davis's lead."

"I had two reasons. One was fear of the weather, which proved justified. The other was that the Constitution prescribes March 4 as the first day of a new President's term, and I desire to observe scrupulously its every provision." Lee reflected on his own hypocrisy. While following all the meaningless minutiae for his inauguration, he aimed to sidle around the much more prominent Constitutional prohibitions against interfering with slavery.

He intensely disliked feeling like a hypocrite, which was both alien and repugnant to his nature. But a show of observance on small matters would help mask his deviation in great ones, and he was resolved to deviate. The success of a man like John Dabney pointed up the injustice of slavery as no abolitionist tract could. Aside from the caterer's undoubted ability, that was one reason Lee had engaged him: if legislators saw a successful black man in action, they might be more inclined to allow other Negroes to seek the same road.

Mildred Lee fastened a last stay. "We're ready, Father," she said.

"Excellent. Then let us proceed."

"I want a lap robe, lest I catch my death," Mary Custis Lee declared.

"Fetch your mother a lap robe, and quickly," Lee said, with a pointed glance at his watch. "The ceremony is to commence at half past eleven o'clock."

Mildred draped the robe over her mother's knees. "Is that fast enough to suit you?" she asked. "Or if I'd taken longer, would you have left without us, the way you used to march off to church by yourself sometimes when we were slow?"

Lee, whose natural sense of punctuality had been reinforced by more than thirty-five years of military discipline, said, "As well you didn't expose me to the temptation." Mildred stuck out her tongue at him. He made an effort at looking severe, but found he was smiling in spite of himself.

Julia started to push Mary Custis Lee's chair, but Lee waved her away:

this was a duty he would undertake himself. Rather than going out to the lobby of the Powhatan House, he headed for the hotel's rear doorway, which opened right across from Capitol Square. His daughters walked proudly behind him, their wide skirts rustling as they glided down the hall.

Chill air smote. Lee's breath puffed from him, as if he had suddenly taken up pipe smoking. His wife pulled the lap robe higher. "There; you see? I should have frozen," she said.

Lee reached down to pat her shoulder. "I am glad you have it."

Capitol Street and the paths through Capitol Square already swarmed with people making their way toward the covered wooden platform which had been erected under the statue of Washington. Marshals with drawn swords—and with AK-47s slung on their backs—briefly halted the tide to let Lee and his family cross. Before he and Albert Gallatin Brown were sworn in on that platform, other ceremonies awaited at the Confederate Capitol.

Marshals helped Lee wrestle his wife's chair up the stairs to the flag-draped entrance to the Capitol. The chief marshal, a plump, superannuated colonel of ordnance named Charles Dimmock, saluted. "Mr. President-elect," he boomed.

Lee inclined his head. "Mr. Chief Marshal."

Congressman Sion Rogers of North Carolina bustled up to Lee. "Mr. President-elect, on behalf of the Joint Committee on Arrangements, it is my privilege to welcome you to the Congress of the Confederate States of America. If you and your charming family will please to come with me?"

He escorted the Lees into the chamber of the Virginia House of Delegates—the Virginia legislature continued to meet in the Capitol, along with the Confederate Congress. Congressmen, senators, members of the Virginia Senate and House, Virginia's Governor Smith, several other state heads, judges, generals, and clergymen packed the hall, along with a goodly number of reporters. They converged on Lee until Colonel Dimmock interposed his formidable person between the throng and the President-elect.

The minister from the United States caught Lee's eye. "Congratulations, General, or rather, Mr. President-elect."

"Thank you, Mr. Pendleton," Lee answered gravely. George Pendleton, a former congressman from Ohio, was a close friend to U.S. Vice President Vallandigham, and had favored peaceful accommodation with the South throughout the Second American Revolution. Lee added, "Let me applaud you on General Sheridan's recent capture of Winnipeg. Your armies continue to perform very well, as does your ironclad fleet on the Great Lakes."

"You are generous to a recent foe." What Pendleton meant by that was thanks for forbearing to comment on the complete dominance of the British fleet on the high seas. Not only had Boston harbor been bombarded again, but a force of English marines had seized and burned San Francisco, then reembarked on their ships and departed before U.S. forces could do anything about it.

"If you will come with me, Mr. President-elect . . ." Congressman Rogers said. Lee obediently followed him to the front of the chamber. Jefferson and Varina Davis, Albert Gallatin Brown and his wife Roberta, and outgoing Vice President Alexander Stephens, a lifelong bachelor, were already standing there chatting. So were Lee's three sons and Joseph Brown; Albert Gallatin Brown's other son, Bob, captured at Gettysburg, had emerged from a Northern prison camp so weak that he had died a year after the war ended.

"There, you see, Mildred, we are the last to arrive," Lee said. His youngest daughter only sniffed. He laughed a little; Mildred was incorrigible.

As he came up, he noticed that, while Varina Davis and Roberta Brown were talking animatedly, their husbands, longtime political foes in Mississippi, still had little to say to each other. "That is a lovely ring, Mrs. Davis," Roberta Brown remarked. "May I see it more closely?"

Varina Davis extended a slim, shapely hand. "Mr. Davis gave it to me upon our engagement. A dozen small diamonds surround an emerald-cut sapphire."

"Lovely," Mrs. Brown said again. "The mounting is also very fine work."

The talk broke off when Jefferson Davis saw Lee approaching and hurried up to shake his hand. Albert and Joseph Brown followed, as did Stephens and Lee's own sons. Lee also bowed over the hands of Varina Davis and Roberta Brown. Jefferson Davis said, "I leave you a nation at peace and secure within its borders, sir. God grant that you may offer your successor a similar boon."

Congressman Rogers, who wore a harassed expression, consulted a scrap of paper he carried in his left hand. "If you ladies and gentlemen will be so kind as to form a receiving line . . . First you, Mr. Vice President, then the Vice President-elect's family, then Mr. Brown himself, then the President's family and Mr. Davis, then the Lees, and finally General Lee himself in the place of honor at the end . . ." He repeated himself several times, and chivvied people about until he had them all where he wanted them.

Dignitaries began filing past, shaking hands and offering best wishes. Lee returned murmured words of thanks, which he wondered if they heard. Finally, Senator Louis Wigfall of Texas broke the routine. Nathan Bedford Forrest's defeated running mate was a burly, broad-shouldered man, with a fierce countenance and a long, thick beard. He growled, "If you think you're gonna turn the niggers loose, General Lee, you'll do it only over my dead body."

"I do hope it won't come to that," Lee said quietly—let Wigfall make of the answer what he would. The Texan stopped, stared, scowled, and, at last, forced by the crowd behind him, moved on.

Lee's arm was tired and his hand sore when Congressman Rogers declared, "The hour now nears half past twelve o'clock. We shall proceed out through the east door of the Capitol to the platform in the following order: first, Chief Marshal Dimmock and his marshals; next, the band, which has—I hope—gathered by the east door; next, the members of the Joint Committee on Arrangements; next, the President-elect, attended by the outgoing President; next, the Vice President-elect, attended by the outgoing Vice President; next, the families of these officials; next, the members of the old and new Cabinets—excluding Mr. Davis, for obvious reasons—and their families, next . . ."

He went on for some time, marshaling his hosts like any good general. Senators and congressmen even lined up in columns of four. The press made up the rear of the procession, behind Masons and members of other benevolent societies but ahead of the generality of citizens.

The band began blaring "Dixie" as Lee made his way toward the east door—Congressman Rogers let out an audible sigh of relief to hear them. Lee remembered the last time he had left the Hall of Delegates. A band had played then, too, for he had just been invested with the command of the armed forces of a Virginia not yet even formally affiliated to the Confederate States of America. His step faltered for a moment as he thought of the changes he had been part of through the past seven years.

Outside, Colonel Dimmock was shouting at the generality of citizens who already crowded Capitol Square: "Make way for President Lee! Without the President, you don't have a show. Make way, make way! Marshals, move them aside."

The marshals did their best. Slowly, the procession began to advance. The journey to the base of Washington's statue took three times as long as it should have. Lee fidgeted nervously as he went along at slow march. Jefferson Davis set a calming hand on his arm. "The crush does not matter, not today. As the good colonel said, without you we have no show." Caught out like a small boy at some naughty act, Lee spread his hands in a show of guilt.

The band, still playing lustily, took its place to one side of the wooden platform after the marshals cleared away the numerous citizens who had thought the area ideal for viewing the inaugural ceremony. That only packed the rest of the square more tightly; crowds spilled out onto Ninth Street and Capitol Street, snarling traffic on both thoroughfares and creating a hubbub which, in both volume and intensity, seemed inappropriate to the celebration about to take place.

Having displaced the improperly situated spectators, the marshals spread out along the front of the platform. There were at most a dozen of them; it was no great show of force. Lee thought of Lincoln's 1861 inaugural in a country coming apart, where sharpshooters peered from the windows of the U.S. Capitol and a battery of artillery remained just out of sight in case insurrection broke out without warning. No such fears disrupted the Confederate States, not today.

Lee and Jefferson Davis ascended to the platform. So did Alexander Stephens and Albert Gallatin Brown. The members of the Joint Committee on Arrangements already stood up there. Congressman Rogers had another list in his hand. "Yes, Bishop Johns, your place is up here, as is yours, of course, Judge Halyburton. Colonel Dimmock, you too, if you please, and the President of the Senate, and the Speaker of the House of Representatives, and you, Governor Smith. For our other distinguished guests, we have seats waiting down here at the front." He pointed to the rows of wooden chairs there, marked off by a gilded rope.

There was only one problem with those wooden chairs—not enough of them had been set out. Senators and members of the Virginia House of Delegates, reporters and congressmen and Cabinet members rowed like Kilkenny cats as they tried to stake out places to sit. Lee watched the unseemly spectacle for a couple of minutes, then turned to Charles Dimmock. "Mr. Chief Marshal, may I beg a favor and ask that my wife be brought up here? Given her infirmity, I fear she may not be altogether safe in that seething crowd."

"I'll see to it, sir." Dimmock leaned over, called a couple of junior marshals to his side. The husky young men pushed their way through the squabbling dignitaries—seeing a minister pull a congressman's beard, Lee wondered how many duels would arise from the day's events—make their way to Mary Custis Lee, whom her children had protectively surrounded, and, with the help of her sons, got her and her chair onto the platform.

"Thank you, Robert," she said. "This is much better for me." A gust of wind tugged at her bonnet. She snatched up a hand to keep it from being blown away.

When all the chairs were taken and those unable to gain them had been banished beyond the pale of the gilded rope, the band, at a signal from Sion Rogers, fell silent. The congressman shouted, "The Right Reverend Bishop Johns will now ask the Lord's blessing on this auspicious day."

The noise from the crowd did not cease, but it did diminish as the bishop, splendid in the glistening silks of his vestments, stepped forward to the edge of the platform. "Let us pray," he said. Lee bent his head, but not before he saw the wind blow off the bishop's miter. Johns made a catch a base ball player would have been proud of, set the runaway headgear more firmly in place. Several people cheered.

Ignoring them, the bishop repeated, "Let us pray. Almighty God, guide and protect us in our efforts to perpetuate the principles which, by your blessing, our fathers were able to vindicate, establish, and transmit to us, their posterity. Our hope remains reverently fixed on you, whose favor is ever vouchsafed to the cause which is just. With humble gratitude and adoration, acknowledging the Providence which has so visibly protected the Confederacy during its brief but eventful career, we trustingly commit ourselves to you, so that, with the continuance of your favor gratefully acknowledged, we may look forward to success, to peace, and to prosperity for our nation. Amen."

"Amen," echoed from the crowd as Bishop Johns stepped back. Judge J. D. Halyburton of the Confederate Court at Richmond strode ponderously forward to take his place. The judge had a Bible under his arm. His voice was a bass rumble that suited the massive frame his black robe could not altogether conceal:

"The President of the Senate of the Confederate States of America having informed me that Senator Albert Gallatin Brown of the state of Mississippi has obtained a majority of the electoral votes cast for the office of Vice President of the Confederate States of America, I now have the honor to invite Senator Brown here to me, to set his hand upon the Holy Scriptures and take his oath of office." Judge Halyburton held out the Bible to Brown. "Raise your right hand, sir."

As his running-mate was formally invested with the Vice Presidency, Lee looked out at the sea of faces, all turned toward the platform. Most were still and attentive, watching and doing their best to hear Brown take his oath. A small commotion a hundred yards away, or perhaps a bit more, drew Lee's eye—several men were trying to elbow their way closer to the platform through the tightly packed crowd. Lee wondered why; most of them were tall enough to see over the heads in front of them.

Judge Halyburton was booming, "I now have the honor to invite General Lee here to me, to set his hand upon the Holy Scriptures and take his oath of office."

Lee took off his hat as he walked over to the judge. The wind kicked up again, blowing his coat open. He tried to keep it in place with his arms, and hoped the chilly breeze would not cause him to catch cold.

"Set your hat down for a moment, if you would," Halyburton said quietly. Lee obeyed, putting his foot down on the edge of the brim so the hat would not fly away from him. His left hand went onto the Bible. At full volume once more, the judge said, "Raise your right hand."

Again, Lee obeyed. Then, phrase by phrase, he repeated the Presidential oath: "I, Robert Edward Lee—do solemnly swear—that I will faithfully execute—the office of President of the Confederate States—and will, to the best of my ability—preserve, protect, and defend—the Constitution thereof." On his own, he added, "So help me God."

Judge Halyburton's plump cheeks got plumper as he grinned and stuck out a hand. "Let me be the first to offer you my best wishes, President Lee."

"Thank you, sir." Lee retrieved his hat. As if that were a cue, the band played "Dixie" again. The crowed cheered and clapped over the music. Lee used those couple of minutes to review his inaugural address. He hoped it would not slide out of his mind the moment he began to speak. He'd spent the last several days working to memorize it, but knew he lacked the lifelong politician's gift for storing away long stretches of prose.

The music stopped. The crowd grew . . . quieter. When Lee decided they were as quiet as they were going to get, he took a deep breath and began, wishing he owned Judge Halyburton's stentorian tones: "The trust you, the people of the Confederate States of America, have reposed in me makes me all too conscious of my own inadequacies. Further, the great achievements of my predecessor, the illustrious Jefferson Davis, founding President of our happy Confederacy, set a standard I despair of emulating. In the face of formidable odds, he secured for us our independence from the government of the United States, which was determined to deny us our right to such independence. He—"

Just then, the fickle wind flicked his hat out of his hand, leaving him with the unpalatable choice of losing his dignity by letting it blow away or losing his dignity by bending to pick it up. It lay at his feet, as if mocking him. He glared down at it. Before the wind could sweep it off the platform, he stooped down and grabbed it.

Something *craack*ed through the space his head had just occupied. *A bullet*, the unsleeping soldier's part of his mind reported. He started to straighten. Another bullet tugged at his coat sleeve, parting the material neat as a scissors.

Judge Halyburton had never seen combat. All through the war, he'd served on the bench in Richmond. But nothing was wrong with his reactions. He swept out a thick arm and knocked Lee off the platform. He stumbled and went to all fours when he hit the ground below. An instant later, the judge crashed down beside him with a cry of pain, blood soaking his robes from a shoulder wound.

Lee leaped to his feet, started to scramble back onto the platform so he could see what was going on—a dignified, even boring, occasion had turned to horror in the wink of an eye. Judge Halyburton grabbed his ankle and held him back. "Stay down here, you damned fool," he shouted. "It's you they're shooting at."

That had not occurred to Lee. Despite reading of Lincoln's assassination in the *Picture History of the Civil War,* he still found the idea of political murder in America as alien as that sideways world wherein the South had lost its war for freedom.

Thinking of that other world, and of having seen those big men elbowing through the crowd, made him suddenly, dreadfully certain who the "they" doing the shooting were. "The Rivington men!" he exclaimed, and tried to break free of Judge Halyburton's grip. "Let me go!" But the judge clung to him, limpetlike, with all the strength in his unwounded left arm.

Bullets kept flying, with the extravagant frequency that marked the use of repeating weapons. Through his own startlement, through the rising tide of shouts and screams from the crowd, Lee noted that these repeaters, whatever they were and to whomever they belonged, sounded different from the AK-47s to which he'd become accustomed.

He also noted that, while the assassins had failed to slay him with their first shots, they were not giving up. All but one of the marshals who had served as ceremonial guards in front of the platform were down, dead or wounded. The sole unhurt man had his repeater on his shoulder, but hesitated to fire because of the crush of people between him and the gunmen, and because of the innocent people behind them. The assassins had no such compunctions.

Lee finally twisted free from Judge Halyburton. He leaped up onto the platform, only to be knocked flat by Jefferson Davis. "Stay low!" the just-become-former President bawled in his ear. As if to underline his words, another stream of bullets buzzed by.

The platform was a charnel house, blood and bodies everywhere. Wounded men shrieked. Mary's chair lay on its side, two wheels in the air. Ice ran through Lee. "My wife," he gasped. He had wanted her to be able to see his moment of triumph. Now— "Mary?" he said again. Davis did not, or perhaps would not, answer him.

The crowd surged like the sea gone mad. Most people were trying to flee the assassins, but some men moved purposefully toward them. Amidst the continued chatter of the strange repeaters, single pistol shots began to bark. A fair number of citizens habitually went armed, and almost all of them had fought in the Second American Revolution. After the initial shock, their instinct was to hit back.

The marshal with the AK-47 fired three quick rounds. Then he reeled backwards; the rifle flew from his hands as he clutched at his neck. A dignitary in frock coat and top hat snatched up the weapon and began to shoot with a confidence that showed he had been a wartime infantry soldier. Within moments, three other men grabbed fallen marshals' rifles and followed his example.

But the assassins kept shooting, too. Lee wondered how that was possible, given the fire now coming against them from every side and their lack of any cover save the panicked folk around them. Yet the repeaters that were not AK-47s snarled on and on; men and women toppled and screamed. More bullets cracked by, some just above Lee's head.

After what seemed forever but was, Lee's pocket watch insisted, only a couple of minutes, the assassins' weapons at last fell silent. Jefferson Davis cautiously raised his head. When nothing happened, he let Lee up.

"Dear God!" Lee groaned, getting his first long look at the slaughter all around. He'd known the aftermath of battle ever since his days in Mexico, more than twenty years before; during the Second American Revolution he'd seen more slaughter than one man had any business knowing. But never in his worst nightmares had he imagined a firefight in the midst of a crowd of civilians—combat was for soldiers, not innocent bystanders.

If the murderers out there had ever heard of that rule, they laughed at it. Men in silk cravats and men in farmers' overalls, women in faded calico and women in glistening taffetas bled and moaned and cried, for nothing more than being in the wrong place at the wrong time. And up on the platform, where the assassins had concentrated their fire—

Lee had trouble telling who was slain, who wounded, and who merely splashed with other people's blood. Then he saw that Albert Gallatin Brown, for one, would never get up again; the new Vice President of the Confederate States had a neat hole above his right eye, while the back of his head was a white and crimson horror of blown-out brains and bone.

Jefferson Davis yanked off his coat, began tearing at it to make bandages to help the injured. Lee knew he ought to do likewise, but he couldn't, not yet—he'd just noticed his wife's skirts, behind her overturned chair. "Mary?" he said. She did not answer, but she might well not have heard him through the groans and wails all around. He hurried to her.

Death had been kind, as far as death ever is. She looked surprised, not hurt, but her staring eyes would never see anything again. Blood soaked her breast and pooled all around her; a single round had gone in one side of her throat and, quite neatly, out the other.

As if from very far away, people shouted, "General Lee, sir! President Lee!" The titles reminded him that public duty came before private pain. He made himself turn his head away from the woman with whom he'd shared almost thirty-seven years. Tears would come later, when he had time for them. Now . . . now someone was yelling, "One of the bastards is still alive, President Lee!"

Even through shock and anguish, that could still surprise him. Like a splash of cold water, it helped clear his head. He said, "Then he must be kept so. We shall have answers for this. Bring him up here at once." While he waited, he leaned over the edge of the platform, down to where Judge Halyburton sat holding his shoulder with his good hand and using some most unjudicial language. "Your honor," Lee said, and then again, more urgently: "Your honor!"

"What do you need?" Halyburton growled.

For this day never to have happened. As fast as the thought appeared, Lee forced it down: no time for it, and no use to it. He said, "I believe, and hope momentarily to confirm, that the men who committed this cowardly atrocity belong to the society that calls itself American Will Break. That society has for some years housed itself in the building across from Mechanic's Hall." He pointed toward the western corner of Capitol Square. Sure enough, through the trees he saw the Rivington men's flag still flying. "Will you grant us a warrant to search those premises?"

"Goddam right I will," Halyburton said. "And if that's where the snakes lair is, sir, I'll tell you to get yourself somewhere else besides here. A good shot could hit you from there."

"He's right, Mr. President," Jefferson Davis said. "Get to cover at once, behind Washington's monument." He did not wait for Lee to argue, but forced him down off the blood-soaked platform and then behind the sheltering marble and bronze. At the same time, he shouted, "A guard for President Lee!"

The guard detachment was surely the highest-ranking in the history of the Confederate States, as a good half of its members were generals who had come to watch one of their own inaugurated. They held bared swords, weapons hardly more likely to be useful than the drums and fifes and horns of the bandsmen who also crowded round to protect Lee.

Despite the guards, despite Davis's warnings, Lee looked around the base of the statue of Washington. More folk than Judge Halyburton alone must have heard what he said about the headquarters of America Will Break, for men marched purposefully toward it through the still-milling crowd.

"This is a hard day for the country," Lee said. "We shall sorely miss Vice President Brown, as well as the other casualties we have suffered.

And—" His voice broke. If he let himself think about *and*, he would not be able to do what manifestly had to be done. *And* would wait, would have to wait. Davis set an understanding hand on his shoulder. He nodded gratefully, said, "I hope—I pray—Mrs. Davis is safe?"

"Yes, she is well, praise be to God—I saw her. Your own loss—" Davis looked uncommonly grim. "We shall have a reckoning for this day, and hang these wretches higher than Haman—a better end than they merit, too."

Lee's sons, big men like himself, forced their way through the guards to him. Blood splashed Custis and Rob; by the way they ignored it, it was not their own. Lee's mouth twisted when he saw Roonie cradling a wounded hand against his other arm. For a moment, he could not help being father rather than leader. "Your sisters, your wives?" he demanded harshly.

"None of them hurt," Custis said, and Lee's shoulders slumped in thanks. Then Custis went on, "But sir, is Mother—?" Tears cut clean tracks through the crimson stains on his cheeks.

"Yes, my dear boys, she—" Lee again checked himself before he dissolved in sorrow with his sons. Just then, a congressman and a fellow in the ragged clothes of a day laborer dragged Konrad de Buys up to him. He knew a crazy kind of relief; duty always pulled him out of his private concerns. How often Mary had taken him to task for that. *Mary*— He scowled and focused his attention on de Buys.

The Rivington man's face, usually bold and boyish, was pale and twisted with pain. He'd been shot in right wrist and left shoulder; blood soaked hastily—and no doubt grudgingly—applied bandages. His eyes widened, just for an instant, when he saw Lee. Then, as best he could through the torment of his wounds, he set his features to reveal nothing. He even managed an ironic nod of greeting.

Lee had always admired de Buys's gallantry; to find it still displayed under such circumstances wrung from him a cry almost of despair: "Why, sir, *why*? What did we ever do to merit such treatment at your hands?"

"You know the answer to that," de Buys said, and Lee remembered Andries Rhoodie's voice, tolling like an iron bell: *I do not threaten. I promise.* Now the Rivington man permitted himself an expression: self-reproach. "Who would have thought we could bugger up this operation against the likes of you?"

"You mind your mouth, you son of a bitch," the day laborer snarled, shaking de Buys like a rat. The Rivington man set his teeth against the agony that must have shot through him—then lashed out with a foot and caught his captor right between the legs. The day laborer collapsed with a groan, clutching at his privates. De Buys did not even try to run. He managed a haggard smile for Lee and another nod, as if inviting him to ask the next question.

Before Lee could speak, gunfire crackled in front of the building that had sheltered America Will Break since 1864. More screams and shouts arose from the civilians still milling about in Capitol Square. Konrad de Buys's smile got wider. "You will not find us easy meat for your slaughter."

"Nor did you find us so," Lee said, which sobered the Rivington man.

Jefferson Davis said, "The snakes in their nest will presently discover, as this one has, that their plot against you miscarried, Mr. President. Again I urge you to repair to a location out of rifle range from that nest."

Lee was about to refuse. Then he glanced at Konrad de Buys, saw the Rivington man watching him in turn. The intensity of de Buys's gaze made him stop and think hard. The offices of America Will Break looked across Franklin Street to Mechanic's Hall, not back toward Capitol Square. As Davis said, whatever Rivington men remained at their headquarters might well have thought their attack successful until armed men approached the building. If he stayed where he was, he gratuitously offered them a second chance to make it so.

"Very well, sir," he said quietly. "Let us return to the Capitol, then, a building easily secured against anything short of artillery." Davis's nod was grateful. Konrad de Buys's face once more revealed nothing save pain and indifference. Most of the Rivington men were good at secreting away their thoughts, but Lee judged from the very blankness of the mask that de Buys concealed disappointment, not delight.

The plan had been for Sion Rogers to escort him from Capitol Square to the Presidential residence after the inaugural address, and for some other member of the Joint Committee on Arrangements to conduct Albert Gallatin Brown back to his rented house. The plan, thanks to the Rivington men, lay messily dead. So did Albert Gallatin Brown. Rogers, Lee thought, was only wounded . . .

Back at the Capitol, Lee sent urgent orders down to the armory and the powder works. There, if anywhere in Richmond, he would be able to lay hands on a decent number of properly trained soldiers. The Confederate capital was a city at peace; who would have imagined it needed garrisoning against its own? Lee stood surrounded by his country's highest commanders, but they had no men to lead.

James Longstreet was saying something to the same effect, an old Indian-fighter's joke about too many chiefs. Lee only half heard him; he was considering the extent of Konrad de Buys's injuries. Shaking his head, he said, "You will need to see a surgeon." Only when the words were out of his mouth did he realize he had been contemplating the best way to preserve the life of the man who, regardless of whether he had actually fired the fatal shot, had just killed his wife.

"A surgeon?" de Buys scoffed. "D'you think I care to live without my arms? That's what he'd do to me, you know."

"There is no other way to prevent the inevitable suppuration of your wounds—" Lee faltered. His surgeons—his time—knew no such way. The Rivington men might well.

But de Buys said, "Hang me and have done. You'll get round to it soon enough, at all odds." The hungry growls from everyone who heard him attested to the truth of that.

Someone tapped Lee on the back. He spun round. It was Colonel Dimmock, but for the bandsmen one of the lowest-ranking soldiers present. A bullet had clipped off the bottom of his right ear; though that side of his tunic was covered with blood, he seemed unaware he'd been wounded. He held out a weapon to Lee. "This was what those murdering swine were shooting with, sir."

Lee took the—rifle? Even as his mind formed the word, he rejected it. The firearm was too short and stubby to merit the name. It reminded him of nothing so much as an AK-47 that had somehow been washed and left on the line to shrink. Even the metal stock, he discovered, folded around against the body of the piece to save space. The gun weighed next to nothing. He supposed de Buys and his henchmen had carried such weapons exactly because they were easy to conceal until needed.

Though de Buys was seriously injured, he held the gun well away from the Rivington man as he asked, "What do you call this thing?"

"Why should I tell you anything?" de Buys said. Then he spat out a short, sharp fragment of laughter. "But what the hell difference does a name make? It's an—" Lee heard the name as "Oozie." Seeing him frown in perplexity, de Buys amplified, "U-Z-I, named after Uziel Gal, the Israeli who designed it."

"Israeli?" Lee frowned again. "Does that mean Israelite? No, never mind, you needn't answer." He turned to the men who had hold of de Buys. "Take him to jail. Make certain he is securely guarded. If he will not see the surgeon, do not compel him to do so; he will, after all, soon stand trial." The soldiers nodded. Like Lee, they knew de Buys would go up on the gallows shortly after the trial was over.

They turned the Rivington man around and started to march him out of the Hall of Delegates. Only then did Lee see the four or five bullet holes in the back of de Buys's jacket. The man had no business being on his feet, not if he'd taken those hits along with—along with the two that had actually wounded him, Lee thought uneasily. "Wait!" he said.

When he asked de Buys about his seeming invulnerability, the Rivington man smiled a nasty smile and said, "I told you we'd not be easy meat, General Lee." Lee reached out and prodded his belly. It was hard, not with muscle but with metal or wood or something of that sort. Lee knew of no armor proof against rifle bullets. The Rivington men evidently did. No wonder the team of assassins had been so hard to bring down. He began to worry. If the Rivington men all wore it, they would be anything but easy meat.

As if to underscore that concern, fresh firing broke out around the building America Will Break used. In a way, Lee supposed that was good news: it meant more troops were coming up to deal with the Rivington men. But it also meant they had not yet been dealt with.

The guards took Konrad de Buys away. The firing went on and on. A messenger dashed into the Capitol. Seeing Lee, he saluted raggedly and panted, "Marse Robert, them sons of bitches—begging your pardon, sir—they won't give up for hell. We got a lot of men down out there, and I don't know but one of theirs we kilt—son of a whore fell out the window he was shootin' from. Can we bring up artillery to blast 'em out?"

"Whatever is wanted to accomplish the task at hand," Lee replied at once. He ground his teeth. But for skirmishes inside Washington, his soldiers had scant experience fighting within the confines of cities. That did not appear to be true of the men of America Will Break. He thanked God that they were confined to a single building. A few hundred such fighters, especially armored like de Buys, might be able to seize and hold . . . even a town like Richmond. The thought was unpalatable but inescapable. He wondered how many Rivington men Rivington actually held.

Other messengers came in, bringing more word not only of the small battle across from Mechanic's Hall but also of the carnage de Buys and his accomplices had worked. Lee's heart sank with every piece of bad news: Alexander Stephens wounded; Judah Benjamin wounded; John Atkins, his choice to replace John Reagan as Postmaster General, dead; General Jubal Early dead with pistol in hand as he tried to attack the assassins; Jeb Stuart wounded. That last report hurt almost as if it had been one of his own sons. Past the bare fact of the injury, the messenger knew nothing. Lee bent his head and prayed the wound was not severe.

A Napoleon roared, and a moment later another. Lee heard the rending crash of twelve-pound iron roundshot battering masonry. He briefly wondered why the gun crews did not come to closer quarters and blast the Rivington men from their holes with case shot. Then he scorned himself for a fool. Even Springfields could murder an artillery crew that got close enough to fire case shot. Against riflemen with repeaters, the ploy was suicidal.

The brass cannon boomed again, and again, but then they fell silent. Small-arms fire continued. Lee paced the Hall of Delegates chamber like a caged lion, waiting for another messenger to come and let him know what was going on. He wished he could lead from the front, as he had in his U.S. Army days. But that role did not suit a commanding general, much less the President of the Confederate States.

At last a messenger did arrive. Lee all but sprang at him, only to recoil in dismay when he gave his news: "Bastards picked off the gunners faster'n they could serve their pieces, even at long range. They ain't all dead, nothin' like that, but most all of 'em's shot."

Lee groaned. Sharpshooters with telescopes mounted above their rifles might have been able to hit artillerymen at a thousand yards or more, but he hadn't thought AK-47s capable of such work. When he turned away, his eye fell on the—the UZI, de Buys had called it. He shook his head, annoyed at himself again. How could he assume AK-47s were the only guns in the Rivington men's arsenal? The answer was simple but painful: he couldn't.

Rifle fire rose to a new crescendo. Forgetting the dignity and importance of his office, Lee started for the doorway to find out what had happened and to take charge. Colonel Dimmock's bulky body blocked his path. "No, sir," the chief marshal said. "Here you stay till it's over."

"Stand aside," Lee ordered. Dimmock did not move. He outweighed Lee by at least thirty pounds, and even the thought of forcibly shoving him aside reminded Lee that, trapped by his duty, he had to obey the chief marshal. He dipped his head to Dimmock. "I beg your pardon, sir. You are in the right."

But waiting came hard, hard. The rattle of small-arms fire slowed, flared, slowed, flared once more, stopped. When the lull stretched to two minutes, Lee tried pushing past Colonel Dimmock again. Again the colonel refused to yield his place. Lee tossed his head like a man trying to bite his own ear. Dimmock ignored the show of temper. Bare moments later, the gunfire began again. Sighing, Lee apologized again.

A new messenger entered the Hall of Delegates. "Sir, it's a hell of a mess out there. If those Rivington sons of bitches had a clear field of fire all around their damn building, we'd never get close enough to shoot at 'em, all the lead they're throwing around. We had us a little truce to move the wounded a while back—that's what the quiet was. Hope you don't mind that."

"No, by no means," Lee said. "We must do what we can for our men.

Press on with the attack, and since the cover of the surrounding structures is proving our principal advantage, be sure to use it well."

The soldier saluted and hurried away. The gunfire from around the AWB headquarters went on and on. It was nearly sunset when the racket peaked in a few seconds of sustained shooting at full automatic that stopped as abruptly as the fall of a headsman's axe.

When yet another messenger came in, Lee pounced on him. The man looked weary but triumphant, an expression Lee had seen on soldiers since before the Mexican War. "The last of them murderin' creatures is dead," the fellow said. A cheer went up from everyone who heard him. He went on, "We finally got some troops into the building. Took some doin'—them Rivington bastards had the door barricaded so we couldn't noways knock it down. Finally some of our boys made 'em keep their heads down while some more went in through the windows. That distracted 'em, made 'em fight two bunches at once. They died hard, but they's dead."

"God bless you, Corporal," Lee said. The messenger's sleeves were bare of stripes. He looked confused for a second, then grinned enormously. Lee turned to Colonel Dimmock. "With your gracious permission, sir—?" The chief marshal stepped out of the doorway.

Officers and bandsmen formed up around Lee as he went outside. He did not want them, but they refused to go away. After brief annoyance, he decided he could not properly be angry with them: they had their duty, too. For that matter—something he thought of too late, had it been true— the last messenger might have been a Rivington man in disguise, aiming to lure him out of the safety of the Capitol.

He hurried west toward the statue of Washington. Capitol Square had emptied of healthy civilians, save for the doctors who moved from one of the wounded to the next, doing what they could. That, Lee know, was pitifully little. No doubt the Rivington men, with their century and a half of added knowledge, could have given more effective treatment—but had it not been for the Rivington men, none of these poor wretches would have lain here at all. A small tincture of guilt colored Lee's rage: had the people not come out to see and hear him, they would not lie here, either.

A four-wheeled military ambulance clattered eastward. Every bump made the wounded within cry out. Lee bit his lip. At least one of those wounded was a woman. War had spared him at least that horror. Now he met it in allcged peacetime, on what should have been one of the high days of his life.

He called to the ambulance driver, "Are you taking them to General Hospital Number Twelve?"

"No, sir, I got to go on to Chimborazo," the driver said. "Number

Twelve's full up." He clucked to his horses, flicked the reins. The ambulance sped up. So did the cries from inside it. Lee's heart went out to those poor hurt souls. Chimborazo Military Hospital, out on the eastern edge of town, was twice as far from Capitol Square as Military Hospital Number Twelve, which meant they would have twice the jolting journey to endure.

It also meant the butcher's bill in the square was small only by comparison to a stand-up fight during the Second American Revolution. General Hospital Number Twelve could take in more than a hundred people. If it was already filled . . . He wondered just how many wounded had had to go to Chimborazo. He promised himself the Rivington men would pay for every one.

He started to go up to the covered platform on which he'd taken his oath of office, but stopped when he saw the dead and injured had been taken away. Only the bloody rills that ran down the timbers of the front and sides told of the chaos that had reigned here a few hours before.

He wondered where they had taken Mary. He wanted to see her, to say how sorry he was for inviting her up onto the stand, to say good-bye. No time now. He hoped she would know without his telling her. She was often sharp-tempered; with her endless bodily afflictions, who could blame her? But after thirty-seven years, she knew him—had known him, he corrected himself, still not truly believing it in his heart—about as well as one person can know another.

The bodies of the five men who had accompanied Konrad de Buys still lay where they had fallen. They were not a pretty sight. All but one had been shot in the head; the sole exception, who looked absurdly peaceful by comparison to his comrades, had bled to death from a thigh wound.

Rips in coats and shirts told of other rounds that had struck without doing damage. Lee's lips thinned—they'd all been armored like de Buys. No wonder they'd been so hard to bring down. With that armor, maybe they'd thought they could escape once they'd done their murderous work. If so, they'd proved mistaken, there as elsewhere.

None of the assassins still gripped his UZI. Lee hoped that meant the guns had been taken to someone responsible—with luck, to Josiah Gorgas, who would no doubt be delighted to have such fascinating new toys to play with. And if not, well, if not, a thief would be able to use the UZIs only until they ran out of ammunition.

"Where now, sir?" one of the bandsmen asked when Lee shifted his direction again.

"To the offices of America Will Break," he said in a voice like stone.

The corner of Franklin and Ninth was another scene whose like Lee had not known since the war. As in Capitol Square, physicians and ambulances swarmed liked bees. Bullet holes scarred and pitted the face of Mechanic's Hall. A Confederate soldier shot through the head hung half in, half out of one window. Across the street was an identically dead, identically placed Rivington man.

The headquarters of America Will Break had taken far worse damage than Mechanic's Hall; the twelve-pounder shot had blown several gaping holes in its brick and marble front. *Only blind luck the building didn't go up in flames*, Lee thought. Fire spread so easily and was so hard to fight. He remembered the charred Richmond of the *Picture History of the Civil War*, and had to shiver. That disaster could have happened here.

He pointed to the roof, above which the red, white, and black AWB flag still flew. "Someone cut that down at once."

A couple of soldiers hurried off to do his bidding. One of them said, "We ought to save it with our captured Yankee battle flags." That had not occurred to Lee; he'd simply wanted the hateful banner cast on the rubbish heap. But the soldier had a point. The Confederacy had won a battle here, but the cost, the cost . . .

Lee followed the men into the building, looked around curiously. Part of the curiosity sprang from his never having been here before; the Rivington men had come to him rather than he to them. But some of his curiosity was also professional: here he had the chance to learn what hard combat inside a building did to it. He shook his head, not liking what he saw.

The trail of blood and crumpled bodies led him to the suite of offices America Will Break had used. Corpses in Confederate gray far outnumbered those in mottled green; the Rivington men had fought like devils— or perhaps they had simply preferred dying in action to the gallows. Brass cartridge cases clinked, an incongruously cheerful sound, as Lee kicked them out of his path.

A door had painted upon it AMERICA WILL BREAK and the organization's three-pronged insignia. Lee stepped over two bodies in gray and one in green, walked inside. The fellow whose head and torso he had seen from the street had fought from a window here. Bullets had chewed up the wall opposite that window; the picture that hung there was no longer recognizable.

One of the bandsmen who guarded Lee looked around and said, "Take away the dead men and it ain't so very peculiar, is it?"

He was right; shorn of carnage, the offices of America Will Break might have housed any fair-sized business or trading establishment. Lee did not know quite what he'd expected. Perhaps, knowing what he knew about the Rivington men, he'd looked for the future to have impinged more visibly on their operation. But the desks, the chairs, the cabinets full of papers here seemed at first glance no different from those in the War Department across the street. Those papers would have to be examined, of course, but their home appeared utterly ordinary.

"You'd reckon anybody nasty enough to do what these bastards done ought to have a place that looks worse'n this," the guard went on.

"That's so," Lee said thoughtfully. The bandsman, whose every word declared his lack of education, had nonetheless touched an important truth. Evil, to Lee's way of looking at things, ought to declare itself openly, to appear as foul as it was in fact. But the headquarters of America Will Break, a group that stopped at nothing, not even indiscriminate murder, to achieve its ends, had for the eye, at least, no taint. Somehow the semblance of normality made even worse the evil it contained.

Lee strode from room to room within the suite. All the furnishings were like those of the chamber through which he'd entered, which is to say, unmemorable. But unmemorable men could not have plotted such hideously memorable deeds.

At last Lee came to a door before which several soldiers stood. "It's locked, sir," one said. "We put a shoulder to it, but it don't want to move."

Excitement flowered within Lee—was this the Rivington men's sanctum sanctorum? "Send for a locksmith, then, if you have not already done so," he said. The soldier hurried away. Lee examined the doorknob. Here at last was something unfamiliar: its shape was like none he had ever seen. He wondered what luck the locksmith would have with it. The door was painted with a smooth coat of gray enamel. He rapped it. It was metallically cold, metallically hard, and gave not at all.

Jingling with tools, the locksmith arrived around half past six, and set to work at once. Five days later, despite his efforts, those of the best burglar in Richmond (released from jail to test his expertise), and a team of men armed with a stout ram, the door remained closed.

Once more, Lee found himself awash in telegrams. He would willingly have forgone the flood of sympathy, and indeed, were it possible, would have forgone the telegrams that had announced his election and set in train that bloody March 4.

From the flood, though, came a few messages he cherished. One, from Springfield, Illinois, in the U.S.A., said simply,

MAY GOD BE WITH YOU AND YOUR COUNTRY IN YOUR HOUR OF SORROW. YOU ARE IN MY PRAYERS. The printed signature read, A. LINCOLN.

Another came from Clarksdale, Mississippi:

REQUEST YOUR KIND PERMISSION TO RESCIND MY RESIG-
NATION FROM CONFEDERATE STATES CAVALRY SO I CAN
LEAD AGAINST THE MURDERERS WHO WOULD SET AT
NAUGHT OUR REPUBLIC AND ITS INSTITUTIONS—N. B. FOR-
REST.

"How shall I respond to this one from Forrest, sir?" asked Charles
Marshall, who had resumed his wartime post as Lee's aide. By his tone,
he wanted nothing to do with the Patriot leader.

But Lee said, "Answer, 'Your country is ever grateful for your service,
Lieutenant General Forrest.' He and I may fail to see eye-to-eye on a great
many issues, but hypocrisy has never been numbered among his vices.
And against the men of America Will Break, I fear we may need the most
able military talent available to us. Do you deny Forrest's native gifts along
those lines?" Marshall shook his head, but his mouth was set in a narrow
line of disapproval as he wrote down Lee's reply and took it to the telegraph
office.

That afternoon, Lee endured his wife's funeral service. Bishop Johns,
one arm in a sling from the wound he himself had taken up on the platform,
spoke of how all-wise Providence had summoned Mary from the world of
men, of how her spirit yet lived and would continue to inspire everyone
who had known her thanks to the courage with which she had faced ad-
versity, of her unshaken confidence in God as her hope and strength, which
all would do well to emulate.

Lee believed with his whole being every word the Right Reverend Johns
spoke, yet the oration brought less comfort than it should have, serving
instead to tear off the scab which had begun to grow over his grief. He
wept, unashamed, as a hearse drawn by six black horses took his wife's
coffin to the Richmond, Fredericksburg and Potomac Railroad depot to
start its final journey to Arlington. He knew she would never have forgiven
him for interring her anywhere else.

A lieutenant came up to him as he was leaving St. Paul's Church. "I
beg your pardon, sir, for disturbing you at such a time, but your orders
were to be informed the moment we succeeded in entering that sealed
chamber. We have just done so."

"Thank you, young man. Yes, I shall go there at once. Have you a
carriage?"

"Yes, sir. If you will follow me—" The lieutenant drove Lee east on

Broad to Ninth, and then down the western side of Capitol Square to the building that had sheltered America Will Break. When he swung right onto Franklin, Lee pointed and exclaimed. The lieutenant chuckled. "We took a leaf from your book, sir. Since that damned door—I beg your pardon again—defeated our every frontal assault, we decided to outflank it."

A ladder leaned against the side of the building. Several masons in grimy overalls stood at the base of the wall. One still held a mallet and chisel. Crowbars and pry bars, along with chunks of stone and broken brick, lay on the sidewalk. They'd broken a hole in the wall big enough for a man to crawl though.

"Has anyone gone in yet?" Lee asked. When the lieutenant shook his head, Lee descended from the carriage and hurried toward the ladder.

The lieutenant sprang down, too, and got in front of him. With the self-conscious voice junior officers use when dressing down their superiors, he said, "With your permission, sir, I shall precede you, in case the Rivington men"—*men* was not the word he used—"have placed a torpedo or some other infernal device in there."

Lee considered that, reluctantly nodded. His courage was not at issue here, and his duty to his country was. "Very well, Lieutenant; carry on."

The young soldier swarmed up the ladder, disappeared into the inky hole. Lee waited with barely contained worry and impatience until he stuck his head out again. "Seems safe enough, sir, though I tripped over a chair and damn near broke my fool neck. Can you bring a lantern up with you? It's still almighty dark inside."

A soldier darted into the War Department across the street, came out with a lantern which he handed to Lee. He and a couple of the masons steadied the ladder while Lee ascended. Lee was simultaneously grateful and offended: they hadn't offered the spry young lieutenant any such assistance. How decrepit did they think he was?

At the top of the climb, the lieutenant took the lantern from him, then helped him through the hole. He held the flickering light on high while Lee got to his feet. Its faint yellow beams and the gray light that came through the hole in the outer wall told Lee at once that America Will Break truly did not belong to 1868, or any year close to it.

"Metal," he muttered. "Everything metal." The desks, the cabinets, the bookcases against the walls, the swivel chairs, all were painted metal, like the impenetrable door that had so long defeated everything the Confederacy threw at it. On this side, he noticed, that door was set well into the wall. Its inner surface was not painted at all, only polished, and cast back at Lee the light the lantern shed upon it.

Above one of the cabinets, a low one, hung a poster blazoned with the emblem of America Will Break. Above the insignia stood the AWB initials Lee had first seen on Andries Rhoodie's coffee mug in camp above Orange Court House. He wondered where Rhoodie was. The big man had not died on March 4, nor had he been at his house when soldiers came that evening, armed with a warrant and with AK-47s set on full automatic. That worried Lee—this side of Bedford Forrest, Rhoodie was as dangerous a man as he could think of.

Below the three bent spikes in their circle stood a pair of unfamiliar words: AFRIKANER WEERSTANDSBEWEGING, and below them, in smaller letters, AFRIKANER RESISTANCE MOVEMENT. Lee cocked his head. He wondered what an Afrikaner was—not an African, certainly, not by the way the Rivington men treated Negroes—and whether the name betokened resistance against Afrikaners, whatever they were, or by them.

He deliberately turned away from the poster, refusing to let inessentials sidetrack him. He walked over to the polished metal door, set his hand on the knob. The lieutenant dashed up and tried to turn it for him. This time, he refused to yield his place. The men on the other side of that door had done everything but fire a Napoleon at it—and they'd contemplated that, desisting only for fear of damaging the room the door guarded. Were it hooked to a torpedo, they surely would have set off the explosive charge.

He worked the knob. It did not turn smoothly—the Confederates had managed that much, at any rate, in their efforts to force it—but it turned. The door was heavy. Lee had to exert his full strength to pull it back, and the massive hinges squealed in protest as he did so, but it opened. A couple of officers standing on the other side stared at him, then grinned and began to clap.

Their applause was joined by another noise, a low, throaty rumble, that began as soon as the door swung wide. They stopped clapping. The rumble went on. Looking about for its source, Lee decided after a few seconds that it was somehow coming from *within* the thickened wall. It sounded mechanical, though not really like a steam engine. He wondered why anyone would want to conceal something mechanical inside a wall.

Behind him, in the hidden chamber, the lieutenant cried out. He whirled, wondering what trap the youngster had sprung. He saw no trap, only the lieutenant's startled face. He saw that very clearly, for several long, thin tubes mounted on the ceiling—he'd not noticed them before; who notices ceilings?—had suddenly started shedding a fine, white light that illuminated the room as well as hazy sunshine might have.

"What on earth—?" the lieutenant said.

Lee did not know what on earth, either, though after a moment's reflection he supposed he should not have been surprised the Rivington men enjoyed better lamps even than gaslight. But understanding all their tricks was another inessential now. The shining tubes let him read the titles of the volumes that packed these secret bookshelves. As soon as he saw the *Picture History of the Civil War* was one of them, the shelves drew him like a lodestone.

He ran a finger lightly down the spine of the *Picture History*, as if to reassure himself it was real. Somehow, finding a second copy of it was far more than twice as strange as finding only one. One was an isolated curiosity, a *liber ex machina*. But where there were two, there had to be hundreds, thousands. All at once, the distant time from which the men of the AWB had come felt nearly close enough for him to touch.

And that *Picture History* proved to be but one of hundreds of books about the Second American Revolution, though they called it the Civil War, or the War Between the States, or occasionally the Great Rebellion. He found memoirs by Joe Johnston, by U. S. Grant, by Jefferson Davis—he shook his head when he saw Davis's were called *The Rise and Fall of the Confederate Nation*—by Jubal Early. He shook his head again; he'd gone to Early's funeral yesterday and knew his former division commander had written no memoirs. Nor, for that matter, had Johnston or Grant or Davis.

He also found studies on the battle of the Wilderness; on Confederate railroads; on black–white relations, North and South, before, during, and after the Second American Revolution; and on Confederate Richmond— one, he saw with wry amusement, was called *General Lee's City*. The amusement slipped when he pulled the book off the shelf and saw on its cover Richmond in flames. He opened the book, discovered it had been published—would be published? would have been published?—in 1987. He also noted that its author was one Richard M. Lee, and wondered if the man was a descendant. If he was, he had an impartiality Robert E. Lee approved of, for he also seemed to have written a book named *Mr. Lincoln's City*.

Lee put the book back in its place. It stood near half a shelf of volumes that looked to be devoted exclusively to him. He left them alone. He already knew who he was. The Rivington men, for all their reference works, plainly did not.

Along with the books on the Confederacy, Lee found several shelves of volumes on South Africa—not a country, so far as he knew, that appeared on the globe in 1868. Some had their titles written in English, but more in the German-looking language that had also produced the phrase *Afrikaner Weerstandsbeweging*.

It was not German. That had been Lee's first guess, when papers written in it turned up in the files of the AWB outer offices. But a professor of

German summoned from the Virginia Military Institute had taken one look and gone back to VMI with his tail between his legs. Lee did not let failure frustrate him—and where the professor gave up, a Richmond merchant, a Jew from Aachen, was able to make fair sense of the AWB's private tongue.

Lee stuck his head out the door, asked the two soldiers in the adjoining room, "Is Mr. Goldfarb anywhere about?"

"Yes, sir, I saw him next door," said one of them, a captain. He turned to his companion. "You want to go and fetch him in here, Fred?"

Fred, who was a lieutenant, went and fetched him. Avram Goldfarb was a medium-sized, heavyset man in his fifties, with curly gray hair and a curly gray beard long enough to obviate any need for a cravat. His nose was more distinctly Hebraic than that of Judah P. Benjamin, and his eyes . . . when Lee looked into those dark, deep-set eyes, he gained a more profound understanding of the Book of Jeremiah than he had enjoyed before. Avram Goldfarb had seen sorrow, for himself and for his folk.

He dipped his head to Lee. "You've found more papers in this *verkakte* tongue for me to read, sir?" At Lee's nod, he rolled those sorrowful eyes. "I will do my best, even if it makes me crazy. This speech, it is not *Deutsch*—German, you would say—it is not Dutch, as I should know, since Aachen lies by the border and before '48 I did as much trade with Amsterdam as with Cologne . . . But enough. This speech, it is not quite anything. It is, you would say in English, a mishmash."

Lee was not sure he would say that, but he got the idea. He stood aside to let Goldfarb into the secret chamber. The Jew blinked when he noticed the extraordinary ceiling lights, but Lee gave him no time to ponder them. He pulled out a book that had *Akrikaner Weerstandsbeweging* in its title, hoping it would tell him more about the AWB.

"*The African Resistance Movement: What It Is*, by Eugen Blankaard," Goldfarb read.

" 'African'?" Lee pointed to the poster on the wall.

"Afrikaner, then," Goldfarb said, shrugging, "whatever an Afrikaner may be." He opened the book to the frontispiece, an arresting photograph of a stalwart young man, his right arm upraised, his left hand on a Bible, standing blindfolded in front of what looked like a firing squad armed with AK-47s. There were a few lines of text under the photograph. Goldfarb translated them: "If I advance, follow me. If I retreat, shoot me. If I die, avenge me. So help me God . . ."

It was not the oath of a group that did anything by halves. Lee let air hiss out through his nose; to his sorrow, he already knew that. Whatever Goldfarb thought of it, his face revealed nothing. He turned the page, then startled Lee by starting to laugh. He pointed to the copyright page. "The printer must have been drunk, sir, and the proofreader too, or someone would have noticed this says the book was made in 2004." He laughed again, louder this time.

"Mr. Goldfarb," Lee said seriously, "I suggest you never speak of this, ah, error to anyone save me. Please believe me when I tell you I make this suggestion for your own safety."

The Jew studied him, saw he meant what he said. Slowly, he nodded. "I will do as you say, sir. Now to the—is *foreword* an English word?"

"The preface, perhaps," Lee said after a moment's thought.

"The preface. Thank you. I begin: 'More than half a *Jahrhundert*'— excuse me, a century—'ago, during the Second Worldwar—' " He said it like that, as if it were one word, so Lee needed a second to understand and another to start to imagine what it meant, but Goldfarb was already going on: " 'a great man, Koot Vorster, said, "Hitler's *My Struggle* shows the way to greatness, the way to South Africa. Hitler gave the Germans a calling. He gave them a fanaticism which causes them to stand back for no one. We must follow this example because only by such fanaticism can the Afrikaner nation achieve its calling." ' " Goldfarb looked to Lee. "This, to me, is nonsense. Do you wish me to go on with it?"

Lee did not understand the historical references either, but he knew that was because the history in question had yet to happen. He also got a stronger feeling for the way the AWB thought: fanaticism, to his way of thinking, was no virtue, yet the Rivington men plainly considered it one. He said, "Please do continue, Mr. Goldfarb."

"If you like." Goldfarb cleared his throat and went on: " 'But no one— hmm—heeded Vorster.' I am sorry, sir, but this is Dutch spelled as if the devil had written it, and I must sometimes guess what it means. 'South Africa threw in with England, and Hitler and Germany were beaten—and so was South Africa. Now we whites are prisoners in our own country, ruined by stupid, evil laws that make all men alike, regardless of their color. Those who cursed our land with these laws call themselves liberal, but they lie. They call us outlaws. We take pride in the name, and call them fools. They have been seduced by outlanders and outlanders' ways, and we will no more stand for it. White power shall yet rise again, and put the kaffir'—I do not know what a kaffir is, I am sorry—'back down into his proper place. The rest of the world be damned, say I. So say we all.' "

"They *are* a tiny group of radicals, then," Lee breathed. Goldfarb gave him a curious look. He took no notice of it.

"Shall I go on?" Goldfarb asked.

"Wait." Lee was thinking hard. If mankind's opinion—"the rest of the world," Blankaard had written—had decisively turned against these self-admitted Afrikaner outlaws a hundred fifty years ahead, then what better, more logical reason for their return to the Confederacy than an effort to build another nation that favored "white power" to become South Africa's friend and collaborator in a changed future? Rhoodie had said as much, and everything the Rivington men had done here fit in with that goal.

The Confederate States of America had not been formed for outlawry: just the reverse. That alone would have made Lee oppose the AWB with everything he had. But the men from the future had given him other reasons. He heard again Bishop Johns's prayers over Mary's casket. "They shall not have their way."

"Sir?" Goldfarb asked.

"Never mind," Lee said. "No, you need go no farther in that book now; I have heard enough."

"Yes, sir." Goldfarb slapped the volume closed, stared all around. "What a strange place," he said, to which Lee could only nod. Goldfarb pointed to an object—Lee knew no better word for it—on one of the desks. "What is that thing, for instance?"

"I cannot tell you, Mr. Goldfarb, for I do not know." Lee had curiously tapped the artifact in question a couple of times himself, as he walked back and forth past it. Its main piece was shaped like a box, taller than it was deep, but it had a thin metal tube projecting upward from one corner of the top. A spiral cord joined the boxlike part to another one which was small enough to be held in the hand.

The front of the boxlike part was covered with switches and knobs. One said ON-OFF. Lee flicked it from the latter to the former. A light went on in the glassed-in upper part of the box. A low hiss, rather like distant surf but more steady, came from a metal-covered grill. Lee moved the switch back to OFF. The light went out; the noise faded and was gone.

"I've never seen anything like that before," Goldfarb said, "but what is it good for?"

"Again, I do not know," Lee answered, though the AWB men doubtless did.

"Or what about this other thing next to it?"

"Still another mystery, I am afraid." Lee ran his hand over the gadget close by the one that hissed. It was hard, but did not feel to the finger like metal, wood, or glass—though glass did seem to cover the large, dark, greenish square that dominated the center of the oyster-gray, upright cabinet.

Connected to that small cabinet by another spiral cord was a low, flat box with letters, numbers, and symbols printed onto upraised studs. For no reason Lee could fathom, the letters were scrambled, and there were two sets of numbered studs, one above the top row of letters, the other off to the right by itself. He poked a couple of studs. They clicked and went down under the pressure of his touch, but otherwise did nothing.

"Maybe it is a qwerty," Goldfarb said, pointing to the nonsense word formed by part of one row of letters.

"Maybe it is," Lee said, quite seriously. Then he pointed, too, at the words beside the sole decoration on the otherwise severely functional device: a stylized apple with rainbow stripes and a bite taken out of one side. "Or maybe it's a Macintosh IVQL."

"I wonder what it is for," Goldfarb said.

"So do I." Lee turned away from the qwerty—he liked the merchant's suggestion better than his own—and found another book with *Afrikaner Weerstandsbeweging* on the spine. "Tell me what this one contains, Mr. Goldfarb, if you would be so kind."

⋆ XVII ⋆

Judge Cornelius Joyner nailed a sheet of paper to the notice board in front of the Nash County courthouse. To Nate Caudell, who watched from the middle of a crowd of silent, grim-faced people, each stroke of the hammer sounded like a bullet slamming home. He squeezed Mollie Bean's hand. She squeezed back, hard enough to hurt.

The justice of the peace tossed aside the hammer. The thump it made against the damp ground reminded Caudell of a dead body falling. He sternly reined in his runaway imagination. Judge Joyner turned and faced the men and women who packed the square. "I know not all of you have your letters, so I'm going to read this out loud for you. You'd best listen and pay heed, too."

He turned back to the notice he'd just posted. His deep voice was big enough that Caudell had no trouble hearing him: "The following proclamation is published for the information of all concerned: By virtue of the power vested in men by law to declare the suspension of the privilege of the writ of *habeas corpus* in regions threatened by rebellion: I, Robert E. Lee, President of the Confederate States of America, do proclaim that martial law is hereby extended over the counties of Nash, Edgecombe, Halifax, Franklin, and Warren (in North Carolina), and I do proclaim the suspension of all civil jurisdiction (with the exception of that enabling the courts to take cognizance of the probate of wills, the administration of the estates of deceased persons, the qualification of guardians, to enter decrees and orders for the partition and sale of property, to make orders concerning roads and bridges, to assess county levies, and to order the payment of county dues), and the suspension of the writ of *habeas corpus* in the counties aforesaid. In faith whereof I have hereby signed my name and set my seal this fifteenth day of March, in the year 1868. Robert E. Lee."

Caudell added his sigh to the dozens that went up around him. Read all at once, as Joyner had read it, the proclamation felt like a boulder rolling over him. He hung his head in shame at having his home country branded throughout the South as a "region threatened by rebellion"—but then, Rivington lay within Nash County. Till word came down of what people were calling the Richmond Massacre, he'd been mildly proud to have Rivington close by, no matter what he thought of some of the men who'd settled there. Now he wished the place were on the far side of the moon.

Judge Joyner said, "Don't go away yet, folks. There's more." He raised his voice again: "Lieutenant General Forrest, commanding Confederate States forces in eastern North Carolina, is charged with due execution of the foregoing proclamation. He will forthwith establish an efficient military police and will enforce the following orders: All distillation of spirituous liquors is positively prohibited, and the distilleries will forthwith be closed. The sale of spirituous liquors of any kind is also prohibited, and establishments for the sale thereof will be closed."

Now the noises that rose from the crowd sounded more like mutters than sighs. Most of the grumbles came from farmers who were used to turning part of their corn into whiskey. The Liberty Bell saloon had a shiny new padlock on the front door, though Caudell suspected that would not keep Wren Tisdale from selling a spirituous liquor or two out the back.

"I'm not done," Cornelius Joyner warned. "You all had better listen to this: "All persons infringing the above prohibition will suffer such punishment as shall be ordered by the sentence of a court-martial, provided that no sentence to hard labor be for more than one month by the sentence of a regimental court-martial, as directed by the Sixty-Seventh Article of War. By command of the Secretary of War. S. Cooper, Adjutant and Inspector General."

"A month working on the roads for selling a man a drink?" Raeford Liles said. "I don't believe it."

"You'd better," Caudell warned him. "That's just what you could draw from a regimental court. If they haul you before Forrest, now—" He let the words hang. Liles turned a faint green. Having met the new Confederate commander for eastern North Carolina, he figured *he* might hang if he violated an order Forrest was charged with enforcing.

Judge Joyner picked up his hammer and stood aside. George Lewis stepped out of the front row of the crowd to take his place. Lewis wore a gray civilian jacket and a shirt to which a three-barred stand collar had been hastily sewn. *Must be none of his old uniforms fits anymore*, Caudell thought, smiling a little.

Lewis said, "I am ordered by General Forrest, and authorized by Governor Vance, to recall to duty Company D, 47th North Carolina Infantry, for a period not to exceed 180 days, said company to serve as military police for Nash County and perform such other duties as may be duly assigned by proper military authority."

Mollie squeezed Nate's hand again. He wondered if that meant she intended to rejoin the Castalia Invincibles herself. He was afraid it did. She'd returned from Richmond wearing a wig that nearly matched the dark curls he'd shorn so she could go there in disguise. She wore it in public all the time. If she took it off, she could easily play the man once more.

Caudell wished she wouldn't. The two of them had stayed together since she'd got back from Richmond. He feared she would take up her old ways if she found herself among so many men. But he feared even more that she would be hurt or killed if she took up a rifle again. His memories of combat were too recent and too horribly vivid for him to make light of its risks, as he had before he signed up with the Invincibles in 1862.

But if she wanted to put the uniform back on, how the devil was he supposed to stop her?

Lost in his own worries, he'd missed some of what Lewis was saying. He started listening again: "—report here for duty tomorrow at noon. Wear your uniforms if you have them still; we'll give out armbands to everyone who doesn't. And we'll furnish weapons."

"Repeaters?" someone asked eagerly.

"That's right. If you're going to soldier, you'll carry soldiers' weapons. I said that loud and clear down in Raleigh." Lewis puffed out his already massive chest, as if to say it was only through his political pull that the Castalia Invincibles had obtained AK-47s. More power to him if that was so, Caudell thought. Lewis went on, "Get word to anybody you know who lives in the county but isn't here in town today. We may give a few days' grace, but we won't stand for deserters."

Caudell stuck up a hand. Lewis pointed at him. He said, "What do we do if we run into Rivington men? God only knows what's going on north of here. That proclamation's dated the fifteenth, but here it is the twenty-sixth, and it's only just now got here."

"I know it." George Lewis's face was rounder now than when he'd last led the Castalia Invincibles, but no less determined. "We aren't called up to go after the Rivington men; we're supposed to be military police. But if you see one of the bastards, shoot him. They've wrecked the railroad track up near Weldon, and they've torn down all the telegraph lines they can get to. Far as I can see, Nate, we've got ourselves a little war here."

All through the town square, heads bobbed up and down. Nate nodded with the rest. As far as he could see, it looked like a little war, too. Probably the only thing keeping it from turning into a big war was that there weren't enough Rivington men to make it one. But even a few would be ungodly hard to get rid of. Uneasily, he remembered the armor Benny Lang had worn under his mottled clothes. It had turned a Minié ball; would it stop a round from an AK-47? He had no way of knowing, but he thought it likely.

Lewis waved to show he was done. Cornelius Joyner went back inside the courthouse. Singly and by small groups, people began drifting out of the square, talking as they went. Caudell started to say something to Mollie. She beat him to it: "I already know what you're gonna tell me, Nate. I don't wanna have to hear it."

He spread his hands in front of him. "But, Mollie, it isn't right. It—"

"Why ain't it? I'm as good a soldier as any o' them others, ain't I?" Her voice was low but very determined. "You know damn well I am, Mister Nate Caudell. 'Sides, I reckon all this is part my fault—leastways, Marse Robert made an almighty much about that book I brung him. That was your idea, too, remember? Wouldn't hardly be right, makin' a mess and then not helpin' put it back together."

"But—" Caudell kicked helplessly at the dirt. Mollie had ruined half the argument he'd had in mind, but only half. Trouble was, he knew no safe way to say the other half.

Mollie did it for him. "You're worried I'll go back to whorin' again, I reckon," she said. He could only nod. He felt his face grow red. Mollie shrugged. "Can't say for certain I won't. But if I do, Nate, then you won't have to have nothin' more to do with me, an' that'll be that." She set her hand on his arm. "I don't want it to end that way, I swear I don't."

"I don't, either. It's just—oh, hell." Caudell kicked the dirt again. Foolish to take chances, he thought—would you use a one-time drunk to guard a whiskey barrel? Well, maybe, if you were sure he'd changed his ways. Was he sure about Mollie? He knew he wasn't, and knew he couldn't say so, not unless he wanted to kill the still-fragile bond between them.

He also knew he had only to say a couple of words to Captain Lewis to keep her out of the muster . . . but that would cost him Mollie, too. He scowled fiercely, first at the street and then at Mollie. She wrinkled her nose in reply. "Hell of a thing," he said.

"What's that?"

"Here I am not even back in the army yet, and I've already lost a fight."

The tunic with the first sergeant's stripes still fit. It was ragged, but it had been ragged four years ago, too. Caudell wore one of his regular pairs of pants and his black felt hat. He laughed at himself as he headed for the square. He didn't look much different from the way he had when he'd got home from the war. No, come to think of it, he'd been missing a hat then.

Some of the men who joined him in front of the courthouse still had their old tunics, some didn't. Only one or two wore proper forage caps. They were a motley band, but hardly more so, Caudell reflected, than when they'd paraded through Richmond in triumph.

The men stood around in little groups, talking about fights they'd seen. George Lewis walked through the square, exchanging banter with them and checking their names off on a list. Not far from Caudell, he paused in perplexity. "I don't recall your serving with the 47th, sir."

Henry Pleasants grinned at him. "No reason you should, Captain. I was with the 48th—48th Pennsylvania, that is." He tapped the silver oak leaf on the Union shoulder strap he'd sewn to his checked flannel shirt.

Lewis's eyes widened. He could read Northern badges of rank, though they differed from those the Confederacy used. Quietly, he said, "I mean you no disrespect, Lieutenant Colonel—you're Pleasants, aren't you? I've heard of you—but only those who served with the Castalia Invincibles have been summoned to duty."

"I don't claim the rank, Captain Lewis, nor seek to raise trouble," Pleasants said. "I would happily join you as a private, so long as I may join. This is my country now, and Lee my President—and if anyone tries to foully murder him, how may I call myself a man unless I help hunt the villains out?"

"Hmm." Lewis rubbed his chin. "You speak smoothly enough, that's certain. Did you command that regiment?"

"Till Bealeton, yes, but as I say, I know I have no rank in the Confederate army." Pleasants waved his hand. "Put it to your other men. If they say no, I'll go home and tend my farm. If they say yes, you'll have one more soldier.''

Like most regiments raised to fight in the Second American Revolution, the 47th North Carolina had always done without much military formality. "By God, I'll do just that," Lewis said. He raised his voice: "Invincibles, shall we admit to our number Henry—it is Henry, isn't it?—Pleasants, who had the misfortune to spend the war wearing a blue coat rather than our good Confederate gray?"

Nate Caudell spoke up at once: "Hell, yes, let him in. If he's crazy enough to want to live here, he'll fit right into this company."

"Thanks, Nate—I think," Pleasants said, laughing.

"Sure, let him in," Dempsey Eure said. "The more we have, the less for each of us to do." Four years of peace had not diluted his soldier's pragmatism.

But Kennel Tant shook his head. "Don't want to let no damn Yankees into this here company." Several other Invincibles echoed that, some of them profanely.

The men argued back and forth for a few minutes. Then George Lewis said, "All right, we'll have a show of hands. All those for letting Henry Pleasants join us—? Those against—?" Looking around, Caudell saw that Pleasants had won the vote. Lewis saw the same thing. He turned to Pleasants. "All right, Private, I'll put your name on the list." More softly, he added, "I may pick your brains every so often, too."

Henry Pleasants came to attention, saluted. "As the Captain wishes."

"You're under my orders too now, Henry," Caudell said, touching the stripes on his sleeve.

"Now *there's* an appalling notion," Pleasants said with an exaggerated shiver. "Captain Lewis, may I please reconsider?"

"I've already written your name. Do you want me to have to scratch it out and make my list untidy?"

"Oh, I suppose not," Pleasants allowed. "Just keep me away from this wild man here."

"I love you too, Henry," Caudell said. He might have gone on teasing with his friend, but suddenly he had no heart for it. Mollie Bean had just walked into the square. She was wearing gray.

Caudell hoped someone, anyone, would speak up and greet her by her right name. It would take only one voice. Then Captain Lewis would have to send her away, and she would stay safe. Several of the men who lived in town stared first at Mollie, then at Caudell. They knew the two of them had taken up with each other. But no one said a word.

Mollie went up to Lewis, gave him a crisp salute. "Melvin Bean reportin',
sir."

"Bean." He went down his list, checked off the name. Then he took a
longer look at her, snorted laughter. "Good God, Bean, haven't you managed to raise a beard *yet*?"

Several Invincibles let out strangled coughs. Mollie turned red.

Hope soared in Nate. Then he saw that George Lewis's plump cheeks
were on the pink side, too. *Why, you son of a bitch*, he thought—*you've
known all along*. The only thing Lewis might not have known, since he'd
spent most of the time since the war down in Raleigh, was that Mollie and
Caudell were together.

Now, though, something about Mollie besides her smooth cheeks caught
the captain's notice. "It says here you're from Rivington."

"Yes, sir, that's so," she said, nodding.

"You're about the only one from the company who is. I'll make you
acting corporal, put you next in charge of skirmishers after Nate here. Most
of the fighting right now is north of Rivington, but along with breaking up
stills and such, I want us to see how closely we can approach the town
from this direction. Maybe Forrest will want to hit the Rivington men two
ways at once, and that's something he'll need to know. Does that suit you?"

"Yes, sir." She walked over to stand by Caudell, grinned up at him.
"That suits me right fine." If Lewis hadn't known they were together, he
did now.

Nate wanted to kick her. He wanted to pick her up and shake her, to
see if he could get some sense into her that way. He wanted to laugh and
cry at the same time. Captain Lewis had ordered the two of them to work
together, which was wonderful. But he'd also given them the most dangerous job the company would have to do, a job that wasn't even properly its
responsibility. Caudell wondered if he ought to squawk about that. He
ended up just standing there, feeling foolish.

He saw more than one soldier eyeing the way Mollie stayed at his side.
He hoped they got the message she wasn't available—and he hoped she
wasn't. Maybe, he thought hopefully, jealousy would make someone give
her away and force Captain Lewis to notice officially that she was a woman.
But no one said a word.

Lewis said, "Come on inside the courthouse and get your rifles."

Dempsey Eure whooped. "I'd sooner get my hands on a repeater again
than—damn near anything." He was looking at Mollie, too, but with a
twinkle in his eye that made it impossible for Caudell to get angry at him.

The AK-47s leaned against the courthouse wall in a row neater than the

Castalia Invincibles were likely to form. Cornelius Joyner, an Invincible himself, stood guard over them with a pistol. One by one, Lewis handed each of his men a rifle and three banana clips heavy with cartridges.

Caudell hadn't touched a firearm since he left the army. His hands, he discovered, still knew what to do. The smell of oil and metal and powder that came from the rifle, the sensuously mechanical glide of the charging handle as he pushed it back to expose the open chamber, made him see the army's old Virginia campground almost as vividly as he did the courthouse where he stood. By the murmurs that rose from his comrades, they also had memories flooding back.

The only memories Henry Pleasants had of AK-47s were unpleasant ones. "I'm glad I'll be on the right end of one of these things for a change," he said. "Somebody'll have to show me what to do with it, though."

"Easy enough to learn." Dempsey Eure had mischief in his voice. "Especially getting the bolt back in."

"I have a feeling, Sergeant, that you're trying to lead me down the primrose path," Pleasants said.

"Me?" Eure was the picture of affronted innocence.

"Sir, if you like, I'll take Henry with me and teach him what he needs to know," Caudell said to Captain Lewis.

"All right," Lewis said. "Teach him quickly, though. You, Bean, and the rest of a squad will head up toward Rivington tomorrow morning. Check the farms you come across, certainly, but I want to know where the Rivington men have their pickets out. As I said before, that's important military information. Send a man back with the word before sunset tomorrow, or at once if you come under fire."

"Yes, sir." Caudell knew Lewis was giving him the option of using Henry Pleasants as his messenger if the Pennsylvanian had trouble getting the hang of the AK-47. Maybe he would do that. On the other hand, if bullets started flying, maybe he would send Mollie Bean back to Nashville to tell Lewis what they'd run into. She wouldn't like that, but she would have to go: she was only acting corporal, while he was a first sergeant.

The conclusion would have made him happier if he'd managed to forget how free and easy Confederate soldiers were apt to be about obeying orders they didn't care for.

"There's nothin' you could call a straight road between here and Rivington," Mollie said early the next morning. The smell of brewing coffee took Caudell back to the war, though this cup came from the Liberty Bell instead of being hastily cooked above a little campfire.

Henry Pleasants methodically stripped his AK-47, reassembled it, then stripped it again. "This is an astonishing weapon," he said, the third time he'd said that this morning and at least the dozenth since he'd got the rifle. "Whoever invented it was a genius, to get so many new things right and put them all together." He'd said that about a dozen times, too.

Caudell sipped his coffee, which was far better than the chicory and burnt barley he'd drunk while he was in the Army of Northern Virginia. Pleasants already handled the repeater with confidence and competence. He was an engineer, Caudell reminded himself, and used to learning to use unfamiliar devices in a hurry. That suited Nate fine. Not only did he admire his friend's knack, but if Pleasants was no liability with a rifle, he could use Mollie as a messenger without—well, with only a few—qualms of conscience.

She was saying, "Easiest way to get from here to there, matter of fact, is to go over to Rocky Mount and take the train on up." She chuckled. "That'd be the easiest way, anyhow, if the line wasn't busted an' if the Rivington men wouldn't shoot you dead for tryin' to use it."

"Let's try another road, then," Alsie Hopkins said. He sounded so serious that the whole squad hooted at him.

Caudell raised his cup, tilted his head back to drain it. He slung the AK-47 over his shoulder. "Let's go," he said.

Ambling east along Washington Street to First hardly seemed like soldiering, though Ruffin Biggs complained, "I forgot how heavy a rifle this was." Caudell frowned; compared to the rifle musket he had carried, the AK-47 was small and light. But compared to no rifle at all—his burden the past four years—it did feel rather like a slab of stone. He decided Biggs had a point.

First Street remained a respectable road until it leaped over Stony Creek. The soldiers' feet drummed loudly on the wooden bridge. Bob Southard said, "What's that fairy tale? The three billy goats guff?"

"Gruff," Caudell corrected him. He waved down at the little stream. "Might could be a few snappers in there, but I don't think Stony Creek's big enough to hold a troll."

A few hundred yards past the bridge, the road split into three narrow tracks, none of which seemed to lead anywhere in particular. "See what I mean?" Mollie said.

"The right fork is the one that goes north and east," Henry Pleasants remarked. "That's the way we're looking for."

Mollie looked at him. "You're right, but how'd you know? You're new hereabouts."

"A couple of my miners, Welshmen, came down and settled on that road," he answered. "I thought they'd work on the railroad with me, but they're content to farm a few acres and hunt a little."

"Haven't seen 'em in town much," Caudell said. "They must stick to themselves."

Pleasants nodded. "They do. Lloyd and Andrew are both like that."

"We ought to have a look at those farms of theirs, then," Caudell said. "Could be anything on 'em—a still, maybe, or who knows what else?"

Lloyd Morgan's place came first, a couple of miles up the path from Nashville. The cabin on it was small, dark, and tumbledown, rather like Morgan himself. He looked anything but happy at having guests, but did not presume to argue with a squad of soldiers with repeaters at the ready. He also smelled powerfully of whiskey. Try as they would, though, Caudell's squad found no still. Nate asked him where he'd got the liquor. He just shook his head and muttered in Welsh.

Finally Caudell gave up. "Lee's proclamation doesn't make it against the law to get drunk. Let's go."

As pine woods screened Morgan's farm from view, Ruffin Biggs grumbled, "I bet he's standing back there laughing at us."

"Could be so," Caudell agreed.

"Can't win all the time," Mollie Bean said. When she was doing what any other soldier might, as now, Caudell found he had no trouble thinking of her as Melvin again. He could not decide whether that was good or bad.

Andrew Gwynn's farm, an hour's tramp from Lloyd Morgan's, made the latter seem a plantation by comparison. Looking at the tiny, weed-infested plot Gwynn cultivated—or rather, did not seem to cultivate—Caudell marveled that he managed to make a living from it. And if he didn't . . . how *did* he make a living? Suspicion rose within Caudell. He said, "We'll look this place over *real* careful, boys."

They looked. Andrew Gwynn came out of the shack by the path to watch them look. Under a shock of dark hair, his face was pale, narrow, closed. Unlike Morgan, he was in complete control of himself. When the searchers again failed to find anything, he gave them a cold nod and went back inside.

Caudell was dissatisfied, frustrated. "I *know* he's hiding one somewhere," he said several times. "I can feel it."

After the squad had moved another couple of miles closer to Rivington, Henry Pleasants told him, "It's back in a little clearing, well off the road. There's no path—far as I know, Andrew never goes there the same way twice."

"Why didn't you say that when we were back there, Henry?" Caudell demanded, glaring at his friend.

"If you'd found it by yourselves, that would have been all right," Pleasants answered. "But Andrew came down here at my urging. I didn't feel right, giving him away before his eyes."

"But our orders were—" Caudell stopped, remembering what he'd thought about orders the day before. He set hands on hips. "You know what, Henry?" Pleasants shook his head. Caudell went on, "You'd better watch yourself, because near as I can see, you're turning into a rebel."

Alsie Hopkins slapped his knee and doubled over laughing. Pleasants didn't look so sure. "Is that a compliment?" he asked.

"Damned if I know," Caudell said.

The road twisted like a snake with the bellyache. Past Andrew Gwynn's farm, Pleasants was as lost as Caudell, who marveled at how strange places just a few miles from home could be. Without Mollie to tell him which turns to make, he knew he might have wandered in circles. A blue jay jeered at him from up in a pine tree.

Before long, they found another break in the woods. Caudell glanced first at Mollie, then at Henry Pleasants. So did the rest of the squad. "Nobody knows who lives here?" Caudell said. "Well, we'll have to go and find out, then."

They stopped at the edge of the woods, peering through brush at the clearing ahead. By the look of things, nobody lived there, though someone once had. The cabin was a roofless ruin, the fields a riot of weeds and shrubs and, here and there, man-high saplings.

Bob Southard tramped off across the field. Alsie Hopkins started after him. Caudell put out an arm to stop him, called to Southard, "You want to be careful, Bob. We're getting close to where those Rivington bastards might be."

Southard shook his head and kept walking. "They got more things to worry about than me. They—" He never said anything else. A burst of fire from the far side of the clearing cut him down where he stood. He spun when he was hit, so Caudell could see the almost comic amazement on his face as he fell.

Caudell's own battle reflexes had not faded; at the first sound of fire he threw himself flat. The wisdom of that was proved a moment later, when bullets probed the place from which Southard had emerged, searching for anyone who might have been with him. "Oh, sweet Jesus, I pissed myself!" Alsie Hopkins wailed. Caudell didn't feel like laughing. Had he not stepped behind a tree not long before, he knew he might have done the same thing.

Bullets slapped trees, smacked branches with a rough hand, again and again and again. Whoever was shooting up ahead, he seemed to have all the ammunition in the world, and he wasn't shy about using it. Caudell turned his head far enough to get his mouth out of the dirt, said to Henry Pleasants beside him, "That's no AK-47 up there."

"What is it, then?" Being a transplanted Northerner, Pleasants was not yet intimately familiar with the rifle he carried.

Caudell shook his head without raising it. "Damned if I know. But the report is heavier, and he's not firing clips, either. Listen—damn bullets just keep on coming." He remembered how far away the trees on the other side of the clearing were, and how fast poor, overconfident Bob Southard had gone down. "Whatever he's shooting, it's got ungodly range."

The firing stopped. "Stay down!" three people hissed at the same time. Mollie Bean added, "He's tryin' to find out just where we're at."

"We've got to spread out," Caudell said. His initial terror at unexpectedly coming under fire was gone now, replaced by the more familiar fear that went with any combat. If he could not master that fear, he could live with it; four years of peace dropped away from him as if they had never been. When he spoke again, he might have been teaching a lesson his students already knew well: "Henry, you and I will slide right. Ruffin, you and Alsie head left. M-Melvin, you stay here, give us some covering fire, and if anything goes wrong, you make sure you get back and give Captain Lewis the word."

Mollie said, "Ought to be me with you instead of Henry, Nate. He ain't that handy with a repeater."

"But you know the country hereabouts best. That gives you the best chance of making it back to Nashville," Caudell said. He made sense enough that she quit arguing. He took a deep breath. "Let's go." He slid backwards, into deeper cover. Henry Pleasants had no trouble staying with him, or staying low. He might have been a lieutenant colonel, but he'd learned to move like a red Indian.

Mollie's AK-47 barked, three or four quick rounds sent in the direction from which the bullets ahead had come. The reply was almost instantaneous, a storm of fire so furious that Caudell realized he hadn't left Mollie in a safe place after all. Against that monster gun, there didn't seem to be any safe places.

Off to the left, Hopkins and Biggs started to fire. The gun hesitated for a moment, then began stuttering out death in a new direction. It chewed away at the brush that screened attackers from it. Caudell noticed he was thinking about it as if it were a sentient entity in its own right, and a malevolent one.

When he said something like that to Henry Pleasants, his friend laughed mirthlessly. "Now you know how I felt at Bealeton."

Now crouching, now crawling, they scurried through the trees, guided by the deep, monotonous patter of the gun—*and the gunner*, Caudell reminded himself—they were stalking. Mollie kept squeezing off shots every minute or two. So did Alsie Hopkins and Ruffin Biggs. For a while, the hidden gunner continued his pattern of swinging back and forth between them. Then, apparently deciding Mollie wasn't advancing and wasn't dangerous where she was, he concentrated his fire on the two moving men.

"Shall we take some of the heat off them?" Pleasants asked, hefting the AK-47 he'd still never fired.

Caudell shook his head. "Not yet. Best way we can do that is get close enough to make sure our shots count."

Pleasants sketched a salute. "Spoken like an officer."

Most of an hour of slow movement went by before Caudell spotted muzzle flashes ahead and to his left. He went flat on his belly and wriggled forward like a cottonmouth. Henry Pleasants was right beside him. For some time, those flashes were all they saw. When at last they drew near enough to make out more, Caudell's lips shaped a silent whistle. "He's got his own little earthwork there."

In back of concealing branches, heaped-up dirt warded the gunner against bullets from front, left, right. Either Hopkins or Biggs fired at him. A burst answered them, keeping them pinned well away. Caudell saw a flick of motion behind the long barrel of the gun that projected over the revetment. A plan shaped itself in his mind. He whispered to Pleasants, "Move away from me, over to that stump there. Next time he starts shooting, we'll both try and take him out."

"All right." Ever so cautiously, Pleasants crawled into place. Caudell himself crouched behind a tree trunk. He waited, waited . . . Mollie fired. The hidden enemy did not reply. Then shots came from the left, from Biggs and Hopkins. A stream of bullets lashed out at them.

Caudell fired. So did Henry Pleasants. They were close enough to hear the enemy gunner's cry of fear and rage. The long barrel swung toward Caudell with terrifying speed. Seen straight on, the muzzle flashes were bright as the sun. Bullets slammed into the trunk, just above his head.

All at once, the bullets were chewing up the treetops, not closing in on him. After a few seconds, the firing stopped. Wary of a trick, Caudell waited several minutes before peering round his sheltering tree trunk. The big, black gun barrel pointed up at the sky. In his mind's eye, Caudell saw the Rivington man who had been back of it hit, saw his dying weight slump down onto the gun and raise the muzzle, saw him fall away so the bullets stopped coming.

Shaking with reaction, he called over to Pleasants: "You all right, Henry?" His voice shook, too.

"Yes, I think so." Pleasants didn't sound any too steady himself, which reassured Nate. "What the hell kind of gun is that, anyhow?"

"Damned if I know. Shall we go find out?" Caudell started to leave his cover.

But Henry Pleasants said, "I don't think that's a good idea, Nate."

"What? Why not?"

"Two reasons. For one thing, we've done what Captain Lewis told us to do: we've found where these bastards have their southern pickets posted. And for two, look how well situated that gun is. Do you think it's there all by its lonesome, or do you think there are more guns farther back, just waiting for us to show ourselves so they can cut us down?"

As if in response to Pleasants's words, a new gun opened up, north and east of the one they'd taken out. Bullets cut twigs, *spaang*ed off stones. Caudell, once more flat on his belly, could see no flashes. Hearing the deep, endless roar was quite bad enough. "All right, Henry, I'm convinced. Let's get out of here."

Getting out was almost as sticky as getting in had been. The sun was low in the west by the time they rejoined Mollie Bean. Ruffin Biggs and Alsie Hopkins were already there; Biggs wore a filthy bandage stuffed into the front of his right shoe. "I got a couple of toes gone, I reckon," he said matter-of-factly. "Here on out, you can call me Gimpy."

"What the hell kind of gun was that you went up against, Nate?" Mollie asked, unconsciously echoing Henry Pleasants.

Caudell could hear the concern she did her best to conceal. It warmed him. He wanted to squeeze the breath out of her, to prove to himself, flesh on flesh, that he was still alive. He couldn't, not now. He said, "Henry here talked me out of going up to see." When he explained why, his companions nodded.

Alise Hopkins said, "That there gun looks to shoot 'bout as far as a Napoleon." He shook his head. "Didn't much fancy gettin' shot at when I couldn't hardly shoot back."

Ruffin Biggs nodded again, this time to Pleasants. "Reckon you was right, Yankee—Cap'n Lewis'll need to know about a gun like that, and so will Hit-'em-Again."

"Forrest, you mean?" Henry Pleasants let out a dry chuckle. "Ruffin, I suspect he already knows."

Guards round the Capitol, guards posted on the grounds of the presidential residence, a guard with an AK-47 in his carriage . . . Lee felt a prisoner of guards. And guards most of all at the corner of Ninth and Franklin, infantry and artillery both, protecting the most important secrets of the Confederacy.

The battered building that had housed America Will Break had changed since Lee visited it just after his men finally succeeded in breaking into the AWB sanctum. The hole in the outer wall of that hidden chamber was bigger now. It needed to be, to let light into the room: the glowing tubes on the ceiling had failed when the thing that chugged in the wall fell silent. A new canvas awning shielded the opening from the elements.

The officer in charge of the guard detachment saluted as Lee's carriage rolled up. "The congressional delegation arrived a few minutes ago, sir. Per your instructions, they are waiting in the outer office of that suite."

"Thank you, Major." Lee got down from the carriage. So did his body-guard. He tossed his head. The only time he had to himself these days was in the privy or the bathtub—and had the tub been bigger, a guard likely would have joined him there. Assassins murdered freedom merely by ex-isting.

The senators and congressmen turned as Lee came in through the entry to the AWB suite. So did Judah P. Benjamin, leaning heavily on two sticks. Luckily, the bullet that had gone through his calf missed the bone; the wound was healing. But the former Secretary of State still moved like an old man instead of with the imposing presence he had once enjoyed.

"Gentlemen, you have my sincerest gratitude for joining me today," Lee said. "If you will be so kind as to come with me, I will show you why you were invited here."

"It had better be good," growled Senator Wigfall of Texas. "When I tried going into that room yonder, the one with the heavy door, the damned guards said they'd shoot me to stop me. I'm not accustomed to our own good Confederate soldiers turning into Hessians, and I don't care for it, not one bit I don't."

"They were but obeying my explicit orders, sir. You will see the reason behind them, I assure you. The guards will admit you now, as you are in my company."

And indeed, with Lee heading the group, the soldiers presented arms to Wigfall and the other senators and congressmen. The officials turned this way and that, staring at the unfamiliar office furnishings within the secret room. Wigfall pointed to the qwerty on one deck. "What the devil is that thing?"

"If you can tell me, Senator, I shall be in your debt," Lee said.

Congressman Lucius Gartrell of Georgia, a Confederate rather than a Patriot in politics, looked toward a hole in the wall not far from the door. "What happened there, Mr. President?"

"The device which made those tubes overhead"—Lee pointed—"give light was housed there. After it ceased operation, we removed it in an effort to discover the principles by which it worked. Our best guess is that it ran out of fuel."

"Can't you just give it more wood or coal, then?" Gartrell said.

"It does not appear to burn either, but rather a combustible fluid of some sort," Lee answered. That was what his military engineers had told him, based on the few drops of strong-smelling liquid left in the tank marked FUEL. Whatever the liquid was, it wasn't whale oil: of so much the engineers seemed certain. Past that point, no certainty existed. Most of the savants working with the HONDA GENERATOR—for so it proclaimed itself to be—believed that what it generated was electricity, but what the stuff was good for once generated they hadn't a clue. The Rivington men had known, though.

Duncan Kenner of Louisiana, another congressman of the Confederate persuasion, said, "This is all very interesting, I'm sure, Mr. President, but why are we here?"

Lee nodded to Judah Benjamin, whose usual small smile never wavered; Benjamin had primed Kenner to ask just that question. Lee said, "The answer, Congressman, reaches back more than four years and has until recently been a tightly held secret. Even now, before I continue, I must require your word of honor, and that of your colleagues, not to divulge what you learn here today without my prior permission."

Most of the legislators agreed at once. Mulish Wigfall said, "Be damned if I'll buy a pig in a poke."

"Very well, Senator, you may go; I am sorry to have wasted your time," Lee said politely. Wigfall glared but, seeing Lee prepared to be inflexible, added his promise to the rest. Lee nodded his thanks, then went on, "In early 1864, as you must all be aware, our Confederacy's prospects in the war for independence were poor. We were outnumbered and outfactoried from the start, portions of our land had been overrun, and the North was beginning to find in Grant and Sherman and Sheridan officers who could bring its full strength to bear upon us."

Even Wigfall had to nod; the staunchest Southern fire-eater remembered how bleak things had looked then. Lucius Quintus Cincinnatus Lamar of Mississippi, newly returned to Congress as a Patriot and as staunch a fire-eater as any ever born, said, "The coming at that moment of the Rivington men and their repeaters always seemed to me to be visible, even miraculous, proof of the favor which divine Providence showed the Confederate States of America." Several other senators and congressmen solemnly nodded.

"I confess that I inclined toward a similar view for some time," Lee said. "I have since been disabused of this notion. We were indeed shown favor, but of a sort neither divine nor miraculous. Hear me out, my friends; the story I am about to tell you may seem implausible, but I assure you it is the truth."

He told the legislators what he knew of the Rivington men and their travel through time to come to the South's aid. Part of what he said was gleaned from Andries Rhoodie, part from the volumes in the chamber where he now stood. As he spoke, he watched Louis Wigfall go paler and paler. That did not surprise him; the men of the AWB must have given Wigfall their own version of this tale. Lee finished, "And so you see, gentlemen, they helped us gain our freedom, not out of consideration for our virtues, but so we might serve as pawns in their game."

Silence stretched when he was through. Finally Congressman Lamar said, "This is an—extraordinary web you spin, Mr. President, so extraordinary that I hope you will not be offended if I say it would be all the better for proof."

"I can offer that, or at least corroboration," Judah Benjamin said. "I heard much of this same tale from Andries Rhoodie's lips, as did Jefferson Davis and, if I be not mistaken, Joe Johnston and Alexander Stephens as well." Benjamin looked around the room. "And unless I am *much* mistaken, my friends, some few of you will have heard it as well. We are not so good at keeping secrets, even important secrets, as we might be."

Since Lee kept secrets without difficulty, he had not thought of that, but by the expressions on several legislators' faces, Benjamin had a point. Lee glanced toward Wigfall. Almost defiantly, the Texan said, "I've heard it, yes, but not through gossip and chit-chat. The Rivington men told it to me and General Forrest, though their interpretation of the events differed substantially from that ascribed to them by Mr. Lee."

" 'By their fruits ye shall know them,' or so the Bible says," Lee answered. He waved to the book that lay open on every desk in the secret room. "To few folks is it given to learn how history would judge them. Thanks to the men of the AWB, we possess that opportunity. I have taken the liberty of marking certain passages in these books, passages I believe to be representative of the whole. By no means do I require you to take these as all-inclusive, however; feel free to browse as you would, to learn how the future thought of some of the issues our Confederacy was in part founded to uphold."

"You mean niggers, don't you?" Wigfall said. "In the end, it always comes down to niggers."

"There, Senator, I find I cannot disagree with you," Lee said, thinking this was one of the few occasions on which he could truthfully say that.

He took a step back, indicating that the congressmen and senators might begin their examination. Instantly, he was reminded of a game of musical chairs, for legislators outnumbered chairs to hold them. His momentary amusement vanished as fast as it formed; just such a contretemps at his inauguration had led him to bring Mary up onto the platform with him and, shortly thereafter, to his becoming a widower.

Unlike the scene in Capitol Square, no unseemly brawl followed here. Some men claimed seats; others stood and peered over their shoulders. All the books had markers inserted at the pages that gave their publication dates. A few derisive snorts arose from skeptical lawmakers, but those soon faded. Many of the volumes were illustrated, and illustrated with photographs and lavish color impossible to match in the mundane world of 1868. And every work had the dizzying effect of being written with the hindsight of a hundred years and more. Within moments, the only sounds in the room were soft grunts of wonder.

Louis T. Wigfall heaved his bulk out of a chair, advanced on Lee. "I owe you an apology, Mr. President, and I am man enough to give it. I thought you'd put together some humbug here to befool us, but I see it is not so. You could not have manufactured so much, and in such detail." Shaking his head like a bedeviled bear, he shambled back to the desk from which he had come and, without complaint, took a place behind Congressman Gartrell, who had occupied his chair.

Lee leaned against the hard, cold side of a closed file cabinet, let the lawmakers look as long as they would. This was the second such delegation he had led into the AWB sanctum; eventually, he planned to allow the entire Confederate Congress to see the books and papers assembled here.

As had happened with the first group of legislators, wonder began to give way to indignation as senators and congressmen moved from one volume to the next, compared one account of the lost Civil War and its aftermath with another. "Every one of these things sounds as if a damnyankee wrote it," Congressman Lamar exclaimed. Someone else—Lee did not notice who—added, "Not just a damnyankee, but a damned abolitionist Yankee."

Where Lee had quoted Matthew, Judah P. Benjamin chose Bobbie Burns: " 'Oh wad some power the giftie gie us, To see oursels as others see us! It wad frae monie a blunder free us, An' foolish notion.' " He did his best to turn his soft accent to broad, harsh Scots. A thoughtful silence descended when he was through.

Into it, Lee said, "Unique among men, my friends, we have been granted that, ah, giftie. We always remained faithful to our peculiar institution despite the censure of those outside our bounds, confident posterity would thank us for that fidelity. But here before us we have the verdict of posterity, which condemns us for maintaining the ownership of one man by another and is convinced that that system, if ever it were justifiable, had in our time long since outlived such justification." This time he picked words from the Book of Daniel: " 'Thou art weighed in the balances, and art found wanting.' Only God knows His judgments, but we may see for ourselves the verdict which history has brought in against us."

"Did you know of this when during your Presidential campaign you spoke of ending slavery?" Congressman Kenner asked.

"No, sir, I did not," Lee said. "Indeed, the Rivington men painted for me quite a different picture of the future, a picture in which white and black remained forever at each other's throats. The pages in this room serve to give the lie to that picture, as I think you will agree, yet it was the one they offered, as Mr. Benjamin and, I think, Senator Wigfall will attest."

Judah Benjamin's massive head moved up and down. Wigfall also nodded, though his expression was anything but sanguine; Lee wondered whether the fierce frown was aimed at himself for having forced the Texan to make that admission or at the AWB men for having misled him.

L. Q. C. Lamar said, "What of the Rivington men, then? If this love feast between Negroes and whites be the way of the future (and so it would seem, startling and, I must say, repugnant though I find it), how do the Rivington men fit into it?"

"Poorly, I suspect." Lee held up a hand. "No, I do not intend to be flippant. By their own words, as rendered into English by Mr. Benjamin's coreligionist Mr. Goldfarb, they show themselves to be zealots at strife with virtually the entire world of their time. Let me offer you an analogy which quite offended Andries Rhoodie: the Rivington men are as mad in their support of whites in their times as John Brown was in support of blacks in ours."

The Confederate legislators looked at each other. One by one, they began to nod. The same thing had happened with the first delegation to see the evidence from the twentieth and twenty-first centuries. Few men were brazen enough to withstand their great-grandsons' scorn.

Louis T. Wigfall came close. "Damn me to hell, sir, if I can stomach that stinking black Republican of an Abe Lincoln being made into some plaster saint. And damn me to hell if I want to live in a country where the man who blacks my boots and curries my horse is my equal."

"A measure of equality before the law by no means creates of itself equality in society," Lee said. "The United States make that abundantly clear. And let me ask you a different question, Senator, if I may: Having seen the means the AWB employs to reach its ends, do you yet find those ends deserving of your support?"

Wigfall's glower grew black as his boots. But he had been in the middle of the Capitol Square massacre. At last he shook his heavy head.

"Nor do I." Lee raised his voice, spoke to the entire congressional delegation: "Am I to construe from this, then, that you shall vote in the affirmative when a bill arranging for the gradual, compensated emancipation of Negro slaves, the terms to be along the lines of those I outlined before becoming President, is introduced into the Senate and House of Representatives?"

Again, the lawmakers looked at one another, some of them as if they hoped one of their number would have the nerve to say no. Lee watched them all, especially Wigfall and Lamar, whom he judged likeliest to oppose him, the one from stubbornness, the other out of principle.

Lamar cleared his throat. Several congressmen beamed. The representative from Mississippi said, "Retreating from a long-held position is apt to be as dangerous in politics as in war; in so doing, I fear I look down into the open grave of any future aspirations. Yet given the evidence you have presented to us today, I have no choice but to support such legislation as you suggest, and justify my vote to my constituents as well as I may thereafter."

Lee's nod was the next thing to a bow. "If not the immediate gratitude of the voters in your district, you will gain your country's lasting thanks."

After the Mississippian declared himself in favor of Lee's program, the rest of the lawmakers fell in line. Even Wigfall nodded gruffly, though Lee, knowing his volatility, did not take that as a firm promise. Judah Benjamin said, "You know, Mr. Lamar, what with the atrocities of March 4 and the insurrection currently being mounted in North Carolina, your vote in favor of emancipation may yet redound to your advantage, provided you make your district aware that in so voting, you reject everything the Rivington men support."

Lamar's features, usually on the brooding side, lit up. "It could be so, sir; with your well-known acuity of judgment in matters political, it likely is so."

"You flatter me, sir," Benjamin said, and he contrived to appear flattered, but flattery, Lee thought, was best defined as overfulsome praise, and, having seen Benjamin in action, he was more than willing to concede the former Secretary of State's reputation was deserved.

Congressman Gartrell said, "How fare we against the rebels, sir?"

"Not so well as I would wish," Lee answered. "The Rivington men are few in numbers, but possessed of the advantage of a century and a half of progress in the mechanic arts, progress we of course lack. The repeaters they furnished us for use against the United States are one example of such progress; unhappily, we have discovered that they are *only* one example. The Rivington men have on the whole succeeded in maintaining the positions they seized when fighting broke out after March 4. Were it not for the AK-47s in our arsenal, I fear they might have managed to do much more than merely hold those positions."

He stopped, scowling almost as ferociously as had Senator Wigfall. The long-barreled, large-caliber endless repeaters the Rivington men used to defend strong points made AK-47s seem like Springfields by comparison. Nor were the torpedoes they buried in the fields between those strong points any bargain, either; after watching the legs blown off two or three men, their comrades grew noticeably less eager to advance.

"We shall in the end defeat them, though?" Gartrell pressed anxiously.

"If we defeated the United States, sir, we shall surely overcome a small band of insurrectionists." Lee wished he were as certain as he sounded.

Bullets snapped past a few feet over Caudell's head, the stream sweeping first left to right, then back from right to left. The wash in which he lay was only about a hundred yards from the gunner. Getting this close had taken him all day. Now that he was here, he didn't know what to do next. Firing a few shots at random was likelier to alert the gunner than to kill him. And the Rivington men still had the rifle grenades they'd used in the trenches outside Washington City. Caudell didn't want them raining down on him.

He turned to Henry Pleasants, who sprawled beside him in the gully. "We can't go forward, not anymore," he said, waving. Pleasants nodded; if they showed themselves, they were dead men. Caudell waved in the other direction. "We can't go back either, not hardly." Eight or nine soldiers lay in the gully with them, the survivors of twice that many or more. Pleasants nodded again. Caudell said, "Well, what does that leave us? I'm looking for ideas, damn it."

"I wish I had one," Pleasants said. "Maybe when night comes—" He broke off with a grimace. By the way they shot at night, the Rivington men could see in the dark like cats. And even if that weren't so, with the brute of a repeater up ahead, if one bullet didn't get you, the next one would, or the next.

Flopped down a couple of feet away, Mollie Bean said, "Can't go forward, can't go back." She wiped her forehead with her sleeve. Since the one was as dirty as the other, that helped her not at all. She still looked good to Caudell. The only way she could have looked better was far away from the fighting. If something happened to her— But she hadn't let Caudell send her away.

He said, "We can't go over 'em: not enough trees, and they'd shoot us out of 'em like boys with squirrel guns. And we can't go under 'em, because we aren't a pack of moles."

He'd been talking as much to hear the sound of his own voice as for any other reason. He almost jumped when Henry Pleasants rolled over and whacked him in the shoulder. Jumping, here, was dangerous. Pleasants's eyes blazed in his filthy face. "The hell we can't go under 'em," he said. His voice shook with excitement.

"Huh? What are you talking about?" Caudell said.

"Going under 'em," Pleasants repeated impatiently, as if to a stupid child. When Caudell still looked blank, he realized he had to explain further: "Nate, I used to be a mining engineer, remember? If we could run a tunnel from here to under that big repeater, set a charge of powder, and light it off— We can do it, I swear we can, and blow 'em high as the sky. The ground around here is soft, the side of the wash will keep the Rivington men from spying what we're up to . . . I'm not crazy, Nate; I swear by almighty God I'm not."

"You mean it," Caudell said slowly, wonderingly. The stream of bullets was right overhead now. Advancing farther against the gun that spat them was only a fancy way to commit suicide, unless . . . Caudell had a sudden vision of gun and gunner both flying through the air. He liked it better than anything else he'd imagined since being so rudely returned to combat.

Pleasants sensed he'd hooked his fish. "I sure do mean it, Nate. If we can bring Lloyd and Andrew up here, and some other men who've dug— you must have some in this state—and their tools, and the timber we'd need to shore up the tunnel as we dig—" He started ticking off on his fingers exactly what he'd need, as if he were sitting comfortably in a mining office instead of hunkered down in a dry wash.

Finally, to dam the flow of ideas, Caudell held up a hand. "All right, I surrender—you've convinced me. But I'm just a sergeant, remember?" He pointed at the stripes on his sleeve. "I can't get you everything you're talking about. We'll head back to Captain Lewis. If you sell him your scheme, too, you'll likely get a chance to try it."

"Let's go." Pleasants turned and started to crawl down the gully.

Caudell grabbed him by the ankle. "Henry, you just swore to me you weren't crazy, and here you go making yourself out a liar. If you want to live to see Captain Lewis, you won't just march off and do it, not from here you won't. Think about where you are. When night comes, we'll try getting out. Till then, we sit tight." Pleasants looked mutinous. Caudell went on, "How much digging did you plan on doing today, anyhow?"

His friend managed a shamefaced laugh. "Sorry. You're thinking straighter than I am, that's plain. But when I see something like this in my mind, I go all on fire to get started on it, no matter what's in my way."

"I know you do." Caudell remembered that that driving eagerness to get the job done, and the matching blindness to anything not directly related to getting it done, had cost his friend his railroad job. After a couple of years as a first sergeant, practicality was his own middle name. He plucked at his beard as he thought. After a couple of minutes, he asked, "If you're not here, can one of your Welshmen oversee this job?"

"Andrew could," Pleasants answered at once. "Lloyd works well enough, but he likes his whiskey too well to make a proper chief."

"Fair enough. Here's what we'll do, then. After it gets dark, you and I and Melvin here will all head back to Nashville. We'll go separately, and—"

"Wait a minute," Mollie Bean interrupted. "What're y'all sendin' me back for?"

"You've spent the last however long listening to Henry and me," Caudell answered. "You know as much about this notion of his as I do, anyway. Captain Lewis needs to hear it. Even at night, it's no sure bet one of us, or even one out of two, will make it back safe out of the range of that damned gun up there. But if I send three, somebody ought to get back."

She nodded, warily. "All right, Nate. Reckon that makes sense." In front of other people, a good deal had to stay unsaid between them. If she'd thought he was sending her back just to get her out of danger—which he very much wanted to do—she'd surely have refused to go. But her pride could accept an order with military reason behind it.

Shadows shifted, lengthened, began to blend into the one great purple shadow of twilight. When full dark came, Caudell turned to Mollie and Pleasants. "I'll go first," he said. "First one through is likeliest to draw fire. Henry, you're next—give me fifteen minutes or so before you start. M-Melvin, you go last, fifteen minutes behind Henry. We'll all meet"—*I hope*, he thought—"at Captain Lewis's."

"Luck, Nate," Pleasants said.

"Luck," Mollie echoed, so softly he hardly heard her.

He wanted to hug her, to kiss her, to be with her anywhere but this miserable spot. All he could do was nod a nod she might well not have seen in the darkness, then scuttle off down the dry wash. His mouth was dry, too; he remembered too well the terrifying confusion of the night fight outside Washington City. Then the Rivington men and their fancy weapons had been allies. Now they were trying to kill him.

The wash got shallower and shallower as it curved away from the endless repeater. He rolled out of it and behind a hollow stump. Doing his best to keep the stump between himself and the gunner, he crawled, scrambled, crawled again. He'd gone several hundred yards before bullets came snarling after him. He threw himself flat—better than flat, actually, for he landed in a hole in the ground. He waited a few minutes, then crawled on. When he decided the pine woods screened him away from the Rivington man at the gun, he got up and walked, steering by the stars till he came to a road he knew.

He'd started only six or eight miles outside Nashville, but the town clocks were chiming midnight when he came into town. Lewis made his headquarters at the courthouse. A sentry gave Caudell, now even filthier than he had been before, a dubious look. "You sure this won't wait, soldier?"

"I'm sure." Caudell put bite in his voice. He discovered he still had his wartime prejudice against anyone in a clean uniform. His growl sufficed to get the sentry to step aside. He went into the courthouse, found Lewis snoring on a pallet. "Captain Lewis, sir? Captain?"

Lewis grunted, then rolled over and sat up. "Who—?" He rubbed his eyes. The torches outside the doorway let him see who. "What the devil is it, Nate?"

As Caudell started to explain what it was, several horsemen rode into the town square, their harness jingling. A man with cavalry spurs on his boots strode into the courthouse. Caudell kept on talking to Lewis: *let the damned courier wait his turn*, he thought. Most of that breed were arrogant, eager to get their ever-so-precious words in first, but this one stood quietly until Caudell was through.

Captain Lewis yawned till his jaw gave an audible pop. Then he said, "If this Pleasants knows what he's doing—and he sounds like he does— tell him to go ahead. Sounds like a good chance to get rid of that damned repeater, and we haven't had much luck with it any other way."

As Caudell saluted, the man behind him spoke for the first time: "Captain, Sergeant, the hell with one repeater. When you're holdin' four kings, you better not just raise a dime."

Caudell whirled. He knew that voice, though he'd not expected to hear it in the Nashville courthouse. George Lewis sprang out of bed and to his feet. He was wearing his makeshift captain's tunic, but only drawers beneath it. He came to attention and saluted anyhow. "General Forrest, sir!"

"At ease, Captain—and put on your pants," Nathan Bedford Forrest added with a chuckle. "I rode in to see how things were on this part of the line around that goddam Rivington place, on account of they'd been pretty quiet till now. Reckon they're gonna liven up some." He rounded on Caudell. "Where is this mining engineer of yours, First Sergeant?"

"He ought to be along any time now, sir," Caudell said uncomfortably. He told again how he, Pleasants, and Mollie Bean—though he remembered to call her Melvin—had set out at fifteen-minute intervals.

Forrest nodded. "Best you could have done, I expect. But if that engineer stops a bullet— Wait. He said one of those other miners could do the job, too, didn't he?"

"Yes, but—" Caudell hopelessly spread his hands. Henry Pleasants was his friend. Mollie was a great deal more than that. Forrest might understand his feelings, but the man was—had to be, by the wreathed stars on his collar—a soldier first. Now that he had an idea, he would carry it forward with or without the person who first proposed it. To Caudell, the people mattered more than the idea. He waited and worried, waited more, worried more.

About three in the morning, when worry was turning to despair, Mollie and Pleasants came into the courthouse together. Caudell let out a rebel yell that likely bounced half of Nashville out of bed. He hugged Henry Pleasants first, which gave him all the excuse he needed to hug Mollie too, longer and more closely. "What the devil happened to you two?" he demanded.

"We got lost," Mollie said in a small, sheepish voice. "My fault. I—"

"I don't care a damn about all that," Nathan Bedford Forrest broke in. He paused a moment to let himself, or at least his rank, be recognized, then said, "Which one of you is Pleasants?"

"I am, sir." Pleasants drew himself stiff and straight. "Private Henry Pleasants, 47th North Carolina, formerly Lieutenant Colonel Henry Pleasants, 48th Pennsylvania."

"Is that a fact?" Forrest took a longer, closer look at the mining engineer. "Decided you liked it better down here, did you?"

"Some ways," Pleasants said, and let it go at that.

Forrest did not press him; he had things other than politics on his mind. "Caudell here tells me you think you can run a mine under that big repeater up in front of you."

"I can blow that goddamned gun just as high as you want it, sir," Pleasants said positively.

"The hell with one repeater," Forrest said, as he had to Caudell and Lewis before. "I want that mine. I want it bad enough to taste it, Colonel." Pleasants beamed to hear his old rank used; Captain Lewis glared a little. Forrest plowed ahead: "About how long would you need to dig it?"

Pleasants's eyes went far away; his lips moved silently as he calculated. He stayed in that brown study for several minutes. When his face cleared, he answered, "Give me the men, tools, and shoring timbers I'll need—and a pump, in case the shaft is wet—and I'll have it done in three weeks to a month."

Forrest clapped him on the back. "You'll get 'em, by God," he promised. "And you'll have your old U.S. rank back as part of my staff, if that suits you."

Now George Lewis glared more than a little. Pleasants grinned from ear to ear. "Thank you, sir! Maybe I should have voted for you after all."

Caudell gulped, wondering how the notoriously hotheaded Forrest would take that. But the general's answer, when it came, was low-voiced and serious: "Sir, if I'd known then what I know now, I wouldn't have voted for myself. I was fooled into thinking America Will Break had the South's best interests at heart, not its own." He shook his head, plainly angry at being deceived. Then he grinned, too, an expression half mischievous, half savage. "Now I aim to fool those Rivington bastards right back."

"How are you going to do that, sir?" Caudell, Mollie, and George Lewis asked at the same time.

"We've just been tapping at America Will Break down here south of Rivington," Forrest answered, still with that predatory grin. "I aim to swing a good deal around to here, start pounding 'em right about where that repeater is. The more men and guns we throw at 'em, the more they'll have to bring in to keep us from crackin' 'em. I'll throw in more, and they'll bring more, and by the time three weeks or a month have gone by, gentlemen, they'll need a sight more than one repeater to hold us back. I'll make them make that spot the linchpin of their whole position."

It was as if someone had struck a match right in front of Caudell's eyes. Dazzled, he exclaimed, "They can bring up all the fancy guns they want, because while they're doing that, we'll be digging. And when we're done—"

"—we'll blow every one of those fancy guns straight to hell," Nathan Bedford Forrest finished for him. "That's right, First Sergeant. Then we'll smash through the gap and go straight for Rivington." Forrest's grin suddenly slid off his face, leaving him looking very grim indeed. "And if the Rivington men get word of what we're up to because somebody blabs, I'll kill the bigmouthed son of a bitch with my own hands. Does everyone understand me?"

The courthouse got quiet for a moment. Even without knowing Forrest's reputation, no one who heard him could have doubted he meant exactly what he said.

Perhaps seeking to ease the tension that blunt threat had left in the air,

Henry Pleasants said, "You know, Melvin, you're the spit and image of Nate's lady friend Mollie Bean. Just how close a relative of hers are you?"

Caudell choked and wished he could sink through the floor. Mollie, though, must have anticipated getting asked that sooner or later, for she answered lightly, "We're right close, Henry—excuse me, I mean Colonel Henry, sir. Lots o' people say we look alike."

"You certainly do," Pleasants said.

General Forrest told Nate and Mollie, "You two go get some sleep; you've earned it. My thanks for coming back with word of this here plan." He turned to Pleasants. "You stay here with me, sir. Sounds like we got ourselves a whole mess o' talking to get through."

"Yes, sir," Henry Pleasants said. "I think we do . . ."

★ XVIII ★

Lee wondered how Jefferson Davis had ever managed to inveigle him into accepting the Confederate Presidency. Even without counting the armed guards who surrounded the presidential residence on Shockoe Hill, he found himself a prisoner of his position. To do everything that needed doing, he should have been born triplets. The one of him available was not nearly enough: whenever he did anything, he felt guilty because he was neglecting something else.

He drank coffee as he waded through the morning's stack of reports. General Forrest was shifting the main effort of his attack to southwest of Rivington, a telegram said. Lee glanced at a map of North Carolina on a stand by his desk, then shrugged. That direction of assault looked no more promising to him than any other, but Forrest usually had a reason for the things he did, even if the reason was not obvious. Often it wasn't; being without any formal military training, Forrest made up his own rules as he went along. And if Lee couldn't see what he was up to, likely the Rivington men couldn't, either. Lee hoped they couldn't.

The telegram also reported that Forrest had appointed a new officer to his staff, a Colonel Pleasants. The name was vaguely familiar to Lee, but he couldn't place it. He reached for a book taken from the AWB sanctum: *Lee's Colonels*, by a certain Robert Krick, a man still a lifetime away from being born. It was a better, more comprehensive list of the higher officers of the Army of Northern Virginia than any from Lee's own time.

It did not, however, mention Colonel Pleasants. Lee looked at the far wall of his office without seeing it as he tried to remember in what connection he'd noticed the colonel's name. He pulled out the *Picture History of the Civil War*, a volume that over the past few months had come to seem like an old friend. Sure enough, Pleasants's name appeared in the index. Lee flipped to page 472.

Reading about the grinding campaign that had not happened in 1864 still made him want to shiver, as if he were going through one of Poe's frightening tales instead. Hard to imagine his incomparable Army of Northern Virginia trapped within siege lines round Petersburg, with the Federals using every expedient they could think of to break those lines.

He read of the mine Henry Pleasants had proposed; of the tons of powder going off beneath the Confederate trenches; of the Battle of the Crater that the Union forces seemed to have bungled beyond belief, for otherwise how could they have lost? Having read all that, he idly wondered how Pleasants had ended up in the South rather than Pennsylvania.

The idleness fell from him. He slammed the book shut with a noise like a rifle shot. "Mr. Marshall!" he called. "Come in here, please. I need you."

"Sir?" Behind his spectacles, Charles Marshall's eyes were worried; Lee rarely sounded so urgent. "What do you require?"

"Send a telegram to General Forrest at once, saying that I order him— be sure to use the word 'order'—I order him not to include the name of the latest colonel to join his staff in any further dispatches, either telegraphic or postal. Do you have that?"

"I—think so, sir." The aide repeated the message accurately enough, though his voice was puzzled. "I confess I don't altogether understand it."

"Never mind. Just take it to the telegrapher immediately."

Marshall shrugged but hurried away. Lee returned the *Picture History of the Civil War* to its place on the shelf. If Henry Pleasants was planning to do now to the Rivington men what had been done to the South in 1864 until those same Rivington men helped change history, Lee did not want them reminded of his existence. If they were tapping the wires between North Carolina and Richmond, and if Pleasants's name seemed vaguely familiar to one of them, as it had to Lee . . .

He shook his head, more than a little unnerved at stumbling over a new complication to fighting the men from the future. Not only did they have armaments and armor his forces could not match, they knew a great deal about the events of his own recent past and the people who shaped them. A mere name might have been plenty to warn them of what Forrest likely had in mind.

Lee set Forrest's telegram aside and read the latest papers from Washington, Philadelphia, and New York. He did not think the British would get the Canadas back any time soon. Vancouver had just fallen to a U.S. force pushing up from Oregon. The *Washington Evening Star* was even reporting that the Russian Empire, alarmed at the progress of Federal arms, had offered to sell Alaska to the United States as preferable to seeing it conquered like the rest of North America. Lee smiled at that—what good were more square miles of snow and ice to anyone?

His smile faded as he read of continued English success at sea. The blockade of the eastern coast of the United States was probably tighter than the U.S. blockade of the Confederacy had been during the Second American Revolution, and the U.S. merchant fleet reduced to desperate straits. Confederate corn production was booming, to make up for the U.S. wheat no longer available to the British Isles.

That led him into the latest report from Julian Hartridge of Georgia, his Secretary of the Treasury. Reparations from the United States had allowed the Confederacy to pay off most of its wartime debts. That was important. The French had installed Maximilian in Mexico, not least because the previous government owed them money, and he did not want to give any European power a similar excuse for meddling in Confederate affairs.

But new debts came every day: the manufactured goods the South bought were worth more and could be produced for less labor than the cotton and corn it gave in exchange for them. Gold kept flowing out of the country. Southern industry had made great strides during the war and Lee wanted to encourage it further, but the Constitution forbade a protective tariff.

He made a rueful noise, half grunt, half sigh. When the historians of a century hence came to write about his Presidency, he suspected they might call him the Great Circumventor, because the Confederate Constitution stood foursquare against most of what needed doing. All the South had wanted upon secession was to be left alone, but the world and the South itself had changed too much since 1861 for a return to the halcyon antebellum days to be possible, much less practical.

Or so Lee believed, at any rate. The proof of that belief lay in a draft bill on his desk, a bill with the deliberately innocuous title of "Legislation Regulating the Labor of Certain Inhabitants of the Confederate States." That word *inhabitants* brought back his smile, though without much mirth to it: he could not have called the people affected by the legislation *citizens*, for under existing law slaves were not Confederate citizens. His bill would see to that—if it passed.

Despite all the startling documents from the captured AWB offices, despite the Richmond Massacre itself, he still worried about that. He thought he had convinced the legislators themselves of the wisdom of his course. But the people back home, despite having elected him, remained unenthusiastic about setting the Negro on the road to freedom. Lawmakers wanted to be reelected, not just to be right and to do right. In their wisdom, the framers of the Confederate Constitution made sure their President would not have to concern himself with that. Lee was pleased to recall a Constitution provision he wholeheartedly endorsed.

His daughter Mary came into the room. She served as hostess during the fortnightly levees he held, following the custom Jefferson Davis had begun. What with his wife's infirmity, much of that duty might have fallen to her in any case. After March 4 . . . he deliberately made himself shove that black, red-stained day out of the forefront of his mind, or as far out as he could. "What can I do for you, my dear?" he asked.

"I have a parcel here for you, from Colonel Rains in Augusta, Georgia." She handed him a small box closed with twine.

He opened it with the enthusiasm of a child getting a birthday treat. "From Colonel Rains, is it? Probably some new munitions." But the box held, inside a protective layer of cotton wool, a corked bottle of pills and a note: "I am given to understand that the Rivington men, before their descent into vicious and brutal madness, prescribed nitrogenated glycerine as a medicine for you. In the hope that the enclosed may be of benefit, I remain your most ob't servant. G. W. Rains."

"I hope they help your chest pains, Father," Mary said.

"They certainly should." Lee paused, looked up at her over the tops of his spectacles. "How do you know what they are for? For that matter, how did Colonel Rains learn I was taking nitroglycerine? I scent a conspiracy."

"I plead guilty. I found one of your old empty bottles and sent it to him, as the label gave the proper dosage to include in each pill. But the idea came originally from Mr. Marshall, who recalled both the nature of your old pills and that Colonel Rains was producing the identical substance. I'm only sorry neither of us thought of it sooner."

"Don't trouble yourself on that account, my dear; I seem to have survived to this point even without the medication," Lee said, touched by their concern. His expression hardened. "I am not sorry to have a supply from a source other than the Rivington men."

Mary nodded, her own face grim. Like her younger sisters, she still wore black to mourn her mother. But for blind luck, she would have been mourning him, too. The new nitroglycerine tablets rattled in the bottle as he picked it up. The Rivington men had been willing, even eager, to help him when they needed him, and help him they had, more than any contemporary could. But when his hopes for the South crossed theirs, they'd tried to discard him as casually as if he were a smeared sheet of foolscap.

He clicked tongue between teeth. "It is my country, not theirs."

"Father?" Mary said. But he'd been talking to himself, not to her.

Thomas Bocock of Virginia, the Speaker of the House, said, "I now have the distinct honor and high privilege of presenting to you the President of the Confederate States of America, Robert E. Lee."

Applause from congressmen and senators filled the House chamber as Lee stepped up to the rostrum. Bocock sat down in back of him. Albert Gallatin Brown should have been beside the Speaker, in his capacity as President of the Senate. But Albert Gallatin Brown was dead, which also meant that, if anything happened to Lee, Bocock would become the Confederacy's third President.

Lee dismissed that thought from his mind as he took a few seconds to gather himself before launching into what might prove the most important speech of his administration. He said, "Distinguished Senators, members of the House of Representatives, I am of course aware of how unusual it is for a President to request of you the privilege of speaking to your assembled number in support of a particular piece of legislation, but I desire that you have my reasons for requesting of you a favorable vote on the bill now before you regarding the regulation of labor of certain inhabitants of the Confederate States."

During the war, the Confederate Congress had usually met *in camera*, its deliberations secret. The policy carried over into time of peace as well. Lee did not altogether approve of it, but this once found it useful: not all of what he had to say belonged in the Richmond papers.

He made that clear from the outset: "All of you, by now, have seen the works the AWB brought back to our time. You have seen how with virtual unanimity the twentieth and twenty-first centuries condemn the institution of slavery with the same sort of loathing we might apply to savage tribes who devour their fellow men."

Several legislators winced at the harsh comparison. Lee did not care; he aimed to state his case in the strongest possible terms. He went on, "The AWB sought to keep us just as we were, sought to freeze us in place forever so we might join them in defiance of what lies ahead, and sought to overthrow our duly elected government when we gave the slightest sign of contravening their desires. Their armed revolt continues to this day. A vote against this proposed legislation is a vote for the AWB and its methods.

You will have seen that for yourselves in the AWB's secret chambers; I wish to explicitly remind you of it here today so that you may retain no doubt as to the issues involved."

He paused for a moment, looked out over his audience. This business of gaining his wishes through persuasion did not come naturally to him, not after a lifetime of simply receiving or giving orders. Save for one or two scribbling notes to themselves, senators and congressmen stared intently back at him. If not persuaded, they were at least fully attentive. That would do. Onward:

"Yet I believe, gentlemen, we should sooner or later have been compelled to confront this issue, even had we gained our independence by our own exertions, even had the AWB never existed."

Had the AWB never existed, the South would not have gained its independence by its own exertions. Lee had known that since he first opened the *Picture History of the Civil War.* The members of Congress knew it too, intellectually: the books from the AWB sanctum made it abundantly clear. But in their hearts, most of them still surely felt their beloved country would have found some road to freedom without the intervention of the men from the future.

Lee went on, "The war itself and its aftermath taught us new lessons about the Negro, lessons, I admit, a fair number of us would sooner not have learned. Yet they remain before us, and we ignore them at our peril. We learned from the United States that colored men might make fair soldiers, a possibility we had previously denied. Let me now state what some of you will have gathered from your readings in the secret chamber: at the time when the Rivington men came to us, certain of our officers had already begun to suggest freeing and arming Negro slaves so they might battle the Northern foe at our sides."

A murmur ran through the House chamber. Not everyone had noticed that part of the record, nor did everyone care to remember how little hope the war had held only a bit more than four years before.

"The arrival of the Rivington men and their repeaters obviated the necessity for such desperate expedients, but the Negro has continued to instruct us as to his capacities. Though the insurrections that so long plagued the Mississippi valley have been reduced to small, scattered outbreaks, the tenacity with which colored men maintained them in the face of overwhelming odds must give us pause if we continue to see those colored men only as the docile servants they appeared to be in days past.

"We have tacitly recognized this change, in that many blacks who escaped from bondage during the upheavals of the Second American Revolution remain at liberty, not least, perhaps, because, once having tasted freedom, they can no longer safely be returned to servitude. Further, during the war several states relaxed restrictions on what the Negro might be taught, the better to benefit from his intelligent exertions. Once having taught him, one may no longer demand that he subsequently forget.

"Yet if the Negro may learn, if he will take up arms in his own defense, if in our hour of peril we contemplated his taking up arms in *our* defense, where is the justice in leaving him in chains? To do so but exacerbates the risk of servile rebellion and gives our enemies a dagger pointed straight at our hearts. I submit to you, my friends, that emancipation, however distasteful it may appear, exists *de facto* in large stretches of our territory; gradually acknowledging it *de jure* will allow us to control its impact upon our nation and will shield us against the excesses we all fear.

"Gentlemen of the Congress, rest assured I do not lightly urge upon you the provisions of the legislation whose introduction I have proposed. I truly believe these provisions shall prove to be in the best interest of the Confederate States of America in the long run, and request of you their passage. The world will little note nor long remember what I say here, but it can never forget what you do here. Let our descendants say that this nation, under God, shall have a new birth of freedom, and let them say that it began here today. I thank you."

He stepped away from the podium. The applause that followed was more than polite, less than warm. He wondered how much of it he would have kept had the Confederate Congress known he was borrowing words from one of Abraham Lincoln's memorial addresses. By all accounts, Lincoln's little speech at Gettysburg had become famous in the world wherein the South's independence had been crushed. Here in the real world, Lincoln and all he stood for were discredited, his words, no doubt, doomed to obscurity forever. Lee had read through that Gettysburg speech at least a dozen times. He thought it deserved to live.

Louis T. Wigfall got to his feet. "Mr. Speaker!" he boomed.

"Senator Wigfall?" Thomas Bocock responded as he resumed his customary place of honor.

"Mr. Speaker, I desire to say a few words in respectful opposition to—"

Bocock's gavel came down on the rostrum with three sharp cracks, cutting through the building spate. "The honorable gentleman is not recognized. He will please recall that we are met in special joint session for the specific purpose of hearing President Lee's address. He will, I am certain, have adequate opportunity to express his opinion of the measures proposed in that address when in deliberation within the confines of the Senate chamber."

Wigfall tried to go on with his speech anyhow; the Speaker of the House gaveled him down. At last, red-faced and sullen, he sat. Lee stared stonily at him. He might not have made his speech, but he had made his point.

Lee's shoulders shifted slightly as he stifled a sigh. If not even the acknowledged voice of the future convinced some people of the folly of their chosen course, what could? *Nothing* was the answer that immediately sprang to mind. He hoped with all his heart such stubborn souls made up only a minority of the Congress.

A deep-toned whistle in the air, not a bird— "Mortar!" Nate Caudell yelled, along with twenty others. He dove into a deep bombproof, a timber-reinforced hole dug into the front wall of the trench. He landed on top of someone. Two more men jumped in on top of him.

The mortar shell burst less than a hundred yards behind him, in the second line of trenches. Dirt fountained skyward; a clod found the bombproof opening and hit him in the back of the neck. Half a minute later, another round whistled past overhead, this one, by the sound, destined for some far more distant target.

The four men who'd taken shelter in the bombproof crawled out—no one could stand inside—made foredoomed efforts to brush themselves clean. Caudell also rubbed bruised ribs. He glared about a quarter seriously at Dempsey Eure. "That's the second time you landed on me the past two days. I'm starting to think you're more dangerous than any damned mortar bomb."

"Long as the Rivington men think the same way," Eure answered with a chuckle.

"How many of *them* have you landed on?" Caudell asked darkly.

His friend said, "Reckon I'll have my chance soon enough—if Henry ever gets that tunnel of his finished. He diggin' under them guns up there, or is he headin' all the way to China?"

The three weeks to a month Pleasants had promised to Nathan Bedford Forrest had already stretched into a month and a half. Proper tools and experienced diggers were in shorter supply in North Carolina than he'd imagined. Caudell had crawled down the tunnel himself a couple of times, carrying boards through blackness toward a flickering candle flame that gave a man with a pick a tiny dollop of light by which to work. He wanted to kiss the dry wash when he emerged, and marveled that some men endured a lifetime down in the mines.

Another mortar bomb went sailing off into the Confederates' rear. "Good thing they don't seem to have a whole lot of shells for that beast," he said. "It reaches almost all the way back to Nashville."

Dempsey Eure nodded. "I was listenin' to some artillery men talkin', and they say it's got more range'n one of our hundred-pounder coast defense guns. Be switched if I know how the Rivington men do it."

"Same way they do the AK-47s, I reckon."

"Whatever that is."

Caudell shrugged. Same way they get books full of photographs—and colored ones at that, he thought. Same way they get books printed in . . . was it 1996? He'd never spoken to anyone but Mollie about the *Picture History of the Civil War* she'd stolen. Who would believe him? He wasn't always sure he believed himself. But getting back in the trenches against the endless repeater and the long-range mortar had undermined his doubts as surely as Henry Pleasants was undermining the bastion up ahead. He'd come to take the AK-47 for granted, but those other weapons reminded him afresh that they did not belong to 1868. They were also one more reason the tunnel was running late.

Captain Lewis walked down the wash. He dipped his head to Caudell and Eure. "Much to my surprise, it's done at last," he said. He sounded annoyed whenever he mentioned the tunnel; seeing Pleasants promoted from private to colonel in one fell swoop still rankled.

"We've been ready awhile now, sir," Caudell said. He waved to the sets of packed-earth steps that led up from the bottom of the wash to the parapet. Excavating a hundred-yard shaft produced a lot of dirt. It had to go somewhere inconspicuous to keep the Rivington men from spotting it and figuring out its source. The steps served that purpose and, when the moment came, would also let the Confederate soldiers quickly go over to the attack.

"Pleasants will touch off the charge at sunrise tomorrow, or is supposed to, at any rate," Lewis said. "Assuming it goes off, you know your orders?"

"Yes, sir," Caudell and Dempsey Eure said together. Eure amplified: "Soon as it blows, we go over. We head straight for Rivington, and we don't stop for nothin'." The orders had come straight from Forrest and were imbued with his driving energy.

"That's it," Lewis agreed. "If it turns out to be that simple, we can get down on our knees and thank God the next time we go to church. But the general's right—the first strike has to be right for the heart. The troops behind us can fan out and take whatever strongpoints are left from the flank and rear."

"What if it doesn't blow?" Eure said.

"Then General Forrest thinks up something new and, unless I miss my guess, Colonel Henry Pleasants turns back into a pumpkin—I mean, a private." But, being a just man at heart, Lewis added, "He's not stinted himself, I give him that. I hope it works as he claims; we shan't have a better chance than this."

"I hope it works, too," Caudell said fervently. If it didn't and the attack went on anyhow, the result would be gruesome, and he would be a part of that result. He wondered whether charging a nest of endless repeaters could possibly be worse than tramping across open fields toward the massed muskets and artillery atop Cemetery Ridge. Maybe not, but it wouldn't be much better, either.

After darkness fell, men began moving forward in the zigzag network of trenches the Confederates had dug up to the dry wash. To help disguise that movement, long-range artillery fire started up. The fire had to be at long range; no matter how well protected cannon were, fire from the endless repeaters murdered their crews when they tried to get too near the Rivington men's lines.

Confederate artillery fuses were imperfectly reliable; more than one shell burst above the soldiers' heads rather than among their foes. But enough came down near their target for the Rivington men to answer with mortar fire. "Damned if I don't halfway hope they hit somebody," Caudell growled to Mollie Bean. "I'm sick of my own side shooting at me." Just then, another shell fell short and made them both throw themselves flat.

Mollie said, "They ain't *tryin'* to kill us, Nate."

"Does that make it better or worse if they do?" he asked. She thought for a few seconds, then shrugged. He didn't know the answer either, but army life was easier to take when you had something to bellyache about—for one thing, it kept you from remembering you might get killed in the next few hours.

He broke a piece of corn bread in half, passed one chunk to Mollie. After she ate it, she rolled herself in her blanket, lay down. "I'm gonna sleep while I can—if I can." The racket from the artillery duel made that anything but obvious.

Caudell wished she were safe in Nashville, but telling her so seemed pointless, since she wouldn't listen to him and, even if she had, she could hardly get back there against the tide of soldiers moving the other way. For that matter, he wished *he* were safe in Nashville, which was just as impossible to arrange. He took a cigar out of a tunic pocket, lit it at a tiny cook fire, smoked in quick, savage puffs. The smoke failed to soothe him as he'd hoped. He tossed the chewed butt into the dirt. By then, Mollie had succeeded in falling asleep.

He lay down next to her, not really expecting to doze off himself. But the next thing he knew, someone was shaking him awake and saying, "Come on; get ready now." He sat up, surprised to see the sky pale in the east. He put on his hat, grabbed his rifle and his haversack. He moved a couple of full banana clips from the latter to his trouser pockets where he could get at them easily. With that, he was as ready as he could be. Beside him, Mollie made the same sort of sketchy preparations.

As darkness faded, he could see farther and farther up and down the wash. There stood Captain Lewis, carefully cleaning his AK-47 one last time. And there—Caudell nodded to himself. He might have known Nathan Bedford Forrest would place himself in the first rank when the fighting started.

Henry Pleasants stood by the mouth of the tunnel he'd proposed and labored so mightily to build, a length of slow match in his hand. He looked toward General Forrest. Forrest was looking from the sky to Pleasants and back again. At last he nodded, a single abrupt motion.

Pleasants stooped, touched the slow match to a fuse that lay on the floor of the tunnel. The fuse caught. Pleasants sighed and straightened. Caudell noticed he was holding his own breath. How long for the flame to run from this end of the tunnel to that?

Before he could ask, Forrest beat him to it: "When will it go off?"

"Shouldn't be long," Pleasants answered. A Confederate shell screamed overhead, making him raise his voice. "In fact, it should be right about—"

Before he could say "now," the ground shook beneath Caudell's feet. He'd heard of earthquakes, but he'd never been in the middle of one before. A roar like fifty thunderstorms left him momentarily stunned. He saw Forrest's lips shape the words "God damn!" but could not hear him through that echoing blast.

He did not know whether he was the next man out of the gully after Forrest, but he was sure no more than a couple of others could have been in front of him. Two or three steps past the parapet, he stopped dead in wonder. He'd never had a good look at that strongpoint while the tunnel was being dug: peering through a firing slit only invited a bullet in the face. And the bastion wasn't there for him to examine anymore.

"God almighty," he said softly. The gunpowder, brought in bag by bag, barrel by barrel, had blown the biggest hole in the ground he'd ever imagined—it had to be fifty yards across, fifty feet wide, and God only knew how deep. All around it lay broken chunks of earthwork, timbers snapped like dry twigs, guns tossed every which way, and twisted bodies in mottled green.

Like him, most of the others emerging from the Confederate works paused to gape in wonder and disbelief. Up ahead of them, Nathan Bedford

Forrest turned, gestured furiously. "Come on, you bastards! And fetch the ladders right now, do you hear me? We ain't got time to waste."

That was true. Not only were the guns in the bastion itself destroyed, but the endless repeaters to either flank had fallen silent, the men at them momentarily stunned by the disaster that had befallen their comrades and doubtless wondering if the ground was about to heave up under them as well.

Caudell dashed forward, shouting for all he was worth. He reached the edge of the crater, slid down into it on his backside. More wreckage lay strewn over the bottom, and more bodies. Some of them moved as he scrambled past. He stopped and stared again, wondering how anyone could have lived through that explosion.

But Nathan Bedford Forrest, disdaining to wait for ladders, was already climbing the far wall of the hole and yelling, "Come on, come on, *come on!*" Caudell hurried after him—a general who went out ahead of his men could always pull them after him.

Forrest, grimy now as any private soldier, reached out a hand and helped pull Caudell up onto the flat ground beyond the crater. Behind them, teams of soldiers were carrying ladders across the bottom of the hole, leaning up against the wall so others could ascend.

Off to either side, the repeaters started their deadly stutter again. But hundreds of Confederates were almost to the crater, inside it, or coming up the ladders. There was Captain Lewis, shouting orders and waving to get the men into a line of battle. "Keep moving!" Forrest shouted. "Come on, keep moving!"

Bullets chewed the grass close to his feet, spat dirt into Caudell's face. That was AK-47 fire from the bushes ahead; the Rivington men had detached fighters to try to plug the gap the Confederates had blown in their line. Caudell dove behind the closest cover he saw: a corpse wearing mottled green and brown, its head and neck twisted at an impossible angle. He fired several rounds before he realized the blank, staring face a few inches from his own belonged to Piet Hardie.

His lips skinned back from his teeth in a savage smile. He gave the corpse a familiar thump on the shoulder. "How many more wenches did you aim to torment to death, Piet? Too bad you won't get the chance, isn't it? Quicker than you deserved to go, too." *Maybe not*, Caudell decided once he'd said that. A noose would have been quick, and if ever a man deserved a noose, Piet Hardie did.

Once out of their earthworks, the Rivington men were vulnerable. The Confederates knew how to attack mere riflemen, and their numbers counted for more than their foes' armor and helmets. Some men in gray rushed forward in small groups, while others fired to cover their advance. Then the groups reversed roles, leapfrogging past one another as they fanned out to get around the handful of defenders.

"So long, Piet." Caudell leaped to his feet and, hunched low, dashed toward a broken tree fifty yards away. Bullets whipped past him as he ran. He sprawled behind the scanty protection the tree trunk gave him, fired to support a double handful of men moving up on his right. Then he was running again, in the direction of a tall clump of grass.

Behind him and to his left, one of the Rivington men's endless repeaters fell silent. A minute later, so did the one on the other side. Rebel yells rang through the continuing racket of rifle fire. Caudell whooped as loud as anyone. With those murderous repeaters out of action, the Rivington men could not hope to keep the whole Confederate army from going not only through Henry Pleasants's crater but around it to either side.

Nathan Bedford Forrest saw that, too. "Forward, boys, with me! They ain't got a prayer of holdin' us back now." He was normally soft-spoken; Caudell had noticed that back in Nashville and in the trenches. But at need, on the stump or in the middle of a fight, his voice swelled to carry as far as he wanted. He pointed north and east. "We're an hour from Rivington. Let's go!" The soldiers cheered like madmen.

Cheers or no, though, Rivington proved more than an hour away. If the Confederates knew how to advance against rifle fire, the Rivington men were artists on defense. They gave ground only grudgingly, in a reverse of the leapfrog pattern their opponents used to move forward. They made stand after stand, stalling the Confederates again and again, surely inflicting far more casualties than they suffered.

But the Confederates had soldiers to spend and the Rivington men did not. The gray line grew ever wider, flanking the Rivington men out of one position after another. Forrest did not, would not, let the advance flag. Whenever a handful of Rivington men held out against everything the Confederates could throw at them, he cried, "Come on, boys, we'll go around. Pull the weed up by the roots and the leaves are bound to wither."

"Nate!"

He whirled where he lay, his AK-47 swinging almost of its own accord to bear on the person who'd startled him. He jerked the barrel down in a hurry. "Jesus God, Mollie, I damn near shot you. Are you all right?"

" 'Cept for you just now havin' your gun on me, sure. You?"

"Yup. How much farther to Rivington?"

She frowned as she thought. Such a serious, involuted, almost harsh expression should have made her face seem more than usually masculine, especially in this warlike setting. But instead she reminded Nate of a girl trying to remember where she'd put her pincushion. He wanted to carry her back to Nashville, a notion as tender as it was impracticable.

"Three, four miles, I reckon," she answered at last. Then she brought her rifle up to her shoulder, fired a couple of quick shots. "Thought I saw somethin' movin' in them bushes up there. Reckon not, though. Come on."

Caudell looked ahead for the next likely piece of cover. He pointed toward a thick stand of pine saplings. He went first, with Mollie ready to open fire on anyone who shot at him. When nobody did, he got down on one knee and covered her advance.

They were still near the foaming crest of the Confederate wave, for they could hear Nathan Bedford Forrest loudly and profanely urging his men on. He was also yelling something new: "We get into Rivington, don't you go burning any houses, you hear me, not even if there's some of these muddy green boys shootin' from 'em. Anybody burns a house and I catch him, he'll wish a Rivington man put a bullet through his head instead, God damn me to hell if I lie."

"What do you suppose that's all about?" Caudell asked. While wanton arson was not a legitimate tool of war, he'd never heard it so specifically and vehemently forbidden.

"Nate, you got to remember I been in them houses." Mollie hesitated. Nate grimaced, recalling how and why she'd been in them. When she saw he would do no more than grimace, she hurried on, "Ain't nothin' like 'em nowheres else. The books, the lights, the cool air that blows—"

"The books!" he exclaimed. The *Picture History of the Civil War* had come out of one of those Rivington houses. If they held more volumes of that ilk, the Confederate authorities had good reason to want them preserved.

"Makes sense to me," Mollie said when he quickly explained his reasoning. "Marse Robert, he was plumb took with the one you had me bring him."

For the next few minutes, neither of them had much chance to talk. The Rivington men did their best to rally. They seemed to be in somewhat greater numbers now, reinforced by their fellows rushing down from the town. Rifle grenades bursting among the Confederates created brief consternation, but after weeks of intermittent mortar fire the small bombs were not so terrifying. And, now that they were forced from their fortified positions, the Rivington men, even reinforced, lacked the troops to halt determined attackers. Determined the Confederates were. The advance resumed.

Someone moaned from behind a clump of beggarweeds. Caudell and Mollie hurried over, ready to help a wounded comrade. But the man back there was not a comrade; his mottled tunic and trousers proclaimed his allegiance to America Will Break. Blood from a wound above the knee soaked one leg of those trousers, turning dark green and brown to black.

"Got you!" Caudell yelled.

Distracted from his pain, the Rivington man whipped his head around. It was Benny Lang. He was utterly defenseless; his rifle lay several feet away. Caudell's finger tightened on the trigger of his AK-47. "Don't," Mollie exclaimed, guessing what was in his mind. "He ain't one of the real bad ones, Nate."

"No?" Caudell remembered George Ballentine. But that memory wasn't nearly all of why he wanted to put a bullet through Benny Lang. It wasn't exactly as if Mollie had been unfaithful with the Rivington man . . . not exactly, but pretty close. But after a few seconds, Nate lowered the rifle a little. If he'd killed Lang here in the bushes, man against man and gun against gun, that was war, and fair enough. Try as he would, though, he couldn't make himself think of blowing out the back of a wounded man's head as anything but murder.

"Thanks," Lang said when he no longer looked straight down the muzzle of the AK-47. "Help me cut my trouser leg off so I can get a bandage—" He was half stunned from his injury and, no doubt, he didn't remember seeing Mollie Bean in uniform, just as Caudell had never seen her in properly feminine clothes until that morning in church. But her voice must have registered at last, for he blurted, "Jesus Christ, Moll, is that you?"

Moll. The pet name made Nate ready to shoot him again. Mollie ground her teeth before she answered, almost inaudibly, "It's me all right, Benny. I soldiered before—I'm sorry I lied to you when you ast me how I got shot. And this here"—she raised her chin, looked defiantly at Caudell, as if daring him to deny it—"this here's my intended, Nate Caudell."

The wounded man got out part of a laugh before it turned into a hiss. "Caudell. Christ, I remember you—I taught you the AK, didn't I? Small bloody world, what?" Caudell, numb with suddenly having to be sociable on the battlefield, managed a nod. Lang had both hands on his wound. Where his trousers looked black, those hands were red. He said, "I'm going to reach for my knife. I'll do that very slowly, and I give you my word of honor I won't throw the knife once I have it—there are two of you, after all, and only the one blade."

Caudell nodded again, now with assurance—this was business. As Lang got out the knife, he scooped up the Rivington man's rifle. He did not relax his vigilance, not one bit; after the Richmond Massacre, could a member of America Will Break be trusted to honor a parole?

But Benny Lang did only what he'd promised, slicing his pants leg so he could see the wound in the outside of his thigh. Had it been to the inside, he would have bled to death in short order. As it was, Caudell, who had enough experience with gunshot wounds to make a fair judge, thought he would recover if fever didn't carry him off.

Lang might have been reading his mind. "I carry medicine to keep wounds from going bad. I'm going to get that now, and a pressure bandage." Again he moved with slow care. The medicine came in a little packet. He tore it open, sprinkled some powder onto his leg, and slapped on the bandage. Then he held the packet out to Caudell. "There's some left. You may need it in a while, or—or your Mollie."

Caudell took the medicine packet, grunted gruffly as he stuck it in his pocket. He didn't want to feel beholden to Benny Lang, not any which way. Gruff still, he said, "Stay here. Someone will take you back to the surgeons pretty soon."

"Spare me that," Lang said. "It's a through-and-through wound, so your doctors won't have to dig the bullet out—not bloody likely you'll take me to one of ours, is it? I know your men mean well, but—" He shuddered at the very idea, then shook his head. "It all went so well for us, till Lee was elected. Since then, everything's been buggered up." He put a hand on the bandage, as if still unwilling to believe ruination could have chosen to visit him personally.

"He's as settled as he's going to be," Caudell said to Mollie. "Let's get moving."

But before they could leave, something in Benny Lang's pocket let out a flatulent burst of noise and then words: "Report your position and status, Lang. Over."

Nate's rifle came up again. "What the devil is that?"

"It's called a radio," the Rivington man answered. "Think of it as a talking telegraph without wires. May I answer?"

Curiosity and caution fought within Caudell. Curiosity won, barely. "Go ahead, but if you betray us, it'll be the last thing you ever do." He jerked the AK-47 to emphasize his words.

"Right." Lang eyed the rifle's muzzle with respect. He took out something a little smaller than a low-cut shoe, extended a telescoping metal rod from one end, spoke into the other: "Lang here. I am wounded and captured. Out."

"You can talk with your people on that—radio, did you say?—any time you want, can't you?" Caudell asked. When the Rivington man nodded, Nate held out a hand. "Give it here."

Lang scowled. Instead of obeying, he smashed the radio against a good-sized rock, as hard as he could. Pieces flew in every direction. He said,

"Do what you want with me. I won't let you spy on us." Caudell's blood had cooled. After a moment's anger, he reluctantly lowered his rifle. If he'd been in the Rivington man's place, he hoped he'd have had the courage to do as Lang had.

Mollie thought of something else: "You've had these radio things all along, haven't you? Ever since you came here?"

Benny Lang nodded again. Caudell saw what Mollie was driving at. "And you never let on, did you? Having these things would have helped us almost as much as our repeaters, I reckon. But you never let on. Why not?"

"If we'd needed to badly enough, I think we would have," the Rivington man answered. "But we always thought it was a good idea to keep a few secrets of our own. You play poker?"

"Yes," Nate said.

"Then think of them as an ace in the hole."

"Fat lot of good they did you." Caudell took a couple of steps toward the crackle of gunfire ahead. Mollie started to follow.

Benny Lang grimaced when he saw that. "You be careful, Moll. Bullets have no chivalry."

"Found that out at Gettysburg," she told him. "I hope you make it, I do." But after that, she quickly turned back to Caudell. "I'm ready, Nate." She left Lang without looking behind her.

As they pushed on, Caudell said, "So I'm your intended, am I?" He thought he kept his voice light.

It must not have been light enough; Mollie turned and looked at him through frightened eyes. "Well, ain't you?"

He wondered how many battlefields had known arguments like this one. *Precious few,* he thought. Then he realized he had to answer Mollie. "Yup, reckon I am," he said, "long as we both come out of this alive."

Her face glowed with that special shine that could make her beautiful, even if she was not particularly pretty. Seeing her expression, Caudell felt himself grinning, too. Now that the words were said, he found he rather liked the idea of being an intended; it gave him a feeling of purpose conspicuously missing from combat.

But he'd said other words as well, and coming out of the fight alive was by no means guaranteed, for him or for Mollie. The woods ended so abruptly that he had to bring himself up short to keep from blundering into open country. Swearing at himself, he peered from behind a tree at the estate ahead.

The colonnaded big house, with wings spreading out to either side, would not have shamed any successful planter in the state. The rows of clapboard slave cabins also argued for extravagant prosperity. But Caudell scratched his head. The slaves had their garden plots, and there was a barn for livestock, but where were the broad acres of corn or cotton or tobacco needed to support such a grand estate?

When he asked that aloud, Mollie said, "The Rivington men ain't all planters, Nate, but they all live like they was. Why not? They got the gold for it, remember, maybe from sellin' all our rifles to the gov'ment."

"Maybe," Caudell said, though vivid memory reminded him the Confederate government had been a lot longer on promises than hard cash in 1864. But however they came by it, gold the Rivington men certainly had; he could almost feel the sweet heaviness of the one-ounce coins he'd got from the Rivington bank just after war's end.

He shrugged: one more answer he'd never know. How the Rivington men got their money didn't matter, not in the middle of a fight. What did matter was that for the moment, anyway, no one was shooting from the big house. Caudell rubbed his chin. The nearest slave hut was hardly more than fifty yards away. He pointed toward it. Mollie nodded. Nate dashed forward, bent at the waist to make as small a target as possible. He dove behind the hut, fetched up against it with a thump. As soon as he was safe, Mollie sprinted up beside him.

They lay there panting for a few seconds, then got to their feet—they still stooped, for the roof was too low to offer much cover—and sidled around toward the front of the cabin. They almost ran into a tall, skinny Negro man hurrying the other way—and almost killed him, too, for Caudell's heart leaped into his mouth and his finger tightened on the trigger of his rifle. By Mollie's gasp, the unexpected meeting frightened her just as badly.

If they were frightened, the slave was terrified. He jumped backwards, screaming like a woman, and threw his hands high over his head. "Don' shoot me!" he squealed. "Don' shoot poor ol' raggedy Shadrach who ain't done you no harm!" Then he seemed to see the uniforms Caudell and Mollie were wearing, instead of merely the AK-47s they carried. His eyes widened till they looked like splashes of whitewash on his black face. "Lawd God," he said, "you ain't them devils what owns us? You gummint so-jers?"

"That's right," Caudell said, thinking that *raggedy* was a word that fit Shadrach like a second skin. Plenty of his first skin was plain to see, for his gray cotton jacket and trousers were little more than rags. By the ladder of ribs thus exposed, Caudell guessed he was fed no better than he was clothed.

Now his eyes got wider still; Caudell hadn't thought they could. "Gummint sojers," the Negro repeated wonderingly. He capered like a stick puppet, then leaped forward to fold Caudell and Mollie into a bony, rank embrace. "I's powerful glad to see you gentlemens, 'deed I is. You kill every one o' them devils in green, you hear me? Kill 'em daid! Every Rivington nigger there is 'll bless you fo' it."

Caudell blinked; he was not used to this kind of ecstatic greeting from a slave. During the Second American Revolution, Negroes had run away from Confederate armies, not toward them. He wondered again what sort of horrors the Rivington men worked on their blacks, though Shadrach's condition gave him a clue. But that, for the moment, was by the way. He pointed toward the big house. "Any Rivington men holed up in there?"

"No, suh," Shadrach said positively. "The massa, he off fightin' 'gainst you folks. Couple other devils run by here a while back"—he gestured vaguely—"but they don' stop. You hunt 'em down, suh, hunt 'em down if'n you has to use dogs. Every nigger here, he never complain about nothin' no mo', not if'n you gets 'em all. You give us guns, we shoots 'em our own selves."

"I believe you," Caudell said. He did, too, where before the war he would have laughed at the idea that Negroes might make soldiers (before the war, of course, no Negro would have been so suicidally foolhardy as to ask one white man for arms to use against another).

"Marse Robert, he gwine set the niggers free like we hear tell?" Shadrach asked.

"A little at a time, yes," Caudell said, which was plenty to set the slave dancing again.

"If that house is empty, we got to get going," Mollie said. Caudell nodded. He glanced back as he trotted away. Shadrach was still capering beside the mean little slave cabins. A couple of women, gaudy in brightly striped skirts and wearing red handkerchiefs on their heads, stepped out of their huts. Shadrach pointed at Caudell and Mollie, said something. The women screeched for joy and started dancing, too. One of them was big with child. Hurrying past the big house, Caudell wondered who had put that child in her.

A few hundreds yards past the clearing, fighting picked up. The coughing snarl of an endless repeater brought Caudell to a respectful halt. Off to the right, he heard Nathan Bedford Forrest yelling, "I see the dirty son of a bitch! We'll git him—he ain't dug his self in yet."

Sure enough, after a minute or so the Rivington repeater fell silent and rebel yells rang out in triumph. Caudell and Mollie moved forward again, past the dead gunner. He had sited his weapon well—say what you would of them, the Rivington men were no mean soldiers—but in this chaotic fighting had lacked time to use the spade. Now he also lacked most of his face.

Mollie and Caudell came up to another palatial mansion, this one also flanked by slave huts all the shabbier in comparison to the big house. Mollie frowned; after some little hesitation, she said, "That there's Benny Lang's place."

"Is it?" Caudell's voice was as neutral as he could make it. He paused for thought, finally found something safe to add: "He never seemed to notice his book was missing."

"You're right," Mollie said. "Reckon with the war over and all, he didn't need to read about it no more." Caudell chewed on that a few seconds before he nodded. As Lang himself had said, everything—the war included—went the Rivington men's way until Lee became President of the Confederacy. And when things went badly afterwards . . . "I think you put all this in train when you took that book."

"Wasn't all me, Nate Caudell," she said, sounding almost angry. "You reckon I'd've ever thought of anything as crazy as goin' up to Marse Robert by my lonesome? Not likely!"

"Maybe not," he admitted. "I won't lose sleep over my part, though. The way I look at it is like this: If the Rivington men are the sort of people who could do something like the Richmond Massacre, they aren't the sort of people who ought to be near the top of the heap. They would have done something else just as bad sooner or later, with us or without us. They need putting down, and we're just the ones who happen to be doing the job."

"Might could be you're right," Mollie said thoughtfully, and, after a moment, "Reckon maybe you are. You got a good way of lookin' at things, Nate."

"Most important thing I want to look at now is the both of us getting through this alive . . . intended." The way Mollie's face kindled made Caudell glad he'd tacked on the last word.

They went by or near several more big new houses; the Rivington men had built far back into the woods from what once was the sleepy little town of Rivington. About a mile and a half from the western edge of what had been the town, the Rivington men made a serious stand. "You want to watch yourself," a corporal warned as Caudell came up. "They got wire with teeth strung out up ahead. You try crawlin' through it, it slows you down an' they shoot you." Bodies hung up at grotesque angles underscored the fellow's caution.

From behind the wire, the Rivington men traded fire with the Confederates. Nathan Bedford Forrest stalked down the stalled Confederate line.

His dark gray eyes flashed with frustration. "We got to keep drivin'. They get a chance to dig in here, we have to start all over again, God damn it." Suddenly he pounded fist into open palm, laughed out loud. Turning to an aide who walked beside him, he said, "Major Strange, I reckon it's about time to send in a flag of truce."

Major J. P. Strange, Forrest's adjutant, was a dark-haired man of about the general's age, with a high, broad forehead, sweeping mustaches, and a graying beavertail of a beard. He said, "The usual message, sir? They'd best surrender, or we shan't answer for the consequences?"

"The very same." Forrest chuckled reminiscently. "Don't know how many times we slickered the Yankees with that one during the war. 'Course, after Fort Pillow they was more inclined to believe it than they had been before."

"Let me scout out some white cloth and a stick, sir," Strange said.

A few minutes later, he stepped out between the two lines waving the parley flag. Firing slowed, stopped. A Rivington man called, "Come ahead and say your say, graycoat. We won't shoot for—say, an hour?"

Strange looked back at Forrest, who nodded. "Agreed," the major said. Holding the white flag high, he walked forward. A Rivington man, almost invisible in his mottled clothes and what looked like green and brown face paint, took charge of him.

Caudell lit a cigar and prepared to enjoy the brief cease-fire. Long before the hour was up, though, he saw the white flag returning. A tall Rivington man accompanied Major Strange. "May I cross to speak with you, General Forrest?" he shouted.

"Come ahead, Mr. Rhoodie," Forrest shouted back. "The truce has a while to run." He waited for the Rivington men to approach, then said, "How do you answer, Andries?" Caudell, listening, realized with a small start that the two men were—or had been—friends.

"I answer no," Andries Rhoodie replied at once. "I know your tricks— I've read of them often enough, remember. You'll not bluff me into giving up."

Forrest's swarthy face darkened further with rage. Few men care to be called predictable, especially men as wily as the Confederate general. "If you think I'm bluffing this time, Andries, you are mistaken. If you do not yield, you will likely die here."

"And if I do yield, what will happen to me?" Rhoodie retorted. "After Richmond, if I'm taken I'll dance on air, which you know as well as I. And we may hold you yet."

"Hold us, sir?" Forrest's laugh sounded more like a bay. "You haven't the chance of a snake in the Garden of Eden of holding us."

"How many battles did you win by bluff?" Rhoodie said. "You won't bluff me."

"I won by bluff when I was weak. I ain't weak now, Andries."

"You say so."

"Want to see my army, so you know what I've got?"

It was Rhoodie's turn to laugh. "How many of them would I see three times, to make you look stronger than you are? You can trick damnfool Yankees that way, but don't expect me to fall for it."

"Git back to your lines, Rhoodie, or you'll find the truce runnin' out a mite early," Forrest growled, taking a step toward the Rivington man. He was ten years older than Rhoodie and, while large, could not match his massive frame. Still, Caudell would have bet on him in a fight—he had a fire, a vitality, the Rivington man lacked.

But Andries Rhoodie, if stolid next to Forrest, was also stolid enough not to be overawed by him. He held his ground, glowering like a big slow bear facing a panther. "How many lives do you want to spend taking us down?"

"Few as I have to," Forrest said. "But when it comes to that, Andries, I got more lives to spend than you. That worked for Grant against Lee till you came along, didn't it? Reckon it can work just as well for us this time."

Most of the Confederates who heard Forrest—even Major Strange—frowned and scratched their heads, wondering what he was talking about. Caudell started to frown with them until he remembered the *Picture History of the Civil War.* If Forrest hadn't seen it, he knew of something like it and knew it was true. Rhoodie knew that, too; for the first time, Forrest succeeded in rocking him. He ground his teeth, once, twice, three times. Then, without another word, he turned and stamped back to his own line.

Nineteen ninety-six, Caudell thought as he watched that broad retreating back. But there was no dream to it; somehow, the Rivington men had slid back through time to change the way the Second American Revolution turned out. And, having changed that, they'd also tried to change the subsequent Confederate government—tried to change it by gunfire. Caudell's hands tightened on his own AK-47. They weren't going to get away with it.

Nathan Bedford Forrest muttered a curse which his mustache muffled. He, too, stared after Andries Rhoodie. When he turned back to his own troops, his eye fell on Caudell and Mollie Bean. His gaze sharpened. "I saw you two back at Nashville with Pleasants," he said, not making it a question. "You're from around these parts, then."

"Yes, sir," they said together. Mollie added, "Matter of fact, sir, I'm from Rivington."

"Are you?" Forrest said, suddenly smiling. "Suppose you could guide a company around east to outflank these works the Rivington bastards are running up here?"

"Reckon so," Mollie answered. "I expect we can march faster'n they can dig."

"I expect so, too." Forrest turned to his adjutant. "Major Strange, gather a force from the men moving up. Take command of it and go with Bean and Caudell here"—Nate envied the general his memory—"around to the right. I want you moving before the hour's up, on account of they're surely digging now."

"Yes, sir," Strange said, adding to his guides: "You two come along with me and help me assemble my force."

"If you do get around them, drive straight for Rivington," Forrest said. "Get into their rear one more time and they're done for."

"Question, sir," Strange said; at Forrest's nod, he went on, "Do you want us to strike for the town once in their rear, or back at the fighting men themselves? Your usual aim is to beat the army; with that accomplished, the place it defended will fall of its own accord."

"Nothing is usual about the Rivington men," Nathan Bedford Forrest answered. "In Rivington they have the engine they use to bring in their weapons—I gather they travel here through it, too, come to that. If it's taken or wrecked, the fighters are done for, too. So this time I want the town."

"You'll have it," Major Strange promised. "Caudell, Bean—do I have your names straight?—come along now. This time I really mean it." Caudell stumbled over his own feet a couple of times as he followed Forrest's aide— he wasn't paying much attention to where he was going. His mind kept chewing on the idea of an engine that ran through time. It made perfect sense; the Rivington men had to come from somewhen that wasn't 1868. But he'd never wondered about how they did it until Forrest set him thinking.

The soldiers he and Mollie helped Strange collect belonged to several different regiments; advance was as likely as retreat to break up an army's neat ranks. When they'd rounded up about a company's worth, the major said, "All right, Bean, get us around them."

"Do my best, sir." Mollie led the impromptu force east, saying, "We'll go most of the way to the railroad tracks before I try and bring us north. There's a little path runs alongside 'em, about half a mile this way."

"Good enough," Strange said. "The line of the railroad itself is sure to be strongly held, but a path . . ." His features were not nearly so mobile as those of his commander, but anticipation sparked in his eyes.

The detachment had not been moving long when firing erupted up ahead. After a few minutes, mortar bombs began falling, *crump, crump, crump*, back around where Major Strange had chosen his men. Caudell said, "I'm not usually what you'd call fond of marching, but right this second, it looks pretty fine to me." Major Strange, who tramped along in front of him, bobbed his head up and down in emphatic agreement.

The din of gunfire faded behind the Confederates. Caudell took that as a good sign, hoping it meant the Rivington men hadn't the men to extend their wired line all the way from the position they'd been defending to the Wilmington and Weldon tracks. If they had— He took a deep breath which had nothing to do with how tired he was. If they had enough men for that, this detachment was going to get chewed up.

Mollie recognized the path when she came to it. Nate would have marched right by; it was so narrow and overgrown that he wondered if it went back to Indian days. That made it harder to follow north, but also raised his spirits: newcomers like the Rivington men might never have discovered it.

No wire with teeth reached out to trap him for enemy guns. The soldiers who marched with him had seen too much war to make a lot of unnecessary noise, but they grinned and checked their rifles. They knew what they were gaining here.

"How close to the town do the woods grow?" Strange asked Mollie.

"Inside half a mile, sir," she answered. The major beamed like a cherub.

As it turned out, they didn't do quite as well as Mollie expected. They came to a new clearing with a half-built big house in the middle of it. On the far side were four or five Rivington men hurrying toward the fighting. They stopped in comic dismay as the Confederates began coming out of the woods. Then one of them raised his repeater to his shoulder and started shooting.

The fierce little fire fight lasted only a few minutes: even with body armor, four or five were no match for a company. Major Strange was rubbing his chin as he trotted north. He waved the detachment to a halt, told off about a quarter of his little force and pointed them westward. "I know the general told me to drive for the town, but the Rivington men have to know we're here now after the racket we just made," he said. "I don't aim to be hit from the side when I'm supposed to be doing the hitting myself."

The men he'd split off from his main command went regretfully, but they went: Strange's order made too much military sense to be disobeyed, even by soldiers who wanted to be in at the kill. They'd all been outflanked at one time or another and didn't fancy ending up on the receiving end of that punishment ever again.

Strange waved once more. "Let's go! Skirmish order." The Confederates formed two lines, the men well separated from one another, and rolled forward. A few shots came from in front of them, but only a few. Nate let loose with a rebel yell as the whitewashed bulk of the Notahilton began playing peekaboo through the trees.

Gunfire crackled, not far off to the left. Mollie pointed toward J. P. Strange, nodded approvingly. So did Caudell: sure enough, the Rivington men had tried to swing back on the detachment. *Always nice to have an officer who can see past the end of his beard*, Caudell thought.

Something went *pop* under Strange. The noise was loud enough to make Caudell, who trotted along perhaps fifty yards to the right of the major, look his way. He saw a black cylinder bounce out of the ground, about to the level of Strange's waist. A split second later came another, much louder blast. The major collapsed with gruesome bonelessness, almost torn in two. A couple of men closest to him on either side also went down. Small, deadly pieces of metal buzzed past Caudell like angry bees.

"Torpedo!" The cry rose from half a dozen throats.

Caudell wished he could glide through the air or, like Jesus, walk on water. But there was no help for it but to run on. "Once we take Rivington, we don't have to worry about torpedoes again as long as we live!" he shouted, as much for his own spirit's sake as for the men around him. He blinked when they raised a cheer.

And there, all at once, lay the town whose name had become a curse all through the Confederacy. Only a handful of men in mottled green were on the street. Caudell fired at one of them. Several other Confederates opened up at the same time, so even though the man fell, he was not sure his bullet had brought him down.

The other Rivington men scrambled for cover. Remembering Nathan Bedford Forrest's orders to poor Major Strange, Caudell yelled, "Watch where they retreat to. That'll be what the general wants us to take out."

Following his own advice wasn't easy. The Rivington men were far from the only people dashing this way and that: a great many shrieking slaves, some white men in ordinary clothes—*the true Rivington men*, Caudell thought—and a handful of women scattered in panic at the sound of gunfire.

"The railroad station!" Mollie said, and that did indeed seem to be where the Rivington men were retreating. One corner of Caudell's mouth twisted down. He'd had a small taste of house-to-house fighting when the

Army of Northern Virginia took Washington City, and he didn't care for it. Of course, nobody ever bothered to ask a soldier whether he cared for the job he was doing.

He crawled down to the end of the horse trough behind which he and Mollie lay, looking for the next piece of cover he'd run to. As he did so, he saw two men in splotched green dart over the tracks. "It ain't the station!" he said, forgetting all his carefully cultivated grammar. "They're making for that shed across the way."

He remembered the shed, and the armed guard who'd prowled around it, from his train trip through Rivington on the way home after the war. But for four years' weathering, it looked the same now as it had then.

"They crazy?" Mollie said. "They can't fight from the shed."

She was right—the only thing that made the shed different from a big wooden box was its door. A determined squad in the train station could have held out for a long time, maybe even until the Confederates brought up artillery. But another Rivington man abandoned the station for the shed. A bullet knocked him sprawling before he got there. He crawled on, leaving a trail of blood behind him, until he made it through the doorway.

Crazy to go from the station to the shed, unless . . . "They must keep their time engine in there!" Caudell said. The men of America Will Break were losing their fight for Rivington, but if they'd come out of a distant time, they might be able to go back again. The idea angered Caudell—it seemed like an unfair escape hatch.

"Time engine?" Mollie said.

"Not now," he answered absently. The tactics the Rivington men were using made him sure he'd guessed their game. The fighters in the train station were a rear guard, holding back the Confederates while their fellows, one by one, dashed for the shed. A couple of them stopped bullets and fell, but most ran the gauntlet of fire.

They knew their business. Even when but one man was left in the station, he kept firing now from this window, now from that, so his foes took a little while to realize he was alone. And he let go a long, sprayed burst before he sprinted across the tracks, forcing enough of the Confederates to duck that he made it to the shed safe. The door swung closed behind him.

Only when silence lengthened did some of the Confederates warily emerge from cover. A lieutenant—in the confusion, Caudell never had caught his name—trotted up to the shed. If any Rivington men remained inside, he was a dead man. But no one fired from in there. He waved his hat, signaling it was safe to approach.

Caudell came up slowly, wondering if things could be as peaceful as they seemed. The young lieutenant started to pull the door open, then thought better of it. He sent several rounds through the rough pine boards. When all stayed silent, he grinned and yanked on the iron handle.

A blast of yellow flame, a roar— The mine literally blew him out of his shoes. But for those shoes, all that was left of him was a great red smear on the ground and the train tracks. The three men behind him also went down as if scythed. So did the facing wall of the station.

"Another torpedo!" Half deafened by the explosion, Caudell could hardly hear himself scream.

Mollie saw something he had not. Pointing, she said, "All the blast came out in one direction. I wonder how they did that." When Nate, head still ringing, helplessly spread his hands, she stepped close and bawled in his ear till he understood.

However the Rivington men managed their hellish tricks, he was just glad he hadn't been right in front of the shed. Along with the four men instantly killed, several others were down, badly wounded. Their cries pierced the thick wool that still seemed to swaddle Caudell's ears.

But the door to the shed was open—open for good now. Caudell glanced at Mollie. She nodded, though her face mirrored the dread he felt. They ran for the doorway together, shouting for all they were worth and firing as they went.

The air inside smelled hot and burnt. Caudell dove and rolled. He bumped up against a stack of crates, neatly stenciled MEALS, READY TO EAT. Mollie crouched beside him. He blinked again and again to make his eyes adapt to the sudden gloom. The shed wasn't as dark as it should have been. Over in one corner, hidden behind more crates, a bright white light shone off the cobwebby ceiling.

Mollie pointed to it with the muzzle of her AK-47. "That's the same kind of light Benny Lang had in his house, 'cept he had 'em all over, not just the one."

"To hell with Benny Lang." But Caudell was already scuttling forward on hands and knees. "Reckon we've got to find out what that is." Mollie went right behind him, and several other soldiers, too. He waved them to a halt when he came to a turn in the maze of crates. "If I touch off another torpedo, no need for us all to go up."

He rounded corners one by one, each time by himself. He didn't think about bravery till long afterwards; at the time, the only thing in his mind was the luckless lieutenant's empty shoes. If he did touch off a torpedo, he'd never know what hit him. Oddly, that helped steady him. He'd seen too many worse ways of dying.

Then he came to the last turn. Ahead of him, the light spilled out bright as day, maybe brighter. One of the men in back of Mollie said, "Where the hell'd all them Rivington bastards get to?"

Caudell turned the corner. Since he had no idea what a time engine was supposed to look like, he couldn't have honestly said the machine took him by surprise. It had a small platform, perhaps three feet square, that glowed almost like the sun. His first quick thought when he saw it was relief that it was no larger—who could say what deviltry the Rivington men might have brought from the future through a *big* time engine?

He blinked so he could squint through the glare, and to make sure he could trust his eyes. On that platform stood a Rivington man, but Caudell could see right through him, as if he were one of the ghosts old Negroes talked about incessantly. While one part of him chewed on that, another brought up his repeater. Before he truly thought about what he was doing, he squeezed off half a dozen rounds.

The bullets passed right through the Rivington man. He did not crumple—he disappeared. The glowing platform went dark, plunging the shed into blackness. The Confederates behind Caudell shouted in alarm; for that matter, so did he. The time engine spat sparks like a railroad car going forty miles an hour with its brakes locked. The wall behind it and the crates to either side caught fire almost at once.

"Let's get out of here!" three people yelled together. The soldiers scrambled and stumbled and cursed their way back through the maze toward the light from the shed's blasted doorway. Caudell, who brought up the rear, was coughing and choking on smoke by the time he made it to the blessed fresh air.

But even as he rubbed his streaming eyes, he wondered what had happened to the Rivington man on the platform when he shot up the time engine. Had the man made it back—or rather forward—to his own year? When the engine smashed to bits, was he rudely dumped into 1882, or 1923, or 1979? Or had he vanished into a limbo of no time at all? Caudell knew he would never find out—or stop wondering.

A brisk crackle of gunfire from the south made him quit speculating in a hurry. Here were the outflanked Rivington men, come too late to save their link to whatever year had spawned them. But they still carried rifles in their hands, and they'd proved themselves fighters as tough as any Caudell had ever run into. If they wanted revenge, they could take a fair-sized chunk of it.

Caudell ran south, away from the burning shed. He flopped down by the horse trough from which he'd fired at the train station, only now on the opposite side. Where was Mollie? There, shooting from behind the steps of the general store. A big knot of fear eased inside him when he saw her.

The shed and the supplies inside blazed fiercely now; he could feel the heat on the back of his neck from a hundred yards away. He looked over his shoulder. The thick column of black, black smoke mounting to the sky came from the funeral pyre of the Rivington men's hopes.

He peeked round the edge of the horse trough for a muzzle flash at which to shoot. He fired twice. Then the AK-47 clicked uselessly—another clip empty. He clicked in his last one, chambered a round. As he did so, he remembered how nearly impossible it was to load a rifle musket while lying down. He crawled along, peeked round the other edge of the trough— maybe someone in mottled green was waiting for him to show up in the same place twice in a row. He hadn't lived through the Second American Revolution by being stupid.

No muzzle flashes—but what was that, flapping from behind a pokeberry bush? "A white flag," he said, doubting his own words while he spoke them aloud. But a white flag it was. A Rivington man stepped out from cover to wave it back and forth. Slowly, firing on both sides died away. The men of America Will Break emerged, one by one, hands raised in surrender.

Even after a couple of dozen fighters in mottled green, all of them rifle-less, came out into the open, Caudell stayed low behind the horse trough. He had trouble believing the Rivington men, after battling so long and hard against everything the Confederacy could throw at them, would give up now. Nor was he alone. Hardly any Confederate soldiers left hiding places to take charge of their enemies.

So the Rivington men kept walking, hands up, heads down. That more than anything else at last convinced Caudell they really were giving up: they *looked* like beaten troops. He got to his feet, ready to dive back to safety in an instant at the least hint of danger. When Mollie made as if to join him, he waved her back, saying, "Keep me covered."

Some of the other Confederates moved with him. Others stayed in place to support them: how many he was not sure, for when he turned around to look, he could see only a couple of them. He also saw the blacks and native whites of Rivington coming out of their hiding places now that the shooting had stopped. A few of them also started toward the men of America Will Break, the men who had ruled their town, ruled their lives, for the past four years and more.

The man with the white flag was the same big fellow who had parleyed with Nathan Bedford Forrest. Caudell searched for his name, found it: Andries Rhoodie. Rhoodie turned his head from one of the approaching Confederates to the next. Finally he made straight for Nate, hailing him with: "You seem to be the ranking soldier here, sir."

"Me?" Caudell's voice was a startled squeak. He looked quickly to either side. Sure enough, Rhoodie was right; no Confederate officers had broken cover—he wondered if any of the detachment's officers were still alive— and no other first sergeants. He gathered himself. "Yes, sir, I guess I am at that. I'm First Sergeant Nate Caudell, 47th North Carolina."

"Then you are the man to whom we must surrender." Rhoodie sounded as if he would sooner have faced red Indians' scalping knives. He wore no sword, but took off a belt that held a holstered pistol, thrust it at Caudell. "Here."

"Uh, thanks." Though no connoisseur of surrender ceremonies, Caudell suspected they could be handled with more grace. Awkwardly, not wanting to let go of his AK-47, he belted the pistol round his own waist. Then he blurted, "What made you just up and quit like that?"

"What the bleeding hell d'you think?" Rhoodie stabbed a finger toward the burning shed. "With our time machine gone, how are we supposed to fight a whole country?" He did not even try to hide his bitterness.

Caudell forbore to mention that he was the one who'd ruined the—time machine, Rhoodie had called it. But, nettled by the Rivington man's tone, he said, "Even when you had it, we were whipping you—otherwise how did we get here?"

Rhoodie glared, then seemed to crumple. His shoulders sagged, the iron went out of his backbone, he stared down at his heavy boots. Behind Caudell, sudden shouts rang out: "Hey, what's that crazy nigger doin'?" "Where's he goin'?" "Look out!" "Somebody stop him!"

As Caudell turned, a short, scrawny black man wearing only a pair of tattered trousers shot past him. The Negro clenched a broken whiskey bottle. With a wordless shriek of hate, he drove the jagged end into Andries Rhoodie's throat.

Blood spurted, spectacularly crimson in the afternoon sun. Rhoodie let out a gobbling, choking scream, brought up his hands to clutch at the gaping wound. But blood poured between his fingers, from his mouth, from his nose. He took a couple of wobbling steps, tottered, fell.

Another Rivington man grabbed for a bandage pack like the one Benny Lang had used, knelt by Rhoodie. "Andries!" he shouted, and then something in a guttural language Caudell did not know. Rhoodie lay still. After a minute or two, the other Rivington man stood up, shaking his head. Under dirt and streaks of green and black paint, his face was white.

The Negro threw down the broken, bloody bottle. He turned to the Confederates, saying, "Massers, y'all do what you want wif me. I 'dured more'n man was meant to 'dure from dat white devil. You look heah." He ran his hands up and down his ribcage, which showed in even sharper relief than that of the slave with whom Caudell had talked outside of town "An' heah." He turned to show his back and the scars, old and new, crisscrossing it. "I ain't no ornery, uppity nigger, massers, sweah to God I ain't—dat Rhoodie, he jus' evil to his boys. I seen him heah, an' I couldn't take no mo'."

Caudell and the rest of the soldiers in gray looked at one another in confusion, wondering what to do next. A black who slew a white had to die; so said generations of law. But if the white was an enemy of the Confederate States, a man who'd led the Rivington fighters, who was wanted in connection with the Richmond Massacre, and who, moreover, had abused the black outrageously? Generations of law said the black still had to die. Generations of custom dictated against bothering with much law.

No one raised a gun against the Negro. After a long pause, Caudell jerked a thumb back toward Rivington. "You'd better get out of here." The Negro stared, then fled as fast as he'd come.

"But—that kaf—that nigger—he just murdered a *blank*—a white," a Rivington man spluttered furiously.

"Shut up, you," four soldiers growled in the same breath. One added, "Reckon the son of a bitch had it coming, by God." Caudell thought the same thing, but hadn't quite had the nerve to say it out loud. That someone did showed the South was indeed different from what it had been in 1861.

★ XIX ★

The door to the Presidential mansion stood open for the fortnightly levee. Moths got in with the people, but to close the door would have made the place stifling: along with June, summer had come to Richmond. More moths fluttered hopefully against the window screen, looking for their chance to immolate themselves in the gaslights within.

Robert E. Lee and his daughter Mary stood just inside the front hall, greeting visitors as they arrived. "Good evening, sir and madam . . . How are you today, Senator Magoffin? . . . Well, Mr. Secretary, what brings you here?"

Jefferson Davis allowed himself a thin, self-deprecating smile. "I just thought I would drop by to see how this house was getting along without me. It seems to be doing quite well."

"You also expressed a certain small interest in hearing the latest gossip, as I recall," Varina Davis said with a twinkle in her eye.

"I?" Davis looked at Lee. "Mr. President, I submit myself to your judgment. Can you conceive of my making such a preposterous statement?"

"No, but then I cannot conceive of your lovely wife lying about it, either," Lee replied.

"I never knew you were such a diplomat," Jefferson Davis exclaimed, while Varina's creamy shoulders shook with merriment. The former President went on, "Had you shown this talent previously, I might have sent you to Europe in place of Mason and Slidell."

"In that case, sir, I am glad I hid my light under a bushel," Lee said, which won him a small laugh from Davis and a bigger one from his wife.

Mary Lee said, "You both seem happier now that you are out of this house."

"Happier?" Jefferson Davis soberly considered that, and after a moment shook his head. "No, I think not. Easier might be a better word, in that the full weight of responsibility now lies on your father's broad and capable shoulders."

"The full weight of thirst now lies on my narrow, parched throat," Varina Davis said. "With your kind consent, gentleman, Mary, I aim to raid the punch bowl." Her maroon skirts, stiff with crinoline, rustled about her as she sailed grandly toward the refreshment table set against the far wall of the room. With a final bow, Jefferson Davis followed his wife.

Once he was out of earshot, Lee said, "Let him claim what he will, my dear Mary—I am certain you are right. I've not seen such spring in his stride since our days back at West Point."

When the stream of guests slowed, Lee claimed a goblet of punch for himself and drifted through the crowd, listening. That, to him, was what was most valuable about the levees: they let him get a feel for what Richmond thought—or at least talked about—which he could have had in no other way.

Two things seemed to be on people's minds tonight: the recent surrender of the last America Will Break rebels down in North Carolina and the continuing congressional debate on the bill that weakened slavery. A plump, prosperous-looking man approached Lee and said, "See here, sir! If we are to set about turning our niggers loose, why then did we shed so much blood separating ourselves from Yankeedom? We might as well rejoin the United States as emancipate our slaves."

"I fear I cannot agree with you, sir," Lee answered. "We spent our blood to regain the privilege of settling our own affairs as we choose, rather than having such settlements enforced upon us by other sections of the U.S. which chose a way different from ours and which enjoyed a numerical preponderance over us."

"Bah!" the man said succinctly, and started to stomp off.

"Sir, let me tell you something, if I may," Lee said. The fellow stopped; however much he disagreed with his President, he recognized an obligation to listen to him. Lee went on, "When I went into Washington City after it fell to our arms, Lord Lyons, the British minister to the United States, asked me a question I have never forgotten: as we had made the Confederate States into a nation, what sort of nation would it be?"

The man had an answer ready: "The same sort as it was before the war, of course."

"But we are not the same now as then, nor can we again become so," Lee said. "As the minister pointed out, commerce demands we play a role in the wider world, and the war was hard on us and harder on our institutions, including that of Negro servitude. I would sooner make some small accommodations now, give the Negro some stake in the South—which is, after all, his country, too—than face, perhaps, servile insurrection in ten years' time, or twenty."

"I wouldn't," the man snapped. This time, he did leave.

Lee sighed. He'd had similar conversations before at these levees. Every one of them saddened him: how could so many people be unable to see past their own noses? He did not know the answer to that, but it was demonstrably true.

He cheered up when Mississippi Congressman Ethelbert Barksdale came over to him and said, "I heard the last part of your talk with that fat fool, Mr. President. Of course he doesn't fear fighting in a slave uprising; by the look of him, he probably didn't fight in the Second American Revolution, either—or don't you think he's the kind who would have hired a substitute?"

"I shouldn't care to impugn the courage or patriotism of a man I do not know, sir—but you may very well be right," Lee said. Sometimes a small taste of malice was sweet. The pleasure swiftly faded, though. "But there are so many with views like his that I fear for my bill."

"It will pass, sir," Barksdale said earnestly. He was a Confederate party man through and through, having backed Jefferson Davis in war and peace and Lee after him (he'd barely kept his own congressional seat in the past election, just riding out Forrest's Mississippi landslide). Now he lowered his voice: "If you'd told him what the AWB was really working toward, he would have turned up his toes."

"With men of his stripe, I wonder even about that," Lee said gloomily. But Barksdale had a point. Without the Richmond Massacre and the books in the AWB's secret room, no bill limiting slavery in any way would have had a prayer of getting through the Confederate Congress. In the aftermath of the murders and of the revelations from the AWB sanctum, his legislation did have a chance, maybe even a good one. "As often happens with those who would do evil, the Rivington men proved their own worst enemies."

"That they did." Barksdale looked left, right, back over his shoulder, let his voice fall even further, so that Lee had to lean close to hear him: "And speaking of the Rivington men, Mr. President, what shall be done with the ones captured in the fighting round their home town?"

"Home base," Lee corrected. "You pose an interesting question, Congressman. They were, of course, taken in arms against the Confederacy: a *prima facie* case for treason if ever there was one. Were we to hang them, not a voice could be raised against us."

Barksdale stared at him. "You mean they might not hang? You startle me."

"Nothing is yet decided. They fall under military rather than civil jurisdiction, both on account of their rebellion and because Nash County, North Carolina, where they were captured, had had the right to the writ of *habeas corpus* revoked and fell under the administration of General Forrest."

"Ah, I see." Barksdale's face cleared. "The question is whether to hang 'em or shoot 'em? I don't much care one way or the other; they'll end up equally dead with either, which is the point of the exercise after all, eh?"

"As I say, nothing is yet decided. But I do want to thank you again for your sterling work in support of the bill regulating Negroes' labor. Have you any idea yet when it might come up for a vote?"

As was his habit, Ethelbert Barksdale licked his lips while he thought. "The vote in the House might be as early as next week. If it passes there . . . hmm. Senators having fewer limits on their debate than representatives, the bill may well encounter considerable delay in the upper house before it goes up or down."

"I mislike delay," Lee said fretfully. The longer legislators had to bury in their memories the Richmond Massacre and the truth about the AWB, the likelier they were to revert to comfortable, traditional Southern thought patterns—into which slavery fit only too well. "I trust, sir, that you will do your best to move the bill forward in the House with the utmost expedition."

Barksdale puffed out the chest of his starched white shirt till he looked like a pouter pigeon. "Mr. President, you may rely upon me."

If he was pompous, he was also sincere. Lee gave him credit for that, replying, "I do, sir; believe me, I do."

The Mississippi congressman preened. Then his eyes narrowed in calculation. "One way to influence the tally might be the well-timed execution of a Rivington man or two."

"I shall bear your advice in mind, I assure you," Lee said. Barksdale swaggered off, pleased and proud to have influenced events. But Lee, though he would remember the advice, had no intention of taking it. He did not object to executing felons; he'd ordered rapists and looters in the Army of Northern Virginia hanged. To kill a man for the sake of political advantage, though—he rebelled at that, however richly some of the Rivington men deserved it.

He talked for a while with a veteran who had a hook where his left hand should have been. "Gettysburg, the third day," the fellow said when Lee asked him where he'd been hurt.

He'd heard that too many times. "I should never have sent you brave lads forward then."

"Ah, well, it came right in the end, sir," the veteran said, smiling. Lee nodded, touched by his devotion. But he would have been equally mutilated had the South lost, without even the pride of victory to show for it. That would have been his bitter portion had the Rivington men not come, just as it was now for thousands of maimed men in the North.

Chatting with a couple of pretty girls helped restore Lee's spirits. He'd always had an eye for women, had corresponded with several for years, but never did anything more all through his long marriage. Now the girls were also eyeing him, with a frank feminine speculation he'd never noticed before. He suddenly realized he was an eligible man once more. His face heated. The idea frightened him more than any two battles in which he'd fought. He retreated to the less intimidating company of Jefferson Davis.

"You're rather flushed," the former President observed. "Perhaps you should have the front door opened again in spite of the insects."

"The heat is not what troubles me," Lee said, with such dignity as he could muster. Davis, though far from a savvy politician, knew better than to ask what did.

As Lee's carriage rolled east along Cary Street toward Libby Prison, it passed a mule team hauling a barge down the City Canal. In the James River, the twin stacks of the light-draft gunboat *C.S.S. Bealeton* sent pencils of smoke into the sky.

The prison was a three-story brick building, cream-colored up to the bottom of the second-floor windows and red above. A warehouse before the war, it had housed as many as a thousand Federal prisoners during the winter of 1863–64. Many of them managed to escape not long after Lee first met the Rivington men, but the chimney through which they'd gained access to the basement was long since sealed up. Moreover, more guards kept an eye on the fifty-one Rivington men on the third floor than had watched all those Yankees.

Lee's own bodyguard nevertheless looked nervous as he preceded his charge up the stairs to the second-floor Chickamauga Room. "I shall be quite safe, Lieutenant, I assure you," Lee said. "Only the one prisoner will be brought in, and not only you but several from the force here will be present to make certain nothing goes wrong."

"Yes, sir," the lieutenant said, eloquently unconvinced. After a moment, he added, "With the AWB men, sir, how do you propose to make *certain* of anything?"

"That is the question," Lee admitted.

"Yes, sir," his guard repeated, fiercely now. "I mean, after what happened at your inauguration—" He broke off, not wanting to hurt Lee by reminding him of the ill-omened day. His expression said he would have executed all the captured Rivington men without a second thought.

The Chickamauga Room, as headquarters for the prisoners' interrogation, had been fitted with a desk by one of its nine-paned windows and a few chairs. Guards snapped to attention when Lee came in. While he settled himself at the desk, a couple of them hurried off to fetch a captive for him to question.

The man who returned between the guards was slim and dark and walked with a limp. In plain gray shirt and pants—slave's clothes, actually; the prison warder saved a dollar where he could—he did not look like one of the fearsome Rivington men. "Good morning, Mr. Lang," Lee said. He pointed to a chair a few feet in front of the desk. "You may sit if your wound still troubles you."

"It's healing well enough," Benny Lang said. He sat all the same. Lee's bodyguard, AK-47 ready to fire from the hip, interposed himself between chair and desk. The men from the Libby Prison detachment stood off to one side, their rifles equally ready. As he looked from one of them to another, Lang's mouth shaped an ironic smile. "I suppose I should be flattered at how dangerous you think I am."

Lee's answer was serious: "The Confederacy has learned, to its cost, how dangerous you Rivington men are." He watched Lang's smile fade, went on, "I also wish to inform you, so you may pass it on to your fellows upstairs, that the House of Representatives yesterday passed by a vote of fifty-two to forty-one the bill regulating the labor of this nation's colored individuals. The way in which you sought to turn us from that course succeeded only in putting us more firmly upon it."

Lang set his jaw. "Get rid of us, then, and have done." The bodyguard's back seemed to radiate agreement with the suggestion.

Lee said, "You must understand beyond any possible doubt that the direction in which you intended to go is not the one we have chosen for ourselves. Those of you who grasp that and are able to fully accept it may yet gain the opportunity to redeem your lives despite your treason."

"How's that?" the Rivington man asked scornfully. "Say we're sorry and go scot-free? I'm not a big enough fool to believe it. I wish to heaven I could."

"You needn't," Lee said. Benny Lang gave a mordant chuckle. Ignoring it, Lee went on, "If you were ever to regain your freedom, you would earn it, I assure you."

Lang studied him. "You're not a man in the habit of lying," he said slowly. "Tell me more."

Lee still wondered if he should. As his bodyguard had said, being certain about anything that had to do with the Rivington men was impossible. Even though they'd been stripped of all their gear from the future, right down to their very clothes, he couldn't be sure that, knowing something of which 1868 was ignorant, they might not yet find a means to escape and give the Confederacy more grief. He felt, in fact, rather like a fisherman who had rubbed a lamp, seen a genie come forth, and was now wondering how—or if—he could control it.

If he could, though, how much good that would bring his country! And so, cautiously, he said, "You know, Mr. Lang, that in capturing the AWB offices here in Richmond and your headquarters down in Rivington, we have come into possession of a large quantity of volumes from the twentieth and twenty-first centuries. Our scholars, as you may imagine, have fallen on these with glad cries and will spend years gleaning what they can from them."

"If you have the bloody books, what do you want with us?" Lang said.

"Primarily, to serve as bridges. A complaint I have heard repeatedly is that your volumes take for granted matters about which we know nothing. I confess that, having seen your works in action, I find this unsurprising: we are speaking, after all, of a gap of a hundred fifty years. You men may well prove of great value by helping us understand—and perhaps helping us use—your, ah, artifacts. Performing that task faithfully and well could, in time, possibly even expiate the crimes of which you are surely guilty."

"You'd use us, eh?" Lang cocked his head. "From your point of view, I suppose that makes good sense. But how would you know you could trust us?"

"There lies the rub," Lee admitted. "I am glad you can see it. We would be taking a risk; with your greater knowledge, you might delude the men with whom you work in the same way you sought to delude the entire Confederacy as to the path the future would have taken without your intervention—and as you tried to do with your speaking wireless telegraph." Learning of that device still irked Lee. He said, "We could have done great things with it in the late war . . . had you seen fit to reveal its existence."

Lang said, "We would have, I swear it, if you'd been in trouble. As it was, as we thought, the AKs turned out to be plenty to win your freedom."

"And so you concealed a potentially vital tool from us, for your own advantage. I promise we shall do our best to prevent any future episodes of that sort. Your Rivington men would be split up, not permitted to know where your fellows are nor, save under most unusual circumstances, to communicate with them. Further, you would be required to explain fully to the scholars or mechanics with whom you will be working every step of every process you demonstrate. Even so, we recognize the risk remains, though we shall do our utmost to minimize it."

Benny Lang made a sour face. "We'd be just like the poor damned German technicians hauled off to Russia at the end of World War II." Lee did not understand the reference. Seeing that, Lang went on, "Never mind. Whatever you propose is better than hanging. I think most of us will be willing to go along. I know I will."

"The reason I chose to put the question to you first, Mr. Lang, is that you are one of the Rivington men likeliest to be chosen to help us comprehend the products of your time. By most accounts, you have comported yourself well here in the Confederate States: you fought bravely on our behalf—and then later, it must be said, against us—and, while living the planter's life in Rivington, you treated your Negro servants relatively well. This lets me hope, at least, you will be able to accommodate yourself to your changed circumstances."

"I'll manage. Given the alternative, you can bet I'll manage," Lang said.

"Yes, that would offer considerable incentive—so much so, in fact, that we shall carefully examine every man's sincerity and credentials before even considering his release. Your sentences may possibly be suspended; they shall not be forgotten."

"You'd be stupid if you did forget them," Lang said, nodding. "The other thing that worries me is, not all of us know the kinds of things you will want to learn. Up in our own time, we weren't professors, you know. A lot of us were soldiers or police. Me, I repaired computers."

"There. You see what I meant about the gap between your time and mine?" Lee said. "I haven't the faintest idea what a, ah, computer is, let alone how to repair one."

"A computer is an electronic machine that calculates and puts information together very quickly," Benny Lang said.

Lee almost asked him what sort of machine he had said, but decided not to bother, as he doubted the answer would have left him enlightened—

the gap again. He chose a simpler question: "What does a computer look like?" When Lang explained, Lee grinned like a small boy—one mystery solved! "So that's the proper name for the qwerty."

"For the what?" Lang's confusion lasted only a couple of seconds. "Oh. You named it for the keyboard, didn't you? That's not bad. Give me a steady supply of electricity and I'll show you things with that machine the likes of which you've never imagined."

Lee believed him. The Rivington men had already shown him—shown all the South—a great many things whose likes had never been imagined. Some of them, he thought, should have remained unimagined. He wondered if the computer would prove to be one such. Time alone would tell. He said, "If the device be as useful as you say, will you teach us to manufacture more like it? We have commenced production of our own AK-47s, you know."

"No, I didn't know that, but it doesn't matter anyhow. General Lee—" Three guards growled at the same time. Lang looked briefly nonplused, then realized his mistake. "Sorry. *President* Lee, if you want me to build you a bloody computer, you may as well hang me now. I can't do it, or rather, you can't do it. You not only lack the technology you need, you lack the technology to make the technology you need, and likely a couple of more regressions before that, too. Give me electricity and I'll show you how to use however many computers you've captured. You can do that until they break down. When they do, they're gone for good."

"But you repair computers," Lee objected. "You just said as much."

"So I do, when I have the proper tools and parts. Where am I to come by those in 1868?"

"And if repairing one becomes a condition for your continued freedom—for your survival?"

Benny Lang stared bleakly at him. "Then I'm dead."

Lee liked the answer; it bespoke a certain basic honesty. If any Rivington men ever saw the outside of Libby Prison, he resolved that Benny Lang would be one of them. For now, though, he said only, "Tell your comrades what I have said to you, Mr. Lang. Before long, you will be furnished paper and pens. I want a complete listing of the types of knowledge each of you possesses. Warn the rest not to lie; you have lied to the Confederacy far too much, and any claim one of you proves unable to substantiate will result in his being considered a full-fledged traitor once more. Do you understand that and agree to it?"

"I understand it. As for agreeing, what choice have I?"

"None," Lee said implacably. "Be warned also that your crimes and your likely trustworthiness will be weighed against what you know when we consider whether to release any of you. Also, Mr. Lang, do pass on to your friends the vote of the House of Representatives. If you are set at liberty, you shall not be permitted to meddle in politics. Is that quite clear?"

The resentment that flared in Lang's eyes showed it was. "You give us few choices."

"Would you, in my position?" Lee said, and Lang would not meet his gaze. He turned to the prison guards. "Take him back upstairs."

As they marched off with Benny Lang, Lee walked back down to the street. His bodyguard said, "Sir, if it was up to me, the only time those bastards ever saw the sun again except through iron bars would be the day we took 'em out to hang 'em."

"Believe me, Lieutenant, I sympathize with you there," Lee said, "but they may yet prove of great value to our country. And it is *our* country, Lieutenant. We shall shape it to our ends, not theirs, I promise you that."

"But if they do meddle, sir?"

"Then we hang them," Lee said. Satisfied at last, the bodyguard raised his repeater in salute.

"Ain't gonna be easy, Nate," Mollie Bean said. The closer the wedding day came, the more nervous she got. She stooped down, tossed a pebble into Stony Creek.

"We'll do fine," Caudell said stoutly, watching the ripples spread. "Your hair is growing out nice as you please; pretty soon you'll be able to pack away your wig and just say you've changed your style."

"My hair's not what I'm frettin' about, an' you know it perfectly well. Ain't gonna be easy livin' in this town with some of the people knowin' I used to be a whore."

"I wish you wouldn't be so blunt," Caudell muttered.

"How come? Don't you like bein' reminded, neither?"

"You know it's not that," he answered quickly; they'd had this discussion before. He continued, "Once we're married, do you want to move back to Rivington, then?"

"God almighty, no!" Mollie threw up her hands. A startled blue heron leaped into the air with a loud *whuff, whuff, whuff* of wings. "In Rivington, everybody knows I was—doin' what I was doin'—till first part o' this year. Hereabouts, it's only some of the men who remember back to the war—leastways, I hope that's how it is."

"Nobody's ever given me a hard time about it." Caudell made a fist. "Anyone who tried, I'd give him this. Now you tell me straight out, Mollie, have you ever had any trouble from the women in town, any at all?"

"No-o," she said; he judged she was telling the truth but didn't quite trust it. As if to confirm that, she went on, "Sometimes, though, I just don't feel like I can look them fine ladies in the eye."

"They're no finer than you are," he insisted, and meant every word of it. "Come to that, do you want me to tell you which ones had great big babies six or seven months after they said their 'I do's'? I can name three or four right off the top of my head."

That won a giggle from her. "Can you? It don't surprise me."

"There, you see?" he said triumphantly.

"Ain't gonna be easy," she said again, brief confidence deserting her.

He took a deep breath. "How's this, then? We'll stay here as long as everything is good, as long as everybody treats us the way they're supposed to. The first time anybody doesn't, we'll pack up whatever we happen to have and move someplace where nobody's ever heard of either one of us, and we'll make ourselves a fresh start."

"You don't want to do that, Nate." Mollie sounded worried. "Hard pullin' up stakes when you've been somewheres a long time. An' you like Nashville; you know you do."

"I like you more," he said, and intended to add, "And I want you to be happy, too."

Before he had the chance, Mollie pulled his face down to hers and kissed him. Her eyes were shining as she said, "Nobody never told me nothin' like that before." Some of her fear seemed to leave her once more, for she looked around and then waved, and this time she surprised no birds. "It's right pretty here—the willow there, the jasmine just across the creek that'll be all full o' sweet flowers tonight . . . Nate! Whatever is the matter, Nate?"

"Nothing, really, I reckon." But Caudell still felt as though he'd seen a ghost; the sensation was almost as strong as when he'd fired through the Rivington man on the time machine platform. After a moment to steady himself, he explained: "I was fishing under that willow when poor Josephine—remember Josephine?—stuck her head out through the jasmine. Piet Hardie had the hounds out after her."

"Him." Mollie's face changed; her voice needed only the one word to turn flat and hard. "I've prayed more than once that he didn't get away when we took Rivington. It ain't Christian, but I done it. 'Fraid I'll never know, though."

"Oh yes, you will." Caudell told how he'd huddled behind Hardie's body after Henry Pleasants touched off the mine outside Rivington.

Mollie clapped her hands together when he was done. "He got what was comin' to him, by God." Caudell felt as if he were a bold knight who'd slain the Rivington man in single combat, not just stumbled upon (almost stumbled over) his corpse. By the way Mollie flushed and pressed herself against him, she had something of that same feeling herself. She looked up and down the creek. Her voice went low and throaty. "Don't seem to be anybody around, Nate—"

"So there doesn't." Grinning, he laid her down on the thick, soft grass, then quickly stooped beside her. With practiced fingers, he undid the buttons and eyelets that held her dress closed; the process would have gone even faster than it did had he not paused every few seconds to kiss the flesh he exposed. But soon she lay bare, and he as well. Their sweat-slick skins slid against each other. "Oh, Mollie," he said. She did not answer, not in words.

He got back into his clothes reluctantly; no matter what a preacher might say, early summer was easier to take without them. He felt at peace with the whole world as he and Mollie kept walking slowly along the creekbank. But after a few paces, she said, "Reckon we can try what you said, Nate. I hope it works, I purely do. But if it don't, I'll be glad for the chance to pull stakes, and that's a fact."

"All right," he answered, pleased and a trifle annoyed at the same time; he might have wished her to stay happy and distracted rather longer.

Before he could say anything (later, he thought that just as well), the two of them rounded a bend in the creek. On the far bank, by a thicket of water oaks, a gray-haired black man sat fishing. He waved with his left hand, called, "How do, Marse Nate, Miss Mollie?"

"Hello, Israel." Nate looked over his shoulder. No, the Negro couldn't have seen him and Mollie cavorting in the grass. Relieved, he turned back. "Catching anything?"

"Got me a couple catfish." Israel held them up. Stony Creek was so narrow, he hardly needed to raise his voice to talk across it.

"How's it feel, workin' for the famous Colonel Pleasants?" Mollie asked.

"Now the fightin's done, Marse Henry, he took off the uniform fast as can be," Israel said. "The railroad he was workin' for, they send a man out to the farm the other day, askin' him to take back his old job at twice the money. He say they make it back by usin' his name, an' I expect he be right."

"What did Henry tell him?" Caudell said, bumping into a new set of mixed emotions. He wanted his friend to do well, but he didn't want him moving back down to Wilmington. As far as seeing him went, that would be almost as bad as if he went home to Pennsylvania.

Israel answered, "He tol' that man to git off his land and never come back, that he had better things to do with his name than sell it to a railroad that hadn't wanted the man who was wearin' it. His very words, Marse Nate; I was there to hear 'em."

"Good," Caudell said. Mollie nodded. So did Israel. Just then, the line the black man was holding gave a jerk. He pulled in a fat little sunfish, let it flop away its life on the bank. Nate added, "As long as that's settled, I think I'll call on Henry some time in the next few days."

"Always glad to see you, Marse Henry and me too," Israel said. As he spoke, he got another bite. "You come tomorrow, maybe some of this nice fish be left."

"I wouldn't mind if there was," Caudell said agreeably. "I won't be going up there just to eat it, though. I want to ask Henry if he'll be my best man."

Taken by surprise, Mollie gasped and clung to him. Israel smiled across the creek at the two of them. "That's fine," he said. "Marse Henry, he always goin' on about how happy you two be, so I know he be happy to do that for you."

"Don't tell him ahead of time," Caudell warned. "I want to do it myself."

"I won' say a word," Israel promised. "Miss Mollie, Marse Henry, he go on too about how much your brother or cousin—I ain't quite sure which—Melvin looks like you. He be at your weddin'?"

"I—don't think so," Mollie answered after a moment's hesitation. "Now that the fighting's done, I don't think we'll see Melvin much around these parts."

"Travelin' sort o' man, is he?" Israel said. "Some folks is like that. Too bad he won't be there to see you wed, though."

"We'll do fine without him." Mollie leaned against Nate again. They started walking along the creek once more. Israel's farewell wave was interrupted by yet another catch. Caudell knew mild envy; he'd never pulled so many fish out of Stony Creek so fast.

Mollie said something. His mind on fish, Caudell missed it. "I'm sorry?"

"I said, maybe it'll work out all right after all. You start talkin' about gettin' a best man and things like that, it makes the wedding start to seem real."

"It had better seem real." He slipped his arm around her waist, pulled her close, kissed her. Israel was no doubt watching from the far bank. Caudell couldn't have cared less.

The upstanding wings of Nate's collar brushed against his beard and tickled. He felt slightly strangled; he wasn't used to the tightness of his cravat. Even without the black silk tie, he suspected he would have had some trouble breathing: few men go calm to their wedding. The still, sultry air inside the Baptist church gave him an excuse for sweating.

As men will, he tried to tell himself he was being foolish—he'd marched into battle with fewer palpitations than he had right now. But the inside of his mouth stayed dry.

Ben Drake was well into the wedding service. The preacher's big voice boomed, "If there be any who know of any reason this marriage should not take place, let him speak now or forever hold his peace."

Caudell tensed. Preachers intoned those words at every wedding. But here—some of the men listening here knew who—and what—Mollie had been. He didn't think anyone held that sort of grudge against him or her, but— The prescribed pause passed. No one spoke. The service went on. Caudell eased, a little.

Much too quickly, or so it seemed, Drake turned to him and said, "Do you, Nathaniel, take this woman Mollie to be your lawful wedded wife, to have and to hold, to love and to cherish, until death do you part?"

"I do." Caudell was used to outshouting a room full of school children. Now he wondered if even Henry Pleasants beside him, resplendent in full colonel's uniform—Confederate, though he had threatened to scandalize everyone by wearing blue—could hear. Pleasants beamed—he must have spoken out loud. He tried on a smile. It fit.

"Do you, Mollie, take this man Nathaniel to be your lawful wedded husband, to have and to hold, to love and to cherish and to obey, until death do you part?"

From behind her veil, Mollie's words rang clear: "I do."

"Then under the laws of God and those of the sovereign state of North Carolina, I pronounce you man and wife." Ben Drake smiled. "Kiss your bride, Nate."

Awkwardly, Caudell moved aside the filmy veil. The kiss was decorously chaste. In the third row of pews, Barbara Bissett started to sob. His landlady cried at any excuse, or none. This time, she was not alone. By the time Nate and Mollie walked up the aisle to the church door, half the women who'd watched the ceremony were dabbing at their eyes. Caudell wondered why they did that. Weddings were supposed to be happy times, but the little lace handkerchiefs always came out.

He and Mollie stood in the doorway while their friends filed past. As far as he could remember, he'd never shaken so many men's hands, hugged so many women, in so short a time. "A beautiful wedding, just beautiful," Barbara Bissett said, squeezing him against her ample bosom. Then she started crying again.

Dempsey Eure came up, his wife Lucy beside him. He slapped Caudell's back, planted a loud smack of a kiss on Mollie's cheek. "Now all you two have to do is wait till the sun goes down," he said, adding mischievously,

"Fool thing to do, too, if you ask me, gettin' married near the longest day—and the shortest night—of the year."

The men who heard him guffawed; the women tittered and pretended they had no idea what he was talking about. Mollie said, "You're terrible, Dempsey."

"Oh, I'm not quite as bad as all that," he answered, grinning.

Just for a moment, some of Nate's joy leaked away. Dempsey had shared a winter cabin with him during the war. He'd also gone over to Mollie's cabin then, a few times or more than a few. Was he reminding her of it now? She might have had a point when she said this wouldn't be easy.

But there by Dempsey stood Lucy Eure, blonde and slim and pretty in a birdlike way. She had one hand on the top of their son's head; a sleeping baby filled her other arm. By the proud way Dempsey smiled at them, he was happy enough right where he was. Caudell decided he worried too much. If he read things into every chance remark, he and Mollie *would* have trouble.

Raeford Liles said, "All them letters you got from this lady here, Nate, and all them times you told me you weren't sweethearts, I reckoned the two of you would join up sooner or later." He cackled.

"You were right, sure enough," Caudell admitted, determined now not to be teased. He put an arm around Mollie. "I'm glad you were."

Two big elms shaded the street in front of the church. The guests stood in small groups there. "Don't anybody leave quite yet," Henry Pleasants said loudly. "You may just possibly have noticed some trestle tables there. Hattie, who cooks for me and my farmhands, has set up a little spread for you all."

"You still talk like a Yankee, Henry," Caudell said. "You're supposed to say that as one word."

"They weren't goin' away anyhow," Mollie put in. "Seems more like they was tryin' to keep from chargin' them tables."

"Hattie will hold them at bay," Pleasants said. Sure enough, the big black woman lashed out with a serving spoon at a man who got too close to a platter of roasted chicken. He hastily drew back.

Hattie used the spoon to beckon to Caudell and Mollie. "De new husband and wife, dey eats first," she proclaimed, as if daring someone to argue with her. Nobody did. Caudell hurried over, grabbed a plate and fork, and foraged among chicken and ham and turkey, corn bread and sweet potato biscuits and beans cooked with salt pork. Carolina fruitcake, peanut brittle, and peaches candied in honey also looked tempting, but the plate had only so much room.

Another trip, he told himself, attacking the ham. His eyebrows leaped up as he tried to figure out what all Hattie had done with it. He tasted brown sugar, mustard, and cloves, molasses, honey, and something that had him puzzled until he finally identified it as the liquor from brandied crabapples. He was sure there were more flavors than he was noticing, too. He took another bite, and another. Pretty soon the ham was gone, but some of the mystery remained.

"Here you go." Henry Pleasants pressed a glass of whiskey into his hand.

"Thank you, Henry." Caudell paused, then repeated himself in a different tone of voice: "Thank you, Henry—for everything."

"Me? What's there to thank me for?" Pleasants waved the idea away. "Hadn't been for you, I'd've just gone back to the life I went into the army to escape. I dreaded having to do that when the war was over, and thanks to you, I had no need."

He would have said more—he'd had a glass of whiskey or two himself, while Caudell was eating—but Wren Tisdale came over to him and asked, "How much do you want for that nigger wench, Pleasants? I'll give you top dollar, by God—the business her cooking will bring into the Liberty Bell ought to make her worth my while pretty quick."

"She's not for sale, sir," Pleasants said. "She—"

"Will you hire her out to me, then? How much would you want for two weeks of her time out of the month?"

"If you'd let me finish, I'd have told you she's not for sale because she's free," Pleasants said. "If you want her to cook at the Liberty Bell, you'll have to worry about making it worth *her* while."

The saloonkeeper's pinched, sallow features darkened with anger. "I ain't no Yankee—I don't hold with free niggers." He stalked off.

"That's peculiar," Caudell said, watching him go. "Hattie's cooking isn't going to change just because she's free."

"True enough, but if he took her on as a free woman, he'd have to treat her that way." Pleasants lowered his voice. "A lot of you Southerners have trouble with that."

Caudell pointed to the three stars on the collar of his friend's gray jacket. "You're a Southerner yourself now, Henry, like it or not, even if you can't say 'y'all,' and come to that, the blacks in the U.S.A. aren't having an easy time of it, either, if you can believe the papers."

"That's so." Pleasants sighed. "If Lee's bill ever gets out of the Senate, it will put this country on the right track, at any rate."

"I can't see why they're taking so long over it," Caudell answered. "Even Bedford Forrest said he wouldn't have voted for himself if he'd known the truth about the Rivington men."

"After politicians listen to their own speeches for a while, they start forgetting what they know, if you ask me." Pleasants tapped Nate's glass with a forefinger. "Can I fill you up again?"

Caudell pointed to a punch bowl. "Why don't you get me some syllabub instead? It should go nicely with the fruitcake." And sure enough, the sweetened mixture of Madeira, sherry, lemon juice, and cream, all spicy with mace and cinnamon, perfectly complemented the candied orange peel, cherries, raisins, figs, and pecans in the cake. When he was through at last, Caudell said, "You can just roll me back home, Henry. I'm too full to walk."

"Or for anything else?" Pleasants asked with a proper best man's leer.

Caudell glanced over at Mollie. Her smile brought one to his own lips. "You needn't worry about that," he said firmly.

When the trestle tables were as bare of food as if an invading army had swept over them, and shadows lengthened toward evening, Raeford Liles drove the newlyweds to the widow Bissett's in his buggy. Everyone pelted them with rice as they climbed up onto the seat. "You have some in your beard," Mollie said.

"I don't care," Caudell answered, but he brushed at himself anyhow. Half a dozen grains cascaded down onto the front of his jacket. The buggy started to roll. More rice flew.

The house was quiet and empty when Liles pulled up in front of it; all the Bissetts were going out to sleep at Payton Bissett's farm, to give Caudell and Mollie one private night. Reining in, the storekeeper said, "You got to pay me my fare now." Before Caudell had a chance to get angry, he explained, "I'm going to kiss the bride." He leaned over and pecked Mollie's cheek.

Caudell slid down from the buggy, held out his arms to help Mollie. "Like I told you back at the church, Mr. Liles, I'm glad you were right and I was wrong."

"Heh, heh." The storekeeper's grin showed his few remaining teeth. "Reckon I don't need to wish you a good evenin', now do I?" He flicked the reins, clucked to his horse. The buggy turned in the middle of the street, headed back toward Liles's rooms over the general store.

"Why don't you come with me, Mrs. Caudell?" Nate said.

He hadn't called her that before. Her eyes slowly widened. "That's sure enough who I am now, ain't it?" she said, perhaps half to herself. "Mr. Caudell, it'd be purely a pleasure." They walked to the doorway arm in arm.

He carried her over the threshold twice, at the front door and again at the doorway to his upstairs room. The second time, he didn't put her down right away, but walked over to the bed and gently laid her upon it. Then he went back and closed the door behind them. As he began to untie his cravat, he said, "One day before long, we'll have to find another place to live. This room isn't going to be big enough for the both of us."

She was sitting up, reaching around to the back of her neck to undo the fastenings of her wedding gown. She interrupted herself to nod. Then she smiled that glowing smile of hers. "Reckon you're right, Nate. But it's big enough for tonight, don't you think?"

He hurried to her. "I'm sure of it." He had no idea whether they would live happily ever after. He'd start worrying about that tomorrow. Tonight, he did not care.

Robert E. Lee angrily jerked his head to one side, as if he were snapping at his own ear. "Twenty-four men," he growled. "Twenty-four men holding our country's future in their pocket—and they will not let it out."

"Our Senate, like that of the United States upon which it was modeled, is leisurely in debate," Charles Marshall said.

"Leisurely?" Lee rolled his eyes up toward the ceiling of his office, and toward the heavens that ceiling hid. "Mr. Marshall, I have been raised from childhood with the firm conviction that the republican form of government is the finest ever devised, but the dilatory tactics I have seen in connection with this bill tempt me to doubt my faith therein. Had the Army of Northern Virginia campaigned in the manner in which the Senate debates, AK-47s would not have sufficed to gain our independence."

"Had the Army of Northern Virginia campaigned in the manner in which the Senate debates, it would have been McClellan's Army of the Potomac instead," Marshall said.

Caught by surprise, Lee let out a short bark of laughter. "I will not say you are wrong, sir, but that is no way for a proper army—or a proper government—to conduct its business."

"The vote must surely come in the next few days, Mr. President," Marshall said.

"Must it? So people have been claiming for weeks now, yet still the debate goes on, and on, and on." Lee's open hand came down with a thump on a pile of the day's Richmond newspapers. "And still this—this twaddle continues to be printed."

Charles Marshall raised a sympathetic eyebrow. "It is pretty dreadful, isn't it?"

"Dreadful? I wish I were a fine profane swearer like General Forrest, so I might more appropriately express my feelings."

Lee whacked the pile of papers again. Every sort of argument the South had devised over the years to justify slavery was coming out anew in the course of the Senate debate—and in the newspapers. Arguments taken from the *Politics* of Aristotle lay cheek by jowl with those borrowed from the Book of Genesis and its condemnation of the children of Ham. Tucked in alongside both were modern, allegedly scientific claims that aligned blacks with the great apes and purported to prove them inferior to whites.

In the papers, the counterarguments adduced by supporters of Lee's legislation seemed feeble by comparison. Those senators had to be circumspect, to keep from sounding like homegrown abolition fanatics. Much of their public argument was based on the evidence of the past few years, evidence that showed the Negro in a light different from that in which he had been viewed before. Could helpless Sambo, they said, have made first a soldier and then a rebel so dangerous that *de facto* emancipation already existed over broad areas of the Confederacy? The answer, they maintained, was obviously no.

But their foes turned that answer against them. If the Negro could make a soldier and a dangerous rebel, why, then, all the better reason to grant him no concessions; indeed, to tighten control on him harder than ever.

The real trouble was, half the arguments in favor of Lee's bill could not be stated publicly. Its backers could rail at the Rivington men, could point out how they had murdered to try to force the Southern government away from any step toward emancipation and had revolted when the murders failed to achieve their purpose. That was fine, as far as it went.

It did not go far enough, though. Lee did not want the lesson of future history paraded through the newspapers for Northerners and Englishmen to read. Those secrets were an ace in the hole against the ambitions of nations larger and more powerful than the Confederate States.

If they did not stay secret . . . Late reports from the war in the Canadas said that some U.S. forces were beginning to carry repeating rifles patterned after the AK-47. That worried Lee. One day before too long, the United States might try a war of revenge against the Confederacy. If they did, he wanted things like buried torpedoes and endless repeaters to stay dark and quiet, the better to surprise the invaders. Trumpeting the knowledge from out of time would only make that harder. In public, then, his supporters had to watch what they said.

He sighed. "When the Second American Revolution began, our bold Southern men said they could beat the North with one hand tied behind their backs. We found out it was not so soon enough. Now I wonder if we can pass this bill while using only one hand." He explained what he meant to Charles Marshall.

His aide thoughtfully pursed his lips. "If the only way to rally popular support for the legislation would be to allow everything to come out, are you willing to do that?"

"Now there's a pretty problem!" Lee exclaimed. "I confess I had not thought of it in quite those terms. Which weighs for more, a nation's safety or justice for its inhabitants?" He considered the question for three or four minutes before continuing, "I believe, sir, the answer must be no. Once a secret is gone, it is gone forever and cannot be restored. But even if my bill fails of passage in this session of Congress, it may be introduced again in future sessions, and one day will surely be approved. How say you?"

"Mr. President, your views generally strike me as sensible, and this instance is no exception. You remind me that you are fighting a war here, not merely a single battle."

"Well put," Lee said. "When caught up in the excitement of a single battle, it is important to bear in mind the campaign of which it forms a part."

"True enough, sir," Marshall said, "although I had not envisioned your Presidential term as analogous to a military campaign." He ventured a chuckle. "I suppose that if I spoke with Jefferson Davis, he would say he had spent a good part of his time in office campaigning against our Congress."

"I do hope to avoid some of the difficulties he had. He was and is a most able man, but also one who sees disagreement as an affront, if not a betrayal. I do not think he himself would disagree with my assessment. I still have hope, at least, that a more conciliatory approach will yield better results."

"And if not?" Marshall asked.

"If not, I shall bellow and froth at the reprobates until steam starts from my ears as if from a locomotive engine's safety valve." Lee caught his aide staring. "I see you do not believe me. Too bad—if I cannot fool you, how am I to deceive the Congress?"

Still shaking his head, Charles Marshall walked out of the office. Lee settled in to his daily paperwork. He had never cared for it, and the Presidency brought far more of it his way than he'd had to deal with even as general. But regardless of whether he cared for it, it was part of his duty, and so he conscientiously undertook it.

A report from the Virginia Military Institute caught his eye. Hendrik Nieuwoudt, one of the Rivington men ordered there, had been found hanged in his room, apparently a suicide. He'd left a note on his bed: "I can't stand being watched anymore."

Lee's mouth tightened. Constant surveillance was the price those AWB men who had been released paid, and would continue to pay, for being suffered to live. That phrase, with its Biblical overtones, echoed in his mind. He'd thought of the Rivington men as captive genies before. Witches, though, made as good a description for them: they had curious powers and they were dangerous. Benny Lang and most of the others appeared to understand and accept that. But Nieuwoudt was the second of their number to kill himself.

Lee had a horror of suicide; to him it seemed the ultimate abandonment of responsibility. Yet the Rivington men were already abandoned like no others in all the world, cast adrift even from their proper time. What had they to live for? He wished he could make their lot easier, but would not put his nation in harm's way for their sake. If that made him partly to blame for their deaths, he would accept the burden. An officer had to learn to do that, else he would never be able to give an order that brought his men within range of the enemy's shot and shell. And now he was not merely general, but commander in chief.

Reminding himself of that brought his thoughts back to the Senate. How easy it would be if he could simply order the men of the upper house to approve his legislation! But he could not; the Constitution did not permit it. They would make up their own minds in their own good time . . . and quite probably drive him mad in the process.

Commotion on the grounds of the Presidential mansion. Lee looked up from a letter he was writing to the British minister. Running feet, a sentry's cry of, "Halt! Y'all halt right now, do you hear me?" After the Richmond Massacre, sentries took their duties more seriously than they had in times past.

Several voices shouted back at the sentry. That garbled any single reply, but one word was repeated often enough to come through clearly. "Vote! The vote!" Lee jumped to his feet and hurried out, the letter forgotten. He'd hoped the vote might finally come today, but past delays had forced caution on him.

Guards stood before the front steps with extended bayonets, holding a squad of reporters out of the residence. The reporters' yells redoubled when Lee appeared in the doorway. "Fourteen to ten," one of them bawled above the general din. "Fourteen to ten, President Lee! What do you have to say about that?"

"Fourteen to ten which way, Mr. Helper?" Lee asked, doing his best to hold anxiety from his voice. "You must be aware your response to that question will have some small bearing on the comments I make."

The man from the *Richmond Dispatch* laughed, which meant Rex Van Lew of the *Examiner* got to tell Lee what he needed to know: "Fourteen to ten *for*, Mr. President!"

Lee's breath whooshed out in one long, happy sigh. He'd had remarks ready for this occasion (and another set ready in case he lost), but they all flew straight out of his head. He spoke the first thought he had: "Gentlemen, we are on our way."

"On our way *where*, Mr. President?" asked Virgil Quincy of the *Whig*.

"That we shall all discover in due course," Lee answered. "But I am heartily glad we have begun the journey."

"You've given up owning slaves yourself, President Lee," Quincy said. "How will the passage of this bill affect you personally?"

"Aside from making me the most relieved man in Richmond, do you mean?" Lee said, which raised more laughter among the reporters. Through it, he went on, "As you may know, the Constitution sets my salary at $25,000 per annum. I aim to contribute the tenth part of that sum each year into the emancipation fund this legislation establishes, to show I favor it with more than words alone."

That quieted the reporters, who bent over their pads to write down his reply. After a moment, Edwin Helper said, "How do you feel about the prospect of no more niggers being born into slavery after December 31, 1872?"

"The date I proposed originally to Congress as the *terminus ad quem* was December 31, 1870," Lee said. "I accept, with a certain amount of reluctance, its decision to delay that day two years further, but I am forced to concede that the additional period will let us prepare more adequately. I am pleased that Negroes will begin to be freeborn during my term in office, and even more pleased that they shall begin to enjoy their full liberty before the commencement of the twentieth century."

Rex Van Lew stiffened at that, like a bird dog coming to point. "There's been a good deal of talk about the twentieth century all through the debate of this bill, sir. Why worry so much about it now—why talk so much about it now—when it's still more than thirty years away?"

"Any conscientious legislator naturally has in mind the future of his country, Mr. Van Lew, and speaking of the twentieth century is a convenient way to indicate our course toward that future." It was, Lee knew, less than half an answer. The twentieth century—and the twenty-first— loomed large in the debate because senators and congressmen were actually able to judge their views, not merely guess at them. But that was a story which ought not to appear in the newspapers.

Van Lew, both clever and persistent, recognized that Lee had been imperfectly frank. He waved his hand again, but Lee pretended not to see him. He pointed instead to Virgil Quincy, who asked, "What will you do with masters who refuse to accept part payment so their slaves can start working to buy themselves free?"

"Congress has passed this bill, I will sign it, and it shall be enforced," Lee said. "I might add that a majority of our citizens, knowing my views on the matter, chose to invest me with Presidential authority. I construe this to mean they will comply with the law."

"Don't you think they voted for you because of who you are rather than your views about slavery?" Quincy asked.

"Who I am includes my views on slavery," Lee answered. "With that, gentlemen, I fear you will have to rest content." He went back into the Presidential mansion.

"What about the Constitution, President Lee?" someone shouted after him.

By then, Lee had already closed the door. He could pretend not to hear the question, and he did. He felt brief shame at using a politician's trick, but stifled it. The plain truth was that his bill violated the spirit of the Confederate Constitution and very likely its letter as well. Opponents of the law had been saying—bellowing—as much for months. He did not care to admit publicly that they were right.

Before he took office, he'd hoped to see Congress get around to establishing a Supreme Court during his term. Now, all at once, he wondered if that was a good idea. Justices would probably overturn the law, or important sections of it, if it came before them for review—and it would. They'd have a harder time doing that if the legislation was well established and working smoothly before they ever got a chance to examine it.

Another politician's trick, he thought; his mouth twisted in distaste. But however much he hated the idea, he was a politician now, maneuvering against his foes in Congress as he had against the Union army. Deception and misdirection had served his strategy then; no reason not to employ them now.

His servant Julia came into the reception room, a feather duster in her hand. She must have heard the reporters: when she saw Lee, she dropped him a curtsy as elegant as any he'd ever received from a highborn white lady. Without a word, she turned and began dusting the bric-a-brac on a table.

Thus she did not see the deep bow Lee gave in return. Most of the nearly four million blacks in the Confederacy remained slaves; that would be so for many years to come. But Lee tried to look into the misty future, to see how his country would change as more and more Negroes gained their freedom.

He was, at bottom, a deeply conservative man; the principal reason he'd supported the slow beginning of emancipation was in the hope that gradual change would lead to less long-range disruption than the periodic explosions of hatred that had to follow any effort to pretend the time from 1862 to 1866 had never happened. He hoped that blacks, once free, would come to be, and be recognized as, good Southerners like any other.

But just what even so simple a phrase as "good Southerners like any others" meant would have to be redefined in the years ahead. Would free Negroes be able to join the army? How would that look, black faces in Confederate gray? In 1864 it had been a counsel of desperation, and averted by victory. Now it would have to be seriously considered.

Would free blacks be able to testify against whites in court? For that matter, would they be able to gain the right to vote? Looking ahead, he suspected those things, unthinkable now, might well come with the passage of time. He wondered how many of the congressmen and senators who had voted with him believed they or their successors would ever have to worry about black voters. Few, he was sure: most thought they were giving the Negro just a little freedom.

"But there is no such thing as possessing just a little freedom," Lee mused. "Once one enjoys any whatsoever, he will seek it all."

"You got that right, Marse Robert," Julia said. He started slightly; he hadn't noticed he was speaking aloud.

He wondered how much change he would get to see himself. When Andries Rhoodie asked if he wanted to learn on what day he would die, he'd answered no without thinking twice. But the *Picture History of the Civil War* and other volumes from the AWB hoard let him know he ought to have only a little more than two years left: not even enough time to see the first black babies freeborn.

Yet he still had hopes of proving the volumes from the future wrong. The world to which they referred was no longer the one in which he lived. Here and now, he had nitrogylcerine pills to lend his heart strength; his hand went to the jar in his waistcoat pocket. That hadn't been so in the other world, the vanished world, the world where the Confederacy went down to defeat.

Watching his beloved South beaten had probably also helped break his heart in the more usual sense of the phrase. He remembered that unbearably somber photograph of him in the *Picture History*. What point could his life have had, lived out among the ruins of everything he'd held dear? Even losing Mary could not be a greater grief.

In truth, though, he had purpose as well as medication. If he took care of himself, why shouldn't he live longer than the vanquished Lee of that vanished world? If God was kind to him, he might yet see Negroes start growing up toward freedom, might even see the end of his term in 1874.

And if not—not. It lay in God's hands, not his own; God would do as He willed, and against God's judgments there was no appeal. Lee would go on doing his best for as many days as the Lord chose to grant him. A man could do no more. When he was gone, however far ahead that might be, others would carry on after him.

He looked over his shoulder toward the doorway in which he'd stood when the reporters brought word his bill had passed. "I shall have given those others a fair foundation upon which to build," he said quietly. Then he started back to his office. Despite the happy nature of the interruption, that letter to the British minister remained to be written.

ACKNOWLEDGMENTS

The Guns of the South would never have been written had Judith Tarr not complained in a letter to me that the cover art for an upcoming book of hers was as anachronistic as Robert E. Lee holding an UZI. That set me wondering how and why he might get his hands on such a weapon. *The Guns of the South* is the result. Thanks, Judy . . .

Special thanks go to Chris Bunch, formerly of the U.S. Special Forces, for advice on the care and feeding of the AK-47. Any inaccuracies that may have crept in are purely my own.

This would have been a different, and I think a poorer, book were it not for the exceedingly kind assistance of W. T. Jordan of the North Carolina Department of Archives and History. Responding to a letter from a writer of whom he'd never heard, Mr. Jordan graciously sent me a photocopy of the rare, long-out-of-print regimental history of the 47th North Carolina, which was written by Captain John Thorp of Company A, with an additional sketch by Lieutenant J. Rowan Rogers of Company I.

Moreover, Mr. Jordan is the current editor of the series of volumes entitled *North Carolina Troops, 1861–1865: A Roster*, volume XI of which contains the detailed roster of the 47th North Carolina. The information contained therein has proved beyond price and given me a great many of my characters.

Thanks to Nashville town manager Tony Robertson for sending me a beautifully detailed map of Nashville. Again, I appreciate the kindness strangers so often show to writers.

Two highly intelligent and well-informed readers, Dan Cragg and Anne Chapman, carefully went over this manuscript after it was submitted. It is considerably improved because of their thoughtful suggestions. Thanks also to Mr. Cragg for the two Minié balls from Fairfax County, Virginia.

And finally, thanks to my wife Laura for her usual thoughtful first reading, for telling me where I'd gone wrong, for suggesting ways to make things better, for splendid help with the research, and just for being who she is.

HISTORICAL NOTES

If my portrayal of Robert E. Lee seems to bear only a small resemblance to the revisionist one offered by Thomas Connelly in *The Marble Man*, it is not because I am ignorant of the latter but simply because, in most instances, I disagree with Connelly's interpretation. Lee's own writings, I think, show clearly enough what sort of man he was. The fragment of a letter which opens this book is from letter number 610 in the collection *The Wartime Papers of Robert E. Lee*, edited by Clifford Downey and Louis H. Manarin.

All persons stated to have served with the 47th North Carolina in early 1864 actually did so at that time, in the companies noted and with their proper ranks. There are only two partial exceptions to this rule: I do not know whether the slave George Ballentine still remained with the regiment then, and I do not know the actual company with which Mollie Bean served.

Mollie Bean did serve with the 47th North Carolina. She was, the *Richmond Whig* of February 20, 1865, tells us (as cited in *North Carolina Troops, 1861–1865: A Roster*), picked up in uniform not far from Richmond on the night of February 17 and sent into the city for questioning. At the provost marshal's office, she said she had been with the regiment for two years and had been wounded twice. The *Whig* story ends, "It will not, we presume, be pretended that she had served so long in the army without her sex being discovered." But such cases, the *Whig* notwithstanding, were far from unknown among both the gray and the blue. I have taken a novelist's liberty in imagining why she joined in the first place.

I have taken similar liberties in inventing occupations for a few minor characters from the 47th when those are not known, but the jobs of most of those who served in that regiment, along with their ages, home counties, and wounds suffered up to the time at which *The Guns of the South* begins, are authentic. The character I have ascribed to each man is a product of those factors and of my imagination (Billie Beddingfield's nature is inferred from his habit of repeatedly gaining noncommissioned rank and then being demoted again).

The town of Rivington, North Carolina, is entirely fictitious, as is everything connected with it, including Mollie Bean's residing there.

The men of the 47th North Carolina could not actually have looked across Washington to see the burning Long Bridge from the position in which I have them doing so. Geography occasionally has to bend just a little to serve the novelist's needs.

The terms of peace between the United States and Confederate States are based upon those set forth in a letter of February 8, 1862, from Confederate Secretary of State R. M. T. Hunter to his European commissioners James Mason and John Slidell, as modified by subsequent events both real and imaginary. Lee's plans for measures limiting slavery are derived from Brazilian constitutional proposals (unfortunately not adopted) of 1823 and from Brazil's free-birth law of 1871 (I concede the anachronism). Brazil's Parliament finally adopted full emancipation in 1888.

For those who are interested in such things, I append detailed returns of the fictitious U.S. Presidential election of 1864 and Confederate Presidential election of 1867. The returns of the U.S. election in particular seem to require some further explanation. The two-party system was not so well established in the 1860s as now, as witness the four-cornered electoral struggle of 1860. Starting a new party and hoping for success was perfectly possible; the Republicans, indeed, had run their first national ticket as recently as 1856. In a country stunned by defeat, as the U.S. was here, new movements would naturally arise.

I might also note that, before I worked out the final tally, I did not know myself who was going to win this election. State-by-state returns were determined as follows: McClellan, the most conservative candidate, was given a percentage equal to half the total Bell and Breckinridge received in each state in the real election of 1860. In states where they had not appeared on the ballot, he was assigned a small, arbitrary percentage. The exception here is his home state of New Jersey, which seems reasonable, as he carried it in the real 1864 election (one of the two states, Kentucky being the other, which he did carry) and later served as its governor.

Lincoln and Frémont are considered to have split a vote percentage equal to the average of Lincoln's 1860 and 1864 actual percentages. This method was designed to reduce the Republican total from what it actually was in 1864 with the war almost won, and in most states worked well. In Pennsylvania, however, where Lincoln's actual percentage *increased* from 1860 to 1864, I reduced the percentage to be divided between Lincoln and Frémont. Frémont's share of the total Republican vote varies by how "radical" I judged the Republicans of each state to be: he scores better in Kansas and New England than in the Midwest.

Horatio Seymour got whatever percentage was left in each state. The percentages for all candidates were turned into popular vote figures by using actual 1864 vote totals. While *The Guns of the South* is, of course, a work of fiction in every respect, I think these imaginary returns do reflect the confused political situation that would surely have existed in a United States that lost the Civil War.

U.S. PRESIDENTIAL ELECTION OF 1864

State	Seymour-Vallandigham Pop.	Elec.	Lincoln-Hamlin Pop.	Elec.	Frémont-Johnson Pop.	Elec.	McClellan-Everett Pop.	Elec.
California	38,649	5	36,108		12,379		19,060	
Connecticut	29,653		35,740	6	11,913		9,652	
Delaware	4,941		4,874		1,218		5,889	3
Illinois	161,233		164,716	16	18,457		3,831	
Indiana	124,372	13	117,089		29,412		9,244	
Iowa	51,716		62,618	8	7,389		4,254	
Kansas	3,151		6,215		11,524	3	691	
Kentucky	59,213	11	12,892		1,473		18,510	
Maine	40,638		46,034	7	23,303		4,821	
Maryland	40,892	7	18,879		2,114		19,900	
Massachusetts	42,468		83,005	12	35,273		14,741	
Michigan	71,070		74,210	8	19,338		661	
Minnesota	15,818		19,465	4	6,615		509	
Missouri	49,147	11	37,356		4,383		13,461	
Nevada	6,814		7,389	3	1,626		591	
New Hamphsire	26,738		30,150	5	11,419		1,323	
New Jersey	49,051		16,350		12,359		50,982	7
New York	333,209	33	293,019		87,687		16,807	
Ohio	219,618	21	197,939		41,002		12,725	
Oregon	6,769	3	5,210		3,064		3,302	
Pennsylvania	228,678	26	217,033		55,652		72,371	
Rhode Island	7,820		8,696	4	5,559		992	
Vermont	11,873		25,083	5	17,391		1,394	
West Virginia	11,754		19,585	5	2,197		1,081	
Wisconsin	68,996	8	66,159		13,590		597	
TOTAL	1,671,580	138	1,638,415	83	436,337	3	287,749	10

CONFEDERATE PRESIDENTIAL ELECTION OF 1867

State	Lee-Brown Pop.	Elec.	Forrest-Wigfall Pop.	Elec.
Alabama	38,933		51,189	11
Arkansas	25,776		28,376	6
Florida	7,063	4	6,238	
Georgia	57,056	12	49,391	
Kentucky	80,565	14	65,651	
Louisiana	24,295		26,215	8
Mississippi	29,711		39,384	9
North Carolina	55,223	12	41,489	
South Carolina*	—		—	8
Tennessee	74,368	14	71,738	
Texas	27,807		35,248	8
Virginia	75,739	13	51,982	
TOTAL	496,536	69	466,901	50

*South Carolina's electors to the Electoral College were chosen by the legislature rather than by popular vote.

ABOUT THE AUTHOR

Harry Turtledove is that rarity, a lifelong southern Californian. He is married and has three young daughters. After flunking out of Caltech, he earned a degree in Byzantine history and has taught at UCLA and Cal State Fullerton. Academic jobs being few and precarious, however, his primary work since leaving school has been as a technical writer. He has had fantasy and science fiction published in *Isaac Asimov's Amazing, Analog, Fantasy Book*, and *Playboy*. His hobbies include baseball, chess, and beer.